REBOOT

REBOOT

PHILL FEATHERSTONE

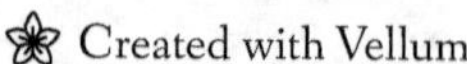 Created with Vellum

REBOOT SERIES 1
PARADISE
A GRIPPING PSYCHOLOGICAL DRAMA OF A GIRL ALONE
GIRL
PHILL FEATHERSTONE

THE OUTLINE OF these hills has barely changed in a thousand years. Until now. Now across the valley the margin of the land is no longer marked by the peaty moor. Instead, wind turbines stalk the skyline. The planners ordered that they should be white, so as not to stand out. It doesn't work. They are too huge. The poles thrust sixty metres into the air and are topped by trios of blades, each the length of an articulated truck. Every day there is wind and every day they turn, like a row of giants pirouetting in a ponderous ballet.

Granddad hated them. Climate change meant nothing to him. He lived here all his life and he saw these intruders as the work of some nameless, capitalist Satan bent on destroying our glorious heritage. His father had not fought Hitler to allow such vandalism in our green and pleasant land.

'It's them buggers in London,' he'd say. 'I bet they wouldn't put up with the bloody things in the south. They wouldn't stand for it.'

Of course, he was wrong. Turbines were built everywhere, and everybody – well, almost everybody – did stand for it. Many people welcomed them. Nevertheless, it would have pleased Granddad to know that the power the turbines are generating as I watch them today is of no use, no use at all. No one will turn on the TV or boil a kettle. No one will switch on a light. The factories will stay silent and the offices and schools dark.

It was like that yesterday and it will be the same tomorrow, and for all the days to come. These diaries tell you why.

1

———

ME

INTRODUCTIONS ARE BORING, but unless I take time to explain things it will be confusing for you. Me first. Not very polite, I know, but it's probably the best place to start. My name is Kerryl – or that's what my family and friends call me. It's a funny name but there's an explanation for it. I'll go into that later. (There, that's a reason for you to keep on reading, isn't it?)

My proper name is Cheryl. Cheryl Alison Shaw. They call me the Paradise Girl. Don't get excited – it sounds sexy but it's not. I'm seventeen years old and still a virgin. I'm not a nun, I've been out with loads of boys – Tim, Mark (two of them), Nathan, Jake, Tristram, Steve – but I wasn't that keen on any of them and they didn't last. The exception was Mark II. He was older than me, fearsomely good looking and he had a nice car. I thought he was really hot. When I wasn't with him I was texting him or phoning him or on Face2Face, and when I wasn't doing that I was thinking about him. But it seems he wasn't as keen on me, and one day my best friend, Josie, told me that he was going out with Monica Woodbridge and saying I was a frigid cow. It seems everybody knew I'd been dumped and I was the last to find out. I felt as though I'd been kicked by my horse, Joey, and I cried for a week, but I was angry too.

The worst thing was the shock. I thought Monica was my friend. As well as that, all the girls in our group had been going out with the same boys for a long time, but I seemed to keep a boyfriend for only a few weeks. Was there something wrong with me? To be honest, I'm not a great beauty. I don't mean I'm a train wreck or anything. I'm not bad looking, but I'm not like Charlene Brooker or Suzy Simmonds. They're electric, both of them. Charlene could be a model, and Suzy's always surrounded by a gang of drooling boys.

They're gone now: Charlene, Suzy, Josie, Monica, all of them.

Sorry for the break there. I had to stop to have a little weep. I'll try not to do too much of that. I suppose I can console myself with one thing: with everyone else dead, I must be the most beautiful girl in the world.

THE PURPLE DIARY (BEFORE)

2
____

ARRANGEMENTS

I'VE ALWAYS KEPT a diary. Not every day. Sometimes I'd go ages without writing anything. Then I'd do five days on the trot. I was talking to Miss Dove, who used to teach us English at St Winifred's, and she said that was a good thing.

'Only write when you have something to say,' she said.

I didn't ask her whether I should apply that advice to the essays she sets us, because if I did there'd be times when I wouldn't write anything at all!

Lander, my brother, used to tease me about my diaries. He resented them because he didn't understand why I wrote them. One of the worst rows we ever had was when I caught him in my room reading one of them. I went berserk. I had a pair of scissors in my hand, and I swear I would have impaled him if he hadn't jumped over the bed and kept it between us. He couldn't understand why I was so mad.

'Why write it if you don't want anybody to read it?' he said.

He called me pathetic and I didn't speak to him for more than a week. Not until he realised how much he'd upset me and apologised. I think he was jealous. Not so much jealous of me writing my diary, but of the diary itself. He liked to think I told him everything, us being twins and all, and here was stuff the diary knew and he didn't.

Lander's not here anymore and I don't know where he is, but I don't think he's dead. They say twins can sense these things. That may or may not be true, but I don't get any kind of death vibe, like I did when our Dad had gone. I have a feeling that Lander's alive. Somewhere.

The diaries I used to write didn't just record things that happened to me. I used them to help me work stuff out, and to say things I couldn't share with anybody, not even Josie, and certainly not with Lander. This diary is different though. It's different from anything I've written before.

Why?

Because I know I'm going to die.

Why?

Because the people I lived with – Gran, Granddad and our Mam – are already dead. So are all my friends and so is everybody else. And if Lander's not dead he might as well be.

Am I scared? The crazy (but true) answer is, 'I don't know'. Sometimes I wake up in the middle of the night feeling that something is eating me from the inside. I have to get up then because going back to sleep is out of the question. But most of the time, in the daylight, it doesn't seem real, even now, and I just get on with things. I can't believe that it won't all come right again, that life won't get back to normal. I mean, they'll sort it out. Won't they?

Anyway, I'm going to write about the things that happen to me now and I'm going to try not to be emotional. I'll tell you what I do, what I see and hear, what I think and what I feel. I'll keep writing as long as I can, until I'm too sick to do any more, and should there be anyone left, perhaps in another country, my diaries will tell them what happened here, in England, and particularly in this tiny corner of it, at this time in the twenty-first century.

I've got two notebooks, a purple one and a green one, and I'm going to use them for two different diaries. In the purple diary, the one that you're reading at this moment, I'm recording what's already happened. That's the part of the story I've called *Before*. My other diary, the green one, is my day-by-day account of what's gone on since then. I'm calling that one *Now*. I'm writing them both at the same time (well, not at *exactly* the same time, but you know what I mean), putting down each day's events in the green one and then catching up on the back story in the purple one. Purple past, green present, get it? Is that confusing? I hope not. Feel free to skip about from one to the other if at any stage you get bored. I'm not going to label the entries in either of them with dates. The passage of time is largely irrelevant now, and it doesn't matter whether something happened on a Monday in May or on a Tuesday in June. Actually, I'm not sure that I'd know to tell you, anyway. One day is very much like another.

3

FIRST NEWS

According to Miss Dove, a writer writes for herself; if she worries too much about the reader she ends up writing what she thinks they want to read instead of what she wants to say. It becomes false and she loses her voice. When she said 'loses her voice' I thought at first she meant like when you have a sore throat or a cold, but then she explained it and I understood. Rudy Fothergill, our other English teacher, didn't agree. He said that people like Dickens knew exactly who their readers were and what they wanted, and there was no question he wrote for them.

Mr Fothergill wasn't actually called Rudy. That was just our name for him because he'd stroll around the tables leaning over our shoulders. He was pretending to look at our work but really he was trying to see down our tops (rude = Rudy, get it?).

Anyway, I'm going to imagine you, my dear reader, so I do know who I'm writing for. I'm going to think of you as tall, dark and mysterious, a bit like Heathcliff. You have a firm but quiet voice and an infectious laugh. Oh, and you have strong arms and an awesome six-pack! Of course, you might not be the way I'm imagining you at all. You might be an old man, or an old woman. You might be somebody ordinary, like me. Should I give you a name? Maybe later.

Lander kept a diary too. Well, it wasn't a diary because he never actually wrote anything in it (writing wasn't Lander's thing). As soon as it became obvious that the Infection was something to worry about he started to collect information about it. Some of it was things like leaflets from the Government, some were newspaper cuttings, but most of it was stuff he got off the internet. There were a whole bunch of them doing it, sharing information. They had their own website: *www.thetruthwillse-tyoufree.net*. They'd post on it, and tweet, and they'd swap messages.

I've kept some of the papers Lander collected. Here's a cutting from *The Times*.

African Ghost Town
by Andrea Ellis

"I first visited the town of Konso in Ethiopia four years ago. Then it was a thriving, bustling place, an administrative and commercial centre and home to some 4,000 people. It had a petrol station, two hotels, a basic clinic, a bank and a twice-weekly market. It had electric power and a telephone system. I visited it again last week to find that it had become a ghost town.

What has devastated Konso is not drought or famine, scourges we have seen many times before in this part of Africa, but something which is even more deadly. Virus I/452 is so new it doesn't yet have a proper name, although the people of Konso call it 'waga', a word they also use to mean a grave marking.

I interviewed Dr Genevieve Amblée, the regional officer for Médecins Sans Frontières, who is coordinating local efforts to combat I/452. 'One of the main problems with this infection,' she told me, 'is the period of incubation. The virus settles in a host and is with them for seven to ten days before there are any signs of illness. This means that there are a lot of secret carriers, people who are already infected but don't know it yet, and all the time they are passing on the virus to others. The chief difficulty in trying to come up with a vaccine,' Dr Amblée explained, 'is that the virus constantly mutates so that what may work against it one day is completely useless the next.'

Scary, isn't it? That's not the half of it. There are some more cuttings in Lander's collection from around the same time, when the Infection was taking hold and becoming a serious problem in Africa but before it had spread anywhere else. There's one from the *Daily Mirror* headed 'Cursed Continent' and another from the *Daily Mail* called 'Africa's Lost Opportunity'. They both accuse African governments and unnamed individuals of pocketing billions of aid money instead of spending it on health, education and hygiene, and the authors imply that the countries have only themselves to blame for what they're going through. That seems to me terribly unfair, to write off the people because of what their leaders have chosen to do.

I can remember Granddad looking at one of the articles and going very quiet. Before, when he found anything that interested him in the news he would read it aloud to everybody in a loud voice, as a preamble to one of his rants about 'them buggers in London', or taxes, or the way farmers were treated, or Leeds United, or the state of Yorkshire cricket. It used to drive Gran crazy. But now when he saw something in the paper that troubled him he'd say nothing. He'd just put it aside and go out to the barn, looking worried.

The Infection – and it was starting to be spelt with a capital 'I' – was closer now and getting more coverage on TV. Lander kept these two reports. The first is from *The Guardian*.

> *Is Africa's scourge our nemesis?* (*Insights* (BBC Events Channel, 9 pm) presented a grim picture of the latest in the catalogue of woes that have often afflicted this great but sad continent. It also contained a stark warning of what might happen to the rest of us, although it was less clear about what we can do about it.
>
> Michael Lockwood, who is rapidly making this Monday evening slot his own, provided a detailed account of the nature and spread of I/452, the World Health Organisation classification of the disease which is now rampant in several sub-Saharan countries. Not much is known about it, and even the singular might not be accurate. It could be that I/452 is several diseases spread by different viruses but sharing common characteristics.
>
> It likely started in Senegal, although some say that Mozambique has an equally strong claim to this dubious honour. It's spread by contact, and there is evidence that it's also present in fauna and is carried by animals and birds, although they are simply transporters and don't show any of the symptoms.

One of the most dangerous aspects of this infection (or infections) is that a human host can harbour the virus for a week or more before starting to feel ill. In that time it's possible to infect scores, hundreds, of others.

Following the initial explanation were harrowing shots of the effects of the disease. Sadly we are starting to become familiar with these: suppurating sores, bleeding babies, heaving hospitals, and desperate people.

So far, so good. What was lacking was any sort of suggested response. There were several questions. What will happen if the disease reaches Europe? How can we guard against it spreading through our cities? How can we help those who are afflicted? All of these turned out to be rhetorical. All right, it's not the programme makers' job to come up with public health policy, but they should at least have provided us with access to the people whose responsibility it is. There were spokespersons from the opposition parties, who had two messages: something must be done, and anyway it won't happen here. There was no one from the Government, but instead a bland and, in truth, insulting statement that implied the easy spread of the virus was Africa's own fault for squandering billions of aid money instead of using it to improve living conditions and build hospitals.

Despite this, the programme was a timely wake-up call. Let us hope that those who should hear it pay attention.

The next clipping is printed from the online version of the *Daily Mail*, on the same date as the one above.

Look, a Wolf!

> Whenever the BBC Events Channel has surplus airtime it sends somebody out to find something nasty to scare us. Last night it was Michael Lockwood's turn. He was dispatched to report on yet another infection rampant in Africa. In *Is Africa's scourge our nemesis?* he told us what he knows about it (not much) and showed us footage of people suffering. His message was, 'Look, this could happen to you.' Well yes, it could. We might also get run over by a bus. Or win the Lottery. Then Lockwood wheeled out some politicians who were expected to have the answers to stopping it. Surprise surprise, they didn't.
>
> More interesting, and definitely more entertaining, was *I married my dad* (*Real People*, ITV 5). This was about an adopted young woman who had an affair with, and eventually married, an older man, only to discover that he was her biological father. As luck would have it, what triggered this revelation was the man's insistence on a paternity test when his young bride became pregnant, whereupon the doctors found out that the couple shared DNA. Naturally, cats were among pigeons and the father...

And there the page ended. Lander hadn't bothered to print any more of the article. I was disappointed because I wanted to know what happened. Either Lander knew, or he wasn't bothered. He never had much time for celeb stuff and gossip.

4

____

FARM LIFE

ME AND LANDER (Yes, I know, Miss Dove, it should be Lander and I, but this is my diary and I'll write it how I bloody well like) were born on the same day on this very farm where I am now. Lander was first and I came out an hour or so later. My, how he traded on that hour! 'I'm the oldest,' he'd say when I argued with him. 'Oldest first,' when we were in line for treats. He'd call me his 'little' sister, 'junior', 'kiddy', and when our Mam gave us jobs to do he'd leave the crappy ones for me. 'That's one for the youngest,' he'd say.

The farm belongs to Gran and Granddad. Our Mam wanted to be with her mam for the births, so she came to stay here to have us. She had a bad time and the births weren't easy. The whole business did her some damage. She never went into detail so I don't know exactly what went wrong, but it meant she couldn't have any more kids.

She stayed on with Gran and Granddad after we were born, and not much later our Dad moved in too. He'd had his own business making bespoke furniture but it hadn't been going well, and he packed it in and came up here. The farm's not big enough to support us all, so some of the time our Dad worked on the land with Granddad and for the rest he had a job as a driver. Our Mam helped Gran around the house and with the hens. She shared some of the cooking (although to be honest she wasn't much good at it!) and she worked part-time at the newsagents in Walbrough, the town at the bottom of the hill.

We were happy. Me and Lander ran wild on the farm. We'd go down into the woods to make dens and up on the moors to look for remains. Lander said you could find dinosaur bones in the peat, but the closest we came was the skull of a sheep. The moors scared me, particularly when it started to get dark or when heavy clouds came over and the light went. Lander said there were sucking bogs on the moors that you couldn't see till you were in them. You'd be walking along and the ground would look normal and then, whoosh, it would give way and you'd be in a sucking bog. They were called sucking bogs because the mud sucked at your feet and trapped you and pulled you under.

On the edge of the moor, out of sight of the farm, there are some giant stones in the shape of a horseshoe, around a shallow pool. Lander said they were haunted, and we used to play around them, hiding and scaring each other and our friends. They're called the Bride Stones and there are lots of local stories about them. One is that they're people who were petrified (I mean turned to stone, not scared) for blaspheming. Another is that they're folk who pissed off a local witch. There's a legend that if a girl sits on the flat slab at the edge of the pool – the Bride Stone itself – on Midsummer's Day she'll see her true love. There's also a story about a bride who went there for her wedding and drowned herself in the pool when the groom jilted her.

Anyway, back to our childhood. As we grew older we began to help with things, particularly the hens and the sheep, and of course at haymaking everybody pitched in. We went to St John's Primary School in Walbrough. Then, when we were eleven, I moved up to St Winifred's Girls' School in Halifax and Lander to King's Heath Boys'. We hated being sent to separate schools – we'd never been apart for such long stretches at a time – but in the end it probably turned out for the best. It meant we became more independent of each other, yet at the same time it brought us closer together. And we were close, even though we used to fight like mad sometimes.

Our Mam and Gran got on well, and our Dad was all right, although looking back I think felt a bit left out and resented what he thought of as accepting charity from his wife's parents (that's how he saw it, I don't think they did). I was talking to Lander the other day about the time when we were kids and used to roam free.

'Bit different now,' he said.

I said, 'Not really, it's still the same place.'

That made him angry. 'Oh yes, of course it is,' he said, 'people dying all around us. It's fucking paradise.'

I sat on the sun-warmed wall and looked out over the fields. The meadow was so full of buttercups it looked as though it had been dusted with yellow powder paint. A pale blue sky rimmed the hills across the valley. The trees at the end of the field were entering their first flush of green and masked the valley town. Beside me a drunken bumble bee made an uncertain landing on a dandelion. Yes, it was still paradise, but was Lander right? Were we losing it?

We'd been reading *Paradise Lost* at school. Not all of it, just some parts that Miss Dove picked out for us. We did the bit where Adam and Eve part for the first time and go in separate directions to work on the land, and Satan gives Eve the apple. Adam comes back and there's this great scene where, although he's horrified at what she's done, he eats the fruit too because he'd rather share her fate, whatever that might be, than go on without her. It's awesome! I learnt some of what he says to her by heart:

> *... with thee have I fixed my lot,*
> *If Death consort with thee, Death is to me as Life;*
> *So forcible within my heart I feel*
> *The bond of nature draw me to my own,*
> *My own in thee, for what thou art is mine;*
> *Our state cannot be severed, we are one,*
> *One flesh; to lose thee were to lose my self.*

Those lines get to me. They make me well up every time. That's the sort of boyfriend I want. I don't expect I'll find him now.

Our dad died when me and Lander were nine. It must have been gruesome, although to be honest I don't remember much about it. There was a lot of fuss and rushing about, and an ambulance, and the police, and my Auntie Madge coming. Everybody looked serious and our Mam was crying. Nobody took much notice of us, and we sat in the corner trying to figure out what was going on. I can remember Lander saying to me, 'Our Dad's dead.' Hearing him say it out loud like that hit me and I started to cry. Nobody took any notice; they were all too busy.

We didn't discover the details until later. Dad was killed in a farm accident, quite a common one it seems. A walker found his body and raised the alarm. Nobody knows for sure exactly what happened, but our Mam told me and Lander what the police and the insurance man thought. Dad was down in the bottom field on the tractor. He parked it on the slope and got out. He can't have put the brake on properly and the tractor started to move. They think he tried to get into the cab to stop it, but he must have got caught on something. The tractor carried on down the hill and rolled over, squashing him underneath it.

'Would Dad have died straight away?' I asked our Mam.

She said, 'Yes, he would. He wouldn't have felt a thing.'

She was just trying to make me feel better. Much later I asked Dr Carmichael and he said our Dad bled to death and it could have taken a couple of hours.

Me and Lander wanted to go and see where it happened. It wasn't that we wanted to see the blood, our Dad's life splattered on rocks, staining the grass, soaking into the leaf mould, but we wanted evidence that he was really dead. It seemed so unreal. That morning when we'd gone to school he'd been in the yard. He checked that we had all our stuff, patted us and told us to have a good day. I didn't know I'd never see him again. I should have given him a kiss and a hug. I should have clung to him and refused to go to school. Then he wouldn't have been able to take the tractor.

5
______

FUTURES

AFTER THE ACCIDENT our Mam seemed angry, all the time, as if what had happened was somebody's fault – Gran's, Granddad's, even our Dad's, as if he'd chosen to get himself squashed and die.

Once the insurance company had paid out, money wasn't a problem for our Mam any more, although she always behaved as if it was. I suppose she couldn't get used to having a bit to spare after all those years of struggling to make do. I was going through her papers the other day and I found she'd got £36,000 in her savings account at the bank, and a few hundred more in her current account. As well as this there were some Premium Bonds and a couple of ISAs, and £12,500 in the farm account. She was rolling in it, but that didn't stop her from acting as if she was skint. I remember the parents' evening when Miss Dove suggested I apply to Cambridge.

Our Mam looked horrified. 'Cambridge?' she said. 'I can't afford to send her to a place like that. All those posh people, you need a fortune to go there.'

Miss Dove told her that the students weren't all posh and it didn't have to cost more than any other university, but Mam didn't believe her.

The school arranged some extra classes to get me ready for the entrance exam. Miss Dove talked to me a lot about what it would be like to be a student there: the lectures, the libraries and museums, and the social life.

'What about Lander?' you say. 'Was he aiming for Cambridge too?' Well, the answer to that is, no chance. Oh, it's not that he wasn't clever. I think he was always brighter than me, and he was fantastic with computers. He just wasn't interested in schoolwork. Apart from gadgets, his other great passion was sport, especially cricket. He was a fearsome fast bowler, with a perfect line and length (whatever that means; it's what people said). He was in his school's first team when he was only fifteen, and even then hardly anyone could deal with him. He played an invitation game for the Yorkshire Colts and took 5 for 16 against a Derbyshire Youth XI. They offered him a place at the Yorkshire Cricket Academy and he was over the moon, but our Mam wouldn't let him go. She said he had to finish his schooling first, so he had 'something to fall back on' if the cricket didn't work out. The Academy people said they'd take care of all that, he could finish his courses and take all his exams with them, but she wouldn't have it.

'It's madness,' she said to him. 'What happens if you get injured? Or if in the end it turns out that you're not good enough to play for them?'

I don't think Lander ever forgave her for that. After, he seemed to lose interest in cricket. The Walbrough Cricket Club offered him some games. They were a good side and had a couple of professionals who'd played for Pakistan, but he wouldn't hear of it. It was Yorkshire or nothing.

As well as giving up cricket he stopped trying at school. He took to hanging out with a bunch of wasters. Our Mam used to go on at him but it made no difference.

'No point,' he'd say when she asked him why he wasn't doing any work. 'There's no point doing anything, because I might not be good enough.'

I was on his side, he knew that, but I felt I had to say something because he was throwing away all his opportunities. 'You've got to try,' I said. 'There's more to life than cricket. And besides, you can always take it up again later.'

We had a terrible row and in the end he yelled at me.

'You sod off to your precious Cambridge if that's what you want,' he said, 'because I'm doing what I want.'

We didn't talk about it anymore after that. Eventually the school threw him out. They didn't expel him exactly, they simply said that they wanted him to take a term off 'to reorientate himself'. He never went back. He helped a bit on the farm, though not nearly enough to satisfy our Mam. Most of the time he'd be in his bedroom, on his computer.

I said I'd tell you about my name, and why they call me Kerryl. Well, as you know, my proper name is Cheryl. So why am I called Kerryl? Simple. When I was a kid I couldn't say Cheryl, and when I tried what came out was Kerryl. I couldn't manage Shaw either, and if anybody asked me my name I'd say 'Kerryl Kaw'. Everybody used to laugh a lot at that. Our Mam thought

Kerryl was a cute name and it stuck. People called me Kerryl right through primary school, until I got to secondary. There my friends would still call me Kerryl but to the teachers I was Miss Shaw, right from Year 7. Miss Dove used to call me Cheryl, but when I was in the seniors and went to see Dr Fawcett, the Head, she called me Alison. I expect she thought Cheryl was a bit common. I don't much care for it myself. I think there was a celeb called Cheryl on the TV around the time I was born and our Mam liked her so she chose that name for me. Some people at school called me Rick. Rick-shaw, get it?

And Lander? A bit the same. His name is Alexander James Shaw (our Dad's name was James). The closest we could either of us get to Alexander was Lander, so that's what he was. Kerryl and Lander. That's the story of our names. It was worth waiting for, wasn't it?

6

———

HERE

I'M SITTING WITH a folder of Lander's cuttings beside me. He must have started collecting them quite early, before the Infection became really big news. Did he know what was going to happen? He couldn't have, but he must have had some inkling, otherwise why collect and save all this stuff?

There are half a dozen clips that date from right back at the beginning, before the Infection got a capital 'I', but they're only short and they don't say much. You've seen the first few that went into any sort of detail. The next interesting one is a long report from *The Sunday Times Magazine*. It has maps and diagrams which show how the virus radiated from what was thought to be its starting point and spread through South and North Sudan to Egypt, and from there to the Middle East and Europe. It's a long report and if I paste all of it into my diary it will fill it up. This extract is what turned out to be probably the most important part.

> An emergency session of the United Nations General Assembly was preceded by a meeting of

26

the Security Council. Unusually the latter was held behind closed doors, but it is understood that several radical emergency measures were discussed to prevent the further spread of the Infection, particularly to the Far East, Europe and the USA. Among the topics on the table were restrictions on international travel.

Sources refused to confirm that Saudi Arabia is under pressure to abandon the Hajj, the annual pilgrimage to Mecca due to take place later this month at the end of the Islamic year. The Hajj is the largest annual gathering of people in the world, and the World Health Organisation has suggested that it might be deferred, along with other major events across the globe. However, the Saudi Ambassador declared that 'the Hajj is a demonstration of the solidarity of the Muslim people and their submission to God' and that postponement was inconceivable.

Alongside the UN activity the President of France, M. Huilac, is convening an urgent meeting of the leaders of Portugal, Spain, Italy, Greece and Turkey (known along with France as the 'Midi Six') to agree on plans for dealing with the possibility of the I/452 virus being carried into Europe by fugitives, migrants and other illegal traffic across the Mediterranean.

A spokesperson for M. Huilac refused to comment on reports that a suspected case of the I/452 infection had turned up in Marseilles.

Lander has highlighted the last sentence. By then the Infection had taken hold in other places in Europe. People were saying it was only a matter of time before it was everywhere, although I don't think anybody realised exactly what that meant: that all of us, everybody, would one day catch it.

There's quite a lot of this stuff of Lander's and I can't include every single bit. There's one thing that needs to go in, though, because it's really important. It shows the abject stupidity of the politicians whose job should have been to protect us against what was happening but who turned out to be incapable of doing anything useful. It's a print-out from Lander's computer, some sort of official memo. I don't know where it came from or how he got it, but I guess he hacked into some site somewhere (he was always doing stuff like that).

 <u>From</u>: Controller, BBC News

<u>To</u>: Director, Media Monitoring Unit, 10 Downing Street

<u>Subject</u>: Interview – Elizabeth Harley (Minister for Health)/Gavin Martin (Anchor, BBC News Review), BBC1, May 29th, 21.30.

Malcolm

I send you herewith a transcript of the interview with Bessie Harley that we broadcast last night.

Quentin

Attachment:

- **Gavin Martin** Good evening. Those of you who watched *Insights* on the BBC Events Channel two weeks ago will have seen our report on the mysterious virus which has ravaged Africa, and you may have heard of the alarming speed at which it seems to be spreading. The Government has been accused of not doing enough quickly enough to prevent the virus from reaching the United Kingdom. Tonight we have with us Elizabeth Harley, Minister for Health.
- **Elizabeth Harley** Good evening.
- **Gavin Martin** Minister, you will be as aware as I am of what is being said. Is the Government doing enough?
- **Elizabeth Harley** Well yes, of course. We are taking all necessary action to protect the people of these islands.
- **Gavin Martin** Can you tell us what that action is? From where I sit it's hard to see what, if anything, is being done.
- **Elizabeth Harley** The Government has been monitoring the situation very closely from the beginning, and some time ago we issued guidance to travellers to avoid many areas. The Royal Navy has played a major part in the Mediterranean blockade which was put in place, largely on the initiative of the United Kingdom, to seal off southern Europe and prevent the virus from being brought over by migrants and others running away from infected areas in Africa.
- **Gavin Martin** The blockade hasn't worked, though, has it? We have cases of the infection recently reported as close as Belgium and northern France. What do you plan to do now?

- **Elizabeth Harley** I agree with you that the situation is serious. This very morning I chaired a meeting of COBRA to discuss our response to these reports.
- **Gavin Martin** And that is?
- **Elizabeth Harley** Well, I think we have to retain a sense of proportion here. The diagnoses from Lille and Antwerp have yet to be confirmed, and we're only talking about one case in each city. If they are confirmed, then we need to establish whether this strain of the virus is the same as the African one.
- **Gavin Martin** And in the meantime, what steps are being taken to stop it coming here?
- **Elizabeth Harley** Well, Gavin, as you know, the Government has been running announcements on radio, television and in cinemas. These provide guidance on hygiene and on keeping homes and workplaces germ-free. We're supplementing them with leaflets which will go to every home in the country. They tell people what to do if they...
- **Gavin Martin** But this seems to be based on the assumption that the virus *will* get here. What are you doing to ensure that it doesn't?
- **Elizabeth Harley** If you'll let me finish, Gavin, the Government must see that people are as well informed as possible about the virus and what to do if they encounter it.
- **Gavin Martin** So you do think it's unstoppable, that the disease will spread to these shores.
- **Elizabeth Harley** I didn't say that, I didn't say that at all. We're working very closely with our European partners to contain matters. The European Health Executive has set up an early warning system to notify members immediately of any new outbreaks.

- **Gavin Martin** But what about travel restrictions? There are calls from the opposition for restrictions on all but essential travel from and to mainland Europe, and for the establishment of screening units at ports and airports.
- **Elizabeth Harley** Yes, well, I notice the opposition is very good at making demands without spelling out the consequences. What's 'essential travel'? Travel that's essential to you might not seem so to me. And if we were to screen everyone coming into the country, think what chaos that would cause. The whole system would seize up.
- **Gavin Martin** Better to be held in a queue than to die in agony, surely.
- **Elizabeth Harley** Now let's not be dramatic. These blanket controls are not as simple as people make them sound. Pulling up the drawbridge isn't the answer. The fact that we live on a group of islands has stood us in good stead in the past. I'm sure it will again.
- **Gavin Martin** I think people would be happier if they thought the Government was relying on more than the Channel to protect them. Are you confident that everything is being done to prevent the disease from coming here?
- **Elizabeth Harley** Yes, I am.

The next one is the last of the clippings in Lander's collection. It may be the shortest but it conveys the bleakness and desperation of what happened better than any of the others. It's simply the whole front page of the *Daily Express*. There's the masthead, the date, and then just two words, in a black-edged box filling the rest of the space:

It's

Here

That's it. No photos, no text, just the headline. After all, what more was there to say?

7

PREPARATIONS

THE NEXT DAY – or was it the day after? – I arrived at school as usual with my friend Josie to find Mrs Pritchard, the Head of Upper School, at the door of the sixth form block. She told us to go to the hall for a full assembly. Full assemblies were rare. The school hall was small, and getting 1,200 girls and the staff into it was a bit of a squeeze. Because of that, they were usually saved for the beginnings and ends of terms, and there were still a few weeks left before the summer holiday. We were to go straight to the hall, Pritchard said. She wouldn't even let us drop off our bags in our form rooms first.

Me and Josie sat with Mandy Ross and some other Year 13 girls, hoping they knew what it was all about, but they were just as much in the dark as we were.

Everybody stood when Dr Fawcett, the Head, came in, and there was a hush as she swept down the hall to the stage. She was a very tall woman with a pointed nose and grey, almost white, hair tied back. She got to the lectern and made a downward gesture with her hand, and we all sat. She waited a long time before she started to speak, as if she hadn't quite worked out what she was going to say, or at least how to start.

'Girls,' she said at last, 'you will all be aware of the serious and highly contagious infection that has taken hold in Africa. You will also have heard, how the disease has spread beyond that continent and is now rampant in Asia and mainland Europe.

'A few days ago,' she went on, 'it was reported that a case has been diagnosed in Kent, and yesterday there was further evidence, from Birmingham and Norwich, that the Infection has arrived on these shores. For this reason the Government has decided that immediate action is necessary to prevent the disease from spreading further. As part of this, all places of education have been ordered to close immediately, until further notice.'

There was a stifled cheer from a group of Year 9. They got the Head's most regal glare. When she continued she said that the closure was a sensible precaution. She was sorry that there had not been time to inform parents, but it had been necessary to act quickly.

'At the end of this assembly,' she said, 'you are to go home. Go straight there. Do not spend time saying goodbye to friends or teachers.'

There was total silence for what seemed an age. Fawcett stood erect at the lectern and surveyed her school, her eyes fixed and her mouth grim. Some of the staff were looking flabbergasted, others were staring at the floor, and an old girl at the back whose name I didn't know appeared to be crying into her handkerchief.

The Head spoke again. 'Your subject teachers will be putting homework for you on the school's website. You are expected to complete it conscientiously. Those of you in Years 11 and 13 will be wondering about examinations. The examination boards have announced today that they are suspending all examinations, and new arrangements will be made when schools resume. I have been assured that performances in the papers you have already taken this summer will stand.'

She wished us well and looked forward to seeing us all together again, happy and well, soon.

I shuffled along the corridor towards the main entrance with Josie, Monica, Charlene and a few others. Just before the door, I felt a hand on my arm. It was Miss Dove.

'I thought you might like these,' she said.

She held out two books. One was *The Turn of the Screw* by Henry James. We'd read *Washington Square* and she'd been talking to us about James's other work and encouraging us to read some.

'It's a ghost story, of a sort,' she said. 'You said you were thinking of writing one. I think this might interest you.'

'By telling me not to bother?' I said.

'By helping you to write a better one,' she said.

The other book was a fat paperback. I read the title. It was called *Mimesis: The Representation of Reality in Western Literature* by Eric Auerbach. I opened the front cover. On the flyleaf was her name, Angela Dove, and 'Girton College, Cambridge'.

'Read it,' she said. 'You're the only one of my students who I think might get something from it.'

I thanked her. I felt really moved. She wasn't waiting for any of the other girls to lend them her books, and I was welling up. 'Where are you going?' I said, thinking that maybe I could cheat the rule and look in on her.

'I'm going to Chepstow,' she said, 'back home to be with my parents.'

'Can I email you?' I said. She nodded and said she'd text me her email address. She smiled at me and her eyes looked moist.

I walked with Josie to the bus stop. 'Are you scared?' I asked her.

'Course I'm scared, you silly moo. Aren't you?'

'I suppose so. I don't know,' I said. 'It doesn't seem real. All those people dying so far away and you and me walking along the road here in the sunshine to catch a bus. It doesn't seem like it's happening.'

'It'll seem real enough when somebody round here catches it,' she said.

I laughed at her. 'You sound just like my gran,' I said.

She gave me a playful nudge. 'Well that just shows what a wise old bird your gran is, doesn't it?' she said.

The bus came and we got on board. We were both of us quiet for a time, then Josie said, 'It's all right for you. You're lucky, living where you do. You'll be safe. There's no way the bugs will make it up the hill to you.'

I hadn't thought about that. Josie's dad was a baker. They had a little shop on a street of terraces in the middle of the town and Josie, her mam, her dad and her kid brother all lived above it.

'You've got loads of room,' she said. 'We're all packed in like sardines. If anybody in our street gets it all the rest of us will. That's for sure.'

I gave her arm a squeeze. 'Come up with us,' I said. 'Please. We've got plenty of space We can make some for you, I know we can.'

Josie pulled out a tissue and shook her head. I could see she was crying. We didn't say any more until we got off the bus in the middle of Walbrough.

'I suppose this is it, then,' Josie said. 'You to your place, me to mine.'

'It'll be all right,' I said, 'I'm sure of it.'

Josie forced a smile. Her eyes were red. 'You always look on the bright side,' she said. 'That's one of the things I love about you.' She leaned forward and kissed me on the cheek. I hugged her. 'We shouldn't meet till it's over,' she said, 'but let's keep in touch.'

'I will,' I said.

8

———

SIEGE

I COULD SEE that it was sensible to close the school until the threat of the Infection was over but I was disappointed. We all grumbled about St Winifred's but I liked the rhythms and routines of the regulated day. I liked the lessons and I liked my teachers. Well, most of them. I was especially gutted because I wouldn't be able to finish my exams. I'd got four more papers to go, and I thought I'd done well in the ones I'd already taken. I wanted to get an A* in everything. It was a challenge. I'd got eight A*s in my GCSEs. Maths and French let me down – I only got Bs in those – and I was annoyed that I hadn't managed a full house. This time I was determined it would be different. I'd been revising hard, doing two or three practice questions every night when I'd finished my jobs around the house or the farm. I tend to write too much (you'd never guess, would you?!), so I was working to get my ideas down in the time allowed.

Lander thought I was mad. 'School shut, exams scrapped, that's paradise,' he said.

I explained that I really wanted to take my exams and he rolled his eyes.

'Smart-arse,' he said, and threw a cushion at me.

'Thick twonk,' I said, and threw it back.

'Twonk?' he said. 'Twonk? What sort of posh twatspeak is that? What's a twonk?'

I didn't tell him that twonk was Elizabethan slang for a dildo, at least that's what Rudy told us, although he might not have been right because he said it with a kind of leer on his face and I tried to look it up but I couldn't find it anywhere. Instead I returned the cushion, which had come my way again, and I was pleased to catch him on the side of the head with it.

Even though the schools closed I didn't expect that everything else would too, but it did. New instructions from the Government came out every day, and we got used to turning on breakfast TV to see what was the latest thing to be shut down or axed. At the same time the schools, churches and other places of worship were instructed to stay locked and to suspend their services.

'They'll never shut everything,' Granddad said. 'There'll be a bloody revolution.'

There wasn't, although there might have been. An imam in Bedford flatly refused to close his mosque. He was on TV saying that life and death were in the hands of Allah and that the faithful had an obligation to attend Friday prayers. The army threw a cordon around the mosque and there were some nasty scenes. Religious groups in other places joined in. It went on for a few days, and who knows what would have happened if the Infection had not eaten into the protesters and the crowds melted away.

Cinemas, theatres and clubs were ordered to close too. There was a club owner in Shoreditch who tried to start a 'Right to Rave' movement. He set up a website and defied the ban, saying it was his duty to offer music to the people ('And to collect twenty quid off each of them at the door,' said Lander). Police in biohazard outfits raided his place, he was dragged away and everybody in the club was arrested. A band calling themselves The Virals set up a free gig in Roundhay Park. There were about 3,000 fans there when the police arrived in riot gear, and that was the end of that. It was widely reported, the same footage playing again and again. Some people posted messages calling the police pigs and fascists but I think they did a good job. The band was crap!

Very soon after that, sports grounds were closed and sporting events cancelled, and all the time the roll of victims of the Infection silently grew. Within a couple of weeks there were cases in every major town and city. Hospitals were full and A&E departments struggling. There were constant instructions not to go out, and to stay at home. The TV offered an endless stream of old comedy shows and blockbusters, just like at Christmas. Off-air or subscription, the channels were all the same. I suppose this was intended to reassure people and keep them in, but it seemed to me more likely to drive them out. I'd seen all the shows and movies before, so mostly I stayed in my room watching moviesticks on my iPad and reading.

I read the copy of *The Turn of the Screw* that Miss Dove had given me. It's a strange story. Are the ghosts real? No, I don't mean that, I know ghosts aren't 'real', what I mean is, who sees them? Of course, the governess does, but does Mrs Grose, the housekeeper? Do Miles and Flora, the children? Can ghosts exist for one person and not for another? Is it all happening inside the governess's head?

I started on *Mimesis* but it was hard going. I've read only a few of the works Auerbach talks about. Some of the early quotes are in Latin, and although there's a translation it puts you off. I've never done Latin and it makes no sense to me! I made a list of the books I need to read to help me understand it. Where would I get them? The libraries are closed. I decided it would be better to wait till the libraries opened again, and I put it aside and went back to the moviesticks.

I settled into our new routine far better than Lander, although he should have been used to having time on his hands. I helped with the animals and did odd jobs around the farm. I've always done the milking during the school holidays and now I took it over completely. It meant getting up early, but even on a chilly morning sitting in the semi-dark in the sweet-smelling barn, my head against Bonnie's or Dolly's ample flank, music on my iPod (I was developing a taste for classical music. Who'd have thought it?) was very soothing. The world of the Infection seemed like another planet. I felt safe. Like most farms we had no near neighbours, there were no callers and we saw nobody. There was plenty of food so we did not need to go down to Walbrough. How could the Infection get to us up here? All we had to do was carry on as normal, sit tight and hope that the people in the valley would be all right too.

Our Mam had laid in a stock of antiseptic wipes, and she made Lander and me go round twice a day wiping everything: doors, furniture, drawer handles, surfaces, anything that anybody touched. I volunteered for the mornings and left the evenings for Lander because he's hopeless in the morning. I didn't think all the wiping was necessary but I did my stint thoroughly to please our Mam. Lander skived off and did his badly.

'What's the point?' he said when I grumbled at him. 'Either we're safe up here or we're not, and a bit of wiping isn't going to make any difference.'

'How do you know that?' I said. I was angry with him and I told him he was a selfish, lazy slob.

'Great,' he said, 'you want to do it, knock yourself out!' and he flung down the packet of wipes and stamped out. I finished off for our Mam.

Lander had a problem: he didn't seem able to settle down. Although the news reports were upsetting and I felt very sorry for the poor people who were suffering, I was content with our lives at the farm. I didn't want it to go on like that for always but I had no doubt that things would soon get back to normal, and while it lasted it was quite cosy. Lander, on the other hand, fretted. He missed his friends and whatever it was they did when they were all together. He didn't want to be here, but there was nowhere he could go.

We had plenty of warnings that the Infection was coming closer. It got to Birmingham, then Derby, Nottingham, Sheffield, Wakefield, Leeds, Bradford, Stafford, Manchester, Oldham. It was like an advancing army, throwing a ring around us. Even though it seemed clear now that it would reach our valley we thought we'd have more time to prepare. We didn't. It was as swift and unexpected as a knife from a stranger in the dark. In the cities it spread amazingly quickly because people lived and worked closely together. One infected person on a tram in Manchester could give it to all the other passengers, and they would take it home and pass it on to their families and friends. The people on the tram wouldn't know they were carrying it and those they met wouldn't know they were being infected. They would all consider themselves fine. Then a week to ten days later the passengers would start to feel ill, and soon after that all their contacts would too.

We all knew the Infection could take hold easily and quickly, but nobody had realised what that meant. So it was all a scramble, and it seemed that everything the authorities did could be described in the same way: a good idea that might have been useful if it had been done sooner, but was now far too late.

Take, for example, the biohazard suits. Apparently there were loads of these, and masks, which had been put into store a few years ago when MI5 uncovered a germ warfare plot and there was a big scare. The problem was that at first no one knew where they were all kept. It took days to locate them, and then even longer to transport them and give them out. And they weren't much use anyway. Because they were old and hadn't been stored properly the plastic of some of them had deteriorated so that they split easily. Also, there weren't enough of them, and a rule was made that only essential workers, people under thirty-five and pregnant and nursing mothers could have them. That meant that me and Lander got one each, but our Mam, Gran and Granddad didn't. I wanted our Mam to have mine but there was no way she would. 'We're expendable,' said Granddad. I don't think he was being bitter. He was just stating what seemed to him to be an obvious fact.

The Government set up Infection Control Centres (ICCs) in every town. These were supposed to take some of the pressure off the hospitals. The ICCs offered first-line care and were meant to give out the bio suits and the literature but they were badly organised and the staff poorly trained. The ICC for Walbrough took over the Health Centre. It commandeered the premises and seized the ambulances and emergency vehicles. However, it was all done in a rush, communications went adrift and orders were misunderstood. The existing Health Centre staff, including the doctors, nurses and ambulance drivers, suddenly found themselves with no premises, no equipment and no jobs to do. They were skilled people but there was no one organising them and they drifted away.

Later, after the Infection had taken hold, the job of the ICC changed to collecting and cremating the corpses. It couldn't do it. There were so many bodies and some were being left to rot. I know this because I saw them.

Every night on TV there were news updates. They were trying to say that the situation was under control and everything would soon be back to normal but we knew that wasn't true. People called each other and QuickChatted and posted online, so it was easy to find out what the real situation was. By now the internet sites were buzzing with gossip about shortages and it was impossible to get online grocery deliveries. Some sites started offering basic things – eggs, milk, bread, cereal, jam, soap – for silly money. Others offered to do your shopping for you, sterilise the packaging and bring it to your door. There was news of people panic buying and there was looting. The police were attacked in Bradford when they were trying to stop a crowd breaking into a supermarket.

One morning I heard our Mam bang on Lander's door. 'Come on,' she said. 'I'm going into Walbrough to get supplies and I need some help.'

There was the usual grumpy Neanderthal grunting from my brother, but he did get up.

'Suits on,' said our Mam, when Lander eventually appeared downstairs. Me and Lander put on our bio suits. I certainly felt foolish and I'm sure he did too, and I felt embarrassed that we had suits and our Mam didn't.

'Ooh, you do look a picture,' said our Mam, reaching to chuck Lander's cheek. He pushed her hand away. We climbed into the Land Rover and Mam drove us down the hill.

'Well, will you look at that?' she said as we approached the town.

There were police and army everywhere, all dressed in orange biohazard suits. Some of them had guns. A lot of the shops had been boarded up and only ones selling essentials were open.

'There's nothing much about, so at least parking won't be a problem,' our Mam said as she swung into the supermarket car park. 'Looks like we'll have to queue, though.'

We joined the straggling line of would-be shoppers waiting patiently outside the store. Some of them were wearing biohazard suits, but a lot weren't.

'Keep apart,' a soldier barked. 'Stay at arm's length from everyone else. Don't close up.'

There were two suited people at the door. One of them gave us hand wipes and told us to cover our eyes and mouth and step one at a time into a sort of plastic tent. 'Stay inside until you hear the buzzer,' she said. As soon as we were inside the tent a flap closed behind us. Me and Lander pulled on our masks, Mam held a cloth to her face and the space filled with a very fine mist. Then the buzzer went off and we walked out the other side of the tent into the shop.

What we found was not a supermarket any more. There was just a long counter across the tills, with some of the shop people behind it, all in bio suits. We weren't allowed to go to the shelves. Mam had to show them her ID and they looked on their computer to check our household entitlement. Then we had to tell them what we wanted, up to the number of points we were allowed, and they fetched it. When we'd finished our Mam paid and we went out by a different door.

'I paid for all that,' said our Mam, 'but I wonder if money's going to be any good for much longer.' I expect she was thinking about her £36,000.

When our Mam told Granddad about our trip he decided to take the tractor and trailer into the town to see what he could find.

'We've got to get what we can while we can,' he said to Gran. 'There'll be no end of useful stuff lying around down there and soon it'll all be gone.'

He took Lander and was away for hours. I don't know what we expected, Gran, Mam and me, but we didn't think he'd come back with the trailer piled high with wooden pallets. He looked pleased with himself.

'Is that it?' said Gran. 'Is that all you could get? What on earth have you brought those for?'

'We found them at the back of Lamb's Sweets,' said Granddad. 'There must be another hundred there. I'll go down again tomorrow for some more.'

Gran thought he was mad and told him so.

'You never know what will come in handy if things go on like this,' said Granddad. 'Pallets are very useful. I can make things out of them. We can use the wood for repairs. We can burn them. You'll be glad of these, mark my words.'

He took the trailer around the back of the barn and I helped him and Lander stack the pallets against the wall. I didn't know then what I would eventually use them for.

9

———————

A VISITOR

I WAS MISSING my friends, especially Josie. After the school closed I talked to her every day on my mobile. I texted her and sent her messages and pictures on QuickChat and iKnowU and we'd spend hours on Face2Face.

Then two days went by and I didn't hear from her and she didn't answer my calls. I texted her and said I didn't care about the Infection, I wanted to come and see her and I'd walk down the hill and we could meet at the park. Within a few minutes my phone rang and I saw it was her.

'Josie?' I said. There was no answer. I thought maybe she didn't want to see me. Then I realised she was crying.

'Don't come,' she said. 'Don't come anywhere near me.'

'Why ever not?' I said. 'What's the matter?'

'My mam's got it,' she said. 'She went down with it yesterday and George (her brother) has got it too and I expect I'll be next.'

I cried too then. It was the worst phone call, neither of us saying anything, neither wanting to drop the call and both of us crying.

I messaged Josie that evening and she replied. She said that I was the best friend she could have and she loved me. I messaged her again in the morning. She didn't respond. I called her number and there was no answer. I tried the landline but got a number-suspended tone. I wanted to go to her house to find out what had happened but Lander talked me out of it. He said I was being selfish.

'What happens if you catch it and bring it back here?' he said. 'Do you want to infect all of us?'

I called some of my other friends. Penny Cross lives on the same street as Josie. She said she didn't know about Josie herself but she'd seen an ambulance outside her house. I said that might mean they were taking somebody to the hospital.

'No,' she said, 'nobody goes to a hospital any more. They're using ambulances for hearses now.'

I asked her what things were like down the hill. She didn't want to talk about it. I called Suzy Simmonds but it went through to voicemail. I went on iKnowU but nobody in my pod had posted for two days. I put out a *Holler*. There was only one reply and that took an hour. It was from Steve, the last boy I'd gone out with. We hadn't really broken up but he'd moved to Ayrebridge along the valley and we'd just not connected since. We did a Face2Face. The picture kept jumping, but I could see he was wearing a black anarchist T-shirt and his hair was a mess. He looked awful. He said everybody there was dying and all the young people were having a 'Death's Doorway' rave and they were all going to dance and drink and shag and get high until one by one they dropped. He said that people were breaking into the stores and taking what they wanted and there was no one there to stop them, no police or army or anything. He said I should join him because if you've got to go that's the way to do it.

He held out his phone and swung it in an arc so I could see what he meant. There were a lot of people in the streets, mostly young but a few adults too. Some of them were half-naked, some had bottles, and some were dancing. Several were lying on the floor, either drunk or even dead. He lingered on a couple who were making out. In the background another girl was puking up. It made me feel sick.

We might have gone on as we were for who knows how long. We might all have survived, because as long as we kept to ourselves up here how could the Infection get to us?

Bryst put an end to that. I don't blame him. He didn't set out with the intention to kill us. He was just looking for some way to help his boy.

I'm going to put this down in detail, even though it means a lot of writing.

I was in bed. It was time to get up but I was putting it off. I'm usually pretty good in the mornings but that day was unseasonably cold. Granddad wouldn't run the heating in the summer, and the house was chilly. I made a cocoon with the duvet and hung on until I could stay there no longer.

I passed Lander's bedroom. The door was open and he was on his back with his mouth open, snoring. Buster sleeps with me now but then he used to sleep on the landing, and as I passed he looked up and his tail thumped the floor. He didn't get up, though. He was Lander's dog and he wouldn't stir till his boss did. I stamped down the stairs but I knew Lander wouldn't hear me. A bomb wouldn't wake him before ten o'clock. Then he'd arrive in the kitchen, rubbing his eyes and expecting breakfast.

I took my parka from its peg and went across the yard to the barn. I remember hearing the wind slam the kitchen door behind me and thinking, 'Good, that'll stir you up.'

Once inside the barn I felt better. I always did when I smelt the sweet hay and the animals. Our three cows were waiting patiently. I gathered the bucket and the stool. Only two of them, Bonnie and Dolly, were giving milk. Molly was in calf but still a few weeks away yet.

I remember exactly what happened. I've rerun it time and time again in my head, wondering if I could have done anything differently. The problem is, I didn't see the danger until it was too late. It just never occurred to me. Does that mean I was to blame for what happened?

Anyway, the story. Bonnie and Dolly are placid animals and don't need to be tied for milking, so I set the stool beside Bonnie, took a cloth, dipped it in a bowl of disinfectant and wiped her udders. Then I began to knead her teats, squirting the milk into the bucket in warm, frothy spurts. When I'd got all I could from her I loosened her and she ambled away. I switched on the cooler and poured in the milk. The barn door was open and Bonnie was free to leave now but she wouldn't. I always milked her first and when I'd done she'd wait until Dolly was finished too. Then they'd both go out together.

After I'd done Dolly I drained off the cooler and filled a minichurn to take to the kitchen. Molly didn't want to go out – cows don't like rain – but I shooed her off after the others and stepped out to close the barn door, and that's when I saw him. He was about twenty metres away and standing perfectly still. I thought he was cradling a bundle of rags, but then I saw it was a child wrapped in a dirty blanket. I thought it must be dead because its limbs were hanging loose and its head lolled back. The man took two paces towards me and I backed into the doorway.

'Stay there, don't come near me,' I shouted.

'Please, please,' he said, 'please don't go. I need help. Please.'

He had a slight accent, middle European, I thought. He took another step towards me and I backed away.

'What do you want?' I said. 'You can't come in.' My voice was hard and he seemed to flinch.

'My boy,' he said, 'he is ill. Please help me. Please.'

The child moaned and rolled its head towards me. The face was pale, the eyes bloodshot, and now he was closer I could see he was shivering.

'I mean you no harm,' the man said. 'We need help, somewhere to rest for a short time. That's all I ask, and some water, that's all. My name is Bryst. I'm a musician. I was on my way to my brother in Manchester when my boy got sick. It's only a cold, it's not the Infection. Please trust me.'

I didn't believe him. I could see the boy was infected and I shouldn't have listened to him. I should have run back to the house and shouted for Granddad or Lander to come and drive him away, but I couldn't. The boy looked to be in pain, and the man who said his name was Bryst seemed so sad. He was desperate, but he wasn't threatening or grovelling, he was dignified. I felt sorry for them. I had to help.

'Follow me,' I said. 'And stay back. Don't come any nearer.'

I led the way towards the house and pointed to a spot in the yard about three metres away from the kitchen door. 'Stay there,' I said.

I went inside and shut the door firmly behind me. Granddad was at the table with a mug of tea, watching the morning news. Gran was frying bacon. I wondered if Bryst was hungry. He must be, he looked starving. His face was so thin and the hands holding his son were long-fingered and bony.

'There's somebody outside. He's got a little lad with him,' I said.

Gran dropped the skillet and our Mam looked horrified. Granddad went to the door and looked out. He didn't say anything to Bryst but he shut the door again.

'The boy's ill,' I said. 'The chap says he's got a cold.'

Granddad went into the hall and came back with one of his shotguns.

'Where are you going with that?' said Gran.

'I'm going to see him off before they infect us, that's where I'm going.'

'You're going to see off a sick child? With a shotgun?' Gran blocked the door to the yard and folded her arms.

For a moment they faced each other, but Gran held her ground and Granddad looked down. 'Anyway, it's not loaded,' he mumbled. He broke the gun and laid it on the table. He looked up at Gran and nodded. She'd won.

'Right,' said Granddad. 'This is what we'll do. Kerryl, you put on your bio-suit. I'll borrow Lander's. You and me'll go out and take a look at the boy to see if it really is just a cold he's got, or if it's more serious.'

'Give you three guesses,' said Lander who'd come into the kitchen to see what all the fuss was. He was happy to get up now the milking was done.

'Well, we'll see,' said Granddad. He gave Gran a long look. 'There've been reports of gangs stealing from isolated homes, so, Lander, take the .22 up to the back bedroom and watch the yard in case it's some trick to cover an attack on us.' He told our Mam to stand by with the first aid kit and Gran to lock the door and stay inside.

When we were suited up and everyone was ready, Granddad eased the door open and led the way out. The man had disappeared. All that was left was the child, lying on the ground in a wet bundle.

I searched around to see if I could find Bryst but he'd gone. Meanwhile Granddad spread some hay in a corner of the barn. Our Mam found some old blankets and we made up a sort of bed. Then Granddad lifted the boy and carried him into the barn. I think that's when he put the split in Lander's suit, because it was so tight on him. We dried the boy and wrapped him up. He had a high fever and the next day the diarrhoea started. Then the cramps came. We tried to help him, easing his limbs to soothe the pain. We tried to get him to eat something but everything we gave him came right back up again. There was nothing we could do. The next day the bleeding began, and then it was all over. It was awful when he died but it was a relief too. His cries had been pitiful.

The boy never spoke to us and we never knew his name. We guessed he was about seven. I thought that maybe Bryst had gone to get more help, but he never came back. Granddad phoned the ICC and they sent an ambulance. Lander and I watched one of the suited men load the boy into the vehicle while the other went through the forms with Granddad. Bryst had left no clue about either of them, and all I could do was tell the man what had happened. He said he'd have to put it down as the death of a male child, identity unknown, and if we discovered any more we were to report it. He said we shouldn't have taken him in and we should expect to hear more about it. He left a card.

After the ambulance had gone Lander turned on me. He'd hardly spoken during the time we'd been nursing the boy but now he was furious.

'What were you thinking of?' he said. 'You must be out of your fucking mind.'

I was angry with him for being angry with me. 'What could I do?' I said. 'Send a sick child away? Is that what you would have done?'

'Too fucking right it is,' he said. 'You've probably infected us all.'

'The boy didn't come into the house,' I said, 'and we had the suits.'

'The suits are useless, everybody knows that,' he said. 'We'll all get it now. Thank you very fucking much, sister.'

Our Mam told him to stop swearing and threw him some wipes. 'If you're so worried, wipe everything,' she said.

Lander was right, though. Or nearly.

10

———

A PARTING

I ONCE READ a magazine article about how to cope with the death of a parent. I'd felt terrible when our Dad died, but I'd never really considered our Mam going. She'd had the odd cold now and then, but I'd never known her to be properly ill. She had always been there and she always would be. So it was a shock when the next day I came down to do the milking and found Mam and Gran already up. Mam was in an armchair, a blanket wrapped around her and her head lolling back on the cushions. Gran was on the other side of the kitchen. Mam's hair was dank and stringy, and when she looked up at me I could see she was sweating and her face was flushed.

'What is it?' I said.

'What do you think?' said our Mam, and she smiled at me weakly. Her voice was feeble and she looked frightened. I moved towards her but she held up her hand. 'No, love, don't come any closer,' she said.

I stood away from her, awkwardly, like being told off at school. She told me how she'd been up most of the night. How she'd had

55

a headache when she went to bed and she'd taken a couple of Paracetamol. She woke up after sleeping for an hour or so sweating, her head feeling worse and her joints aching. She shuddered. Gran wanted her to go to bed but she wouldn't.

'I'm all right here in the chair,' she said. 'If I lie down I won't ever get up again.'

Just then Granddad came in from the yard. 'It's all done,' he said.

He'd been getting a space ready for Mam in the barn, where Bryst's boy had been. 'A sort of isolation ward,' he said. He'd moved an easy chair across from the house, and a little table for her to put her things on, and he'd rigged up a light. He'd hung a curtain across the end of the stall to give her a bit of privacy, and brought a few of her things from her bedroom. There was a jug of drinking water, a bowl and toiletries for washing, and a little jar of flowers. It must have taken him a long time to get it all organised like that. He shook his head when I asked if there was anything I could do to help.

'Don't come and see me,' said Mam, getting up. She moved like an old woman as if it hurt her. 'Nor Lander neither,' she said. 'Don't come near me, either of you.' She blew me a kiss. 'It's nothing,' she said. 'I expect it's just a bit of 'flu, that's all. I love you.'

I stood in the kitchen and watched her hobble across the yard. The Infection was here, now, embedded in our family and attacking someone I loved. I felt completely useless. I wanted to get on the phone for help, or take her down the hill in the Land Rover. But there was no point trying to get treatment. Where would we go? The ICC would just send us away and tell her to go to bed. Anyway, it was a criminal offence for someone experiencing the symptoms of the Infection to deliberately go out in public. If we were caught we would be locked up and forgotten. There were even reports of infected people seen out of their homes being shot, along with their carers.

Once our Mam was settled Granddad sent me to get Lander, and the four of us sat in the front room. Granddad told us that he did not doubt that our Mam had the Infection and that she would die.

'No point beating about the bush,' he said. 'We've got to face the facts.'

Lander and me were the two with biohazard suits. Granddad had taped up the tear he'd made in Lander's suit but he didn't want to risk it splitting again, so it was agreed that Gran and me would put on the suits and take it in turns to nurse our Mam. That way someone would always be with her. Lander and Granddad would have to talk to her from the door.

She was too weak to say much, but she tried her best to smile at Gran and me whenever we came in to be with her. I sat on the milking stool at her side and watched her, lifting the water that she couldn't get enough of to her lips and wiping her brow with a hanky splashed with rose water, her favourite. I remembered when she'd done the same for me when I'd had scarlet fever. Her hair was plastered to her forehead with sweat. I moved it aside and thought about how, when I was younger, she used to brush and plait mine before I went to school. I've got a lot of hair, thick and long. She doesn't plait it any more but on a Saturday night if I was not going out I'd wash it and she would brush it for me while we watched the TV together.

After the fever came the vomiting, and then the diarrhoea. Me and Gran had a real struggle to keep Mam clean. Everything we took off her we put into bags, took round the back of the barn and burnt. Next were the cramps. They were awful. All her muscles knotted. She couldn't breathe, her body arched, her jaw locked and her sinews stood out like cords. She gripped my hand and squeezed it so tight I thought she would break my fingers. It hurt enough to bring tears, but I didn't mind. I thought that if I shared her pain it might make it easier for her. Crazy, I know. When the spasm passed she'd lie panting, too weak to do anything except wait for the next one.

Towards the end of the third day she entered what I knew from the descriptions would be the final phase. The cramps eased but she had no strength. She coughed blood. She couldn't swallow so was unable to eat or drink. She could hardly speak. A lot of the time she slept, and when she wasn't sleeping she seemed disconnected, far away.

It was hard. The hoods and masks and gloves took away any possibility of closeness. It seemed that the last contact our Mam would have with us would be through layers of latex and plastic. It wasn't enough that the Infection racked the body, it punished a sufferer with isolation too. Loneliness can be a terrible affliction. I didn't fully understand then how terrible but I do now. I also know now that although extreme loneliness is a partner of death, it isn't reserved only for those who are dying. You'll see that when you get to the green diary.

It was because I didn't want our Mam to feel she was alone that I took a decision, and that was when Lander and me had the last of our big rows.

It was clear that our Mam was getting close to death. She'd gone through the vomiting and the diarrhoea and the cramps. Then a strange calm came over her. She was very weak and barely conscious. It was my turn to be with her. Lander came into the barn and stopped in the doorway like he often did. I was holding her hand and dabbing her mouth with a tissue, wiping away the blood-tinged saliva. I'd taken off my bio hood, my mask and my gloves, and they were on the floor beside me.

'Jesus Christ, Kerryl, what are you doing?' Lander shouted at me. 'Your mask! Your hood! For fuck's sake put them on, now, before it's too late.'

'I expect it's too late already,' I said. The shouting had roused our Mam but she didn't look to be with us. I got up from the bed and went out into the yard. Lander followed me, keeping a distance between us.

'I don't want to live like this,' I said, 'afraid of people, avoiding them, not able to touch anybody without being wrapped in plastic. If this is all that's left for us, I don't want it.'

'So you decide to kill yourself? To commit suicide?' Lander said. 'And on the way infect the rest of us too. Wouldn't it have been an idea to talk to us about this first? To talk to me, your twin? Who gave you the right to decide something like that?' He was quivering with rage, as angry as I'd ever seen him.

'I'm sorry,' I said, 'I can't help it. I don't want to say goodbye to her trussed up like a mummy. I don't want that stupid mask to be the last she sees of me. Isn't dying bad enough without having to do it on your own?'

'Everybody has to do it on their own,' he said. 'You're a mad, selfish bitch.' And he walked off.

Do you think I'm a mad, selfish bitch? Do you think I'm cold, the way I'm writing all this down? Perhaps, but you have to understand how it was for me, for us all then. It isn't that I didn't feel things, but the sharpness of the pain that comes with the ending of a life lessens the more times you see it. When death is rare it affects you more deeply than when a lot of people are dying. I've read that this can happen in wartime. People get so used to the killing and the dying that a kind of numbness sets in and they begin to take the violence and the deaths for granted. It isn't that they don't hurt any more, it's just that you become desensitised, immune to the pain.

That's what happened with the Infection. The reports of the first deaths in Birmingham and Norwich were long and detailed. There were videos of the funerals and there was footage of grieving families and friends, mounds of flowers, interviews. The TV, QuickChat, iKnowU and YouTube were full of it. For the second wave of deaths, there was less coverage. As the volume of cases grew the focus shifted away from individuals and their grief to numbers. There was just too much for anybody to take in, and the dead became simply tables of statistics.

Granddad rang the ICC and told them about our Mam, and the ambulance collected her. The next day Lander went down to Walbrough in the Land Rover to collect her ashes. I would have gone with him but he was still angry with me, so he went on his own. He brought them back in a little urn made of shiny black plastic. It looked cheap, the sort of thing you might see in a pound shop or on a stall at the seaside. Was this our Mam? Was this what she'd come to? It was grotesque.

It was soon after this that Lander went. By 'went' I don't mean he died, I mean he went away. Just like that. He'd carried on at me about not talking to him about taking off my suit when I was with our Mam, but did he discuss with me whether he should leave? It's Lander we're talking about here, so there are no prizes for guessing the answer.

11
____

LANDER

THE FIRST INDICATION that Lander was going to do something dramatic came that evening. I went into the front room to have a minute or two alone with the ashes. Granddad had put the urn on the mantelpiece, with the printed condolence card from the Government that everybody got. I think we all thought that there wasn't much point in doing anything special with the urn because the rest of us would soon be gone too. I didn't turn on the light but stood before the urn in the gloom, thinking about our Mam. I was about to leave when I heard a noise behind me. It was Lander, sitting in a corner, alone. There was a long silence while each of us waited for the other to apologise. I gave in first.

'What are you doing here in the dark?' I said.

'What does it look like?' he said. 'I'm just sitting here. I don't need a permit, do I?'

I didn't want another quarrel so I didn't answer.

After a minute he said, 'I'm just thinking how totally bloody pointless all this is.'

'What is?' I said.

'All this,' he said. 'Us, the farm, trying to go on like normal, like nothing was happening.'

I didn't know how to answer. I mean, it wasn't pointless, was it? He'd been angry with me when he'd accused me of trying to commit suicide, so how could he say that trying to stay alive and carry on was pointless? I sat down too. The grandfather clock ticked heavily. Neither of us spoke.

Then Lander said, 'I can't do this. I don't like dealing with sick people.'

'Nobody does,' I said, 'but it's not their fault, they don't choose to be sick.'

'What happens when you get sick yourself?' he said, 'and Gran, and Granddad, and me? Who'll look after us then? Who'll look after the last one left? Who'll turn off the lights?'

'I don't know,' I said.

I sat with him for a bit longer in the dark. I could see from his face that he was in a state – his jaw was working and his brow twitching – but I didn't know what to say to help him. He blew his nose loudly, and that made me think that before I'd come in he'd been crying. Then he stood up. 'I love you,' he said. I was astonished, but before I could say anything back he was gone.

I should have been touched but instead I felt a prickle of unease, a premonition that something was wrong with him. We're twins, and we're close like twins are, despite all our rows. But it was completely out of character for Lander to come out with something like that. What was bothering him? What was going on?

The next morning I came back from the barn expecting to see Lander at the kitchen table like usual, bleary-eyed and waiting for Gran to give him his breakfast. Instead, Gran asked me where he was.

'I don't know. Should I?'

'I thought he was with you,' she said.

'Why?' I said.

'Well, he's not in his room,' she said. 'I thought he must have gone with you to help with the milking.'

'Help with the milking? Fat chance!' I said.

I ran up the stairs and looked in his bedroom. The bedclothes were in their usual tangle but the bed was empty. I checked the bathroom, and our Mam's room, but he wasn't there either. There was no sign of him. I went back to his bedroom. His backpack was gone, and so were his biker's jacket and his trainers. I came downstairs and went out to the shed. His motorbike and helmet were missing.

'Where do you think he's gone?' said Gran.

'Oh, he's probably just gone for a ride around,' I said.

'I don't think so,' said Granddad, who had just come in. 'I didn't hear him leave, and that means he rode down the hill without starting his engine. He didn't want us to know he was going. I think he'll be away for a bit.'

I was suddenly angry. 'Well, at least it's one less mouth to feed,' I said, 'and it's not as if we'll miss his work because he does bugger all.' Gran frowned. She doesn't like me swearing.

After breakfast, while Gran cleared up and Granddad left to see to the sheep, I went up to Lander's room. I was feeling softer towards him now and I wondered whether to change his bed for when he came back. I flicked back the screwed-up sheets, and there was a note. Lander had beautiful handwriting, better than many girls. He'd written, 'Sorry. This is for the best. Take care, and good luck. L.' And two kisses.

I was numb. I couldn't understand why he would leave just like that. I cried a lot, all through the afternoon milking, tears running down my face and dripping off my chin as I rested my head on Bonnie's warm flank. She looked round at me and gave a cud-laced sigh, as if she knew.

We talked about Lander again that evening. 'Where do you think he's gone?' I said.

Granddad didn't answer, but Gran said, 'Don't worry, I'm sure he'll come back.'

But he didn't. And even though later I found out the reason why he left I haven't forgiven him for it.

12

ALONE

THERE'S ONE LAST thing to write about in this purple diary, and it's very hard. It's hard because it's how I came to be finally alone. Funnily it feels worse remembering it now than it did going through it at the time. At the time there was such a lot to do and no opportunity to think, and it was just a matter of coping.

Gran and Granddad were upset about Lander taking off. He'd said goodbye to me, sort of, but he'd said nothing at all to them and it was a real shock to them to find him gone. It wasn't that he was needed on the farm. We could easily cope without him. What hurt Gran and Granddad was that they felt he'd blown them off, given them two fingers.

They talked endlessly about where he might be, and Gran blamed herself for driving him away by nagging at him too much. It shows how little she knew him! Nagging never made any impression on Lander. He was able to blank it out so well that I don't think he even heard it. In the end, Granddad said he thought he must have decided to go because he couldn't stand to be here after our Mam had died. That idea seemed to help them both.

They might have carried on and on talking about Lander if they hadn't got ill themselves. It was about a week after he'd disappeared and I came in from the morning milking to find the kitchen empty. Gran was the queen of the kitchen and every single morning of my life she had been there in charge, at the table, at the sink, at the stove. Today she wasn't. I called upstairs. I'd never known Gran or Granddad oversleep, but they might. It was then I heard a sound from the front room. I tried the door but it wouldn't open.

'Don't come in, love. Stay back,' I heard Gran's voice say.

I knew straight away what was wrong and my insides turned to lead. Ever since our Mam died I'd been waiting for the rest of us to start the symptoms. But a day went by, and then another, and another, and a week and we were all still healthy. A week to ten days for incubation, they'd said. A few more days and we'd have passed that. We'd be all right, we'd have dodged it.

'Gran,' I called, 'let me in.'

There was silence. Then I heard Granddad say, 'We don't want you to come in here, love. Your Gran and me, we're not well.'

Whenever anybody said that there was always the silly, irrational hope that it wasn't the Infection they'd got, it was something less serious. It never was, but I still said, 'Let me get you some Paracetamol. It might be just a touch of the 'flu.'

There was no answer.

'Look,' I said, 'let me in. I want to help you. I feel fine, I can look after you.'

'You mustn't come near. We don't want you to get it too,' said Gran.

'I'll wear my suit,' I said.

I took it out from its sterilising wrap and put it on, although it seemed pointless. If they had got it they'd have been infectious for days and there wasn't the slightest chance that I'd escape.

'There, I've got my suit on,' I called. 'Let me in, please.'

There was a click, the door opened a crack and I squinted through the gap. Granddad was in a chair by the fireplace. He looked awful. He was covered in blankets and he was shivering. His face was flushed and shiny with sweat. His eyes were closed.

'When did it start?' I said to Gran. She was standing by the door. She looked better than he did, but not much.

'Middle of the night,' she said. 'He got the shakes and he said his knees and hips hurt. Then he got coughing and I saw there was blood on his pillow. Not a lot, just a few little specks,' she said, as if that made it less worrying. She gestured towards Granddad in his chair. 'He's been like this ever since,' she said.

They must have been here, in the front room, when I went out to do the milking. I remembered that Buster had been whining softly at the door. I'd just thought he wanted to go in and sleep on the couch, one of his favourite spots, so I'd ignored him.

I helped Gran to a chair near Granddad and made her sit down. 'What about you?' I said.

'Oh, I'm all right,' she said, but I could see that she wasn't.

I took off my mask and slipped out of my suit. Gran started to protest but I said, 'Look, we've been sharing a house. If I'm going to get it, I'll get it. A poxy bit of plastic won't stop it.' I screwed up the suit and put it in the rubbish basket. Then I gave Gran a hug. She held back at first, as though still worried about contaminating me, but then she relaxed and kissed me on the cheek.

'You're a good girl,' she said. 'I expect you're right. Oh, Kerryl, what a business. That we should all end up like this.' She shook her head and let out a long sigh. 'It's God's punishment for all our wickedness, that's what it is.'

I couldn't believe that. What had Bryst's boy done that was so wicked? And Gran, well, there was no one less wicked than her. She was kindness itself. Everybody said so.

'Then let's make the most of it,' I said. I took the bottle of sherry that they kept on the sideboard and some glasses and poured a tumbler full. I looked at Granddad but he'd fallen asleep, so I gave it to Gran and poured another one for me. I don't like sherry, I'm more of a vodka kind of gal when I do go for it, which isn't often, but I knocked that sherry back fast enough.

I helped them upstairs and made them as comfortable as I could in their bed. They lay with the curtains closed, their arms around each other. They didn't want anything apart from water, which they drank and drank because of the fever. I dragged a rocking chair from our Mam's room and sat with them. I held Gran's hand for a long time, but I kept dozing off and nearly fell out of the chair. They both seemed asleep, so I kissed them and went to my room. I was thankful they didn't seem to be in pain, suffering like our Mam had. I lay on my back in the dark and tears ran over my cheeks. Gran and Granddad were gone, there was nothing I could do to save them. I wondered when the symptoms would start with me and which I would feel first. The headache? The aching joints? The cramps? I moved my knees and hips and shoulders and elbows. Did I feel a twinge? I wasn't sure. Did my head hurt? It might have been the sherry. I fell asleep.

I woke in a sweat with my bed covers in a tangle. The horrible certainty struck me that it must be the fever, but I sat up and was surprised to find that I felt all right: no aches, no pains, and the headache had gone. The only symptom was that my mouth felt as though it had been stuffed with polystyrene granules, so I drank some water and felt better.

I got out of bed and went to Gran's and Granddad's room. They both looked to be asleep. I tip-toed away, splashed my face, and went down to do the afternoon milking. Actually, they must have been dead already, because when I went back upstairs an hour later I reached for Gran's hand and it was stone cold. Granddad was the same.

For about an hour I didn't do anything. I was tearful and I cried a bit, but it wasn't as if their deaths were a shock, and mostly I was grateful that they'd not suffered as much as some people had. It's embarrassing to admit it, but I also felt sorry for myself. What would happen to me now? There was no one left. Everybody had gone. I was on my own.

I went downstairs and made myself a coffee. I sat at the table, cursing Lander for being away and wishing that he would come back. I needed him. Buster padded across to me and nuzzled my hand. At least I had him. And Joey, my poor neglected horse that I only briefly saw now and hadn't ridden for weeks. And the cows, although conversation with all of them was limited.

There were two dead people in the house and I didn't know what to do. They'd died so quickly, not over days like our Mam had but in hours, and there'd been no time to prepare. I went upstairs. Of course, I hadn't expected Gran and Granddad to move, but for a second I was surprised they were both exactly as before. When I'd found them their eyes had been shut as if they were sleeping, so I was spared having to close them. It looks so easy when you see people do it in the movies but I don't think it would have been. Their faces looked purplish in the dim light. Was I sure they were dead? The line between living and dying is such a fine one, perhaps they were still on this side of it. There was a loose feather from a pillow on the floor and I held it at Gran's mouth and nose. It was still.

I returned to the kitchen and took down the *What to do when someone dies* leaflet from the pin board. I got my mobile and started to tap the number for the ICC. Suddenly I began to tremble, so much that I nearly dropped it and could hardly hit the right spots on the screen. I remembered that Lander had put the number in the memory of the landline phone so we could speed-dial it. I'd told him he was being macabre and he'd thrown a cushion at me and told me not to use posh words just because I was going to Cambridge. My eyes started to water.

The number rang for a long time before an automated voice asked me for 'the full name and the National Insurance number of the person whom you wish to report deceased', and for the address and postcode of the location of the body. The zombie voice told me that the information had been recorded and a collection would be arranged as soon as possible, but that given the unprecedented demand there was likely to be a delay. It sympathised with my loss.

The system could only cope with one name at a time, so I did Gran first and then had to dial again and queue again and repeat the whole process for Granddad.

I put the phone down and wondered what to do while I waited. I cleaned the kitchen and the bathroom and tidied the front room.

The ICC men came mid-evening, two of them, one short and one tall. They looked spent. It wasn't their faces, which I couldn't see well through their masks, but the way they stood and moved that made them seem worn out, used up. The tall one carried a folding stretcher and the other a large plastic equipment case.

'Where's your suit and mask?' said the short one as I met them at the door. 'Do you want to kill yourself?' He didn't wait for an answer but pushed past me.

'We'll be back for you next,' said the other one. 'Upstairs?'

I took them up to Gran's and Granddad's room. I don't know why I'd shut the door; somehow it had seemed respectful. When I opened it there was a smell that knocked me back. The taller of the men noticed my reaction and put his hand on my shoulder.

'Best if you stay out here, love,' he said.

The ICC crew were brisk and businesslike. They covered Gran in a plastic sheet and rolled her over so the sheet wrapped around her. They sprayed something with a strong antiseptic smell into the bag they'd made and sealed it. Then they did the same to Granddad. They lifted both bodies onto the floor, bundled up the bedding and sealed that too in a plastic bag. Then they carried the parcels that were my Gran and Granddad downstairs, one at a time, to the ambulance. When they opened its doors I saw that it was fitted with racks for stretchers, five on each side. They were all full, so they had to put Gran and Granddad on the ambulance floor. They hooked a webbing strap around them so they wouldn't slide about.

Although they were tired and busy, the men were sensitive and gentle.

'I'm sorry for your loss, love,' said the tall one. 'Who were they? Family?'

'My Gran and Granddad,' I said.

He gave a sympathetic tut. 'They'll be cremated tonight,' he said. 'I have to tell you that while the emergency regulations are in force families can't attend the cremations. Nobody can, they're done behind closed doors.'

The short one was filling in something on a tablet. 'It's a rotten business, this,' he said. 'Fingerprint here,' he said, and handed me the tablet. I hesitated, trying to understand what it was. 'It's just your agreement to release the departed to us,' he said. 'They'll be ready tomorrow. You'll get a text to say when you can collect them.' He meant the ashes.

'Are you going to be all right?' said the tall one. 'Is there somebody up here with you?'

'Yes, my brother,' I lied.

Somehow the night passed, although I can't remember how I got through it. I felt an awful emptiness. The house was so quiet. Before, even when we were in different rooms and no one was making any noise, I could feel that other people were there. Now there was nobody, just stillness and silence. I heard scratching and went to the door. It was Buster. I knelt and hugged him. He put up with it, a puzzled frown on his face. 'I'm going to need you, my old friend,' I said. He tried to lick my face.

I started to pass the time with games on my tablet, but that seemed somehow disrespectful so I put it aside. I found a classical music station on the radio, but they were playing something really gloomy and it made me feel worse. I found an old recording of a chat show online but that didn't work either. It had been made before the Infection and it seemed so trivial, the things people were talking about insignificant compared with what was happening now. I stood on the landing for a long time, watching the full moon. At one stage I got an antiseptic spray and drenched Gran's and Granddad's mattress. Then I thought,

Why? Nobody else is ever going to sleep on it. I thought I might burn it if I could get it downstairs. I wished Lander was with me. Buster rubbed his wet nose on my hand and I stroked his ears.

I went to my room and took from a drawer the two notebooks: the purple one and the green one. I opened the purple one and wrote the title 'Before'. Then I started on an account of what had happened, right from the beginning. I thought it was important to leave a record of my story. I didn't know how important writing the diary was going to become for me.

13

____

DEAR READER

SO THAT'S IT. That's how things got to be the way they are now, and it's the end of my purple diary. If, my dear, patient, imaginary friend, you've stuck with me this far and you want to find out what happened next, move on to the green one. If you've had enough, go and do something more interesting. But before you do either I need to flesh you out a bit. That includes giving you a name. I can't keep on calling you 'my imaginary reader' for the rest of my diary, however long or short that turns out to be.

I've thought about you a lot, and since early on I've had a clear picture of you. If you've cheated and looked at the green diary, you'll already know what I decided. If not, this is how I got to settling who you are.

The first thing was to establish your gender. You had to have one. You could have been gay or bisexual or trans, but that might have made you more interesting than me and I couldn't risk that! So the question was, whether to make you a straight male or a straight female. If you were female you'd be a friend to chat with about girly things and exchange gossip with. Except there wouldn't be any exchange, it would just be me telling you, and I don't know any girl who could stand being constantly quiet while I did all the talking! Of course, having you as a girl would mean that I could say things to you that I couldn't or wouldn't to a boy, but in the end the idea of you being male is more exciting. You'll have to turn your back when I undress and stay outside when I go to the bathroom, but apart from that you can be with me all the time. And there's always the chance we might develop a romance!

I knew from the start what you look like: fair-haired and hunky. You're broad, but not too much – I don't want to be seen out with a barn door. You're muscular, though, and strong. You've got powerful shoulders and great pecs. You can pick me up and carry me – and I promise to lose some of my lard to make that easier for you. You're clean-shaven and have hardly any body hair, I don't like bears. You're tall but not too tall. I'm five foot eight and I can't have you shorter than me. At the same time, I don't want you to be towering over me. Six foot seems right, a four-inch difference between us. We'll look good together, and if there is a romance it's a handy height for snogging! You're white but tanned, you have a strong chin, high cheekbones and twinkly blue eyes. Your hair is quite long and has a bit of a curl to it. Your voice is deep enough to sound manly, but not ridiculous, like a voice in a TV ad. Most of the time you wear jeans and T-shirts (plain, no logos or messages). You look good in shorts because of your muscular legs.

That's the physical bit done. Now, what about your personality? Well, I've got to know you a bit now and I think you are kind and generous. You've got a great sense of humour and a happy-sounding laugh, the sort that makes me want to laugh too. You're intelligent, but not as smart as me. In fact, you're a bit in awe of how bright I am. You play the guitar. You're interested in animals, reading, clothes, the same bands that I like, and cooking. I'll let you have some lads' stuff too: cars, motorbikes, football. Not computers though. I got enough of that stuff with Lander.

The last job is to give you a name, and that's hard. It has to be timeless without being old-fashioned. I thought about Mick, but that sounds Irish. Not that I've got anything against the Irish, I just don't see you as being Irish. I quite like the name Mark, but I've been out with two Marks: one was a dork and the other an arsehole. I flicked through a few of the romances Gran had got from the library. The love bunny in the first one is called Jake. I quite like the sound of that, except when Lander was little and wanted a pee he used to tell our Mam he wanted a jake, so it can't be that; I'd just be laughing at you all the time! Another from the romances is Brad. That has kind of an Australian twang but it doesn't seem classy enough. Sam might be a possibility, except there was a girl called Sam in our form at school and she was a bit weird (well, she was a lot weird actually!). Tod, Simon, Martin, Matt – maybe, but none of them seems quite right.

Then it comes to me: Adam. You're called Adam. It's short, virile, and strong, and it fits you perfectly. So, Adam, meet your Eve.

THE GREEN DIARY (NOW)

14

ASHES TO ASHES

My new diary starts today. That's because it's different now. Up till two days ago there was always somebody else here asking, giving, ordering, wanting, or just being there. Now there's no one. I'm on my own.

I collected my grandparents' ashes. No urn for them – maybe the ICC had run out – and they were in white cardboard boxes. I put them on the table and stare at them for a long time. I open them and look at the grey powder. There's about the same amount in each, but there's so little of it. The urn that holds our Mam's ashes has a screw top. I've never looked inside and it feels so light that for a wild moment I think it might be empty. I undo the lid. What's inside looks just the same as what's in the boxes. I know that the human body is more than half water, but surely there's not as much in here as there should be. Is this really all a person is? Have they given me all of them? Or just a bit, a sort of token? Is the dust I'm looking at really my Gran, my Granddad, our Mam at all? The ICC must be dealing with so many bodies, hundreds and hundreds of them. How do they know which is which? How do they keep them separate? These could be the ashes of total strangers and I'd never know. And would it matter if they were? The Prime Minister said when he made a broadcast just before everything collapsed, 'We're all in this together.' He was right, but I don't think he meant all in the same ash can too.

I don't know what I'll do with them. Bury them? People talk about scattering ashes, but where would I scatter these? Wouldn't scattering them be like just throwing them away?

I feel as though I'm being crushed by a colossal weight. I must do something to cheer myself up. I switch on the kitchen TV and scan the channels. There's news (depressing), movies (old), soaps (also old), reality shows (older still), panel games (even older than those), sitcoms and chat shows (dull and out of date). I switch to the ads channel. The blend of seductive voices, bland slogans and chirpy tunes is soothing. I suppose that's why a channel that shows nothing but ads is popular.

I must face up to the question that's been with me all the time since our Mam got ill. When will it be my turn? The best I can hope for is that it will be over quickly. I look at the leaflet that lists the symptoms. One thing the cold catalogue doesn't mention is fear. The prospect of the Infection is terrifying. It's like facing a death sentence. There is no appeal, no possibility of mercy. So why not save all the pain and finish it now? I'm not short of means. There are two shotguns in the cupboard in the hall. They're good ones: Purdeys, Granddad's pride and joy. There's a .22 rifle as well, that Lander used. It can't be that difficult to shoot yourself, look at some of the dickheads who manage it. And it would be quicker than the Infection.

I sit stone still while I consider it. Load. Click. Bang. Gone.

Easy. But is that what I want? Am I so desperate that I want to give up the little bit of life I have left? And suppose I botch it and die slowly and in agony over days? That's no improvement on the Infection.

Everything feels more intense. The breeze from the open window on my face is sharper, the air is clearer, the scent of the fields sweeter, and the light brighter. Buster is at my feet, his head leaning against my ankle, and I can feel every single hair of his muzzle where it touches my skin. A bird sings at a thousand decibels. The sun shines. I can't kill myself. It's not that I don't have the guts. It's that I don't want to. Despite everything that's happened, despite what's in store for me, life, the world, is still precious.

15

FIRST DAYS

I open my eyes to the sun blazing through my bedroom window. The dark thoughts of last night have gone. I slept well, and I get up with energy and a sense of purpose.

How long have I got? A day? More? Incubation is seven to ten days. I check the calendar. Today is Wednesday. I reckon I've probably got till Sunday, so I'm going to make the most of it. I need a plan. Buster nuzzles my hand as if he knows what I'm thinking and agrees. There's a roll of kitchen paper in the drawer. I tear some off, spread it out on the table and take a felt tip pen from the jar by the phone. I draw a circle in the middle of the paper and at the top write DAILY JOBS. Then I fill it with a list of the things that are most important.

- Morning milking (must do that)
- Afternoon milking (that too)
- Hens – check their run's secure (essential, there are a lot of foxes around)
- Hens – check nest boxes for eggs (nice, I like eggs, but not essential)

- Joey – feed; groom; ride (poor old Joey, he deserves some attention and I'd like to spend some time with him)
- Buster – feed; walk; feed some more (he wags his tail to show he supports that)
- Go running on the moor (okay, maybe; I used to enjoy that, it was part of my 'fight the flab' routine, but I haven't done it for ages)
- Cats – feed (where are the bloody cats? not seen them)

I draw another circle for each of the days I have left and write in it the other things I have in mind to do.

- <u>Wednesday</u>
- Dispose of ashes – Mam, Gran and Granddad (some sort of ceremony?)
- <u>Thursday</u>
- Move my stuff downstairs. Bring down my bed and mattress & set them up in the front room. (Easier for me to get to the rest of the house when I'm ill; also easier for the ICC people to deal with what's left of me.)
- Clean the house. (Okay, no one will see it, but I owe it to Mam, who seemed to spend all her life tidying up.)
- <u>Friday</u>
- Prepare a kit for when I'm ill – plenty of water, Paracetamol, spare PJs, washing stuff & towels, bowl (to catch vomit), phone, torch, and notebook (for important last thoughts).
- <u>Saturday</u>
- Text goodbye to all my friends.
- Do a farewell message for my iKnowU wall.
- Free Joey & the cows & the hens.
- Turn sheep loose.
- Buster?

* <u>Sunday</u>.

Yes, Sunday. Crunch day. If the Infection hasn't got me before, it surely will have by then.

NEXT DAY

This morning I took some cash from our Mam's wardrobe. I've always known where she keeps – kept – it and it was not unknown for me (and Lander) to help ourselves from time to time. Not lots, just the occasional fiver to see us through. We thought she didn't know, but I think now she probably did and didn't care. There wasn't as much there as I'd expected; then it dawned on me that Lander must have taken some when he left. I don't mind. I took £40. Then I put on my bio-suit and drove down to the ICC to get some urns for gran's and granddad's ashes. I realised something was wrong as soon as I swung off the road and into the car park. The ICC was closed, doors shut fast and boards back on the windows. A few people were hanging about on the steps, angry and confused. None of them was wearing a protective suit. A woman was crying.

'It's fucking shut,' a man said. I asked him why and he said how the fuck did I expect him to know? Clearly a man of few words. Well, one, really.

'Is it shut for good?'

'I don't fucking know,' he said. 'Who do you think I am, the fucking prime minister?'

'No, I don't think you're that,' I said. He glared at me.

'They've got my Derek in there,' the woman whimpered. 'They can't keep him like that. I want him, he's mine.' She began keening, a drawn-out, desolate wail growing in volume and intensity. The man stared angrily at her.

There was no point staying and I turned away.

It was a shock and a disappointment. I'd decided that it was disrespectful to keep my grandparents' ashes in cardboard boxes, and that was why I'd gone for the urns. I felt guilty I hadn't done so before. I climbed into the Land Rover and came home.

So, no urns. I think I'll just scatter the ashes. It seems a better idea than trying to do anything fancy. There's a corner of the back field where cowslips grow. Our Mam always liked them so I'll scatter her there. Granddad told me that he planted the ash tree at the end of the lane the year he and Gran were married, so I'll put him there. Where shall I leave Gran? She loved sitting on a summer evening on the little wooden bench at the edge of the yard, where you can watch the sunset and see the lights coming on in the valley. That seems a good place for her. Then I change my mind. Gran and Granddad were together for a long time, much longer than they were apart. Shouldn't they be in the same place? I could mix the ashes and divide them, and put half by the tree and the rest by the seat. But that can't be right. It must be bad karma, splitting up a person's remains, like carving up their soul. I'll keep the ashes separate and have a ceremony for each.

How do you die? I don't mean the process of your soul parting from your body, if that's what happens. I mean how do you manage it? You can't just let go of your life, put it down like a bag of shopping that's got too heavy, can you? There ought to be more to dying than that. You should do something special to mark the second most significant thing that ever happens to you. I suppose that's why the deaths of kings, queens, emperors and so on were like shows, with people clustered around their deathbeds straining for their last words. There'll be no one to cluster around mine, but even so, I want to make some preparations.

I'd put in my plan that I would text goodbye to all my friends. I've scarcely thought about them in the last few days, but suddenly contacting them becomes the number one priority. Except I don't want just to message them, I want something closer than that.

I'd called Josie before and got no reply. I know there's no point trying her again. I call Natasha, Charlotte, Suzy and Penny Cross. I even try Monica Woodbridge. None of them answer. I call Steve. His phone goes to voicemail.

'Hi Steve, it's Kerryl. I just wondered how you're doing. Still partying? I'd love to talk to you. Call me.'

I don't know why I say that last bit. I've never been that keen on Steve, and if you'd asked me before, 'Do you want Steve to be the last person you speak to?' I'd have said no. Now it's different. Loneliness kicking in, I suppose.

I'm feeling desperate for human contact, and I do something I told myself I never would. Weeks, months ago I was having a tutorial with Miss Dove. She left her phone on the table when she slipped out. I hesitated for so long that I thought she'd be back and I'd miss my chance, then I picked it up. I wasn't snooping, I didn't want to read her messages or anything, I just wanted her number. The school didn't allow pupils to have the private numbers of staff, but I could get hers now. There was no password, and her phone woke up as soon as I grabbed it. I clicked on 'my phone' and jotted down the number, telling myself that I'd never use it and that simply having it in my contacts was enough. Now I choose it and press 'call'. It rings for a long time, and then a man answers. 'Yes?' he says.

I'm surprised at the male voice and I don't know what to say. 'I'm sorry,' I mumble, 'I must have the wrong number.'

'Who do you want?' says the man.

I'm tempted just to cut off but I say, 'I was trying to get hold of Miss Dove.'

There's a pause. 'You have the right number,' says the man. 'Who are you?'

'My name's Cheryl Shaw,' I say. 'I'm one of her students at St Winifred's.'

'Oh,' says the man. There's another pause, so long that I think he might have put the phone down and gone to get her. Then he comes back on. 'I'm Miss Dove's father,' he says. 'I'm afraid you can't speak to her. She passed away last week.' There's a catch in his voice.

I can't answer him. I can't even say that I'm sorry. I disconnect.

I sit still, the phone in my lap, while the light fades. The banal sounds of the ads channel come from the kitchen next door.

LATER

I run my fingers along the books on the shelf beside my bed. Most of them are set books for our English course. I pull out the letter I keep between two of them. I've read it so often – at least once a day to begin with – that I know it by heart. It's from Cambridge, telling me I've got a place. I look at it for a long time. Then I tear it into pieces. There's no point in keeping it. Whatever happens about the Infection I know I won't be going to Cambridge now.

16

A NEW NORMAL

I still haven't moved my things downstairs, but last night I slept on the sofa anyway. When I woke up I had backache and a headache and I thought, *All right, this is it.* I hadn't made all the preparations I'd planned but there was no time for that now. Buster sat on the floor beside me and licked my hand. I fell asleep.

When I woke up I looked at the clock on the mantelpiece and couldn't believe it: three o'clock, the middle of the afternoon! The other amazing thing was I felt better. I stretched cautiously, feeling for the tell-tale stiffness, but my joints were fine. I got up, and decided I was more than all right; I was good. I dressed and went over to the barn to milk Bonnie and Dolly. They were very reproachful at being missed earlier. I threw some food into the hen run, had a few words with Joey and gave him some carrots. It was so wonderful to see them all again, after thinking only that morning that by now if I was not actually through death's door I'd be standing on the welcome mat.

I spent the evening watching old movies on the TV. I couldn't understand why I was so tired after sleeping most of the day. It was only then that I realised I couldn't remember when I'd last eaten. I thought about it. I didn't feel hungry. If I wasn't hungry I didn't need to eat. That would be a good thing because I could do with losing some weight.

NEXT DAY

I got up feeling stiff and cramped. I make myself some coffee, proper coffee using Granddad's grinder and percolator, not the instant that Gran would make. 'If I'm heading for the end of the world I might as well have a decent cup of coffee on the way,' I say to Buster. I'm talking a lot to him now. He leans against my legs and licks me. I give him a biscuit (not chocolate).

I go upstairs to get the rest of my things. Before I start I open the door to Lander's room. I've not been in there since he left. The place is a tip. Every surface is covered with mess. There are clothes dumped on the bed and on chairs. There are magazines, books, tissues. Some of the magazines are about computing and some are lads' stuff, with huge-breasted girls in tiny bikinis on the covers.

I don't throw anything away. I put the magazines in piles. I go through the heaps of clothes on his chair and his bed, and the ones thrown in the bottom of his cupboard. Those that smell bad I put to wash, and the others I hang up, or fold and put away in his drawers. I straighten the sheets and make up his bed. I don't like things not to be tidy, and I want his stuff to be ready for him when he comes back.

I go downstairs and put on the ads channel. I find it comforting. It's like having people around me but it makes no demands. It's all I want. I don't want news bulletins or useless statements from the Government about how to manage something that everybody knows is already beyond control.

I fill the kettle. In a minute I'll have a shower, but first I'll make a cup of tea. The ad for Guy's fragrance comes on the TV, the one with Jason Ford with his shirt off. I put the kettle down to watch.

There's a small click and the picture and sound vanish. 'Fuck,' I say out loud. I try the switch, turning it off and on again, but although the green light comes on the screen stays blank. I fiddle about with the wires at the back but they all seem properly connected. I try the TV in the front room because that gets its signal from a satellite and not over broadband. That doesn't work either. I flick through a dozen channels and they're all the same: snowy screen, hissy sound.

I have a think. I wonder if there's a power cut. We have solar panels and a wind turbine, and they make most of the electricity we need during a normal day, so provided they were producing enough to power the TV and boil the kettle I wouldn't notice if the public supply went down.

I go across the yard to the barn where all the power stuff is: the inverter, controller and meters. Granddad dealt with all that after Dad had gone. I frown at the dials. I wish I paid more attention to how it all works.

As far as I can see, everything is all right. There's energy coming from the solar panels and from the turbine. Some of that is being fed into the mains, which must mean it's working. The problem, therefore, is that there's something wrong with the TV. Not our TV sets, but the TV broadcasting system. All of it.

I go to my bedroom to get my radio. At least I can listen to that. Except I can't. I turn it on and scan through the stations, but on all of them there's only hissing. I switch from FM to DAB. Nothing there either. What's happened?

An emptiness sits in my stomach. It's as if I've been cast adrift and the rest of the world has disappeared.

NEXT DAY

The TV and radio going off means that something is seriously wrong. I mean, at a time like this wouldn't the Government do everything it could to keep the broadcast networks going? If it can't do that it can't communicate and it's lost control. I didn't expect my iPad to connect to the internet but I tried it anyway. I couldn't connect to anything with my phone either.

It sounds stupid, but I can't do anything except try to be normal. I mean, if I don't do the normal things, what do I do? So I do the milking and the feeding. When I get back in the house I hook my phone to my Bluetooth speakers and put on some music, very very loud. Buster reclines in a corner. I don't think he really has his paws over his ears, I think it's just the way his head's lying.

I decide to go for a ride. Joey needs the exercise and Jesus, so do I, and it could be my last chance. I saddle him up and take him for a canter around the bottom fields. We both enjoy it, but we don't see a soul. On a normal Sunday there'd be plenty of people on the path that winds up the hill beside the farm – walkers, mountain bikers, people taking their dogs and children out – but today there's nobody.

I get back, unsaddle Joey, rub him down and go back to the house. I am not sick. I am not sick! I haven't been near enough to anyone else to be infected since our Mam went, and the time is almost up. If I get through tomorrow without any symptoms it proves I'm safe. I will have survived. **I WILL HAVE SURVIVED.** I wonder who else has. Where is Lander?

It's a lovely day and I don't feel ready to go in yet. I put on some boots and take off up the hill behind our house. When people first come to our farm they think it's the top of the world, but it's not. There's still plenty above us. Buster's up for a walk and he trots along beside me.

For no particular reason, I decide to make for the Bride Stones. It's only about half a mile to the stones but it's a tough climb. Buster races ahead of me and rushes back so many times that he covers the distance at least twice.

The semicircle of monoliths is on one side of a shallow, peaty pool. On the other is a horseshoe of rock, about ten metres high. At some time in the past the face has been quarried, and there are rejected stones around its base, some of them the size of a horse. How did they move such enormous objects back in the days when this quarry was used, when there were no motors, and pack horses tracked the hills?

The Bride Stones themselves are seven huge pillars. They look like a prehistoric monument, dolmen driven into the earth, but they're not. They're natural, some geological freak created when the glacier that once filled the valley retreated at the end of the Ice Age. Local lads scale the stones, treating them as a challenge. Lander once told me that he could climb all seven but I never saw him do it.

I clamber up one of the easiest of the sun-warmed stones and sit on its top. It's too high for Buster to jump and I'm not going to lift him, so he whines at the bottom. I look out at the spread of moorland on the hills across the dale, and Walbrough laid out like a toy town below. In the far distance is more high ground, the faint edge of the Derbyshire peaks. Normally from here you can pick out the landing lights of the planes coming in and out of Manchester airport, tiny pinpoints of light like fireflies, but today there are none. Normally the sky would be laced with vapour trails; there are none of those either. A road, a railway, a river and the canal jostle for space through the narrow valley. All are idle, still.

It's only when I'm up here that I know why I had to come. It was to prove that I am still able to manage the climb up the hill, and because if I do succumb tomorrow to this sodding, evil plague, this is the last time I'll see the glorious landscape that has been the background to my life.

I look down at the pool, dark, with a few reeds at its edge. In the library at school there was a copy of a picture. It was a girl in a long dress lying on her back in water. She was holding flowers at her chest and she was dead. I'd seen the original on a school trip to a pre-Raphaelite exhibition in Leeds. It was supposed to be Ophelia, who had drowned herself because Hamlet had dumped her. If you wanted a pool to drown yourself in, I thought, this one here would be a good choice. A bit shallow, perhaps, but water's water, and that's all you need.

I remember the legend that from this rock you could see your true love on Midsummer's Day. Is it Midsummer's Day today? No idea. I've lost track of the days. I scan the moor around the rocks. No one. I sit on the stone until the sun lowers and I feel chilly. Then I go back to the house.

17

WEEK TWO

A bad night. Despite my euphoria yesterday, I'm still scared of the Infection. I woke up what felt like every five minutes expecting to be sweating and for my limbs to be aching. I got a savage cramp in my leg. It was probably only the result of scrambling up to the Bride Stones yesterday, but in the silent darkness it felt fatal.

The verdict this morning is that I'm okay but I'm knackered. I look in the cupboard for breakfast. There's plenty there but I don't fancy any of it. I'd love to get some fresh bread, like Josie's dad used to make. I wonder if there's any in the town. It's a lovely sunny morning and I'm all right. I could go and look for some.

The trouble is, I don't feel like doing anything, not even reading. I always have a book on the go, but not at the moment. That's crazy. I have a lot of books, and there are books I should be reading for Cambridge. No, correction: there is no Cambridge. There is no exam or syllabus to read for now. Maybe there's no reason to read at all, and never will be again. Has the line of fiction, the chain of creative narrative that is unpicked in

Mimesis, ended? Will nobody ever write a story again? And if they do write, who's to read it? They don't all have you, Adam.

I pick up one of Mam's old magazines but I don't fancy it. Our Mam only read gossip and celeb stuff. Granddad read *Farmers' Guardian* and books about the wars. Gran was a bit of a dark horse and she'd get bodice rippers from the public library, but it would take her ages to read one, weeks and weeks. Whenever anybody asked me what I wanted for a birthday or Christmas I'd say a book. Sometimes they'd buy me one, sometimes they didn't, and sometimes they bought me a book that maybe they'd liked when they were kids but was now ancient.

One of the things I liked most about moving up to St Winifred's was the school library. It was open at lunchtimes, and I'd go there every day to read. I'd even sneak in my packed lunch, although it was against the rules. Girls who'd been excused from PE and games spent those lessons in the library, so I used to nag our Mam into writing me sick notes.

'You're the only girl I know who has her period every fortnight,' said our games teacher, 'and it's always at its worst on games days.' I don't think she minded really. Unlike Lander, I was crap at games and she was probably glad to be rid of me.

I used the library as a refuge, and the characters that peopled the books were a diversion from the things that troubled me during the rest of the day. I became the girls I read about: Anne of Green Gables, Rebecca, Jane Eyre, Scout Finch, Hermione Granger, Katniss Everdeen. It was through the library that I first got to know Miss Dove. She didn't teach me English then but I saw her almost every day because she'd come in most lunchtimes. Once she got used to me being there she'd look to see what I was reading. Sometimes she'd comment, or ask me what I thought of a book. She seemed to have read everything! Then she started suggesting books to me. It was Miss Dove who got me into Jane Austen. And Kate Mosse. And Margaret Atwood.

'Well, I don't think there's any doubt what you ought to be doing,' she said. 'I think you must join my advanced English group.'

So I did, and I carried on reading, right up to the Cambridge exam, right through everything until now. Now I've stopped, even though there's plenty on my shelves waiting for me.

Do you read, Adam? Most boys don't, at least not as much as girls. I've not got you down as a Philistine, though. I think you have a sensitive side. I think you'd read. Anyway, you'd better read this diary, because nobody else will.

Looking back over some of the things I've written I can't believe how normal they seem. Chatty, jokey even. 'How could you feel like that?' you say. But I don't, not most of the time. Most of the time I'm depressed as shit and near to tears. But when I write it's different. It's as if I become somebody else and another girl is speaking through me. So don't judge me too harshly, Adam, if you think I'm not treating what's happened seriously enough. How would you react in my shoes? It's only writing that's keeping me sane.

NEXT DAY

This is scary. After loafing about yesterday and not settling down to anything, I resolved this morning to get a grip. I'm not dead and I'm not going to die (yet). I don't have the guts to kill myself, and besides, I don't want to (yet). Therefore I have no choice but to keep on, and I need to start doing things. So I decided to make a trip down to Walbrough. I wish I hadn't.

I thought the town would be in a bad way, but it was even worse than I expected. I once saw a movie about the end of the world. There'd been a nuclear war and everybody was dying from the radiation. There was this shot of a city. The buildings were abandoned, the streets deserted, and the pavements are broken and empty. There were wrecked cars, and there was litter blowing like ghosts in the wind. Well, when I got into Walbrough the litter was there all right and so were the wrecked cars, but there was something more, something that the movie couldn't convey: the smell! It hit me as soon as I got to where the buildings start.

How to describe it? Well, one day me and Lander were helping Granddad round up the sheep to bring them in from the moor for the winter. Lander was a way off and suddenly he let out a yell and made as if to throw up. He beckoned me over.

'Have you ever smelt anything so gross?' he said.

I hadn't. 'What is it?' I said, and he pointed for me to look over the wall.

All I could see was a dirty grey pile of wool that looked to be mixed up with some slime. Then I examined it more closely. It had been a sheep but a lot of it had turned to liquid. The pinkish bits that were left seemed to be moving and I saw that what remained of the animal's flesh was heaving with maggots. The stink was unbelievable. I'd tell you Walbrough was the same as that but it wasn't; it was worse!

There was nobody around, there weren't even any bodies that I could see, and all the shops were shut. Some of the windows had been smashed and bits and pieces of stock scattered in the road. There were the burnt-out remains of half a dozen cars, and along the road two vans were at crazy angles. In the middle of the High Street was a dead animal of some sort. I couldn't make out what, because it was heaving with dogs, tearing at the carcass and snarling. As I watched the struggle one of them, a really big one, backed away tugging something long and elastic in its jaws.

When I looked around I could see there were dogs everywhere, slinking along the pavement, hanging about on corners, and skulking in doorways. Some were in packs, some on their own. They were a restless, bad-tempered bunch, growling and snapping. I was glad I'd decided against bringing Buster with me.

I drove round the corner to Newell's Supermarket. There was more rubbish in their car park and two more abandoned vehicles. I parked the Land Rover as close to the front of the store as I could. The plate glass windows were smashed, and although the interior was dark I could see that the place was in chaos.

I opened the door of the Land Rover and the rotting sheep stink hit me harder than ever. It was so gut-churningly gruesome that I could barely take a breath without gagging. I thought I would have to give the supermarket a miss, but I held my breath and picked my way in.

The smell inside the store was differently nauseating. There was a heap of mouldy oranges on the floor, and a cloud of green spores erupted when I poked them with my toe. There was a bank of light switches on the wall and I tried them, but nothing worked. There hadn't been time for the staff to clear the fish and meat counters before they left, and all the surfaces were covered in mounds of glistening grey I-don't-know-what. Sticky streams oozed from under the doors of chiller cabinets and freezers. I could see that people had been in there raiding because dry stock had been dragged off the shelves. Packets, tins and jars were scattered in the aisles. Some of the jars had broken and some of the packets were split open.

The raiders had been choosy. The section where batteries and small electronic items used to be displayed had been cleaned out, and the wine and spirits section was nearly empty too. I went along the food shelves. There were lots of tins and jars but I didn't fancy any of them. I've got plenty at home anyway. I don't need anything, and coming on top of the stench the thought of food was making me feel queasy. I helped myself to some hair products and cosmetics. I found some perfume: Summer Girl. Normally I wouldn't have touched it with a barge pole because it smells like a tart's boudoir, but I splashed it all over me regardless.

I was going along the shelves and stowing in my backpack the few things that looked any good when I heard a noise from the front of the store. I moved away from the end of the aisle and crouched behind a display rack. It didn't give much cover but there was no time to find anything better.

The visitors were trying to be quiet but they were making a poor job of it. One of them looked ill, and as soon as he came inside he flopped down by the door and sat with his head propped against the wall. The others left him and made straight for the wine and beer shelves, only one aisle over from me. I kept very still. It seemed as though they might have been there already because they looked and sounded half pissed. I remembered that I'd left the keys in the Land Rover. However, even though it was right by the door the intruders didn't seem to have paid any attention to it on the way in. I prayed that they'd ignore it on the way out too. If they ever left. They looked to be settling in for a long session. Two of them were on the tiled floor, gulping at bottles, clearly starting on a serious drinking spree, although the choice of booze on offer didn't seem to impress one of them. He picked up a bottle and flung it across the store, swearing. It smashed against the wall. One of the others shouted at him. I could see that the shouter was holding a shotgun. It looked old and battered, not clean and well-oiled like Granddad's Purdeys, but I had no doubt it would work. I didn't intend to give him a reason to try it so I stayed behind my stack, very still.

One of them wandered to the end of the aisle where there was a stand loaded with gift cards: iTunes, Amazon, MusicMash, Red Letter Days, and Deezer.

'Fuck,' he said, 'look at all these.' He grabbed a handful of the cards and stuffed them into his pocket.

'What the fuck are you doing?' said the gunman.

'I'm taking these,' said the first one. He held one up. 'Look at this,' he said. 'A day driving a Ferrari at Brands Hatch. Sharp, eh?'

'You mad bastard,' said the gunman. 'They're worth nowt. They're just plastic. You'd have to take them to a till to get 'em activated and there ain't none of them. Anyway, where're you going to spend 'em?' he said. 'Brands Hatch? It'll be just as fucked as here.'

'Dim twat,' said the third.

The one with the gift cards was embarrassed. Anger offered a diversion. 'What did you call me?' he said.

'I said you're a dim twat,' the other replied. 'You're a wanker an' all.' He was up for a fight.

They moved towards one another and the gunman stepped aside to give them room. Then he saw me.

'Well, what have we here?' He came forward and stood over me sneering, superior, threatening, as if he was in control and could do what he liked. I was scared.

The two fighters dropped their fists and turned around. The gunman grabbed me by the hair and pulled me to my feet. He stood back and ran his eyes over me, lingering on my tits and my legs. 'Not bad,' he said. 'Not Miss World, but she'll do.' He turned to the others. 'You sort out your business and I'll do mine,' he said, and winked at me.

The others had lost interest in fighting. They came closer. All three were staring at me now.

'Finders keepers,' said the gunman, warning them off. 'This little girl's mine. You two can have what's left.' He leant the shotgun against the shelves, undid his belt, pulled it from its loops and wrapped it around his hand, buckle outwards. It was now a weapon. 'Knickers off, love,' he said.

I hesitated.

'Come on,' he said, 'we haven't got all day.'

I'd put on a skirt to come down into the town. I don't know why I'd bothered to dress up like that instead of keeping on the jeans I always wore. Our Mam always expected me and Lander to be smart when we went into town with her so I guess it was habit. It gave me an idea. I put my hands under my skirt and took hold of my knickers. I wiggled my hips as I eased them down and crouched to slip them over my trainers. I made a show of this because I wanted them all to be distracted, and they were. All the time I was staring at the gunman, trying to look smouldering and raunchy, although that was the last thing I felt.

I'd noticed that there were some aerosol spray cans on the floor. I positioned myself so that as I squatted my skirt belled out and covered one of them. I took it in one hand and hoped it was something nasty. With my other hand I twirled my knickers. They weren't the sort I usually wear, they were a scarlet, lacy pair that I'd got from Victoria's Secret in Manchester one Saturday when I was feeling flush and flighty. Again, I don't know why I'd put them on today but I think something must have been looking out for me.

The sexy underwear certainly caught the men's interest. Suddenly I tossed the knickers at the gunman. Reflexively he made to catch them and in the second his attention left me I gave him a long burst from the spray can, full in the face. I was taller than him so I got a good angle. He let out a raging howl and his hands flew to his eyes. He stumbled backwards into the shelves and the gun clattered to the floor. I squirted him again.

'Christ! Fuck!' he yelled, his hands rubbing at his eyes. One of the others came at me and I let him have it too. He screamed and dropped to his knees.

The third man seemed paralysed. 'Throw some water on them,' I shouted. He came to life then and rushed towards a shelf of water bottles. Both the others were bent in two, blubbering and wailing. I picked up the gun and ran for the door, chased by their curses: 'Fuck! Christ! Bitch! Cunt!'

I hurled the shotgun into the Land Rover and myself after. My whole body was trembling so much I could hardly start it, and then when I had I couldn't get it into gear. I reversed and hit one of the abandoned cars. There was a thump that jarred my neck and a crunch of metal and glass. I slammed it into forward, floored the pedal and raced out of the car park, crashing the box as I changed up. I glanced at the spray can on the seat beside me. Oven Cleaner. *Oh my God, I've blinded them*, I thought.

I'm not a cruel person. I hate seeing people or animals hurt – Lander says I'm too soft for a farm girl – but I was glad about what I did to the two men. They deserved it, and I wished I'd got the third one as well. They were all infected, I was sure of that, and the one by the door looked almost dead. Had they infected me? The gunman was the only one who had touched me. He'd pulled my hair, and I'd picked up the gun he'd been holding. But he was the one of the three who'd seemed in the best health.

Perhaps he was clean. I dreaded another two weeks of anxiously waiting to see if I developed symptoms.

Back at home, I put all my clothes in the washing machine on a hot programme. Then I scrubbed my hands till they were nearly raw, showered, and washed my hair. I dressed again and went out to the yard, where I drenched the Land Rover in disinfectant. After that I was exhausted. I made myself a cup of soup and sat on the sofa. I fell asleep before I could drink it, a nervous reaction I think. The last I remember is a silly playground jingle going round and round in my head.

> Lost your knickers, you silly mare,
> Showing the boys your underwear.
> Lost your knickers, you silly cow,
> Bet you're in the fam'ly way now.

I wish you'd been there to help me, Adam. I could have done with a bit of extra muscle.

18

────────

ALONE

I'm not going into the town again. What happened in the supermarket shook me up more than I would have predicted. I won't go down the hill again until I'm sure that there's nothing bad going on. Even if I'm not attacked, somebody might see me going back up the hill. They could follow me and find out that I'm here on my own. That thought makes me shudder. The window in our Mam's bedroom gives a good view of most things in the valley, and I've spent a lot of time looking through Granddad's field glasses to see if anything is moving. I've seen plenty of dogs and other stray animals, but nothing human. Even so, I don't want to make it obvious I'm here. I won't switch on lights at night, I'll use candles and oil lamps instead, and I'll draw the curtains.

LATER

I need to do something about gran's and granddad's ashes. Two boxes. Or perhaps one, with a division down the middle, so they can be together. It will give me something to do. That's why I'm lardy, because I don't do anything. I get up and milk the cows, see to Joey, feed the hens and look for any new eggs, check the sheep. Then there might be a bit of cleaning and tidying, and that's the day taken care of. The rest is mine. I don't have the TV but I can play games and watch moviesticks on my iPad. I'm still not reading, but there's my diary and I spend a couple of hours a day on that. The trouble is, all this involves sitting on my arse. I've always been inclined to put on weight, and I have an ongoing battle with my spare tyre. I look in my bedroom mirror and pinch my stomach, and pull a face. I need to do something energetic, something that will burn off the fat. Or maybe I just need to eat less! Do you like chubby girls, Adam?

NEXT DAY

My diary's become so important to me that I feel a kind of ache if I haven't written anything for a bit. Yesterday I was grumpy, grumbling at Buster, slapping Bonnie's rump harder than I needed to, and shooing the hens away. I didn't realise till bedtime that it was because I hadn't done my diary. I don't know why not, I just didn't. So this morning I'm sitting down straight away, before breakfast even, and writing. Perhaps I'll skip breakfast. That would be good for me, although I woke up thinking how nice it would be to have some porridge, made with Bonnie's lovely creamy milk.

So what's new in the forty-eight hours since I last wrote? Well, I'm trying to dry Bonnie off. She's been in milk a long time and I know it should be done because Granddad used to do it, but I'm not sure how. Every day I take a bit less milk from her to encourage her to stop lactating and I think it's working. After that there'll just be Dolly. It will be a relief to have only one cow producing. I have too much of the stuff. I drink a little and Buster loves it, but there's always plenty left over. I could make more cheese, and butter, and yoghurt, but the fridge and freezer are stacked full already. There's rice, semolina, and tapioca in the pantry and I've got Gran's recipe book, so I could make some milk puddings. I don't fancy them, though. I used to love them, but now even thinking about them makes me feel pukey. So I pour a lot of the milk away. I hate doing that and I think how our Mam would have gone ballistic about the waste. I wonder if I could get another freezer up the hill. The problem would be how to get it onto the trailer. I might be able to go down in the tractor and use the bucket to lift it in, and I could unload it and put it in the barn. Then I could store some more.

I don't need another freezer. I have more than enough of everything. I could do absolutely nothing for ages and still have all the food I can eat. It's a life of luxury really. Everything I need without having to work for it. Paradise.

LATER

If there was anybody else left alive I'd know by now, don't you think?

It's not just that the valley's dead, that's only this immediate area, but if there were people left in other places I would surely have seen some sign – a plane or a helicopter or something. Or the TV or the radio would have come back on, suddenly blaring and scaring me to death. My mobile would have started up (I still keep it charged), and there'd be pages of notifications, texts, messages and missed calls. But there's been nothing, not even a reply to the voicemail I left for Steve.

I must think about this. Mr Armitage, who used to teach me philosophy and logic so I'd be ready for the Cambridge exam, told me to deal with a big question by breaking it up into smaller ones, arranging them in order and reaching an inescapable conclusion. So here goes.

- <u>Big question</u>: What evidence is there that every other person in the UK is dead?
- <u>Smaller question 1</u>: Have I seen anybody in the past week?
- <u>Answer</u>: No, just the four guys in the supermarket, and one of those was almost dead. I bet by now the others are too.
- <u>Smaller question 2</u>: Do I have any of the usual signs that there are other people alive somewhere else?
- <u>Answer</u>: There's no TV, no radio, no internet and the phones aren't working, so no.

I don't think there's any need to go on. I think the conclusion is that without any evidence for the existence of another living person, everybody else has gone. Does that apply to the whole country, to the whole of England, Scotland and Wales? Well, it seems crazy, but it probably must. I can't imagine London being dead, with all the houses and the hotels and offices and government buildings closed and empty, the large stores just vastly bigger versions of Newell's. Imagine not just Walbrough's few thousand, but eight million people dead! God, think how that would smell! But what other reason could there be for there being no sign at all of life anywhere?

The news bulletins had been obsessed with how incredibly quickly the Infection was spreading once it had taken hold over here. We already knew that it was rampant in mainland Europe, and that it got there having devastated North Africa and the Middle East. So pretty much every bit of this segment of the big orange was affected before everything went off. The TV news was all about what was happening here, not much about anywhere else, but I remember a dispatch from America that said the Infection was getting serious over there too, that the President and Congress had moved out of Washington to secret locations, and New York and L.A. had practically shut down. But America is vast, huge stretches where there are no people at all. Wouldn't the wildernesses act as isolation corridors? Surely the Infection couldn't have spread everywhere there, could it? And what about the rest of the world? Russia, China and Australia? What about the islands?

Lander said the Infection can be carried by birds. Birds fly thousands of miles, across lands and oceans. Birds could take it anywhere, and if you touched something an infected bird had landed on you'd get it. There were rumours that some animals might be hosts as well. I don't think the Government wanted that spread; they must have been worried about people turning on farm animals and murdering each other's pets. Are Bonnie and Molly and Dolly carriers? Is Joey? Buster? The cats? I have no way of finding out.

One of the last news reports I saw said that the Russians were accusing the Americans of spreading the virus to destabilise them. The Americans were saying it was terrorists, probably helped by Islamic State, Al-Qaeda, the Kremlin, you name it. Before the TV died the accusations and counter-accusations were turning into threats. America said it would go to any lengths to defend itself and Russia said the same. Did Russia and America finally nuke each other? Did some potty outfit like North Korea decide it was going to do something spectacular? Have I survived the Infection only to perish from radiation?

Anyway, having examined the matter fully, Mr Armitage, here's my judgement:

- 1. I should have caught the Infection long ago. I should by now be dead. Why aren't I? I nursed our Mam and I deliberately took off my biohazard suit and sat on her bed and held her hand. Lander bawled me out and said I was bound to catch it, but I didn't. Gran and Granddad got it, but not me.
- 2. No one else is left. If you'd suggested that to me even three months ago I would have said you were terminally stupid. But now I think it could be true. If there were people alive in the USA, or Russia, or China, don't you think they would have come here by now? You might say, why would they? They must know what the situation is, and what could there be here of any use to them? But even so, they'd come to find out what was going on. Wouldn't they, if they could?

So, the reason I haven't caught the Infection is because... I'm immune. There, I've been thinking about it for a while and now I've said it. I could be the only person in the UK, maybe in the whole world, who isn't susceptible to the virus. I could be the last human being left alive. And Lander too? After all, he is my twin.

Maybe I ought to be pleased about that but I'm not. It's not a privilege, it's a curse. I am alone, and nothing I can possibly do will make any difference to anything.

Fuck, I get depressed at this time of night. I stay up late, writing rambling rubbish by candlelight and I get morbid. I'm going to bed. But I keep thinking: is there anybody else? And if not, why me? Why me?

I wish you were real, Adam. I could do with a cuddle, something to take my mind off it all.

19

———————

PROBLEMS

I'm thinking of cutting off my hair. It will be hard because it's my best feature. It's the colour of dark chocolate, wavy and luscious, everybody used to say so. I've always been proud of what Granddad used to call my tresses, and I tried not to be smug when my friends told me how much they envied me. My hair's thick and long... and there's the trouble. It would be a lot easier to have it short. I tie it up but it gets in the way and sometimes it falls down. If I'm busy with something messy and my hands are filthy, that's a problem because I can't tuck it back. It can be dangerous, too. I burn the household waste because if I leave it out it attracts animals. I take one of the wooden pallets from behind the barn, toss it into the old slurry pit, drop the rubbish on top, douse it with petrol and chuck in a match. Yesterday I did that and it went up like a rocket. My hair was loose and it almost caught fire. One side got singed and there was a horrible smell. It scared me. There's also the risk of it catching in something. I remember there was a girl at our school who was practically scalped because her hair got caught in the flywheel of a grinder in her dad's workshop. It ripped it all off and for a time she had to wear a wig.

I feel sorry for women who have to hide their hair. I can remember when I was little asking our Mam why some of the girls I saw in town covered their heads with cloths.

'It's to do with their religion,' she said.

That didn't seem to me to be a very good reason. 'Why?' I said.

'They're Muslims,' she said.

I spent a lot of time wondering what was under the headscarves, and thinking that it must be something truly awful if it had to be kept out of sight. There were Muslim girls at our school, so I don't know why I didn't just come out and ask them, but I didn't. Instead, I concocted a fantasy that they were concealing something terrible, like a hole in their heads so you could see right through their skulls into their brains. I had nightmares about it.

Of course, I'd grown out of these nightmares by the time I went to St Winifred's. Then I just assumed that a Muslim girl's hair must be dull and boring, if she had any at all. Then, when I was in Year 8, I went into the toilets and found Minal Akram. She was in my form and I knew her quite well but I'd never seen her without her hijab. Now she was, standing in front of the mirrors with her head bare. I didn't think she'd be bald but I never expected what I saw. Her hair was beautiful, gorgeously black and glossy. I was astonished.

I said, 'Minal, I never knew your hair was like that. It's lovely. What a pity that you have to keep it covered up.'

She said, 'It's what a lot of Muslim women do.'

At the time I was flirting with different faiths, trying them on. Our Mam was vaguely C of E, Gran and Granddad lukewarm

Methodists, but none of that impressed me. One problem was that I didn't like the idea of some supreme being watching me all the time, scoring my behaviour and deciding whether I should be rewarded or punished. I had school for that! I'd just got around to considering Islam. I liked its simplicity and compassion and charity, but after my conversation with Minal I dismissed it. I like to think that wasn't just because of vanity about my hair.

Until the Infection I washed my hair at least once a week. I can't always do that now, but I try. I love to shampoo it in the bath, and rinse it and put on a bathrobe and sit by the fire brushing it out and drying it. It keeps things normal. Every time I run the bath, though, I wonder what would happen if the solar panels stop working. I suppose it's not so much 'if' as 'when'. It must be ten years since our Dad put them up on the roof to give us free hot water. I have no idea what their lifespan is, but when they do break down I won't know how to fix them. Getting hot water then will be a lot more difficult. At least I've got enough shampoo to last me for the next 400 years.

I know that the sensible thing to do would be to hack off all my hair and shave it back to my scalp. No tangles, no chance of lice, and no risk of an accident. Yesterday I sat at the mirror for a long time, winding it in my hands, pulling it back and trying to imagine what I'd look like without it. I might look a wreck. Or maybe it would look cool. The thing is, I don't want to. It really would be like slamming the door on the past. It would be confirming that things will never again be the same as they were. Of course I know they won't, but as long as I've got my hair I can hope there might someday be something more than this. I can't bring myself to cut it off. Not yet.

NEXT DAY

Molly is huge. I looked this morning at her vast, rounded flanks. I could see her calf moving inside her. I think that gives me a little time because Granddad said that calves go still before they're born.

I'm nervous about this. It might be simple, it might all be straightforward. It's not Molly's first so she'll know what's going on. But suppose something goes wrong.

In English we did a Ted Hughes poem with Rudy, about a sheep trying to give birth. The lamb was coming out head first, not feet first like they're supposed to, and Ted Hughes writes how he had to reach inside the sheep and cut the unborn lamb's head off. Then he pushed the stump of its neck back inside her so that he could reach in and get the legs and pull the dead lamb out.

It was awful. It made one girl sick and she had to run out of the classroom. I felt a bit churny myself. I think Rudy did it deliberately. He'd sold Ted Hughes to us by saying that he'd written a lot of poems about animals, and we read *Thought Fox* and we all liked that. This one was different and Rudy enjoyed the effect it had on us.

When I looked at Molly I remembered that poem. What if that happens with her calf? I couldn't do what Ted Hughes did, I know I couldn't. Would I have the strength to get the .22 and put Molly out of her misery?

20

WEEK THREE

I managed to get through to bedtime yesterday without eating anything at all. Aren't you proud of me, Adam? Yeehaa! I expected when I woke up this morning that I'd be starving and ready to eat the first thing I set eyes on, but not so. I feel okay.

I've taken against mirrors. We have so many of them. It never occurred to me before, but we must have been a very vain family. I have two in my room, there are two in the bathroom and another two in our Mam's bedroom and en-suite. (Why don't I sleep in her room? It's nicer than mine, and I could use the en-suite. I might move.) Back to the mirrors; that's six so far. There's one in what was my grandparents' room, two in Lander's room, one on the landing, one in the hall, and a little one in the porch that our Mam would use to check her hair and make-up before she went out. There's another over the mantelpiece in the dining room. I think that's all but I can't promise I haven't missed one. Anyway, that's thirteen mirrors for what were five people. Hang on, fourteen – I'd forgotten the one in the downstairs loo. Fourteen mirrors, just for me. This means that I see myself a lot, and I don't like it. Sometimes I catch the reflection of a movement out of the corner of my eye, and even though it's only me (well it must be, mustn't it, there's no one else here) it makes me jumpy.

This morning, after I'd done the milking and seen to Joey, I went round the house and took down all the mirrors and turned them to the wall, leaving only the one in the bathroom that's on the cabinet.

I was getting tubby again before the Infection, but once it started Gran and our Mam, and me too, forgot everything we knew about a balanced diet. We were eating potatoes a lot because we had plenty and they're easy. We were eating pasta because it's quick and simple. Gran went on a bake-a-thon and made loads of cakes, and we were drinking Bonnie and Dolly's creamy milk and eating their cheese. The night our Mam was taken ill I found a packet of éclairs in the freezer and I ate them all in one go before they'd properly thawed out. I didn't even offer one to Lander, I just sat in the corner of the barn and guzzled them. I told myself that I was under pressure and I needed the extra energy, as if that would make it all right and it wouldn't just all turn to blubber. The next day I found a box of chocolates at the back of our Mam's wardrobe. She must have been keeping them as a present for somebody, and I ate all those too. Then I made myself sick. Don't be shocked, I know about bulimia and I'm not bulimic. I hadn't wanted the chocolates but I couldn't stop myself from eating them, and once I had I felt an irresistible urge to unload them. It was like I'd blundered into a cycle of behaviour that belonged to somebody else, not to me. I won't do it again, I promise.

On top of all the gorging, I've not been doing any exercise. On school days I used to walk to Josie's and then with her to the bus stop, and back home up the hill in the evening. I was never into games or PE, but sometimes Josie and I would go for a run around the park, especially if there were any of the boys we fancied playing football. Now after my chores I just sit on my butt.

I'll miss the mirrors because I talk to myself in them. Is that nuts? Often when I passed one I'd wave to myself, or I'd pull a face, and say hi. Sometimes I'd stand in front of one and ask it a question. Sometimes I'd read out a poem: Sylvia Plath, Adrienne Rich, Emily Dickinson, Carol Ann Duffy. I know some off by heart. Elizabeth Barrett Browning wrote one for us, Adam.

> How do I love thee? Let me count the ways.
> I love thee to the depth and breadth and height
> My soul can reach, when feeling out of sight.

Isn't that gorgeous? It makes me go all goosebumpy. I like Keats, too.

> My heart aches, and a drowsy numbness pains
> My sense, as though of hemlock I had drunk
> An hour since and Lethe-wards had sunk.

Isn't lethe a lovely word? Lethe, lethe, lethe. I just love the sound of it. I told Josie that if I ever had a daughter I'd call her Lethe.

She said, 'Well if you want everybody to know what a mad cow you are, why not?'

I suppose she had a point, but anyway it won't happen now. I don't believe in virgin births.

I like Andrew Marvel, too. Or I like *To His Coy Mistress*, which is the only poem of his I know. We read that with Miss Dove. I wonder what he was like, Andrew Marvel. Was he as hot as his poem? He was an MP, so probably not.

I've just looked back at this, and all the stuff about eating is a bit embarrassing. It's certainly not sexy. I thought about tearing the page out, but then I thought I'd leave it so that when I've slimmed down we can laugh at it together.

NEXT DAY

I'm in a bad mood today, so you'd better stay back, Adam. I didn't feel hungry yesterday but I do today, and I always get grumpy when I'm hungry. But I think it's working already. Mam's scales say I've lost five pounds! Already!!

I'm wandering round the house trying to think what to do and I see that the liquid gas tanks are nearly empty. They're for the kitchen cooker and the gas fire in the front room. When they're gone that's it. I'll have to get by without. I saw some in the valley, four big ones outside a factory, but they're too heavy for me to move them on my own.

Electricity isn't a problem so long as I'm careful. I've got the turbine and the solar panels. They're enough to keep the fridge and freezers running, charge up my iPad and phone and give me some light. Sometimes there's a day when there's no wind for the turbine and it's so overcast and dim that there's little from the panels. Then I just carry on and do my best to conserve the batteries. I use candles and oil lamps at night. I could use electric lights – we've got energy-saving bulbs everywhere – but I don't want to draw attention to the house by lighting it up like an ocean liner. I know there's probably nobody out there, but I prefer the candles and lamps, anyway.

The taps don't work any but I can get water from the spring in the yard. I found a whole box of water-purifying tablets out the back and I used those for a bit. Then I forgot and nothing happened, so ever since I've been drinking the water straight from the spring. Every day I fill a couple of buckets which I use to flush the loos.

I'm not looking forward to the winter. We get lots of cold winds up here, and sometimes we're snowed in. Keeping warm is always a problem in the winter. I must make sure I've got plenty of logs split for the fire.

At this time of year the cows are outside, but from November, when they're inside all the time, I'll have to muck them out. Lander used to do that with a hose (see, he did have his uses!) but I'll have to carry buckets from the spring. I wonder if they really need to come in. The sheep stay out all year, so why shouldn't the cows? I'll have a word with Bonnie about it. She's the most sensible of them.

Do you need to know all this, Adam? Of course not, I'm just thinking aloud.

21

______

FIRST LOVE

I'm looking through my things, trying to fight the boredom by finding something to do, and I come across my love letters. Five of them. From Federico Garcia Lorca. I start to read them and I think how terrific they are, how much I like them. Well, I should; I wrote them!

It was the Easter holiday in Year 10. The term had been miserable for me because I was being bullied. You'd think I would have got used to it because it had been happening ever since Year 9. Three girls were behind it: Donna Dugdale (she was the main one), Tamsin Sharpe and Jessica Parker-West. They were all September birthdays, and so although in the same year group as me they were almost a year older. They were physically much more mature, too. Donna was tall and blonde and very curvy, and Tamsin and Jessica were well-developed, too. There were some bystanders and hangers-on, but these three were the ringleaders. They all had rich parents. The Dugdales had a fleet of trucks; you see them often on the motorways, or rather, you used to. The Parker-Wests own Medbourne Hall, an up-market hotel and conference centre. I don't know what Tamsin Sharpe's

118

family did, but they were loaded too. These girls seemed special. They got away with things that the rest of us weren't allowed to do, like wearing make-up and jewellery to school. They had the latest phones, tablets, and laptops. They were brought to school in cars, Donna sometimes in her dad's Bentley. Josie and me, on the other hand, came to school on the bus.

They didn't take much notice of the rest of us, so I suppose I brought it on myself by sticking my head up. There was always an admiring, awe-struck gaggle around them, and for reasons that now embarrass me, Josie and I took to hanging around on the fringes of this flock. One day I mistakenly pushed myself to the front. I can't remember exactly what I said, but I was trying to get Donna's attention to impress her. I mentioned seeing one of her dad's trucks and I referred to his business as haulage.

She gave me a withering look. 'It's not "haulage",' she said with a sneer. 'It's logistics.'

I felt a complete idiot. I suppose I'd seen the word logistics on the trucks but I had no idea what it meant.

The bullying started soon after that. They found out I live on a farm, and whenever I came into a room where they were they'd say things like, 'Phew, can anyone smell cow poo in here?' Or, 'Look, it's the girl from udders feeled!' (Huddersfield, get it? Or they'd pass me in the corridor and start singing 'Old MacDonald Had a Farm'.

It was low-level stuff and I didn't really mind. It went on for the rest of the term until they found somebody else to plague and it eased off. Then a few months later it started up again, and this time it was nasty.

I'd always been a tubby kid, but as I moved into my teens I got worse. 'Lardy-arse', 'Jelly-belly' and 'Nelly' were their favourites, and when it got too much for me and reduced me to tears, 'Blubber-tub'. They got a damaged chair from somewhere and put it in my place, and when I sat on it and it collapsed they couldn't stop laughing, even though I hurt myself.

I could have put up with the name-calling, the tricks they played on me and the stories they spread. What got to me was when they took it online. That way it wasn't just our year that knew about it, it was everybody. Somebody got a photo of me and superimposed it on the body of a hippo. There was a supersize porn star called Melissa McStrange and they got a still of her in action and put my face on that too, together with my mobile number. That was awful. I had to change my SIM, but it still got to the stage where I was scared to look at my messages or my pages because of what I might find there. I used to cry myself to sleep every night.

Josie tried to help me. She told them to leave me alone, but then they started on her too, stuff about her having buns in the oven (because her dad's a baker – or was), and she had to back off. She encouraged me to go on YouTube. There was this guy who called himself Sweet Cheeks. He had his own channel, where he helped people with their problems. I did look, but he was in America and it was all high school stuff and meant for laughs: 'A boy I like is in the football team and I'm a cheerleader but he looks at the other girls and not at me. What can I do to get his attention?' and Sweet Cheeks's reply was, 'Take your clothes off'. I didn't think he'd be able to help me so I never contacted him.

Lander knew there was something wrong, even though he went to a different school. One Sunday evening just before the last week of the term he came into my bedroom and found me crying. He asked me why and I told him I wasn't going to that school any more. He pestered and suddenly it all came out and I told him what was happening.

He had a solution straight away. 'You need to distract them,' he said.

'How?' I said.

He thought for a minute. 'Well, you can point them at somebody else instead of you,' he said.

It was tempting, but I didn't know how to do it. And I couldn't bring myself to, it wouldn't be fair to the other person. If I did that I'd be just like the bullies.

'That wouldn't be very nice,' I said.

'Well then, you need to find something else about you for them to talk about, something that's more interesting than your lardiness.' Lander was always one to call a spade a spade.

The answer came to me in bed that night. I needed a boyfriend! He had to be romantic, exotic even, and he had to be somebody Donna and her mates wouldn't know or expect to meet. Suddenly all the details arrived in a rush, and I began to build a story. He was foreign, Italian. He was over here for a visit. Our Mam, Lander and me were going to Scarborough for a few days in the holiday to stay with Auntie Madge and Uncle Ernest. That's where I'd meet him. There would be an intense whirlwind romance and then we'd have to part. It would be so romantic.

The first thing I needed was some photographs. I spent ages trawling the internet. There were plenty of suitable candidates from model agencies but all the pictures were stamped with watermarks so were no good to me. Eventually I found an unstamped face that would do. There were several shots of him. He was about the right age, seventeen or so, good-looking, with floppy hair, a frank gaze and dimples when he smiled. The problem was his hair was fair and his eyes blue and he simply didn't look Italian. Then I had a flash of inspiration. He was only *half* Italian. His father was Italian but his mother was English. That's why he was in Scarborough, visiting her family before going back to Verona (we'd been doing *Romeo and Juliet* at school). It was because of this link that he could speak good English. I printed some of the photographs and I posted one on my iKnowU page with the message that I'd seen this terrific-looking boy and I thought he fancied me.

He had to have a name, and I couldn't think of one. Apart from Romeo, I could only think of Mercutio and Tybalt and they wouldn't do. I did a Google search and there were millions, so many I couldn't choose. I asked our Mam for some Italian boy's names (I needed them for a project at school, I told her) and she came up with Giovanni, Giuseppe and Lorenzo, none of which I fancied. I went into a bookshop and started browsing the shelves and there I found it, on the spine of a book: Federico Garcia Lorca. *Perfect*, I thought. My boyfriend would be Federico Lorca, Ricci for short. I didn't find out till later that the real Federico Lorca was a famous playwright, and was Spanish anyway!

I'd now got his name and some photos and I started concocting the story online about how we'd met. It had been love at first sight. He had seen me sitting alone in a coffee shop in Scarborough, and asked if he could join 'the lovely English rose'. We talked and talked, and when we parted he asked if he could see me again. I said yes and he kissed my hand.

Several of my friends posted back, intrigued and envious, and a girl called Amber, one of the Dugdale mob, replied: 'Really?? Tell me more.'

I knew I needed more than a few photos. I needed something concrete to demonstrate that Ricci was real. I told Lander what

I'd done. I expected him to tell me I was stupid, but he thought Ricci was a cool idea.

'If you need something more to show them, when we get home write yourself a love letter from him,' he said.

'Nobody writes love letters any more,' I said.

'Maybe Italians do,' he said.

I didn't wait till we got home. I wrote a love letter that afternoon. I had to do it on my iPad and print it because I would have to show it around and I couldn't risk anybody recognising my handwriting.

My dearest darling Kerryl, I wrote. *How I miss you. Being apart from you breaks my heart. My arms ache for you. I long to see your smile, to bathe in the pools of your lovely eyes, to hold you under the moon and stroke your beautiful hair...* and so on. Yes, I know it's cheesy but I was only fourteen. I wondered whether to make it raunchy and thought not. Ricci is a good Catholic boy and doesn't go in for casual sex. I put the printed letter in an envelope, addressed it to myself at the farm, and posted it. The Scarborough postmark was important.

That night I wrote four more letters. I really enjoyed doing it, although reading them now I'm appalled at what I put. I looked up some Italian endearments (*cara mia, ti penso, ti voglio tanto bene!, bellissima* and so on) and scattered them in my text. I put each letter in an envelope addressed to me. Then I stamped the envelopes and gave them to Auntie Madge. I asked her to post them to me one at a time, when I phoned her and said so. I told her it was for a project we were doing at school on the Royal Mail and girls were getting people from all over the country to post letters to them. (It's amazing what parents and relatives will believe if you tell them it's educational!)

My scheme worked. On the second day back at school I took in the first of my letters. I made a big show of trying to keep it secret and then reluctantly giving in and showing it. Donna Dugdale's crew were like a flock of birds. They rose into the air, circled and when they came down again they were grouped around me, not her.

My hot, Italian boyfriend was the main interest in our year group for several weeks. Have you called him? Have you texted him? Has he written? When I felt that interest was beginning to wane I phoned Auntie Madge and asked her to post me another of the letters. Sure enough, it arrived the next day. I passed it around and the whole affair was rekindled. My size was forgotten. The important thing about me now was that I was Ricci's girl.

I'm not sure that Donna Dugdale herself ever really bought it. She wasn't stupid, and she examined the envelopes with their Scarborough postmarks very carefully. I'd got Lander to sign the letters and write the addresses, but I think she was still suspicious.

'How come we only ever see photos of him,' she said, 'and not of the two of you together?'

I explained that we'd been alone, and I'd taken pictures of him on my phone and he of me on his.

'Ever heard of a selfie?' she said. 'And this one, there are palm trees in the background. That doesn't look like Scarborough.'

'It was taken in Italy,' I said. 'He messaged it to me.'

Whether she believed me or not, she could do nothing about it. The other girls had all swallowed the bait and were hooked.

I made up stories about Ricci, things he'd told me, things we'd talked about on the phone. I put a PAYG SIM in an old phone of

Lander's and texted myself messages from Ricci. I even had him chuck a girl he'd been seeing in Italy for me. It was like a soap, with all the girls waiting for the next episode.

As the weeks passed the curiosity of my audience waned, and so did their interest in me. They transferred their bitchy attention to somebody else and I was free. Besides, I was making a determined effort to lose weight and I was keeping to a strict diet. No way was I Miss Sylph, but it was showing and there were now other girls almost as tubby as me, one of them being Donna herself!

I met Donna after she left at the end of Year 11. She was waiting for her lift and was nice as pie.

'Whatever happened to that Italian hunk of yours?' she said.

'Oh, we broke up,' I said.

'Whatever for? He was gorgeous.'

'It was the distance,' I said. 'We were just too far apart.'

Why go into all this? Well, Adam, it's just so you know that you're not my first imaginary boyfriend. Ricci beat you to it.

22

STRANGE HAPPENINGS

Something really weird has happened. It's so strange I don't know what to make of it. I don't even know whether I should write it down because you might think I'm losing it. Of course, there could be a perfectly reasonable explanation but at this moment I can't think of one. See if you can.

I'd been reading through the first part of my diary, the purple one that I wrote to give you the background to where I am now. I wanted to check that I'd put down everything you need to know. I'd been sitting so long at the table that my back was aching, so I put the diary aside and went out. I thought I'd saddle up Joey and go for a ride. I started by cleaning out his stable and then I fetched him from the paddock and put on his saddle and bridle. He seemed edgy and kept scraping the ground, and I had to work to calm him down. I thought it might be the weather – it's quite close today – or maybe some stray animal had come by and scared him.

I decided to ride around the edges of the fields. The grass is long and I was thinking that I would have to decide how to handle the haymaking. It should have already been cut by now because the seeds are falling, and that's where the goodness is, in the seeds. The problems are how to do it, and what to do with the stuff I don't need.

I'm not sure how to do it. I can drive the tractor, no problem, I've been doing that since I was twelve, but I've never used the mower or the baler. Granddad and Lander always did that. I'll have to learn. It can't be that hard. Can I shift a couple of hundred bales, load them onto the trailer and stack them in the barn? Well yes, I can. There are forks on the tractor to lift the bales and an elevator for stacking them, but it will be hard work and it will take me a long time. It's not something I'm looking forward to. All good for fighting the flab, though.

I rode into the top field, turned Joey, encouraged him into a canter and headed for the low stone wall separating it from the bottom field. He took it easily. He's a great horse and was enjoying being ridden.

I was keeping alert. Loads of animals have gone feral and they can be threatening. They must have been let out when their owners got ill, or maybe they broke loose: rams, pigs, cows, goats, dogs, even bulls. A farm further along the hill kept alpacas, and I saw one of those ambling around the other day. It looked comical, with its dozy expression and silly haircut, but I know they can bite. The countryside's turning into a sort of safari park. The animals leave you alone, apart from the dogs. The dogs are different. Half starved and wild, they go around in packs and they're scary. I've only seen a few up here but I don't let Buster run out like he used to.

I digress (again). I'm just putting off writing about this strange thing that happened. I know I have to tell you, but I'm worried because I think you might not believe me, and you'll think I'm mental.

Deep breath. I was trotting across the bottom field, keeping Joey near the edge so that we didn't trample down the grass, and then I saw it: the gate from the field onto the lane was *swinging wide open*!

'Is that all?' you say. 'What's the big deal about that?' Well, the big, fucking huge, enormous deal is that this gate is always kept locked. Always always always. Locked with a padlock and a chain, through hoops so it can't be slid off. It's been like that for as long as I can remember. Granddad kept it locked to stop walkers from going into the field for picnics because he didn't like the mess they left. This time, though, the gate was wide wide open. More than that, the chain and padlock were gone.

'Maybe it's been unlocked for some time and you just haven't noticed,' you say. 'Maybe Lander unlocked it before he left,' you say.

Stop trying to be smart, Adam, because you don't know what you're talking about. It's three weeks since Lander went and it can't have been open all that time. I *know* the gate was shut and locked because last week when I went into Walbrough I took the Land Rover down the field track and came out through this gate. I came back the same way and chained it up again. And yes, even though I was freaked out by what had happened in the supermarket I am *sure* I locked it behind me. I can remember stopping and doing it because my hands were shaking so much I could barely fit the key into the lock. I was careful to fasten it properly because I was worried that the men might be following me, so I tested it. I remember too that when I got back to the farm I didn't put the key where it normally lives in the kitchen with the others, I put it in the ammo box in the Land Rover so it would be handy when I needed it again.

I headed Joey straight back to the farm, opened the Land Rover and looked in the box. Empty. So who opened the gate? And how did they know where to look for the key? And what have they done with the padlock and chain? And given that the Land Rover was open with its key in the ignition, why didn't they just nick that?

In a way it's creepy, but I'm puzzled rather than scared. I'm also a bit cheered. Might it mean that I'm not the only one left? That somebody else is still alive? That I have company? Ah, but what company?

Granddad always used to lock the doors every night when we went to bed. I haven't been bothering with that. I shall tonight.

NEXT DAY

I wish you'd been here last night, Adam, beside me in my bed. Not for that! (although it would have been nice!) No, I wish you'd been here because I heard noises. I know what you think; it was my imagination running wild after discovering the open gate. But it wasn't. I know the usual night-time noises. The countryside isn't as quiet at night as townies think. There's always a lot going on, and since so many animals have been roaming around loose the disturbances have been more frequent. They wake me up, but they don't bother me.

Last night, though, was different. It was too rhythmical and deliberate for it to be stray animals. Buster could hear it too, and he was making that low-level, under-the-breath growling he does when he's worried about something.

I was scared. I got up and went to the window, hiding behind the curtain in case anyone was there. There was a moon, not full but bright enough to light the yard. I watched for a long time but I couldn't see anything. I went back to bed but I didn't sleep. I just lay there, listening for more of the noises and thinking about the gate.

This morning the sun is shining. I've been out to the barn and looked around the yard and there's no sign of anything amiss. In the broad daylight last night's noises seem unreal.

How to describe them? Well, it's hard because they weren't like anything, except somehow they seemed human. It was almost as if someone was chanting my name rhythmically – Kerryl, Kerryl, Kerryl – but very quiet and very low, not clear enough for me to hear it properly.

Am I having hallucinations? Am I going bonkers? It wasn't you, Adam, was it?

LATER

Dr Fawcett used to say that we were very lucky girls because we went to one of the best schools in the north of England. If she was right and St Winifred's Girls' School was one of the best, then God help the others. Although other people must have thought it was good too. When I went to Cambridge for my interview, Dr Smith said, 'Ah, St Winifred's,' in the sort of tone that suggested that not only had she heard of it but that she thought well of it. Of course, other girls had gone from there to Cambridge in the past, so perhaps she did. It got rated outstanding in so many inspections that the inspectors stopped coming.

When I told my family that Girton had offered me a deferred place to give me time to 'broaden my experience' Lander said,

'It's because you're a thick farm girl. Will a year be enough?' We had a fight, but a friendly one, not serious.

Well, my experience certainly is broader now.

If I'd gone to Cambridge, what would I have done? Miss Dove wanted me to become a writer. She said I have a talent for description and storytelling. I was co-editor of the school magazine. We changed its name from 'The St Winifred's Magazine' to 'Winefride' (the Saint's original Celtic name) and gave it a feminist slant, and we published a couple of my own stories. But I don't think fiction is me. I would have liked to have been a journalist, a correspondent. Perhaps if the Infection had come later I might have been in Africa, in Senegal where it first broke out. I could have described it, what it did, and maybe given everybody a warning. If governments had been persuaded sooner to take it seriously perhaps people would have survived and not all died.

I might have been a lawyer. There was a courtroom drama on TV that I used to like. It was called *My Learned Friend* and it was about this gay couple who shared chambers in one of the London Inns of Court. When they worked together they always won their cases but sometimes they ended up on opposite sides and then they were constantly trying to put one over on each other.

So yes, I would have liked to have been a barrister. I like the idea of standing up in court and defending the poor girl who's accused of something she didn't do. It's plain to everybody that she's guilty, except to me. I believe in her innocence and at the last minute, just as the case is swinging away from me, I discover this vital piece of evidence which proves she couldn't have done it and shows how wrong everybody else is. Besides, I rather fancy the gown and the jabot. (That's the name for the ribbon thing they wear at their throats. Did you know?) Of course, I'd have had to cut my hair to get the barrister's wig on, so it might not have worked out for me after all. I wouldn't have wanted to be a judge, though. I don't think the judge's wig suits a woman.

I told Lander I was thinking about being a barrister. He said, 'It's easy, but the pay's rubbish.'

I said, 'Don't be daft, barristers get paid a fortune.'

He said, 'Don't you believe it. Go down to Costa Coffee and you'll see loads of staff with 'barista' on their shirts, and they're all on the living wage.' Then he fell about laughing. He thinks he's so funny.

All this rambling! I can't help it. It takes my mind off the spooky stuff like the gate and the noises. The only explanation I can come up with is that it was me that left the gate open. I was so flustered after my narrow escape in the supermarket that I didn't lock it properly and my memory's playing tricks on me. I've almost persuaded myself of that, but it only deals with half the problem. Where's the key? Where's the padlock and the chain? And I still can't explain the noises.

LATER STILL

I go across to the barn for the afternoon milking. Bonnie and Dolly are already waiting outside to be let in. Molly's been in all day. Her calf is due any time now, and she spends all her time lying in her stall, except today she's standing up. I think that's a sign it might be soon. I go over to her and rub her neck and make soothing noises and she makes that hollow sighing noise that cows do. I wish I felt confident about this.

I get the other two in. Bonnie's really jumpy. That's unusual, she's generally so placid, but I put it down to the fact that I've been taking less milk from her, and perhaps her udders are over full and that's causing her discomfort. Perhaps it would be kind to take a bit more, but I want her to give up.

I'm just getting her into position when I catch a movement out of the corner of my eye. A cat? A rat? No, bigger than those, but nothing clear at all. It's more a change in the light than a shape. It's nothing. I get the stool and settle into the milking. Then I'm aware of it again, the edge of a shadow curling round the door. I jump up, knocking over the milk, startling the cows with the clattering bucket, and I run outside. I look down the length of the barn and catch it rounding the far corner, elusive as a wisp of smoke. I run to the end of the building. Nothing. No sign of anybody or anything. I call, shout to come out, but my words die on the wind.

I go back into the barn, shut the door and put the bar across. My pulse is racing and I lean against the wall till I feel calmer. I stay still for a long time, listening for any sound, but all I hear is the wind. The cows stare at me patiently.

There are no more disturbances and I finish the milking. Were there any to begin with? Did I see anything at all? Was it just a trick of the light, passing clouds, the effects of a sleepless night? Then I have an idea: Bryst. Perhaps it's Bryst come back to see how his boy is, to get him. I go to the corner of the yard by the gate and shout his name, Bryst, over and over again. Rooks billow and caw in the trees down the lane, but there's no other response. I shiver, although it's not cold.

I'm sure I saw something. When I come over to milk tomorrow I'm bringing a shotgun with me. The cows don't like Buster, Molly in particular is fidgety when he's around, so I've been leaving him in the house because of her calf, but tomorrow he comes.

Perhaps it was you, Adam. Perhaps instead of shouting for Bryst, I should be calling your name: Adam. Adam. Adam.

23

PRECAUTIONS

I've written before how much I was dreading Molly's calving. I know that most of the time cows calve on their own, but I was scared stiff there might be a complication. It's not just the sheep poem. I can remember that once when one of our other cows gave birth Granddad had to pull the calf out with a rope. Suppose Molly's was to come out back feet first. That's not unusual, I know, but the cow often needs help with it. Suppose the calf dies inside her. What will I do? There's no vet to phone.

I looked at some of Granddad's old books on stock management and they made me feel worse. They talk about scary things like an undilated cervix, uterine inertia, and there are photos showing people using things called 'calving chains'. We don't have one of those and I don't think I'd be able to use it even if we had. I'm strong but I can't heave a cow around. I wish I'd looked up all this stuff on the internet before it went down. Videos on YouTube would be a lot more helpful than fuzzy photos in old books, most of them in black and white. I wish I'd paid more attention to how Granddad handled a difficult calving, instead of just burying myself in my books or my iPad.

But Molly didn't need me anyway. She managed it all on her own, good girl. I slept like a log and heard nothing during the night – probably a reaction to my broken sleep the night before – and I went over for the milking, shotgun in my hand. Buster was at my side, in guard dog mode and wagging his tail, pleased to be needed.

I could sense something was different before I got to the door. Molly was resting in her stall and beside her was her calf! It's lovely – tiny, shiny, coffee coloured and perfect. You'd love it, Adam. It stood on its spindly, wobbly legs and looked at me with big, innocent eyes. Molly licked it. Bonnie and Dolly were leaning over the gate, for all the world like a pair of friends visiting the maternity ward.

I did the milking, feeling huge relief. Joy, too, at this new being, this demonstration that the world is not coming to an end, that despite everything life is going on. It may not be human life, but it is life.

I have to admit, though, that the calf is a problem; or rather he will be, because it is a 'he'. He looks sweet as a doughnut now but he could be a handful when he's older. Little male calves grow up into bulls, and the last thing I want is a rampant, randy bull to cope with. Granddad would castrate it but I don't know how to do that, I wouldn't know where to start. Well, I would know where to start but not how to start, if you see what I mean. Anyway, I don't think I could bring myself to do it.

I don't want Molly's calf, but I don't want it to be harmed either. I'll keep it for now. Molly will look after it, and at least I won't have to milk her.

LATER

I've spent a long time today just sitting on the milking stool in the barn and looking at Molly and the calf. It made me think. What would I have done if there had been complications and Molly had been in terrible, endless pain? It would have been obvious what was the right thing to do, but could I have done it?

Another thought is what would happen if it wasn't a cow in trouble but me, if I needed a doctor? I don't mean the Infection, I'm sure now I'm not going to get that, but there are other things. I dreamt a few nights ago that I found a lump in my breast (all right, I don't put everything in the diary, not at first anyway). I had to get up and check myself. Of course, there was nothing there, but I couldn't get back to sleep again. Suppose I did find one. Or I got something else. Or I had an accident, like Dad did. He bled to death when there were loads of people around. With nobody here I wouldn't stand a chance. And what about the shadow I saw in the barn? Suppose it's someone – or something! – that means me harm.

Back in the kitchen I write myself a list of things to do or avoid to keep me out of trouble. This is it (with annotations). If you can think of anything I've missed, feel free to suggest it.

- Don't walk around outside in the dark. (The Baxters' eldest came home late one night drunk from a party and fell into the slurry pit. He didn't drown, but it was very nasty.)
- Always put things away – don't leave tools or kitchen stuff around, especially not on the ground. (Charley McMichael's mum left a kitchen knife on the floor beside her chair after she'd been peeling apples and walked on it and cut her little toe off.)
- Make sure that everything electrical is switched off when it's not in use. Check wires and plugs regularly.

Don't touch any of the supply equipment without throwing the isolator. (Granddad got a heck of a shock one day off the regulator in the shed. He said he might have been killed if he'd not been wearing rubber boots.)

- Don't leave candles or fires burning unattended. (We've got smoke alarms, but who would hear them?)
- Make sure ladders are securely fixed before climbing them. (Obvious.)
- When using tools or machinery concentrate on what you're doing and don't daydream. (Obvious again, but daydreaming is my thing – it sort of goes with digressing.)
- Lock the doors at night and never leave the house without a loaded gun.

There must be lots more, but these are the ones that come to me first and I'll start with them. I skewer my list and fix it to the kitchen pinboard.

I worry that I'm relying on guns. Carrying a shotgun around with me feels strange. I never touched one before – in fact, I hated them. I'm still not keen, but a gun gives me a feeling of security. It's not just the open gate or the night noises or the whatever-it-was in the barn (no repeats of the latter, I'm glad to say) that have made me edgy. I'm also scared of the dogs. There seem to be more of them every day, and they're getting bolder. I often see them skulking around the edge of the yard or chasing and fighting in the fields. They growl and bare their teeth, but so far they haven't come near me. I know that one day one of them will, and then we'll see if I've got the guts to pull the trigger. Oh, I wish you were here, Adam. I do so wish you were here.

24

———

WEEK 4

I get up late and I spend some time with Molly and her calf (any ideas for a name for it?), and suddenly I'm at a loss. What shall I do next? I have nothing to add to the diary because I haven't done anything. I don't want to read or play games on my iPad. I don't want to go for a ride, although Joey would like it. There's no cleaning to be done. I don't need any clothes washed or anything ironed. What I want to do, the thing that would be top of my list if I could choose anything, is to talk to somebody: Josie, Miss Dove, our Mam, Gran, Granddad, Lander even.

It's not that I don't use my voice. I talk all the time. I talk to Buster, Joey, the cows, and even the hens. I used to talk to my reflection in the mirrors until I turned them round. I talk all the time to you, Adam. What I don't get is hearing anybody reply. I don't have conversations. The closest I come are the movies and shows on my moviesticks that I play and play and play. I've got about thirty and I know practically all of them off by heart so that I talk along with the characters. Sometimes I play more than one part, using different voices. I've got quite good at this, particularly for some of the older ones: *Friends*, *The Office*, *The Simpsons*

(Granddad loved them, Gran hated them), *Batman*, *Star Wars*, *Twilight*, the High School Musicals. If I'd known what was going to happen I'd have got a whole lot more moviesticks and recorded everything I could.

A terrible, hollow feeling comes over me. I may never hear a living voice again. I didn't know that loneliness could feel like this. It's a hurt, a physical pain that I can't locate because it comes from everywhere and is deep inside me.

It's some time before I realise that I'm crying. Then I get cross with myself. 'Snap out of it, you stupid cow,' I tell myself. 'You are alive when everyone else is dead,' I say. 'Count your blessings and stop whingeing.'

Then inspiration strikes. It's been a while since the supermarket incident. There can't possibly be anyone still around in Walbrough. I'm sure it will be safe by now. I'll go and find some moviesticks. I'll saddle up Joey and ride him down to the town. Joey will get some exercise, and so will I, and if I'm on Joey I'll be able to get away quickly if there's a problem.

Moviesticks came after DVDs. Every TV has a slot to take one, and when I was a kid lots of stores sold pre-recorded ones. At some stage, people stopped using them because they found it easier to watch movies and shows online, and you could get absolutely everything on one of the streaming services. There was a second-hand market for the sticks, though, because I've seen them on market stalls and in charity shops. I might try those. Perhaps the vandals haven't hit the charity shops as hard as the other places because they'd not expect to find much they'd want in them.

I change out of my scruffy jeans into smart ones. I seriously think about wearing a skirt because that saved me last time, but it wouldn't be as easy on Joey. Then I get Lander's air pistol from his bedroom. I've scanned through the binoculars and not seen anything down in the town, but you never know. The air pistol is easier to carry than a shotgun and it looks like a proper automatic. It wouldn't do much damage, although a pellet from it would sting and it might be enough to scare somebody off. But as Granddad used to say, 'A gun's no substitute for being careful', so I'll have to keep my eyes open.

LATER

Another disaster only just averted. What is it about me?

Joey seemed happy to be out and was eager to go. I made him wait while I locked the front door. I wouldn't have bothered but while I was upstairs changing I heard a noise downstairs. At least, *I think* I did. I was singing along with my iPad so I can't be sure. 'Catch the Rain' by Far Sighted, since you ask. Do you like them? They used to be my favourite band, although I'm going off them a bit now. I wonder if they survived. I reckon stars and celebs must have, don't you? I mean, with all their money they must have been able to buy things to protect them. But where are they?

Anyway, back to the noise. It was quite loud and sounded like a chair scraping on the kitchen floor. I came downstairs with my heart pounding, holding the gun out in front of me like they do in the movies, and found... nobody! There was no one in any of the rooms and no signs of entry. All the doors and windows were shut and locked. Buster must have heard it too, though, because he was in the middle of the kitchen, hair bristling, growling softly. It was probably only another dog in the yard, but it was the fourth thing that had made me feel queasy: the gate, the noise in the night, the shadow in the barn and now this. So I took the time to look around the yard carefully before I went out, and locked the door behind me.

Despite telling myself to keep calm, my spine tingled as we came down the lane to the open gate. Except it wasn't open any more. Had I shut it? I'm not sure. I didn't think I had but it was closed now. Perhaps I did. Or the wind took it. I couldn't remember. Something as simple as that and I couldn't fucking remember! It's not as if there was a lot of other stuff to fill my head. I think I must be going crazy.

As I'd expected, Walbrough was deserted. There was even more mess, more litter, more rubbish and I think more broken windows, but there were no people and, strangely, no dogs. The smell was still there but not as bad as before. I took Joey along Canal Street towards Chez Annette. That's where my prom dress came from. They usually had something nice in there, and it being expensive was no longer a problem. The front of the shop had been caved in, like all the others, and stock thrown about and trampled on, but there still looked to be some stuff inside. There were a few very classy bags on a shelf but I couldn't see any point in taking them. What would I use them for? I started searching the rails. There was a really nice skirt, aquamarine with splashes of orangey reddish circles. I glanced around – you can't be too careful – and slipped out of my jeans. The skirt wouldn't do up! Even though the label said it was my size!! Must be a mistake. I tried another. A bit better but not ideal. I took off my shirt and stood in front of the only mirror that wasn't broken in my bra and knickers, and took a good, honest look. I'm too fat. I turned sideways on. No point pretending, I am. (I'm only putting this down, Adam, so that later when I'm skinny we can look back on it and laugh.)

Right, I thought, *I've been eating less but it hasn't worked. Now I've got to get serious.* I grabbed the nice skirt, and half a dozen others in a size down from my normal one, and a couple of dresses and some tops, and I stuffed them in plastic bags. I put on my jeans and T-shirt and stamped out of the shop, promising that I would starve myself until I could get into the things I'd chosen. I climbed back onto Joey and whispered in his ear an apology for the extra load I'd become.

Quite close to the centre of town is Almond Street. It's a row of newish, detached houses set back from the road, homes favoured by successful small businessmen or middle managers commuting to Manchester. I thought they were the sort of places that might still have some moviesticks around somewhere. Joey took a bit of persuading to go up the path to the first one and kept shying back. Somebody had already been in there because the door was forced open and the doorframe was splintered, so I wasn't holding out much hope. Still, it wouldn't hurt to look.

I slid off Joey and walked towards the door, holding out the air pistol. I stepped over the broken glass in the doorway, and almost threw up. The smell was unbelievable. I took another crunching step and froze. There was a horrible growling, and the biggest dog I'd ever seen was between me and the door. It was huge, black and ugly. It went for me. I didn't think, I just pointed Lander's air pistol at it and fired. I snatched the trigger so much you would have thought it was a certain miss, but I must have hit it somewhere because it yowled and ran off, yelping like a puppy. I charged out, scrambled onto Joey and urged him away. I didn't slow his gallop till we were well out of the town and on the track towards home. Then I reined him in to a walk and took several long, deep breaths. My heart was racing and the blood pounded in my head. Oh my! That. Was. A. Fucking. Big. Dog.

After a few minutes I began to calm down. Wouldn't it have been a thing, to survive the Infection that wiped out the whole world, only to be killed by a poxy dog! Miss Dove would have called that anomalous. It's from a Greek word meaning uneven, she said. She told us lots of tragedies were based on anomalous behaviour:

the loyal hero Macbeth killing his king, selfish Lear giving everything away, Othello murdering the woman he loves more than anything else in the world, and the whole scene in Elsinore. I don't want any anomalies, thank you.

I am not going back to that shitty town again! Not ever. It's a death trap. The houses contain decomposing bodies (and possibly dogs), and that's why they smell so frightful. They must be hotbeds of germs and disease. And there are too many things hanging about waiting for a chance to attack you.

There is another reason that I don't want to go back. I felt awkward going into that house on Almond Street. It doesn't seem right to help yourself from what were people's homes. I know that whoever lived there doesn't need their things any more, but picking over their stuff seems disrespectful. I wouldn't like the idea of snoopers raking through my belongings and taking what they fancy, even when I'm dead. Raiding the stores is different. That's just like shoplifting, and we've all done that. Haven't we?

25

PARADISE

I woke this morning with my bedclothes damp, my chest tight and my whole body wired. It felt like somebody'd wrapped me tightly in wet towels. I think I'd been crying in my sleep because my cheeks were wet and there was a big dribble stain on my pillow. I went to the bathroom and examined my face in a mirror. I looked awful. My eyes were puffy and red, and I had a smear of dried snot on my cheek that made it look as if it had been varnished. I couldn't remember what I'd been dreaming but I was so aching with loss that I began to well up again. I wrote so glibly the other day about everybody being dead and me the only person left. Then I felt detached, as if the Kerryl who was doing the writing was not me but another girl, someone in a story. Now I've collided with reality, and I feel alternating waves of misery and panic. They are gone: all my family, all my friends, everybody I knew. I will never see, hear, or touch any of them again. I may never see another living soul. I am alone. Can I go on? How can I go on? What's the point? I felt wretched, bleeding.

I looked out of the window. The farm was surrounded by a mist so dense I could barely see the edge of the barn a few metres across the yard. There was no way through it, no way out of it. It echoed how I felt: blind, imprisoned, trapped in a landscape without features or landmarks. In a fog like that you could walk for hours and only go in circles.

Reluctantly I dressed and went over to the barn to see to the cows. Molly and her calf were fine. He's got great big eyelashes and a cute, bewildered expression, as if he doesn't know what to make of all this newness around him. He's gorgeous. I wish I knew what to do with him. I milked Bonnie and Dolly but the yield was way down. Perhaps soon both the cows will be dry. I'll be pleased. I have no use for the milk. Dairy products make me fat, so I end up pouring it away.

I went back to the house. The mist hadn't lifted at all and the claustrophobia was getting to me. I grabbed my jacket, whistled for Buster (always up for a walk) and set off up the hill. Cloud like this is quite common when the valley warms up after rain, although mostly it goes quite quickly and here at the farm it's usually below us. This morning, though, it seemed to be everywhere and lingering. I hoped that by climbing the hill I could get above it and into the sunshine.

I walked out of the yard past bales of sweet-smelling haylage. There are a lot of them, shiny and black like enormous stubs of liquorice, stacked three high. Our land produces more hay than our few cows need, and Granddad used to bale the rest and sell it. There's no one to buy it now. I think I might just get a knife and slash through the plastic, letting out the luscious fodder for whatever comes around to enjoy.

The path up to the moor is paved with flat slabs of stone. It's an old packhorse track, made in the days before the valley roads when ponies would fetch and carry fleeces and rolls of cloth between the upland dwellings. The paving has been smoothed by centuries of use, and in places there are twin grooves worn by the iron-rimmed wheels of narrow carts.

The mist soon thinned and I emerged above it, as I'd expected. I kept on walking, getting higher all the time, and as the sunlight filled me my spirits rose. Buster seemed glad to be out of the murk too, and he ran about sniffing and investigating. At one point he disturbed a pheasant that startled us both, exploding from the heather in squawking protest. When he was younger Buster would have chased it but now he doesn't bother, and he watched it flap away with disdain.

I was heating up, and I took off my jacket and dropped it to pick up on the way back. No one was going to nick it, were they? I wished I'd put on shorts instead of jeans. At the top of the hill where it bends over onto the moor proper I stopped for a breather. The sky up here was bright blue. There were no signs of human life, apart from the line of wind turbines on the opposite hill. The sun-splashed gold down the shafts and on the blades, still uselessly turning. The valley was a white-topped basin and looked as though it had been filled with mashed potato.

On the way up the hill Buster had been shooting off in elliptical runs, overlapping search patterns with me always at the centre. Now he walked by my side. I wondered if he'd smelt or heard something that made him cautious, but he seemed happy to go on. I scanned the moor around us, on the lookout for feral animals. All seemed well. Perhaps he was just taking a break.

I hadn't set out for the Bride Stones but that was where I ended up. The old rocks looked mellow and less sinister than usual in the sunlight. I sat down on one, the Bride Stone itself, where girls would wait, hoping for a vision of their true love. Buster flopped down alongside me. How many before me had been in this very spot? Had any of them ever seen anything? I peered into the distance, screwing my eyes against the glare. Buster's nose twitched and his paws flickered as he hunted in his sleep.

I took off my trainers and put my feet in the peaty water. It was startlingly cold but wonderful after the hot climb. I lay back, my head on my hands, and let the sun bathe me. The stone was flat and smooth, hard but not uncomfortable. Far away a sheep bleated, and nearer a curlew called. Somewhere high above a skylark sang, its bubbles of sound falling to earth.

The sun was really hot now, and the cool water inviting. Even though I knew there was nobody to see me I glanced around to check. Then I unbuttoned my shirt, slipped it off, and undid my bra. The fresh air felt good. I stood up, dropped my jeans and wriggled out of my knickers. I took off the band holding my hair and shook it down. I spread out my arms, letting the sun stroke me while I revolved slowly on the stone. Not for a long time, not since I was a young girl, had I been naked in the open air and the sensation was wonderful – liberating and erotic. A light puff of air brushed me, delicate as a feather. I squatted on the rock and lowered myself into the pool.

The water came up to my knees and I gasped from the chill. I took a couple of steps in, then I crouched and launched myself forward. It was only just deep enough for swimming. I did one circuit, a slow breaststroke, then climbed back onto the stone, shivering while I dried myself with my shirt. The cold water had hardened my nipples and I caressed them, working them gently with the palms of my hands.

Suddenly my rising enjoyment froze and I felt a rush of adrenaline; I was being watched! I know it sounds ridiculous, but I was sure of it. I untangled my wet shirt and wrapped it around me, bending over and keeping my legs together. Then I scrambled into my jeans, struggling a bit because my legs were wet. I did up my zip and buttons and looked around. I could see no one, but there are a lot of places to hide, in the bracken or behind the rocks. Hurriedly I stuffed my feet into my trainers and put my bra and pants in my pocket.

Buster looked up sleepily, stretched and wagged his tail. He didn't seem at all bothered. He can pick up people approaching long before I can, but he hadn't reacted. Does that mean there was no one there? I was certain there had been. Knowing you're being looked at is a sort of sixth sense. I don't know if boys can feel it, but it's something all girls pick up. It's what tells you when the boy on the bus or the man in the pub is checking you out, even when he's behind your back. You just know it. That's what I had felt. Had I imagined it? It was so strong. Was it just my over-active imagination again? My heart was thumping as I hurried back to the farm.

I'm not going to write any more diary today. I need some space to think about things. Despite Buster's lack of response, I am certain that this morning up at the Bride Stones I was not alone.

Was it my true love? Was it you, Adam?

———

NEXT DAY

Okay, Adam, I agree; leaving the farm doesn't work. I just scare myself. I'm best staying here. Nice of you to point that out to me now! I came to the same conclusion myself last night while I was watching an ancient *Strictly* on the video recorder. The doors were locked and I'd lit a fire, because although it's only August the evenings can be chilly. I'd made myself some nettle tea. I didn't use honey like I prefer, but sweetener. I don't have much of that, so it will have to be honey or sugar when I run out, because sure as shit I am not going down to the shops again.

Right: doors locked, old feel-good show on the TV, log fire, the room lit by candles, sprawled on the sofa with a mug of something hot and sweet, and Buster asleep with his head in my lap. Time to take stock. I've been concentrating too much on the minuses. I may be all on my own and I'm certainly missing people a lot, but on the plus side, there's nobody to answer to or to try to please. The only demands on me are those made by the animals, or ones I make myself. I should be content. I'm free.

On my way back from the Bride Stones I came round the far side of the shed and saw the blackboard, rain-rinsed but still legible: Welcome to Paradise Farm. It set me thinking about one of the lessons on *Paradise Lost* we'd had with Miss Dove. Jocasta Short, who was always a bit full of herself, said that she thought that Milton's paradise sounded boring, and if she'd been Eve, or Adam, she'd have been only too glad to get out of there.

Miss Dove went around the group and asked each of us for our own definition of paradise, what the word meant for us personally. There was a range of answers. Monica Woodbridge said that paradise for her would be having a life of luxury, with everything you could possibly want, like being a celeb. Miss Dove sighed and moved on. Minal Akram said that the Islamic view of paradise was the state of being closest to God. Miss Dove said that could describe Milton's paradise too. Somebody else said that paradise for them would be a place where there was no evil and people were always kind and good to each other. When it came to my turn I said that complete freedom would do it for me. My paradise would be the freedom to do anything I wanted without ever having to ask for leave or permission, and for there to be no need to please anybody but myself. Miss Dove said that a complete lack of responsibility to or for other people sounded like extreme selfishness, which would be the opposite of what most people thought of as paradise. We argued.

We had English again after break, this time with Rudy. When I came into the classroom he said, 'Ah, the Paradise Girl.' It seems that Miss Dove had told him about our discussion over coffee. After that he'd often use it. 'What does Miss Paradise think?' he'd say. Or, 'Paradise Girl, would you mind collecting up the essays?' I didn't like it. He said it with a sort of sneer that I thought was creepy and it made me feel awkward.

I can see now that Miss Dove was right. I am my own boss now. I can please myself. I can do exactly what I like and I don't have to do anything I don't want to. I can get up and go to bed when I like, think what I like, say what I like, and wear what I like. I can walk around all day naked, like Eve, if I want to. There's nobody to tell me to do anything, and nobody expects anything of me. I have the paradise I described. But this isn't paradise at all. You see, I left the main thing out. Milton wrote, 'Solitude sometimes is best society', but he was wrong. The main thing that turns an ordinary place into paradise, as the biblical Adam well knew, is having someone to share it with. Without that it's not paradise at all; it's hell. And that's where I am.

SICKNESS

I didn't feel well when I woke up. There was a rawness at the back of my throat and I had the snivels. My head felt thick and I had no energy. The Infection? Of course, that was the first thing that occurred to me too. However, I was sure it was not that. My joints weren't achy, I didn't have a temperature and I certainly didn't have diarrhoea – the opposite if anything. Besides, how could I possibly have become infected? There's nobody left to infect me.

I would have stayed in bed if I could, but the bloody animals needed seeing to, didn't they? I milked Bonnie and Dolly and let them out to pasture, Molly and her calf too. Then I opened up the hens. I didn't look for eggs. To be honest, I couldn't give a toss if they lay or not. I've got loads of eggs in the fridge and bowls of them in the pantry and I'm not eating them. I'm not eating anything.

When I'd done my jobs I boiled some water, put in it a splash of lemon juice and a slug of Granddad's rum and took it to bed. I planned to stay there for the rest of the day. I've not had anything to eat and I hardly had anything yesterday and I'm not hungry. If this goes on I might soon get into those clothes I took from Chez Annette.

LATER

My throat was sore, and even though I was comfortable in bed I didn't sleep. Things turned over in my head and I got to thinking about hobs. When I was a little girl Gran would tell me stories about them.

'Hobs,' she used to say, 'are small, like dwarves. They're covered in shaggy hair and have huge feet. They live in hob holes and have got super strength.'

Hobs used to fascinate me, but they scared me too.

'No need to be afraid,' Gran would say. 'A hob won't harm you. It will help you if you treat it right.'

'Where do they come from? Where do they live?' I asked.

'Well,' she said, 'nobody knows where they come from, but a hob finds a farm that it fancies and makes that its home. Then, once it's settled in, it will work in secret to help the farmer.'

She seemed to believe this, because if there was a problem, like a sick sheep or a cow with mastitis, Gran would say, 'We could do with a hob now', and Granddad would say things like, 'This looks like a job for a hob.'

There were indeed times when problems that had seemed serious suddenly evaporated. Like when our Dad was all set up to finish the hay. It had been cut and tedded and was ready to be baled and stored, and the tractor wouldn't start. He said something on it was seized up and it needed new parts, which would have to be ordered. It would be out of action for several days, by which time rain was forecast and the hay would be ruined. And then, just like that, the tractor started. Our Dad hadn't done anything to it; the seized part had freed itself. The baling was done and the hay got in. Gran said it must have been a hob.

'Mm, a hob with a City & Guilds Certificate in Agricultural Engineering,' Dad said. He didn't believe in hobs and said all that stuff was country rubbish fancied by people who spent too much time on their own.

You were never to let on you knew the hob was there. Gran told a story of a farm in the Dales where a hob saved the harvest and the farmer thanked it by leaving a leather jerkin out for it. The hob took offence and from then on it changed from helping to causing mischief.

'Why, Gran?' I said. 'They were only being nice to it.'

'Ah, but the hob didn't see it like that,' she said. 'Hobs are proud. A hob's a spirit, and it belongs to no one. It does what it does because it does what it does. If you thank it, even worse if you try to reward it, it thinks you're treating it like something you own or employ, and it takes offence.'

I believed in hobs when I was a kid. I'd always be wary when I was out on my own, especially if it was dark. If anything mysteriously nice happened, like the time I found a litter of puppies in the barn, I'd know it was a hob that had done it, but I'd be careful to avoid appearing grateful or thanking it. When I got older I agreed with our Dad; hobs are just stories. Or are they? Could it be a hob that left the gate open? Did a hob help Molly with her calf? Was it the shadow of a hob I saw in the barn?

Don't be stupid, Kerryl. Get a grip. A hob would be useful now, though. Gran said that some hobs were supposed to have extra special powers and could cure children of whooping cough and worse. I could do with one of those hobs. My throat feels as though it's been sandpapered.

LATER STILL

I slept for a long time. In the afternoon I went down and did my chores, and then I came straight back to bed. I think I'm feeling a bit better, but I don't have any energy. I don't want to read or use my iPad. My head feels thick and I'm only writing this because I get withdrawal symptoms if I don't.

NEXT DAY

I spend the whole day sliding in and out of sleep. I don't dream of anything, not even of you, Adam (although I'd like to).

When I wake up it's pitch dark and I reach out for the matches to light a candle. Buster watches me, standing at the end of my bed with his tail thumping my mattress. 'Sorry, old sport,' I say. 'We're not going for a walk. I'm staying here and so are you.' He understands, because he sighs and lies down on the rug, his chin on his paws.

I leave the candle burning for comfort. Having slept all through the day I'm wakeful now, and I lie for a long time listening for any sounds outside. It's a thick, late summer night – hot and heavy. I open the window. Unusually for up here, there's no wind. If that lasts it will be a concern because my wind turbine won't work and I'll be struggling for electricity. It won't, though. A very still period like this is always followed pretty quickly by high winds and rain.

I hear an owl hooting and somewhere a dog yelping, but not the distant planes and trains and traffic I would normally have expected on a night like this.

I conjure up an image of Adam and begin to touch myself. (You're not to read that bit, and if you do you're to forget it immediately!)

27

A VISITOR

For the last couple of days I've been getting up for just long enough to milk Dolly and feed Buster. I've slept most of the time, with occasional vivid dreams. I've drunk a lot of water and a little milk, but I've eaten nothing.

My throat feels better, but when I got out of bed I was very wobbly. I had a cup of milky coffee. Then I made myself a slice of toast, but I couldn't eat it. Too scratchy.

Now I'm at the kitchen table writing this. My headache has gone and so has the fever. I got so hot in my own bed that I had to throw my duvet on the floor and go and lie on Lander's. My bedclothes must be really smelly, because even Buster's abandoned my room! I'll try to wash and dry them today.

I have my slice of toast beside me and I've only taken one small bite from it. I don't want it. I won't have anything else to eat today. I look down at my midriff. Definitely thinner but my tummy still shows through my PJs. When I have a bit more energy I'll try on some of my old clothes, the ones I'd pushed to the back of my cupboard, and see if they fit me. I won't risk the new ones yet because I'll be so disappointed if I haven't reached my target.

What I need is a table where I can record my progress towards the weight I want to be. I turn to the back of my diary and rule three columns. I head them:

<u>Date</u> <u>Weight - (or +!)</u>

I fill in the first few lines from memory. From now on I'll weigh myself at least once every day and write down the result in this table. Then I can easily check how much I'm losing, and if I'm not losing I can do something about it.

I look up from my notebook and gaze out of the kitchen window at the side of the hill that rises above the farm. In the early hours the weather broke and rain lashed the bedroom windows. It's stopped now and has been replaced by another dense mist. It's as if the farm has been packed in cotton wool. Or put in a white plastic box and the lid closed. I hate it, but at least it's an excuse not to go out. I'm not going up to the Bride Stones this time!

Tomorrow is August 31st (at least, I think it is) and that's my birthday. I hope I'm properly better for it. Not that there's anyone to celebrate with, apart from Buster. And of course you, Adam.

It's just as I turn my head away from the window and go back to my notebook that a movement catches my eye. I look up, and I see something on the path. It's a man! Even as I try to focus the mist wraps the figure and hides it from me.

I get up and rush to the window, leaning forward and straining into the white haze. Was there someone there? Did I see him? Did I really see him? My head's spinning. Tiny, multi-coloured dots swirl in front of my eyes. I feel dizzy. I grip the sill. Then the cloud parts once more and I see it – him – again. He's on the path no more than fifty metres away. He stands with his thumbs hooked in the pockets of his jeans and he's looking at the house, and at me. He's there for no more than a few seconds before the mist takes him again.

I stand at the window for ages waiting for the mist to part, but it doesn't. My heart thumps and my legs are trembling. Who is he? Did he see me? Where is he now? I'm frozen, expecting to hear some movement in the yard or a rap on the door. The man had been young, and he wore a black T-shirt and jeans. He'd had a bag hooked over his shoulder. He looked well-built and fit. In the glimpse I had of him, he looked friendly, not threatening. Despite that I was nervous.

I come away from the window. My fingers are aching from gripping the sill so tightly. My dressing gown has slid off my shoulder and I'm freezing. I ease it back on and go to the cupboard. I'm not a great drinker but I need a slug of vodka. This is medicine, not pleasure. While I'm trying to pour it with dithering hands I feel Buster's wet nose snuffle my leg. It occurs to me how strange that is. Usually, if anybody he doesn't know comes within a hundred metres of the farm Buster will go to the door and bark, and if he feels especially put out he'll growl. But he's not done any of that. He's just stayed in a lazy, doggy heap on the mat beside the boiler cupboard, the warmest place in the house. That means either that he hasn't registered the stranger (impossible; Buster's got the sharpest ears and nose of any dog I've ever known) or the visitor is somebody he knows. Also impossible.

LATER

I keep going to the window. Gradually the mist thins, and then it clears completely, but I see nobody there. Should I go out and search? I get dressed and put on my boots. What if the mysterious stranger is still close, hiding in a nook in the yard, waiting to jump me when I go out? I get one of Granddad's shotguns and slide a cartridge into each barrel. I don't know if I'm shaking so much because I'm scared, or still cold, or it's the hangover from the 'flu I've just had. God help me if I have to aim at anything.

I unlock the door and ease back the bolt, making as little noise as I can. Then I change my mind and lock it again. I go from room to room, looking out of every window. Then I do the same upstairs. Doing this I can see the whole of the area around the house: the yard, the front terrace and both sides. Obviously, I wouldn't be able to see anybody behind the barn or in one of the sheds, but everything close is visible. Buster trails after me, puzzled by what I'm doing. I spend a long time at each window, keeping myself concealed so I won't be spotted, but see nothing. Then I go round the house and do all the rooms again. Still nothing.

I go upstairs and sit on my bed in an agony of indecision. Part of me is elated that another human is being close by, another person who's survived the Infection. Another part of me is more cautious. The person I saw was male, young and strong looking. That's both exciting and worrying. He's not done anything to suggest he might mean me harm, but there would be little I could do to stop him if he did. Should I hide? Or should I go out and try to make contact? And of course, the question I'm almost too scared to allow: was it real? was there anyone there at all?

Time passes and I wait. In the afternoon I go downstairs to write this.

I drink a glass of water. Sooner or later I'll have to go out. I should already have been to milk Dolly. She'll be all right, she's been giving less and less anyway. I'll have to see to her tomorrow morning. I'll have to go out then, cross the yard to the barn, whatever the risk.

NEXT DAY

Today I am eighteen. Or I think I am. A couple of weeks ago I let the battery in my phone run out and for some reason it wouldn't start up again. I had to do a reset and it lost all its data. Normally it would have picked up the date and time online, but I had to set it myself according to what I thought they were. So I may have missed a day, but it's near enough. Anyway, nobody's going to remind me, or turn up to my party on the wrong day!

Eighteen. An adult. Old enough to serve on a jury. Old enough to vote, if there were anyone to vote for. I think I'll vote for Buster. I pat him and give him a dog biscuit. He thinks being a politician is a good idea.

It took me ages to get to sleep last night. I was thinking about the guy on the path. This morning I wanted to lie in, but I could hear Dolly complaining and I had to get up to go and relieve her. I took the shotgun and eased the door open. I had a good look around and all seemed clear, so I ran across to the barn and dived inside. It was only then that I thought I should have checked before I burst in. I should have done what they do in the movies: position myself beside the door with my back to the wall, swing round, kick the door open and stand in the doorway holding out my gun. Lander used to go on about how stupid that was. 'Imagine,' he'd say, 'standing in the doorway like that, against the light where you'd make the best possible target!' Anyway, it didn't matter. The barn was empty. I got Dolly in and she looked accusingly at me. 'Where were you yesterday?' she was saying. She was fine, though. So were the others. Molly's calf is growing and looking fit.

After I'd done the milking I went back to the kitchen. There was an envelope with my name on the table. Nothing mysterious this time. It's a birthday card I've written for myself. Well, I've got to have at least one! Even though I know what it looks like and what it says inside, I open it and stand it on the table.

HAPPY BIRTHDAY, KERRYL
YOU'RE THE ONLY GIRL IN THE WORLD
ALL MY LOVE
ADAM
XXXXXXXXXXXXX

I cook a birthday breakfast for Buster and me: tomatoes, beans, eggs and some tinned ham which I fry. Even though I'm off meat I hope it will taste like bacon. It does a bit, but once I've loaded my plate I don't want it. The look and smell of the food make me feel sick. I give it to Buster and he finishes it in about three seconds. Then he goes to sleep on the rug, alternately snoring and farting. I loaf on the couch and read some magazines. I've read them all before, every word, front to back and back again to the front, and they're getting tatty. It's tempting to risk another trip into town to see if I can find something more recent, but not today. I've decided I'm not going to do anything today that isn't essential, so when I get bored with the magazines I watch some old episodes of *Carla's Secret* on my iPad until it runs out. Then I pick up my diary and start writing again. I've almost finished the purple one, the account of how things got to be like this.

LATER

I've got writer's cramp. I drop my pen and shake my fingers. I push the notebook aside and stretch. I don't fancy coffee and I'm short of tea, so I make some nettle tea and put a spoonful of honey in it. I know, honey! But I can't slim on my birthday, can I? Anyway, I didn't eat breakfast.

I sit in the window, watching the rain swirl across the fields. I'm bored. I look for my iPad to play a game or watch a moviestick but I can't find it. I was using it earlier, I'm sure. I look in the kitchen and under the cushions on the couch but it's not there. Where did I have it last? Perhaps I left it upstairs. I'll get it later.

It's still raining. I wonder if I might see again the figure I saw yesterday. I keep looking, hoping I will, scared that I might, but the hillside is empty.

I do the afternoon milking and give Dolly and Bonnie some cow cake in honour of the day. I go to the stable and give Joey some oats. I spend some time with him, rubbing his muzzle and patting his neck. He whinnies a bit and paws the ground. I think he's lonely, too. A horse like Joey needs exercise, and my 'flu means I haven't ridden him for several days. I'll take him out tomorrow. I'll go up to the Stones and gallop him across the moor.

I go back inside. The evening's come on early because of the bad weather, and I draw the curtains and light a fire. It takes me a while to get it to burn properly. The chimney's getting smoky. I can't remember when it was last swept. I watched the sweep do it once and I think I know how to do it. I just need the kit. They called the sweep Sooty Morgan. Perhaps his address is in Granddad's notebook. If I can find it, I could go to his house and borrow his brushes. But that would mean leaving the farm again.

I make some more tea and open a tin of Dundee cake I've been saving. I've got some candles, too, and I arrange eighteen of them around the top. Buster ambles into the kitchen and looks hopeful. I give him a handful of dog biscuits and he wolfs them. I don't think he would have appreciated candles, although he does like cake. I light them and take the cake into the front room. I blow out the candles and wish. I can't tell you what I wish because that would prevent it from coming true, but you can probably guess. I cut a piece of the cake and take a bite but I don't like it. It tastes like sweet sawdust. It makes me feel ill. I go to the sink and spit it out, on the verge of retching. I throw the cake in the bin.

I didn't know loneliness could be like this. Before the Infection, I had the reputation of being quite a solitary person. I had a lot of friends but only one of them, Josie, was what you could call close. With full days at school and Lander, Mam, Gran and Granddad at home it was a relief to be on my own. I used to spend hours reading in my bedroom and resented being dragged out to do something on the farm. But being alone is different from being lonely. Loneliness hurts. Yes, it does. It's a physical pain in every crack and cranny of your being. It's a hurt that can't be eased or subdued, that no tonic will relieve. Sometimes it gnaws and sometimes it tears. There may be moments when you're distracted by something else, but it never goes away and it will come back stronger than ever, seizing you by the throat and demanding attention. I ache for the sound of a voice, the touch of another person. I think I would go completely mad were it not for Buster. And of course you, Adam.

It's because I'm lonely that I've looked out of the windows today, like, 500 times. By the 350th time my mood has swung from dreading seeing somebody out there to desperately wishing I would. Oh, where are you, man on the path?

I lie on the sofa and close my eyes. None of the things I could do appeals. I don't want to read, listen to music, or watch moviesticks. Anyway, I still haven't found my iPad. I throw one of the cushions at the wall.

'It's my fucking birthday,' I shout, 'and I'm on my own and I'm miserable and I'm bored.'

There's silence. Just the crackling of the fire and the ticking of the clock that I still wind religiously every day. I sink back on the remaining cushions. Buster regards me anxiously. I close my eyes.

Perhaps I dozed off, I'm not sure, but suddenly it was later and a noise made me jump.

Now I'd better warn you, this is weird. It's so very weird it seems mental to write it down. But I'm not going crazy, it really did happen. The sound that woke me was familiar to me but strange, a sound I know so very well but haven't heard for a long time. It was my mobile phone. It vibrated and it chimed. That's the alert to notify me that I have a text!

I was flabbergasted. I couldn't understand it. Then it dawned on me what it meant, and my heart leapt. I rushed to the window expecting to see the town below lit up, houses ablaze, street lights burning, life back to normal, but it was as dark as ever. I flicked on the TV, and the radio. The TV was dead, the radio just noise. Nothing had changed. I was trying to understand what was going on when my phone chimed again, the reminder that the text hadn't been viewed. It was only then that I looked at it. The screen was startlingly bright and there was a single message. It said,

TXT ME.

I cradled the phone in my hands as if it was an injured bird. What does it mean? It must be evidence that someone else is out there. Who is it? The man I saw yesterday? It can't be, it has to be somebody who knows me well enough to have my number. Does the sender also know it's my birthday? Is this a birthday message? I stare at the thing. The lack of information is infuriating. There are just those two words, **TXT ME**. There's no sender ID. I tap the Who? key and see the words 'new contact'. Big help!

My mind is a maelstrom. I want to acknowledge this contact, to reply, but there's no number listed so how can I? Do the obvious, Mr Armitage would say, so I do. I touch the 'reply' arrow. Then I key in my message:

WHO R U?

My fingers are trembling so much that it takes me several goes to hit the right letters.

I press 'send'. I expect it to fail, there's no one to send it to, no network to send it on. There's a whooshing noise while the message pad spins. Then it morphs into a smiley face and shows the notice, 'message sent'.

I place the phone carefully on the table and wait. I watch it expectantly. All the time I think I'll see the stupid bouncing ball that will tell me the message has failed, but I don't; just the words 'message sent'.

28

HENS

Nothing more happened last night. I waited for hours by the phone but it was dumb. When at last I went to bed I put it under my pillow, desperate not to miss a message, but it stayed silent. I kept looking at it to check the battery hadn't run down. It was fine, just dumb.

I woke up this morning still thinking about the mysterious contact. In the daylight it somehow seemed less dramatic than it had last night. I checked the phone several times to make sure I hadn't dreamt it. It was exactly as before.

TXT ME.

and my reply

WHO R U?

The reply looked stroppy, challenging. Had I been too abrupt? Had the texter taken offence? Don't be daft, Kerryl. Whoever it was had bothered to text you, so do you think that's going to put them off?

I went to let the hens out of their run and that was when I got another shock. There were none there. They were all gone. I looked in the coop, expecting they'd be huddled together inside, but that was empty too. Nothing. No hens, no chicks, no eggs, nada. Okay, maybe I've not been looking after them as well as I should, what with not being well and all, but there was plenty for them to eat and a warm, safe, dry place for them to go.

My first thought was a fox had got in. That had happened before. I was about seven, and I still remember it. I walked into the field and found Gran in tears, holding her head in her hands. There was blood everywhere. It looked like something from a Tarantino movie. The fox had started to eat two of the hens, and the rest had been dismembered, every single one of them. Bits of chicken, savaged and barely recognisable, were scattered around the run: feathers, flesh, sinews, feet, heads. That's the trouble with a fox, Granddad said, it doesn't just take what it wants to eat, it kills the lot. This morning it was different; there was nothing left at all. No feathers, no blood, nothing.

I looked in the area around the run and the coop and couldn't see anything amiss. The wire netting was sound and the doors were still securely fastened. I looked for traces of digging because Granddad told me once that sometimes a badger will try to tunnel its way into a hen run, but there was no sign of that either.

Could somebody have stolen them? When? Why? Who? Is it the person I saw on Friday? Or whoever it was who texted me last night? Might they be the same? Don't be ridiculous. *If* there was anyone else around, why on earth would they take my hens? Hens are plentiful, there are thousands of them running free. I feel sad. The hens were Gran's. She liked them and so did I, poor gentle, dumb, things. Now I feel I've let her, and them, down. I hope they're not dead. I feel a lump in my throat.

I stand in the doorway to the run, take a deep breath, and summon up the spirit of Mr Armitage. The question is, what do I do now?

The possibilities seem to be:

- <u>Option 1</u>: Catch a few wild hens and a cockerel and restock the run.
- <u>Downside</u>: If I did that I'd feel compelled to watch it day and night to make sure that whatever has happened today doesn't happen again.
- <u>Option 2</u>: Do without keeping my own hens, and when I want poultry for food go and shoot a wild one, or a pheasant or a grouse, because there are plenty of all of them about.
- <u>Downside</u>: I wouldn't have eggs. Does that matter? I used to eat them a lot but I can't remember when I last had one, and I've got hundreds of them. Buster likes them, though.

There's a third option: go vegan. Part of me thinks that would be a good idea because it would avoid killing stuff. Granddad used to snap the hen's necks. He did it swiftly, just a quick flick, and he said they didn't feel anything, but it was awful. He'd drop them on the ground and their legs would twitch and their feet scrabble as if they didn't know they were dead and were trying to carry on. It's not only the killing that's horrible, it's the plucking and gutting. Ugh!!!

I leave the hen run door flapping open – no point closing it now – and go back to the house. On the way I scan the fields and the hill, looking for stray hens and wondering if I might see my watcher again. There's Joey in his paddock and the cows are peacefully grazing. There are a few ragged looking sheep on the edge of the moor, and the inevitable mangy dog hanging around on the fringes of the yard. Nothing that looks unusual.

In the kitchen I take out my phone and stare at it, willing it to come to life. It's mockingly unresponsive. **TXT ME**. What does it mean? I don't understand. I feel nervous, apprehensive. If this person can reach me by text, why don't they call me? Why don't they talk to me? They have my number, so why can't I hear their voice?

I can't settle to anything. I go and see Joey. He trots across his paddock to me and I rub his nose.

'Did you see what happened to the hens?' I ask him.

His big brown eyes gaze at me from under their long lashes. It's as if he's saying that he does know and he would tell me if only he could.

I milk Dolly and give Molly and her calf the rest of the cow cake. The calf's not up to eating it yet but seems to enjoy licking it. Bonnie and Dolly look on forlornly. I don't have enough for them. My supplies are running low. 'Nursing mothers and children only,' I tell them. There's a feed merchant along the valley where I'm sure there'd be some. However, restocking cow cake is not on my list of priorities at the moment. Sorry, gals.

Out in the yard, I look at the spot on the track where the guy I saw was standing. There must be rational explanations for all the odd things that have been going on: the gate, the noises, the strange feelings, the sighting, the text, the hens. I am as certain as I can be that I am the only person alive around here, but I know nothing of anywhere else. The major services have gone down, but that doesn't mean no one's left in other places. Perhaps there are a lot of people unaffected by the Infection but we just can't communicate with each other. Perhaps some of them are looking around, searching for others. The big mystery isn't that somebody else might have survived, but how a text message could appear on my phone when, as far as I can tell, the mobile network is dead and has been for weeks. Wearily I go back into the house. I take my phone from the table and rouse it. The two texts are still there.

There are no answers to my questions. I lie down on the sofa and fall asleep with the mobile on my chest.

29

BLACKOUT

Buster woke me by licking my face. For a second or two I couldn't work out what was happening, there was just this wet mess and his tongue going right into my ear. I pushed him away. His breath was foul. Memo: clean his teeth.

My eyes were prickly and my mouth was dry. It was still dark and I turned over to go back to sleep, but Buster started licking me again and wouldn't leave me alone. I shoved him away, more roughly this time, and he started whining. I swore at him and sat up. It was pitch black and I reached out to the switch for the standard lamp beside the sofa. Nothing happened, it wouldn't work. I groped my way towards the light switch on the wall. That didn't work either. We keep a torch in the top drawer of the sideboard and I shuffled towards that, stubbing my toe on a chair leg and cursing. The torch was feeble, but it gave enough light for me to light a candle and find my trainers.

None of the light switches worked. I opened the door to the yard. There was a strong wind and the turbine should have been pushing out plenty of power. The torch beam was just bright enough to pick out the pole at the end of the yard and to show the blades stationary. Perhaps it had jammed – it did that once before – but there should have been power in the batteries. I was still fuzzy from sleep, but I grabbed my coat and shuffled over to the barn, where the inverter and the rest of the stuff for the electrical system are fitted. I shone the torch on the meters. They were all on zero! There was no power. Nothing was coming from the mains (obviously), nothing from the solar panels (it was the middle of the night), nothing from the turbine (I'd just seen that it wasn't going round), and the fourth display told me that the batteries were flat. Just then there was a beep, warning me that the backup that keeps the meters working and remembers the power management settings was low too.

I went back to the house and lit some more candles. I have plenty, and I put extras in the hallway and up the stairs, around the kitchen and in the front room.

I'm sitting at the kitchen table now, writing this and trying to figure out what's gone wrong and what to do about it. When did I last check the meters and the electrics? I didn't. It was always Granddad's or Lander's job and I never thought to do it. It's been overcast for the past few days, so the solar panels won't have been doing much. Was the turbine working yesterday? I didn't notice. I'm so used to it being there I don't see it any more. It could have stopped generating days ago and as long as there was power in the batteries I wouldn't have noticed.

I can't do anything till daylight, but I don't feel like going to bed. Buster pads after me to the kitchen, making hopeful, attention-seeking noises in his throat. I open a tin of Dog Star (beef in jelly, his favourite) and tip it into his bowl, dodging his wild tail. I wince as I stand up. My back's stiff from sleeping on the sofa and I do a few stretches. I've brought the bathroom scales downstairs and I step on them. I've gone down again. I write the new number in the back of my diary. I'm pleased with the progress I am making, but there's still a way to go yet. I return to the table to await the dawn.

I remember my phone and retrieve it from where it's slipped down between the sofa cushions. Yesterday's message thread has another entry.

TXT ME and **WHO R U?** are now followed by

????.

The timing is 2.34 am, an hour ago.

My hands tremble. Is that a response to my question? Does it mean my message was received? Am I having an actual conversation with somebody? A row of question marks; perhaps it's just an error message.

I tap the 'reply' arrow and begin to key in. I've just started when there's a red slash across the screen followed by the notice 'Your device is running on reserve power and will now close down' and the whole thing dies. I scream in anger and frustration, and come close to hurling the fucking thing away. I have a booster, but of course it's empty. I can't charge the phone until daylight and the solar panels start working, or I get the turbine going again. There's somebody out there who has not only sent me a message but now responded to mine, and I can't contact them. I scream again. Buster looks anxious.

There's nothing to do but wait. I go back to the kitchen. I can't even make a cup of tea. Hang on a minute, I can. We've got a paraffin stove in the cupboard under the stairs. Do I have any paraffin? Don't know. Can I be bothered looking? No. I open a packet of peanut butter cookies, take a bite out of one and toss the rest in the bin. I don't like them any more. Buster looks at me as if

I've just destroyed the *Mona Lisa*. He loves peanut butter cookies (well, actually he loves all cookies) but if I gave them to him he'd inhale the lot and make himself sick.

How bad a problem do I have? If I can't fix the turbine I'll be dependent on getting at least a bright day to have any power, if not a sunny one. And winter's coming, when there'll be less daylight. I suppose all I really need electricity for now is to run the fridge and freezers and to charge up my phone and iPad, and as I still haven't found my iPad that means just my phone.

Doesn't the dawn take a long time to arrive when you're waiting for it? I remember all those schooldays when mornings seemed to hurtle in at warp speed, and way before I was ready it was time to get up. Now, waiting for and wanting the sunrise, it takes forever to arrive. At last, the sky lightens enough for me to go out into the yard and investigate.

LATER

Right, report.

I think the turbine may just be stuck. When it did that before, Granddad got a ladder and levered the blades free with a tommy bar. There's a further problem, though, because our ladder got nicked from the barn about a year ago and we never replaced it. We have a shorter one but it won't do. If the turbine had stopped with one of the blades aligned with the pole, i.e. at six o'clock, I could have just about got to it, but it's stuck with one blade at four o'clock, another at eight o'clock and the top one at twelve. I can't get anywhere near them.

It's daylight now and the panels are charging the batteries, but I don't yet have enough power to boil a kettle. There's warm water in the tank so I can take a shower and I go up to the bathroom for a long one. I stand in front of the mirror and look at myself. I'm moderately pleased. I'm definitely losing weight. I've not been eating much at all. I'm not really hungry, either, and when I do feel hungry and try to eat, as soon as I taste it I don't want it. But that's a good thing, isn't it? It means I'm getting somewhere.

While I was in the shower I had an idea. I think it's a good one. There's an elevator in the barn that Granddad used to lift hay bales into the loft for storage. If I hook it up to the tractor I can back it under one of the turbine blades. I might then be able to climb up it and reach the blade. It's totally off the rails safety-wise – Lander would say it has A&E written all over it – but it's worth a try.

It's sunny today so I have enough power from the solar panels. That gives me breathing space, and time to think. It would be daft to rush into anything.

It also means I now have enough juice to get my phone going.

30

ACCIDENTS

I managed yesterday to get my phone charged up again. There were no more messages. I'd asked the sender to say who they were but all I'd got back were the question marks. What does that mean? It means that he/she doesn't want to say who they are. Why not? Why are they being so mysterious? Maybe I have to make the next move. I tap in

MY NAME IS KERRYL

and hit 'send'. There's the whoosh, the spin, the smiley face and 'message sent'. Again I can't believe it. Sent where? How? Who to? (Oh all right, to whom?)

I wait and stare at the screen, desperate for it to come to life but it doesn't. It's agony. The closest I've come before to this feeling of excited frustration was when I had a date with this really hot guy and we'd arranged to meet under the market clock and I was there first and he was late, only a few minutes but it seemed like hours and I thought he wasn't coming. Of course, the person I'm texting could be hundreds of miles away, thousands, maybe on a different continent. That's it. They're in a different time zone and that's why replies are slow coming.

I open a game on my phone but the screen's too small for it to be interesting. I need to find my iPad. I search the whole house, even our Mam's room and Gran and Granddad's, although I know I haven't been in there. I check the barn, though God knows why I would have taken it over there. Anyway, I hadn't. It's gone. Surely it can't be far away. I must just have put it down somewhere and forgotten. I'm definitely losing my marbles, as Gran used to say. I expect I'll suddenly come across it when I'm looking for something else, but I wish I could find it. I miss it.

LATER

I've checked out the bale elevator. It's an adjustable, trough-shaped ramp, with a chain conveyor fitted with spikes running up the centre. When it's working the spikes catch on the bales and pull them up. It seems firm enough and should be easy to climb. I'll have to watch the spikes, though, because they're savage and if I were to slip I could end up with a nasty cut. I was tempted to have a go right away, but I was tired so I decided to leave it till later. I was early in bed last night and despite everything that's happening I slept well. In the past I didn't allow Buster to sleep with me, mainly because he always wants to be right in the middle of the bed and I have to arrange myself around him, but since Gran and Granddad went I've been letting him sleep at my feet – on them really. He spends the nights gradually easing himself up the bed a millimetre at a time, like some big hairy quantum experiment, so that by morning he's in a good position to lick my face. It's comforting feeling him there, makes me feel less alone. But I'm not alone now. Am I?

LATER STILL

I thought about staining this page with blood, just to highlight the drama! It certainly gets a row of scowly faces, all of them in pain. Writing's not easy but I can still manage it, so here goes.

I succeeded in hooking the elevator to the tractor. That was hard. The elevator was too heavy for me to pull, and it took me three goes to get the tractor into the right position to fix the coupling. Then I towed it out and backed it up to the turbine. That wasn't as difficult as I'd expected, and I got it right underneath the blade that was at four o'clock. The only problem was that the ground around the bottom of the turbine was uneven and I had to shore up the elevator with flat stones to get it level and stop it from wobbling. When I was happy that it was firm I climbed up. Hairy, or what? The base was solid but the sloping bit (the trough) that takes the bales swayed about. There was nothing firm to stand on because of the spikes. Besides, the thing is made for hay bales, not for a human, and it protested. It creaked and wobbled about and I thought I was going to fall off. I was wetting myself. I'm not good with heights.

I managed to wedge myself near the top of the trough, with my knees braced against the sides and in a position where I could reach the blade. I stretched out and the elevator lurched scarily. I wasn't helped by Buster deciding at just that moment that he'd climb up too and help me. I thought he was going to have us both off and I had to shoo him away. He watched the rest of the performance from the edge of the yard, looking rejected and upset.

I caught hold of the turbine blade and tried to move it. Although it did give a little, it wouldn't turn. It was well and truly stuck. My thigh muscles were aching from pushing against the trough. I gave the blade a big push and the elevator lurched. I flung out my arm to steady myself and caught my hand on one of the bale spikes. I screeched in pain and watched with horror the blood running down my arm.

I spent the next half hour getting myself down from the top of the elevator and washing and sterilising my hand. The gash stung and I think it probably needs stitches, but there's no chance of that. I cleaned it as thoroughly as I could and applied pressure. After a while, the bleeding stopped and I rummaged in the first aid box to find some germicide. There were no butterfly plasters but there were some bandages. Have you ever tried to bandage your own hand? Definitely a two-person job. Even Buster couldn't help, although he offered. I don't think dog lick is much use as an antiseptic.

I'm now writing this while I calm myself down and wait for the throbbing in my hand to stop. Luckily it's my right hand that's hurt and I'm left-handed. As soon as it settles down I'll change. My T-shirt and jeans look as though I've just come off a shift in an abattoir.

Maybe what's stopping the turbine going round is a problem with the hub. The hub has a cover and if I take it off I might be able to see if anything is jamming the works. It would make sense to leave it for today and let my hand heal a bit, but I've got this far and I want to resolve the situation. I want to get the thing going, or I want to know for sure that it will never work again. If it's that, I'll have to make plans to manage without it.

EVEN LATER STILL

It took quite a long time for my hand to feel better enough for me to have another go on the elevator. When it did I went back to the shed to get a selection of tools. I was so busy thinking about the turbine hub and hoping I'd cleaned my wound enough and that my hand wouldn't become infected that I forgot to take the shotgun with me. I left it leaning in a corner by the sink, where

I'd put it when I came in. One of my safety rules, remember? Never leave the house without a loaded gun. Well, this time I did.

Driving the tractor one-handed was a bit of a challenge and it took me a while to move the elevator forward from its original position. Then I backed it until the slopey bit (hope you don't have trouble with these technical terms, Adam) was leaning on the turbine pillar. I wedged it in place by using stones to stop the wheels moving and womping them with a sledgehammer, again one-handed. I tell you, if I go on like this I'll be a contender for Miss Universe! Anyway, the elevator was much more stable in its new position because the pillar stopped it from swaying.

When I was happy that it was firm I crawled up the trough again. This time I'd thought to use some old rubble sacks to cover the chain and spikes. It didn't make the spikes completely safe but it gave some protection.

I got to the top and stood up on the wobbly ramp, hooking my right arm around the pillar to steady myself. I could see straight away what the problem was. The rotor shaft was snagged with baler twine, a lot of it. If you don't know – and I suppose that if you're a townie, Adam, you might not – baler twine is a thin cord used to tie up bales of hay. When Granddad was a boy it was made from hemp and the bales were tied by hand. Now it's spun from strands of plastic and a machine compacts the hay and ties it up like a parcel. Except sometimes it gets it wrong. It misfeeds, and then instead of you getting a tight pack the thing falls apart. Other times you'll pick up a bale and it collapses. In both cases, and in several others, you're left with lengths of redundant loose twine. In Granddad's eyes it was a major crime to leave this lying on the ground. He was always meticulous about picking it up and he insisted that we did too because it can foul machinery or choke a grazing animal. So where did all this on the turbine come from?

I got a spanner from my tool belt to loosen the nuts that secure the housing. It was hard trying to keep my balance on the unsteady ramp while undoing the fixings with my good hand and holding on to the elevator with my other arm, but I did it. I even managed to catch the housing as it came away and stop it from falling to the ground.

Next, I got a cutter and started to hack away at the twine. It was wound round and round and round the hub, several metres of it, effectively jamming it tight. I don't think that could happen by chance. I suppose if one end had got caught on the spinning shaft it might have done it, but how could it get up there in the first place? It looked more as if the job had been done deliberately to sabotage the thing, but that was nonsense. How could anybody get up there without me seeing them? And even if they could, why would they? I'd made several cuts and the twine was coming away when disaster struck. The wind had been buffeting me while I'd been working and the turbine began to move. Immediately the shaft broke free. I was astounded at the power of the blades, there was no way I could stop them. One of them struck the elevator, the whole thing swayed, rocked off its support and I lost my grip. Part slipping, part falling, I landed hard on the ground on my left foot. Pain shot through my ankle and up my leg and I collapsed, cursing and shrieking. I barely noticed that the turbine was now whirling like crazy above me.

I lay on the ground, teeth clenched and sobbing, waiting for the pain to ease. I sat up and tried to assess the damage. I didn't think I'd broken anything, but it hurt. I was wondering how I could make it to the house when I saw something in the corner of the yard. At first I thought it was another dog, but as it came closer I saw that it was a worse problem than that. A large boar was snuffling along the barn wall. Either it was a wild one or an exotic domestic breed because it had tusks. At first, it didn't notice me, but then it did.

I froze. I know boars are dangerous. Granddad always used to say that he'd rather face a bull than a boar any day. It stared at me with cold, piggy eyes. It was massive, bigger than a man. The tusks were huge and its ears flopped over its eyes. Its hide was covered in spiky black hair. It gave an arrogant snort and trotted towards me. It didn't at that stage look threatening but I couldn't be sure. I had a screwdriver and the twine cutter, but what use would they be? Besides, I had a bad hand and I didn't think I could stand up. The boar stopped a metre or so away to take stock. Then it lowered its head. I picked up a stone and flung it at the animal. It shied away and the stone glanced its flank. It looked affronted, grunted and came for me.

Suddenly all hell broke loose. A snarling, barking furious whirlwind called Buster hit the boar like an express train. He circled it, snapping at its flanks. The boar looked pained at the distraction and turned away from me. Buster sank his teeth into one of its back legs. It squealed, twisted and caught the dog with one of its tusks. Buster yelped in pain and bit again. The boar made to fight back, thought better of it and ran away, snorting and squalling. Buster chased it to the edge of the field, snapping at its heels. Then he came back to me. I couldn't stop trembling and Buster was sure that the best way to help was to lick me. I hadn't the will or the energy to push him away, and I lay on my side until he'd finished, when he settled down beside me, whining gently. I ruffled his ears and stroked his nose with my good hand and he snuggled closer. I patted him and he yelped, and it was then I saw the damage that the boar's tusk had done. There was a nasty, weeping tear in his flank, just above his rump. It needed seeing to.

Somehow I got across the yard to the house, Buster limping along with me. Once in the kitchen I dragged a chair to the sink and flopped onto it. It clearly hurt Buster to have his wound touched, but he seemed to know I was trying to help him, and he sat mostly still while I bathed it and put on some of the cream I'd used on my hand. As soon as I let him go he started licking it off, but I couldn't stop that. I reckoned that it might do him good from the inside too. I limped to the freezer and got an ice tray, which I tipped out into a tea towel to make an ice pack for my ankle. All through the whole operation I was in a storm of pain. Every movement was agony, which didn't slacken until I'd been sitting with my leg raised and the ice pack on my ankle for some time. Buster went to check his bowl, which I took as a good sign.

For the rest of the day I've been using one of Granddad's sticks to get about. It would have been easier with two but I can't manage a stick in my bad hand. I must look a proper sight and sound worse, a snivelling, drivelling wreck. I don't bother trying to hold back my sobs and yelps of pain, or to wipe my running nose. There's no one here to impress.

I'm feeling better now. I'm writing this in bed. I have a bad hand. I have a bad leg (my ankle's wrapped in a cold, damp towel). I have a very affectionate dog (lying as close to me as he can get). We're both of us feeling very, very sorry for ourselves, but it could all have been so much worse. My ankle could easily have been broken and it's not, and that's a mercy (Gran used to say that, but I'm not sure what she meant). I could have hit my head when I fell, and knocked myself out. I could have been lying in the yard unconscious when the boar came. Buster could have been shut inside. If he hadn't gone for the boar I'm sure it would have attacked me, and if he hadn't had the guts to keep on fighting it even when he'd been gored it could have killed us both. Thanks to him I got off lightly.

My hand's a worry, though. I think I managed to clean it all right, I certainly applied industrial quantities of antiseptic to it, but if everything had been normal Mam or Gran would have been pestering me to go along to the clinic for an anti-tetanus jab.

There is one good thing that's come out of this; I now have a working turbine. Before I came to bed I was able to hobble over to check the read-outs and all is well, power is being generated, and the batteries are charged up. Then I hauled myself up the stairs, but before I did I locked and chained the door to the yard.

31

———————

CONTACT

I didn't write this down yesterday even though it shook me up. My hand and my ankle were enough to think about. Also, it's crazy and you, my beloved Adam, might think I've jumped totally off the bus. You probably do anyway – I've been telling you about some weird shit – but this was stranger than anything yet.

When Buster chased the boar away from me there was a second when it turned round, as if it was going to take him on, before it veered away and ran off. In that instant it didn't look at Buster, it looked straight at me. It had a really sad expression, disappointed and hurt. The obvious question: how can a boar's face show an expression? The not-so-obvious answer: it was not the face of a boar that looked back at me; the face was human.

There you are. I told you that you'd think I'm a nutter. Is it because I'm lonely and starved of people that I had this creepy hallucination? Or is it because I'm not eating? I know that since I went off food I've been having peculiar dreams. Perhaps this was just another one of those, except wide awake and so scarier. Perhaps the animal really was a person. Perhaps there are some people the Infection doesn't kill and they are morphed into other creatures. Now come on, Kerryl, get down out of that tree! Not a bad idea for a story, though. It would make a terrific movie.

LATER

I didn't think it would be so easy to stop eating. Now I can understand how Tracey Blackburn did it. People who say that dieting's hard are wrong. It's the simplest thing in the world. You just stop stuffing food into your mouth.

The first couple of days after I decided to fast I didn't want to eat. The next few days I was starving and would have hoovered up anything in sight (that must be how Buster feels all the time!). That was tough. I was thinking about food every waking minute. It took a lot of willpower to stop myself from bingeing. Then one morning I woke up and out of habit my first thought was breakfast and then I thought, *I don't want anything. In fact, not only do I not want food, but if I do try to eat something it will make me sick.* It's been like that ever since. It's as if eating was a habit, like smoking, and I've got over it. I can't fill in my weight table because I can't balance on the scales on one foot, but I certainly *feel* thinner. I pinch my stomach and the fat roll seems to have more or less gone. I bet a lot of my clothes fit me now.

I've been here in bed since yesterday and that's where I am now, reading, dropping off, reading again, and in between writing this. Buster's been sleeping at my feet, except at one point early this morning when he tried to sleep on my bad foot and I hit the roof. He's been downstairs several times and I think he's checking his bowl. I'm pretty sure he's not into dieting and so I'll have to go down soon and refill it.

Getting upstairs yesterday was a real performance. I sat on the bottom step, held the mug of tea I'd made myself in one hand and used the other hand and my good leg to hutch me up to the next stair. I did this, one tread at a time until I got to the top. Buster was keen to help me but didn't know how, so he just got in the way and at one point he almost knocked the mug out of my hand with his tail. I shouted at him and he went away. He spent the next hour curled up in the corner of my bedroom, sulking. It would have been funny if my leg hadn't hurt so much. It would have made a great clip for *You're the Star*. If there'd been anybody around to video it, or to watch it. *You're the Star* was one of Gran's favourite TV shows. It was a half-hour collection of homemade phone or camera clips of people (and animals, and children) having disasters, falling, bumping into each other, knocking things over and generally doing silly things. She used to look forward to it all week.

Why bother going upstairs? you say. Why not sleep on the sofa, like before?

I'm not really sure. It's a bunch of things. For one, sleeping on the sofa gives me a bad back, and I can spread out in my own bed. More than that, I just feel safer upstairs. I don't know what I'm afraid of, and I can't explain why being upstairs makes me feel less threatened, but it does.

LATER STILL

I fell asleep again. I expect it's shock that's making me sleep so much. I woke up and Buster was whining. I assumed he was hungry, so I got out of bed to go down and feed him. 'I must teach you how to work a tin opener,' I told him. 'Then you can feed yourself.' Then I thought, *No, not a good idea. You're a lovely dog but let's face it, you are greedy, so I don't think self-service would work.*

I felt really wobbly. Going down the stairs was easier than coming up yesterday because I didn't have anything to carry, and I swung on the handrail, hopping on my good foot. I hobbled into the kitchen to get the dog food from the dresser. I fed Buster and thought it would be a good idea to take a few cans and an opener upstairs, to save me coming down every time he needed feeding, except I didn't think I could bear the smell of the dog food in my bedroom. I could feed him on the landing, but that would mean I'd have to get out of bed anyway.

I was wrestling with this problem when I caught sight of my phone where I'd left it on charge. At that very second the screen sprang to life and there was the buzz of the vibrator and the chimes for an incoming message. I jumped and dropped the pack of dog food.

There was the message I'd sent yesterday before all the fuss with the turbine: **MY NAME IS KERRYL**

Under it was a reply:

I KNOW

32

PUZZLES

I'm in bed, but I haven't been sleeping. I couldn't get to sleep at all last night. I tried reading to take my mind off things, but I couldn't concentrate. Every couple of minutes the realisation would beat in my head – somebody knows my name! somebody knows my name! somebody knows my name! – and when that happened I'd be seized by a fit of trembling. At first I couldn't believe what I saw on the screen. I thought it must be some fault with the phone, or perhaps a virus. Do phones get viruses? A phone's a kind of computer, so I suppose it could.

When I first read the message I took the same energetic and decisive action I had after the first one: I sat down and looked at it for a long time and wondered what the fuck was going on. Then I hobbled round the house and made sure (again!) that all the doors were locked. Then I climbed back upstairs.

Now I've decided I'm not happy lying in bed. Between ourselves, I've been here for so long that my bum is getting sore. Also, I've changed my mind about being upstairs and decided that I feel more vulnerable up here than I do sleeping in the front room. I know that in theory I could stand at the top of the stairs and if anyone tried to come up I could whack them with something heavy, but downstairs I have a better idea of what's going on. So I'm going to get dressed and go down.

LATER

I've put on jeans (no trouble at *all* doing up the waist – in fact, I'm having to wear a belt!). I've also put on one of Lander's shirts, nice and loose in case I have to move quickly. My ankle feels better but I couldn't run yet. I can hobble, so long as I don't lean on it too hard. I've drawn all the curtains. I hate that, it's like living in a cave, but the idea of somebody out there peeping in at me gives me the creeps.

Okay, I'm scared, but lolling around here in a shaking heap won't achieve anything. I must be rational. Summon Mr Armitage's training again and set out the situation logically.

- 1. Somebody is able to send me text messages and receive them from me.
- 2. This is even though the whole mobile phone network seems to be down, along with everything else that could communicate.
- 3. The sender knows my name. (Well, of course they do because I told them, but they say they knew already – or do they just want me to think that?)
- 4. The number of individuals who know/knew my name must be limited to a hundred at the most: family, friends, some of the girls and teachers at school, a few people in the town, the tutors at Cambridge who interviewed me and dealt with my application.
- 5. As far as I know all those people are dead. Of course, I can't be certain. Maybe someone's survived. I have.

- 6. Only a very few of those who know/knew my name would have my number.

So the big question is, does whoever it is who knows my name also know where I am? I have to face that possibility. That's why I'm scared. But why should I be? Why should I think of them as a threat? Well, what they've done so far doesn't fill me with confidence. If they're friendly, why not send me a full text introducing themselves properly, instead of two-word messages that seem designed to freak me out? Why not call me and *talk? Why not just come round and knock on the fucking door?* It's as if they're deliberately trying to spook me.

The use of the 's' word does bring up another possibility, and I hesitate to mention it. All these weird things that have happened – the gate, the shadows, the hens, the man on the path, the turbine and the text messages – are being caused by something supernatural.

There, I've said it. It's been in my head for a while but I've not admitted it in case you think I'm a complete fruit cake and go right off me. I don't believe in ghosts, or I didn't. Gran did. She was sure she kept seeing a strange woman in old-fashioned clothes around the farm. Lander and Granddad pooh-poohed it. I'm not sure what Mam thought. I don't think she could make up her mind, and neither can I now. The figure I saw on the path didn't *look* like a ghost. I don't mean that it should be something in a long white shroud, but he looked so, well, *solid.* And he was fit. I think of ghosts as being ancient and flakey. This guy was young, and a hunk. Another thing is my mobile. I've never heard of a ghost sending text messages, have you? Here, now, in broad daylight, the idea of poltergeists or spirits or hobs is ridiculous. But in the dark, when the house feels desolate and the wind whistles outside, it seems perfectly possible. It's scary, even though I leave candles burning all night (breaking my own safety rules).

I've loaded Granddad's two shotguns and hidden them (one's on the floor under the sofa in the front room and the other's behind the coats in the hall, in case you're looking). I keep Lander's air pistol close at hand, wherever I am. His .22 is in the cupboard, and that's loaded too.

I wish you were real, Adam. I could just do with a useful bloke around at the moment. Not to defend me, you great lunk – what do you think I am? – but to fight alongside me, if it comes to it.

LATER STILL

Of course, there's yet another explanation for the texts. It's that the sender is Lander. That must have occurred to you, too. He knows my number, and I wouldn't put it past him to be able to figure out some way to make texts work on my phone. He's gone off somewhere for reasons only Lander would know, and he's decided to get in touch.

However, I don't think so. Make no mistake, Lander would love the idea of freaking me out, but I don't think he'd go to these lengths. I don't know where Lander is or what's happened to him, but he's not the texter. How can I be so certain? Well, this won't seem very convincing to you unless you're one yourself, but it's the twin thing. We're not identical, but for the first nine months of our lives we shared the cramped living space of our Mam's womb, and since then we've rarely been apart for more than a few hours at a time. For as long as I can remember I've always had a rough idea of what Lander was up to. If Lander was close, I would know it. If he was trying to contact me, I would know it. It's not Lander.

I ponder what to do. I can't spend whatever's left of my life surrounded by guns and with the curtains drawn and the doors locked. I have things to do. In the long term I need to work out how I'm going to start building myself a life, because I can't go on like this, moping about, seeing things, living from day to day without any clear plan for the future. Some jobs need to be done straight away. I have to put the cover back on the turbine, do something about the hay, make the yard safe from stray creatures, and look after the animals. The animals! Oh shit!! The cows!!! Joey!!!! In all this mess I've forgotten them. I haven't done the fucking milking!!!!!

EVEN LATER THAN THAT

As soon as I remembered the animals I dropped my diary. I got my bad foot into a boot. That hurt. I picked up one of the shotguns and called for Buster. Then I limped across the yard to the barn, feeling hugely guilty and expecting the worst. I couldn't understand why Dolly hadn't been making a fuss. Usually when a cow needs milking it bellows enough to crack the windows, but I've heard nothing. I noticed that Buster was limping too, probably out of sympathy, and he wasn't running about like he usually does. He keeps worrying at his back, where the boar got him. I've put a bandage on it to try to stop him licking off the antiseptic ointment and he looks a dufus, quite comical in fact. The wound must have been bothering him and I promised him I'd have a look at it after the milking.

I opened the barn door expecting, well, I didn't know what, but I was prepared for some sort of trouble. However, everything was normal. The cows were in the barn, Molly and her calf in their usual stall, and Bonnie and Dolly in theirs. They watched me with only a casual interest. There was fresh straw on the floor and they looked totally happy. I grabbed a bucket and the milking stool and started massaging Dolly's teats, but there was nothing there. It seemed that my neglect had forced her to run dry – or she'd been milked already. I went to the cooler. There was milk in there, fresh and still warm. Somebody had been in the barn. Somebody had done the milking.

My blood literally ran cold. I didn't understand what that cliché meant before, but I do now. It's the feeling that your spinal cord has been flash-frozen. I took the gun and limped around the end of the barn to the paddock. Joey was there, calmly nibbling grass. He didn't even come over to me when I leant on the fence. It was obvious he wanted nothing. Buster whined. He couldn't understand it either.

Is this the work of a hob, you ask? Hob my arse! I stamped back to the house, as well as I could stamp with a bad foot. I was fed up with all this creepy stuff. Whoever was doing this and the texter were one and the same, I was convinced of it. I was going to take him on, whoever he is. I was going to challenge him. How do I know it's a 'him'? I just do.

I took off my boots. I stuffed Lander's air pistol in my waistband (with just a momentary feeling of satisfaction that it fitted so easily). I sat down and took out my phone. Underneath the last message, I entered a new text:

WHERE R U?

33

———

CLOSE

I was too wired to sleep last night. This morning I'm wrung out, and dizzy when I stand up. I feel as though I've been hollowed out. See what you've done to me, Adam.

This is what happened. This isn't for you because you were there so you know, but it has to go down in the diary, for the record. All right?

Okay. Last night. I came in from the barn and warmed myself a can of soup. It tasted watery and I only had a couple of spoonfuls. Nothing else appealed so I went through to the front room and curled up on the sofa. I spent ages there, listening to my music and waiting to see if there was any reply to my text. Buster wheezed on the rug beside me and made occasional whimpering noises in his sleep.

At last, it must have been well after midnight, I forced myself to go upstairs (yes, I'm sleeping – or trying to – upstairs again, and yes, I know, I'm pathetic because I keep changing my mind). I fancied a bath, so I ran the tub. There was a flask of Eau d'Amour on the window sill. It was Mam's favourite and I haven't been using it because the scent of it makes me think of her and that upsets me. Besides, it was expensive and nowhere in Walbrough was posh enough to stock it so I don't know whether I could ever get any more. Then I thought, *Oh, what the hell. Here's to you, Mam,* and I tipped in a generous slug.

I lay in the silky water for ages. My ankle and hand are better but they still hurt a bit, and I flexed them in the warm suds. It was so calm and cosy lying there in the candlelight, my Bluetooth playing quietly in the background. It seemed so normal, like it had always been. I could imagine Mam and Gran downstairs watching the TV, Granddad reading his paper, and Lander in his room on his computer. Perhaps they were there but in a different dimension. Perhaps if I concentrated hard I could slip through the membrane that divides theirs from mine and join them. As long as I stay here and don't move they will remain.

I closed my eyes. When I opened them again the bath was stone cold. I clambered out, shivering, and wrapped myself in a towel. My playlist had finished and the house was silent.

I took a candle into our Mam's room and turned her big mirror around (you remember I faced all the mirrors to the wall because catching sudden sight of reflections spooked me?). The girl I saw was like a creature in a vampire movie. My arms and shoulders were boney. My eyes were sunken and had dark rings around them. Panda eyes, Lander would call them. My lips had been sore for a couple of days but I was surprised to see how dry and cracked they were. I bared my teeth. My gums were red and bleeding. What was wrong with me? I bent towards the mirror to get a better look, and that was when I saw a figure. It was at the end of the landing, beside the door to Gran's room. For a nanosecond I thought it was Lander back. It was wearing a T-shirt and skinny jeans, and looked fit. The face and hair were in shadow. It looked at me and I clutched my towel to me. Then I turned, and it had gone!

I ran to the top of the stairs and peered down into the gloomy hall. I listened. The grandfather clock ticked and Buster snored in the corner of my room. Had I been dreaming, still dozy from my bath? The figure had looked so solid. And when I went to where it had been, where it had stood and watched me, I thought I could smell a man's cologne. It was one I knew, one that Lander sometimes used – Boss or Armani or something like that. There must have been someone there.

Of course, I couldn't sleep. The strange thing is that I wasn't scared, not at all, but I was wired up. What had happened? Who had I seen? Was it you, Adam? Who else could it have been? But the doors are locked so how did you get into the house? Where are you now? Are you watching me?

All these questions and more made such a clamour in my head that sleep was out of the question. So this morning I feel like a zombie. Perhaps I am a zombie, one of the undead caught in the daylight. Perhaps I did get the Infection and my corpse has been reanimated. Eek!

LATER

There's another problem and it worries me, a lot.

I thought Buster hadn't been himself and I took a look at his shoulder. I've been putting it off because of my hand, and when I did examine it I felt guilty because it's badly infected. It must be hurting him but he can't tell me. He whimpered while I was seeing to him, but he stayed still and let me take off the dressing, bathe his wound with disinfectant and water and apply more ointment and a new bandage. When I'd finished he licked my hand, his way of saying thank you, and I rubbed his ears. Then he went to lie down again.

I'm worried about him. The gash smells bad. It's swollen, and when I pressed it puss came out. I've used loads of antiseptic on it but God knows where that tusk had been. He needs a vet but there's no chance of that.

Please please please let Buster be all right. I can't bear the thought of him in pain, or of being without him. 'I'm sorry, old friend,' I told him. 'I'll look after you better, I promise.' I think he understood.

LATER STILL

OMG. I've had a reply.

I was trying to tidy up a bit, part of my plan to take control of my life and get busy, when my phone vibrated. It was in my jeans pocket and it made me jump.

The text I sent yesterday was **WHERE R U?**

It was meant to be a challenge, to force the texter out into the open. The reply throws it right back at me. It's one word.

CLOSE

34

———————

A LETTER

If whoever's sending these texts meant to give me yet another sleepless night, they surely managed it! The text coming right after the apparition (was it?) on the landing, I couldn't clear my head of either.

I tried all sorts: reciting poetry in my head, reliving visits I'd made to places, imagining the walk up to the Bride Stones, but none of it worked. I'd distract myself for a few minutes but then the thoughts would push back. Finally, I gave in and got up. I picked up a candle, and because I'd been thinking about him I wandered into Lander's bedroom.

I wish I'd found his message sooner. I can't think how I missed it, but how did he think I'd know it was there? He could have left something to alert me. That's typical of Lander, expecting everyone else to be in step with him and able to read his mind.

I've been in his room a few times since he left, to tidy up and to put away the clothes I'd washed, and I don't know why I didn't see it then – thinking about something else, I suppose. To be fair to Lander, the message was pretty obvious: a memory card taped

200

among the posters on his wall with a big arrow in red felt pen and a large 'K'.

I powered up his computer and mounted the card. It contained a single text file. I opened it.

Hi Kes

I was going to say that if you're reading this it means you've not caught the Infection and you're still alive. Then I thought that sounds naff, and I can hear you saying, fucking duh. I have some stuff to tell you. You're going to find it weird, but I haven't time to explain properly so you'll just have to trust me and go with it.

When the Infection came it just didn't make sense that everybody who was exposed to it died. The virus is a parasite and it can only live for a limited time outside a human body. How could it carry on if it killed all its hosts? It was against all the rules of evolution and survival. Well, I wasn't the only one who thought that. I went on the dark net and found accounts from quite a few people who claimed to have caught the Infection and got over it. The trouble is, most of them seemed complete nutters. Not all, though. There was this guy called Anton, in Belarus, who ran a forum. He did a regular blog and I signed up as a follower. He had over a hundred of them. They seemed just like you and me. They'd all been mega-exposed to the Infection and all their family and friends had caught it, but for some reason they'd not. They called themselves The Selected, no kidding, and they thought they were special. They seemed to be clustered in southern

Asia: Kazakhstan, Afghanistan, Nepal, and places like that. They swapped news of where they'd been, what they'd been doing, and why they thought they hadn't been got by the bugs. Their reasons went from being super-holy and chosen by God, to bathing in special rivers, to eating weird food. Some of them were completely gaga. There was one guy who only ate berries, and another who made pills out of yak dung! It was a hoot. A few of us started a sub-net to share the crazy stories.

Somebody suggested that the survivors should all get together to found a new civilisation, but nobody could agree on where, or figure out how to arrange it or how to get past the travel ban. Then something started to happen. To cut a long one short, it seems it wasn't that these people had escaped the Infection, just that they'd caught it in a different way. One of the guys in the group is a doctor and he explained it best. He said the intention of the virus, if you could call it that, is to find a human host, occupy its brain and live there. The human nourishes it and transports it so it can spread to others. That's what's supposed to happen in the second stage of the Infection, after the fever and the cramps. The problem (for the virus) is that most people die before it can get itself lodged in their brains. So if you shiver and cramp up and shit your insides out and die, then the virus has fucked itself and has nowhere to go. If you don't get those symptoms, or if you do and you survive, then it can move in upstairs. But that's rare. According to the doctor, that's why it's evolved to mutate like it does and to be so easy to transmit, because it needs lots of goes before it finds somebody who lasts long enough for it to be able to move on to the next phase. Now there's a new strain, where the initial symptoms are a lot milder, not much more than a cold, and you get over them and it's easier for the virus to settle in your head.

I wanted to know how you'd see if it was happening to you and if the virus was living in your brain. Then Anton started writing about it on his blog. He said he'd been infected but had got through. At first he thought he was back to normal, but then he started seeing people who weren't there. Alongside this, he was doing things and forgetting he'd done them, so that he thought there was some other dude there with him. He figured this out because as an experiment he listed every single thing he did as he did it, throughout the day. When he read it back there were things on his list that he had no memory of doing, none at all, and when he'd discovered them he'd thought they'd been done by somebody else. It was like he'd become two people. The same thing was happening to other dudes and they all found it tough to deal with. One loony-tune said the virus was aliens come to take us over and this was how they were doing it, by occupying our minds. Another said he was going to top himself and he must have because he didn't post any more. Anton stayed quite clear and calm throughout, even when things got bad for him. He said that his head was full of all these imaginary dudes, more every day. He could see them and hear them, but they weren't real. He proved it by making videos of him having conversations with them, but there was nothing there, only him talking in an empty room. Then the site went down and I couldn't follow Anton any more.

I started to see things myself, guys I used to hang out with who couldn't possibly have been there (e.g. Bryan Fry and his dad, who drowned when their boat turned over a couple of years ago). I found that things were being changed around in my room. I accused you of doing it and we had a row. Remember? After that, I fixed the lock on my door so I could keep you out but stuff still got moved around so it could only have been me. What clinched it was when I saw our Mam walking across the yard, two days after she'd died. Ghosts are rubbish, so I knew it must be the virus that had got into me.

I got scared then. Before Anton's site closed one guy posted how he was regularly visited by a dude who called himself The Master, and he ordered him to kill his father and somehow he couldn't refuse so he did it. I wondered what would happen if one of the people I was seeing ordered me to kill you. Or Granddad, or Gran. Or if I just lost it and went on a rampage. I couldn't risk that, so I've decided to go away. If I can I'll get to Anton's group and see who's left. I'll try to figure out what's going on and find the guys who've been working on the treatment. Then I'll come back for you. That's a promise, so keep out of trouble!

I hope this stuff doesn't happen to you. All the people posting on the site were blokes, so perhaps chicks don't get it in the same way. I hope it's like that. Anyway, that's all. I can't remember ever writing so much before! Pity it's not a school essay. Fucking A*, yeah?

Keep safe. L.

P.S. I've taken my iPad. You can have my computer. I've cleaned off the porn. Just kidding!

So that's why Lander went: to protect me, to protect the rest of us. That's typical of him. Tears were in my eyes by the time I'd finished reading. I want to hug him. I want him back.

35

────

WEEK 6

There were no texts yesterday and there've been none so far today. I keep checking but there's nothing since that single word. **CLOSE**

It hasn't wobbled me as much as you might expect. You'd think it would totally freak me out, the idea that some monosyllabic stranger was stalking me and was near, wouldn't you? Because that's what it is, stalking, isn't it? I'm okay with it, though, because I know that the texter isn't threatening. I thought he was at first, and I still keep the doors locked and the curtains drawn, and I still make sure there's a firearm close by, but I'm positive he doesn't mean me any harm. If he'd wanted to hurt me he could have done it by now, he's had lots of chances. He could have smashed a window and got in, or jumped me on the way across to the barn. And what about the other night? He was only a few feet away and I had nothing on but a towel. He could have done what he wanted. Why didn't he? Because he's Adam, and Adam is my friend. That's why I'm not scared.

There's one thing that does bother me, though. What if there is no Adam? What if my brain's infected like Lander said, and all the weird things that have happened – the field gate, the hens, the shadow in the barn, the watcher on the path and on the landing – are either in my head or things I've done myself?

The problem with that is there are some things on my list of the weird and creepy that I couldn't possibly have done. For example, there's no way I could have got downstairs on my own with a bad ankle, hobbled across the yard, milked the cows, put some fresh straw down and then gone back to bed again and forgotten all about ever doing it. For those couple of days it was torture to put any weight at all on that leg, and walking was sheer agony. So believe me, if I'd done all that I would have known! Then there was the damage to the turbine. How could I have done that? If it was Adam who did it, he's no friend, he's a bastard! Sorry, Adam, if you read this and it wasn't you. But if it was you, you deserve it!

LATER

I've been looking at the texts again. I took the word 'close' to mean 'near'. However, it could be 'close' meaning 'close down' or 'end'. Perhaps Adam is telling me that the exchange of texts is over. Perhaps it's a sign-off. This makes me feel let down and crappy, like I've been dumped.

LATER STILL

This afternoon I've been napping on the sofa in the front room. I don't seem to have any energy. I don't want to do anything and even writing my diary is an effort. I suppose I ought to eat something but I don't feel hungry. When I got up this morning I weighed myself. I've lost over twenty pounds since my top weight before the Infection started! Twenty pounds!! I came down and tried to drink some milk, but it tasted horrible, greasy and sour, and it made me gag. The only thing I do fancy is chocolate, but I don't have any and I don't intend to go down the hill to look for some. Tonight I'll make myself eat something. Promise.

EVEN LATER

I wake up and Josie and Miss Dove are sitting in the armchairs in the front room. They look really well. Miss Dove's hair is in a French plait and she's wearing a powder blue top with a greenish scarf, the colour of her eyes. Josie is in her school uniform. She has pink cheeks and a red nose. I want to hug them both but I can't get up.

'You're all right,' I say, 'you've survived.'

Miss Dove smiles at me – she really does have the most fabulous smile. 'Yes,' she says, 'we have, and I can see that you're all right too, although you look a bit pale.'

'I'm fine,' I say. 'It's great you're here.' It doesn't occur to me to ask how they got in through locked doors.

'We came to tell you about school,' says Miss Dove.

'We're all going back,' says Josie.

'But it's still the holiday,' I say.

'No matter,' says Miss Dove. 'The Governors have said we should go back now because the school closed early, before the end of term.'

'We start again tomorrow,' says Josie. 'Isn't it great?'

'Yes,' I say, 'it's fantastic.' It really is. I can't wait. 'What about the other girls?' I say. 'What's happened to them?'

'They're all fine too,' says Josie.

'We'll all be back together again tomorrow,' says Miss Dove.

Miss Dove and Josie get up. Miss Dove bends over and kisses me on the forehead. Her hair brushes my face and I smell her perfume. Josie puts her arms around my neck. She smells of the bakery. 'See you, Kes,' she says. 'Take care.'

They go out through the door to the hall and close it behind them. I sit there and touch my forehead where Miss Dove kissed it.

EVEN LATER STILL

When I wake up again I'm cold. The curtains are closed but I can see it's still dark. I stand up and stretch, and have to grab the back of a chair to steady myself. I don't seem to be able to get up nowadays without feeling giddy. I go through to the kitchen and stare at the fridge. There's nothing in it apart from milk, a bit of cheese and the remains of a loaf. None of it appeals, although some toast might be okay. I pull out the loaf. It's covered in green blobs. I bin it. I look in the pantry. There are lots of tins: beans, stewed meat, soup, rice pudding, peaches, plums, pears, tomatoes, sardines, sweetcorn. I can't face any of it.

I pick up my phone. Does what Josie and Miss Dove said mean that everything is back to normal? I go through the usual trials but nothing works. I can't connect to the internet. The TV screen stays blank, all the channels dead.

There's no further message on my phone. Did 'close' really mean 'end'? What are you playing at, Adam? I text again.

R U STILL THERE? WTF'S GOING ON?

Of course, there's no reply. I didn't expect there would be. I put some food down for Buster but he doesn't seem interested in eating either. He doesn't get up, just looks at me and wags his tail, feebly. His dressing will need changing but I don't want to disturb him now. I'll do it in the morning.

I lie on the sofa, drifting in and out of sleep. I don't worry about the milking and seeing to Joey. Someone will have done it.

Sometime later I'm suddenly awake. I'm freezing cold. I look at my phone. There's another message, although I hadn't heard the alert.

I SAW U SKINNY DIPPING. NICE!!

Oh no! Jesus! Fuck! I feel myself blushing and my hands tremble. I *was* being watched. He was there! He was looking at me, ogling me like a peeping Tom. I tremble so much that I drop the phone and it thumps on the carpet. I roll onto my back and stare at the ceiling. My teeth and fists clench and I feel a surge of anger. Who does this prick think he is? How dare he? Then another emotion kicks in. When I think about it it's like a scene from one of the Greek myths we read with Miss Dove: the nymph, naked on the rock, and the mortal looking at her from behind one of the Stones.

It's a bit of a turn-on. If I'd known at the time that he was gawping at me I'd have given him more of a show!

36

A DATE

OMG, what a dream. If it was a dream. I'm not sure what it was. All I know is that I woke up with my sheets in a complete tangle. I'm hot and wet. I mean not only sweaty wet, but wet down there, too. My lips feel swollen, my breasts are tender and I feel as though something's hit me between the legs. At the same time I feel easy, as though a weight's been lifted off me. I lie there for a long time enjoying the memory of my dream. If this is what being ravished feels like, I like it.

When I came upstairs last night for some reason Buster didn't come with me. He usually does but all he wants to do at the moment is lie down by the boiler cupboard and sleep. I put an extra blanket down for him and he seemed to like that. I think his wound's bothering him. I wish he could tell me where it hurts and what makes it feel better. I lit a candle on the landing in case Buster wanted to come upstairs in the night. Then I stripped off and lay in bed, thinking about the latest text. **I SAW U SKINNY DIPPING**

At some point I dropped off. I don't know how long I slept, but suddenly I was wide awake again. There was something different about my room, although I couldn't see what. I rolled over in bed and touched something warm. I shrieked and leapt out, calling for Buster and ready to run downstairs. Then I heard this voice. It was deep and musical, calming and reassuring. 'Come here,' it said. 'Don't be afraid. Sit here.'

They were invitations, but at the same time they were commands. I had to do what the voice said, there was no choice. I grabbed the sheets to cover me and sat on the edge of the bed, ready to take off at any moment.

'How's your ankle?' said the voice.

I swallowed. 'All right, thank you,' I said. 'It's getting better.'

'I'll take a look,' said the voice.

He rolled off the bed and knelt at my feet. It was a single movement, fluid and athletic. There was enough light from the candle still burning on the landing for me to be able to see the top of his head, the blond curls. He was on one knee and was wearing nothing except for a pair of white briefs. He took my foot and flexed it gently. His fingers were firm and his hands were strong, but also tender. I watched the muscles of his shoulders rippling under his skin. He began to massage my ankle between his thumb and his fingers. What he was doing ought to have hurt but it didn't, it felt wonderful. He ran his hand up my calf to my knee. His hand was smooth and soft, but solid. I felt myself flush. I was breathing faster.

He stood up and I saw the bulge in his trunks. *OMG*, I thought, *I think this is it.* He stooped, put one arm under my knees and the other around my shoulders, and picked me up as if I weighed nothing. He laid me on the bed, gently, spreading me like something sweet and special. He lay beside me, his head propped on one arm.

'I'm Adam,' he said.

'I know,' I murmured.

Gently he put his hand flat between my breasts. 'Your heart's racing,' he said, 'and you're trembling. There's nothing to be afraid of.'

He leaned over and kissed me on the nose. 'You're very beautiful,' he said. Before I could make the protest that any well-brought-up girl should his mouth was on mine. His tongue flickered on my lips. I parted them and I answered his tongue with mine. He eased himself on top of me and my hands wrapped around him, feeling the strength in his shoulders. One of his hands buried itself in my hair. His other hand stroked my thigh. His knee rose smoothly between my legs and I settled onto it. My body was like a bowstring. I knew that this, whatever he was going to do, was what I wanted, and that I wanted it more than I had ever wanted anything before.

The whole night wasn't so gentle. Once we got going we twisted and writhed, locked our limbs and wrestled. At one stage I felt as though I was being electrocuted and I flung myself back and yelled. Then I felt him jerk, and shudder all over, and we were still. We were both panting and wringing wet. For a while he lay on me, heavy, while our breathing and the throbbing of our pulses eased and I felt his hair, his back, his bum. He rose on his elbows and gave me one more kiss, long and slow, as he withdrew from me. I had never felt happier, or more relaxed. Everything was marvellous and my world was rimmed with gold. I gently nibbled his ear and he gave a contented sigh. I felt drowsy, and slowly we sank into sleep.

When I awoke I felt for him. I wanted him again. I wanted to talk to him. I had so many questions. But he wasn't there. I felt a rush of disappointment. I had felt his body against mine only seconds before I woke up, I was sure of it. I called, 'Adam.' There was no answer. He had gone as quickly and mysteriously as he had arrived.

I waited for a long time, drifting – asleep, awake, asleep, awake – feeling my body where he'd touched me, yearning for him to come back. Late morning I got up and had a shower. I dried myself and put on a little make-up and one of the dresses I took from Chez Annette, because he might return at any time. Then I went downstairs and made some tea. I put out two cups. Does he take milk? Sugar? For the first time in weeks I was hungry. I spread some crispbreads with jam. I was just starting on one when I noticed something was missing. Where was Buster?

I called, expecting to see him padding round the door, his claws clicking on the tiles. He didn't come. I called again. Maybe he was locked in somewhere. If so I should have heard him whining, but the house was silent.

Perhaps he went out with Adam. How did Adam leave when the house was locked? I'm thinking about this as I go to the front door, and there's Buster. He's lying on the doormat. He looks to be asleep. I squat down to stroke him. He's cold and stiff. His usually wet nose is dry. He's dead.

I let out a howl of misery. MY BEST FRIEND IS DEAD. With trembling fingers I check him over, looking for damage, but there's no obvious indication of what's killed him. It can only be the tusk wound. It must have been worse than it looked, worse than I thought. I lie on the floor in my pretty dress and put my arms around his neck and I weep. I haven't been looking after him. I'm a selfish bitch. I've been so wrapped up in myself, my moods, my own hurts, the texts, Adam, that I didn't give him the care he needed, the care he deserved. While I was busy upstairs with Mr Universe, my dog was down here dying.

When I've finished crying I'm angry. I spread a towel over him and go looking for my phone. It's on the dresser, where I left it last night.

I grab the thing and hammer in a message.

WOT HAVE U DUN TO MY DOG?

The reply comes almost at once.

???? NOTHING. NOT ME.

THEN WHO? I WANT ANSWERS.

There's a slight pause, then the reply.

OK. MEET ME, I'LL XPLAIN IT ALL.

I hesitate. Meet him? I so desperately want to see him, to hold him again, and there's the promise of an explanation. At last I'll know what this mess is about. I send,

WHEN? WHERE?

There's another pause. Then,

**BRIDE STONES. TOMORROW. NOON.
B.READY**

37

LOVERS' MEETING

He told me to meet him 'tomorrow' but it might as well have been light years. Time passes so slowly. I can't face using my own bed with its rumpled sheets and the smell of him, so I sleep downstairs on the sofa again, or rather I try to. Several times I get up and go to where Buster lies under his towel in the hall. Every time I look at him I cry. I can't believe he's dead. I keep expecting him to look up and wag his tail and slurp me with his big, sloppy tongue.

The Bride Stones. Shall I go? I must, but why there? Why not here? Perhaps there's a reason he's selected that place. Does he know its romantic associations? Does he know it's a place for lovers? **B READY** the message said. Ready for what? I feel a quiver of anticipation that this is the place Adam has chosen for us to meet again.

Eventually I can't put up with lying on the sofa any more and I get up. It's 5.30; six and a half hours to go. I scramble into a pair of old jeans and a sweatshirt, then I go across to the shed to get the wheelbarrow. I don't bother any more with the gun or locking the door; I know I'm safe. I bring the wheelbarrow back to the house and somehow manage to get Buster's body into it. I try to be gentle with him, but it's hard because he's heavy. All the time I'm alternately crying and cursing.

When I've got Buster in the barrow I wheel him behind the barn. The rest of the pallets that Lander and Granddad had fetched up from the town are stacked against the wall, next to the old pit. I throw four or five of them in. Then I get the barrow to the edge and roll Buster on top of them. I go to the barn, fill a bucket with diesel from the tank and splash it all over Buster and the pallets. I hate doing it. I can hardly see through my tears, and as the oily liquid soaks his coat I have to keep telling myself that he's dead and he can't feel it. I wish I could manage a better send-off for him. He was a good dog.

I go upstairs and run a deep bath, thanking our Dad yet again for installing the solar panels all those years ago. While it's filling I scrub the diesel off my hands. Then I wash my hair and wrap it in a towel. I tip plenty of Eau d'Amour into the bath and wallow. I shave my legs, my armpits and my bikini line. I get out of the bath, towel myself dry and rub myself all over with that really expensive lotion Gran and Granddad gave me for Christmas. I dry my hair, adding some *Screengirl* and brushing it till it shines. I take the tweezers and pluck my eyebrows. I apply some foundation to my face, just a little, and a little blusher. I dab a trace of gold on my eyelids and run some eyeliner round them. I eyebrow pencil my brows and stiffen my lashes with mascara. Finally, I put on some lipstick, pouting and blotting.

I stand in front of the mirror and check myself out. Do I look good enough for him? I've lost a lot of weight. Am I too skinny now? Am I still curvy? I'm pleased that my skin looks smooth. When our Mam went on her diet she lost so much weight that her skin sagged, so it looked like it belonged to somebody else and she'd just slipped it on for now. I'm young enough for my skin still to be elastic and there's no sign of sags.

I'm still sad about Buster but I'm excited about the meeting.

My phone sounds. Another message.

R U READY?

I text

ALMOST.

At once the reply comes back,

CAN'T WAIT TO C U. COME 2 ME.

My hands are shaking as I text the reply.

B PATIENT. I'LL B THERE. XXX.

I've decided that if I'm meeting a mysterious someone at the Bride Stones I'm going to dress for it. I put on my sexiest underwear, including suspenders and stockings (when did I last wear those?). Then I get into my best dress. It fits me easily now.

I take another look in the mirror. Do I feel ready for my wedding? Do I look like a bride? It's an odd wedding where the bride doesn't know the groom, like one of those arranged marriages that Minal's sister had. I do know the groom, though. He's Adam. He's my Heathcliff and I'm his Cathy, and we will come together on these moors, just like they did.

There's one more thing. In a box on our Mam's dressing table is her wedding ring. I slipped it off her hand before they took her away and it's been in the box ever since. I put it on my finger, the third on my left hand. It fits me. Now I truly am a bride.

Downstairs I put on some flats and a rather smart gabardine that our Mam bought just before everything fell apart. I tie on a headscarf, tuck in my hair, take a box of matches from the kitchen and go round to the back of the barn where Buster lies on the pallets.

The matches won't take in the wind, but I crouch behind the wall where I can light a paper spill. I toss it on the pyre and it explodes in a tower of flame. I jump back and watch it for a few moments. I'd meant to say a few words for Buster, but the flames are too quick. They leap and blacken his hair and I can't bear to look any more, so I come away. Buster used to be Lander's, but then he was mine and he knew I thought he was the best dog in the world.

Back at the house, I check my make-up to be sure it hasn't smudged. I pick up a pair of beige heels and put them in a bag. I'm writing this last entry. Then I'll put my diaries in the bag too, and go to the Bride Stones to meet my groom.

AFTER

38

RECONNAISSANCE

SURVEY AND RECONNAISSANCE Unit (SRU) NW14, based in York, was nearing the end of its tour of duty. The six-person crew had been tasked to scour a segment of West Yorkshire, and for the past five days had been working their way through the string of towns along the Calder Valley. The status of each had to be recorded, every street videoed, and major buildings photographed. The aim was to find out what remained of the life that had existed before the Infection, and to report back to the clear-up and reconstruction teams. They had not been told specifically to look for survivors, although the possibility of finding someone who had escaped the plague was always in their minds. The hope of that had receded after each day of fruitless searching.

The driver, Sandy Lisle, sighed as she brought their vehicle, a specially equipped Toyota Avatar, to a stop in the last town on their list. They'd been at it since four that morning, done two towns and this was their final call. With luck they'd be finished by noon and on the road back to York, to a long bath, a good meal and some leave. She rolled her shoulders to loosen the knots and looked at the desolation that surrounded them.

'My God, what a hole. Where are we?'

Jackson Pollard, seated behind her, read from the briefing sheet. 'Walbrough. Market town and civil parish. Former mill town, now a commuter area for Manchester, Bradford and Leeds. Local employment mainly light engineering, services and agriculture; major employer Lamb's Sweets and Confectionery. Three primary schools, one secondary. Pre-Infection Population 12,002.'

'Any flags or alerts?' said the unit commander, Charlene Adams.

'None I can see.'

'All right. This is the last one. Let's get suited up and go. Maggie and Jacko, you take the blue sector. Chris and Mahmood, you take yellow.' She handed them pads which showed Walbrough divided into coloured sections. 'Sandy, you stay here with me. When the others get back we'll do green. It's the usual drill, folks: check in every fifteen minutes, look out for stray animals, and if you come across any dogs that look as though they might have rabies, shoot them. Don't enter any buildings, even if the object of your dreams is beckoning you from a bedroom window. Wear your suits and hoods at all times, and if by any remote chance you do find any humans alive, avoid contact. No heroics. Remember, we're here to look and report on what we see. If there is anybody still alive, they'll have managed on their own until now and a few more hours won't hurt them. Any questions?'

Pollard raised a finger.

'What is it, Jacko?' Charlene asked, although she knew what his answer would be.

'Do we have to do this?' Jackson had a whiny voice that irritated Charlene. 'We've spent the last three weeks going all along this God-forsaken valley. We've stopped at every smelly little town and village. We've been down every street and examined every rat hole and dog kennel, and look what we've found. Broken windows, smashed doors, burnt buildings, looted shops, starved animals and rotting corpses. This place is just like all the other dumps we've been to, worse if anything. I mean, look at it. I say we drive round, take some video and get our arses back to base.'

Charlene sighed. This was Jackson's standard speech at every stop they'd made for the past week. 'You know that's not on, Jackson. If we're ever to get things back and running again, we have to do this. The authorities need to know the situation on the ground, otherwise how can the reconstruction begin? We're all tired, but we're going to do as good a job here in Walbrough as we did on the day we came out of the arks and started this work. We'll do a proper survey, and then we'll go home. Anybody else?'

Nobody spoke.

'Very well, then, get going. And remember, take care. These streets may not be inhabited, but they are still dangerous.'

The pairs checked each other's suits and hoods and tested their communicators. One took the video camera and an emergency kit, the other an automatic weapon, and they started across the square.

Charlene watched them go, then climbed into the front seat of the Avatar beside Sandy. 'Do you think he'll do it?'

Sandy laughed. 'Who, Jacko? Fuck no. He's a lazy bastard. He'll cut more corners than a blind tailor. He'll go out of sight, smoke a vape or two and then come back. You should have sent me with him.'

Charlene shook her head. 'Maggie's with him. She's all right. She'll keep him up to the mark. Besides, I want you here. We need to talk.'

Sandy groaned inwardly. She thought she knew what it would be about. However, she was wrong, Charlene didn't want to talk about their 'relationship'. Instead she said, 'You know, Jacko's right. All this is pointless. Everything's smashed up. There's nobody here. Same with the other RSUs. Every night we check in and the reports are identical. Mess, stink, squalor, damage, death, decay. Nobody and nothing has survived. All the places are the same. We might as well just drive away and leave them to rot. Look at that.'

Sandy peered through the windshield at the desolate square. The doors of the surrounding shops had been broken, their windows smashed and the raided contents dragged out. There were rags that had once been clothing, there were split cartons, smashed bottles, a fridge, a mattress, two vacuum cleaners, a TV. Everything was covered in mud, grit and slime. It was the same everywhere the unit had been. As the Infection had taken hold, order had broken down. Those who had not at first been smitten had taken comfort from the surrounding horror by indulging in a bonanza: free food, free goods, free booze, free everything. There had been arguments, fights, and fatalities as people tried to grab what they could. Then, one by one, they all started to feel the probing fingers of death. They went to their homes and locked the doors, to sweat, to vomit, to cramp, to bleed and to die.

'Do you think there's nobody left to find, then?' said Sandy. 'Do you think everyone's dead?'

Charlene watched a starved dog limp around the corner of what had been a market stall. Its back was arched and its shrivelled hide stretched like a drum skin over its ribs. It sniffed at something it had found and bared its teeth. No, she didn't think they'd find anyone. Jackson's view came from laziness, not reason, but she agreed with him. However, she recoiled from the bleakness of that message so she said, 'Well, we got through it, didn't we?'

Sandy leant towards the windscreen and rubbed at a smudge with her thumb. 'We survived because we were sent into the arks. If we'd not, we'd be as dead as they are.' She pointed to a confused heap of rags against the wall.

Charlene raised her binoculars and saw that it was, had been, two people. They were wound together. Male? Female? One of each? Had they fallen while fighting? Or were they lovers who, on the threshold of death, had locked each other in a final embrace? Impossible to say. They were questions that, like many others, would never be satisfied because nobody who knew the answers had lived to report them. Those who had been sent into the arks – a network of sealed pods originally constructed to protect key personnel in the event of biological warfare – had gone in with orders to maintain a strict silence, so that their existence would remain secret. There had been no contact with the outside world so they knew nothing. All they could do was emerge when the tests said it was safe, to search, investigate, and start the long process of rebuilding a ravaged civilisation.

Time passed. At one stage Sandy lowered the window to get some air, but the sickening stench forced her to close it again. She was hot and uncomfortable in her bio-suit. She undid the zip. It was against standing orders, but Charlene wouldn't mind.

She rested her head in the angle formed by the headrest and the side window. Both the women dozed. They were exhausted, the whole unit was. They did the overnight watch in pairs, taking turns, which meant that one night in three they got no sleep.

Poppers would fight the fatigue for just so long, then they ceased to have an effect. They'd passed that point a week ago.

'The simulations were wrong, weren't they?' Sandy said.

'Not half,' said Charlene. She laughed but without humour. 'Remember Operation Dinosaur?' she said.

'Do I just?' said Sandy. 'Building shelters out of sticks, lighting fires with a flint and steel? They were supposed to train us for Armageddon, but nobody foresaw anything like this,' she said. 'This is paradise, or it will be.'

Charlene was shocked. 'Paradise? You think?'

'Yes, I do,' said Sandy. 'Just consider: there were 4,000 people sent into the arks. That means that now the Infection's over there'll be 4,000 people living in a country built to support sixty-five million. Okay, there was a lot of looting and things were smashed up, but that's only in the town centres. There's plenty of stuff in storage. There's enough tinned and packaged food to keep us for a century. There's ample space to grow crops, and fresh meat running wild, there for the taking. There's clothing, furniture, machines, and electronic equipment, together with all the spare parts we'd ever need to last our lifetimes and beyond. There are complete factories that just need to be started up again. All 4,000 of us could drive flash cars and live in mansions. We'll have to clear up the mess and get the basic infrastructure working first, but it's all still there. We'll have everything we want. In the end, it will be paradise.'

Charlene didn't look convinced. She gazed out of the window. 'I suppose that depends on what it is that you do want.'

Sandy gave her long look. 'What's bothering you?' she said.

Charlene turned to her friend. 'Why do you think we were given places in the arks? Why did they choose us?'

'It was a random draw,' said Sandy. 'They said so.'

Charlene snorted. 'Random draw my fanny. Look at the people who were in our ark, and in all the others too. What do you notice? I'll tell you. We're all young adults. I haven't seen anybody under twenty-five or over thirty. Is that random?' Sandy shrugged. 'What's your specialism?'

'You know this. Before the Infection I'd just completed my medical training. I'm a doctor.'

'And what's mine?'

'You have a PhD in metallurgy.'

'And Mahmood?'

'Software systems developer.'

'Jacko?'

'I'm not sure. Some kind of engineer, I think. What's your point?'

'My point is that between us we cover a wide range of skills, and we're all highly qualified in our specialist areas.'

'All right, we were chosen for our expertise,' said Sandy. 'What's wrong with that?'

'Nothing,' said Charlene. 'It's essential if we're going to try to get things going again, but there's something else. What do you notice about our unit?'

'A bunch of idle wasters?' Sandy shook her head. 'I don't know what you're getting at.'

'Yes, you do,' said Charlene. 'You, me, Maggie, Chris, Jacko and Mahmood. Four women and two men. In the arks, the ratio was the same, with about twice as many females as males. If there were 4,000 of us allocated places, that's getting on for 3,000 women to not much more than 1,000 men. Do you think that proportion came about as the result of a random draw?' Sandy didn't answer. 'No,' Charlene went on, 'neither do I. We've been saved so we can rebuild the population. A thousand Adams and 3,000 Eves. The men will be required to work and to fertilise the women, and the women will be required to breed, and to breed, and to breed. Again and again and again. We'll be machines in a baby factory. That's a funny paradise.'

Sandy was silent while she took this in. Then she laughed.

'What's the matter?' said Charlene.

'They obviously didn't know. We should have told them. We're gay.'

'Do you think they'd care?' Charlene said. 'So long as we each produce a baby a year they won't give a shit whether we're gay or straight. And if we don't produce they'll have no use for us.'

39

SEARCH

IT WAS OVER two hours before the two reconnaissance pairs returned, arriving within a few minutes of each other. Charlene and Sandy put on their hoods and slid out of the Avatar so they could spray the others.

'Anything?' said Charlene when they were all back in the vehicle.

'What do you think?' said Jackson, and stared out of the window.

'Use the correct form to report,' Charlene snapped. Then she added more gently, 'Come on, Jacko, we're all tired.'

Jackson, who had bristled at the first reproof, relaxed. 'All right, sorry.' Charlene held out the voice recorder and nodded for him to speak. 'Reconnaissance report, Jackson Pollard and Maggie Phillips, town of Walbrough, West Yorks. Blue sector. All streets surveyed and videoed, file WB45112. No signs of recent human activity. All shops have been entered and show evidence of random looting. No mains water or electrical power. Roads and railway intact, although some roads are currently blocked by vehicles. Some fire damage, but most buildings appear sound.

Town Hall and Health Centre are intact. Contact posters left on each street. No survivors seen.'

He handed the recorder to Mahmood. Apart from the different names and sector, his report was the same.

'Can we go now?' Jackson said.

Charlene shook her head. 'We haven't done green sector. That was for Sandy and me.'

Jackson groaned and, for the first time so did the others. Charlene could smell mutiny. Would they miss anything by not doing the green sector? No.

'All right, you win. Let's get out of here.'

Everybody cheered. Charlene nodded to Sandy, who started the Avatar and gunned it across the square, scattering some evil-looking gulls.

'Stop!' shouted Mahmood. 'Just a minute!'

Sandy braked the Avatar.

'What is it?' said Charlene. 'This is not the time to need a pee.'

'No,' said Mahmood, sounding excited. 'Look up there. Isn't that smoke?' He was pointing to a small group of buildings on the flank of the hill, high above them.

'Yes, it is,' said Chris.

'Must be a fire,' said Mahmood.

'No shit, Sherlock,' said Jackson.

'Hang on,' said Charlene, 'somebody might be trying to signal.' She got out her iPad and studied it for a moment, glancing up at the column of smoke, which was growing as they watched and was now thick and black. 'It's this farm,' she said, pointing to a spot on the map.

Sandy leaned over. 'Looks like it.'

'We'd better take a look.'

Jackson howled. 'Jesus no, please. You know what it'll be. A fault in solar panels or a turbine, or the sun burning through some glass. We've seen it all before.'

Charlene turned and gave him a scathing look. 'Well, Mr Clever, you might not have noticed but there's been no sun today. There hasn't been any wind, either. It's been dull and still, a bit like you, so there's no chance a turbine would have been turning, solar panels wouldn't have been doing much and the glass option's out, as well.' She looked back towards the smoke and raised her field glasses. 'Anyway, I can see the smoke's coming from behind an outbuilding.'

Mahmood was looking at his iPad. 'There may be a problem. It looks as though that place the smoke's coming from is red-flagged.'

Charlene spread her fingers and enlarged her map. There was a red marker on the edge of the town that she hadn't noticed before. 'Yes, it is.'

'What's that mean?' said Maggie.

'It means it's to be left alone, we're not to go near it,' said Jackson.

'Correct,' said Charlene. 'A yellow flag designates an object of scientific study. A red flag an object of *special* scientific study. This is a red.'

'So we leave it,' said Jackson.

'But why the fire?' said Sandy. 'There must be somebody up there to have lit it. Perhaps they've seen us and are trying to signal. Perhaps they need help.'

Charlene made a decision. 'We're going to take a look,' she said. Jackson moaned.

'I don't know how to get up there,' said Sandy. 'You'll have to direct me.'

Charlene returned to her map. 'Okay, go out of the square and back the way we came. A few hundred metres along there's a road on the right, opposite the park, then a lane on the left.'

Halfway up the hill they took a wrong turn and found themselves facing a gate. The farm was across the other side of the field. The smoke was still billowing from behind it.

'Across?' said Sandy.

'Better not,' said Charlene. 'We don't know the terrain, and there's no need to take a risk. Don't want to find ourselves in a hidden ditch. The track goes round the side of the field, let's stay on it.'

'Look,' said Jackson, pointing. In the paddock beside the farm was a large brown stallion. He looked sleek and well-fed.

'That horse has been cared for,' said Charlene. 'Come on, I think we might have something here.' Her heart started to beat faster. Were they going to find somebody alive at last, after all their searching? Would her unit be the first to locate survivors?

The track led them around the back of the farmhouse into a yard. The smoke was thicker here. No one said anything but they were all on edge. What went on at a site of special scientific study? What was being studied? Who was studying? What would they find? There was no clue outside the building. The door to the house was shut.

'Right,' said Charlene, 'we do this by the book. Suits and hoods tight, tool up, communicators on. Sandy, you stay here, video everything and open up a communications channel to HQ, tell them where we are and that we're investigating because we think there's an emergency. Keep the engine running in case we need to get out fast. Jackson and Maggie, one on each side of the yard. Maggie, you cover the barn, Jackson the house door. Have your weapons ready but don't wave them about. We want to be alert but not threatening. Chris, round the back of the barn and check out the fire. Mahmood, go to the front. Don't show yourself, just look and tell me what's going on. If anything looks iffy, no heroics. Get the hell out!'

They climbed out of the Avatar. Charlene took a loud hailer from its clip. 'Attention, attention please.' The metallic voice rattled around the yard and bounced off the hill above the house. 'We are a reconnaissance unit sent by the Provisional Directorate for the North of England. We have seen your signal and are here to help you.'

They waited, breath held, pulses raised. Nothing happened. The house door stayed shut, smoke drifted idly across the yard. In the distance, a curlew called. Charlene raised the loud hailer again.

'Please show yourselves. We are here to help you, and the Government requires you to cooperate with us.'

Charlene looked at her watch and timed two minutes.

'Anything from HQ?' she said.

Sandy shook her head. 'No contact. The signal's been patchy all along the valley and there's nothing here. I can't get through.'

Charlene was uncomfortable. A red flag was a red flag. They probably oughtn't to be there at all, and they certainly should go no further without proper authorisation. On the other hand, they might be about to encounter somebody who had survived the Infection without the shelter of an ark, and that person might need help. There was a crackle in her earpiece. 'Chris, what you got?'

'Not much. No one here. The fire's still burning. It's quite a big one and it's been lit deliberately. Lots of timber and stuff, all piled up, like a beacon.'

'A beacon?'

'Yes, you know. Like the ones they had when we were kids, to signal special occasions. They'd build them on hilltops.'

'You're sure it's human-generated, not just a heap of old stuff that's somehow caught fire?'

'Sure. It's mostly pallets, and petrol's been used as a starter, I can smell it. Something's in the fire. It's a dead animal, maybe a large dog. I think somebody's built the fire to burn the body.'

'Jesus,' muttered Jackson. 'It's like finding life from space.'

'Let's hope not,' said Charlene. 'Mahmood, anything from you?'

'No, boss. The door on this side's shut and there's grass all around it. It doesn't look as though it's been used in a while.'

Charlene thought for a moment, then gave her orders. 'Okay, that's good. Chris, take some pictures, then come round here. Keep to the wall, don't make yourself a target. Mahmood, come back. You and me will take a look at the house.'

Sandy gave her a warning look. 'I know,' said Charlene, 'red flag. Orders. But what if we just went away and there was somebody in there in desperate need.' She tried the house door. Locked. 'Right. I'll go in with Mahmood. The rest of you wait out here, side arms at the ready but not obvious. Remember, if there is someone here it's because they're immune. We're not, so wear face masks and don't handle anything without gloves. Sandy, keep trying to raise HQ. If you get through tell them what's going on and request authorisation to investigate. Oh, and ask for backup. Jacko,' she said, 'time to show us how strong you are. Get Thumper.'

Jackson took the heavy ram from the back of the Avatar. He lined himself up, swung it back and crashed it into the door. It held firm. 'It's a good one,' he said.

'Again,' said Charlene.

The doorframe splintered, and on the third blow it gave. They were in.

'Careful now,' said Charlene, 'it could be booby-trapped.' She led the way in.

Charlene didn't know what she'd expected to see, but it was nothing like what she found. Everywhere they'd been they'd seen mess and destruction, decomposition and decay. But here everything was so ordinary. The place was clean, tidy and well-stocked. The kitchen was modern, with a stainless steel fridge, cooker and microwave. Clean dishes were stacked on shelves. Saucepans hung from hooks on the wall. On a draining rack beside the sink were a single plate, mug and knife. A large pantry contained provisions for a siege: tins, cleaning materials, toilet rolls, containers full of rice, flour, dried peas and beans, pasta, jams, sauces. Charlene flicked the switch on the wall. The lights came on.

'Mm, everything seems to be working.'

She opened the fridge. It was empty except for milk and a large bowl of eggs.

They went through to the hall. There was a grandfather clock which was going, a rack with three or four coats. Charlene picked one up and sniffed the collar. There was a long, brown hair on the shoulder. The other coats seemed a similar size. Next to the coat rack was a sturdy-looking cupboard, with a key in the door. Charlene opened it. There were two shotguns, a .22 rifle and an air pistol, all clean and oiled. Every slot was full, all the guns present. On the bottom of the cupboard were boxes of ammunition.

'Well,' said Charlene, 'this seems pretty organised. I wonder where she is.'

'She?'

'Yes. Only one person is living here. A young woman.'

'How do you know that?'

'Single place setting on the kitchen drainer means one person. The coats on the rack are women's. I recognise the perfume on them. It's *Bitch*. That's a young person's fragrance, not something an old lady would buy.'

Mahmood was impressed.

'You check out the rest of the downstairs,' said Charlene. 'I'll do the bedrooms.'

'Be careful, boss. Don't you want me to cover you?'

Charlene smiled. 'No, I'll be all right. I don't think we've got anything to worry about.' She ran lightly up the steps.

'WHO IS HE?' said Charlene.

'I don't know,' said Sandy. 'He waved his ID but it's a foreign name and I didn't get it. Says he's from the Department of Information, whatever that is. You'd better go see him. He seems seriously pissed off.'

Sandy had managed to raise HQ and had reported their location and what they were doing. As Charlene had instructed, she'd asked for authorisation to investigate the site but the duty officer had been out of his depth. He told her he didn't have the authority to agree to what she'd requested, but he would refer it up. Meanwhile, he'd arrange for backup. So Charlene had decided to go ahead anyway, and they'd continued searching the house and its surroundings, trying to get some clue about its mysterious occupant.

'Okay, better see what he wants,' Charlene said. 'What's he like?'

'A serious hunk,' said Sandy. 'Tall, good looking, fair hair, muscles. Almost enough to make me turn.'

'Almost.' They laughed.

'Seriously, though, if they want to use us for baby farming he can be my first mate.'

'You think? What we get will be out of a test tube.'

Charlene led the way downstairs. The young man was in the front room, standing beside the mantelpiece and looking at the urn and the white boxes. He was casually dressed in a check shirt and black chinos. His face was tanned and his hair a nest of blond curls. His eyes were a dazzling blue. The only thing about him that looked official was the leather document case under his arm. He was not wearing white gloves or a face mask.

'They're ashes,' said Charlene, taking off her own mask. 'From cremations.'

'Yes,' said the young man. 'I know that.'

He was probably not much more than twenty, Charlene thought. There was a hint of middle Europe in his accent. Also a hint of chubbiness in his face. It was okay now, but give him a year or two...

He gave Charlene a hard stare. 'And you are?'

Charlene showed him her ID and the young man studied it carefully. He grunted what might have been disapproval and handed it back.

'Likewise,' she said.

The young man took out his wallet. He'd meant it to be a quick flash and fold, but Charlene stopped him while she read the words beside the photo.

· · ·

Przemysław Adamski

Field Agent

Department of Information

'Right,' she said. 'Introductions over, what can I do for you?'

Przemysław Adamski put his document case on the table and folded his arms. 'You can start by telling me why are you here,' he said.

The young man's manner was hostile but Charlene answered calmly. 'I am in command of a survey and reconnaissance unit, from York. There are six of us. We've been along the whole of this valley. We were on the point of leaving Walbrough when we saw smoke coming from up here. We came to investigate. We think someone's living here and was trying to signal.'

'You need to go,' said the young man. The women didn't move. 'Now.'

Charlene resented his attitude. She was a unit commander. Who did this guy think he was? 'What do you mean, go? A young woman has been living here, recently, and we need to locate her.'

'No you don't,' said the young man. 'You shouldn't be here at all. It's a Site of Special Scientific Study.' He unzipped his document case, flipped open a tablet computer and read from the screen. '"Sites of particular interest or importance are designated by red or yellow flags. Such sites must not be approached or entered without special authorisation from the Department of Information." This place is red-flagged. You have no right to be here.' He snapped the pad shut. 'Well?'

'Standing orders,' said Charlene. 'Yes, I have some of those, too.' She looked at the ceiling and recited. '"The task of a Survey and Reconnaissance Unit is to carry out thorough searches of given areas. All premises and property are to be evaluated and assessed. Units must pay special attention to the possibility of finding survivors, and in the event survivors are located must be prepared to take whatever action the Unit Commander considers appropriate to preserve life." This is our designated area. We've found a survivor. I think the appropriate action is to provide her with assistance.'

The two faced each other for a few seconds. The young man gave ground first and his expression softened. He let out a huge sigh. 'Cock up,' he said. 'Left hands not knowing what the right hands are doing. We need to get you away, though, before Kerryl returns.'

'Who?'

'Kerryl. The girl who lives here.'

'There is no one here,' said Sandy. 'The place was like this when we arrived.'

'Except the door wasn't smashed in,' the young man said, icily.

'Look, Mr Adamski,' said Charlene, 'we seem to have got off to a bad start. Of course we'll leave if that's what's required, but why do we have to do that before this Kerryl comes back? She probably hasn't seen a living soul for weeks. We should stay and help her.'

The young man sat down at the table and motioned to the women to do the same. 'Call me Adam,' he said. 'Mr Adamski's too formal and most people find my given name unpronounceable.' Charlene and Sandy sat.

'The person who lives here is a young woman called Kerryl Shaw,' Adam said. 'You need to understand that she's very special, unique even. Not because she's survived exposure to the Infection, several thousand people have done that, but because we can find out from her things we can't learn from anybody else. How much do you know about the virus?'

'Mutating organism, strain I/452,' said Sandy. 'Deadly, easily caught and easily transmitted. Causes severe symptoms which usually result in death. I thought it was universally fatal, but you seem to be saying differently.'

'It is usually fatal,' said Adam, 'but not invariably. A small number of the people who catch it survive. In the last few months, we've learnt a lot more about it and how it has been developed to spread through the body. The Infection has two stages. The first is the one everybody knows: a high fever followed by severe cramps, diarrhoea and haemorrhaging. Most people don't get beyond this stage, but a few do and they move on to phase two. By this time the other symptoms have receded, therefore the subject may now appear normal. However, they're not; the virus is still in them. It's migrated to the brain, where it lives on and reproduces.'

Charlene shuddered, cringing at the notion of some alien thing, a parasite, dwelling in a person's head. 'This is what's happened to Kerryl? She's got to phase two?'

'Yes, she has. And she's got there without apparently going through the symptoms of the first stage.'

'And that's what makes her special?'

'Oh yes. It means the virus may be evolving and adapting. But there's something else that makes Kerryl special. She's a twin.'

'What, you mean there's somebody else here too?'

'Not here,' said Adam. 'Her twin brother is called Lander Shaw. He was arrested six weeks ago for attempting to travel illegally, and taken to a DoI centre in Oxford. At first, we thought he was just like the rest of the survivors. Then he told us about Kerryl, and we realised we had a unique opportunity. You see, all we could do up to then was study the other survivors by observing them, interviewing them, scanning their brains, and putting them through tests. That's helpful but it can't tell us how they might react in the real world. With Kerryl and Lander, it's different. They aren't identical twins but their DNA is extremely close. And they've had very similar upbringings. The bonus is that they were together when the Infection spread, so they were likely to have been exposed to the virus at the same time and it will be at the same stage in both of them. That means we can scan Lander's brain and spot any changes that take place, and we can observe Kerryl to establish how these changes affect her day-to-day behaviour, her ability to look after herself, solve problems and live a normal life.'

'So you've been spying on her,' said Sandy.

'We've been *studying* her,' Adam insisted. 'A scientific investigation. The original plan was to watch her remotely and we planted cameras in the house. We hid them in the mirrors, but she must have realised something was amiss because she turned them all round and we couldn't use them. So I've been observing her directly.'

'Without her knowing?'

'That was the intention. I've tried to keep out of sight, but a couple of times she might have seen me.'

There was a long silence. Then Charlene shook her head. 'I can't believe you've been doing this. I can't believe you've been happy just to watch this young woman... how old is she? Twenty?'

'Eighteen.'

'Just to watch her struggling, trying to manage on her own, thinking she's the only person left. How could you do that without stepping in to help her? What sort of a creature are you?' She was gratified to see that Adam at least had the grace to look uncomfortable.

'It's a scientific study,' he said. 'So we can learn how the virus affects people and how we can help everybody. Besides, I have looked after her. I've made sure she's been all right. For example, she had a bad fall and hurt her ankle. Luckily it wasn't broken, but if it had been I would have been here to deal with it. While she was laid up I did things for her, like milking her cows.'

Charlene wasn't impressed. 'I don't think milking a few cows cuts it. Being here all on her own must have been a nightmare. If it were me I'd have gone mad.'

'That's why we've been setting her challenges.'

'Challenges?'

Tasks designed to enable us to assess her rationality and her response to problems. They also keep her occupied.'

'What sort of tasks?'

'Some of them have been very simple. I left a gate open that she would have expected to be locked, to see how she dealt with a phenomenon that had no obvious explanation. Then we removed her hens to test her reaction to a disturbance in her routine. Others were more complicated. We wanted to know how she would deal with a major survival issue, so we created a fault in her wind turbine.'

'I don't believe this!' Sandy exploded. 'Spooked her with a gate? Took her hens away? Messed with her turbine? Who are you? Don't you think this poor girl has suffered enough without you playing tricks on her?'

'They were not tricks,' Adam insisted stiffly. 'They were tests, so we could study her responses. Kerryl and her brother are extraordinary. They are giving us insights into the effects of the virus that we wouldn't otherwise have. We must learn everything we can from them.'

Charlene and Sandy made no response. They could see what he was saying, but they were not going to agree with him.

'You really must go now,' he said, 'before she comes back. I can cover the damage to the door, but it would cause a major trauma if she found her house full of strangers.'

Charlene got up to leave. 'A few minutes ago, when you were telling us about the virus, you didn't say it had developed to progress through the body. You said it had *been* developed.'

'Yes,' said Adam. 'Our people think that this virus was grown in a lab somewhere.'

'You mean it was created by humans?' said Charlene.

Adam nodded. 'We think so.'

'Why? As a bio weapon?'

'Maybe. We're not sure why, it could have been innocent, but it seems it was probably an experiment that somehow went out of control and got loose into the population.'

The two women looked at him in stunned silence. 'My God,' said Sandy.

'One more thing,' said Charlene. 'You'd better have this. We found it in the kitchen. I don't expect there's anything on it, the phone system hasn't worked in ages. Anyway, we can't open it.' She put Kerryl's mobile on the table in front of Adam.

'There's a password,' he said. He tapped the screen a few times and the phone came to life. He studied it and a look of disbelief spread across his face. 'Holy shit!' He took an iPad from his case and put it next to the phone. 'Look at these. What do you see?'

Charlene and Sandy peered at the two devices. 'They're text messages,' said Charlene. 'How can that be? Who can she have been texting? And who's been texting her?'

'Exactly,' said Adam. 'Who? Look at the two threads.'

Both screens looked identical, one just a larger version of the other. 'They're the same,' said Sandy.

'No, they're not. Look again.'

Sandy peered at the screens. Then she got it. The messages that were marked 'sent' on the iPad were marked 'received' on the phone, and vice versa. She didn't understand. 'You mean these two things have been sending texts to each other? Whose is the iPad?'

'It's Kerryl's. She's been texting herself.'

Charlene was incredulous. 'You mean she's been exchanging messages between her own phone and her own iPad? How? Why?'

'The how is easy,' said Adam. 'The networks packed in weeks ago, so these must have been sent and received over the local Wi-Fi here on the farm, which is still working.'

Charlene still couldn't believe it. 'Let me get this straight. She's been sending lovey-dovey texts and then pretending to be someone else and answering them.'

'She's not been pretending. As far as she knew at the time, she *was* someone else.'

Sandy put her index finger to her temple and made a screwy sign.

Adam shook his head. 'Remember what I told you about how the virus affects the brain? One of the phenomena we've seen at Oxford is what we call "acute personality dislocation", APD. A sufferer seems to have two – sometimes more – distinct personalities that they switch between. Often the switches are random but in a few cases they seem logical, planned even. Like here. One of the texters is Kerryl herself; the other is an imaginary correspondent, a boyfriend maybe. She becomes that other person in order to send messages from them.'

'And she doesn't know she's doing it?'

'The "real" Kerryl thinks that she's sending messages to a stranger, and the stranger is replying. She's completely unaware of what her other persona is doing.'

'And when she replies?'

'Then she is somebody else, another person distinct and separate from the real Kerryl.'

'But that's incredible.'

'Not really. People on their own often talk to themselves. There are plenty of examples of APD in cases where prisoners have been placed in solitary confinement. This is just an extension of those. In solitary confinement it usually takes a long time for APD to manifest itself. In this case, the stress of her situation, maybe compounded by the virus, has accelerated the process. Fascinating. Fascinating.'

Adam looked at the texts again. Suddenly he leapt up. 'Jesus! Why didn't I notice it? I know where Kerryl is.' He rushed from the room.

41

____

THE BRIDE STONES

A COLD WIND pierced them as they crested the hill. They could see nothing ahead but the bare, black rocks and it looked as though the Bride Stones were deserted. Until they got close. Then they saw her.

Kerryl was lying on her back, in the centre of the pool and slightly below the surface. Her hair made a halo in the water and her dress ballooned around her. They ran the last few metres to the bank and Jackson and Mahmood waded in. Between them and with help from Charlene and Sandy they pulled her out.

Sandy knelt beside her, feeling her neck, wrist, and ankles.

'Shouldn't we be giving her the kiss of life, or something?' said Jackson.

'Too late,' Sandy said. 'There are signs of rigor mortis in her hands, face and neck. She's been dead for at least a couple of hours.'

'She's drowned herself?' said Adam.

'Looks like it,' said Charlene.

'Mm,' said Sandy. 'It's possible but I'm not sure. I can't see any marks or signs of a struggle on her, so it doesn't look like she was forced under the water. There's no indication of an attack by an animal, and it doesn't look as though she fell in as the result of an accident. But it's very difficult to kill yourself in a flat, shallow pool like this. As soon as you get water in your throat your reflexes kick in and you cough it out. You can't hold yourself under long enough to make yourself drown.'

'So what happened?'

'She might have fainted after coming up the hill, but there's another option. She looks extremely undernourished. It's possible she went into an anorexic coma. If she was standing in the pool at the time she'd just collapse, and that would be it.'

They looked down at Kerryl. Her eyes were closed as if she was sleeping. She wore a pale, ankle-length dress with thin straps, and a design of flowers and birds embroidered across the breast. Her skin was marble white, and her hands together on her chest. She looked like an effigy on a tomb in some ancient cathedral. Where the wet fabric clung it showed her ribs and hipbones, sharply angular beneath the silk. Her arms and shoulders were skeletal.

Charlene pointed to her left hand, where a band of gold gleamed. 'That looks like a wedding ring. She wasn't married, was she?'

'I don't think so,' said Adam. 'No, I know she wasn't.'

'So why is she wearing it?'

Adam thought for a moment. 'These rocks are called the Bride Stones. They have romantic and supernatural associations for local folk. The texts invited her to meet somebody here. She's dressed herself like a bride and put on a ring. I think she came here expecting to meet her groom.'

'And who was that supposed to be?' said Sandy.

Adam shrugged. 'I think her alter ego, the other texter.'

'Poor girl.'

'I found these,' said Jackson, who had been exploring the rocks. He gave a plastic bag to Adam, who took out two notebooks: one green, one purple.

It took some time to deal with the body. While they waited for the support to arrive they continued searching the area around the Stones and found a fleece and the shoes Kerryl must have worn to walk up from the farm.

When the recovery team arrived they were brisk and business-like. They zipped Kerryl into a body bag, lifted her onto a stretcher and took her to where their helicopter waited. Charlene, Sandy, Jackson and Mahmood left to walk back to the farm.

Adam watched the helicopter's rotor spin up and the machine rise, bank and head south. He waited until it was a distant speck, then he sat down on the flat stone where, not long before, Kerryl had undressed for her swim. Even then she'd looked emaciated, scrawny. Shouldn't he have foreseen what was coming? Couldn't he have done something to save her? His orders had been unambiguous: keep your distance, don't interfere, don't let her know she's being observed. But he'd had discretion. He could have done more.

He took up the green notebook. It was almost full, every page densely packed with her neat script. He turned to the last entry.

· · ·

I am here for you. You promised you would come to me, but you have not. Now I think you never will.

What shall I do? I cannot go home.

There is nothing for me there without you.

There is nothing for me anywhere if you are not.

To lose you is to lose myself.

I shall stay here. I shall rest in this pool, where a bride once rested before.

I shall close my eyes and I shall think of you, remembering last night and all the times we have been together.

Goodbye, my love.

Kerryl's misery and pain were beyond bearing and Adam had to blink away tears. He flicked the pages of the notebook and was astonished to see his own name.

He froze. He was there. She was addressing him, writing for him. Had she known about him all along? He fingered the cream paper. He could see her now through the farm window, bent over her task, the breathless, loopy script spilling from page to page, transported on the swell of her coursing thoughts.

He put down the green book and opened the purple one.

'You should read this one first,' the flyleaf said. So he began.

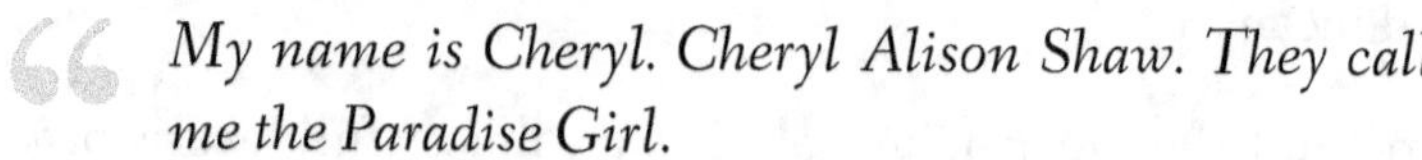

> *My name is Cheryl. Cheryl Alison Shaw. They call me the Paradise Girl.*

REBOOT SERIES 2
AFTER SHOCKS
A SEARCH FOR TRUTH IN A WORLD BECOME CHAOS
PHILL FEATHERSTONE

1

—————

LEAVING

LANDER REVIEWED THE items he'd spread out on his bed. It was the fourth or fifth time he'd checked them. There were:

- His ID card: essential in case he was picked up by a patrol.
- Chocolate bars: also essential, but for a different reason.
- Maps: he knew where he was going but he intended to avoid main roads, so they would be important.
- A Bowie knife in a sheath: because you never knew.
- His favourite fleece: it was probably cold in Belarus, and in any case summer was ending.
- A pair of binoculars: useful for spotting patrols, with luck before they saw you.
- A torch: electric power was becoming less reliable.
- A compass: he could usually find south during the day, but at night it might be different.
- A water bottle: obvious
- An envelope containing two hundred and seventy-four pounds in notes and coins: also obvious

Money was probably not much use any more, but having it was a comfort. Some of it was his own savings, but most had come from the tin he'd found in the bottom of their Mam's wardrobe. It was where she kept her cash. He felt bad helping himself, even though she wasn't around to ask. He'd been scrupulous in taking no more than half, leaving the rest for his sister, Kerryl. Their Mam would have wanted that.

When he'd stowed all the items in his backpack there was one more thing left on the bed: a USB flash drive.

Lander tossed it in his hand. He was trying to decide what was the best thing to do with it. It had taken him a long time to compose the letter it contained. Writing was not his thing, that was more Kerryl's scene, and putting it together had been hard work. Where should he leave it to be sure his sister wouldn't miss it? Not downstairs; their Gran might clear it away before Kerryl saw it. He might put it under her bedroom door but she might miss it. Besides, he couldn't be sure she was asleep and he didn't want her to know about it until after he'd gone. It had to be somewhere she'd see it and want to investigate, so that she would read it and understand why he had left them all.

He took a reel of tape and stuck the USB drive to the notice board over his desk. He chose purple (her favourite colour) so it would catch her attention, and to make sure he pinned a sheet of A4 next to it and with a black marker wrote a big letter K, filling the paper. Then to be on the safe side he added an arrow pointing to the drive. There. He knew that she'd come into his room to look for him and there was no chance of her missing it when she did. He was assuming she'd be curious enough to put it in her computer right away.

Suddenly there was a sound on the stairs: his grandparents were coming to bed. Quickly he pushed the backpack under his bed, lay down, shut his eyes, and pulled the duvet up to his chin.

The loose board on the landing creaked. Then his bedroom door opened a crack and a shaft of light striped the bed. It was Gran. In the few days since the death of their Mam, she'd taken to looking in on him and his sister the last thing before she settled down herself. She didn't do anything, didn't come in to straighten their bedclothes or give them a goodnight kiss, she just stood in the doorway. He didn't know why. Mam had stopped doing that when they went to secondary school, but Gran seemed to think it was a good idea. She closed his door gently and moved on to Kerryl's room next door.

He lay still. He couldn't risk leaving the house until he was sure his grandparents were asleep. They had been talking downstairs for so long that he wondered if they were ever going to bed. Their voices had been too muffled for him to hear what they were saying but he could guess. It would be about the Infection. That's the only thing anybody ever talked about now. What else was there?

There was the usual coming and going to the bathroom. Teeth were cleaned, the lavatory flushed, and Granddad let go his nightly, world-class fart. Normally Lander would have thought that funny, but not tonight. He was about to leave everything he knew, so there was not much that could make him laugh tonight.

The door to his grandparents' bedroom closed and there was silence. He'd been hot, lying fully clothed under the duvet, and he was glad to throw it off. It was nearly midnight. He told himself to wait for another quarter of an hour, just while everything settled down. The minute hand on his watch moved with glacial slowness. After a while, he heard the rhythmic rasp of Gran's snoring, but he knew better than to trust that. She was the lightest of sleepers. Granddad always said a mouse belching would wake her. Was Kerryl asleep? He'd heard nothing from her room for ages but he knew she often spent hours reading. Maybe she was doing that now.

At last the minute hand reached a quarter past the hour. He got up from his bed and took the spare pillows from the bottom of the wardrobe. He arranged them under the duvet to make a lumpy shape. It wouldn't pass close inspection, but to a casual glance in the dark, it might look as though he was sleeping.

He stood in the doorway and took a last look at his room. There were only a few things he'd miss. His laptop, of course. There was no point taking that. There was the match ball from the time he'd played for Yorkshire Colts. That had been a day. He'd taken 5 wickets for 16 against a Derbyshire Youth XI, and they'd given him the ball as a souvenir. They'd also offered him a place at the Yorkshire Cricket Academy. He'd been over the moon for a while, but he needed their Mam's consent and she'd refused to give it. 'You need to pass your GCSEs, get some qualifications behind you,' she'd said. 'Then you can think about playing games.' They'd rowed about it for days but she wouldn't budge. He'd given up on school after that. He'd done it to punish her, and it had only recently dawned on him that really the one who was being punished most was himself. That was particularly true now that Kerryl was all set to go to Cambridge. Not that he'd want to go there anyway. He'd better things to do than rub shoulders with a load of toffs. The ball was small enough to take and he was tempted to slip it into his pocket, but he told himself no. It was part of his old life, a life he was leaving behind; at least for now.

He slung his backpack over his shoulder, took his trainers, and tiptoed onto the landing. The squeaky board was right in the middle and he was careful to avoid it. He bent to look under Kerryl's door. There was no chink of light, but that didn't mean anything. She might be Snapchatting on her phone, or listening to music on her earbuds, or she might be reading by torchlight. He pressed his ear to the door, straining for any sound. At first he could hear nothing, but then he picked out the sound of steady breathing. She was asleep, all was clear.

There was a sudden snort from his grandparents' room. He froze in case it was a prelude to other nocturnal activity, but everything stayed quiet. It was a timely nudge, though; stop messing about and get moving.

He could have gone down the stairs with his eyes shut, but faint moonlight through the landing window made it easier. He knew that the third and seventh treads creaked, and he was careful to avoid those.

Buster looked up as Lander entered the kitchen and gave a welcoming whimper. He rose from his basket and stretched. Lander bent and fondled the dog's ears and tried to still his tail, which was beating a noisy tattoo on the cupboard door. Clearly, Buster had high hopes of what this nocturnal visit might mean: a walk? an early breakfast? both? His tail wagged even more vigorously and Lander heaved the animal's swaying rump aside.

'Sh. You'll wake the whole house,' he murmured.

Buster was Lander's dog and a good friend. He would miss him. He'd thought about taking him, but decided that although he could imagine him being useful, the upheaval wouldn't be fair on the old dog. Besides, it would be harder for him to hide from the authorities with a big sloppy Labrador in tow. And he would be another mouth to feed.

Lander squatted. 'No, mate, you've got to stay here,' he said.

Buster looked disappointed. Lander opened a tin of Dog Star beef and jelly, his favourite, and filled his bowl. That would keep him busy while he slipped out of the house.

'See you, boy,' he whispered, patting him. 'Look after everybody. Kerryl will look after you, and I'll come back. I promise.'

He crept out of the kitchen.

For as long as Lander could remember the door to the yard had not been locked at night. Grandad said there was no point. 'Who's going to bother coming up here to thieve from us? Anyway, we've got nowt worth pinching.'

That had changed. The Infection had made everybody cautious, and for the last few weeks Gran had insisted on it being secured. 'You never know. There are all sorts of strange folk about now,' she'd said.

He took the key from its hook, slid it into the lock and turned it gently. He wouldn't be able to lock the door behind him but that didn't matter. By the time the others noticed he'd be well on his way.

The air was chilly and he shuddered. Summer it may be, but over a thousand feet up in the hills the nights could be sharp.

He tiptoed quickly and quietly across the yard and let himself into the barn. He took out his phone and turned on the torch, shielding the beam with his hand to avoid the light spilling outside. Their three cows watched him lazily as he went to the far corner, where there was a heap of sweet-smelling hay. He knelt and rummaged. He'd hidden his two motorbike panniers there. He'd packed them three days ago. In one were clothes – a spare pair of jeans, socks and underwear, three or four t-shirts and a couple of sweatshirts. Was that right? Would it be enough? It was difficult to pack for a trip to another country, one that you'd barely heard of let alone located on a map. Anyway, if he was short of anything he could probably find it somewhere.

There was plenty of stuff in abandoned stores. And of course, he had money to buy things, if that still worked.

He turned to the other pannier. In that were his waterproof jacket, his sleeping bag, a groundsheet, his washbag, and a spare pair of trainers. The rest was taken up with food. For the past week he'd been sneaking tins and packets from the store in the pantry. He'd felt a bit guilty about this, but their Mam always used to say that Gran kept enough food to feed an army, and he was sure the rest of the family wouldn't need the little he'd taken. He'd probably be able to get plenty of food on the way too, but it was best to have something put by in case there was a problem.

The cows studied him with mild curiosity. How was it that cows managed to look as though they understood everything that was going on, when in fact they were as thick as gateposts?

He was satisfied, and pleased with himself. Had he forgotten anything? He told himself that if he knew that it wouldn't be forgotten, would it? He smiled at his joke. One of his school reports said that he needed to pay more attention to planning. Well, take a look at this lot for planning, Mr Teacher.

He took a pannier in each hand and went out to the yard. He was careful to be very quiet as he passed Joey's stable. Horses don't sleep much, and the last thing he wanted was for Joey to whinny. He was Kerryl's horse and she could hear him from a mile away. If he did sound off she'd be sure to wake up.

Beyond the stable was the shed where he kept his motorbike. It was a 125cc Yamaha that he'd got almost a year ago, soon after his seventeenth birthday. He loved that machine. At least once a week, sometimes more, he gave it a good clean and polish and the chrome shone in the torchlight. He took out his knife and cut off the L-plates. He was a superb rider, he just hadn't taken his test yet. Having to show the plates was demeaning in normal times, and these weren't normal. If he ran into the law the lack of plates would be the least of his problems. He was glad to be rid of them.

He clipped the panniers to the bike, rocked it off its stand, and wheeled it out of the shed. The moon was higher now and brighter, and Lander kept in the shadows. He was well aware that his Granddad never got through a night without getting up several times for a pee. If he were to do that at this moment and look out of the landing window there was a good chance he'd see his grandson in the yard, so her needed to move.

At the edge of the farmyard he got astride the bike but he didn't start the engine. Instead, he pushed with his legs and scooted towards the top of the track down to the valley, where he stopped and looked back towards the house. There were no lights on and the building was a dark shape against the sky. All clear. Phase one is complete. He'd got away without anyone noticing.

He was sad, but he was also excited. He'd lived on Paradise Farm all his life and he couldn't imagine being anywhere else. He felt a choke in his throat and he was tempted to turn back, but he knew he couldn't. It was for their good, Kerryl's and his grandparents', that he was going. He owed it to them to get away as quickly as he could. He'd explained why in the letter on the USB stick. He hoped they'd understand. Would he ever know?

He took a deep breath, pushed forward, lifted his feet off the ground and the bike picked up speed. He'd often free-wheeled down to the town but that had been for fun, not because of a need to leave in silence.

The first part of the track was easy because he could see well. Further down the moonlight didn't penetrate the tree canopy and it was hard to make out the road surface well enough to be sure where he was going. He slowed down for fear of hitting a rut that would send him tumbling down the embankment and into the stream below. Years ago their Dad had gone over the edge on a tractor and not lived to tell of it.

Ahead of him a pale shape fluttered across the path; an owl seeking a kill. That afternoon he'd seen three roe deer grazing in the field. How strange it was that wild things seemed to be carrying on as normal, untouched by the menace that was clearing out their human rivals.

He reached the bottom of the track where it joined the main road into Walbrough and waited, checking to make sure that there was no one around. The last time he'd been into the town was when he'd collected their Mam's ashes. The place had smelt bad then, but now it was worse: a mixture of failed drains, excrement and decay. There was also a whiff of something burning, and over to the south towards Manchester he thought he could see a red glow in the sky. He pulled a scarf over his mouth and nose and pressed the bike's starter.

The racket as the engine exploded into life was deafening in the quiet night. They'd hear it in Leeds! Previously Lander had liked the noise his bike made. He'd even tinkered with the silencer to make it louder, but now in the still of the night when he wanted to sneak away it was a curse. Best to move on quickly, before he woke the whole town.

He pulled onto the road and revved away. The sound of the engine bounced off the blank walls of the buildings, rattled around the streets, cannoned off the steep sides of the valley. With luck that would make it harder to locate his precise position. It was helpful that the brightness of the moon meant he didn't need lights; they would have been a dead give-away.

He roared out of the town, leaving behind the only life he had ever known.

2

———

NIGHT

ONCE OUT OF Walbrough, Lander opened up the bike and did a wheelie. He didn't feel in high spirits, far from it, but he wanted to exit the bottleneck of the valley as quickly as he could and that meant giving the Yamaha its head. He was used to slowing down for the speed cameras but nobody was going to bother about speed limits now and he shot past the first one, giving it a middle finger as he went.

He began to relax. He was confident he'd be well clear before anyone had time to wonder what the din in the middle of the night was. Of course, there was always the possibility that some busybody would report him as a nuisance on the citizens' response line and a patrol would be ordered to look for him. That was a risk he had to take.

The moon had gone behind clouds and he needed his lights, so he switched them on and settled into the saddle, prepared for a long ride. He loved being on his bike and was enjoying the prospect of travelling through the night to Hull, even though it was taking him away from his home. At the coast he would find one of the illegal ferries that his internet contacts said made regular trips to the continent. Then he'd slip out of the country and across the sea. He hoped he had enough money. According to the online chatter the ferry prices had been going up and up, which seemed crazy because money was of less and less use now. What was the point of having cash if there were no shops, no entertainment, no services, and nothing to spend it on?

He didn't hear the car over the noise of his bike but suddenly it was there, racing towards him on his side of the road. It wasn't showing any lights. Lander swerved at the same time as the driver saw him and they missed each other by a whisker. It was a big convertible, a white BMW with the top down. He caught a glimpse of three passengers, at least one of them a girl. They turned and shouted at him as the car shot past. They might have been friendly but Lander wasn't inclined to find out; he gunned his bike to get away.

He was on a long straight section of the road and starting to think that the BMW wasn't interested in him when he saw in his mirrors twin headlights spearing the dark. Was it the BMW? Or was it a patrol? If it was the BMW it meant that whoever was driving it had turned around to come after him. It was hardly likely they'd just want to say hello. The fact that now they didn't seem to care about being lit up like a Christmas tree was troubling. These were people who weren't afraid to break the rules about being out after curfew.

He twisted the throttle as far as it would go. The little bike screamed, but the headlights behind him were gaining fast. Whatever the vehicle, it was certainly in a hurry. Now he could see the broad spread of the beams sweeping the road at either side and beyond him. It was the BMW, no doubt about it.

Perhaps that was all right. He'd only had the briefest glimpse of the driver but he hadn't looked any older than Lander himself. They were only kids. They wouldn't be a problem, would they?

He didn't want to find out. His mind raced. How could he dodge them? He could do a U-turn, but even if he could get past the car would only turn and come after him again. How could he escape?

The Yamaha was at its limit, he could get no more out of it. The highway was level and smooth, and the BMW was way quicker. It would only be a few seconds before it caught him. Then he remembered. On the left at the end of this straight was a lane. Somebody Lander had known at school lived up there. It was a narrow, twisting track and the surface was so rough that only a four-by-four or a tractor could manage it easily. A four-by-four, a tractor, and a dirt bike.

The BMW was now just a few metres behind. It could have overtaken him, driven him off the road, but it seemed to be taunting him. His heart raced. The car's horn blared a fanfare. He swerved across the road and it followed. They were going to run him down! He knocked his mirror to deflect the dazzle and peered ahead, searching for the entry to the lane. It must be close. Had he passed it? No, there it was. He might just do it.

He delayed braking until the very last second and skidded sideways, speedway fashion, as he aimed for the corner. He almost lost control but he hung on and raced up the hill, bouncing over the ruts, spitting stones behind him. Taken by surprise, the BMW shot past the turning. It might come back but even if it did it would take time, and Lander knew that the car would find it hard to get up the track. He eased off the throttle and killed his lights. Suddenly he began to tremble, so much that it was hard to keep the bike straight. He came to an open gate, and with a feeling of immense relief went through it and into a field. He killed the engine, leant the bike against the stone wall and sank beside it. He was still shaking, but gradually he calmed down. He got to his feet and closed the gate, leaving the bike where it was, hidden from the track by the wall so that anyone looking over would have to peer down to see it. He retreated to a clump of trees further along the field's edge.

It was a few minutes before he saw the headlights down the lane. Now, though, the BMW was moving slowly, its lights leaping like a kangaroo as it bounced over the bumps. It seemed an age before they drew level with the gate. The driver had no idea how to drive on a surface like this, and his answer to wheel spin was to rev harder, so the car wallowed and slid and the tyres threw up rubble and grit that rattled on the underside and fizzed along the track. There was a smell of burning rubber.

The occupants were shrieking and squealing and the stereo blared. They were all young. Lander guessed they must be high on something. What did they want with him? Just a bit of fun? Probably, but you never knew. Things had changed since the Infection, and the usual customs were out of the window. Once you would have ignored a stranger, or acted with guarded friendliness. Now strangers were fair game, an entertainment, butts and receptors of whatever you wanted to inflict on them.

He waited while the noise of the car receded up the hill. His pursuers had taken no notice at all of the gate, probably not even seen it. He guessed they'd go on to the end of the lane where it met the hilltop road. There'd be an argument about whether the Yamaha had gone right or left. They might choose one, or they might simply lose interest and carry on to wherever they'd been going in the first place. In either case, it was unlikely they'd find their way back here. He felt relief for the first time since the beast had come hurtling around the corner at him.

The darkness was easing and he could make out a small copse a little way across the field. The trees were feathery silhouettes against the faintly lightening sky. He checked his watch. It was just before 4 o'clock. Three hours since he'd left the farm. It seemed longer than that, but at the same time shorter. Soon it would be dawn. Dawn! Lander couldn't remember when he'd last been awake early enough to see the sunrise. Mornings were definitely not his thing.

He thought about home. Kerryl was always up first. She'd go across to the cows, Dolly and Molly and Bonny, and milk them before anyone else stirred. She did the mornings, he did the evenings. That was the way they'd arranged it. It was strange that they were twins but so different in something like that, him a night owl and his sister liking to rise with the lark. Although when he thought about it, Kerryl seemed easily able to do what their Gran called 'burning the candle at both ends'. She could manage on just a few hours of sleep a night, whereas Lander needed a solid eight at least, preferably more.

He had a choice: he could continue for another hour or so, or he could call it a day – well, call it a night really – and hole up until it got dark again. It was tempting to go on, to get closer to Hull, but the daylight would increase his chances of being spotted by a patrol. And if not by a patrol by somebody else, perhaps by another load of idiots like the ones in the BMW. No, better play safe. Besides, he hadn't slept for twenty hours. He was knackered. He needed to rest.

The mate he'd known at school who lived nearby was called Simon. His house must be close, probably no more than half a mile away. Should he drop in and see if he could sleep there? Simon had been the wicket keeper in his school's first eleven, and in the year above him. He'd not really been a mate, but Lander had visited his house once. It had not been a success. It turned out that Simon was gay. That had been a surprise. On the whole, the gays at King's Heath Boys' School didn't try to hide their orientation and everybody knew, but Simon had kept his dark. However, it seemed that he had made a miscalculation. Lander had missed all the signs and it had been an embarrassing encounter for both of them.

That wasn't what put him off calling, though. The thing that did was that since the Infection struck nobody wanted a surprise visitor arriving on their doorstep. It was a visitor who had brought the disease to his own home. The man who had turned up with his sick boy asking for help hadn't meant them any harm but by coming to the farm he had killed their Mam. No, Simon and his family wouldn't welcome Lander suddenly appearing without warning; assuming they were still alive themselves. And if they weren't, he didn't want to go into another house of death. Over the past few weeks he had discovered that the chances were that he was not going to die from the virus that was killing everyone else. And probably neither was Kerryl. But he didn't want to put it to the test. The sensible option was to bed down here.

He took his groundsheet and sleeping bag from one of the panniers. From the other, he got a tin of beans, his water bottle and a packet of chocolate biscuits. It seemed best to get away from the road so he went over to the copse. He decided not to venture too far into the trees in the dark because you couldn't be sure what you might find in a place like that. Anyway, it was choked with brambles so he sat down on his groundsheet at the field's edge. He opened the beans and tipped the tin into his mouth as if drinking. He alternated mouthfuls of beans with bites of chocolate biscuit as he watched the sky lighten. When he'd finished he filled the empty bean tin with small stones and pushed it into a hollow at the base of the nearest tree. It was a beech. He knew that from the smooth bark and the mast around it. He could recognise beech; he also knew oak, ash, silver birch, holly, but not much else. Kerryl, who knew every plant, flower and tree that ever was, often ridiculed him. 'Call yourself a country boy and you don't know what that is!' she'd jibe when he failed to identify something she thought was obvious.

He took a swig of water and belched. He felt better for the food. He was weary, but he didn't feel sleepy. Nevertheless, he thought it best to prepare for when he did drop off. He didn't want to experience dream walking here.

He spread out his bed. It was hard to find a comfortable spot because of the stones and the roots, and he wished he had a foam roll-up. Eventually he found a space where the ground was not too bad, the vegetation gave him some cover, and he could keep an eye on his bike.

'Dream walking'. That's what the online people called it. It sounded cool. Sexy even. But it wasn't. Dream walking was the way some – just a few – responded to the Infection. Dream walkers were deadly, either to themselves or to others. It was because he was afraid he might be one that Lander had decided to leave home.

There was a reel of elastic in his backpack. It was from their Gran's sewing kit and he'd taken it because, as Gran would say, 'A bit of elastic is always useful.' He cut off a couple of metres, anchored one end to the beech tree and knotted it firmly. He tied the other end around his wrist. He took some time to get the tension right, so that the elastic was secure enough not to slip over his hand and firm enough to wake him up if he tried to move, yet not so tight that it would cut into his skin and block his circulation when he slept. He'd been doing something similar at home for the last few nights. There was not much harm he could do dream walking here, but who knew where he might end up?

When he was satisfied with his arrangements he made sure his knife was tucked underneath him where he could get at it quickly. Then he rested his head on his backpack and closed his eyes.

IN DREAMS

SLEEPING IN THE daylight wasn't usually a problem for Lander. His bedroom was on the sunny side of the house but he never had any trouble snoozing till lunchtime, even in the summer, even with the curtains wide open in the way their Mam always left them after she'd been in to wake him. She always used to say that Lander could sleep for England, anytime and anywhere. However, today was an exception. Perhaps it was the effect of walking out on his home and family in the middle of the night. Perhaps it was the adrenaline still pumping around his system after the brush with the BMW. Perhaps it was the hard ground and not being able to find anywhere free from the tree roots and sharp stones which seemed to be competing to bore into his back, his hip, and his shoulder. A bed roll would have been great, but they'd used the only one they had for their Mam. She'd lain on it in the barn when she was sick. It had got spattered with her blood and smeared with her vomit, and after she'd died their Granddad had burnt it.

As if the hard ground wasn't enough, there was a surprising amount of noise. Lander had assumed that the Infection would keep everyone indoors. Besides, everything was closed now so there was no reason for anybody to go anywhere. And of course, there were the government warnings against any sort of travel. By rights there should have been a funereal quiet; but no, on the contrary, there was no end of activity.

There were vehicles on the valley road – not lots, nowhere near as many as there would have been a few months ago, but more than he expected. There were emergency sirens. There was a train – he'd thought they had all stopped. Somewhere along the hillside a tractor was working. He wondered why. Was someone really tending the land in the expectation that they'd still be alive and farming next year? Nearby a dog barked; then another, further away, answered. Sheep bleated. A donkey brayed. A horse whinnied. It sounded just like Joey. For a second he thought it might be Kerryl, who'd ridden after him to give him an earful for slinking off like a thief in the night, but that was crazy. One horse sounded very like another, and how would she know where he was? Late in the morning a police helicopter passed over, flying low in a series of big sweeps. Was it looking for him? Don't be daft. The police wouldn't send a helicopter to search for one teenager, not with everything else that was going on. Anyway, who would have reported him?

Eventually, things quietened down and he managed to arrange himself in a position where he could avoid most of the lumps. However, sleep still eluded him. He got out his phone and brought up Kerryl's number. His thumb hovered over the call icon. Should he call her and explain? Perhaps no one had missed him yet. Perhaps they thought he was having a lie-in and had decided not to disturb him. Possible, but unlikely.

He thought of his home – the comfortable farmhouse with its cosy kitchen smelling of Gran's baking, its tidy yard, Buster, Joey, and the cows. What would they all be doing? Gran would be busy with housework. Granddad would be out and about in the barn or the fields. Would they be OK without him? The farm barely scraped by. Granddad was getting on, and over the past year he had been depending more and more on Lander to do the heavy work. How would he manage on his own? Kerryl would be all right. By now she would have done the milking and she would be in her room skyping, QuickChatting, or perhaps writing her diary. She seemed to spend ages doing that. She wouldn't be at school, the schools had all shut. Lander remembered how upset Kerryl had been when St Winifred's closed. She'd told him about the assembly where the head had announced it to them all, and some girl had done a soppy reading and everybody had cried. It had been different at his school. At King's Heath Boys' the news of the closure had come in a simple note taken to all the classrooms; no assembly for them. He laughed to himself, imagining the reaction if there had been. There wouldn't have been any tears there. Instead there would have been cheers you could have heard a mile away. Lander had been right that there was no point in school. The Infection had proved as much.

His phone still had plenty of charge and there was a good signal. He opened his browser and clicked on the top tab in his list of favourites. It took him to a home screen, anonymous, just a throbbing light in the centre of the screen, and below that a log-in box. He wondered if the site was still live. One way to find out. He put in his user name and password, and clicked. For a second nothing happened. Then the light shuddered and grew. It swelled, and words began to hurtle towards him, one by one: *the ... truth ... will ... make ... you ... free!*

He knew the site well. As soon as it was obvious that the Infection was serious, Lander had wanted to find out more about what was going on. Kerryl had accused him of being gruesomely fascinated by the whole business, but he'd told her that the more you knew about what was happening the better your chances of staying alive. That was why he got annoyed when their Mam grumbled at him for spending so much time on his computer. He was doing it for them. It was what Dad would have done.

To begin with he had restricted himself to collecting online reports and clips from news broadcasts. Then he'd started to follow breadcrumbs, and they'd led him further afield, into chat rooms and issue groups. That was how he'd found *www.thetruth-willmakeyoufree.by*, or just *thetruth*, as its members called it.

The content was all in English, so at first it didn't register with him that the *.by* suffix stood for Belarus. When he did find out he had no idea where Belarus is but it sounded pretty exotic. The site seemed to be only lightly curated and made no concessions. There was no welcome, no explanation, no guidance to lead you in. You simply applied for admission, waited a few days, then got a password and went straight to it, making of it what you could. It had taken Lander several long sessions to tap into the key forums and bulletin boards and to learn what it was all about.

As far as he could see the users were all men. The thing that made them special was that every one of them claimed either to have had the Infection and recovered or to be immune to it. There was a single rule: members must avoid hearsay or speculation. You could only report and comment on things that had happened to you directly, or that you had witnessed first-hand. Many of the accounts were of casual and accidental contact with the virus, like Lander's own, but a few members actually courted it, deliberately trying to get infected to prove that they couldn't. However, what emerged from all these stories was that there was no such thing as immunity; everyone who was exposed to the virus caught it. Everyone. But not everyone reacted in the same way.

Their Mam had died of the virus. It had been awful, as bad as people said. No, worse. He'd fully expected that sooner or later the rest of the family would go the same way, probably Gran and Granddad first, then Kerryl and him. He waited for the symptoms, but time went on and nothing happened. Now *thetruth* was telling him it might never. The realisation that he might survive this thing that was killing everyone else was like having a death sentence removed. He had been ecstatic, but not for long.

Four days ago he'd got an alert. It was a message from someone who said he represented a group of people who called themselves *The Chosen*. They had formed a 'Community of the Immune', and they invited him to join them. In Minsk. Lander didn't even know that Minsk was a place. It sounded to him more like a name you'd give to a soft toy. Or something you got. Where was it? He looked it up. Fucking miles away, that's where. Go to Minsk? No way! Besides, travel was restricted and movement illegal. Train and bus services had all been stopped, and vehicles were regularly intercepted by army patrols. Anyway, moving around was dangerous. He'd seen on TV a report of a Nottingham family who'd left their home to look after a relative in another town. Local people accused them of coming in from an infected area and a crowd attacked them. They set the family's car on fire and chased them away.

Then the next bombshell hit, the one that convinced him that whether he went to Minsk or not, he had to leave the farm as soon as possible.

The Chosen started posting accounts from people who had all had the same experience. It was a kind of sleepwalking, but with a difference. The sleepwalkers looked to other people to be wide awake. While in that state they did extraordinary things, but afterwards they had no recollection of what. Some of them had tried to investigate what was happening. One managed to leave a video camera running and record a whole episode. It showed him in bed. Then without warning he got up. He looked to be wide awake and started to move about his room. He went to a dresser and started to pick up items and drop them on the floor. Some of them smashed. Then he grabbed one of the drawers and upended it. This went on for a few minutes, after which he got back into his bed and resumed normal sleep. The video ended by cutting to him talking to the camera. It panned around the room and showed the damage he'd done. He explained that he had no memory of it, that the same sort of thing had happened to him several times before, and that the incidents only started after he'd been exposed to the virus. It was as if another version of him, a ghost of his normal self, was doing things independently of his will. He called it "dream walking".

A couple of days later Lander noticed that some of the things in his bedroom had been moved. The plastic car models were gone from the shelf where he kept them. They'd been tossed into the waste bin and some of them were broken. He was furious. He'd had some of those models since he was a kid and a few of them were worth a bit. He'd been thinking of selling them but he hadn't got around to it. He certainly wouldn't just chuck them out. He stormed into Kerryl's room and accused her of being responsible. She denied it, and they had a huge row.

He was sure it was Kerryl's fault – who else could have done it? – but she'd looked so surprised when he blamed her, so hurt. He remembered *thetruth* bulletins and decided to do an experiment of his own. Overnight he locked the door to his room. The first few times nothing happened and in the morning the place was just as he'd left it. Then one day he found that things had been moved. There was only one key and no one else could have got in. It had to be he who had done it while he'd been sleeping, but he just couldn't remember it. He had become a dream walker.

He logged into *thetruth* and went to the bulletin board to report what had happened to him. There was a new and frightening post. It told him that some people, only a few, responded to the virus in a way different from the majority. For this group, instead of causing the terrible and familiar cramps, vomiting, bleeding, and the failure of the nervous system, the virus settled in their brains where it launched a different type of destruction. They called the condition it created D.I.D., 'dissociative identity disorder'. Episodes occurred when the sufferer was asleep, and resulted in outbreaks of extreme violence. It was lethal; not to the sufferer, but to those around him.

He'd been trying to decide what to do about this when there was a ping, and another post appeared. This one was the most harrowing of them all. It was another video. It opened with shots of four bloody corpses. It was clear that these people had been brutally murdered, hacked to pieces. All of them had had their throats cut. The arm of one had been almost cut through, fingers were missing from another. A stomach had been opened. The floor was awash with blood. The video showed all this in ghastly detail. The author of the post came on next. He was hysterical, hardly able to speak, but he managed to get out that the dead were members of his own family. The night before they had all gone to bed as usual. He had felt strange and been restless, but at last he had fallen asleep. He had woken up to find himself covered in blood with the bodies all around him. In one hand he held a carving knife.

'I killed them,' he wept. 'All of them. I couldn't help it. I didn't know what I was doing. I was asleep, and I killed them.'

This was what convinced Lander that for the sake of Kerryl, Gran and Granddad he must leave. That's what he had said in the note he had left. Had Kerryl found it yet?

4

HELP ON A TRACTOR

LANDER WOKE AND the sun was low. He sat up, blinking and trying to work out where he was. He looked at the long shadows of the trees stretching across the grass. Then he remembered. He was running away, and he was in the middle of a field. He was stiff and sore. The ground certainly hadn't got any softer while he'd been sleeping and it was now getting cooler. He stretched and looked towards the lane. Something was missing. His bike!

He shook himself out of his sleeping bag and dashed across the field to where he'd left it beside the gate. He spun around, half expecting to find it further along the wall, but of course it wasn't. There was the flattened grass where it had been. And the field gate was open, whereas he could clearly remember shutting it. Somebody must have come along, looked over the wall and seen it. Like a fool, he'd left the key in place. He just hadn't thought it would be a problem, that anyone would be around to nick it. But they had.

'FUCK,' he shouted. 'BASTARDS. FUCKING FUCKING BASTARDS,' louder with each iteration. He didn't care if somebody heard him.

Whoever had taken his bike had come in through the gate. Had they also seen him?

He went back to where his sleeping bag lay crumpled under the trees. His backpack was there because he'd been using it as a pillow. But his phone! Where was his phone? He remembered reading the post from *thetruth*, but then he must have dozed off. Had it fallen from his hand? He turned the sleeping bag over, lifted it, shook it. Nothing; the phone was gone. So were his trainers! An almost new pair of Arco Sport Professionals that had cost him two months' allowance. His spare pair was in one of the panniers, and that had been on the bike.

'SHIT. HELL FIRE FUCK!'

The panniers had also contained all his food. His stomach grumbled even as he took this in. He picked up a stone and threw it as hard as he could at a tree. It rebounded off the bark and bounced into the undergrowth.

Lander flopped onto his sleeping bag and buried his face in the crook of his arm. He was the closest he'd been in a long time to tears, but he hadn't cried when their Mam died and he was fucked if he was going to cry now. He wiped his face on his sleeve, sat up and forced himself to take stock. What did he have?

He had his backpack, which held some of his clothes. There was also a forgotten chocolate bar, which he immediately ate. He had the little money that had been in his pocket, and some basic information about *thetruth* people. It didn't help at all in finding the exact location of the group, or the address in Bruges where he could connect with the network. He had the roll of elastic. He had his knife, binoculars, compass and torch. He had his water bottle, now empty. He had a black felt-tip pen. He had a map. It was a large-scale motoring version that covered the whole of the north of England. It wasn't any use for minor roads but it showed the way to the coast. He had his sleeping bag.

What did he not have? He had no food. That was a problem but only a temporary one. There'd be plenty of places – vandalised shops, abandoned houses – where he'd be able to get things to eat. Same for water, and in the meantime he'd just have to risk the streams. He had no phone. He had no ID; he'd put that, together with most of his money, in a compartment in the bottom of one of the panniers because he'd thought it would be safer there. Finally – and he was beginning to think this was the worst of all – he had nothing to put on his feet. Until he could do something about that he was more or less stranded.

A little way down the field he'd noticed a large white sack which had blown against the wall and lodged there. It was the sort used for building materials – sand, gravel, rubble, that kind of thing – woven from thick stands of plastic and very tough. They had lots of them back at the farm. They weren't returnable but Granddad wouldn't throw them away. He'd tie them and put them in the barn in case one day they'd "come in". Well, this one had "come in" now.

He dragged the sack back to his camp beside the trees, sat down, unsheathed his knife, and spent the next half hour fashioning himself some footwear. He started by cutting one of the side panels from the sack. That gave him a sheet of material about a metre square. He put his foot on the edge and drew loosely around it with the felt tip. Then he began to cut out the outline with the knife. It was harder than he expected, but with a combination of hacking and sawing he managed. Next, he used the shape he'd made as a template, and drew around that until he'd filled the whole of the plastic sheet with feet, more than twenty of them. He cut these out and gathered them into two equal piles.

He took three pairs of socks from his backpack and put them on. Then, using the roll of elastic, he strapped half a dozen of the plastic shapes to the soles of his feet. He cut a strip from the remainder of the sack and tied it tightly around each one. He stood up and hobbled a few steps. Not too bad. He wouldn't be running a marathon, but he could walk. He was not sure how far, but he hoped it would be far enough to reach somewhere he could find a pair of replacement trainers. He stowed the rest of the plastic in his backpack and put away the other things.

He thought for a moment about going home but immediately rejected the idea. The only thing to do was to stick to Plan A and keep going. There was no chance of getting in touch with Kerryl or his grandparents now that his phone had gone. He'd have to see if he could get hold of another phone somehow so that he could find out how they were and let them know he was safe. He left the field and walked out to the track.

He decided to carry on up the hill, reasoning that because the main settlements were in the valley the hilltop road wouldn't be as busy and so there would be less chance of being spotted. The downside was that there would be nowhere near as many opportunities for finding transport, footwear and food.

It wasn't too bad. The ground was rough and sometimes sharp stones dug into his feet but he reached the head of the track with his makeshift footwear still more or less intact and turned right. The road was too small to be marked on his map but it was going in the right direction. He knew that if he followed the general line of the M62, away from the setting sun, he would eventually get to the east coast.

Progress was slow. The knots in the plastic strapping kept working loose and needed frequent attention. Then the binding on his left foot slipped right off and the whole assembly came apart. It seemed he was having to stop every few minutes. And it seemed as though all the sharpest stones had lined themselves up just for him. He walked for an hour, and it was obvious that his foot protection wouldn't last much longer. He could understand why this style of footwear hadn't caught on. The four-inch heels Kerryl had bought on her last trip to Manchester would have been more comfortable.

He guessed he'd gone less than two miles when he heard the unmistakable sound of a tractor. At first he thought it must be in a field, but then he saw its lights on the road behind him. They were a long way off. Should he try to hide? Or just carry on as normal, looking as though he knew what he was doing and had every right to do it? It couldn't be anything official. The police or the army patrols wouldn't be going around in a tractor. No, it had to be a farmer. Most of the farmers he knew were like Granddad, not well-disposed towards the authorities. It was unlikely that a farmer would report him as a vagrant. He might even help him.

The noise grew louder. The road was narrow with high stone walls on each side, and there wouldn't be much room for the tractor to pass. He stopped by a niche in the wall and squeezed himself in so that it could get by. Except that it didn't; it stopped right beside him.

It was big and green with yellow wheels, a late model John Deere, and it was pulling a cattle trailer. The driver leaned down from the cab window.

'Out late, lad,' he said.

Lander said nothing. Yes, he was. Who was this guy? A specialist in the fucking obvious?

'Yer looks as though yer needs a lift.'

He was an old man, probably as old as Granddad, red-faced, with grey hair poking from under a greasy cap. He looked friendly. He wouldn't be going far, but a lift for even a short distance would be very welcome.

Lander nodded. The farmer opened the door and he climbed in. He pulled his scarf over his mouth and nose.

'What yer doin', lad?' said the old man. Lander looked at him with a puzzled expression. 'Wi' yer face. Why are yer doin' that?'

'I'm covering my mouth and nose. To protect you from the Infection.'

'There's no need for that,' the man said. 'If I'm going ter get it I'm going ter get it. At my time o' life it makes no odds.'

Lander let the scarf fall. A tired old collie was sitting on the jump seat. The farmer pushed it off and it settled resentfully at the back of the cab. There was a clunk and the tractor moved forward.

'Where yer makin' for?'

Lander thought it best to tell the truth, or something close to it. 'I'm heading for the coast. I want to see if I can get a boat over to Belgium. I've got friends there.'

'Makin' for t'coast. Well, I can get yer as far as Knottingley.'

Lander had never heard of it. 'Where's that?'

'T'other side o' Castleford.'

This was good, much better than Lander had expected. It was well on his way. He wondered why the farmer would be going so far.

'I'm teckin' some beasts,' he said, nodding over his shoulder towards the cattle trailer. 'I've got three steers.'

'Oh,' said Lander. He thought that it was a bit late to be delivering cattle, but it seemed rude to say so.

The tractor cab was cosy. Lander looked down at the road, picked out by the lights. The collie decided to see whether he was friendly, stood up and sniffed him. Lander patted it and remembered Buster. Would he know he'd gone? Kerryl would look after him, and he'd be good company for her. Would he miss him? Probably not. As long as Buster got his four square meals a day he'd be happy.

'What's up wi' yer feet?'

'What?'

'Yer feet. Yer've got bandages on 'em.'

Lander laughed. 'They're not bandages.' He lifted a foot where the farmer could see it. 'Somebody nicked my trainers while I was asleep in a field back there.'

'Never! The buggers.' The old man tutted. 'What's it all comin' to?'

'I had to make these out of an old sack I found, but they don't work too well.'

The farmer thought for a moment. Then he said, 'Look in t' back there. There's an old pair o' boots.'

Lander found them. They were wellingtons, indeed old and quite smelly, but they seemed sound and looked to have plenty of wear left in them.

'Teck 'em if yer want.'

'Really? Are you sure?'

'I've got five pairs o' boots and only two feet. If yer wants 'em, teck 'em.'

Lander slid the bindings off his feet and put on the boots. Without the extra socks they would have been too big, but with them they were fine. He felt a great relief. With no shoes his options had been severely limited. Now, with something on his feet and a lift to take him closer to the east coast harbours, things were looking up. All that was left was to find something to eat.

'Ay up.' The farmer pointed.

Lander saw bright lights in the road a couple of hundred yards ahead.

'Roadblock. Army I shouldn't wonder.' The farmer rummaged on the cab floor and tossed Lander a blanket. 'Get thissen down, an' cover thissen wi' that. An' say nowt.'

The blanket was old and smelt strongly of dog. It was clearly the collie's, but Lander had no choice. He squeezed into the footwell and covered himself. A minute later the tractor came to a stop and the farmer turned off the engine.

'You do realise it's past curfew,' said a crisp voice.

'Aye, I do that,' said the farmer. 'I've got an Agricultural Movement Permit.'

'Have you now? So where are you going and what's the purpose of your journey?'

'I'm going to Knottingley wi' some beasts.' The farmer reached under his seat, took a plastic wallet and climbed down from the cab. Lander made himself as small as he could, shrunk himself into the confined space, and looked out under the blanket through a small Perspex window. The area was bright with floodlights. He could see the farmer's back and an army Land Rover.

'A bit late to be moving cattle, isn't it?' said a different voice.

'I'm teckin' 'em now 'cos it's safer. Last time I took some beasts in daylight they was nabbed.' The farmer laughed, but without humour. 'I don't know what's got into folk sin' all this plague business started. You can't sell steers for love ner money, nobody wants 'em, but when you try to move 'em some bugger thieves 'em. So it's best to go at night.'

The guards seemed satisfied, and there were a few muttered courtesies. It seemed to be all over when Lander suddenly felt a cramp seize his leg. He straightened it, he couldn't help it, and he knocked a spanner which was on the cab floor. It made a scraping rattle.

'What's that?' the voice said. 'Have you got somebody in your cab?'

'Nay,' said the farmer. 'It's on'y me dog.'

Lander heard the door open. He froze. He was in agony but he had to keep still. If the roadblock found him he'd be in trouble, and so would the farmer. The collie got up and stuck its head out of the cab door.

'See?' said the farmer, reaching up and fondling the animal.

'All right,' said the guard. 'On your way.'

The old man climbed back into the cab and started the engine. Lander stayed down in the footwell until they were some distance along the road. Then he got back into the jump seat. Irritatingly his cramp had vanished as soon as they pulled away from the checkpoint.

'Thank you,' he said.

The farmer shrugged. 'Yer welcome.'

Lander thought it would be polite to introduce himself. 'My name's ...'

'Nay!' The farmer cut him off, holding up his hand. 'It's as well I don't know yer name. I don't know who y'are, where yer goin' or what yer up to, and it's best we keep it that way.' He paused, then added an explanation. 'Suppose yer told me yer name was George, an' then a patrol stopped me and asked me if I'd come across some'dy called George. I'd have to tell 'em yes. But if I don't know yer name, I can't tell 'em owt, can I?'

There was no answer to this logic. Lander watched through the window as the walls and hedgerows passed by. His stomach growled and he wondered where he could get something to eat, and when.

5

———————

A CHOICE

LANDER RECKONED HE had a good two hours of travel time left. After that it would be too light for him to still be about. The farmer had dropped him at the gateway to a farm just past Knottingley. He'd tried to thank him but his benefactor didn't seem to want that and had driven off with the briefest of goodbyes. They never knew each other's names.

There were few dwellings and the villages were far apart. He walked through one, unlit and deserted, and saw no one. The only sign of life was a nasty-looking dog, mangy and drooling. It snarled at him, but its heart wasn't in it. Lander threw a stone at the animal and it ran off.

There should have been signs of dawn, but there was thick cloud and it was still very dark. He decided he'd keep going. The farmer's boots were not the most comfortable footwear he'd ever had but they were all right, certainly a vast improvement on the plastic sack, and he settled into a mindless plod, an almost trance-like progression that allowed his mind to wander. His thoughts were miles away, so the woman's voice startled him.

'Are you my knight in shining armour?'

Lander jumped, looked around and located the speaker. 'What?'

She was sitting in the garden of a small cottage at the roadside. The building was unlit and the hedge in front was high so that he would have walked past without seeing her at all if she hadn't spoken.

'I wished for a strong young man to come along to help me. I think you must be he.'

Lander looked more closely. It was an old woman, and she was definitely crazy.

'I don't think so,' he said, and started to move off.

'Please,' she said. 'Give me a moment of your time. You have so much of it and I have very little. It's not a lot to ask.'

Lander paused. 'What do you want?' he said, guardedly.

'Ah,' said the woman. She rose stiffly from her chair and came closer, and Lander could see that she was even older than Gran. 'I need a favour,' she said. 'I need your help with a task.'

'What?' She probably wanted something shifted or lifted. Lander would help her because in similar circumstances he'd like someone to help his Gran, but he couldn't afford to stop for long.

'I can see you are eager to continue your journey,' she said. Her voice was not exactly posh but it was educated, a bit like some of his teachers. 'What I'd like you to do won't delay you greatly. It's not dangerous, at least not for you, but I have to admit it is something you might find difficult.'

Lander doubted it. He was used to heavy work on the farm and there wasn't much he was unable to tackle.

'Come into the house,' she said. 'I'll make us a cup of tea and I'll explain.'

Lander hesitated. The prospect of tea was welcome, and there might be something to eat with it.

'Come, do,' she said, walking towards the door. 'There is nothing here that will harm you.'

Still Lander hesitated. The woman seemed to be all right, but the house could be infected. There were lots of warnings about going into unfamiliar buildings. He reached for his scarf again but something told him that the old woman might see covering his face as rude so he didn't pull it up.

'I have cake,' she said. 'Carrot cake. I hope you like carrot cake.'

That swung it. Lander had been checking out the house, looking for tell-tale signs of movement inside, but there were none. An old woman, a very old woman, couldn't be a threat, even if she did seem a bit weird.

He followed her through the door into a small kitchen. The woman indicated for him to sit at the table while she put a kettle on the hob. Neither of them spoke while it boiled.

'How do you like your tea?' she said.

Lander liked tea the way his Granddad drank it. 'Milk and four sugars, please.'

The woman raised an eyebrow and poured the milk with a hand that trembled slightly. She pushed the sugar bowl towards him. 'Help yourself,' she said.

She went to a cupboard and took out a large cake. Lander watched as she cut him a very large slice. She took a smaller piece for herself.

'Carrot cake used to be one of my late husband's favourites,' she said, 'and my son's. I see you like it too. I have a Rayburn and I'm still able to bake while my oil supply lasts. Once it's gone I'm afraid that will be the end of it.'

The woman took a seat opposite Lander and watched him while he ate. When he'd finished she didn't bother to ask but cut him another slice. She hadn't touched her own piece.

'Now, please tell me your name,' she said when he'd finished.

'Lan... I mean Alexander.' He thought this woman deserved his proper name; the carrot cake was excellent. 'Shaw,' he added. 'Alexander Shaw.'

'Alexander. A noble name. A Greek name. My name is Louise Fisher. I used to be Professor of Classics at the University of Bristol. There is some of my work.'

She pointed to a shelf holding half a dozen impressive-looking hardbacks. Lander scanned the spines and read her name and some of the titles. *Feast and Famine in Minoan Crete. Athens, Sparta and the Struggle for Peloponnesian Supremacy. Socrates and the Birth of Modern Thought.* Lander couldn't see himself reading any of them. They seemed more like Kerryl's cup of tea than his.

'This is my most recent work,' said Louise, picking up a volume and putting it on the table.

It was called *Luck, Chance and Fate in the World of Homer.* Was she expecting Lander to read it? Was that the favour she wanted? Some hopes! She'd said that what she had in mind wouldn't take him long. This was a thick book. Reading it would take forever. And it could be dangerous, a serious case of brain strain.

'The Greeks had some interesting ideas about chance and fate,' she said. 'You have read Homer?'

Lander shook his head. At least he knew enough to understand she was talking about the author of the Trojan War, not one of the Simpsons.

'Well, that is a treat you have to come,' said Louise. 'In Homeric Greece one of the words for fortune was moira, meaning a portion or a share. The concept of providence as a share is an interesting one because it implies there is a whole to be divided. It also implies that if one person has a larger share of it, there is less left for others.'

She pointed her knife at the remains of the carrot cake. 'Consider this cake. You may cut it into equal slices so everyone gets the same size piece. Or you can do what I did and make the slices different sizes, some large, some small. Now imagine the cake represents good fortune. Some people get larger slices. Very nice for them. But that means that there's less of the cake left, so others will get smaller slices. The cake is a finite size. If my portion is larger than the average, someone else's must be smaller to compensate. Very good fortune for me means slightly less good fortune available for sharing among everyone else.'

Lander hadn't expected a lecture on ancient history, but what the woman was saying was interesting. It would have appealed to his grandfather, who was a rampant socialist and raged against inequality and privilege.

'I think everybody's slice must be smaller now,' he said, 'after the Infection.'

'Ah,' said Louise, 'an interesting point. However, what the Infection means is that the whole cake is smaller. It doesn't affect the proportions of the individual slices.' She looked at him steadily for several seconds before going on. 'I think that my slice of the cake has been generous. Born into a well-to-do family, happy childhood, happy marriage to a wonderful man, a good career and two lovely children. Yes, I think a pretty fat slice, don't you?'

Lander agreed.

'So,' she said, 'tell me about you. What has your portion been like, so far? Happy home?'

'Yes.'

'Enough to eat and drink, caring parents?'

'Yes. My dad died a while back, but yes.'

'I'm sorry to hear that.' She looked away. 'Would you say you've had a good education?'

'I suppose so. I don't like school much.'

'Ah, well, I can't say whether that's their loss or yours, but you seem to me to be an intelligent young man, so who knows? You're too young for me to ask you about unrealised dreams, but I assume you have some?'

'Yes.'

'So, despite the sad loss of your father, a pretty good share of the cake for you too, up to now.'

'Yes.'

'Would you like another slice?'

She was looking at the carrot cake, and Lander certainly would have liked another piece of that. However, he had the feeling that he was being tested so he said, 'No thank you.'

'Good,' said Louise. 'I think it's right that we should recognise our good fortune and not take more than is necessary, don't you? No need to panic, I'm not coming on to you with religion, telling you to count your blessings, all that sort of thing. In reality I'm a devout atheist, but I think it's good for us to review the balance of our lives from time to time.' She stood up. 'I want you to meet someone whose slice of the cake is somewhat smaller than yours or mine. Come this way. Please.'

She waited for him at the door, holding it open. Lander hesitated. Should he go? Was this the reason she'd waylaid him? Who was he to meet? He had to follow her, it would have been impossible not to.

He stepped into a small room lit by a single candle. It was stuffy and cramped and had an antiseptic smell. There was a bed in the centre, and a lifting device like a beige crane. Beside the bed was a hospital table covered in plastic boxes and jars. There was somebody in the bed. Lander leant forward to get a better look at the figure. It was a boy, perhaps his own age, maybe a little older. The head turned slowly and a pair of large, grey eyes gazed at him.

'This is Spencer,' said Louise. 'Spencer, this is Alexander.' The figure in the bed made no response. Louise stroked his head, the lock of hair falling over his brow. 'I always talk to him,' she said, 'even though he can't hear me. And even if he could, it's doubtful he would be able to understand.

'Spencer is my grandson. He's nineteen. Three years ago he'd been to spend an evening with one of his friends. He was cycling home when he was hit by a car. Two young men in a souped-up Golf, out to impress their girls and going too fast. The driver had been drinking and said he didn't see Spencer because he was not showing any lights. That was ridiculous; Spencer always used lights when cycling, during the day as well as after dark. The people in the car got away with minor injuries, but Spencer's skull was shattered and his back broken. He was in intensive care for three months and came out like this. He can see and he can breathe. He can swallow but he can't chew. He can move his head but nothing else. He needs constant care throughout the day and the night, all day, every day. The car driver was disqualified from driving and sent to jail for eighteen months. Spencer's sentence is much longer. He is imprisoned in his own body for the rest of his life.'

Lander was struck by the emptiness in Louise's voice. Spencer's plight was similar to that suffered by other young people he'd heard of, but he'd never met any of them. Now he did he felt the terrible unfairness of what had happened to the boy in the bed, the blind injustice of it. Louise had said the favour she wanted would only take a moment or two, so she couldn't want ongoing help with his nursing. Was it something quick, like toileting? Feeding?

'What do you want from me?' he said. He was dreading the answer, but the one he received jolted him to the core.

'I want you to kill him,' she said.

It was so unexpected, such a hammer blow that Lander couldn't answer. Was she serious?

'I've shocked you,' she said, 'but please hear me out. Spencer's brother and sister, and his parents, my son and daughter-in-law, are dead. All his relatives are dead, victims of the Infection. For reasons I cannot fathom, he and I are not. I've tried to infect us both, even putting the linen from his mother's deathbed on our own beds. To no avail. We, Spencer and I, seem to be immune, and I guess you are too. That's not the blessing it might seem for any of us. It's a burden which reduces the size of our slices of the cake by quite a bit.

'I am the only carer Spencer has. I am eighty-seven. I have rheumatoid arthritis. I've had two heart attacks and I've run out of my medication. I could die any day. What will happen to Spencer if I do? When I do?'

Lander had no answer, although he knew there must be one.

'What will happen to Spencer then is a slow death. He will starve, but it will probably be thirst that kills him. He will die from dehydration, wrapped in a parcel of his own faeces and urine. It will take some time. He may be in a near vegetative state but he can feel pain. He will suffer. If you kill him, he will be spared that. And I can then put an end to my own life too.'

Lander shook his head, trying to bring some sanity, some reality into this crazy room. 'I can't. If you think it's right, why don't you do it yourself?'

Louise smiled ruefully. 'I've tried. I have a shotgun which would do the job swiftly and painlessly, if a little messily. I have carving knives. I have aspirin in the cupboard. I have brought all of them into this room at various times, and not been able to go any further.' She stroked Spencer's head again. 'He's my grandson. I played with him when he was a baby. I changed his nappies. I lifted him onto my knee and read him stories. He would always come to me if he had any worries or problems. I cannot do it. Could your grandmother kill you?'

Lander knew she couldn't, whatever the circumstances.

'You're all right here,' he said. 'Why don't you wait till the Infection's over and the authorities will look after you? You can even ask them to come now. Phones are still working. You could use my mobile, except it was nicked.'

Louise looked sadly at him. 'Do you think that after all that's happened an old woman and her paralysed grandson will be on anyone's list of priorities? The 'authorities', as you call them, will have much more pressing things to attend to, and rightly so.'

She turned to the corner, where a shotgun rested against the wall. She picked it up.

'You've used one of these before?' she said.

Lander nodded.

'And you've killed things with it?'

'Yes, but only magpies and rabbits, and once I had to slaughter a calf.'

'We could have a long debate about the value of human life, even one as reduced as Spencer's, against the value of all the things you've shot, but there is no time. I promised that what I wanted of you would only take a moment, and it will. A second to pull the trigger, that is all. Then you can go. It will be a mercy, a service to Spencer and to me, a favour we can never repay.'

Lander was torn. He could see the reasoning behind what Louise was saying, but could he bring himself to contemplate what she was asking of him? Surely there was someone else she could go to.

She could see him wavering, and spoke again. 'Solon, the Athenian statesman and poet, said, "Judge not the measure of anyone's good fortune until they are dead". My grandson's slice of the cake was once larger even than your own, but on that night three years ago it was reduced to a mere sliver. By a simple act you could increase the volume of Spencer's good fortune, and mine. And although you might not think it now, your own too.'

Still Lander hesitated. Did Spencer understand what his grandmother was proposing? There was no sign that he did. The grey eyes moved from him to Louise and back again, but sluggishly and not, as far as he could see, in response to anything.

'There is another thing,' said Louise, and Lander thought he detected a new edge to her tone. 'Now that you know what I have told you, I think you are confronted with a moral dilemma, a quandary which leads to an imperative. If you are not prepared to do us this service, to end the life which is a trial to Spencer and a burden to me, then your only ethical course is to remain here and look after my grandson yourself.'

Was that right? It was like being hit in the face by a slamming door. This was blackmail. He couldn't stay. It was impossible. Technically he could do what she wanted. He was a good shot, but he wouldn't need to be. Both barrels in Spencer's mouth, pull the trigger, and it would be done. She was right, it would be over in an instant. The boy would feel nothing. He wouldn't even know what was going on. It wouldn't be murder, it would be mercy killing, like putting down a stricken animal. It would make a terrible mess. Shotguns close up did; he remembered the calf. Should he then help Louise clear up? Help her bury him? She hadn't asked him to do that.

Louise handed him the gun. 'The safety catch is on. You don't mind if I don't watch.'

She went back into the kitchen, pulling the door closed behind her. Lander weighed the gun in his hands. It was a good one, well-balanced. There was a cartridge in each barrel. Spencer's hand was limp on the duvet. Lander took it.

'I'm sorry, old pal,' he said.

Was it his imagination, or did he feel the tiniest, gentlest of pressures from the inert hand? He looked into the eyes, grey and steady on his. Killing was the right thing to do in the circumstances, Louise had convinced him of that. And now Spencer had convinced him of something else. If it were to be done, it should be done not by a stranger but by somebody who knew him, who loved him. It must be done by Louise.

He opened the door to the kitchen. Louise was sitting at the table and looked up at him in surprise.

'I can't,' said Lander. 'I'm sorry, I can't do it. It has to be you. There's no one else.'

He walked out of the front door, leaving the gun against the wall.

It was light now but still early, the morning bright and fresh. He set off along the road, his pace brisk but his heart heavy. Always before – at home, at school, hanging out with his mates – he'd known what had been the right thing to do. He'd not always done it, but he had always known what it was. This time there was no right thing, and he bled for the pair he'd left behind.

He'd gone a hundred yards when he heard the percussive thump of a gunshot. He stopped and waited, and then, a moment later, there was another

He didn't go back.

6

DESERTED

LANDER SPENT THE day under a hedge. Even though it was only early autumn it was cold and he slept badly. It was not only the cold, the uneven ground and the daytime noises. It was the vivid images of the carnage in the cottage that plagued his imagination. The helpless boy and his wise, troubled grandmother haunted him. He wondered what Louise had thought as she looked at Spencer and pulled the trigger, as she took away the meagre life he had left. Should he have done what she asked of him? That would have spared her having to do it herself, but he couldn't. Shooting birds, small animals, even the bull calf he and Granddad had slaughtered had been one thing. Murdering another human being was different. The Infection had made life even more precious, and he knew now that he was not a killer.

It was a relief when dusk came and he was able to continue his journey. It meant he could get on with things, instead of going over and over in his mind what had happened in the cottage.

The land was flat, nothing like the hills and valleys of the Pennines, the home he'd left what seemed like months ago. He thought that if he walked briskly he could probably cover ten or twelve miles before he needed to hide again. Something to eat was a problem. All he'd had for twenty-four hours was a chocolate bar and two slices of carrot cake. His stomach had stopped growling and all he felt now was a gnawing ache. He drank a pint or more of water from a stream and that helped, but he needed something to give him energy.

He'd not gone far when he came to a fork in the road. One signpost said Goole. He knew that was close to his final destination. He'd not been there, but he thought it was probably quite big and so best avoided for now. The other signpost was to a place called Snaith. What sort of a name was that? It sounded slithery, like a snake. He'd never heard of it, but it was in roughly the right direction and it was much closer than Goole. He might find food there.

He took the Snaith road and half a mile later came to a painted welcome board: Parish of Snaith. Beneath the name was the legend pop 3779. Using spray paint, somebody had crossed out the 3779 and written instead 24. Then, presumably later, the 24 had been sprayed through and replaced by the figure 0. To Lander, always one to spot and point out an illogicality, that was absurd. The population couldn't have been zero. What about the person doing the spraying? Pleased with himself at that thought, he set off down the gentle slope into the town. He passed what a sign told him was The Robert Mellor Secondary School, but the gates were locked and the building showed no signs of life.

The streets were very different from what he was used to in Walbrough. There they were all stone, grey-black and stern. Here everything was warm brick, apart from a few buildings that had been washed with pastel colours. The biggest difference, though, was in the overall appearance of the place. The valley towns he'd left behind were desolate. Windows that weren't boarded up were smashed. Graffiti defaced every surface, there was rubbish, there were stray animals, there was the odour of putrefaction and the smell of death. Snaith was completely the opposite. It was clean, tidy, well cared for and picture perfect. There were no signs of decay or destruction. So where was everyone?

His watch said it was just after nine o'clock, and you might have expected there to be at least somebody about, but the doors and windows were closed and the curtains drawn. He came to a convenience store, the sort that would normally be open from first light until well into the evening. It was shut up. He looked through the window. On the shelves were magazines, cans and bottles of drinks, and dried and tinned food. He could see packets of cereal and biscuits, and his stomach churned. In a corner were beers and wines. There were even neat racks of face masks and plastic bio-suites that some places had started to stock when the Infection first approached. The amazing thing, though was that the place was intact. Nobody had broken in, there had been no looting, everything was as it should be. In Walbrough the shop wouldn't have lasted five minutes.

What to do? He was ravenous, and behind that window was food. To the side was a high gate, which presumably led to a yard behind. He looked around. There was nobody in the street, no tell-tale curtain-twitching in the houses opposite. He gave the gate a push but it was locked. It would be simple to climb over, smash a window and get in. But he hesitated. There was something odd about the place. Suppose it was a trap. Suppose there was an alarm and people came running from all directions to set upon him. Where was everyone? Then he remembered the zero on the roadside sign. Did that really mean there was no one here? If so, where had everybody gone? They couldn't all be dead. Surely these buildings weren't housing corpses. But they might be. He left the shop. It would be better to explore a bit more before he did anything he might regret.

He continued further into the town. Everywhere was the same; shops, homes, a primary school, offices were all shut up, all lifeless, like on Christmas Day. The curtains on most windows were closed, those with shutters had them drawn. He passed a pub, a fish-and-chip shop, a chemist, a newsagent and a post office, all in the same state. Another unusual thing struck him: there were no stray dogs. Every street in Walbrough had its pack, all of them hungry and many savage. Here there wasn't so much as a cat. It was a ghost town.

He glanced down a side street and saw a close of prim-looking homes, four and five-bedroom detached houses, goals of an aspiring middle class. One at the far end caught his eye. It was in prime position and the only one with a double garage. Go for the top, he thought, and he walked towards it past the other, silent buildings. He expected that at any second there would be hostile shouts and he would be accosted, but everything stayed quiet.

There was a short, tarmac drive and a concrete path across a lawn to a smart-looking front door. He tapped on it and listened. Nothing. He pressed a bell push and heard a chime from inside. Still nothing. He tried the knob. The door was locked, as he'd expected. It looked solid, impregnable. Might the garage offer easier entry? There was no handle on the door, nothing to get hold of. Presumably it was one of those electric up-and-over jobs. To the side of the house was a gate. That was unlocked and he went through to the back.

The garden was neat, with a patio, a few bushes, a children's swing, and a small shed and vegetable patch at the far end. Then he saw something very interesting; one of the windows was open. It was an upstairs one, and a top pane. He could see from the ground that it was too small for him to get through, but there was a casement below and he thought he might be able to reach in far enough to open that. The best bit was that it was over the garage.

Making it onto the garage roof was easy enough. PE had been Lander's best subject at school, and jumping to grab the edge of the roof and pulling himself up was no problem. Getting into the house was harder. It meant getting to the narrow window sill and squatting there while he reached inside to undo the fastening for the casement. At first he couldn't reach it, but after a struggle he managed to get his fingers to the handle. This was the sort of house that would have window locks, he thought, and he prayed there wouldn't be one here. There was not. The catch turned, and he eased the window open and crawled through.

He was in a bedroom, obviously a girl's. There were posters of boy bands on the wall, make-up on the dressing table, a floral bedspread, a purple rug with an image of a unicorn, and a couple of soft toys on a neatly-made bed. There were books – school texts and fiction – furry slippers, and a pink bathrobe on the door. It could almost have been Kerryl's room. Thinking of her brought a pang of sorrow. He missed her. He missed his grandparents. Had she found the memory stick yet?

There's something about an empty house that gives off its own vibe. If it had been occupied Lander would have felt it, but he knew from the start there was no one in. He opened the door onto a large landing with more doors. One of them was ajar; a bathroom. He used it, then went downstairs, not bothering yet with the other rooms. He went to the back door. There were bolts top and bottom and a key in the lock. He wondered about opening it. Might there be an alarm? He told himself that was silly, because if there was an alarm he would have set it off by now. He opened the door and retrieved his backpack from where he'd left it outside. He didn't lock the door again; if somebody came to the front he might need to make a quick exit.

The hallway was spotlessly clean. Nothing had been left out, there were no marks on the carpets, no dust. It was perfect, like a show house or those room mock-ups you see in IKEA. On one side was a huge sitting room, with two sofas in cream leather, a white faux-fur rug, and a massive TV. On the other side was a kitchen/diner. There wasn't much in the kitchen. The fridge was empty apart from a sealed carton of long-life milk and two eggs. He broke the eggs into a glass, sniffed them and decided they were OK. He whisked them up with most of the milk and added some sugar. He drained the concoction in half a dozen gulps and gave a burp of appreciation. The larder cupboard wasn't much better. He found some rather soft cream crackers in a plastic box, and some tins of sardines. He opened one and ate the fish with his fingers, wiping the juice off his chin with his sleeve. There were a few more cans on the shelf – grapefruit segments, passata, beans, and new potatoes. Who eats tinned potatoes? Gran would have a fit. He was going to try them but he couldn't find an opener, so he had some more sardines because they opened easily with a key that came with the tin. He ate some cream crackers, drank two glasses of water, and then went back upstairs.

The master bedroom was luxurious: an enormous bed with a comfy-looking duvet, a vast en suite, and another TV. There were a couple of built-in wardrobes, and one of them was full of men's clothes. There were suits, jackets, and business shirts. They had no interest for him, but there were also some plain t-shirts and a pile of pressed pairs of jeans. He recognised Gucci and Armani, but he'd never heard of the other brand names. There were also four pairs of trainers. They would come in very handy, he'd gone about as far as he could in the farmer's boots.

He lay down on the bed. Why was this place deserted? Everything was so ordered; that meant that the people hadn't left in a hurry. Neither were there the sad signs – the stained sheets, the soiled clothing, the human mess – that there would have been if large numbers of them had perished from the Infection. It was as if everyone had simply walked out, and recently too. There were cars on the drives, so what had they left in? Would they all come rushing back, pouring out of buses and marching down the street?

The bed was heaven. His last resting place had been hard and uncomfortable, and he soon fell into a deep sleep. It was late afternoon before he awoke, suddenly sitting bolt upright and wondering where he was. There was a rattling sound downstairs. Had somebody come in? He rolled out of bed, tip-toed onto the landing and crouched behind the bannister. At the foot of the stairs was a large ginger cat, looking primly up at him. He placed the rattle; it had been a cat flap. The cat slowly mounted the stairs and wove itself around his legs. He stroked its head and it purred, rolling onto its side. It was sleek and well-fed. Another mystery.

He went to the en suite, turned on the shower and waited for it to run hot. It didn't. Still, better than nothing. He got under the spray, poured soap on his head and scrubbed himself. The water was wickedly cold and he could stand it for no more than half a minute. There were plenty of towels, dense fluffy ones, and he rubbed himself dry. Then he helped himself from the wardrobe to fresh undershorts, a t-shirt and a pair of jeans. They were a bit short in the leg but not a bad fit, and anyway, who was there to see him? He left his own clothes on the floor. They were showing that they'd been well worn and he certainly wasn't going to wash them. He stuffed some more clothes into his backpack, including several pairs of socks to make up for the ones he'd worn out.

Downstairs he opened two more cans of sardines, gave one to the cat and ate the other himself, with the rest of the crackers. There was a phone in the kitchen. He picked it up and heard the familiar purr of the dial tone. It was so reassuring that again he marvelled at how normal things seemed to be here. His fingers hovered over the buttons. Should he call home? It was tempting, but what would they think if he suddenly contacted them now? Besides, if they tried to persuade him to come back, to dissuade him from what he was meaning to do, he would find it hard to refuse. It would be better to wait until he was at the coast, or even across the Channel. Then he could tell them exactly where he was going and why. Of course, they would already know that from his letter on the memory stick. If they'd read it.

The wall clock told him it was 5.30, time to get ready for the next leg of his journey. With luck he'd be at the coast by morning, especially if he could find some transport. He looked out of the window. He weighed up whether to go outside and see if one of the cars parked out there was unlocked. Not yet. Perhaps after dark, although ideally he'd rather be gone by then.

There was a door in the kitchen that he guessed led to the garage. He was right. Half the double space was empty, but in the other was a car. It was an Audi, low, sleek, and red. He could be at the coast in no time in that. He tried the door. Locked. There was no sign of any key anywhere. He wished he knew how to break into a car and start it. Kevin, a lad at his school, had claimed he knew how to do it. Lander wished he'd had a teach-in.

He might not be able to start the car, but there was something in the garage that he could use. In the corner was a mountain bike, a bright yellow Specialized Stumpjumper. It was in beautiful condition, almost new. It had front and rear suspension, disc brakes and custom gears. Lander reckoned it had probably cost the thick end of three grand. That would certainly get him to the coast. Even better, it would make no noise, and he wouldn't have to risk attracting the attention of anyone who might be watching by opening the garage door. Not that he thought anybody would be. Apart from the cat, he hadn't seen a single living thing all the time he'd been in the town. It was like a film set, just that there were no actors or technicians. If he was into sci-fi he might have thought he'd slipped into another dimension.

He decided to leave it another hour before setting off. It wouldn't be properly dark even then, but it would be good enough. Besides, there were no lights on the Specialized and the twilight would help him to get a good start.

In the pantry he found a carton of custard, and he ate that. He put the last two tins of sardines in his rucksack, and some cartons of beans and soup. It was too heavy, so he put the sardines back. The cat looked relieved.

A little before 8 o'clock he wheeled the Specialized through the kitchen and into the back garden. He put on his rucksack, propped open the side gate, mounted the bike and set off along the close towards the road, all the time glancing from side to side for watchers from the houses. He was so engrossed that he rounded a corner and almost rode into it: a large, white van the size of an ambulance, with blue emergency lights. It was stationary, its engine off, and standing one on each side of it were two people in white biohazard suits and masks. They looked like Storm Troopers from Star Wars.

Without slowing, Lander did a U-turn and pedalled back up the close, fast. He'd seen a narrow path beside the house. He had no idea where it went, but the ambulance – if that's what it was – wouldn't be able to get along it and the Storm Troopers wouldn't be fast enough to catch him.

His heart was thumping. It was not only the surprise, it was the shock of seeing the people. Biohazard suits! Did that mean the area was infected? Was that why there was nobody around?

He came to the end of the path, turned onto the road, and there was another vehicle, exactly like the first one. It couldn't be the same, there wouldn't have been time for it to get there. Inside were two other people, also in masks. As soon as he appeared blinding searchlights flooded the street.

Across the road was another jitty. He dropped the bike and ran for it. It was narrow and in places seriously overgrown. He sprinted for a hundred yards but there was no sign of anyone following and he stopped, leaning on the fence, gasping for breath. Who were these creepy dudes? Were they really after him? Why hadn't they followed him? He soon found out.

The top of the fence was just above his head and he scrambled up it to see what was on the other side. Allotments. Excellent, there'd be huts where he would be able to hide. He hauled himself over and was straightening up when he heard a whispering, whirring sound, like moth wings. He looked up. Above him was a drone, a white one. There was another a little further away. And a third coming across the allotments to join them. He turned to vault back over the fence, and there was a fourth, two metres away and head height. It had two stereoscopic lenses that observed him like the eyes of some giant bug. There was a tube pointing at him. A gun barrel.

In the second that he realised this the drone fired. It shot him full in the face. At point-blank range.

7

————

CAUGHT

THE SAME FIVE questions, again and again and again.

> *Who are you?*
> *Where are you from?*
> *Where are you going?*
> *Why?*
> *How did you know about Snaith?*

The questioning didn't start immediately. To begin with he spent what he later learnt were three days recuperating. The drone had sprayed him with a nerve agent. He'd felt panic when they'd told him that, but they assured him that the substance used was very mild and he would quickly make a full recovery.

At the start it had been awful; pain all over and great difficulty breathing. This lasted forty-eight hours, by which time he was so weak he could barely move. After that the pain receded, leaving him exhausted and with sore eyes, a weeping nose, and a headache. Then quite suddenly he felt better, and he was able to take in his surroundings.

He was in a white room that had all the trappings of a hospital ward, but he was the only person there. He had tubes running into his arm, another up his nose, and some sort of sensor with a wire to his chest. For most of the time he was left alone but in the afternoon a nurse came in, or maybe it was a doctor, he wasn't sure because in their bio-suits and hoods they all looked the same. She stood beside the bed and checked the machinery that seemed to be monitoring him. Then she bent over him and in turn raised each eyelid and examined his eyes, shining a pen torch into the pupils. When she'd done that she took off her surgical gloves and removed her hood.

'Well,' she said, 'the good news is that you're not infected. All your blood work has come through clear.'

That was no surprise to Lander. He could have told them that. 'I know. I'm immune,' he said.

The nurse raised an eyebrow. She had a friendly face and looked strong and capable. She reminded him of his mother.

'Are you now?' she said. 'That may be. A few people are immune, I know that, but they can still carry the virus. You don't appear to be a carrier either.'

'Good. So what now? Can I go?'

'Not my decision,' she said, 'but I very much doubt it. I'm afraid you're in trouble.'

This was unwelcome news. He'd heard the broadcasts telling people to stay at home, and he'd ignored those when he decided to start his journey. But that wasn't really serious, was it?

'Trouble? What sort of trouble?' he said.

'It's bad. But not as bad as it would have been if you were a carrier. My advice is to get some sleep and eat some food. You'll need all your strength.'

The next day the questions started. He made no answer but they just repeated them, so to combat the boredom he made things up.

> *'Who are you?'*
> *'The Doctor.'*
> *'Where are you from?'*
> *'Mars.'*
> *'Where are you going?'*
> *'To the Moon.'*
> *'Why?'*
> *'To see the man there.'*
> *'How did you know about Snaith?'*
> *'A little bird told me.'*

The drill was always the same. He was taken into a bare room where three people would be sitting at a table. He was made to stand in front of the table. One of the three would put the questions to him and another would write down his answers, while the third looked on. Sometimes it was the same people, sometimes different ones. No matter what he said, the three interrogators received his answers without comment. Then he would be returned to the cell he'd been put in when he left the hospital ward, and half an hour later they'd bring him back to the interrogation chamber and ask him the same questions again. He tried giving different answers from the ones he'd given before, or the same ones, or a mixture. Whatever he did, they would hear them without responding, he would be taken away, and after another half hour he'd be subjected to the very same ritual again. This went on constantly, throughout the day and into the night.

He asked where he was but they ignored him. He asked if he could make a phone call because in all the police dramas he'd seen on TV that was a given. They ignored him. He asked if he could have a lawyer. They ignored that too. They ignored him completely except for the questions. Over and over and over again, every half hour. They interrupted his meals to ask them. They woke him up to ask them.

By the end of two days he was dizzy. By the end of the third he was so tired he could barely stand. By the end of the fourth he was delirious. He never saw daylight, and the harsh white light in his cell and the interrogation chamber was always the same. He had no idea whether it was day or night.

Sometime during day five he collapsed. He'd been escorted to the chamber, led to his usual place before the table, then somebody took hold of a corner of the room and turned it upside down.

He came round lying on the bunk in his cell. A woman was sitting beside him, a man was leaning against the wall.

'Ah, you're awake,' said the woman. Lander blinked. His eyes felt as if they were full of sand.

'Who are you?' he said.

His question was ignored.

'We're not going to stop this,' said the woman. 'We can't. We will go on asking these questions until you answer them truthfully.'

Lander felt as if his head was made of kapok. 'Why?' he said. 'What do you want from me?'

'We've told you. We need to know who you are, where you are from, and what you were doing.'

Lander couldn't understand. The whole situation was insane. Who did they think he was? Why was it so vital to them to know? With the Infection raging all around, didn't they have better things to do?

'I'm nobody important,' he said. 'I'm just a boy from a farm. Why won't you leave me alone? I wasn't doing any harm.'

The woman made a clicking noise with her tongue. 'Oh yes you were doing harm,' she said. 'You were doing a great deal of harm in Snaith.'

Snaith. The empty town. 'What's so special about Snaith?'

'We were hoping you might tell us that.'

Lander was lost. He felt bereft and alone. 'But I don't know,' he said, helplessly. 'It was just a place I came to. I'd never even heard of it till I saw the name on a signpost.'

'So why won't you answer our questions? They're very simple, and we shall go on asking them until you do.'

There was something in Lander that hated being told what to do. That had been one of his problems at school. It was the same characteristic that made him good at sports: he refused to give in.

'What if I don't?' he said.

'Then you will die, but first you will lose your mind.'

Lander's blood ran cold but he said nothing.

'You will die if we have to keep this up,' the woman continued. 'You haven't thought of that, have you? Human beings cannot manage for very long without sleep. If we keep you awake like this, in the end your brain will shut down, your bodily functions will cease, your blood pressure will fall to critical levels, you will relapse into a series of comas of increasing severity, and eventually you will die. It may take some time, but it will happen. That is unless you cooperate.'

Lander was scared. He did not doubt that the woman was serious.

'And what if I do cooperate?' he said.

'Then your life will continue.'

The man by the wall spoke for the first time. 'It's a no-brainer, literally,' he said, and laughed at his joke.

They both left. Lander forced himself to focus on what the woman had said. He couldn't remember ever having been so tired. He felt as though his brain had already shut down. Everything was woolly. He felt sick, a trembling ache in the pit of his stomach. Would they really kill him? Why? What had he done to deserve that?

Twenty minutes later he was roused and a single guard took him to the interrogation room. There had been two guards to start with. Lander was aware enough to realise that he was now in such a weakened state that he was no longer considered a threat. He was led to stand before the usual table and the guard withdrew to the door.

'What is your name?' said one of the interrogators.

'Alexander Shaw,' said Lander.

Two members of the panel looked at each other. 'Do you have any other names?' said the one who had spoken before.

'James,' said Lander.

'James Alexander Shaw? Or is it Alexander James?'

Lander felt he was in a madhouse. They were talking nonsense. His head was reeling. He was going to faint again. 'Yes,' he said.

'Which? Which is it?'

'Alexander James,' he managed to say.

'Very good. That's a start. Next question: where are you from?'

'Walbrough. It's in West Yorkshire.'

'Where in Walbrough?'

'I live on a farm. Paradise Farm.'

The interrogator nodded. 'And where were you going?'

'The coast,' Lander said. His mouth was so dry he could barely get the words out.

'Why?'

'I'm trying to get across the channel.'

'Why?'

Lander shook his head. He couldn't get into all *thetruth* stuff. His brain was too befuddled to explain it. He just stood there before his torturers, trying to remain conscious, trying to stay on his feet.

'Never mind,' said the interrogator. 'Tell us how you knew about Snaith.'

'I didn't know about it. I'd never heard of it. I just saw it on a signpost.'

'So why did you go there?'

'I needed food, and somewhere to rest.'

The interrogator muttered something to the notetaker but Lander didn't catch it.

'How did you get there from Walbrough?' said the interrogator.

This was unfair. They'd told him that if he answered their questions they'd stop. He had, and now they were asking more.

'I had a motorbike. It was stolen, so then I got a lift. Then I walked.'

'Who gave you a lift?'

'I don't know.'

The interrogator looked sceptical. There was a long pause.

'It was a tractor,' said Lander. 'The guy didn't tell me his name.'

'Why don't you have your ID card?' This was the third member of the panel, who hadn't spoken before. The question was fired at him, sharper than any of the others.

'It was stolen. When my bike got nicked.'

There was another pause, even longer than the first one. Lander was on the point of collapse.

'Take him away,' said the interrogator. The guard opened the door and Lander stumbled after him.

His captors kept to their bargain, but only in part. He was allowed to sleep. He slept for a long time, and that was good. When he awoke he was given a bowl of meaty broth and some bread. That, too, was good. Then he was taken out into a small, enclosed courtyard. There was daylight. There was grass, trees, and birds singing. Lander sat on a bench and savoured the pale sunshine washing over his face and limbs. He felt better, although he still had a headache. They'd said that if he cooperated he would be able to carry on with his life. What did that mean? Would he be freed? Would he be able to continue his journey?

He soon learnt that a night of sleep, a meal and a walk in the garden was as far as it went.

For the rest of the day he was left alone. The following morning he woke up, used the lavatory in the corner of his room and crawled back into his bunk, looking forward to another lie-in. He was just dropping off again, when without warning his door opened and a different guard came in. He was brisk and abrupt. He dropped some clothes onto the bench, and a second guard placed beside them a plate of what looked like scrambled eggs.

'Eat that and get dressed,' said the guard. 'You've got twenty minutes.'

Lander was ready sooner than that. He was in a buoyant mood. They were going to let him go. He would be able to carry on towards the coast. Or go back home. That was tempting, but the original reasons why he'd left hadn't changed.

In the event neither of these options was available. What did happen was that he was taken out to a car and made to get in the back. Alongside him was yet another guard, a very burly looking one with a ring of tattoos around his neck. Lander asked him where they were going but his question was ignored. It was only then that he realised where he was. There was the Minster, there were the walls, there was Clifford's Tower. He was in York.

The car drew up outside a yellow brick building and Lander was ushered inside. He was led down a long corridor and through a heavy door at the end. He was astonished to find himself in what he could see straight away was a courtroom. There was the bench, on a platform with a large chair like a throne in the middle and smaller chairs on each side. There was the witness stand, just like he'd seen on TV. There were half a dozen other people at the front of the room. They were in suits and gowns, and they had their arms covered in plastic sleeves and their hands in surgical gloves. The combination looked ridiculous. They were sitting with wide spaces between them. All of them turned to look at him as he came in, and their eyes followed him to the dock.

The dock? What was going on?

He had only just sat down when the door behind the bench opened, a woman came in and everyone stood up. She, too, was wearing a black gown over a business suit, and she had the bio gloves that seemed to be a part of the uniform in there. She sat in the large, middle chair. Everyone else sat down too, apart from Lander, who had never got up in the first place.

The woman spoke.

'This court is convened and will operate under the abbreviated procedures set out in Section 4 of the Emergency Powers Act. We have one case before us this morning. Would the defendant please stand?'

Nobody moved. Then the guard who had settled himself in the dock next to Lander jabbed him with his elbow and Lander realised that the woman was talking to him. Defendant? What was that about? Was he on trial? What was he supposed to have done? He wasn't a criminal.

A man at the front of the court stood and faced him, a sheaf of papers in his hand.

'Alexander James Shaw, you are accused on three counts under the Emergency Powers Act. One, that you committed the crime of vagrancy by wilfully and without permission leaving your place of residence, your place of residence being defined as an area within one square kilometre of your home. How do you plead? Guilty or not guilty?'

Lander didn't respond. What was this guy talking about?

'Do you plead guilty or not guilty?' said the man, rather sharply.

Still Lander didn't reply. This was unbelievable. Guilty? Of what?

The woman, he assumed that she must be a Magistrate, spoke. 'You must answer the question put to you by the Clerk of the Court. Did you or did you not leave the town of Walbrough without permission?'

He supposed he had. He'd heard you weren't meant to travel, but that was about going to work or to school or to things like gigs. Surely it didn't apply to what he was doing. Anyway, how did you get permission? Who did you ask?

'Well,' said the Magistrate, 'did you do that?'

'Yes, I suppose so.'

'You suppose so, ma'am.'

'I suppose so, ma'am.'

'Enter a plea of guilty,' the Magistrate said.

The Clerk spoke again. 'On count two, that you were in public areas without a valid Identity Card. Do you plead guilty or not guilty?'

'I don't know. I mean I'm not sure,' said Lander. What did they want him to say? He didn't have his ID when they'd picked him up because it had been stolen, but he'd had it when he left home.

The Magistrate sighed. 'Mr Shaw, you must try to understand what is being said to you and to reply. Otherwise this business is going to take a very long time and the Court will lose patience with you. When you were apprehended by the authorities did you or did you not have an Identity Card?'

'No,' said Lander, 'I didn't. But I did have it when I started out. It was nicked, along with my other stuff.' Why weren't they trying to find who'd robbed him, rather than blaming him for something he couldn't help?

'He pleads guilty,' said the Magistrate.

The Clerk smirked. 'On count three, you are accused of entering and being at large in a classified area. How do you plead? Guilty or not guilty?'

They must mean Snaith, thought Lander. That was where they'd picked him up. What was it about that place?

'Do you mean Snaith?' said Lander.

'Of course,' said the Clerk. 'Were you there or were you not?'

'Yes, you know I was. Shouldn't I have been there? How was I supposed to know that? There wasn't anything to say it was off limits.' Lander was beginning to feel angry. This was ridiculous. It was like Alice in Wonderland.

'Take that as a further plea of guilty,' the Magistrate said to the Clerk.

'Very good, ma'am.'

The Clerk sat down and Lander started to do the same, but the guard poked him so he remained standing.

'You have pleaded guilty on three counts,' said the Magistrate. 'All of them are serious offences. Any one of them would merit a custodial sentence. However, you are a young man, and I shall take your age and inexperience into account. On count one, the count of vagrancy, you are sentenced to eighteen months detention. On the count of not having a valid ID, you are sentenced to six months detention. On the count of entering a classified area, you are sentenced to five years detention. All three sentences are to run concurrently. Take him down.'

The Magistrate rose and so did everyone else. Lander exploded. Five years in prison for doing nothing? This was unjust. It was beyond belief, ridiculous, a farce.

'What the fuck?' he shouted at the back of the Magistrate as she turned to go through the door. 'I haven't done anything. I didn't do anybody any harm. I was just trying to get away. You're all bloody mad!'

By the end of the speech he was screaming. The guard grabbed him from behind and got him in an arm lock, forcing his head forward and banging it on the rail. The Magistrate turned to him.

'Be very careful, Mr Shaw,' she said. 'In the circumstances, I have been very lenient with you. One more word and I'll hold you in contempt of court. That will mean an even longer sentence.'

She went through the door and it slammed behind her.

8

______

SPRUNG

IT ALL HAPPENED very quickly. Lander was driven to what he assumed must be a prison, although it didn't look like the pictures of prisons he'd seen on the TV. Those had tiers of cells on separate floors, but this one was small, just a single subterranean corridor, and he seemed to be the only inmate. His cell was barely two metres square. He'd been expecting to share because he'd seen that on the TV too, but he was the only occupant. It had a bed bolted to the floor, a table, also bolted down, and a plastic chair. In one corner there was a stainless-steel lavatory with no seat or lid. On the floor beside it was a roll of very coarse toilet paper. There was nothing else, but despite the sparse furnishings there was hardly room to move.

He'd only had time to test the bed and conclude that it was probably the most uncomfortable one he'd ever encountered, when the cell door opened and two people came in. Both were wearing biohazard suits and masks.

'We're going to run some tests,' one of them, a woman, said. 'We need to find out if you're infectious.'

Lander sighed. 'I'm not,' he said. 'I've already been tested. I don't have the Infection and I'm not a carrier.'

Her companion, a man, leant forward until his face was only a few inches from Lander's.

'Shut your fucking gob, arse wipe,' he said.

They put a needle in his arm and took some blood, they swabbed his mouth, they poked a thermometer into his ear, they felt his pulse, and then they went.

The rest of the day he was left alone. There was nothing to do, no TV, not even anything to read. For some of the time Lander slept. Then he did some stretches, some squats and some press-ups, all he could manage in the tiny space. For the rest, he lay on the bunk and stared at the ceiling. Five years of this? Did they mean to keep him in this room for five years? He would go crazy. Nobody knew he was there, and that frightened him even more. They could do what they liked to him and no one would have any idea.

Halfway through the day a guard brought in a plate of fish and chips. Lander asked for ketchup but the guard gave a humourless laugh. The meal wasn't bad. At least he was being fed.

The next morning the man and woman came back, this time with a third person. As before they were in full biohazard gear, complete with face masks, and one of them was wheeling a metal trolley with various items of equipment on it. He was told to lie down and the trolley was pushed close. He had a moment's panic as the word 'torture' flashed through his mind, but it wasn't like that.

They fitted sensors to his chest and connected them to one of the machines. They shaved the hair from his temples, fixed more sensors there and connected them too. One of the trio studied a screen on the trolley, and a printer beside it whirred. They took his temperature again. They took more swabs from his mouth and several more blood samples. Finally, they uncoupled him from the machines and gave him a flask.

'Fill this,' the woman said.

Lander looked at it with puzzlement. Fill it with what?

'Pee in it, dimbo,' said one of the men. 'Over there, in the corner.'

'Don't worry, we won't look,' said the woman.

The three turned around and Lander went over to the lavatory in the corner. He found peeing to order difficult, but he managed a splash in the bottom of the flask. Sheepishly he handed it over and the three left.

The rest of the day he was again on his own, and he lay on his bunk, wondering what all this was about. Why all the medical stuff? They must know he was immune from the Infection, so what were they looking for?

He soon discovered that by far the worst thing about being in prison was boredom. Three times a day two guards came in with his meals and to check on him. One of the guards would be carrying a plastic tray of food, and the other would be holding what looked to Lander like a cattle prod. The tray would be placed on the table, where it would remain until the next one was brought in and that in turn taken away. The fare wasn't bad. Cereal and buttered toast in the mornings; cold meat with salad for lunch; chicken or fish, with chips or mashed potatoes and greens for supper. The cutlery he had to use was plastic. At the start the guards would both be in full biohazard gear, but after a few days they swapped this for white coats and sterile gloves, so he concluded that all the tests they'd done confirmed what he'd told them: he was clean.

For two hours each day he was allowed out of his cell to exercise in an enclosed yard. He found an old tennis ball in the corner and spent most of the time hurling it against a wall and catching the rebound. Then he'd do some sit-ups, star jumps and burpees. Back in his cell, he'd lie on his bunk, wondering how things were back on the farm. He tried to talk to the guards but they must have been under orders not to have anything to do with him. He asked how many other people were in the prison. No response. He asked if he could have a TV. Cold shoulder. He thought he had the right to make a phone call and asked the guard he judged to be the friendlier of the two if he could. He was told that it was out of the question. The other one added that the Infection was getting worse, and all telephone lines and cell phone circuits were reserved for the emergency services. He was lucky to be in here, they told him.

He didn't feel lucky. He thought he would go mad. All the days were running into each other. How long had he been there? He understood now why prisoners made marks on their walls to record the days. He simply had to keep some sort of record of the passing days. At the next meal he kept back the plastic fork and hid it under his pillow. The guards didn't seem to notice, and after they'd gone he used it to scratch the wall low down by his bed. He didn't know how many marks to make but he put seven. That was a starter. Seven days. One week. How could he manage five years of this? Why had he left the farm? Why had he abandoned his family? What good was he doing here?

He'd scored another seven tally marks on the wall when one morning his cell door opened – nobody ever knocked – and an elderly woman came in. She was pulling a battered wooden trolley behind her.

'I'm Marjorie,' she said. 'You are?'

'Lander,' he answered. There was no way you could not answer this lady.

'What?'

'Alexander.'

'Right. I shall call you Alex. I am the prison librarian. I shall come to your cell at this time each week for you to choose some books from my trolley. You may select up to three.'

Three books, thought Lander. What would he do with three books? That was more than he'd read in the last three years! Kerryl was the reader, not him. But at least it would be something to do.

Marjorie mistook the reason for his hesitation. 'Don't worry,' she said. 'All the books are sterilised between uses. You won't catch the Infection from them.'

Lander looked at the selection. He hoped there might be something on computing there. Or a copy of Wisden. Or a lads' mag or two. But they were all rather battered-looking hardbacks, and there was nothing that seemed less than a hundred years old.

'Spoilt for choice, are we?' said Marjorie. 'Well take your time. I'm in no hurry.' She walked over to the lavatory, looked in it, sniffed and pressed the flusher.

There was a book called *Middlemarch*. He could remember Kerryl talking about reading that, but bloody hell, it was the size of a brick! There was *Moby Dick*. He remembered Kerryl mentioning that one too, and Granddad saying that moby dick wasn't something you read but something you caught if you weren't careful. Lander had laughed, but Gran hadn't thought it funny and she'd said he ought to wash his mouth out.

'I'm not one for reading,' said Lander. 'I'd rather see a movie.' He felt he should apologise for this rejection. 'I'm sorry.'

'No need to be,' said Marjorie. 'It's your loss. No time like the present to start a good habit, though.' She took the copy of *Middlemarch* from his hands and gave him another book in its stead. Lander read the spine: *A Tale of Two Cities*. 'Try that,' she said. 'You don't have to finish it, and if you don't like it you can change it for something else when I come back next week.'

She left, and Lander sat on the edge of his bunk holding the book. This one was enormous too. He flicked to the back. Almost 500 pages. Published in 1859. What was it about people in those days? Where did they get all the time for this stuff? Didn't they have anything else to do? He opened the book, read the first sentence... and carried on. The language was old-fashioned and some of the sentences were very long, but somehow it drew you in. When the lights of his cell went out at 10 he was still reading.

Lander was not going to turn into an avid reader overnight, but he did read some more of the book the next day, and again he became absorbed. The ornate and convoluted language grew easier to follow, and although he didn't fully understand some of the vocabulary he got enough of it to be able to keep moving forward with the story and to get involved with the characters. How about that Dr Manette? Put in prison not for five years, but for eighteen! How could he stand it? Lander felt he had another point of contact with this character: his name was Alexandre. He had a fit daughter too, and that was a definite plus.

He found that with care he could skip pages without losing track of the story. It did need care because you could miss something crucial, but with a bit of thought he managed to get into the rhythm of the book and spot when Dickens was going to say something important and when he was coasting. If Kerryl had learnt to do this – and he bet she had – why hadn't she let him in on the secret? He felt resentful. There she'd been, setting herself up as Princess Bookworm and she'd probably only read half of all the stuff she claimed she had. Was that what Advanced English was all about, picking up the gist of a book and then talking as if you'd read every word of it?

He looked at how much he'd got through. Close to half an inch. He set himself the target of finishing the book before Marjorie came next. That would surprise her. He liked Marjorie, she seemed a decent old bird. He wondered why she didn't wear a biohazard suit, like the guards. Too tough, he thought. The virus would never get through that hide.

He never got the chance to finish *A Tale of Two Cities*, at least not then. Neither did he see Marjorie again. All at once his stay in prison was over.

He was finishing his breakfast – porridge, so it must have been Sunday – when there was noise in the corridor and his usual pair of guards came in, this time wearing their full anti-germ apparel. They were followed by two soldiers, also in protective clothing. Oh my god, he thought, something's gone wrong.

'Time to go,' said one of his guards. Then, when Lander didn't move, 'On your feet, pretty boy. Chop chop.'

'What's going on?' said Lander.

'You're getting out of here, that's what,' said the other guard.

'Right enough,' said the first one, when Lander still didn't move. 'You're to accompany these fine gentlemen to Oxford.'

'Why?'

'They must have decided to do something about your education,' said the second guard, and they all laughed.

'You're being sprung,' said the first one. 'You're out of here.'

'Friends in high places,' said the guard. 'You're clearly too important for the likes of us.'

'Time to pack up.'

Lander had nothing to pack. Everything had been taken from him. He had no clothes other than prison fatigues and the underwear he was wearing. The toothbrushes and grooming gear they allowed him were in a locker in the washroom, and anyway they were disposable. He picked up *A Tale of Two Cities*.

'Leave that,' said the guard, sharply.

'Prison Service property,' said the other. 'Besides, you don't want Queen Marjorie to come after you, do you?'

Lander was fairly sure that Marjorie wouldn't object if he took the book with him, but he put it on his bunk, took a final look at his cell and followed the two soldiers along the corridor.

9

GWEN AND ADAM

'CALL ME GWEN.'

That was not what Lander had expected. The plaque on the door said *Dr Gwendolyn Matthews, Director of Special Programmes*, and he thought as he knocked that the person behind it would be old, serious, and formal. Instead he found a striking-looking black woman who was probably not that much older than he was, and who greeted him with a massive smile. She motioned to the chair in front of her desk.

'Please sit,' she said.

'Call me Gwen' was wearing the white coat which seemed to be uniform for everybody in the Oxford hospital. She also had a sterile face mask which was tied loosely around her neck, and she had the latex gloves they all wore. Lander hadn't been given any of this kit and he was feeling left out, as if everybody else merited protection but not him.

'I expect you're wondering why you've been brought here.' Gwen had such a broad, open smile that it would have been hard not to smile back, and Lander did.

'Well yes, you could say that,' he said.

'I just did,' said Gwen. Lander immediately liked her. She had his own sense of humour. 'I suppose you can guess that it's about the Infection. What isn't? So let's start from the beginning. How much do you know about the virus?'

'Enough,' said Lander. 'I watched my mother die from it.'

'Yes, of course you did. I'm sorry, that was insensitive of me. The tragic thing is that everybody one meets has lost someone, often their whole family. It's easy to become blasé about what are terrible personal losses.'

'That's all right,' said Lander.

His remark about his mother had come out differently from the way he'd meant it. He hadn't been digging for sympathy. What he'd been trying to convey was that after seeing somebody consumed by the virus he didn't think there was much more to learn about it.

'All I know is that sooner or later just about everybody gets it, and hardly anybody gets over it,' he said.

Gwen nodded. 'Let me give you some background. The Infection caught everybody by surprise. We knew about Ebola of course. We, that is medical and health professionals, have been fighting that for years, but although this one has similarities it's in a different league.'

'But it came from Africa, didn't it? Like Ebola.'

'Yes, it did, but only incidentally. We think, and this is only theory mind, that this virus was created in a laboratory.'

'You mean somebody made it?'

'We believe so. We think it was developed as a weapon of biological warfare. Something so devastating that it would be comparable to the H bomb. The ultimate deterrent.'

Lander couldn't believe it. 'Who would do that?'

'It's hard to say. There are only a few countries with the capability to do it. It wasn't us, or so our government says, and there are only three or four others it could have been.'

'So what is it?'

'This virus, its official label is I/452, we think is derived from Ebola, but its effects are even worse and it's harder to stop. The reason why so many people catch colds and influenza, and why those who have 'flu jabs need them renewed each year, is because those viruses change all the time. They evolve, and that gives the body's immune system little opportunity to develop the antibodies to combat them. As fast as the immune system learns how to counteract one mutation, another appears. We think that whoever designed I/452 took a virus of this type – it may even have been a cold or 'flu virus – and somehow spliced it with a particularly powerful strain of Ebola. As an added extra, they managed to make this virus mutate much more quickly than any of the influenza or cold viruses we've met so far.'

Lander was flabbergasted. The idea that human beings could make something like this was incomprehensible. 'But why Africa?' he said. 'Surely it wasn't an African country that did this.'

'Heavens no. We think the originators are certainly from the northern, 'civilised' hemisphere. It appeared in Africa because whoever designed it wanted to test it. They couldn't do that in their own backyard. An outbreak of something that looked like Ebola in Moscow or Beijing or New York would arouse too much attention. Where better to test something that looked like Ebola than in a place where Ebola is endemic? And where lives are cheaper.'

Lander caught the bitterness in Gwen's last remark. Maybe her origins were in one of those places. 'You mean they released it amongst real people on purpose? Just to see if it worked? That's unbelievable.'

'To the likes of you and me, yes,' said Gwen. 'To any decent person, it's completely unbelievable. But to the twisted minds that go in for this sort of thing, there's a perverse logic to it. Where it all came unstuck was that the "cure" they thought they had for it didn't work. They probably meant to try it in a single village, and when they'd observed it and were satisfied they'd learnt all they could, to snuff it out. However, the thing got out of the test area and developed a momentum all of its own. It slipped from the grasp of its controllers...'

'...and look what happened!'

'Yes, look what happened.'

Lander sat for a moment in silence, digesting the awful account Gwen had given him. Would people really do something like that deliberately? Well, they'd dropped the Atom Bomb on a living city, hadn't they? Twice. And fired gas into World War I trenches. And blanket bombed Dresden. And executed six million Jewish civilians. And blown up children, women and men going about their ordinary lives in arenas, mosques and marketplaces. So yes, some people really would do it deliberately. But what did it have to do with him?

'Why tell me all this?' said Lander. 'There's nothing I can do about it.'

'The reason I've told you is the same reason we've had you released from prison and brought you here. And that's because we think there is something you can do about it. Or, rather, something you can help us to do about it. I'd like you to meet my colleague.' She leant across the desk and pressed an intercom button. 'Andrea, would you ask Adam to come in.'

A minute passed while Lander waited. He felt awkward. It was not only the awful account Gwen had given. It was also that she was a very attractive woman, and she seemed to be staring at him. He didn't want to simply stare back, so he looked at the floor, the wall, the picture behind her desk, her stapler. At last the door opened and a young man came in. He was dressed in a white shirt and black chinos. His face was tanned and his head was covered in blond curls. Lander noticed he wasn't wearing either surgical gloves or a face mask.

'This is Przemysław Adamski,' said Gwen. 'We call him Adam for short. He's one of our research team.'

Adam held out his ungloved hand and Lander took it. That was unusual. Shaking hands had vanished as a means of greeting since the virus arrived. He pulled up a chair beside Lander and sat down.

'I've been telling Alexander here what we know of the origins and nature of the virus,' said Gwen.

Adam grinned. 'Alexander, eh? Using your Sunday best name now, are you? I think I'll call you Lander.'

Lander nearly fell off his chair. 'How do you know my name?'

'I know quite a lot about you,' said Adam. There was a hint of middle Europe in his accent. Polish? Czech? 'Don't look worried,' he continued. 'You've not been spied on or anything like that, but I had to find out about you to be sure you were who we thought you were, and that you were in a position to help us.'

'And I am?'

'Yes, I – we – think you are.'

Lander wasn't sure he wanted to cooperate with people who'd arrested him, tried him and jailed him, and now apparently investigated him, but he'd give them a hearing.

'How?' he said.

Adam looked at Gwen, who nodded.

'My team has been studying responses to the virus,' he said. 'As I expect you've realised, the vast majority of people have no defence against it. This is particularly true of the very young and the very old, who contract it most easily. Mature adults succumb more slowly, but well over ninety-five per cent of those who are exposed to the virus develop the Infection and die. That means that most of the UK population is now dead, or soon will be. The same is true in Europe, the USA and, as far as we know, the Russian Federation, Africa, the Indian sub-continent, and south and east Asia. Actually, the whole world, although since communications have become dodgy it's hard to know exactly what's happening where. The virus doesn't discriminate and it has no mercy. It cuts across all ages and all ethnic groups. It penetrates all income groups, even getting into the bolt holes of billionaires, although the better off do have more places where they can hide.'

'You said over ninety-five per cent,' said Lander. 'That's not everybody, then. What happens to the rest?'

'The rest fall into two groups. Some of them initially show only a mild reaction to the virus – headaches, joint pains, sore throat and sniffles, bleeding gums. Then they get better, or they appear to.'

'But they don't,' said Lander. 'The virus attacks their brains.'

Adam looked surprised. 'You know this?'

'Yes. Before I left home I was in contact with an online group. They told me all about it.'

Adam looked at Gwen. 'Did they? What else did they tell you?'

'Well, people who posted said that the effect was like a split personality, kind of two people in one. The two don't know about each other, and they behave separately. One of them can do something without the other being aware of it. They said that usually it's harmless, but it can be violent. Sometimes one of the personalities will attack other people, sometimes it will think it's attacking somebody else but it will be turning on itself.'

Adam shook his head. '*Dr Jeckyll and Mr Hyde.*'

'What?'

'It's a book,' said Gwen. 'By Robert Louis Stevenson. Dr Jeckyll, a good man, invents a serum that turns him into Edward Hyde, an evil murderer, and back again, so he can live two lives.'

'Oh,' said Lander. He had heard of it. He wondered if Kerryl had read it.

'I wish I'd known about this online forum of yours,' said Adam. 'Their information might have saved me a lot of work.'

Lander was going to point out that he'd been on his way to join the group when he'd been arrested, but he thought better of it.

'Anyway,' said Adam, 'people who respond in this way are, as far as we know, all males. We haven't yet come across any women showing a similar reaction, although of course there may be some that we just haven't found.'

'What's the other group?' said Lander.

'That group consists of people like Gwen and me. Young adults, under thirty, fit and healthy. We have a certain immunity in that our bodies seem able to dodge some of the strains of the virus. However, only some. We can go on with our lives but it's Russian roulette. Sooner or later the chamber will be loaded, we'll encounter a mutation that we're unable to cope with and then we'll join the rest. Unless a means of stopping it can be found first.'

'Which group do you think I belong to?' said Lander.

'Neither,' said Adam. 'You and Kerryl are a group on your own.'

For the second time Lander was thunderstruck. What did he mean by a group on their own? And how did he know about Kerryl?

'What are you talking about? Have you been spying on my sister too?'

'Calm down,' said Adam. He took out a mobile phone and swiped through some pictures until he found one and handed it to Lander.

Lander was astonished. 'That's our house,' he said. 'Where did you get this?'

'I took it.'

'When?'

'A couple of days ago. Scroll on to the next one.'

He did. It was the house again, but from a different angle. Somebody was crossing the yard.

'That's Kerryl,' he said.

'Yes. Keep swiping.'

There were eight more pictures, and Kerryl was in several of them. They must have been done on different days because she wasn't wearing the same clothes in all of them. In one of the best ones she was on her horse, Joey. It was taken from quite close, she had no riding hat, and her hair was loose. She looked happy. Lander felt an actual physical tug. They had often had rows lately, but despite that he missed her. Oh, how he missed her.

'Why did you take these? Do you know Kerryl? Are you some sort of Peeping Tom pervert or something?'

Adam smiled. 'Hardly. I'll tell you what I've been doing and why, but first I want you to know that your sister is safe and well. Sadly, I don't have the same news about your grandparents. I'm sorry to have to tell you that they are both gone.'

It was painful to hear, but Lander was not surprised. He'd expected that Gran and Granddad would catch the Infection at the same time as their Mam had. They hadn't, and when he'd left he'd been hoping that they'd managed to escape, and that if no one else came to the farm spreading the virus they'd be able to hang on. But in his heart of hearts he'd known that it was unlikely he'd see them again.

'I'm sorry,' said Gwen.

Lander sniffed. He wasn't one for tears, but the mention of his grandparents and their fate, together with the pictures of Kerryl apparently normal and healthy, had brought on an almost intolerable homesickness.

He nodded to Gwen. 'Thanks.' Then to Adam, 'So if you're not a Peeping Tom, why have you been watching her and taking pictures of her?'

'For a very good reason,' said Adam. 'When you were first spotted the army thought you were just some vagrant seeing what he could steal. You didn't appear dangerous so they let you be. Then you went into a restricted area…'

'Snaith.'

'Yes, Snaith. They thought then that you must be up to no good, so they arrested you and put you in jail. From our point of view, and I think yours and Kerryl's too, that was an excellent thing. The authorities need to know whether a prisoner is infectious, so everybody who's committed to prison is screened for the virus. They did some tests on you, the basic stuff – DNA swabs, blood samples, pulse, temperature and urine checks.'

'I remember them,' said Lander. 'Then the next day they came back and did some more.'

'Yes. That was because when they analysed your samples they found that there was something odd about them, and so they did another batch, more extensive and elaborate this time. They confirmed what they at first thought. That was when they called us in, and we had you brought here.'

Lander began to tremble. Confirmed what? What had he got? This was going to be something terrible. 'What's wrong with me?' he whispered.

'Oh, nothing's wrong with you,' said Gwen. 'Everything is right with you. You see, you're immune.'

'I'm what?'

'Immune. The most thorough tests were done and it's clear. There is no trace of the virus being active anywhere in your system, although there are signs that you've been in contact with it.'

Lander pondered this. He'd been exposed to the virus, he knew he had. His mother and grandparents had caught it, so it must have been around in the house.

'Are you sure?'

'Yes. Completely sure. You see,' said Gwen, 'it seems that your system can produce antibodies unusually quickly. Unlike the rest of us, you can respond to each new strain of the virus almost immediately.'

'What does that mean?'

'For one thing,' said Adam, 'it means you won't die of the Infection. Not this one, anyway. You can go anywhere, do anything in safety.'

'How did you find out about Kerryl?'

'We ran your DNA through our database. You may have lost your ID, but you can't lose that. It told us about you, and your sister.'

'Is Kerryl the same as me?'

'Yes. She's your twin.'

'But we're not identical, our Mam said so.'

'What she probably meant is that strictly speaking you're not. You have a Y chromosome and Kerryl doesn't. But your DNA is so close that there's barely any difference.'

Lander's mind was racing. What was the significance of all this? What did it mean for him and his sister? He was sure he'd been infected and he knew he'd started to show the split personality symptoms. He'd checked with *thetruth* and the behaviour he'd seen discussed there fitted with what he'd been experiencing. He'd had hallucinations. Bad dreams. Periods when he was sure he'd done things without realising it.

'But I've had the split personality thing, I know I have. They call it "dream walking", when you behave like a zombie.'

Adam looked surprised. It was a term that was new to him.

'Interesting. However, you were observed while you were in prison, and your case looks to be mild. Several nights you got up in your sleep, but all you did was stand for a few minutes before getting back into bed. You seem able to control your condition, and while you can it won't result in any danger to you or anyone else.'

Lander wasn't aware of any such control. As far as he knew the business was random. 'How do I manage that? How do I control it?'

'At present it seems to be involuntary, a sort of safety device that you've developed unconsciously. We wonder if you might be able to learn to control it voluntarily.'

'You mean switch it on and off, like taking Dr Whatsit's potion?'

'Yes.'

'Are there any others like us?'

'We've not found any in this country yet, although these online people you talked about might know more. When it became clear that the Infection couldn't be stopped the government set up several isolated areas where people could go to be safe from exposure to the virus. They call them 'arks'. Four thousand people have been selected to fill them. The idea is that they'll stay there until the Infection dies out…'

'…or a cure is found,' Gwen interrupted.

'Of course. Then they'll come out and it will be their job to rebuild the country, and to repopulate it.'

Lander had heard rumours of the arks but had never been able to discover anything concrete about them.

'All the arkies, as we call them, are in Adam's and my age group,' said Gwen. 'Every one of them was tested and they were all found to be like us, semi-immune but not completely so. Just FYI, Snaith had been set up as a reserve ark. The whole place had been isolated, sterilised, and prepared for extended occupation. That's why people were so upset when you wandered in there.'

Half an hour ago Lander had thought his future was plotted. He would find a way to carry on to Belarus, and once there he would wait with others for the time when his disordered personality would kill him, or when he would be removed because he'd become too dangerous to live with. Now everything had changed.

'If I'm immune,' he said, 'and Kerryl is too, I can go home now. We can live on the farm.'

Gwen and Adam glanced at each other.

'You could do that, in theory,' said Gwen. 'But don't you think it would be rather selfish?'

'How do you mean?'

'You and your sister are the only two people we've found who have this particular characteristic. That means there must be something in your genes that the rest of us don't have. If we can isolate what it is, we might be able to find some way of replicating it and protecting people.'

'There's also the possibility,' Adam added, 'that we may be able to use what we can learn from you to engineer the DNA of the babies that the arkies will have so that they produce children who are immune to the virus from birth.'

There was a long pause.

'So,' said Gwen, 'will you and Kerryl help us? What do you say?'

10

EXPERIMENT

THE IDEA THAT the virus had been released as some ghastly experiment was almost beyond belief, but even worse was the thought that struck Lander in the small hours.

He remembered that in the months leading up to the Infection, a hot topic had been the pressures on the earth's resources placed by an increasing global population. In fact, it had replaced climate change as the top environmental issue. There had been a conference of world leaders in Tokyo, which had concluded that if the human race continued to grow at its present rate, within less than fifty years the planet would be unable to sustain it. It wasn't just food. Resources of all sorts simply wouldn't go round. The outcome of the conference was that there was a strong possibility that human society would simply implode.

Of course, there were the usual sceptics – the *Daily Mail* ran a piece with the headline "Tokyo Joke-yo" ridiculing the whole thing – but on the whole people seemed to take the issue seriously. Lander remembered a General Studies session at school where the teacher had asked the class to come up with solutions to the problem of too many people. The boys made a range of suggestions, most of them fascistic: compulsory sterilisation, limiting life by requiring euthanasia after fifty years, aborting foetuses that showed signs of malformation or other problems. Finally somebody said, 'Why don't we just reintroduce The Black Death?' Everybody had laughed, but suppose that's what had happened. Suppose the Infection was not a test that had gone wrong, but a deliberate stratagem to remove a huge number of people. Granddad had often said that the world was run by a secret bunch of anonymous, faceless zillionaires, and that politicians were simply their puppets. Lander had thought it was just another of his rants, but it made a sort of insane sense. It kept him awake most of the night.

In the harsh light of morning, he returned to what Gwen and Adam were proposing, and when he saw them again he gave the only answer he could. Yes, he would do what they wanted. He would have preferred to consult Kerryl, but communication systems were down and there was no way of getting in touch with her. He wanted to bring her to Oxford, where he thought they'd want them both for the tests, but Adam and Gwen had other ideas. Gwen put it to him that the two of them being in different environments offered a unique opportunity to study their behaviour.

'Both of you are in sterile surroundings,' she said. 'Provided Kerryl stays at home she won't be exposed to the virus. Neither will you, as long as you remain in this hospital. What we can do is give a new strain of the virus to both of you...'

She held up her hand as Lander began to protest.

'...You know you're immune. We can introduce the virus to you both, and while your bodies are coping with it we can in Kerryl's case observe how that affects her ability to function in day-to-day practical situations, while in yours we can see what's happening inside your head.'

'Observe how?'

'Well, we have equipment that can look into your brain and nervous system and see exactly what's going on. As far as Kerryl's concerned, we'll watch her.'

'Who's "we"?'

'I'll do it,' said Adam. 'I'll monitor her from a distance and keep a record of what she does and how she is. Don't worry, she won't know I'm there.'

'And how will you infect us?'

'It's best if you're not aware of when or how you're in contact with the virus,' said Gwen. 'If we're to make a fair comparison between you and Kerryl we'll have to expose you both at the same time and in the same way. We need to think about how to do that, but be assured you'll know nothing about it.'

'If you cooperate with us in this,' said Adam, 'there's a good chance that we can learn enough about the virus to enable us to defeat it.'

'And thereby ensure the survival of the human race,' said Gwen.

'It really is as big as that,' Adam added.

Lander knew he had no choice. 'How long will this go on?' he asked. 'How long will you need for these tests?'

Adam said six months; Gwen said three; Lander settled on two.

'At the end of two months I want this all to be over,' he said. 'I want Kerryl and me to be together.'

'All right.'

'Also I want to be able to talk to her.'

'Not possible,' said Adam. 'For one thing, all the phone systems have collapsed – landlines, mobiles, the internet, the lot. More important for the programme, though, is that you don't communicate. The best thing would be for neither of you to know that the other exists. That can't happen in your case, but we need to keep Kerryl totally in the dark about you.'

'We don't want anything to happen that might affect the way she responds to the challenges of her situation,' said Gwen. 'And remember, it is only for two months.'

'Don't worry,' said Adam. 'I'll keep an eye on your sister. I'll have to stay in the background because it's vital she doesn't know she's being observed, but I'll make sure she comes to no harm. And each time I go to the farm I'll take photos and videos so you can see for yourself that she's all right.'

The programme began the next day. Lander was collected by a white-coated technician and taken along the corridor to a consulting room where Gwen waited.

She started with an apology, of a sort. 'I'm afraid you're going to get bored with this, because we plan to carry out these procedures every time Adam goes to your home to study your sister. Then when he comes back we can compare his observations with what we've learnt from you.'

'When do we get the new viruses?'

'They'll be introduced to both of you at the same time.'

'How?'

'That's still under discussion but it will probably be by means of an aerosol spray, administered to you and Kerryl on the same day.'

'All right,' said Lander. 'What do I have to do and when do we start?'

'You don't have to do a lot. We'll need the usual samples – blood, urine, and faeces. A technician will deal with collecting those, and we'll need them every time. We'll also need a semen sample.'

'What, really?'

'I'm afraid so. We have to check your sperm count. A technician will deal with that, too. A male one,' she added, enjoying Lander's embarrassment. 'Apart from those, all you have to do is lie back and relax. Right now we're going to do some neuroimaging.'

'What's that?'

'It's using magnetic resonances to build a map of your central nervous system, including your brain and the way it works. You've probably heard them referred to as MRI scans and CAT scans.'

'Will you be doing them?'

Gwen smiled. 'No, I'm not a radiographer. I'm going to love you and leave you.'

'And is Adam going to watch Kerryl?' He almost said 'spy on', because that was still how he thought of it.

'He's already gone,' said Gwen. 'He left at crack of dawn. Enjoy your day, and I'll drop by when the tests are over.'

It wasn't as easy as Gwen said. The first procedure was gruelling. Lander had to change into a hospital gown and was told to lie down on a gurney in front of a long tube. He knew what it was – a scanner – because he'd seen them on the TV, and he'd taken part in a fund-raising event at school as part of an appeal to buy a new one for the hospital in Halifax. What he hadn't bargained for was the loud noise the machine made, and the terrible feeling of being shut in as the gurney rolled into the tube. Claustrophobia had always been a thing with him, and he felt a surge of panic as he was drawn in. But the radiographer was a girl, Janice. She was attractive, and Lander was anxious not to look like a prick in front of her. However, it took him a huge effort of will to overcome the urge to press the help button she'd given him.

Janice had told him to stay completely still so he did, while his mind wandered over the life that, until very recently, he'd taken for granted. He couldn't communicate with Kerryl, that had been made clear, but he wondered if she had any idea of what was going on. Maybe she had a notion of what was happening to him. He was sure she'd know he was alive, just as he knew she was.

What would their future be now, after all this was over? There'd be no Yorkshire cricket team to play for, and he'd not found anything else that appealed to him as much. Earlier in the year Kerryl had been offered a place at Cambridge to study English. He didn't know much about it, but why would anybody want to spend three years reading? He'd looked up Cambridge on the internet and it seemed full of old buildings, not his cup of tea at all. Besides, in the Boat Race he'd always rooted for the other side, the dark blues, Oxford. Kerryl had been keen to go, but would there be any Cambridge anymore?

Not for the first time he wondered where his sister had got her brains. Not from their Mam, that was for sure. Celebrity TV and

Hello magazine were her style. From their dad? They'd only been children when he'd had the accident that killed him and so they'd been too young to judge, but he seemed to know a great deal. Granddad read a lot – non-fiction and newspapers mostly. He knew about politics and events, and he would launch into monologues on a range of subjects – the way farmers were treated, prices, taxes, the march of the wind turbines over his beloved moors, the management of Leeds United. 'Aye up, he's off on one,' their Gran would say when he started on a diatribe. Now he came to think of it, she was probably the sharpest of any of them. True, she watched rubbish television, but often she'd say something that seemed to be so right that he was left wishing he'd thought of it.

Suddenly the machine gave a rattle louder than anything so far, his bed vibrated and he was rolled out of the tube. He sighed with relief and took the ear protectors off.

Janice came into the room. 'My, you didn't like that, did you?' she said, looking him up and down. 'Your heart was going like a road drill.'

He realised he was wet through. He'd not been conscious of feeling hot but he'd been sweating profusely. His gown and the sheet covering the gurney were sodden.

'Jesus, it looks like I wet myself,' he said.

'And didn't you?'

'Course not.' Lander felt himself redden.

'Says you,' said Janice, with a wink. She pointed to the door. 'There's a shower in there. Help yourself.'

'Will I have to do this again?' he asked as he swung his legs off the gurney.

'Probably, though I don't expect they'll need a scan every time. Gwen will tell you. I don't have the full programme.'

'I'm supposed to give a semen sample. Will you be doing that too?' said Lander.

'In your dreams, lover boy,' said Janice. 'Now get yourself showered and dressed.'

For the rest of the day Lander drifted around his corridor or watched old recordings of soccer matches on the TV. The following morning he was taken to a small room with a single desk. He was told to sit down and a man, who didn't introduce himself, gave him a series of test papers to complete – maths, verbal reasoning, comprehension, general knowledge, and logic puzzles. Each took half an hour. Lander thought it worse than being in school.

As soon as he'd finished them he was taken back to the neuroimaging department. For a few awful moments he thought they were going to put him in the MRI scanner again. However, this time it was a different machine. Only his head went into it, and so long as he could move his limbs he was happy. He looked out for Janice but she wasn't there. This scan was over very quickly. After lunch he was given another five test papers to complete on the same topics, and then his head was scanned again.

'How was that?' asked Gwen, meeting him as he left to return to his quarters.

'Terrible,' he said. 'If those were exams I think I failed.'

All the days while Adam was away were similar to this. The tests stopped when he was there and they spent a lot of time together, playing table tennis, cards, PlayStation games, or simply talking guys talk about nothing in particular. Adam introduced him to squash, which Lander liked and was good at. Adam stuck to his promise to keep him informed. He told him that Kerryl was fine, and described what he'd seen her doing – milking the cows, riding Joey, walking Buster, going up to the rocks on the moor. He showed photographs and short videos of her in the fields, working in the farmyard, or simply sitting on a wall looking at the moors.

Lander enjoyed the time he spent with Adam; however, he didn't like the feeling of being a guinea pig, the subject of an experiment, and he found the constant investigation and scrutiny irksome. He disliked the scans and hated the monotony of examinations and tests. In comparison, lessons at King's Heath Boys' were high excitement.

Over the days the boredom anaesthetised his senses, and it was only slowly that he became aware that the reports from Adam were changing. His accounts of what Kerryl had been doing were rarer and less detailed. There were no videos, and the photographs he was shown were all at a distance and many of them were blurred. Except for one. It was a shot of her crossing the yard. Her hand was bandaged and that troubled him, but worse was her appearance. She was limping, and was noticeably thinner than when he'd last seen her.

'What's wrong with her?'

'You mean her hand,' said Adam. 'She caught it on a piece of machinery.'

'What machinery?'

'The elevator you use to lift hay bales.'

'What was she doing with that? She can't have been making hay.'

'It was an accident. It's all right. It's a clean cut and it's healing well.'

'But she looks to be walking with a stick.'

'She slipped and hurt her ankle. It's just a sprain. Again, it's not a problem.' Adam put his arm around Lander's shoulder. 'She's fine.'

Lander wasn't so sure. 'I need to go and see her,' he said.

Adam shook his head. 'You know you can't do that, and you know why.'

'I can do what you do. I can hide, look at her from a distance without her knowing I'm there.'

Adam frowned. 'I don't think that would work. Your sister's all right, honestly. Anyway, the two months will soon be up and then you can join her.'

Despite Adam's reassurances, Lander was still troubled. Kerryl had not looked at all herself in those pictures. She'd lost a lot of weight and her face was pale. He had a suspicion that Adam wasn't being open with him. What was going on?

He didn't sleep much that night. He lay awake for a long time turning things over in his head. Something was wrong; he could feel it. He had to find a way to see Kerryl and ensure she was safe. If she wasn't allowed to come to him and if Adam wouldn't let him go to her, he would take matters into his own hands. He would go back to Paradise Farm on his own. He would have a quick look, satisfy himself that everything was all right, and then come back.

On impulse, he got out of bed and walked across to the door to his room. He tried the handle. It turned, but it wouldn't open. He tugged. No movement. It was locked. It hadn't been before.

He banged on the door with his fist, anger and frustration welling inside him. Why was he locked in? What right did they have to do that? They must have guessed what he was thinking of doing. Had he been talking in his sleep? Had he been dream walking? Adam had some questions to answer. He'd have it out with him in the morning.

11

ESCAPE

ADAM WASN'T THERE in the morning, so the tests carried on. Two orderlies collected him from his room, walked him along the corridors to Radiography, and waited while he was scanned. Then they took him back to his room and locked him in. He thought about trying to make a run for it, but the men were big and he didn't think he'd have much chance. He demanded to know what was going on, and why he was being treated like a prisoner, and he was told that it was necessary for the programme.

Alone in his room, he fretted increasingly over what might be happening to Kerryl, and he thought more and more about escape. But how could he do that? He saw no one except the guards, the orderlies who brought his food and the medical staff who administered the tests. Janice seemed to have gone; the other medics weren't as friendly as she'd been and they avoided talking to him. It was like being back in jail.

Then, abruptly, the scans and the tests stopped. Lander expected that meant Adam was back, but he didn't appear. Instead, two days passed when he was left completely alone. He waited but no one came, and he spent his time playing video games or trying to find something worth watching on the collection of moviesticks in the day room. He asked the woman who brought his lunch if he could go out for some air, and she said she didn't know. He said could she ask, and she said she didn't know that either. When the guard came on his evening rounds Lander told him he wanted to see Gwen. 'Don't we all?' was the reply.

On day three he got up early, showered, dressed, and lay on his bed waiting for his door to be unlocked. He had decided when it had clicked shut the night before that he needed to take some decisive action. He'd thought about a hunger strike, but that would take a long time to have any impact, and in the short term would anybody notice? The best course would be to make a complete nuisance of himself until he got an audience with Gwen or Adam; then he could demand to be told why everything had ground to a halt and what the fuck was going on. They'd done this topic at school about Gandhi and passive resistance. He would try that and see if it would get some results. He couldn't shake off the continuous, nagging worry that something had happened to Kerryl.

He waited and waited, but nobody showed up. His watch said it was nearly nine, well after the time he was usually collected for the scans or tests, or let out to try to entertain himself in the day room. Eventually he got to his feet and crossed to the door. He bent to take off a shoe so he could pound on it, reached for the handle to steady himself, and found that the door opened.

He was perplexed. He hadn't heard it being unlocked. Had it been locked at all? Maybe it had been like that all night. Perhaps that meant that Adam was back.

He was not in the day room, where they usually met. He wondered if he'd already been in and he'd missed him. A woman came in with a vacuum cleaner and plugged it in.

'Is Adam around?' Lander asked.

The woman shook her head.

'Where's Gwen?' he said.

'She's away.'

Lander looked out of the door and along the corridor. There was no one out there. Could he just leave? He didn't know the geography of the hospital. Most of it seemed to be empty and closed off, but he thought he could probably find his way out. There must be somebody in charge, somebody more important than Adam or Gwen who should be able to give him some answers. Maybe he could find out where they were and see them.

The woman finished her cleaning and went. Lander couldn't sit down or settle. Something was wrong. It was not only that Adam and Gwen seemed to have vanished. He had a persistent feeling of dismay, a sensation as if a ball of lead had lodged in his gut. He struggled with it for most of the morning. Then he reached a conclusion. He had to go north now. He had to go back home.

But how? He had only the hospital scrubs, a smock and pants, that he was wearing. He had no money, no ID and no transport. And there was the minor snag of getting out of the hospital without being stopped. He looked from the window at the street below. There was no one out there and no traffic in sight. The whole of Oxford seemed dead. Even if he managed to leave the hospital, what would he do?

He went on to the landing. At the end of the corridor were stairs down to a foyer. There were a couple of men in white coats standing by a window marked Reception. They were deep in conversation and took no notice of him as he walked towards the large glass doors that marked the entrance.

An ambulance drove into the car park, reversed up to the building, and two paramedics in biohazard gear got out. Lander hid behind a vending machine and watched them walk slowly, casually even, to the rear of the vehicle and open the door. There was a trolley in there with a covered patient on it. They manoeuvred it out and wheeled it towards the automatic doors, which slid open. They were in no hurry. This wasn't an emergency; it was a corpse.

They pushed the trolley across the foyer and into a lift, and the door closed. The two men who had been in conversation when Lander first arrived had now gone. One of them had left his white coat on the desk by the reception window. Lander hesitated. Could he just walk out? Was it as easy as that? He waited. There was silence. But not quite; the ambulance engine was still running.

Lander didn't think about it. He didn't consider where he'd go. He simply stepped from his hiding place, went to the desk, picked up the white coat and put it on. Underneath it was a stethoscope. Even better. He hooked that around his neck, walked out of the hospital door, climbed into the ambulance, pushed the gear lever into drive, and moved away.

'Not too fast,' he told himself, 'not too fast.' He didn't want to do anything that would attract attention. He was simply a medical vehicle on routine business.

How long did he have before the crew realised that their ambulance was missing? What would they do when they did? Had anyone seen him drive away? What should he do next?

He couldn't go all the way from Oxford to Yorkshire in an ambulance, that was ridiculous. Or was it? The fuel tank was almost full, and the ambulance would look official. Perversely it might arouse less curiosity than a car. He was starting to realise that there wasn't anything like the surveillance that there'd been before the Infection. It would be some time before they worked out who had taken the ambulance and guessed where it had gone. It was time that would be wasted if he stopped to look for some other means of transport. His best bet would be to get out of the city as quickly as he could, and then decide how to go on from there.

The street was empty. He didn't know Oxford but he saw a sign for the M40 and he knew that would take him in the right direction. Use that to get clear, and then divert onto minor roads where there'd be less chance of being noticed.

He glanced up at the row of switches above the windscreen. One was labelled 'lights', another 'siren'. Dare he? His hand hovered over them, then he thought better of it. Using them would be cool and it was something he'd always wanted to do, but now was not the time. Now he had to get north without causing a fuss, and find out what was happening to his sister. With the thought of her, the awful, corpse-like weight of anxiety settled on him again.

He kept following signs for the M40, ignoring those for Lytham, Wolvercote, and Kidlington. They might have led him by a less exposed route, but he didn't know these places and it could be they'd take him out of his way. He planned to follow the motorway north and look for an opportunity to strike out across country.

He made good progress. There was little to slow him, apart from the fact that none of the traffic lights worked and he had to reduce his speed at each junction so that he could check for things coming the other way. The chances were that there would be nothing but it was best to be careful. A stupid accident at a blind junction was the last thing he needed. He saw only two other vehicles, one a car and the other an army Land Rover. Neither paid him any attention. He supposed that in his hospital clothing and white coat he looked pretty genuine, although they might wonder why he wasn't in a bio-suit. When he got to a spot where it seemed reasonable to stop he'd check in the back to see if there was a spare one.

After about twenty minutes he reached a roundabout: the M40. Bicester and Birmingham were one way, High Wycombe and London the other. He took the northbound carriageway, towards Birmingham.

The motorway was as empty as everywhere else, and it took him only five minutes to reach the next junction. Birmingham straight on, Brackley and Northampton by another route. It would be dangerous to get too close to Birmingham, so he took the exit. This new road was duelled, but it was slower than the motorway because there were frequent roundabouts. They were all littered with damaged or dead vehicles which must have been dragged there to get them off the highway. On one there were some people camping; two women, a man and a small child standing in front of a shabby tent. They tried to flag him down and he began to slow, but then something warned him not to get involved and he accelerated. One of the women stood in the road to stop him and only jumped aside at the last minute. He saw them in his mirror, shaking their fists and giving him the finger. It was probably a set-up, an ambush, he thought. On the other hand, they might have been in trouble. He should have stopped. It could have been the child, and the mother thought he was a real medic and would help them. But there was nothing he could have done. If he'd picked them up, where would he have taken them? Even so, he felt bad. Kerryl would have stopped, for sure. She thought and expected the best of everybody, and she was always ready to help someone in trouble. She would have called him a selfish pig for driving on. But it was for her sake that he was doing it.

He passed Brackley and saw a sign for Silverstone. He knew about that; there was a motor racing circuit there. He'd seen it on TV. Where was it? Could you drive on to it? It would be a hoot to do that, to go round the Silverstone track in an ambulance, siren screaming, blues flashing. What speed would this thing do? But he told himself not to get distracted, and he pushed the temptation aside.

He didn't know how big Northampton was but he thought it might be quite large and therefore best avoided, so before he reached it he turned onto a side road. Even though he'd had no breakfast he wasn't hungry, but he thought he should eat. The question was, where could he find something? From past experience, it seemed that a private house would be his best bet. Apart from the ones in Snaith, all the stores he'd seen had been raided and nothing decent was left. If he could find a house that was hidden away he'd have a better chance. Everything in the fridge would have gone off, but there'd be packets and tins in store cupboards. Finding another Snaith would be terrific, although on reflection that hadn't turned out well.

He came to a tiny village. It was no more than a hamlet really, just a small church and four or five cottages clustered around a green. It was picture postcard England, and it was easy to forget the tragedy laying waste to the country and the world.

Nobody was around so he parked the ambulance and set about exploring. The first house he tried had been wrecked. The door had been forced, and it swung loosely on ruined hinges. A window had been smashed, and when he looked inside he saw rubbish and toppled furniture. He moved on. The next house had also been entered, but somebody had tried to repair the damage. Cardboard had been taped over the inside of a broken window pane, and the door was firm. He tapped on it. There was no sound or sign of movement from inside, so he tried the door. It was loose but something was stopping it from opening. He shook it and there was a clatter as whatever had been holding it fell away. He eased it ajar and crept in.

The door gave on to a small sitting room. It was so crammed with furniture he wondered how anyone could possibly live in there, but it was clean and tidy, with brightly coloured rugs and cushions neatly arranged. There was a faint scent. Lilac? Gran liked that. There were two other doors. One opened directly to a staircase. The other seemed to lead to a kitchen. He pushed the kitchen door and stepped through into another neat little room.

He was bending at a cupboard to look for food when there was a flash of light, his head exploded, his vision blurred and he fell forward, curling in a ball.

Through his pain he heard a shrill shout. 'I'm not going, you bastards!'

He twisted to see someone standing behind the door. It was waving something, a short wooden cudgel with a bulbous end. That must be what had hit him.

'I'm not going with you. You're not taking me,' it shrieked. The voice was strident and pierced him like an arrow.

The figure wasn't showing any sign of coming nearer and Lander eased himself into a sitting position. He dabbed his scalp and expected to see blood on his fingers, but they came away clean.

Nevertheless, he was hurt. He felt as though his head had been split in two.

His attacker was a woman. She didn't move but her eyes never left him. She was elderly. A streak of grey hair hung across her face. He marvelled that she could have hit him so hard. Oh God, not another old crone as nutty as Louise, he thought.

He raised his hand in what he hoped would be taken as a gesture of peace. 'I don't want to take you anywhere,' he said.

'Why are you in my house, then? You're not taking me to the hospital.'

What was she talking about? Who did she think he was? 'I'm not here to take you to the hospital.'

'Then what's the ambulance for?' Her mouth was set in a firm line and her chin jutted forward defiantly.

Ah, the ambulance. Is that what this was about?

'I'm nothing to do with the authorities,' he said. 'I stole the ambulance to escape from the hospital. They were keeping me prisoner there.'

The woman nodded, as if to say, I told you so. 'Prisoner?'

'Yes. They were doing some tests on me. I took the ambulance to get away.'

'But you're wearing hospital clothes. You look like a doctor.'

'These are the clothes they gave me,' said Lander. 'They took my own.'

The woman looked doubtful, wondering whether to believe him. The arm holding the cudgel relaxed a little, but she didn't put it down.

'If you're not from the hospital, what are you doing here?' she said.

'I'm going north, to find my sister. She needs help. I thought these houses were empty. I was looking for food. I've not eaten since yesterday. I don't mean you any harm. If you'll let me pass I'll go on my way and I won't bother you.'

The woman's expression changed, she looked less suspicious. 'Not eaten since yesterday?' she said.

Lander shook his head and immediately wished he hadn't. He closed his eyes and waited for the throbbing to subside.

'Well we can't have that,' said the woman. 'Go through there and sit down. I'll bring you something.'

She stood away from the door. She was calmer now, but she still kept well clear of him and she still had the cudgel. Lander edged around her. She was tiny, not even up to his shoulder. Her face was grey and wrinkled, and her skin had the same soft puffiness as Gran's. She had the same seriousness and determination too. He could easily have knocked her over, but he didn't want to do that.

'There,' she said, pointing with the cudgel to one of the two sofas. It had its back to the kitchen. He chose the other, the one that faced the door; he wanted to see her coming.

He sat down and held his head. He felt sick. Gingerly he examined where he'd been hit. A large bump was forming. His vision had cleared and although he had a headache he didn't think there was any serious damage. From the kitchen there were the sounds of implements being moved around, and water running.

The woman came into the sitting room.

'Here,' she said, holding out a damp flannel. 'Bathe it with that.'

He noticed that she hadn't given up the cudgel, she wasn't yet ready to trust him. She went back to the kitchen and there were more sounds of movement.

Lander applied the flannel to his head. The compress helped and the pain became less intense.

After a few minutes, the woman returned. This time she wasn't holding the cudgel, it was dangling from her wrist on a cord. She was carrying a bowl and a plate, which she put on a low table beside him. Whatever was in the bowl looked good but the smell of food made his stomach churn.

'Pea soup,' she said. 'I made it myself. I'm afraid it's cold, but it still tastes good.' She pointed to the crispbreads on the plate. 'I've run out of bread. I make my own once a week, on a Tuesday. There'll be some more the day after tomorrow.'

Lander thought he ought to eat, although he didn't feel like it. However, once he'd forced himself to start he felt better. The woman sat on the other sofa and watched him. The soup was tasty and he got through it quickly.

'More?' the woman said.

Lander was improving all the time and would have liked some more, but he couldn't take all this old lady's food. 'No, thank you,' he said.

'Nonsense,' she said, getting up and taking his bowl. 'A fine young man like you, of course you'll have more.' She paused in the doorway. 'My name's Mrs Turner,' she said, 'but you can call me Maisie.'

When she returned to the sitting room it was without the cudgel.

12

————

MAISIE

LANDER STAYED WITH Maisie for three nights. She insisted on having him that long to be sure his head was all right. He was anxious to continue on his way, to get home to Kerryl, but he welcomed the relief from the tedium of the hospital. Besides, until well into the second day he felt groggy; he certainly didn't feel like driving – or running into any further problems.

He soon decided that he liked Maisie, despite their violent introduction, and she seemed to warm to him. She told him that everyone else in the village had died from the Infection. The last ones to go had been her immediate neighbours, and she'd nursed them through their final days. After their deaths there had been a couple of visits by vandals. They'd ransacked next door, and Maisie had waited, hiding with her cudgel while they'd tried to break into her cottage. To her relief, they'd lost interest and gone away. They'd done a bit of damage but they hadn't stayed long, and more importantly, they hadn't come back.

'So you're the last person left here,' said Lander.

'Yes. I was the oldest inhabitant, and it looks as though I'll be the last one to go. I can't think why I've been spared. Perhaps this virus thingumabob doesn't like old meat.'

After his meal on the first day Lander had wanted to go to sleep but she wouldn't let him.

'Not good after a bang on the head,' she said. 'You've got to keep awake. The doctor told me that after my Jimmy fell off his bike.'

Jimmy was her son, a soldier who had been in Afghanistan training the Afghan army. She'd heard nothing from him and she assumed he was dead. She also had a married daughter living in Northampton and she hadn't heard from her either.

The bump on Lander's head was still sore and there was an occasional ringing in his ears but rest, good food and Maisie's care were all helping his recovery. He was soon thinking of her as another Gran; maybe his father's mother, the grandma he'd never known. She was ninety-three, she told him. 'I was born in the village and I've lived here all my life. I've lived in this cottage since I was wed seventy-four years ago.'

Lander didn't at first say much about himself and Maisie didn't pry. She seemed happy to take him at face value, but Lander felt he owed her an explanation of why he'd entered her house and where he was heading, and so he gave an account of what had happened to him. He didn't tell her the real reason he'd left home – he didn't want to spook her – so he just said that it was because he'd gone to find help. He described getting arrested and sent to jail. He said they'd decided to use him for some investigations and taken him to a hospital where he'd been subjected to tests. He'd seen his chance to escape in an ambulance and had taken it. Finally, he said he'd been told his grandparents were dead and he was going back home to be with his twin sister. Maisie had listened in silence and she didn't say anything when he'd finished, but when she got up and passed him on her way to the kitchen she squeezed his shoulder. He was beginning to think that he had a talent for charming old ladies.

Every morning Maisie went over to the church. On days two and three Lander joined her. The building was light and airy, and there were fresh flowers on the altar. Maisie knelt at the altar rail, recited The Lord's Prayer, and then prayed silently for a few minutes. Lander, whose concept of God was something between a rather strict teacher and a football referee, wanted to ask her what she thought He was doing to let things get like this. Perhaps He'd looked away, or nodded off. Could she really believe in a God who would allow the devastation and suffering that were destroying the world? A God who would sit back and let His supreme creation inflict such terrible suffering? Surely if there was a God, He'd do something about it. But Lander held his tongue. He didn't pray, although he did feel a great sense of peace from being beside this kind old woman in that quiet, ancient place.

'Why do you think you haven't caught the Infection?' he asked Maisie as they walked back to her cottage. He was wondering whether to let her in on some of what he'd learned from *thetruth* and been told by Adam and Gwen.

'I don't know, dear,' she said. 'The Lord will have a reason for sparing me. He must have something in mind for me. Meeting you, perhaps.'

Lander decided to leave it.

Maisie fed him like a prizefighter. She said he looked peaky, and she loaded his plate three times a day. He felt guilty taking her food and protested, but she said she had plenty.

'I don't eat much,' she said. 'Anyway, at my age I'm not going to need much more, am I?'

It turned out that it was the ambulance she'd been afraid of. When her neighbour died it had been an ambulance that had come to collect her body. The crew took not only her but her husband as well, even though he was still alive. He didn't come back.

'I thought you'd been sent to get me so I could be finished off,' she said. 'You know, mop up the old ones, clear 'em out of the way. That's why I hit you. I'm sorry.'

'That's all right,' Lander said. 'You thought you were protecting yourself.' He felt his bump. 'That stick you've got packs quite a punch.'

'Yes,' she said. 'That's Titan. That was my husband's name for it. He was called Jimmy, too. He was a gamekeeper at Juniper Lodge, that's a big house just a few miles up the road. He'd had no end of bother from poachers. They'd come four or five times a year and they'd take no end of his birds, and Jimmy would get it in the neck from his boss. One night he caught two of them at it. One got away but Jimmy hit the other with Titan. He didn't hit him hard, but the man fell and hurt himself. He died. The police arrested Jimmy and took him to court. He pleaded self-defence and got off, but it was a nasty business and it went on for a long time. He lost his job, and some of the people around here were really horrible to him. He decided it would be best to work away for a bit, and he got a job on an oil rig. Good money, but I rarely saw him.'

'That must have been a hard time. Was he on the rig for long?'

'A few years. Two months before he was due to retire there was an accident with a winch and he was killed. The company was found to be negligent and they had to pay me compensation.'

'I'm sorry,' said Lander.

'Quarter of a million pounds I got,' said Maisie. 'An absolute fortune. Everybody said how well the company had treated me, although their money couldn't bring him back. I've still got most of it. I'd planned to leave it to the family, but I can't do that now. Anyway, money's no good any more. I'd give it to you but I can't get at it, it's in the bank.'

Lander shook his head. He didn't want Maisie's money.

On her insistence, he drove the ambulance around the side of the church and parked it out of sight of the road.

'I shouldn't think there'll be anybody coming here to see it,' she said, 'but then, I didn't expect you, did I?'

On the third morning Maisie came into the sitting room where Lander had been sleeping and gathered up his hospital scrubs.

'This way, young man,' she said, and set off up the steep, narrow staircase. At the top she opened a door. 'Jimmy's room,' she said. 'There are lots of clothes in his drawers. You're about his size. Help yourself to anything you fancy. He won't be needing them. Those you don't put on you can pack in this.' She indicated a plastic hold-all on the bed, and left him to it.

It was the smallest bedroom Lander had ever seen. Most of it was a bed, which filled a raised platform running right across the room from one side to the other. There was just enough space for him to stand beside it. He wondered where everything was; then he saw that there were deep drawers under the bed platform, three of them. One was full of t-shirts, vests and boxers. Jeans, chinos and cotton shirts were in another; the third contained shoes and socks. Jimmy must have been a little shorter and slighter than Lander so some of the clothes were tight, but he managed to find things that fitted him fairly well.

Taking Jimmy's clothes was difficult. He knew that he wouldn't be coming back for them, and if Lander didn't use them they'd just stay in the drawers until they rotted, or somebody came and nicked them. Nevertheless, it was awkward.

'How are you going to get home?' Maisie asked him as he showed her what he'd chosen.

'In the ambulance,' said Lander. 'It's got plenty of fuel.'

'You'll stick out like a sore thumb. You'll be stopped in a jiffy, mark my words.'

'Maybe, but it's all I've got. It's that or nothing.'

Maisie thought for a moment. 'Come with me,' she said, heading for the back door.

At the end of the neat little garden was a rickety old garage. Maisie pushed the door open and Lander followed her in. It was dark and spidery, and in contrast to the rest of the house this place was a tip. There was an old bike, a rusty toolbox, tubes, wires, a hosepipe, garden implements; and in the middle there was a Mini Countryman. It was an old one, tiny, not like the more recent Minis which in comparison were huge. It was the colour of putty and had wooden cladding on the rear half. It was covered in dust.

'There,' said Maisie, with a note of pride. 'Jimmy and I used to go everywhere in that. Skegness, Hunstanton, Rhyl. We even went to The Lakes once. He loved that car, but I don't drive so it's not been used in a long time. I was always going to sell it but I never got around to it. Why don't you take that?'

Maisie was right: the ambulance would be very conspicuous. In this, he could nip along back roads, and dodge trouble. In a lot of places the roof of the car would be below the hedge tops.

'Will it start?' he said.

Maisie put her hand on his arm. 'Now there you have me,' she said. 'It always used to start first go. But that was Jimmy. He used to spend hours on it, cleaning it, servicing it, what he called tuning.'

Lander eased around the side of the car. Somebody had had the foresight to put it on axle stands, so he expected the tyres would be all right. He opened the door. No interior light came on. That was a bad sign. The keys were in the ignition. He turned them. Nothing. The battery was dead. He popped open the bonnet. Everything looked in order. The big question was, how do you charge a car battery when there's no mains electricity? He went to the back of the car, opened the rear doors, and there was the answer: a pair of jump leads. They looked to be in good condition, but would they be long enough? Could he get the ambulance close enough for them to reach?

There was only one way to find out. He fetched the ambulance from its hiding place under the trees behind the church and managed to get it along the rough track that ran past the back of Maisie's cottage. With a bit of manoeuvring, he worked the nose into a position where he could just manage to connect the jump leads. He restarted the engine, then went back and sat in the Mini. He waited. Then he turned the key again, just one click. A light came on the dash and the fuel gauge kicked slightly, but it stayed on zero.

'Is it all right?' said Maisie, who'd been watching all this.

'We need some fuel.'

Maisie pointed. There were three large jerry cans against the garage wall. 'Young Jimmy put them there last time he was here. He said he thought that the way things were going there'd be fuel shortages and I might need them.'

Lander couldn't believe his luck. Old fuel, either stored in cans or the car's tank, probably wouldn't be much good, but if this lot was only a few months old it should be fine.

He got one of the jerry cans and emptied it into the Mini's tank. Then he sat down again in the driver's seat. He took a deep breath and mentally crossed his fingers. His hand was trembling as he turned the ignition key. The Mini gave a reluctant grunt, then the engine spun, but it didn't fire. He tried once more. Still no luck. If it was really dried out it would take a while for the fuel to get through, he thought.

'Let's give it one more go,' he said. 'This time, for sure.'

Maisie waited, looking anxious. Lander turned the key again. The engine fired, spluttered, and then caught. He jabbed the accelerator and it revved.

'Brilliant!' Lander yelled. 'Absolutely gob-smackingly brilliant!' He got out of the car, leaving the engine running, and gave Maisie a hug. 'Are you sure this is all right?' he said. 'For me to borrow it? I'll bring it back.'

'You're welcome to it,' said Maisie. 'It's no use to me, I couldn't even get it out of the garage, and it just sits there reminding me of better times. Don't worry about bringing it back, although it would be nice to see you again.'

Lander disconnected the jump leads.

During the next hour he jacked up each corner of the car and removed the axle stands. The tyres looked a bit soft but not very, and he was sure they'd be good enough to get him to the farm. He left the engine running all the time to charge the battery, and then he got into the driver's seat and turned it off.

'Crunch time,' he said to himself. If the alternator wasn't working the battery wouldn't have charged. He'd still be able to use the car once he got it going, he just wouldn't be able to restart the engine if it stopped. 'Oh well,' he said, 'nothing venture...'

He turned the ignition and the Mini started. He got out and punched the air. Then he put the other two jerry cans in the back of the car and returned to the cottage.

Maisie was in the kitchen, preparing an evening meal for them. She'd been baking that day. There was wood smoke in the air, and the house smelt of fresh bread. Lander's mouth watered.

'Tell you what,' he said, putting his arm around Maisie's waist as she stirred something on the stove. 'Why don't you come with me?'

Maisie stopped stirring. 'Are you propositioning me, young man? Come with you where?'

'Come home with me, to the farm. You'll get on well with Kerryl and she'll love you. And you say yourself there's nothing for you here.'

Maisie smiled up at him. 'That's very sweet of you,' she said, 'but what would I do in Yorkshire? And you know what they say about two women in a kitchen.'

'Well let me at least take you to Northampton. We can go to your daughter's place and you can stay there, or if...if...' he struggled to find a kind way to say it, 'if there's nothing for you there I can bring you back.'

She shook her head. 'You need to get on your way. It's best for me to stay here. I'm not comfortable anywhere else. I've lived in this village all my life and this is where I'll die.'

Lander meant to set out early the following day, but he and Maisie stayed up late into the night talking. She told him something of her life, of being a young woman in World War II, of Jimmy the elder being conscripted into the army, even though the authorities knew he was a farm labourer. She told of the worry while he was away, of her dread of the postman's visits, and her joy at his sudden and unexpected appearances when he returned on leave. She talked about the younger Jimmy, and her daughter, Jenny, who was a doctor's receptionist. Lander told her more about his life in the valley, his interest in computers, and the way that before the Infection he'd felt bored and frustrated because there was so little going on. He told of his dreams of playing professional cricket.

'I hope one day you'll come back here,' Maisie said, 'but even if you don't I know people will hear of you. You're an outstanding young man. You'll make your mark, I'm sure of it.'

Nobody had ever said that to Lander before, and he was so touched his eyes watered. Not even his mother had expressed such faith in him.

He thought of Maisie's words as he drove out of the village the next day. He was leaving much later than he'd intended, but he had to go. The longer he stayed with this good-hearted old lady the harder it would be to continue his journey, and if he didn't get going today he might just stay forever. Besides, Kerryl needed him. All his life he'd had a sense of connection with her, even when they'd been apart. He didn't have that now, and it worried him.

He kept to the back roads. He didn't recognise many of the place names and he didn't have a map. It hadn't occurred to him to ask Maisie if she had one, and he could have kicked himself for the omission. However, there was a dash-mounted compass in the Mini, and he reckoned that if he kept heading roughly north he'd eventually come to somewhere he'd recognise. The little car went well, and he was near Derby when he pulled in and ate two of the sandwiches Maisie had packed for him.

It started to rain, and it was then that he discovered the only fault he could find with the Mini: the windscreen wipers didn't work. He managed for a while, peering through the drops, but the rain got harder and it was when he almost went into a ditch that he decided he'd have to stop. He pulled into a farm gateway, getting the car as clear of the road as he could. He waited for a while but the rain was hard and it looked as though it had set in for the rest of the day. He'd stay here. The Mini was fairly well hidden, and if he kept his head down nobody who saw it would think there was anyone inside; it would be just another abandoned car. Hopefully, he'd be able to carry on when the weather improved.

The Mini didn't make for comfortable sleeping but there was no other option. He'd seen no more than half a dozen other vehicles since he'd left Maisie's, and only one of them was travelling on his road. He'd be all right. There were some ancient tape cassettes in a box – Jethro Tull, Genesis, Abba – none of it his thing, but he put one on softly and wrapped himself in the rug Maisie had given him. It was hard to settle and he was awake for a long time before he eventually dropped off.

13

THE SHED

LANDER WAS DREAMING of the farm. He and Kerryl were children. They were at the Bride Stones, the unusual formation of rocks on the moors above the farm, where they would often play. They'd been enjoying a game of hide and seek, taking turns to conceal themselves amongst the wild outcrop while the others searched. The trick was to anticipate the arrival of the searcher so you could leap out and scare them before they found you. Then the dream soured. This time, instead of Kerryl being the seeker, Lander was hiding from a nameless, black shape. He couldn't describe it or avoid it, and it terrified him.

Suddenly there was a loud noise and he fell to the side as the car door he'd been leaning on was jerked open. Before he could react, he was seized by the collar and dragged out onto the ground. A torch shone in his eyes. Was it one person or more? He tried to shout out something but a fist came out of the brightness and hit him in the mouth. His lip split and he tasted blood.

Whoever had him was strong. They pulled him away from the car, rolled him over and put their knee in his back. Lander couldn't move to fight back. His chest was being squeezed against the wet road and he could hardly breathe. It flashed through his mind that the last time he'd been attacked it had been Maisie, and that had turned out well. Perhaps this would be all right too. He tried again to speak but the knee twisted, pressing him painfully into the tarmac.

His arms were yanked behind his back and his wrists taped together. Then a rope was looped around his neck and something was put over his head. It was a sack, a hessian sack. It smelt of the henhouse and made him want to vomit. He had to shut his mouth and his eyes to keep the dust out. He licked his lip and tasted blood.

He thought he was going to pass out when his captor at last got off him, but he had only a second to enjoy the relief because his wrists were grabbed and he was heaved to his feet. The movement twisted his arms behind him and was so excruciatingly painful that he cried out, but a kick on his shin told him he mustn't do that. The rope pulled him forward and he felt himself being led away from the car. His eyes were tightly shut because of the hessian dust, but they ran with tears of rage. The Mini had been a tiny jewel, a symbol of Maisie's warm thoughtfulness and his passport back to Kerryl; being snatched away from it was unbearable.

There was a hard shove in the small of his back and he staggered forward. He had no idea where he was going, it seemed to be along a track. It was rough and uneven, and his feet sloshed into puddles so that his trainers were soon soaked. His foot caught on something and he tipped forward. Without his hands to break his fall he landed hard on his knees and hurt them. Wary of another kick and of his arms being twisted again he choked off the cry that rose in his throat and struggled to his feet as quickly as he could.

His captor said nothing coherent, but he grunted and swore a lot. Lander limped on, each step painful. The rain beat down, and the bag over his head was now so saturated it dripped cold water down his neck. It was hard to breathe. Was this what being waterboarded was like? No wonder people would do anything to make it stop. He was choking and he felt panic rising.

His progress was halted by a jerk on the rope. There was the unmistakable stink of a farmyard, so strong it overrode the chicken-shed stench of the hessian. It wasn't the healthy, wholesome smell of Lander's farm, his home. This was the rancid reek of a poor farm, a neglected farm with over-full slurry pits and ailing animals.

He heard the grating scrape of a metal door being slid open and he was pushed inside a building, an outhouse of some sort. His right arm was seized and what felt like a metal brace was put on his wrist. He winced as it was squeezed tight, pinching his flesh. He could feel the weight of a chain attached to the brace. Then the tape binding his wrists was cut roughly. He was pushed again and he heard the door slide shut behind him. There was the unmistakable rattle of a padlock being fastened into a hasp.

His right arm was encumbered because of the chain but his left was free and he used that to snatch the wet sack off his head. He was in a big room. He could tell that from the way sounds reverberated and from the sense of space, but he could see nothing. It was completely dark, with not a chink of light anywhere. Gingerly he fingered his split lip. A couple of his teeth had been loosened too. He rubbed his wrists and picked off the remains of the tape. He'd felt the knife cut him and he pressed on the wound to stop any bleeding.

He had no idea where he was: some sort of farm building obviously, but was it a shed? A stable? The stench of slurry was strong and there was a smell of urine too. Was there a pit for animal waste in the middle of this space? He turned towards where he guessed the door to be but the chain wouldn't let him go in that direction, so he shuffled carefully backwards until his heels came to a wall. He turned and ran his hands over it. It was ribbed metal, cold and damp. The chain would allow him to go in only one direction, away from the door. If he tried to go the other way something held him back, although he didn't get the impression that it was a firm fixing; whatever it was had some give.

He went the way the chain allowed, keeping his back to the wall, feeling along it with his hands and extending his leading foot cautiously, wary of dropping into the imagined slurry pit. The chain became slacker as he moved. His foot came against something fixed to the floor and he bent to investigate. It was a metal ring, with the chain running through it. He knelt – his sore knees protesting – and pulled at the restraint. Again there was resistance. He was too shaken up to explore further. His shoulders were painful from where they'd been wrenched and his knees and wrists hurt.

He sat on the floor beside the ring to try to work things out. He'd been taken prisoner again, but who had done that, and why? Where was he this time?

The surface of the floor was rough, like concrete. It was also damp. So was he. He was more than damp, he was sodden. He was cold and he was shivering. He'd heard people say they'd been so perished their teeth had chattered, and now he realised what they meant. He drew up his knees and hugged them. His back and his chest ached from where he'd been knelt on. The side of his face was sore from its contact with the road. His mouth hurt from where he'd been punched.

Another shower of rain came, even harder this time, hammering on the metal roof so that it was like being inside a drum pelted with pebbles. He hitched himself forward to get away from the chill of the wall, and felt an obstruction in front of him. He explored it with his fingers. It felt like a bale of hay. Beside it was another. He groped for the binding twine, eased it off the bale, and pulled out handfuls of the sweet-smelling grasses. He spread them to make a bed. He loosened the other bale, lay down on his makeshift mattress, and pulled more hay on top of him until he was cocooned. Within a few minutes he was feeling warmer, although he would still have been hard pressed to name a part of him that didn't hurt.

The rain stopped. The din it had made on the roof had been deafening and now it was gone there was an eerie quiet. He could hear another sound. It was a sort of quiet snuffling. For a second he thought it was a rat, but it was something bigger than that. There was an animal in the shed with him! It was not the noise a cow or a horse would make. What was it? A sheep? A pig? A pig would at least account for the bad smells. He felt the chain move very slightly. Was the animal also attached to it? Was he fastened to one end and a pig to the other? He didn't mind pigs but he didn't like them. They stank and were stubborn.

He was about to give the chain an experimental heave to see what happened when he heard more sounds, this time from outside. There was the rattle of the padlock, the screech of the door sliding back and a light appeared. It was from a hurricane lantern carried by an enormous man. He had a bushy beard the size of a shovel and a huge belly. Lander guessed it was the same man who had pulled him out of the car. No wonder his back hurt from where he'd been knelt on; the guy must weigh a ton! The lantern was in one hand, and in the other was a billycan and a plastic bag.

He put all three items down against the far wall and returned to the door.

'Dinner is served, your majesties,' he said, with a mock bow. He went out and slid the door shut behind him.

Majesties? Plural? Lander looked around. In the dim light from the lantern he could see that the chain ran through an iron hoop set into the concrete near the wall, and there was indeed something on the other end. It was human. He – or was it she? – was also lying on a pile of hay. It had its back to him and all he could see was a filthy t-shirt. It had short, black hair and there was a red mark high on one arm. The figure rolled over and regarded him. Its eyes were big and dark. There was a bruise on one cheek. It sat up, so skinny and flat chested that he thought it must be a boy, but then he realised it was actually a girl.

The shed was big. At the far end, just discernible, was an old tractor and some other bits of scrap machinery, and there were more hay bales. He was relieved to see there was no slurry pit, but there was a shallow channel running across the middle of the space, leading to a small hole in the wall. The slurry pit would be out there, hence the smell. The concrete floor was pitted, and stained with what could have been oil but was more probably animal excrement.

The girl began to move, edging towards the billycan and bag. Lander felt a tug on his wrist and saw that she had reached a point where the chain was preventing her from going further. He didn't want to leave his bed, but he realised that she was stuck unless he gave her some slack. He shuffled nearer to the hoop. What now? The girl reached the bag, extracted two plastic bowls and put them on the ground. Next, she took out a hunk of bread. She measured this with her eye and tore it roughly in half. She gripped one of the halves under her arm and put the other in one of the bowls. Finally, she filled the other bowl, the empty one, with liquid from the billycan. It was all done mechanically and with precision, and it seemed to Lander to be a routine familiar to her.

She picked up the full bowl and came over to the hoop, and Lander beside it. At first he thought she was intending to give the food to him, although he couldn't think why she'd do that. She didn't. She squatted beside the hoop and started to eat, taking slurps from the bowl and stuffing bread into her mouth. She wolfed for a moment or two and then pointed at the billycan and bowl. She meant for him to go and get his own food. That was why she'd come to the hoop, so that there was enough slack in the chain for him to reach it. Lander crawled painfully over the floor to where it was. The shed was lofty and there was plenty of room to stand, but the chain seemed to dictate how he moved.

He investigated what was on the menu. The billycan contained a grey liquid. He sniffed it; it smelt of cabbage. He poured what was left into the remaining bowl and took that and his half of the bread back to his place.

He wondered if the girl would retreat, now the purpose of her coming to the hoop had been served, but she didn't. She remained where she was, not looking at him but squatting on her haunches a few feet away. Her back was against the corrugated metal of the wall, careless of the cold. She'd finished her ration and was wiping her bowl with the remains of her bread.

Lander sipped the liquid. It was awful, thin and very salty. He took a bite of the bread. It tasted of mould. He didn't want any of it. He put the bowl and the bread down. He thought fondly of the food parcel Maisie had given him for his journey, with sandwiches made from one of her home-baked loaves. It had been in the hold-all in the car. Where was it now? Where was he? He was weary of being imprisoned. What was it this time? Who was his captor? How long would he be held in this unspeakable hole?

The girl was staring at the food Lander had rejected. She looked at him directly for the first time, and an eyebrow twitched. Lander pushed it towards her and she snatched it quickly, as if she was afraid he might change his mind. She ate it quickly, cramming the bread into her mouth and washing it down with the sludge.

Lander studied his companion while she ate. Now he was closer he could see that she was older than he'd at first thought, perhaps in her middle twenties. However, it was hard to tell because she was so emaciated. Her arms were stick thin, her shoulders and elbows bony. She seemed to be wearing nothing under her t-shirt and her breasts were tiny, mere bumps, with hard little nipples. He could see now that the red mark on her arm was a burn, and quite a nasty one. It was fairly recent because there were still blisters.

She finished eating and wiped her mouth on the back of her hand. She got up, picked up both the bowls and walked over to the empty billycan and the lamp. The chain rattled behind her as she went. For a second it reminded Lander of a movie they used to watch at the farm every Christmas, the one where the ghost of a miser has to drag around a chain forged from the bad things he'd done during his life. The memory of happier times was painful. He'd give anything to be back there again, watching the TV with his family. He even missed his chores and their Mam's nagging.

The girl licked out both bowls, shook the crumbs from of the plastic bag into her hand and lapped them up. Then she returned the bowls to the bag and took that, the billycan and the lamp to the sliding door.

Lander thought she'd be coming back to the hoop but instead she went to a battered bucket in the corner. The chain would only just reach. She turned her back on Lander, let down her muddy jeans, squatted over the bucket and urinated in a steady stream. When she'd done she pulled them up and came back to the hoop. She sat down in her former position and stared at him. Her eyes were wide, dark and steady. The bruise on her cheek looked to be from where someone had hit her, and maybe had once been a black eye.

Who was she? She looked like one of the refugees he'd seen in pictures on the TV. Or somebody from a concentration camp. She was skinny enough. Was she an illegal immigrant? How did she get here? Why were they both chained up?

Lander cleared his throat. 'Do you speak English?' he said.

There was a long pause before the girl responded, as if she was deciding whether or not to reply. All of the time her eyes remained fixed on him. At last she spoke.

'My name is Magda,' she said. 'What's yours?' Her English was perfect.

14

———

WORK

LANDER THOUGHT THAT learning Magda's name might be an ice breaker, the start of a conversation, but he was wrong.

'I'm Lander,' he said.

Magda frowned.

'It's a nickname,' he said.

'Right,' she said, turned her back on him and shuffled away to her pile of hay. She lay down, still with her back to him, and seemed to be settling to sleep. There was so much Lander wanted to know: Who was she? Where had she come from? Where were they? How long had she been there? Who was the fat man who'd caught him and brought in the food? What did he want?

Some of these things he learnt the next day. For others he had to wait longer.

His bed of hay was surprisingly comfortable, and after some adjustment he got into a position where the chain wasn't digging into him. At last he was warm, and with the rain rattling again on the roof it was strangely cosy. He was hungry and he wished he'd persevered with the sloppy goo and the bread, but despite this, he dropped off to sleep.

He was roused by the rasp of the door sliding back and the beam of a torch. He blinked against the light. The fat man was standing in the doorway.

At once he was wide awake. 'Why have you put me in here?' he shouted. 'What have I done to you? Let me go.'

The fat man came towards him. He looked dangerous, menacing, and very bad tempered.

'You shut the fuck up, pretty boy, or I'll bust your lip again.' He stared at him and Lander looked away. Slowly the man went back to the doorway, picked up the bag, the billycan and the lamp and left. The door slammed shut and it was pitch dark once more.

Lander wondered how long he'd been asleep. It was then he realised that his watch was missing. Strange he hadn't noticed it before. Had the fat man taken it? When?

He lay awake for a long time, listening to the rain. At one point he called out. 'Magda? Are you awake?' There was no response. In the end he lapsed into an uneasy doze, almost asleep but not quite, with images of his home, his family, and his room, all scrambling around in his head. Why had he left the farm? It had seemed right at the time but he could see now that it was a dreadful mistake. He might have predicted that Gran and Granddad would die from the Infection. That meant that he had left Kerryl to manage on her own. How was she coping? Was she coping at all? He had no idea whether she was well or ill, happy or sad. She might not be immune after all; she might have died, all alone. Was that the reason Adam had stopped meeting him? Because she was dead?

He seemed to have been asleep for only minutes when he heard the scrape of the door again, the usual herald of their jailer.

'Good morning, love birds,' the man shouted, and banged hard with a stick on the metal wall of the shed. 'Rise and shine.'

Magda jumped up and hurried over to him, her chain scraping after her.

He turned to Lander. 'Get your arse over here, you lazy bastard,' he shouted.

He beat on the metal again; the din was ear-splitting. Lander saw that what he was using was not a stick but the handle of a whip. He hurried over.

'Hope this little prick hasn't been molesting you, my dear,' the man said to Magda, and winked. He had such a brutal voice, such a heartless manner that even endearments sounded coarse.

'No, he was fine, Mickey. I know how to defend my honour,' Magda said, and she winked back.

The man, Mickey, roared with laughter, but it wasn't real. It was a taunt, a savage, mocking sound. A sound that said he was in control and they were at his mercy. Lander did not doubt that here was someone capable of doing him great harm.

He started with Magda. She'd been chained by her right wrist, like Lander. Mickey now put another shackle on her left wrist. This was joined to a lighter chain which ended in a fetter, and he locked this on her ankle. Then he undid her right wrist from the longer chain.

'You wait here, pretty boy,' Mickey said, and he led Magda out of the shed, locking the door behind him.

Lander's heart leapt. With no one on the other end of the chain he might be able to escape. Then he realised what a stupid idea that was. How could he run away, manacled like this? The chain weighed a lot. Always assuming he could get out of the shed, he wouldn't be able to drag it far enough or move quickly enough to find freedom. The only thing he could do was wait to see what happened.

There was a small stack of hay bales close by and he sat on one to wait. Fingers of daylight poked through gaps in the roof and he could see the layout of the shed more clearly. It would be useful to know how things were organised, in case he had to move about in the dark. Presumably, Mickey was going to come back for him when he'd delivered Magda to wherever he was taking her.

He was right. It wasn't long before the door opened again.

'Come on then, squire. Hands off your cock and let's rock.' Mickey laughed once more in his cruel, humourless way.

There was another short chain and fetter on a hook on the wall, and Mickey repeated on Lander what he'd done with Magda. For a second Lander wondered if he could swing the chain hard enough to knock Mickey out, or maybe loop it around his neck and squeeze. But Mickey was strong, and he knew that if he failed and only managed to hurt him, he would be dead.

When the small chain was fixed and the long one lay on the ground, Mickey stood back and looked at Lander. The whip was prominent in his hand. It was a savage-looking thing with a thong of plaited leather. A blow from that would rip the skin.

'Right then, it's off to work we go,' he said, offering Lander a grim smile. His two front teeth were missing. This was a man for whom violence was the norm. 'You can start with the bucket. I don't think emptying shit and piss is a job for a lady, do you?'

Lander didn't reply.

Mickey leant forward until his face was inches from Lander's. He tapped the whip on his cheek, ominously. 'Well do you, arsehole?'

'No.'

'So answer me when I talk to you, fuckbrain. Go over there and collect the marmalade pot.' He pointed the whip in the direction of the night bucket and Lander crossed to it. It stank so much it made him gag. In the daylight he could see that there was a lid on the floor beside it. Next to that were two short planks, which he guessed were to lay across it to make a rudimentary seat, although Magda hadn't bothered with these the night before. The toilet suite was completed by a few torn newspapers on the floor.

'Pick it up and follow me,' Mickey said from the door.

The bucket was about half full and couldn't have been emptied for several days. Lander carried it to the door. It was heavy, and encumbered by the shackles it was hard to move without slopping its contents. Mickey led the way around the side of the shed. Lander's guess had been right. There was a slurry pit there. It was almost full.

'In there,' said Mickey.

Lander tipped the contents of the bucket onto the slimy surface.

'Any bother from you and you'll go in after it,' said Mickey. 'Now put that shit pot back in the shed and come with me.'

As he followed Mickey, Lander had his first opportunity to look around. They were on a rough track, and he was made to walk towards a small, dilapidated farmhouse at the bottom of it. Behind him was a farm gate which led onto a road. The shed was about halfway between the two. The light was raw, and Lander concluded it couldn't be much after 6 o'clock.

As they neared the house he saw that it was in as bad a state as everything else. It was red brick and at one time had been covered in a cream render, but much of that had fallen off, leaving gaps like scabs. There were white deposits on the exposed bricks, and the paint had peeled from rotten window frames. The place was surrounded by rubbish: an old trailer, broken pallets, a rusty washing machine, a bedstead. A few ragged chickens pecked in the yard around Maisie's Mini. Its door was open and one of the birds hopped inside. Lander felt a mixture of anger, frustration and regret. Maisie had given him her car to help him, and look how he'd thanked her. Why hadn't he set out for the north earlier, so he could have done the journey in one go? Why had he stopped beside the road instead of finding somewhere less obvious? He had hung about, left his departure too late, parked carelessly, and as a result here he was.

Mickey took Lander around the side of the house, where there was a tumbledown brick building that might once have been a garage. It had no roof and one wall had collapsed.

'Here,' said Mickey. He picked up a lump hammer and a rusty cold chisel and held them out. 'Well, get hold of 'em!'

Lander took the tools.

'Your job is to clean up those bricks. Knock all the old mortar off 'em so I can use 'em again. When you've done 'em, pile 'em there.'

There was a small stack of smooth bricks to the side of the building, presumably Mickey's work. Or, it occurred to Lander, maybe he'd had a predecessor. He looked at the fallen wall and the jumbled pile waiting to be done. There were hundreds of them. It would take ages.

'Ever done this before?' said Mickey.

'No,' said Lander.

'Well it'll be a fucking first for you, then, won't it? I'll be back in a bit to check on you, and when I do you'd better be fucking working. And remember, I want all the mortar off every brick, every single fucking bit of it.'

Mickey strolled away in the direction they'd come, swinging his whip.

Again Lander thought of escape. How far would he get, manacled the way he was? The chain wasn't long enough to allow proper movement. Walking was hard, running would be impossible. All the land around the farm was open and it would be easy for Mickey to spot him. A better opportunity would surely come. He wondered about Magda. Where had Mickey taken her? What was he making her do?

He picked up a brick and started to chip away at the mortar. Some of the bricks were straightforward to clean because the mortar was brittle and came away easily. Others weren't; the mortar was solid and seemed fused in place. He quickly decided to leave the trickier ones, and he threw them aside. He'd go back to them later, when he'd got better at it. Some of the bricks broke, and he tossed those away too. It was slow work, and hard on his hands, which were soon sore. To make the whole business even more difficult the chain constantly got in the way. The extra weight made his arm ache and that, plus the restriction it imposed, slowed him down. If Mickey needed bricks why didn't he go and look for new ones? There must be millions of them on building sites, there for the taking.

He'd probably been working a couple of hours when somebody appeared around the side of the house. It wasn't Mickey, but a woman. She had a pinched face, and wisps of ginger hair escaped from around a patterned headscarf. She was carrying a plastic dish with a lid. She put it and a plastic spoon on the pile of bricks and walked away. She didn't speak or even look at Lander. The legs below her brown overall were puffy and laced with varicose veins.

Lander took the lid off the dish. It contained a thin, watery porridge, still slightly warm. In normal circumstances Lander wouldn't have touched it, but he was by this time so hungry he would have eaten wallpaper paste. He dipped in his finger and tasted it. It was quite sweet and not too bad. He ate it all, getting what he could with the spoon and then licking out the container, wiping his finger into the corners. He'd felt derisive the night before when Magda had licked the bowls; now he realised that it didn't take much to make a person behave in ways that they would previously have scorned.

He put the bowl and spoon back on the brick pile and carried on. His hands were by now rubbed raw, which made the work even more difficult. The pile of cleaned bricks had barely grown, and when Mickey returned Lander felt a tremor of anxiety. It didn't look much for a morning's work.

Mickey sneered. 'Is that all you've done, Nancy boy?'

Lander nodded.

'What?'

'Yes.'

Mickey sighed. 'Fuck me. A right bloody slacker you are. I'm going to be hard-pressed to afford to feed you if this is the best you can do.'

'It's this chain,' said Lander. 'It makes it hard to do the job. If you took it off I could get on more quickly.'

Mickey gave a contemptuous snort. 'Oh yes, and why don't I order you a fucking Uber while I'm at it, so you can get right away? Do I look fucking stupid?'

He did, but Lander couldn't tell him so. 'No,' he said, 'but you could tie my leg to something.'

'Could I? I have your royal permission to do that, do I? Well, thank you, your fucking majesty.'

'Anyway, I could do better if I had work gloves,' said Lander, holding up his red hands.

Mickey looked incredulous. 'Work gloves! Ah, diddums.' He reached forward and roughly seized one of Lander's hands. 'What are you? Some kind of fucking fairy?' He spat on the hand and dropped it. 'You'd better have done a lot more by the time I come back.'

The day wore on and Lander worked and worked. In the late afternoon the sun came out and it grew warm. Lander took off his shirt, as far as he could with the chain on his wrist, and wrapped it around the hand that was hurting most. It was now so sore that it was bleeding, and the makeshift bandage helped.

The sun was well down – it must have been after seven – by the time Mickey returned and led Lander back to the shed. He was bone weary and just wanted to collapse on the hay. Magda was already there, on her hay pile and attached to her end of the chain. She watched as Mickey removed Lander's shackle, chained him up and left.

Lander flopped down on the bales. There was just enough light coming through the holes in the roof for him to see Magda. She watched him for a few minutes, then got to her feet and clanked across the concrete to him. She stood in front of him and bent down to take one of his hands. He let her. She turned it palm up and examined it.

Without speaking she went to the wall, where there was an enamel jug and a mug. She came back with both, filled the mug, took his hand and gently splashed water on it. To begin with it stung, but then it felt better. She did the same to the other hand, then returned the mug and jug while Lander sat on the bale and his hands dripped. They felt less angry after the bathing but they were still throbbing.

'Thank you,' he called to her.

She nodded and went back to her hay.

They stayed like that for some time, at opposite ends of the chain, umbilically connected but apart. Then there were footsteps outside, the door screeched and Mickey came in with the lamp, billycan and bag.

'Dinner for one tonight,' he said, putting the lamp and food in the usual place. He gestured at Lander. 'This fucker hasn't done enough work today to earn his.' He spat towards Lander and went back to the door.

It smelt like the same concoction again. There was only one bowl and, Lander guessed, probably only half as much as before. Magda went to the can, filled the bowl and took that and some bread back to her bed in the hay. She drank the soup and wiped the bowl. Then she went back to the billycan and poured what was left into the bowl. She took the rest of the bread and brought them both to Lander. She put them on the floor in front of him.

'What's this?'

'It's your share,' she said.

'No, it's not, it's yours. You heard him, there isn't any for me.'

'Don't be daft. If you don't eat you can't work. He knows that. There was the same amount as last night but only one bowl. He was just making a point.'

Lander wasn't sure whether she was telling the truth or sharing with him what should have been all hers, but he wasn't going to argue. He was famished and he ate quickly. Remembering what Magda had done the night before, he put the empty, licked-out bowl in the bag beside the billycan. Mickey clearly ran a regime with routines that he expected to be followed, and Lander didn't need to be told the importance of not upsetting those.

Magda watched him all the time. He thought about going to sit beside her, the chain would have allowed it, but he returned to his half of the shed and lay on the hay. He was achingly tired but not sleepy. His hands were hurting too much for sleep, anyway. He thought Magda might speak but she said nothing, just watched him. He felt something was expected of him but he didn't know what. Looking at how starved she was, she must have been here for a while. You'd think that given the opportunity she would have taken all the food for herself, rather than sharing.

'Do you want to talk?' he said.

'What about?'

'I don't know. You could tell me who you are.'

'I have told you. My name's Magda.'

'I know that, but I mean who are you? Where are you from? How long have you been here?'

'Why do you need to know that?'

'I don't need to know it. But we're shut in here together and we have to live with each other. I mean, you can't even go for a pee unless I cooperate by moving so you can get to the bucket. Same for me. And the same for reaching the food. We're fixed like conjoined twins. I just think it would be good to know something about you, and you me.'

Lander waited but Magda said nothing.

'All right,' he said. 'I'll start.'

He talked. He began by describing his home on the farm, and the life he'd lived there with Kerryl, their Mam and their grandparents. He talked about what they all used to do, and where they used to go. He talked about the virus coming and all their friends dying, then their Mam and, so he'd heard, Gran and Granddad too. He told her about leaving, heading south, being arrested, tried and imprisoned.

He was moving on to being let out of jail and taken to Oxford when he realised that Magda was asleep.

15

———

MAGDA

LANDER'S HANDS HURT so much that, exhausted though he was, sleep was out of the question. Several times he dropped off, but then he rolled onto a hand or the chain and woke himself up. Despite the pain and discomfort, morning came too soon.

The next day was the same as the one before. Magda was taken away first, and then Lander was collected, made to empty the bucket, and put to work on the bricks. As he passed the Mini he saw that the door was still open and there were now more chickens inside it. Maisie had treasured the car for years, it was a classic and Mickey was just letting it go to ruin, the same as he'd done with everything else he touched.

The state of his hands meant that Lander worked even more slowly than he had on the first day. Every brick was torture. He loosened his shirt and pushed his hands into the sleeves so he could use them for protection, but it was awkward, and soon the fabric wore through. His shirt stank. He was wearing the same clothes he'd had on when Mickey had dragged him from the car. Where were his others? They wouldn't fit Mickey, so why couldn't he have them? He daren't ask. He'd already learnt that Mickey didn't like questions, and he was wary of the whip. He soon discovered that he had good reason to be.

Mickey didn't come to him at all during the day, just the woman with the porridge. The weather was much colder now and Lander would have been glad to put his shirt on properly, but he preferred to use it to protect his hands. The work went slowly because he was having to stop frequently. When at last Mickey appeared around the side of the house he was furious.

'Jesus, is that all you've done? I don't fucking believe it,' he bellowed. 'What the fuck have you been doing all day? Sitting on your arse wanking?'

He swung the whip and the thong snapped across Lander's thigh. It was like being cut, a burning, searing pain, but he managed to avoid crying out. Something warned him that any reaction would provoke Mickey further. He hobbled away from the brick pile, Mickey swinging the whip ominously behind him.

Back in the shed, Magda bathed his hands again. This time she had what looked like an old tea towel and she used it to dab them. Lander sat on a hay bale, his palms and fingers screaming and his leg throbbing from the whiplash. When she'd finished the bathing she went to her hay pile, rummaged in it and came back with a small jar. She opened the lid and held it out to him.

'What is it?'

'It's skin cream. Take some and rub it into your hands. Gently.'

Lander extended a finger, loaded it with the cream and applied it to his palms. It smarted, but it also soothed.

Magda went back to her pile and returned with something else. 'Here, take these,' she said. Lander was astonished at what she was holding out to him: it was a pair of gloves, made of black leather. He tried one of them. It was small and a tight fit, but the cream helped him slide it on. Once in place, it seemed to hold everything together and it helped with the soreness. If he wore these he'd be able to handle the bricks more easily. He was touched.

'Where did you get this stuff?' he said.

'I stole it. From Edna.'

'Who's Edna?'

'She's Mickey's woman. The old tart with the ginger hair. My job is to help her in the kitchen and around the house. That's what I do when you're working on the bricks. I found them in a drawer in their bedroom.'

'Won't she know they're gone?'

'Edna? Never. She's rarely on this planet, and if she does notice she'll blame Mickey. Don't let him see them, though.'

'No, of course not. Thank you,' said Lander. 'Thank you for everything — for bathing my hands, sharing the food, and for the cream and the gloves.'

Magda smiled. It was the first time he'd seen her do that. Her teeth were yellow but the smile was warm. 'You're welcome,' she said.

Lander thought it might be a good moment to get answers to some of the things that had been chasing each other around in his head. 'Is there only Mickey and Edna? Does anyone else live here?'

'Do you think anyone else could stand it? No, just those two. And us.'

'Yes, and us. How long have you been here?'

She pointed to some tally marks, scratched in groups of five on the side of the shed near her hay pile. There looked to be a lot of them.

'Sixty-one days,' she said.

'My God,' said Lander. He looked at her. Two months of this and he'd be like her, and she would probably be gone.

'We've got to get out of here,' he said.

'Don't I know it. I've been thinking about that ever since I got here, and I have a plan. I think that your arrival might be just the distraction I need.'

Lander wanted to ask her what her plan was but he was prevented by Mickey's evening visit. This time there were two bowls.

'See? I've taken pity on you,' he said to Lander. 'Though fuck knows why. Well, what do you say?' He advanced on Lander with the whip poised.

Lander put his hands behind his back to hide the gloves. 'Thank you,' he said.

'Thank you who?'

'Thank you, Mickey.'

'I should fucking think so. You just make sure you work your balls off tomorrow, or else you'll feel my tickler again.' He laughed and turned away. He looked at Magda. 'You'd like to feel my tickler, wouldn't you, sweetheart?'

'Depends which tickler you mean,' said Magda, and winked at him.

'You just be ready and you'll find out,' said Mickey. His tone was heavy with innuendo, and threat. He stared at her for a minute, then left, pulling the door closed behind him.

It was sickening, thought Lander. How could she behave like that towards someone like Mickey? He waited until he was well clear, then said, 'Does he often talk to you like that?'

Magda laughed. 'All the time. But not when Edna's around.'

'Why do you let him?'

Magda smiled again. 'I have my reasons.'

'Has he, you know?'

'What, jumped me? Don't be daft.'

Was it daft? 'Not in all the time you've been here by yourself?'

'He hasn't got the balls. I've met a lot of blokes like him. Loud. Foul-mouthed. They're all the same, all talk. Besides, if he tried anything with me Edna would murder him.'

Lander had a vision of the wispy-haired, thread-veined woman alongside her blustering, pig-paunched partner.

'Really?'

'You bet. She has a knife under the mattress on her side of the bed, a sharp one. Now, why do you think she's got that? And why keep it there?'

It was hard to think of Mickey as a dominated husband but that was what Magda was suggesting. She sat down on the bale next to him.

'Magda. That's a German name, isn't it?' he said.

'Is it? My family's German but I was born in Swindon.'

She looked across the barn and Lander thought her eyes were watering. 'I was living in a coven, a sisterhood.'

'You mean like a convent?'

She laughed. 'No, not at all like that. It's a community of women. Don't you know about them?'

'No.'

'There are quite a few. Groups of women who've banded together so they can support and look after each other. The groups all have names. They call themselves after famous women, and they specialise in different things. There's the Nightingales, they're into health and looking after people. The Pankhursts, they're very political. The Brontës are mostly creative arts and writing types. They're making a record of everything that's happened. There are others, too. Those are just the ones I've come across.'

'And they're all women?'

'Mostly. I think some of them may have a few men who identify as women.'

'Which of them were you in?'

'None of those. I was in the Bonnies.' Lander looked blank. 'Anne Bonny was a female pirate. A couple of hundred years ago.'

'So your lot nicked stuff.'

'Not exactly. As the Infection has taken hold there's been a lot of looting. People haven't just taken what they needed, they've taken more, much more, and they've trashed the rest, like a fox in a chicken coop. We Bonnies are trying to conserve what we can. We concentrate on saving things that are either unique, or hard to make and repair. We go out looking for anything useful and serviceable. We have a big warehouse where we store what we've preserved, so it will be ready for when it's needed.'

'Was it raided, then? Is that how Mickey got you?'

'What, the warehouse? Oh, no. We keep that under armed guard. No, I was in a scavenging party with two other girls. I got separated, somebody banged me on the head, and the next I knew I was here. Mickey's guest.'

'A bit like me really,' said Lander. 'I was in a car, I fell asleep and he dragged me out.'

'That Mini. I know. Mickey told me.'

Lander was surprised. He hadn't thought of Mickey holding a conversation. It seemed that the relationship Magda had with Mickey was very different from Lander's.

They sat in silence on the hay bale. Lander liked Magda. At the start, he'd thought she was distant and aloof, but now that she was opening up he saw she wasn't like that at all. In reality, she was friendly and kind. She'd looked after him. Bringing the cream and the gloves for his hands was especially thoughtful. She should have been one of the Nightingales. He glanced sideways at her and tried to imagine her in different circumstances. Beneath the surface she was good looking. Her nose turned up slightly and her eyes were huge and dark. But the toil and inadequate diet had taken their toll. Her face was pinched, her frame scrawny and she had spots. And she was filthy. And she smelt. He expected that he did too, and he couldn't think what he must look like in his dirty shirt, his jeans thick with brick dust and his hands in black gloves.

'Do you know that people started it?' Lander said.

'Started what?'

'The Infection, the spread of the virus. People did it on purpose. It was some kind of germ warfare thing that got out of control.'

'Where did you hear that?'

'They told me when I was in hospital in Oxford. One of the people there said the virus had been developed in a lab and released in Africa to see what would happen. They were going to try it out and then kill it off, but it got loose. It was somebody pretty high up I got this from, so I think they must be right.'

'Jesus. Who would do something like that?'

'The Russians? The Americans? The Chinese? Us?'

Magda sighed. 'People seem to spend all their time thinking up new ways to kill each other. Crazy.'

'It's not the people. It's the politicians.'

'OK, but the politicians do it because that's what the people want. That's what gets the politicians into power, and it's what keeps them there.'

'I don't think people want to kill each other that much, do you?'

'Don't you? Try being an immigrant. You should hear some of the things my dad's been called. Kraut bastard. Russian arse licker. Fuck off back to where you came from. We had a shop, a delicatessen, and the windows were always getting smashed. A week after the Brexit vote somebody tried to set the place on fire. So some people certainly wanted to kill us. And what about Mickey? Wouldn't you like to kill him?'

Lander hadn't thought about it like that. Mickey was a cruel thief and a slave driver. He had treated him badly, and Lander would certainly like to pound him with his fists, but kill him? Although that was what Mickey was doing to them. If he carried on working them and starving them the way he was doing, they wouldn't last long. Magda was little more than skin and bone already.

There was a pause, then Magda spoke. 'Is your sister like you?'

'We're twins, so yes, in a lot of ways. In others, we're very different though. I'm into sport and she's not. I like computers and computer games, and that just bores the knickers off her. I'm not good at school and she's a real keeno.'

'Brainy, is she?'

'She's going to Cambridge University. Or she was.'

They sat in silence for a little longer. Lander shuddered. The night was cooler than before and there were lots of gaps in the metal cladding that let the wind through. Magda got up and dragged her chain over to her hay pile.

'You can come over here with me if you like,' she said.

Lander hesitated.

'Nothing funny,' she said. 'I just thought you might like some company. And we can keep each other warm.'

He walked across to her and they lay down on the hay a little awkwardly, back to back. It took some adjustment to get themselves arranged around the chain. Despite the conditions, despite the ripe smell of his companion, Lander had to admit it was greatly preferable to being on his own.

'You said you've got a plan for getting out of here,' he said.

'Yes.'

'Tell me about it.'

'Maybe later,' she said, 'when I'm ready. It would probably shock you. For now, if I tell you to do something please do it. Don't stop and think about it. Just do it, even if it sounds weird.'

'Yeah. All right, if you say so.' Lander wondered what she had in mind. Mickey never came near them without his whip or a stick, and they were chained all the time. He didn't undo the loop chain until he'd got the shackles on, and vice versa. He dealt with them separately and kept them apart while he was doing so. Overcoming him seemed out of the question. But what she'd said sounded mysterious and indicated she'd certainly got something in mind. He just wished she'd tell him what it was.

He rolled over and put his arm across her. She didn't move away so they stayed like that, a pair of strays cuddling against the cold. They woke each other several times during the night, getting entangled in the chain as they turned over. At one point Lander had to get up and go to the bucket. When he came back Magda had turned over and this time she put her arm around him.

Towards dawn she nudged him.

'Hey.'

'What?' Lander felt he hadn't slept long enough and his head was fuzzy.

'Wake up. It's nearly morning. Better get back to your own bedding. If Mickey finds you over here with me he'll use his whip on you.'

'Why would he do that?'

'Don't worry about why. Just take it from me that he would.'

Lander shuffled across to his hay on the other side of the shed, the chain dragging behind him.

'Don't forget,' Magda called over to him. 'I may do some things you think are peculiar. Just go with it, and do what I tell you.'

'Very mysterious,' said Lander.

'Promise?'

'All right.'

'Good. Because I think I can get us out of here, but it won't be pleasant.'

A little later Mickey came in to collect Magda.

16

____

MAGDA'S PLAN

WITH THE HELP of the gloves and the cream, Lander's hands improved. Magda's balm also lessened the pain in his wrists and ankles, sore from the fetters. Best of all, Mickey set him to a different task; he spent the next two days sawing logs. That was hard on the arms and shoulders but gave his hands something of a rest and the chance to heal. And it made a change from the boredom of the brick pile.

The log store was on the other side of the house, so not only did Lander get a change of scene, but he was also able to see more of what went on. He caught glimpses of Magda at work. She'd hang out the washing, and fetch water from the well and the trough. She opened windows and shook out mats. She waved to him when no one was looking. He also saw Mickey leave in the Mini, his huge bulk crammed behind the steering wheel, and come back a couple of hours later. He was pleased that the chickens had been turned out and that the car still worked, but resentful that Mickey should be using it.

He followed Magda's example of making a mark on the shed wall for each day he was there. He'd made six marks but it felt as though he'd been there forever. Hunger was a constant companion, a permanent biting ache. He drank lots of water to try to lessen the pangs, but that meant he needed to use the bucket several times in the night so he never got uninterrupted sleep. He was exhausted and he wondered how long he could go on. What would Mickey do if he – if either of them – became too weak to work? He could guess.

On the morning of the seventh day, he awoke at what he thought must be the usual time. Magda was snoring gently beside him and seemed dead to the world. He hurriedly got up and returned to his hay pile to await Mickey. However, Mickey didn't appear, and Lander dropped once more into sleep.

He woke again, and this time he could tell it was late. The light coming through the broken roof was different and the shed was warm from the sun. Magda was still sleeping. He thought he must have missed something and at any minute Mickey would be there with the whip, bawling at them for not being ready. He got up, the chain rattling.

Magda looked up blearily from under the hay. 'What's up with you?'

'Look! It's late! We have to get up. Where's Mickey? What's happened?'

Magda lay on her back and stretched. 'Easy, easy,' she said. 'Don't panic. I forgot to tell you. It's day seven.'

'Day seven?'

'Yes. Sunday. Or I think it must be Sunday. Every seventh day we get the morning off. Mickey likes a lie-in and he doesn't get us up till later. I should have said. I'm sorry.'

Lander felt his anxiety drain. He sighed and let himself down on the hay again.

'What happens on Sunday, then?'

'It's very civilised,' she said. 'We're allowed out to wash ourselves and our clothes in the trough in the yard. If Edna's feeling generous we might even get a bit of soap. Then we'll get some of her wonderful oatmeal. We'll be left for a bit to rake up the old hay and put it in the corner over there, and we can break open a new bale. Then we'll be taken out to work for the afternoon. At least, that's what's happened to me so far. I guess it will be the same for you.'

It was. Mickey arrived about half an hour later – it was hard for Lander to know exactly without his watch. He seemed in a buoyant mood, almost jovial, and for once he didn't have his whip with him.

'All right, you lucky people. Enjoyed your lie-in? Good good good.' He undid their chain but didn't fit the shackles. 'This way then, campers.'

They followed him out of the shed and down the track to the farmyard. For the first time since he'd arrived there, Lander was free of chains. The sense of liberty was wonderful; it felt like walking on air. He was thinking about how he might take advantage of his unchained state when he saw, tied to the fence, a dog. It had a mean face and a lot of teeth. Rottweiler? Pit Bull? Lander wasn't well up on dogs. The only one he knew was Buster, but Buster was a lazy old Labrador; this dog looked nasty. Where had it been? He'd not noticed it around before. Mickey untied it and it looked at Lander and licked its lips, as if savouring the possibility of a juicy mouthful.

'This is Bullit,' said Mickey. 'Try anything funny and he'll bite your balls off. Or in your case, sweetheart,' he said to Magda, 'guzzle your tits. Not that you've got that much.'

'Don't worry about that, handsome,' said Magda, cocking an eyebrow at him. 'My other bits work just fine.'

'Do they now?' said Mickey. 'One day I'll have to find out. You're a bit scrawny for me, though. Nothing to get hold of. I like 'em chubbier.'

'Well whose fault is that?' said Magda. 'You'll have to feed me up. Anyway, have you never shagged a skinny girl? You'd be surprised how good we are.'

Once again Lander was uncomfortable at the smutty banter between these two. Magda seemed to encourage Mickey. Surely she didn't enjoy this sort of stuff.

Magda had a handful of garments with her. Presumably, she was going to wash these, but Lander didn't have any clothes other than the ones he was wearing.

'Here,' said Mickey. 'You might as well have this back.' He had Lander's hold-all and he threw it towards him. 'All this clobber's too poncy for me. Won't fit me anyway.'

Lander opened the hold-all. Its contents had been turned over, but it was still full.

'Get your kit off and get cracking,' said Mickey. 'The missus has donated some soap.' There was the slimy-looking end of a bar on the edge of the trough. 'I'm going for a shit. Bullit'll be here to look after you. If you try to leave this yard he'll have you.'

He ambled away to the house. Edna regarded them from an upper window, one hand holding back the curtain. She looked angry, her thin face drawn into a beak so she had the appearance of a bird of prey staring down at them. She let the curtain fall back and disappeared from view.

Bullit had been left untied and watched them closely, its teeth slightly bared. Magda patted its head and the dog wagged its tail.

'Do you know this brute?'

'He's all right. He lives in the house mostly and he's supposed to be protection for Edna when Mickey's out. He's right, though. If you do something unexpected he'll go for you. Now I'm going to take my clothes off, so turn your back.'

Lander had lost count of the number of times he'd seen Magda use the bucket, and for the past five nights he'd slept alongside her, so her coyness now seemed unnecessary. Nevertheless, he did what she told him. There was a sharp intake of breath – the water must be freezing – and the sound of splashing, the smell of soap.

'Well you are a good boy,' said Magda. 'You can turn round now.'

She was sitting on the edge of the trough. She'd put on a fresh t-shirt and jeans, and she was drying her hair on a threadbare towel. She held it out to him.

'Here, you'll have to share this. It hasn't dawned on Edna that there are two of us now. I've tried not to get it too wet. Don't get it dirty though, it's me who has to do the washing.'

Lander took the towel. It was a sorry object, the fabric so thin that in places it was almost transparent. He wondered why there was nothing better. He remembered the soft cotton ones their Mam liked so much, and the ones in the house in Snaith. There must be thousands of towels in hundreds of places. Why hadn't Mickey helped himself to some new ones? Why make do with this old thing, even for people he was using as slaves?

He took off his shirt and jeans and dropped them on the yard. There was no point washing them, they were gone. He got into the trough. It was perishing, but the sensation of the water was so good he put up with the cold. He splashed himself with water and lathered himself. He rubbed the stubble on his face. He hadn't shaved since Oxford and wished he could now. He rubbed soap into his hair. Magda didn't turn her back but watched him.

'Do you like all that stuff?' he said.

'All what stuff?'

'That stuff with Mickey. The way he talks to you. The way you answer him, all that sexy shit. Why do you go along with it?'

'You jealous or something?'

'No, of course not. Although I don't mean you're not attractive or anything. I mean... I...' Lander petered out in confusion.

Magda laughed. 'I'm teasing.' She came closer and lowered her voice. 'Mickey's a slob and he turns my guts, but I'm encouraging him for a reason. Just remember what I said.'

Lander rinsed his hair and climbed out of the trough. He rubbed himself down, put on some clothes from the hold-all, and sat beside Magda. He closed his eyes. It was wonderful just to sit there in fresh clothes, slowly drying off in the autumn sunshine, not having to work, not needing to be fearful of Mickey suddenly arriving and expressing with his whip his dissatisfaction with the amount or quality of what he'd done.

It didn't last long. Too soon Bullit jumped up, wagging his tail, and Mickey came out of the house. He looked even grumpier than usual. He didn't say anything, but took them back to the shed, fitted the shackles and directed them to their labours, Magda to the house and Lander to the log pile.

That evening Lander was taken off work later than usual. He had no way of knowing the exact time but he could tell by the sun that it was well after the time Mickey normally came for him, and he was wondering if he'd been forgotten and, if so, how he'd get through the night.

That's the way it goes, he thought. You get the morning off but you have to work late to make up for it. So much for Mickey being generous.

Mickey did come for him, but he seemed flustered and preoccupied. He didn't take Lander back to the usual shed but instead led him to a smaller brick building on the other side of the track.

'Where's this?'

'It's your new fucking mansion, squire,' said Mickey. 'I can't have you two fuck buddies together anymore, so you're in here now.'

Mickey left Lander's work fetters in place and padlocked them to an iron rod bolted to the wall. Then he left, and locked the door.

Lander stood in the semi darkness, taking stock. Obviously, Mickey didn't want him in the big shed with Magda, but why not? He had a nasty feeling that this new arrangement was because Mickey was up to something, and he had a good idea what that might be. He was fearful for Magda. She wasn't strong and was certainly no match for Mickey.

There were no haybales but there was some sacking on the floor. The arrangement with the fetters and the rod meant that Lander couldn't lie down. The best he could do was lean with his back against the wall, his arms held awkwardly above him. However, after a few minutes they began to ache and he had to stand up again. Then his legs hurt and he needed to squat. Then his thighs cramped and he was forced to keep up a constant fidget to ease the discomfort. How long would Mickey leave him here? Surely not all night. Probably until he'd finished what Lander suspected he wanted to do with Magda. Would she really let him? How would he react if she tried to stop him? He did his best to push these thoughts aside. He was in no position to affect what happened in the shed, but he made a promise that if Mickey hurt Magda he'd make him pay.

Would there be any supper? Mickey's got more than catering on his mind, Lander thought ruefully. He was so hungry that even the cabbage soup and stale bread would have been welcome. Time went by. This place was in better repair than the cowshed and only a little light got in from the outside, but night came and even that faded. Lander waited in the dark, wondering what was going to happen. Was this part of the plan Magda had mentioned? What was she doing and how was it going to help them? He tried to make himself comfortable on the sacking but there was no chance of sleep. Even if he could lie down, a wind had sprung up and there was a persistent rattle from the roof flapping and the shed door shaking.

It was well into the night when he heard a key in the lock. Supper at last, he thought. Mickey must have finished. But it wasn't Mickey. The wind snatched the door open and it was Magda. She had a hurricane lamp.

'Come on,' she said. 'Hurry up.'

She was trembling and seemed tearful. Her clothing was smeared with dark blotches.

'Is it Mickey? What's the bastard done?'

She didn't answer but fiddled with some keys on what looked like Mickey's bunch. After three or four tries she found the one that unlocked Lander's wrist, and then the one for his ankle. The chain dropped away and he rubbed his sore limbs. He could barely stand and she helped him up. Then he saw what the dark blotches were.

'My God, you're bleeding. Are you hurt? What's happened? Where's Mickey?'

'Mickey's in the shed.'

'Jesus. How did you get his keys? Is he asleep? Won't he wake up?'

Magda shook her head and her voice cracked. 'No, Mickey won't ever wake up. I've killed him. Mickey's dead.'

17

GETAWAY

MAGDA DIDN'T SPEAK. Perhaps she couldn't. Lander wanted to know what had happened in the shed but she didn't answer. She seemed catatonic, staring fixedly through the windscreen and hardly moving, except that every few minutes she would have a fit of trembling.

When she'd come to unlock Lander's fetters she'd been shaking, but she'd seemed in control. She helped him stand and ushered him out of the door and towards the yard, where the Mini was parked.

'Get in and let's get out of here,' she said, collapsing into the passenger seat and tossing Lander the keys.

He ached all over. His hands, his wrists, his arms and legs, his neck and back were all agonising. He doubted he'd be able to drive. He turned the key and was relieved to see that there was still plenty of fuel in the Mini's tank. He started the engine and put the car in gear, ready to pull away, wincing at every move.

Suddenly the house door crashed open and Edna came charging out. She had a shotgun and she levelled it at them. Instinctively Lander dived across Magda and braced himself for the impact, but at that moment Bullit rushed from the house and ran at the car, leaping up at the window, claws scraping on the door, barking, snarling. Edna couldn't shoot without hitting the dog and she let the gun fall. Lander saw his chance, put his foot down and gunned the car up the track, the wheels scattering mud and grit. Once on the road he sped up, trying to get away as quickly as possible from the hell that Mickey had made for them.

He kept the car's lights on until they were well clear of the farm, and then he slowed down and switched them off. There was a big moon, huge, almost full, and it was easily bright enough to drive by so long as he didn't go too fast. He didn't discuss with Magda where they were going. He'd already decided that; he was taking her to his home, back to Paradise Farm, back to Kerryl. If she was still there.

Magda was drained. He couldn't imagine what had gone on in the shed, or how this slight woman had got the better of the strong, powerfully built Mickey. What exactly had happened? She said Mickey was dead. How did she know? What did she do? Was she sure? He didn't know whether it was best to talk to her or to say nothing. He stole a sideways look at her. The moonlight drained the colours so it was not easy to see whether what covered her was mud or blood, but he suspected it was the latter. He'd seen in the lights from the house the crimson and brown on her face, her hands, her arms, her clothes. One side of her, the side nearest him, seemed to be soaked, with dark patches on her t-shirt and jeans. He had a sudden and alarming thought. He'd assumed that this was Mickey's blood, but suppose it was hers. Suppose she was bleeding to death beside him. He slammed on the brakes and the car slid to a stop.

'Are you all right? Are you bleeding?'

Magda shook her head. Which question was she answering?

'Are you all right?' he repeated.

She nodded.

'Not bleeding?'

She shook her head.

'Tell me what happened.'

That was the trigger. She began to cry, quiet sobs at first, and then it was as if a dam had burst. She let out a shuddering howl and there was a torrent of tears. She cried as though her world had ended. Lander wrapped her in his arms and held her until the shaking stilled and the yowl subsided to a whimper. Gradually, slowly, she became quiet. He stroked her hair. It felt matted and sticky.

She pulled herself away from him and wiped her nose on the backs of her hands. There was a box of tissues Maisie had given him on the back seat and Lander pulled out a handful and gave them to her. She blew her nose loudly and sniffed.

'I'm sorry,' she said. 'I don't usually cry. I'm not one of those girls who blubs all the time.' She sniffed again. 'It's just that I've never killed anybody before. I'm not used to it.' She smiled ruefully.

Lander had expected Mickey to clear out or trash everything in the car, but he hadn't. There was some chicken manure, but that was the only damage. The rug and two big water bottles Maisie had given him for his journey were still there.

'Here, get that shirt and your jeans off. You can clean up and then you can tell me about it.'

Lander helped pull her t-shirt over her head. It was wet and stiffening. He threw it out of the window. She got out of the car, took off her jeans and dropped them beside the shirt. She wasn't wearing any pants and she started to shiver again.

Lander took one of the water bottles. 'Sorry, this'll be cold,' he said.

He tipped water over her, while she dabbed at the bloody marks with the shirt. Then he helped her wrap herself in the blanket and get back into the car. He rinsed his own hands and got behind the wheel again. She was still shaking and he turned up the heater.

'I'm going to need some clothes,' she said.

'Yes. We're going to where you can get some.'

It was easy to find the way. The place names on the signposts were now ones that Lander recognised, and he knew where he was going. Once he saw lights moving along a side road, but apart from that there was no traffic. None of the houses they passed or saw in the distance was showing any signs of life. All the streetlights were out.

There was so much Lander wanted to know, but he didn't want to start her crying again. He couldn't imagine what it must be like to kill somebody. He'd tried to when he'd held the gun and looked at Spencer. He'd seen plenty of fictional killings in the cinema and on TV. He'd blasted countless humans and aliens on his XBox, scattering blood, bone and body parts over screen after screen. He'd seen some real deaths on the TV too, news reports from war-torn areas. And of course, he'd shot animals – pests, an unwanted bull calf, usually as a mercy to end suffering, very occasionally for fun. Mickey was an animal, but could Lander have killed him? He didn't know, and he was in awe of Magda's courage in taking him on.

'I never thought it would be so hard,' she said. Her voice was so quiet that Lander could only just hear her over the noise of the engine and the rumble of the tyres.

'I bet,' he said. 'I don't know how you screwed yourself up to do it.'

She made a sort of hissing noise. 'I don't mean that,' she said. 'I wanted to kill him. He was a bastard. He was brutal, he was working and starving us to death and he was trying to rape me. He deserved it. I've wished him dead a thousand times and I'm glad he is. What I mean is that I didn't know it would be so hard to make him dead.'

Lander waited for her to go on.

'I've been prick teasing him, you know that. That's what all that mucky talk was about. Thanks to his hard rations I don't have the figure I once had so I can't pretend I was mega-tempting, but I figured that if all Mickey had was Edna he wouldn't turn his nose up at an easy fuck. I knew that sooner or later he'd come to the shed. So I stole the knife from under Edna's mattress. I knew I didn't have long because she'd miss it, so I ramped up the tempting. I was hoping he'd try it with you there in the shed, make you watch. Then you could have helped me. But he didn't. He locked you in the other shed and then he came to me. There was no messing, he just took his pants down and got on top of me. I tried to make him stop, told him I needed time because I wanted to do it properly, but he wouldn't. I panicked then, because I couldn't reach the knife where I'd hidden it under the hay, but after wriggling around a bit I got my fingers on it. I stabbed him. He didn't stop, though, just kept on pounding, so I stabbed him again. The knife was slippery and my fingers slid down the handle and I cut myself. I think I shrieked and that was when he pulled out of me, so I stabbed him again, three or four times in the neck. He was twisting about and swearing at me and it was hard to hit him properly. He got his hands around my throat and started squeezing. I thought I was going to pass out and I kept jabbing at him with the knife. Then it skidded out of my hand and I thought that was the end, he'd strangle me, but all of a sudden his hands slackened and he went limp. I got myself out from under him and felt for his pulse, but his neck was just a mass of blood. There was no pulse. He was dead.'

'Oh My God,' said Lander. Halfway through Magda's speech he'd stopped the car and turned off the engine. It was hard to comprehend the horror of the situation: the two of them wrestling in the shed, then Mickey lying there in a pool of his own blood. 'Jesus, what a nightmare. Are you all right? Did he hurt you?'

'Yeah, a bit, you know, going in when I wasn't properly ready. And my throat hurts, especially when I swallow. And my fingers are sore where I cut them, and I've got some bruises. But no, I'm all right really. Just glad it's over, that's all.'

Lander sat for some time, still struggling with the enormity of what Magda had faced, what she'd done.

'Thank you,' he said. 'For getting me out too. It was a good job he had his keys with him.'

'I knew he would. He always kept them on his belt, he never went anywhere without them. The car keys were a lucky break, though. I thought they might be in the house and we'd have to face Edna and the dog to get them, but they were in his pocket.'

Lander started the engine again.

'Where are we going?' Magda asked.

'I'm taking you to where I live. It's remote, so we'll be safe there. You can meet my sister.'

Lander drove on. Neither of them spoke, and he thought perhaps Magda was sleeping again when she clutched his arm.

'Stop here,' she said.

'Here? What for?'

'I need to pee. Quickly. Here,' she said and shook his arm again.

They were beside a war memorial in the centre of a village, a tall cross with the statue of a soldier at its base.

'It's too conspicuous,' said Lander. 'Can you wait while we go on a bit? I'll find you a field.'

'No,' said Magda, with surprising intensity. 'No. I can't wait. It's got to be here.'

Lander didn't want to seem insensitive. It might be some woman's thing, a reaction to what had happened to her.

'All right, if you must,' he said.

Magda gathered the blanket around her and went behind the memorial. She reappeared a few moments later.

'Better?' said Lander.

'Loads,' she said.

He drove on. It wasn't until later that he realised how significant that stop had been.

18

———

HOME

LANDER WAS NOT surprised that Magda slept for the rest of the journey. The driving was easy, even though he had to rely on the moonlight, and the Mini was going well. He loved that little car. In another hour they were entering the bottom of the valley and heading towards Walbrough. They'd be at the farm in half an hour.

He had told Magda that he was taking her to meet his sister, but he was not sure she was there. For as long as he could remember he and Kerryl had always known what was happening to the other. It wasn't telepathy or anything like that; neither could tell what their twin was thinking. It was more a matter of feelings, an awareness of the other's mood, an emotional resonance. When Kerryl was being bullied at school during what Gran called her 'puppy-fat days', he had known she was going through something that was hurting her and he'd helped her to deal with it. And when their Mam had put her foot down to stop him from going to the Yorkshire Cricket Academy, only Kerryl properly understood how desperately unhappy that made him. They had a constant, low-level connection with each other, in the background but always there. Except not now. Now it was as if he was on one end of a phone call but he'd lost the connection. It had been like that since Adam had vanished back in Oxford, and he couldn't help thinking that the two things were connected.

The valley road was a narrow funnel with only limited avenues of escape and he'd been anxious about the possibility of running into a patrol, but there was nothing. He felt a moment's trepidation when he reached the spot where he'd met the BMW, but the road was empty.

Day was breaking as they drove into Walbrough. The town was far worse than when he'd left it. The damage then had been serious, but now the devastation was complete. There were signs of the start of a clean-up – rubbish had been bulldozed into piles, a few of the gaping shop windows boarded over – but there was a huge amount still to be done. Nothing seemed usable any more. Would it ever be put right? Granddad would have said not. Lander could imagine it now, him grumbling that 'them buggers in the south' would be too busy mending things in London to bother with a place like Walbrough.

They passed the market square. There was what looked to be a llama by the drinking fountain, abandoned and bewildered. Further on there were goats in the park, and a few sheep were lying in the middle of the main road. They moved grudgingly to let the Mini pass. And there was the usual complement of dogs, bad-tempered and starving, worrying at one of the rubbish heaps, tearing at anything they thought they might be able to eat. A single dog ambled over to the car. It was so big it could look at them on a level through the Mini's window. There was foamy, yellow spittle around its muzzle, but it didn't look aggressive. Lander wasn't prepared to chance it, and he drove on.

Magda was still asleep when he turned up the lane to the farm, but the bumpy road woke her.

'Where are we?'

'Nearly there.'

'What, at your farm?'

'Yes. It's not much further, just up this hill.'

'I'm a mess,' Magda said, trying to smooth her hair. 'I should have cleaned up to meet your posh sister.'

'You mean you should put on something from your wardrobe full of gowns? Anyway, Kerryl's not posh. Anyway, she might not be here.'

'Oh.' Magda sounded disappointed. 'Why's that?' And then, 'Are you all right?'

Lander nodded, although he was feeling a dread that grew worse as they reached the top of the hill. What would he find? Their grandparents were dead; was Kerryl too? Was that why he no longer felt any connection with her? And if she was there, how would she greet him after he'd walked out on her?

At last he could see the farmhouse across the fields, the grey stone bathed in the amber glow of the rising sun. There was a horse in the paddock. It was Joey! Lander's heart leapt. Kerryl must be there, she must be all right.

He stopped the car by the field gate and whistled. Joey ambled over, looking pleased to see them, and Lander stroked his neck and his muzzle. When he looked at the animal more closely he could see that he needed some attention. In normal times Kerryl brushed Joey most days until his coat shone, but now it was dull, and his mane and tail were tangled. He had an open gash on his leg. It was weeping, and a magnet for flies. Kerryl would never allow Joey to get like this. Lander's sick feeling grew. She couldn't be there.

The dread got worse when he drove into the farmyard. The place didn't look like his home. It was a mess. There were two bin bags which had been tipped over and their contents strewn about. There were empty cartons, tin cans and plastic all over the cobbles. In the corner there was a heap of empty bottles. A couple of windows had been broken and covered with cardboard. Some of it had gone soggy and showed the jagged glass beneath. The clutter and disorder were completely out of character with the tidy Kerryl. There was another oddity: a battered-looking Lambretta was propped against the wall of the barn.

'Jesus,' said Lander. 'It's a dump. It's as bad as Mickey's place.'

The back door of the house had been smashed, and crudely repaired with scraps of plywood. They'd not even been sawn to fit, but just snapped off and fixed with duct tape.

'Stay here,' said Lander, getting out of the car. 'There might be trouble. I need to find out what's going on.'

'I'll come too.'

'What, wrapped in a blanket? Don't be daft. Stay here.'

He got out of the car and pushed the house door. It opened, creaking loudly. It was dark inside, but there was enough light from the door to see where he was going. He tried a light switch, but nothing happened. The house was as untidy as the yard, and it smelt. There were spills on the kitchen worktops, dirty pots in the sink, and clothes on the floor. Somebody was living here, but it wasn't Kerryl.

The front room wasn't as bad as the kitchen but it hadn't been cleaned in ages. There was thick dust on every surface and a smear of mud on the carpet. There was a black plastic vase on the mantelpiece. He recognised the urn that contained their Mam's ashes. He could remember collecting it from Walbrough after her cremation. It was only a few months ago, but it felt as though it had been in another life. Next to the urn were two white cardboard boxes with something written on their lids. He read the inscriptions; they were the names of their grandparents, the dates of their births, and of their deaths. So here it was, proof that what Adam had told him was right. Gran and Granddad were gone. But where was Kerryl? Had she been here when they'd died? She must have been, because who else would have collected these boxes and put them there? He felt a stab of anger. Why had these things been left on the mantelpiece? Why weren't their grandparents' ashes in proper urns instead of these tatty boxes? Why hadn't they been laid properly to rest? But then he remembered that he was in no position to complain; he'd walked out, and something awful must have happened to Kerryl to prevent her from dealing with them.

'Oy. What do you think you're doing?'

The shout startled him. There was a figure silhouetted in the doorway to the hall. It was a boy, about his own age and he was pointing a shotgun at him. Lander could see it was one of Granddad's Purdeys. He was worried that the guy might not know what he was doing and might fire it by accident, so he raised his hands and very slowly backed away. The gunman came into the room and looked hard at Lander.

'Hey, I know you,' he said. 'Aren't you Kerryl's brother?' He lowered the gun.

'Yes. And I know you, too. Didn't Kerryl used to go out with you? Steve?'

'Yeah. Lander. Hey, dude. Good to see you.'

Lander winced as Steve let the gun fall to the floor and grabbed him in a rough hug.

'What are you doing here?' said Lander, untangling himself.

He was annoyed, partly because Steve was treating his Granddad's expensive gun so carelessly, but mainly because he guessed that the mess in the house and the yard was down to him.

'Hey, where you been, man?' said Steve, patting him on the arm. 'Nobody was here so I came in. I'm crashing. You don't mind, do you?'

'Where's Kerryl?'

Steve looked uneasy. 'She's not here. The place was empty when I got here.'

Kerryl not here? Then where was she? He wanted to ask but he was afraid of what might be the answer. He went to the window and pulled back the curtain. 'Jesus, you allergic to daylight or something? Anyway, the last I heard of you was that you were partying in Bradford.'

'Oh, yeah,' said Steve. He looked rather shamefaced. 'The "Death's Door" thing.'

'That was it. What happened? What are you doing here?'

'Oh, you know. It was great while it lasted. There was loads of people there and some top DJs – RAM40, Punk Daddy, Dr Acid. We were all chilling and popping pills and smoking, and there was loads of shagging. Not me,' he added quickly, 'but pretty much everybody else was doing it, right out in the open.'

'Sounds wonderful.'

Steve didn't pick up Lander's sarcasm. 'Yeah, it was, but then people started getting sick, the virus. Some of them got it bad, right there, and that freaked people out so much they took off. In the end there were just a few of us left and it went tits up, know what I mean? I'd been messaging Kerryl until the system went down, sending her pics and that. I wanted her to come over but she said she didn't fancy it, so when I left Bradford I came to look for her.'

There was a voice from behind them.

'I'm Magda.'

She was standing in the doorway, still in her blanket. Steve did the proverbial double take.

'Holy fuck. What happened to you?' he said.

'A long story,' said Lander. 'What she needs now is a shower and some clothes.'

'There's hot water,' said Steve. 'Loads of it. The solar panels still seem to work fine for that. I expect Kerryl's clothes are where they always were. I've nicked some of yours, but I haven't touched hers.' He sniggered.

Lander didn't know Steve and wondered whether he was going to like him. He'd certainly made himself at home.

Lander showed Magda where the bathroom was, and Kerryl's bedroom. He told her to help herself to Kerryl's things. He was sure she wouldn't mind – if she came back, that is. It was a jolt to see his sister's room again. It was clean and neat, and looked as though she might have only just left it. There were her posters and pictures on the wall, her books on the shelves. There were some magazines, and a box of moviesticks. There was make-up and other goodies on the dressing table, including a bottle of perfume. It was Eau d'Amour, their Mam's favourite. He and Kerryl had given it to her last Christmas.

Last Christmas. How long ago that was. Last Christmas was another life. The Infection had been hardly known then, just a rumour from a faraway land that most of the time didn't even merit a news tailpiece. What would they all have done if they'd known what was going to happen? Lander remembered asking their Granddad this question and he'd said he'd have set off for the Scottish islands, the Outer Hebrides. 'Safest place,' he'd said. 'Pull up the drawbridge and wait till it's all over.' Would they have done that? It's easy to think so now, but leaving everything behind, would they? Is that what Kerryl had done? Had she thought that if her twin could take off, so could she? Should he look for her in Scotland?

'What happened to her?' said Steve as Lander came back downstairs, leaving Magda in the bathroom. 'She looks as though she's been in a fight.'

'She has in a way,' said Lander. 'She had a run-in with an animal.' He supposed that was fairly accurate, and if Magda wanted Steve to know more she'd tell him.

'Fuck, I'd like to have seen that. There's blood all over her.'

'Yeah, well. She's washed some of it off. You should have seen her before. Anyway, you said Kerryl wasn't at home when you got here. Where's she gone?'

Steve looked uncomfortable.

'I need to tell you a few things,' he said. 'About what happened and why I came here.' He sat on the edge of the kitchen table. 'There was this mate of mine at Death's Door, and he said that if anything happened to him I could have his Lambretta. Well it did, happen to him I mean, so I took the Lambretta and I headed here. We, me and Kerryl, got on well when we was going out – I don't know why she dumped me, but she got off with that big jerk Mark Radshaw, the one with the flash car. Anyway, I was at Death's Door and we was messaging, and neither of us seemed to be getting the Infection, so I thought we could get together. Like I said, I wanted Kerryl to join me but she wouldn't, so I thought I'd come here. Know what I mean?'

Lander knew why Kerryl had dropped Steve. She'd told him it was because he was a knobhead. But maybe she'd changed her mind. Or perhaps she was just lonely. When most of the friends you've known are dead your standards are bound to drop somewhat. He wanted Steve to get on with the story.

'So you came here, and smashed the door in,' he said.

'No, easy, man. I didn't do that. That was not me.'

'Who was it then?'

'Well, I was on the Lambretta and I was just coming out of Walbrough when a helicopter came over, real low. I thought it might have spotted me but I was under the trees and it went straight over. Know what I mean? Anyway, I watched it go up to the edge of the moor and it landed. There's a load of big rocks up there, and it landed near them.'

'The Bride Stones,' said Lander.

'Yeah, well, it landed there and some guys got out, but I couldn't see what they was doing so I carried on up the hill. When I got nearer to the farm I could see something was kicking off. There was a couple of army vehicles in the yard. There was a Toyota Avatar, like the patrols use, and another, much bigger, like an ambulance but khaki. Anyway, I was watching them when this car came flying up the track. It was a low sports jobby, and it was bouncing on the bumps like tits on a trampoline. I bet he fucked his suspension right royally, know what I mean? Anyway, it was a good job I'd got the Lambretta off the track or he'd have seen me.'

Lander was getting impatient. 'So where was Kerryl?'

'I'm getting to that. I hid the Lambretta and went up the side of the field and when I got nearer I found a spot where I could see what was going on. The helicopter took off and went off in the direction of Manchester. Then a bunch of dudes came down from the moor and went off in the Avatar. After a bit some more came out of the house, all in bio gear, and they went in the ambulance. The sports car was still in the yard but there was no sign of the driver so I moved in. It was unlocked, and the dumb dude had left his briefcase on the passenger seat. So I took it. I mean, he'd smashed your door in, hadn't he? And anyway, it was the fucking government, wasn't it?'

Steve paused, as if waiting for Lander's approval.

'For Christ's sake, what has this got to do with where Kerryl's gone?'

'Ah, well, this briefcase. There was nothing much in it, a few government papers, all official like, and some personal stuff. And these.'

Steve opened a drawer and took out two notebooks. One was purple and one was green. 'They'll tell you what's happened to your sister,' he said. 'Better than I can.'

Lander knew the books were Kerryl's. He'd seen them before, seen her writing in them.

'You might want to read them on your own,' Steve said.

'Why?'

'You just might, that's all.'

Lander felt a twinge of anxiety. Steve was hiding something. He took the notebooks upstairs.

His room was very much as he'd left it, except tidier. His clothes had been put away and the shelves straightened. The USB stick he'd taped to the wall was gone, so Kerryl must have found it. His laptop was on his bedside table. He'd told her she could have it because he thought it might be useful to her, but she'd not taken it. She'd once told him that she liked the physical process of writing things out by hand. Really? Nuts! Writing was a pain, and anything that made it easier got his vote every time.

He sat on his bed and put the two notebooks beside him. He knew they were diaries, and because of that he knew they'd be special. One of the worst rows he'd ever had with Kerryl had been when she'd caught him looking at one of her diaries. He hadn't meant any harm, he'd done it without thinking. But she'd accused him of prying and had said what she'd written was private, and the row had gone on for a long time. So he was wary of these books now, and of what they would tell him about his sister.

He opened the green notebook. It was filled with Kerryl's handwriting, page after tumbling page, all in her neat script. At one point she'd changed the colour of her pen, but apart from that the pages were all the same. There were no doodles, no sketches, just words. Pasted into the purple book were some of the press cuttings he'd given her about the Infection.

On the flyleaf of the purple book Kerryl had written 'You should read this one first'. So he did.

19

EXPLORING

LANDER SKIPPED MOST of the purple book which covered
the build-up to the Infection arriving at their home because he'd
been there, although he remembered some of what had happened
differently from the way Kerryl described it. He felt guilty when
he got to the part after their Mam died. And the feeling of
loneliness that came through from her account after he'd gone
brought a lump to his throat.

It was as he went through the green diary that his anger grew. He
reached the end and read Kerryl's last words, and slumped
forward on his chair. The notebook dropped from his hand. He
stayed there immobile, while rage built inside him until the dam
burst and he exploded. He jumped up, tipping his chair over. He
let out a howl, picked up his laptop and brought it down hard on
the stone window sill; and again – three, four, five times –
demolishing the case on the granite. He looked at the mangled
wreck and dropped it. He picked up one of his most important
treasures, the ball from the cricket match with Derbyshire. He
looked at it for a moment, then ran down the stairs, taking them
two at a time, out into the yard and hurled it, as if throwing in

from the boundary. He watched the scarlet sphere rise in an arc, hang for an instant, and fall. It hit a rock and bounced into the heather. He wiped his eyes with his sleeve and walked back towards the house.

It was Adam. Adam had done this. Adam was the reason why Kerryl wasn't here.

'The fucker,' he snarled. 'The total, complete bastard.'

He went to the front room and slumped down on the sofa, facing the urn and the boxes of ashes on the mantelpiece. There should be some for Kerryl. Where was she? What had they done with her?

He tried to piece together exactly what had happened. At first in Oxford Adam had kept him up to date with events on the farm. Then his accounts became vaguer. Lander pressed him for details, and he had confessed to setting up "little puzzles" for Kerryl to solve to see how she would respond. But sabotaging the turbine that provided her electricity? Letting out her chickens so she lost one of her food sources? Come on! And then there was what Lander could see was an eating disorder. Kerryl had had problems with food before. At one time she'd been quite tubby. As she'd grown older she'd become more conscious of her figure, but she always found managing her weight difficult and she would see-saw between obsessive dieting and letting herself go. It seemed that the strain of extreme loneliness had driven the whole business completely out of hand and she had become totally fixated on her weight.

Why hadn't Adam done anything about what he must have seen was happening? He'd promised he would look after her. Lander couldn't work out from the diary exactly how Kerryl had died, but he was damn sure something could have been done to prevent it. Might she have imagined some of what went on? Did

Adam really do all the stuff she described? No wonder he'd scuttled off like a rat, rather than face Lander with the news.

He lay back and took deep breaths, forcing himself to calm down. Smashing things wouldn't achieve anything. He needed to compose himself, and focus.

Magda came in. 'Penny for them,' she said.

Lander shrugged. 'Maybe they're not worth that much. I was thinking about that fucker I was with in Oxford, the one I told you about who was conducting the tests.'

She sat down on the couch beside him and tucked up her legs. He caught a whiff of Eau d'Amour; She smelt very different from the way she had in the shed. She looked different too.

'Adam, you said his name was.'

'Yes.'

'What about him?'

'I want to kick the shit out of him.'

'Why?'

Lander raced upstairs, got the green notebook and tossed it on the sofa beside her.

'Read that. Then you'll see why.'

It was well into the following day before Lander saw Magda again. During this time he continued to seethe. His sister had been used, and so had he. Adam was responsible for her death; would he have got rid of him too? His first impulse had been to go to Oxford and beat Adam to a pulp. He still wanted to do that, but he also wanted to know why he'd done what he had. What sort of a sick pervert would stand by and watch a girl kill herself?

Then he had some more thoughts, and these were extremely uncomfortable because they concerned his own behaviour. He, Lander, was guilty too. If he hadn't left, if he'd not become obsessed with some internet garbage but stayed at the farm with Kerryl so that they faced the isolation together, there would be no Adam, either real or imagined, and his twin would still be alive.

Whatever, he needed to get to Oxford and confront Adam. The problem was, how? He had only the vaguest idea of the situation nationwide. He'd seen evidence of some attempts to tidy up and get things working again, but they were few. There was chaos everywhere and repairs would take a long time. And who would do them? Most of the people you'd expect to be working on this sort of thing were dead. He'd been held by Mickey for two weeks and nothing seemed to have changed in that time. There was still no mains electricity. Lander could charge his phone from the power generated by the wind turbine or the solar panels, but he couldn't find a cellular network and there was no internet. He checked these obsessively, because he assumed that whatever government there was would give the highest priority to things like that. The only sign of anything organised was a single FM radio station, all bland music, with a recorded announcement every few minutes saying that the Provisional Government was working to restore services as soon as possible, and listeners should remain where they were and stay tuned for further information and instructions.

The big issue in getting to Oxford was transport. It must still be illegal to travel. The Infection had petered out but the authorities wouldn't want people going around and risking spreading it again. If he were simply to set off down the M1 he was sure he'd be stopped. He might find himself back in jail. He guessed the powers that be would want to keep a handle on who went where, at least to begin with.

On the positive side, Steve had laid in a good stock of provisions. Or perhaps that was Kerryl. Or maybe even their Gran, who never liked to see an empty larder. There wasn't any fresh stuff, but there were lots of tins and packets. The turbine had kept the fridge and freezer working, and there was cheese (but no milk), frozen sausages, burgers, pizzas, lasagne, peas, and various vegetables. Naturally, he couldn't take the cold provisions with him, but he could stoke up before he left.

He went out to the yard and examined the Mini. It seemed none the worse for its stay at Mickey's, although there were a few feathers around and chicken shit on the rear seat. Thankfully the two petrol cans he'd got when Maisie had given him the car were still in the back and still full. The Mini was frugal, and there would be easily enough in the cans to get him to Oxford. That was good, because filling up on the way probably wouldn't be possible.

He went into the barn. The stalls where their few cows had been were empty, but the honcyed smell of hay remained, a bitter-sweet reminder of past times. When he and Kerryl were kids they used to play in there, jumping from the loft onto the soft piles of fodder. It was here that their Mam had died. When she got ill she had insisted on moving into the barn so as not to infect the rest of them. Granddad had fixed up a bed for her. Lander could remember looking at her from the doorway, and sounding off at Kerryl for getting too close. Maybe it was Kerryl who had carried the germs into the house and infected their grandparents. He couldn't bear that idea and he forced the thought away.

Their Land Rover was at the far end of the barn. The keys were under the seat where they were always kept. It was almost empty of fuel but it didn't matter, he wasn't going to use it. What he was after was Granddad's battered old road atlas. He found it rammed at the bottom of the front scuttle.

He took the atlas back to the house and began to work out a route which would stick to minor roads and avoid towns. It would take much longer, but it would be far safer.

'You're going to Oxford?' It was Magda, who'd come in and was standing behind him.

'Yes.'

'Good. I think that Adam guy's a bastard. What he did to your sister was murder.'

Inexplicably Lander found himself defending Adam. 'Yes, but I don't think he meant her to die.' Lander had liked Adam and had got on well with him during the short time they'd been together. He didn't seem like a killer. But then, neither did Magda.

'All I know is that if he'd treated my sister the way he treated yours I'd be after him with a hatchet. I think you should go.'

'I am. I'm going to go find him. It's just that for now I'm giving him the benefit.' Lander was surprised. He was certainly going to challenge Adam, but why was Magda pushing so hard?

'I'll come with you,' she said.

'What?'

'I'll come with you to Oxford.'

'Why?'

'How many reasons do you need? I'm an excellent map reader. I've travelled a lot and I'm good at finding my way around. I can do some of the driving. And despite you being such an arse, I like you. So I'll come. If you want me to, that is.'

Lander did. He'd assumed that Magda would have plans for putting her life back together and he'd expected to be going to Oxford on his own. He'd be delighted to have her with him. He put his hand over hers on his shoulder and looked up at her. Something in her eyes reached out to him. He stood up, and there was a moment's pause before she stepped into his arms. He held her. She was so bony, so skeletal there was hardly anything of her. A good squeeze would break her. He wondered again at how she'd managed to overwhelm a brute like Mickey. He turned his head and their lips met.

It was not great, but she was the first girl he'd kissed in many months. After a moment she pulled back.

'This doesn't mean anything,' she said. 'It's just for now.'

He didn't understand her message but he said, 'Okay.' He let go of her and moved away. Then he said, 'You can show how good you are with maps by working out a route that gives a wide berth to Mickey's farm.'

'Oh, I can do that. There's no way we're going anywhere near that place. When are you planning to leave?'

'As soon as we can. As soon as we're ready. There's no point hanging around here.'

'Right. We'd better warn Steve. We'll need to take some of his food.'

Lander thought that the food would have been there before Steve arrived so wasn't actually 'his', but he let it go.

Steve was out. When he came back, his reaction to the news of their trip to Oxford was a surprise.

'I'll come too.'

'What?'

'To Oxford.'

Before Lander could answer, Magda said, 'Great. Join the party,' and hugged him.

Lander was torn. There was no doubt of Magda's fire and spirit, but after her imprisonment and ill-treatment she was physically fragile; whereas Steve was beefy and strong. That could be useful. But there was a worry. Steve hadn't caught the Infection. What if that meant he was a dream walker? That was a worrying possibility. Steve would have to be watched. Nevertheless, it would be good to have another male with them.

'Welcome aboard,' he said.

'Great,' said Magda, and she kissed Steve on the cheek.

It was Steve's idea that they should go by boat.

'People don't realise it, but you can get almost anywhere in this country on the canals, and they're in much better nick than the roads. There'll be lots of places to hide – in tunnels, under bridges, in cuttings – and there won't be anyone else using them. There's still a travel ban, there are notices about it all over the town. But the army and the police will be watching for vehicles, they won't be thinking about the canals.'

Lander wasn't sure. 'But don't the canals go right alongside the roads in places? I know the one in the valley does. If there was something on the canal you'd see it from the road. And what about the locks? There are hundreds of them. Won't it be obvious we're using them? Anyway, going by canal will take ages.'

'We'll travel at night mostly,' said Steve, 'and we should be able to keep up a fair speed. We'll take the Rochdale Canal and then go on to the Ashton. There are not many locks at all on the Ashton, so we'll be able to make good time there. The worst bit will be Marple locks. There are fifteen of those, but once we're through it'll be plain sailing again, straight down the Trent and Mersey to Birmingham, and then to Oxford. If we can do some of the less exposed sections in daylight too we should get there in just over a week.'

'Sounds good to me,' said Magda.

Steve's estimate was lower than Lander had expected, but even so, a week was a long time. He wanted to track down Adam sooner than that if he could. Steve was making it all sound too easy, and he was suspicious. 'How come you're such an expert?' he said.

'My Mam and Dad used to do a lot of canal cruising. We even had our own barge.'

'Great,' said Magda, 'where is it?'

Steve shook his head. 'It's moored in the basin at Rochdale, but we can't use it. It's too big and noisy. There'd be much more risk of being seen in that. We need something smaller, something lighter and more manoeuvrable.'

'Right,' said Lander. Where were they going to find a boat like that?

'One good thing,' said Steve, 'is that we've got a really good engine, and it doesn't make any noise.'

'Have we?' said Lander. 'Where?'

'That bloody great horse out there in the field.'

'What, Joey?'

'Is that his name? He looks strong, and once he gets the boat moving it will be easy for him. Canals are flat. It's not as if he'll have to pull us up hills.'

'Cheap on fuel, too,' said Magda. 'He runs on grass.'

Steve left the room and Magda said, 'He seems to have this all figured out.'

Lander was more doubtful. 'I hope so. I was meaning to get to Oxford in less than a week, but I can see the sense in what he's suggesting.'

'Sounds the best way to go to me,' said Magda. 'And it will give you time to think through what you're going to do when you eventually meet up with this Adam guy.'

Steve came back with an armful of beer cans, Final Reckoning, a strong lager that was one of Lander's favourites.

'I found these in the off-licence in town and I've been saving them,' he said. They popped a can each.

It seemed to be all settled. The atlas showed the canals as well as the roads, and Magda, with Steve's help, started working out a route. Lander was happy to leave them to it. He took his lager and ambled around the house and the yard, revisiting things he'd never taken much notice of when they'd all lived there. He had a sad moment behind the barn when he looked at the remains of a fire and saw charred animal bones. He knew from Kerryl's diary that they'd belonged to Buster. He also came across a board with the name Paradise Farm still just legible on it. So little had changed, but then so much had too.

He returned to Magda and Steve. They had got as far as the route around Birmingham. He took another can.

He had another lager after that. Then he and Magda found some lamb chops in the freezer. He had another lager while they thawed them out, and then another while they lit a fire in the grate and cooked them in Gran's old frying pan. Then he had one more to accompany the meal. Then he lost count.

Later he was vaguely aware of Magda helping him to bed. When he woke in the night his throat was parched and his head felt as though there was an imp inside his skull hammering to get out. He was in his mother's double bed. Magda was asleep beside him.

20

PREPARATIONS

LANDER FELL ASLEEP again, and when he next awoke Magda had gone. He found her in the kitchen, washing up. He sat down at the table and put his head in his hands.

'Did we drink all that?' he said, surveying the litter of empty cans.

'You and Steve did.'

'Come on, Miss Goody. I saw you having some too.'

'A couple of cans, that's all,' Magda said. 'There was no way I could keep up with you two. Drinking for England, you were.'

Lander groaned. 'Did you put me to bed?'

'I did indeed.'

'Thank you. Did you have your wicked way with me?'

'Fat chance. There was absolutely nothing about you that was capable of standing up last night. Now, how about a full English breakfast? Sausages, greasy bacon, fried eggs, fried bread, black pudding...'

'No, don't,' Lander protested, his stomach heaving at the thought.

'OK.' She laughed. 'We don't have any of that stuff anyway, so instead you can help me clear up this mess.'

Lander began to gather the empty cans and drop them into a plastic sack. His head was pounding and each can landing on the others was like a blow. He tried to place them gently, but that meant bending into the sack, which was just as bad. It was the same whenever he had a hangover; the unanswerable question, why did I do it?

He couldn't recall much of the previous evening, but he had a recollection of getting into an argument with Steve.

'Was I obnoxious last night?'

'No more than usual.'

'I seem to remember yelling at Steve.'

'You did.'

'Why?'

'Don't ask me. You and Steve are the ones who were shitfaced.' Magda came away from the sink and dried her hands. 'You asked Steve if he and Kerryl were planning to get together again, and he said he'd been hoping so because your sister was hot, despite looking like you, and you said he didn't deserve her and he had better keep his filthy hands off her, and he said you were only saying that because you wanted to shag her yourself, and you took a swing at him and missed and fell over, and so did he. I don't think I've left anything out, except that you both seemed to have completely forgotten that the poor girl isn't with us anymore.'

Lander was ashamed. He'd decided he didn't like Steve. He was aggrieved at the way he'd made himself at home in their house and helped himself to anything he fancied. He suspected him of wanting to help himself to Magda too. He hadn't liked the notion of him being with Kerryl, and what Steve had accused him of had been way out of order; he'd been quite right to take exception to it. But on the other hand, Steve was trying to help them, and he probably didn't mean any of what he said. He was thick, that was all.

'Sorry,' he said.

'It's probably Steve you need to be sorry too, he's the one you tried to lay out. But I think he owes you an apology too.' Magda came beside him and put her arm around his waist and her head on his shoulder. 'It's all right. I guess you both needed to let off steam.'

'Is he still in bed?'

'I expect so. Unless he's run away. I haven't seen him, I slept with you. Not that you would have noticed.'

'He must have been up, though. There are two mugs on the table. One's yours, the other must be his.'

For an instant Magda looked confused. Then she said, 'Well you've got it wrong this time, Sherlock. They're both mine.'

'Really? One's got white dregs in it and you take your coffee black.'

Magda looked irritated and moved away. 'I poured it by mistake. There was milk already in the mug and I didn't realise. Anyway, who are you? The coffee police?' She tossed him a tea towel. 'Dry those things on the draining board.'

The cutlery and pans on the stainless steel made a noise like a foundry, and the scraping of the crockery was like tectonic plates moving, but he stuck at it.

In the earlier, pre-lager part of last evening they'd agreed that Lander and Magda would spend the next day getting together everything they'd need for the trip, while Steve would go down the hill to search the canal for a suitable craft to take them there. Steve didn't think this would be a problem because he had an idea of where to look. But he didn't get up until the late afternoon, and after his efforts with the tea towel Lander needed a rest, so none of this happened.

However, the following day it did. All three of them were up early. Lander felt better and so, it seemed, did Steve. They shook hands.

'Okay?' said Lander.

'Okay,' said Steve.

'Right then,' said Magda. 'Let's get to work.'

Steve went off on his Lambretta, and Lander and Magda started on their own jobs. Magda took control. She was very methodical. She packed food into plastic crates while Lander raided the kitchen drawers and Granddad's tool bench for anything that he thought might come in useful – torches, knives, cable ties, duct tape, basic tools, rope, and so on. When they'd got it all together, Lander backed the Land Rover out into the yard and they loaded it with the things they'd gathered.

Next, they both went into the field to find Joey. Lander was worried that he might have wandered off because the fence was broken and there was nothing to stop him, but there he was, in the middle of the pasture, grazing. He was wary of them but Magda had some carrots she'd found in the cellar and they drew him over. They'd started to sprout but Joey didn't appear to mind. Magda seemed to have a way with horses, and while Joey ate she got a halter around his neck. They led him up to the yard and put him in his old stable. He seemed happy to be home.

'Here,' said Magda, 'you hold him steady while I look at that gash on his leg.'

The wound was nasty but it was healing. Magda bathed it gently and applied some antiseptic cream. Joey stamped and tossed his head, but he seemed to know they were helping him and he stayed calm.

'What did your sister use when she groomed him?' said Magda.

'It's all there,' said Lander, 'in that bag on the shelf.'

Magda took the brushes and the combs and got to work on Joey. She brushed him until his flanks began to show some of their previous gloss, and she combed his mane and tail.

'You've done this before,' said Lander.

'Yes. I used to have a pony. Before the Infection.'

'What happened to it?'

'I don't know. Somebody broke into our stable and she ran away.'

By the time they'd finished, Steve was back. He was excited.

'Good news,' he said. 'Top good news in fact. I've found the perfect things to get us to Oxford. Just behind that big factory on the main road, the one that backs onto the canal...'

'Yes, Masham's, I know it.'

'...whatever, anyway there they were, inflatables, two of them. Good sized ones, really tough and in good nick. They'll be perfect. They've got a shallow draft so they don't need much water.'

'Why is that good?'

'The canals might be low in some places, too low for a standard barge but fine for these. We can hook them together, put our gear in one and ride in the other, and the horse can pull them both. We can take turns leading Joey along the towpath. And the best bit is they have, like, these wooden runners fixed to the underneath. Know what I mean? Some of the locks have, like, grass ramps up the sides, and with the runners we might be able to haul the boats up instead of using the lock, and that could save time.'

It sounded good news, and over coffee they told Steve what they'd achieved.

In the evening all three of them sat at the kitchen table and they ate cheese on toast, using the last of a loaf and some cheddar that Magda had found in the freezer. During the meal they talked about the journey. Lander felt a mixture of excitement and caution. Magda had written down the route in detail and marked it in the atlas, so that when they got to junctions there would be no confusion and it would be clear which way they were to go. What they didn't know was who or what they might meet on the way.

'There are bound to be patrols around,' said Lander. 'They seem to be checking on everything. I expect they'll be made up of arkies.'

'What?' said Steve.

'Arkies. It's the word they use for the people who have sat out the Infection in the government's protected areas. They call them arks. They'll have been isolated for weeks. They won't have much idea of what's been going on and they might also be a bit scared.'

'From what I've seen the patrols are around only during the day,' said Steve, 'so if we travel at night we should miss them.'

'And they'll mainly be interested in the towns,' said Lander. 'We need to avoid those as far as we can.'

'Can't avoid them all,' said Steve. 'The canals run right through them, that's why they were built. But in the big places, like Manchester and Birmingham, they go through the industrial areas and there won't be anything going on there.'

'Some of the survivors could be a problem,' said Lander. 'You'll remember from my letter in Kerryl's diary that some people, men, who thought they were immune weren't really. They'd caught the virus but in a different way, and it damaged their brains.'

'Yes. And that can make them unpredictably violent,' said Magda.

'You mean they take a swing at you for nothing at all,' said Steve, looking hard at Lander.

Lander rounded on him. 'It wasn't nothing, what you said about me and Kerryl...'

'Now now, you two,' Magda said sharply.

'Sorry mate,' said Steve.

'All right,' said Lander. 'All I'm saying is that it's not only the patrols we'll need to watch out for. We could come across some of these other weirdoes too.'

'There might be kids as well,' said Magda.

'Kids?' said Steve.

'What about them?' said Lander. 'I thought most of the kids had caught it.'

'Most did,' said Magda. 'Children were particularly vulnerable to the Infection and not many of them survived. But a few did. Some of them are on their own and they're slowly starving to death. That's mainly the younger ones. The older ones have formed into gangs and they're completely out of control, they'll do anything. They'll be watching out for the PG too, and they might well be keeping away from towns and roads like we plan to. So we could run into them, and they could be dangerous.'

'What, kids? Dangerous?' said Lander.

'You'd be surprised,' said Magda.

'How come you know all this?' said Steve.

'The covens are trying to find lost kids so they can take them in and look after them. I came across a few when I was with the Bonnies. We were caring for about a dozen kids and I talked to some of them.'

'Bonnies? Covens? Are you a witch or something?' said Steve.

Magda laughed. 'Coven just means band or group. It's usually used for witches but it doesn't have to be.'

'Magda was a member of a women's group before we met,' Lander explained. 'There are several of them.'

'What, gangs of women? Where? Lead me to them.'

'They call themselves covens in memory of all the innocent women who have been victimised in the past,' said Magda, icily.

'Will they help us?' asked Lander.

'I don't know,' said Magda. 'I think my lot, the Bonnies, would but they're not near where we're going. Some of the others might. I can't speak for all of them, they're not all the same. And just because one would doesn't mean the others will. Some covens don't get on with some of the others.'

'Typical women,' said Steve.

Magda glared at him. 'Those "typical women" are doing useful things the authorities are neglecting. Things that could well save your life.'

Steve looked chastised, and changed the subject.

'If we're trying to spot trouble, there are the stray animals too,' he said. 'Some of the dogs are insane. One nearly went for me today in the town. Got me in a doorway and stood there growling. Luckily there was a brick I could chuck at it. There's other stuff too – wildcats, boars, all sorts, know what I mean? I think we should take the guns.'

Lander could see the sense in that, but he could also see a problem. 'I don't know,' he said. 'The patrols will be armed, and they'll probably be jumpy. If they see us with guns they might think we mean trouble and take a pot at us.'

'That's a risk we'll have to face,' said Magda. 'I think Steve's right. We don't know what we're going to come across. We should take the guns, but we must keep them out of sight and only use them if there's a real emergency.' Magda pushed her plate aside and replaced it with a notepad. 'Right,' she said, 'let's check. What have we got and what else might we need?'

They spent the next half hour brainstorming, while Magda's list grew. It was hard to get Steve to focus because he kept making suggestions that he thought were funny but were really just irritating: Xbox, condoms, bubble bath, dartboard. Lander and Magda tried to ignore him, and eventually he took the hint. When the list seemed complete, Lander read it out.

'I think we've got everything pretty much covered,' he said.

'Yes,' said Magda. 'But we don't have enough food to last us for the whole trip. Maybe we should add some more.'

'I don't think the inflatables will take it,' said Steve. 'They're not very big, and we need room for all our personal stuff – clothes, sleeping bags and that.'

'In that case, we'll just have to forage on the way,' said Magda.

Lander was doubtful. He'd seen the state of some of the stores he'd passed. They'd be fine if most of them were like the ones in Snaith, but if they were more like the ones in Walbrough, where everything decent had been taken or trashed, they might find nothing. However, there seemed to be no other option, so that's what they agreed to do.

'We're OK for bedding,' said Magda. 'You've got your sleeping bag, Lander, I've got Kerryl's. Steve, think you'll be all right with just a duvet?'

'Sure. The nights are getting colder but we can huddle together, know what I mean?' He nudged Magda. Lander tried to ignore it.

'One more thing,' Steve said. He got up and went to pick up a large canvas bag he'd left by the door. 'When I was in the town today, not only did I solve our transport problems, I also got these.' He unzipped the bag and tipped out its contents with a flourish. 'Ta-da!'

What Steve had found were army fatigues in brown-green camouflage.

'Where did you get those?'

'In the discount store. There's been a fire and not much is left, but there's a store room at the back that's untouched and there are piles of these on a table. I reckon they look close enough to the uniform of the patrols to pass, don't you? I hope I've got the sizes right.'

Lander's irritation with Steve evaporated. He may be stupid, he may be irritating – he was both – but he did have some good ideas sometimes. He could forgive him a lot for finding the inflatables, and now these. He clapped him on the shoulder.

'Hey, dude, that is fucking brilliant,' he said. 'Let's get 'em on.'

A few minutes later and they were in the fatigues and ready to go. Lander took a last look at the cosy kitchen. It was tempting to put off leaving for another day, to open the bottle of Vodka he'd seen in the sideboard, maybe light a fire against the late summer chill, but he knew that the sooner they left the sooner he could catch up with Adam. And the sooner he did that the easier it would be to put to rest the thoughts that plagued him about the fate of his twin.

21

――――――

TRAVEL

BEFORE LANDER HAD finally dropped out of school he had started a course in Sociology. It involved more essay writing than he was happy with, but the ideas were interesting and he liked the discussions, and especially the practical assignments. One of these was when the teacher divided the class into small groups and gave each a task to complete. There were only two rules: one was that there were to be no leaders, and the other was that each member of the group was to undertake a different job. The teacher videoed it and the class watched the videos and talked about them. One thing that came out was how quickly and easily the group members assumed roles, picking them up without direction. And once they'd taken on responsibility for a function they stuck with it, even defending their right to it.

Lander was thinking about this as they settled into their journey towards Oxford. Without any debate, Magda took charge of map reading and navigation. She sat in the front boat and alerted them to what lay ahead, particularly places where the canal came close to major roads and built-up areas. Steve had taken on controlling the boats, including handling the locks and dealing with some of the intricacies of the canal system. Lander managed Joey. This involved leading him along the towpath, making sure that when morning came he had access to good grass, that he was comfortably but securely tethered so he couldn't run off, that the harness wasn't chaffing him, and that the gash on his leg was healing. Each of them had their work and they got on with it with minimum reference to the other two.

Steve's idea of hauling the boats up the grass banks beside the locks was a non-starter. Without unloading them they were far too heavy to lift out of the water, and it would have taken longer to take all their stuff out and reload them than it did to pass through the locks in the conventional manner. However, it meant that during these times they were exposed and at their most vulnerable.

Travelling by night was easy, even when there was no moon. It wasn't as if they could stray off their route; they just followed where the waterways took them, and when they came to a fork or junction it was usually obvious which way they should go. Sometimes there were even signposts. They'd stop every hour or so for Magda to study the maps by torchlight and alert them to what was coming.

Travel by night, sleep by day; it should have been a simple recipe but it was not. The idea was that as dawn approached they'd find a suitable tunnel or bridge, and Steve would check the boats and make them fast while Lander saw to Joey and Magda sorted out their rations. Then they would settle down in the boats to sleep the day away. And there lay the problem. Steve and Lander took one boat and Magda the other, but the cold from the water struck through the flimsy hulls and chilled them to the bone. After an hour or so of this Magda came from her boat to theirs and lay between them. The three huddled together, but even so, they were cold and sleep was fitful.

On the second night, when he realised he was never going to get warm, Lander crept out of the boat and lay down on the canal bank. It was not long before he was joined by Magda.

'You can't sleep either,' she said.

'No, too cold. It's fucking freezing under that bridge and the water's like ice.'

'Right. How do you think it's going?'

'What, the journey? Not bad. Actually, I'm quite enjoying it. It's restful, just the clop of Joey's hooves, the gentle splashing of the water and the slowly unrolling landscape.'

Magda gave him a nudge. 'Get you. Who would have thought you had a poetic streak?'

'Not you, obviously,' said Lander. He looked around. 'What do you think of Steve?'

'How do you mean? He's all right. A bit of a laugh really.'

'I mean his behaviour. Have you noticed anything funny about him?'

'No, should I?'

Lander wondered whether he should tell her what he knew of the dream walkers. All sleeping together in the boat, they'd know if anything happened. Perhaps the dream walking only occurred during darkness, and if Steve was a walker he might be escaping the symptoms by being awake and busy then. He decided to leave it.

'Thank goodness there's nobody much about,' he said.

'Yes. We seem to be on our own. There were lights on in a couple of the houses in a town back there, but all the others were dark.'

'Yeah, and there were emergency beacons on the M62.' He remembered looking up and seeing blue flashing lights on the hillside high above them, then realising they must be on the motorway. 'Heaven knows what they were about. There can't be enough traffic for a motorway pile-up.'

'Mm.' Magda thought for a moment, then she said, 'We're not getting on fast enough.'

Lander agreed. He wanted to get to Oxford and sort Adam out, but he hadn't set the pace they were following. 'It was your idea to stop early,' he said. 'You thought we oughtn't to get caught in the daylight in the middle of Manchester, and it would be best to leave it till tonight and get right across the city in one go.'

'Yes, I know I did, but we're going more slowly than I expected.'

'Well, poor old Joey can't gallop!' Lander laughed at the vision of the horse galumphing along the towpath, dragging the boats behind him. 'All we can do is take the risk of doing some of the journey in daylight.'

There seemed to be no alternative. When they put it to Steve he was against it, but Lander and Magda overruled him. They agreed that they would push ahead across Manchester the next night, and once they were clear of the city and in open country they would carry on for a couple of hours after daybreak.

'A lot of the Trent and Mersey goes through Staffordshire,' said Steve. 'From what I remember that's fairly rural, so there won't be many people around. We should be all right.'

Lander's main concern about the new plan was not that they might be seen, it was overworking Joey. 'He's got to have time to rest and eat,' he said. 'He's a big horse and he needs a lot of grass.'

'We've got paddles,' said Steve. 'Some of the time we'll use those and he can take breaks.'

When Lander had been in Oxford he'd asked what things were like in London. He'd been told that it was a no-go area, an anarchic nightmare choked with the dead and the barely living, impossible to enter safely. He'd expected that Manchester would be the same, but the city was quiet. They saw hardly anyone, and those they did see paid them no attention. That included a patrol that cruised by quite close to the canal but ignored them. The result was that they got through the city quickly and without mishap.

On the other side of Manchester the canal went under a railway line. They were moving towards it when they heard an approaching rumble and saw an enormous train of fuel tankers. They hid under the bridge while the train rumbled overhead. Lander was cheered by the sight. This stuff was going somewhere. The fuel would be used to power vehicles, generate electricity and contribute to the long process of restoring normality.

'Wish,' said Magda.

'What?'

'Wish. My Nan used to say that you should wish if you were under a bridge when a train crossed over it.'

Magda closed her eyes and screwed up her face. Lander didn't know what to ask for. Before the Infection he might have dreamt of playing for Yorkshire, or scoring with Charlene Brooker, a really hot girl at Kerryl's school. But now? There was no Yorkshire cricket any more, and all the girls he'd known were probably dead. Nevertheless, he said, 'Okay,' and shut his eyes too. But nothing would come and all he did was pretend, while he listened to the thunder of the waggons overhead.

The train passed and they kept going, even though it was now broad daylight. The land was flatter here and there were fewer locks. The countryside was open and there was no sign of life. The villages were deserted but they always knew when they were getting close to one because of the unmistakable odour, the stench of things rotting. Manchester had reeked of smoke and chlorine; that had been unpleasant but this was worse. It was a unique smell, sickening and pervasive.

There was a brief scare when they went into a short tunnel and found a man there. He was leaning against the wall and mumbling. He watched them as they passed him.

'Horsey, horsey, I've got a horsey,' he called after them. 'Horsey, keep your tail up. A wail of a tale. I've seen a horse fly. Bet yours can't.' He cackled with delirious laughter.

'Mad fucker,' said Steve. 'Been on the zombie juice I expect.'

'More likely it's the Infection,' said Magda. 'He's a dream walker. He's survived the fever and the virus has got into his brain and tipped him over. We're lucky that at the moment he's in happy land and not violent.'

'Doesn't look as though he could do much,' said Steve. 'He looks a wimp to me.'

'You'd be surprised,' said Magda. 'Men who get affected in this way develop a sort of nervous strength. They can be very difficult to deal with.'

'Men,' said Steve. 'Don't chicks get it too?'

'Not so far as we know.'

Lander said nothing, but what Magda was saying surprised him. Where had she learnt about dream walking? As far as Lander knew it had been discovered by *thetruth* people only when the Infection was well established. Adam had known about it, but nobody else he'd met seemed to. Magda was talking as if she was an expert on it.

They kept going until around midday, and stopped when they found an inviting looking barn close by a bridge. The bridge offered scant protection, but by tying the boats side by side they were able to conceal them from a casual sighting. A bonus was that there was plenty of hay and straw in the barn.

'We can sleep on that,' said Steve.

Lander remembered the last time that he and Magda had slept on hay.

'Joey's happy,' said Steve, as the horse attacked a bale.

'Good for him,' said Magda. 'Better watch he doesn't eat too much, though, or too fast. Come on, gutsy.' She took Joey's bridle and nudged him away. 'It's a pity we humans can't eat hay. We're getting low on food.'

'What, really?' said Lander. 'Already? But we had loads.'

'Yes, and you've eaten it. You two are like bloody vultures. We're getting short of water, too.'

They'd been prepared to wash in canal water, and so long as they chose the spot carefully that had been all right, but none of them fancied drinking it.

'What shall we do?' said Lander.

'Well, Einstein, I think we'd better get some more,' said Magda.

'OK, Ms Einstein,' said Lander. 'How? Oh, I know. I'll just pop along to the shops.'

'There are fish in the canal,' said Steve. 'My dad used to catch 'em.'

'What are they?' said Lander.

Steve shrugged. 'Carp? Roach? I dunno.'

'Did you eat them?'

'No, he used to throw them back. But I expect you could. Eat them, I mean. I'll try to catch some tomorrow.'

'I don't want to be rude,' said Magda, 'but I don't fancy eating anything that might live in this water. I've seen some of the stuff people have thrown into it. The next town we come to we'll go on a raid.'

Steve picked up the atlas. 'There's one not far ahead,' he said. 'It'll be best to go while there's still some light, so we can see what we're doing, know what I mean?'

'That's a good idea,' said Magda. 'We don't want to be trying to find our way around a strange place in the dark.'

'We can't all go,' said Lander. 'Somebody should stay here with Joey and the boats. Why don't I go with Steve?'

'Why?' said Magda. 'You think this is a job for the men and a mere girl couldn't manage?'

'Course not,' said Lander. 'But I do think we can carry more than you can. I'm not being macho, it's just that you're still not fully recovered from your holiday with Mickey. Anyway, if somebody comes along the canal bank you'll be better than Steve or me at talking your way out of any problems.'

Magda didn't look convinced but she agreed. 'Oh, all right,' she said.

'You'd better have a gun,' said Steve. 'You never know who could turn up and you might need to defend yourself.'

He left the barn and returned a few minutes later with one of the shotguns. They'd been well hidden in the bottom of the boat and this was the first time on their voyage one had been brought out.

'Do you know how to use this?'

'Yes,' said Magda, rolling her eyes.

'Don't be afraid to, and if you do, wait until whatever you're firing at is fairly close. Squeeze the trigger, don't snatch it.'

'Thank you,' said Magda, fluttering her eyelashes. 'You're such a big strong man. Can you show me which is the trigger? Is it this little bit sticking out here?'

'All right,' said Steve, resentfully. 'I was just saying.'

'You might leave me the box of cartridges too. In case I miss the first time, being only a girl and that.'

'All right, all right,' said Steve.

'Yes,' said Magda, 'it's a good job that I thought to bring them, seeing as neither of you two geniuses did.'

It looked from the map as though the small town they had in mind was about two miles away, a brisk walk along the canal towpath, and Steve and Lander set out at the end of the afternoon. They thought they would be able to get back well before dark. On the way they decided that they'd hide whatever they found and pick it up when they came along the canal that night with the boats, rather than try to carry it back.

Ever since they'd left Walbrough Lander had been concerned that the roads, the railway and the canal were often close together.

'It's because they were all built to follow the easiest route,' said Steve.

'Yeah, but it means it's hard to keep out of sight of the road. We've been lucky so far but I'm bothered that somebody official might see us. We haven't got any ID, or at least I haven't.'

Lander's fears were realised when they still had half a mile to go. They were on a straight part of the canal with the road only a few metres away and nowhere to hide when they became aware of movement beside them. It was a bus.

'Shit,' said Lander. 'Act normal. Just keep walking.'

They did, marching along as if they had every right to be there. The bus slowed, and they could see that the passengers were wearing army uniforms. There were about twenty of them, in full battle kit, and armed. They were all looking at Lander and Steve, and several of them were holding rifles at the ready.

The bus stopped and one of the soldiers stood in the open doorway. He had a sergeant's stripes and was talking into a field communicator.

Steve gave a wave.

'For fuck's sake, what are you doing?' snarled Lander, horrified. 'Do you want to get shot?' He was trembling. He'd heard tales of patrols firing on people suspected of being vagrants.

'Nothing to lose,' said Steve, calmly. 'Act normal, you said.'

'I didn't say stick your fucking neck out. You're out of your mind.'

They kept walking, Lander expecting at any moment to hear a shouted order to halt, or perhaps even the staccato stutter of gunfire. Neither of these things happened. The figure in the doorway went back inside, and the bus moved off and disappeared down the road, away from the direction they were heading.

Lander let out a huge sigh. 'Jesus, that was scary.' His legs were trembling. 'I never thought we'd get away. Why didn't they stop us?'

'Maybe acting normal worked,' said Steve.

'More likely they got another call. They left pretty fast.' Lander's heart was still racing, and there was a cold patch of sweat in the small of his back. 'Where did the bus come from? I never heard it till it was on us.'

'It must be an electric one,' said Steve. 'I'd heard they were using them, and it makes sense if petrol and diesel are short. They must be able to get power, though.'

'What, really?' said Lander.

Steve didn't get the sarcasm. 'Stands to reason,' he said. 'They'd need electric power to charge it, know what I mean? There were a lot of them on it. I wonder how far they can go between charges.'

Lander didn't care. The technical specifications of the bus were irrelevant. What mattered was that they'd been seen. What would happen now? Surely the unit would know that despite the fatigues the two of them were wearing they weren't in the army. Somebody somewhere would check who was authorised to be in the area. He had no doubt they'd be back.

'We'd better move,' he said. 'Magda and Joey are in the direction they've gone. Let's find what we came for and get back as soon as we can. Then we need to get the hell out of here.'

They saw no one else. The visit to the town was a success, although Lander was still too keyed up to do a proper job and forgot some of the things Magda had told them to look out for. The town reminded him of Snaith. There were no people, neither was there the reek of death that afflicted most other towns, but there were signs of damage and destruction. They found a store which still had bottled water and plenty of tinned food, and, to Steve's delight, beer.

'Dancing Vicar,' he said, picking up a can and looking at the leaping clergyman on the label. 'My dad used to like this. It's an old man's drink but it's better than nothing.'

On the edge of the town they'd passed a deserted cottage and Lander had spotted a wheelbarrow in the garden. They'd taken it and now they loaded it up. Steve was for pushing it back to the boats but Lander insisted they stick to their plan, so they left the barrow hidden where they could pick up its contents later. They each took a Dancing Vicar and one for Magda, and jogged back along the towpath.

22

____

CHALLENGES

'FOR FUCK'S SAKE, how many's that?' said Lander, heaving on yet another lock gate. 'You said it would be easy once we were through Manchester.'

'I'd forgotten this bit,' said Steve.

'*The Trent and Mersey is one of the earliest canals built by Brindley,*' Magda read from an information board at the canal side. '*Passing through pleasant countryside it climbs from the Cheshire plain through a series of locks.*'

'Too bloody right about the locks,' said Lander. 'But this is not what I call pleasant countryside.' Every bit of him ached, legs, arms, shoulders, back.

'It says here there are thirty-one of them,' said Magda, 'and the series is sometimes referred to as "Heartbreak Hill".'

'Great. More like back break hill. It's the last time I listen to you,' he grumbled at Steve as they dragged the boats into the next lock. 'I thought you knew these canals.'

'I didn't remember this part. It was ages ago we were here. I was just a kid.'

Lander made a noise somewhere between a snarl and a growl.

'At least all these stops mean Joey's having a good day,' said Magda.

It wasn't worth harnessing the horse to pull the boats from one lock to the next so they were doing it by hand, which meant that Joey was redundant and could enjoy the waterside grass, ambling amiably from one lock to the next as they rose through the tier.

'Cheer up,' she went on. 'Only two more and then it's the tunnel.'

'The what?'

'It says here there's a tunnel,' she said, reading again from the board. 'It takes you under Harecastle Hill towards Stoke. How's your claustrophobia? Because it's over a mile and a half long and it's narrow. Better hope we don't meet anything coming the other way.'

'I suppose you don't remember that, either,' Lander said to Steve.

'Oh yes, I remember that. It's creepy. My dad told us there was a ghost in there. Some woman who was murdered in the tunnel and now she haunts it.'

'Great. Now you tell us.' Lander didn't believe in ghosts but he disliked cramped spaces, and the idea of having to go through a tunnel was worse than any threat of haunting.

'Yeah, it's all coming back to me now,' said Steve. 'Her head was cut off and she walks up and down on the water looking for it. My dad said that some boatmen take long detours to avoid having to go through the tunnel. He said as well that sometimes more boats go in than come out.'

Magda was still reading. 'It doesn't say anything about that here, but it does say there's no towpath, so how are we going to get through?'

'Same way as we've done the bridges and the shorter tunnels,' said Steve. 'We'll paddle. Two of us can take the boats through while the third goes with Joey over the hill to meet us at the other end.'

It was inevitable there would be an argument about who the third would be. Steve said he should go through the tunnel as he was the canal guide, and besides, he'd done it before. Magda said that if they thought she was going to look after the horse just because she was the girl in the group they had another think coming. As for Lander, although the last thing he wanted was to go into a pitch-black hole, he would seriously lose face if he looked to be hanging back, so he had to pretend to be keen on going in the boats too. They settled it by tossing a coin. Magda lost, which meant that she took Joey.

Lander and Steve picked up a paddle each and began to move the two inflatables along the narrow approach to the tunnel entrance. It looked like the wall of a house and the mouth was a rectangle, but as soon as they'd gone through this the roof became arched in the way Lander had expected.

His stomach felt unsteady as they exchanged the brightness of the day for the damp, cold dark. Steve rested a torch on the prow of the boat so that it shone ahead and they could see where they were going, but all it showed was a dull, straight passage boring into the hill. The walls were lined with bricks, millions of them, stained with brown from the ores that oozed through the earth. Periodically there were numbers sprayed in yellow paint on the wall; Lander guessed these were distances, probably in yards.

What had Magda said? More than a mile and a half? How many yards was that? It would take forever.

As far as he could tell the tunnel seemed to be dead straight, but he couldn't see the exit. It was too far away, he supposed. The paddling was hard work and despite the chill he was soon sweating. He thought about the ghost, but there was no sound apart from their laboured breathing and the lapping of the water.

'Stop a minute,' said Steve. 'I just want to cool down.'

Lander took hold of Steve's paddle while he pulled the top of his fatigues over his head. He turned to put it behind him and a sleeve flapped the torch. Lander saw what was going to happen an instant before it did and lunged to save it, but he was too late. The torch rolled off the edge of the boat and plopped into the water.

'Shit,' Lander shouted. The word bounced around the tunnel and echoed back to them.

They both leant over the side. There was a faint light below, where the sunken torch glowed through the brown water. Then it went out. It was like a switch being thrown, like having your eyes suddenly covered. Several hundred yards behind was the tiny bead of daylight that was the tunnel's entrance; ahead of and around them was inky dark.

'Fuck,' said Lander. 'What did you do that for?'

'I didn't do anything,' said Steve.

'You caught the torch with your sleeve, you idiot.'

'It was you trying to grab it. You knocked it off.'

'I fucking didn't, I was trying to save it.'

The row reverberated in the confined space.

'We'd better head back,' said Lander.

'Don't be daft,' said Steve. 'What good would that do?'

'We can't go on in the dark.'

''Course we can. It's a straight line. We just keep paddling till we see daylight.'

It was Lander's worst nightmare. He'd been locked in a small cell, but there had been daylight. He'd been wheeled into a scanner, but Janice had been there and he'd had a panic button that would have got him out in an instant. He'd been chained in a lightless shed, but there had been space around him. Here he was in a narrow space, and the darkness was total. His arms trembled so much that it was hard to hang on to the paddle. A clammy sweat soaked his back. His pulse raced.

Bizarrely, it was the difficulty of what they were trying to do that kept his fear under control. Steve had said that all they had to do was to keep the inflatables going in a straight line. That sounded easy, but how could they establish that line when they couldn't see anything ahead? They collided with the brick walls of the tunnel again and again, bouncing from side to side, the boats slewing. At one stage the rear boat, the one they should have been towing, got in front of the one they were in. Steve's response seemed to be that the greater the disorder the harder he should paddle, and it was impossible to undo the tangle until it occurred to Lander to use the pinpoint of the tunnel's entrance, behind them, as a marker to realign the boats. Once this was done they managed to straighten themselves out and resume their progress. At one stage Lander allowed himself to look back over his shoulder. The tunnel mouth was barely visible. He forced himself to slow his breathing and concentrate on the rhythm of paddling to keep the claustrophobia at bay.

Suddenly there was a wailing sound. It was obvious at once that it was Steve, but even so it made Lander jump.

'I'm a headless ghost,' Steve warbled in a quavering voice.

Lander sighed. 'Fuck off, will you?'

'All right,' said Steve. 'I was only trying to cheer you up by adding a bit of drama.'

'Well don't.'

Lander didn't need any phantom to chill his spine or curdle his blood: the thought of the millions of tons of rock and earth heaped over their heads did that on its own. Were they halfway through yet? A quarter? How long would this torture last?

The end of the tunnel was at first so indistinct that Lander couldn't be sure that he was seeing it. It was faint as a distant star. Was that it? Was that the exit? He strained into the blackness. Yes! There it was. No more than a speck, but definitely, definitely daylight. His spirits rose and he began to paddle harder.

'Steady,' warned Steve. 'You'll tangle us up again.'

It probably took no more than twenty minutes to complete their ordeal, but it seemed much longer. As they approached the end of the tunnel the light seeping in increased, growing brighter and brighter until at last they burst into the glare of glorious day. There was green, there was birdsong, and there were Magda and Joey, waiting for them on the canal side.

'My God, you really did see something in there, didn't you,' said Magda as Lander slumped over his paddle and Steve made the boats fast. 'You're as white as a sheet.'

They rested just long enough for Lander to calm down, to tidy up the boat and harness Joey, and then they carried on towards Stoke.

Joey was refreshed and pressed on willingly, and they got on well. However, there seemed to be more going on here than they'd seen before. There were troops, vehicles and machinery clearing the streets. The air was thick with dust, and smoke from piles of burning rubbish. Although all the working personnel seemed to be occupied and weren't looking in their direction, they were worried they'd be spotted.

'What do you think?' said Steve.

'Best to hole up,' said Magda. 'Go back to travelling by night until we're through here. I suggest we find somewhere to hide till nightfall and get some rest, so we can crack on once it's dark. What do you think, Lander?'

Lander had been in a stupor since emerging from the tunnel.

'What? Oh, yeah,' he grunted.

Magda gave him a long look. 'Well thank you for your contribution,' she said.

They found a bridge under which they could hide. This time, because of all the additional activity, they decided that rather than bed down on the bank it would be more sensible to go back to their original plan of sleeping in the boats. Or trying to. They all three huddled together against the cold. Lander swaddled himself in his sleeping bag and wrapped a blanket around him, tucking it under his feet, but to no avail. Another obstacle to rest was that in his imagination he kept returning to the terrifying, sightless confine of the tunnel. He pictured roof falls, things lurking in the water, simultaneous pursuit from both entrance and exit trapping him in the cloying, stifling blackness. He looked at his two companions. Steve had dropped off immediately. Magda, too, seemed now to be sleeping. They were in each other's arms. He felt a twinge of jealousy.

Carefully, so as not to rock the boat, he disentangled himself from his bedding and crawled out. He sat on the grass bank beside the canal and put on his trainers; no shoes in the boats was Steve's only rule. He needed some exercise to stretch his legs, so he left the canal and went towards what looked to be a public park. He knew there was a chance he'd be seen, but he would rely on his uniform fatigues and a suitably confident air to deflect any casual enquiry.

There were no signs of life in the park but there were none of death either. To warm himself up he jogged over to some trees on the far side, then turned to run back.

He'd just started the return when there was a thwack, and he felt a sharp sting on his arm. At the same time, he heard laughter. He turned around but could see nothing. Then he heard the sound again, and felt another impact, this time high on his thigh. The trees formed a thick copse in a horseshoe at the corner of the park. Whoever was shooting at him, because that's what it was, was in the trees.

'Oy!'

He spun towards the sound, and as he did so there was another blow, this time followed by jeering and sniggers. Then a figure came out of the trees, followed by another. Lander sensed danger and turned to move away, only to find two more blocking his path.

He judged they were eleven or twelve. He counted six of them, but maybe there were more in hiding. Two were girls, the rest boys or indeterminate. They surrounded him, the closest a couple of metres away. He remembered what Magda had said about gangs of older children.

One of them was holding a catapult, obviously the source of the stinging missiles.

'What're you doin' 'ere?' he said. The voice was harsh and surprisingly deep.

Lander didn't reply and the question was repeated more aggressively.

'I'm talkin' to you, shitface. This is our spot. What're you doin' 'ere?'

Lander knew he couldn't take them on. Although he was bigger than any of them he was well outnumbered. All he could do was bluster.

'Are you talking to me, you little pillock?' he said.

One of the girls giggled and one of the smaller boys shuffled up to his larger neighbour and made to pull him away. Lander pressed ahead with what he took to be an indication of advantage.

'I'm securing this park for the army,' he said. 'Now you lot clear out, or I'll have my unit bring you in.'

There was a pause but none of the children moved. They were weighing him up.

Then the catapult holder said, 'He's full of shit. There's no unit here. He's on his own.'

There was a relieved surge and they moved closer, tightening the circle.

'Tek another shot, Nev,' said another one. 'Bet yer can't get him in the nuts.'

Nev raised his weapon and aimed it at Lander's groin.

'Empty 'em,' he said.

Lander didn't move.

'Empty yer pockets or I'll knock yer nuts off.' He tensioned the rubber.

'We'll have yer neck chain too, and yer trainers,' said another.

Lander thought fast. He had his Bowie knife on his belt. If he could jump aside and dodge the projectile, he could maybe draw the knife and get the catapult holder in the same move. He seemed to be the dominant one; with him down the others would probably run. But it was a long shot, and there was an older girl on the periphery of his vision who looked dangerously detached. Maybe she was the true leader.

'Warned yer,' Nev sang, and lined up for the shot.

Lander braced himself and was poised to jump when there was a shrill whistle and a shout from behind.

'Pigs at five o'clock,' one of the children yelled.

Two women, both in uniform and armed, were running towards them. The group scattered. One of the women raised her weapon and fired. The rubber bullet bounced and hit a child, who shrieked and fell. The rest melted into the copse.

The shooter went to the edge of the trees and grabbed the stricken child, who was rolling on the floor and wailing.

'Are you OK, pal?' the other said to Lander. The name Holmes was written on her tag.

Lander nodded. 'Yes. No thanks to this lot, though.'

'Attack you, did they?'

'They were trying to. One of them, name of Nev, is a crack shot with a catapult. Who are they?'

'Ferals,' said the woman. 'They live in the woods. Get by from raiding and general thievery. They're a pain in the arse.' Her radio issued a burst of static, which distracted the two just long enough. There was a blur of movement and the injured child twisted free and dashed into the trees. The woman who'd been holding him didn't bother to follow.

'We know who they are. We'll get 'em sooner or later,' she said.

'You on the clean up?' said Holmes.

Lander improvised. 'Yeah.'

'Where's your unit?'

Lander thought fast. With everything in turmoil, communications wouldn't be good. Even in the relative order before the Infection one branch of officialdom couldn't be relied on to know what another was doing. He took a risk.

'We're on a five-two-five,' he said.

'Oh.' The other woman, whose name tag said Hussain, nodded. 'A five-two-five. And what might that be?'

There was a hint of suspicion in her tone. Lander had hoped they would just accept it as something else that was going on, but unfortunately they were curious. He improvised some more.

'Don't you know?' he said. 'Haven't you been briefed?' The women looked momentarily disconcerted and he might have got away with it, but he pushed too far. He adopted what he hoped was an authoritative frown and said, 'Perhaps you don't have the necessary clearance.'

'Oh, I think we do,' said the woman called Hussain, 'but I'm not sure you do. Where's your field equipment? You look a bit young for a patrol unit, anyway. Where are your insignia? You've got no name tag or unit decal.'

Lander wondered if he could make a break for it. But a bullet, even a rubber one, would be a lot worse than a catapult pellet. He might get into the copse, it looked pretty dense, but then he might run into the children again. He could only go on.

'But five-two-fives require anonymity,' he said, and tried to sigh as though battling with an impossible fusion of ignorance and incompetence.

'Call it in,' Hussain said to her companion, and she unhooked handcuffs from her belt.

Holmes tilted her lapel mic. 'This is SU7,' she said. 'We have an unidentified in Rollins Park. Male, late teens-early twenties, no ID.'

There was a pause. Then the gods of fortune smiled on Lander. The speaker crackled and a tinny voice said, 'Abort that, SU7. We need you back here, sharp.'

Hussain gave Lander a long look.

Holmes put the handcuffs back on her belt. 'It must be your lucky day,' she said. 'Vanish. I don't want to see you here again.'

'And lose that fucking uniform,' said the other. 'Impersonating army personnel is a criminal offence.'

Both women turned and marched quickly away.

Lander was shaken. It was not safe to be out. On the whole he thought that the children might have turned out to be worse captors than the two patrol officers, but he didn't want to test either. He hurried back to the boat. As he approached it Magda and Steve disentangled themselves from each other.

485

23

BRAVE NEW WORLD

AS SOON AS it was dark they moved on.

They had now left the more built-up areas and were back in the open country. It had begun to drizzle and Lander was not happy that he had to walk with Joey on the towpath instead of sitting under a waterproof tarp in the boat. Steve sat with Magda, one arm working a paddle which he used to fend the boat away from the canal bank. His other arm was around Magda. Lander was glad he was in front with the horse and they were behind him, so that he didn't have to witness their petting.

There weren't as many locks to delay them on this stretch of the canal and they got on well. The only interruptions were the few bridges where there was no towpath. At these Lander would unhitch Joey and lead him over the top, while Steve and Magda paddled the boats through the bridge to meet him on the other side.

After an hour they came to a fork where the canal branched. The rain had stopped and the broken clouds allowed a quarter moon to give just enough light for them to see the junction.

'I remember this,' said Steve.

He took the maps and traced their passage with a finger. Magda looked too, her chin on his shoulder and her cheek against the side of his head. Lander walked away and left them to it. He felt shut out.

'We take the right fork,' said Steve. 'That will get us to Birmingham. I'm sure of it.'

'What about the other?' said Lander. 'Where does that go?'

He didn't fancy Birmingham. He knew that the canal went right through the middle of the city and he was worried it might be like London. He'd also noticed that as they got further south more parties were cleaning up the streets and repairing the buildings. He figured that the chances of them being seen and stopped in Birmingham were significantly greater than they had been further north.

Steve pursed his lips. 'Well, we could go that way, but it's much further. It will take us longer.'

'How much longer?'

'Quite a bit. Here, look.' He offered Lander the map.

'I think it has to be Birmingham,' said Magda. 'I'm sure we'll be all right. If anyone sees us they'll simply think we're army and take no notice.'

Lander was doubtful. He hadn't told them about the incident in the park, but that had proved that their 'uniforms' weren't near enough to the real thing to bear scrutiny. However, he said nothing. Steve and Magda seemed to be organising this between them, so let them.

Besides, he didn't care what happened. If they got caught, well so be it. He still had a serious score to settle with Adam over what he'd done to Kerryl, and he was looking forward to an opportunity for that, but the passing days had tempered his sorrow; the anger and grief were still there but their intensity had eased. Revenge is a dish best served cold,' he'd heard somebody say once.

Taking the right fork meant getting Joey to the opposite side of the canal to pick up the towpath, and Lander led him back and over a bridge. When they came down the ramp, Magda was waiting. As she bent to attach Joey to the boat's line, Lander was struck by how much better she was looking. When they'd left Mickey's barn she'd been wasted, a walking corpse. Her skin had been slack and pale, her hair greasy, her face spotty and sallow. Now she was showing the benefits of rest, fresh air, and a nourishing – though often unconventional – diet. She was still thin, but no longer starved-looking. Her hair was untidy but cleaner and healthier. She had colour in her cheeks and her spots were mostly gone. Lander supposed he must be looking fitter too. Heaving all those bricks and logs had been an extended workout, and the bad treatment hadn't continued as long for him as it had for Magda. He felt strong and well.

Joey now knew the drill and he no longer needed to be led. As soon as the rope was fixed to his neck he resumed his casual stroll. Lander walked behind him, in a position to keep an eye on the rope and guard it against snags.

Instead of getting back into the boat with Steve, Magda fell in beside Lander. They walked side-by-side in silence, just the plod of Joey's hooves on the paved path and the slapping of the boats in the water. Magda had asked Lander if she could take the bottle of Eau d'Amour she'd found in Kerryl's room, and she was wearing it now.

After a while she moved closer, and Lander felt her arm on his waist, her thumb hooked in the back of his jeans. He didn't know how to respond. Was she trying to indicate that although she might have a thing going with Steve, she and Lander were still friends? He ignored it. There was a lock ahead. It was in their favour, the gate open. Lander disengaged himself, loosened Joey, and pulled Steve and the boats into the lock. He closed the downstream gate, and Magda opened the sluice at the other end. They stood together watching the lock fill.

What happened next was unexpected. Magda tugged him back so they were out of sight of Steve, who was still at the bottom of the lock. Then, more quickly than he could register what was happening, she was facing him. She pulled him into her and her face lifted towards his. He couldn't help it, his arms wound around her and their mouths met. It was a quick peck, then deeper and more enthusiastic. He realised how long he'd been wanting to kiss her, ever since they'd clung together for warmth under the hay in Mickey's barn. But this wasn't right. Not twenty minutes ago she'd been snuggling in the boat with Steve.

He let go of her and pushed her away. She looked puzzled.

'What?'

'No,' said Lander.

'Why not?'

'Steve. You were with Steve. I mean, I thought you fancied Steve.'

'I was and I do, but I fancy you as well.'

Lander hesitated, trying to take this in.

'I can fancy both of you, can't I?' Magda said.

Lander had no answer. Ever since he'd become aware of the mysteries of mating, since before that really, the rule had been one person to one other, usually one female to one male. If you wanted somebody else, the decent thing was to finish with the person you were with first. Among his group at school there had been admiration for a boy who had more than one girl 'on the go', but girls who were guilty of 'doubling up' were called sluts. Some of the young men he knew in Walbrough had been involved in serious fights when one thought another had even looked at 'his' woman in the wrong way.

'Things aren't like what they used to be,' said Magda. 'The old ways of people owning each other don't work anymore. It's time for something new.'

She leant towards him again, but the lock was now almost full. Steve and the boats were level with them and Lander pulled back.

'But you were with Steve,' he said. 'You were making out with him. I saw you. I mean, I wasn't peeking or anything but I couldn't help it.'

'So? I can fancy both of you, and I can have both of you. Same for you. You can have all the girls you like, but you can still have me.'

Steve had pulled the boat to the side and jumped out. He joined them.

'You see that, don't you, Steve?' she said.

'Yeah,' said Steve.

Lander didn't share Steve's enthusiasm. The women in the Shaw household – his mother, Gran, Kerryl – had all held monogamy and faithfulness in high regard. He could remember when Kerryl had been going out with a boy called Mark. She really liked him, but she discovered he was at the same time dating one of her friends. She'd broken with him even though it hurt her to do so, and she'd cried for days. Like most young males there were plenty of girls he fancied, but he'd always made a point of regarding any girl who seemed committed to somebody else as off limits. Magda presenting herself to him in this way was something his brain couldn't handle. And the fact that Magda knew he'd seen her and Steve and was completely open about the situation made it worse.

'Life has changed,' said Magda. 'Previous generations, with their male dominated moral systems and their rules and restrictions, totally screwed things up. All that's gone. We have an opportunity to reboot the planet, in every way. It's more than a reboot, it's a complete rebuild because there's the chance to renew everything. I mean everything. Now that almost all women are infertile we need to think again about how the genders interact.'

'What?' Lander wasn't sure he had heard her right. 'How do you mean almost all women are infertile?'

Magda looked puzzled. 'Didn't you know? I thought they would have told you that in Oxford. It's another outcome of the Infection. All the women who contracted the virus and didn't die of the fevers and the gripes have stopped producing eggs. Their ovaries have just dried up. It's like the menopause but quicker, and sooner.'

Lander hadn't heard this. He was astounded. 'And that's happened to you? You can't have kids?'

'Yup. I stopped having periods months ago. I thought I must be pregnant, but when I got to the Bonnies they told me the truth. The authorities are trying to keep it to themselves because they're afraid there'll be mass panic, but of course they can't do that for long.'

'But how are we going to survive? How are we going to repopulate the country? The world?'

'Exactly. That's one for the boffins, but there are also social implications. Monogamy is a system designed to support the family unit and provide for the raising of children. If there are no children it becomes irrelevant. Generations of women have been brought up to believe that breeding and looking after children are the most important things in their lives. That's not true now, even if it ever was. And there are advantages to being infertile: no more condoms, no more pills, no more coils, no more morning after, no more unwanted kids, no more abortions.'

Even though he had a twin sister, Lander had never really thought about the woman's side of the sex equation. There was a lot more to it for them.

'So while the politicians and the white coats figure out what to do about it, I'm going to enjoy myself.'

Steve got back in the boat, they hooked up Joey again and moved on. Magda put her arm around Lander, and after a few steps he, tentatively at first, put his around her. She squeezed him and he squeezed her back.

'Were you jealous when you saw me and Steve?'

'No, 'course not,' said Lander.

'Bet you were, really. I'm just trying to keep him on our side, that's all. You don't like him, do you.'

'He's an arsehole.'

'Agreed,' said Magda. 'And if he says "know what I mean?" one more time I think I'll kill him.'

Lander laughed. It was a mannerism that irritated him too.

They moved on; past locks, under bridges, towards the city. Little by little the urban environment became denser. After a while Magda left him and got back in the boat with Steve. When he took a peek they were kissing. He was reminded of a phrase the lads at school had had for loose girls: they "spread the honey". The attitude of his contemporaries at King's Heath to them had been complicated. They'd been reviled, but at the same time they'd been desired. Was that how he felt about Magda?

The voice of Steve roused him from his thoughts. 'It's getting lighter. We'd best look for a place to hide.'

They didn't have to look far. Ahead was a short tunnel. Magda unhitched Joey and removed his harness. 'I'll take him back there along the bank,' she said. 'We passed a meadow where he can graze.'

Lander was doubtful. He didn't like Joey being out of their sight for long. He might stray, and there was the constant threat of feral animals. Or he might simply be taken by somebody. He was a tempting target, a strong, fine-looking horse which, at a time when powering machinery was a problem, could be made to work. But there was no choice, Joey had to eat and there was nothing for him here.

While Magda led him away, Lander and Steve pulled their bedding out of the boat and spread it on the bank. Lander noticed that it was starting to smell. He hoped they'd be in Oxford soon.

'What do you think about this?' said Lander. 'All this stuff Magda was saying?'

'You mean about chicks doing it with anybody?' said Steve. He grinned. 'If that's what they want, it's all right with me. Know what I mean?'

Lander sighed. This was, after all, somebody whose response to the end of civilisation had been to go to a massive rave where sex and drugs had been the palliative.

'Kerryl told me once about a book she'd been reading,' said Lander. 'I think it was called Brave New Life. No, *Brave New World*, that was it. There was free sex in that, and the state kept everybody quiet by giving them drugs. Do you think that's what we're heading for?'

'I dunno,' said Steve. 'Could be worse.'

'Do you like Magda?'

'She's all right. I prefer blondes though. And a bit curvier, know what I mean?'

'I mean, do you like her as a person?'

Steve looked surprised, as though this had never occurred to him. 'I suppose.'

'Because I do. I like her as a person.'

Steve gave him a long look. 'Look, she told you what she thinks, how it's going to be. The scientists are going to have to come up with some way of getting more sprogs, aren't they? Till then we all do our own thing.'

Lander wanted to take the discussion further, to explore what the future might be for them all, but he wasn't sure Steve was capable of doing that. He sat on the bedding in silence. There was a plastic bottle floating in the water and he started to throw pebbles at it. Steve joined in and it became a competition between them.

It dawned on Lander that Magda had been gone for some time. The field he thought she'd meant was only a couple of hundred yards back. She'd had plenty of time to take Joey, secure him where he could graze, and return to their tunnel. She should have come back by now.

He was about to go looking for her when he saw two figures stumbling through the early light. One was Magda, and she was helping somebody else along. He jumped up and ran towards them. Steve stayed put.

Magda's companion was another young woman, and she was in a bad state. Her face was drawn and she had a hunted look. She could hardly walk and was in the sort of hospital gown Lander had worn in Oxford, except that this one was filthy and stained with blood. She reminded him of how Magda herself had looked when they got away from the shed, and for a second he thought this woman must have been Mickey's prisoner too, but of course that was impossible; Mickey was dead.

'Help me get her to the boats,' Magda said.

Lander took the girl's other arm and she collapsed between them. She tried to walk but she could scarcely put one foot in front of the other, so they half carried, half dragged her.

Lander's mind was racing. Had the pair of them been attacked by strangers? By a patrol? Surely they'd not run into some more feral kids.

'What happened?' he said. 'Are you okay?'

'Yes, I'm fine.'

'Who is she?'

'I don't know.'

'Where did you find her?'

'I led Joey into the field and I was tying him to the fence and she came out of the woods. She ran towards me and fell flat on her face. She won't say anything. Let's take her to the tunnel and see if we can get her to take some food. Then we need to work out what to do with her.'

'How do you mean? We can't take her to Oxford with us.'

'We can't leave her on her own.'

'Why not?'

'Take a look at her.'

Lander glanced down at the slight figure dangling from their arms. She was undernourished and she seemed shattered, but despite the stains on her hospital gown she didn't appear to be injured and there were no broken limbs. Then he noticed the unmistakable swelling of her belly.

'Oh my God. She's pregnant.'

24

LISA

HER NAME WAS LISA. She was exhausted, and it was some time before she could speak, let alone tell a coherent story. Magda persuaded her to try to eat some crispbreads and tinned ham, and she sorted out some clothes from the things she'd taken from Kerryl's room. Gradually as the day progressed Lisa's story emerged.

She and her twin sister, Becky, had lived in a small village near Hereford, with their elderly parents and a much older brother. The others caught the Infection, but Lisa and her sister survived.

'Everybody in the village died of it. Everybody. People we'd known for years were gone, just...just...gone,' she told them. 'All our friends. We tried to call them and we went round their houses, but nobody answered and nobody was in. Then all the phones went dead. And the TV. We was real scared at first, being on our own and that, but after a bit we got used to it. It sounds bad to say it, but in a way it was good. Nobody bothered us and we had enough to get by. I was expecting and Becky was there to see to me. We was all right.'

Lander understood what Lisa was saying. Parts of her story were like his own and Kerryl's; twins surviving, the rest of the family and all their friends being struck down. The way they had felt detached from everyone else, even those closest to them, echoed his experience too. Was there something about twins that made them better able to resist the virus?

Lisa had fallen silent. Steve prompted her to go on.

'So what went wrong?'

'A lot. One day a patrol came to the village. It was sunny and me and Becky was in the garden sunbathing, and we heard this noise. It was a car engine. We was so excited we rushed out into the road, jumping up and down because we thought we was being rescued.'

'And you weren't,' said Magda.

'Well we was in a way,' said Lisa, 'but then not. Or not what we expected it to be. They said we was lucky to be alive and we needed to be taken in for some tests, to make sure we was all right. I was hardly showing then and I didn't see why they'd got to test us, but we had no choice. They took us to this hospital in Wrexham. When we got there we saw they had some other girls too, and a few older women, and we heard children but we never saw them. There was no blokes, apart from some of the doctors and these people they called nurses, but who was really guards. They told us that more women had survived the Infection than men and that we was particularly useful to their research because we was twins. But that was a lie, because they split us up. They took Becky away.'

Lisa stopped and Magda gave her a tissue and put her arm around her. They waited until she felt able to go on.

'To start with I was all right,' she said. 'They just left us alone and I spent the days talking with the other girls. It was great to know we wasn't the only ones left. They had electricity at the hospital so we could watch videos. They'd said there'd be tests but there weren't none. It was all right. Then they found out I was pregnant. I think one of the other girls must have told them.'

'How far on were you?' said Magda.

'About three months, I think. I hadn't been to a doctor but there was only one time it could have happened, at a party with a boy I hardly knew. Anyway, they got very excited then, and they did start to do tests. They took blood, and they did scans, all sorts. They took some bone marrow from me too. That hurt. Not at the time, they put you out, but afterwards I had backache and I felt stiff all over, and I got headaches. I couldn't sleep and I lost my appetite. They said all this was normal and not to worry. Then they started to do tests on Becky too.'

'She wasn't in the club too, was she?' said Steve.

'No, don't be daft. But they did the same tests on her. It all calmed down after that. And then Becky disappeared.'

'They took her away?' said Magda.

'They said they wanted to check on her results, but she didn't come back. I asked them where she was and they said they'd taken her to another clinic because she'd volunteered for some extra tests. I knew that wasn't right. She wouldn't have done that without telling me first. They said she'd be back in a day or two, but she wasn't. She'd vanished. I started to get worried then. I said I wanted to see her but they brushed me off. I knew the baby was really important to them, so I told them that if they didn't take me to see her I'd abort it. 'Course I never would, but that's what I told them.'

'Can you do that?' said Lander. 'Abort yourself? Is it possible?'

'Maybe,' said Magda. 'Desperate women have tried all sorts of methods: knitting needles, doing belly flops onto a hard surface, starving themselves, douching with chemicals. They all can work but they're painful, and dangerous.' She turned back to Lisa. 'What happened? Did they take you to Becky?'

'No. But they got really worried, though. They took me away from the other girls and locked me in a room on my own. There was nothing there except a bed and a chair and a telly. There was nothing sharp, not even a teaspoon. So I stopped eating, and after a few days of that they took me to this really important woman.'

'Do you know who she was?' said Magda.

'Another doctor, but a top one.' Lisa frowned. 'A black lady. She said her name was Gwen something or other.'

'Gwen Matthews,' said Magda.

'Yes, that's it,' said Lisa.

'You know her?' said Lander. He was surprised that Magda would.

'I know of her. Anyway, what did Gwen Matthews have to say to you?'

'She said that Becky was all right but she'd had a negative reaction to one of the tests and it would take her a few days to get over it. Then she said that the authorities had a responsibility for repopulating the country. They wanted to do that as quickly as possible and people like me, women who was pregnant before the virus attacked, was very important. They wanted to take some sort of cells from me. They said they'd be for an ovary pool.'

'Stem cells,' said Magda. 'They must have been intending to harvest oogonial cells.'

'What are they when they're at home?' said Steve.

'They can be used to produce oocytes, immature egg cells. They could freeze them and preserve them for fertilisation later.'

'Like a baby bank,' said Steve.

'Yes, kind of,' said Magda. 'What did you say?' she asked Lisa.

'Well, they said it was my patriotic duty to cooperate and I couldn't say no. I asked her what would happen if I didn't do it. There was a bloke with her and he said that to refuse cooperation would be treason, and anyone who did that would be turned out with no money, food or ID. Also, I should think about the effects on Becky. So I said fair enough, but I wanted to see Becky first. They didn't seem to like that, and that was what made me realise that there was something wrong. I got upset then and I yelled at the woman, and they took me away.'

Something occurred to Lander. 'This bloke who was with Gwen Matthews, was he young, good looking, curly blonde hair? Name of Adam?'

Lisa looked surprised. 'Yes,' she said. 'I don't know his name, but that's what he looked like.'

Lander had almost forgiven Adam for what had happened to Kerryl. The experiment had gone wrong, but sometimes they did. It was heartbreaking, but it was understandable. However, he was coming to see that Adam wasn't just the affable, squash-playing mate he'd pretended to be in Oxford. He was driven to find ways to rebuild the population. That was praiseworthy, but in pursuing it he would go to any lengths, and that included sacrificing others.

The individual was expendable if that led to the greater good, and there wasn't a pie safe from his probing fingers. Lander's anger returned.

'Tell us how you escaped,' said Magda.

'That was weird,' said Lisa. 'And easy, really. When they took me away from this doctor woman I was struggling and kicking and they must have knocked me out. I felt a jab in my neck and I went down. I came to in my room, and the door was open and there was a terrible din coming from down the corridor. Shouting, screaming, furniture – those metal chairs – being thrown about, whistles. I had an awful headache but I had to see what was going on. There was another girl in the corridor and she was scared, trembling like a leaf. "What's going on?" I said and she said there'd been a lecture about how they were all going to help repopulate the country and there was no choice and they had to do it and some of them said they weren't going to be no baby farmers and some of the guards started to get heavy, and then people started throwing things. I could see into the big room at the end of the corridor and there was like a real big fight going on. I saw one of the guards get his helmet pulled off and he was hit with a bottle. Just then something rolled towards us and it started to fizz and smoke, so we ran, right out of the door at the other end. Two of the guards come after us and they grabbed the other girl but I got away.'

'Wow,' said Lander. 'Some escape!'

'What did you do then?' said Magda.

'I hid in a drain in the grounds. I heard people searching, and dogs, but they didn't find me. I was there all day, I was perished. When it got dark I came out. One of the other girls had told me there was a women's group near Stafford, like a refuge where people could go. They call themselves the Nightingales. I thought they might help me with my baby so I decided I'd try to find them. But I had no food and I didn't know the way to go and I got lost. I must have walked miles and I'd reached my limit when you found me.'

25

____

LAKE MANOR

'HOW COME SHE KNOWS so much about all this?' said Steve.

'How come who knows so much about all what?' said Lander.

'Magda, all this baby stuff. Oomegoolie cells, or whatever they're called.

'Oogonial. I've no idea. Perhaps she's had some medical training.'

'I thought you'd know.'

Lander thought maybe he should have, but when he considered it he had to admit he knew very little about Magda. They'd been confined together, shackled at opposite ends of the same chain; they'd eaten together and slept together, in the literal sense; they'd each had to use the same lavatory bucket in full view of the other; they had jointly murdered a man, or rather Magda had with Lander an accessory. Yet the flow of information had been one way. He'd told Magda about Kerryl, the farm, his family, his dream of playing cricket for Yorkshire, *thetruthwillmakeyoufree*, everything. She'd listened, she'd asked questions, but all she'd given him was a very brief account of being in the Bonnies and getting caught by Mickey. He knew nothing of her life before that. Was she hiding something?

Magda had said that Lisa was too weak to travel and needed several days of rest and food before she could. Lander was frustrated, impatient to carry on to Oxford, but there was no choice.

'She needs help,' said Magda. 'We can't just leave her, and we can't take her with us. It's best we get her better and then point her in the direction of the group she wants to join.'

Although they were well into an urban area and there were frequent sounds of human and machine activity, their hiding place under the bridge was a good one. No one was using the canal or the towpath, and they'd only once heard traffic on the bridge. Joey had plenty of grass in his field and he could get water too, so he was happy enough.

It should have been a good opportunity to rest but it didn't work out like that. It was hard to get back to sleeping at night again after being used to doing that during the day. Lander had never experienced jet lag, but he supposed this disturbance to his body clock must be what it was like. Noises from Steve and Magda in the other boat didn't help. Eventually he got up.

They'd made a bed for Lisa on the embankment but Lander found her sitting beside the bridge, her face pale in the thin moonlight. He sat beside her. He wanted her to tell him about her plan to seek out the women's group.

'You know this place near Stafford that you're trying to get to? Do you know anything about it?'

'Not much,' she said. 'Only what one of the girls told me. It's supposed to be a big house, in the country, and there's a bunch of women living there. She said there are women's groups all over the place, and all of them go in for different things. Some make stuff, some do studying, some look after kids and teach. They have different names. The one I'm looking for is called the Nightingales. They're supposed to specialise in medical things and in curing people. I thought they'd be the people to go to to have my baby.'

Lander agreed. It sounded as though these women should help. But where were they?

'Do you know any more about them? I mean, a big country house near Stafford is a bit vague. I expect there are a lot of those.'

Lisa rummaged in her pocket. Lander noticed that she was wearing a pair of jeans with a butterfly embroidered on the thigh. They were Kerryl's. The grief was not as intense as it had been, but occasionally seeing something that had been hers gave him a little stab, like now.

'This is all I've got,' she said, handing him a piece of paper.

It was grubby and folded and almost illegible, but Lander could make out the words Lake Manor, which he supposed was what the house was called, and below that the name of a village and a postcode. The postcode was no help, the house name not much better, and he'd never heard of the village. Lander had expected a stately home, somewhere like Shugborough, where the Earl of Lichfield lived and which he and Kerryl had been taken to visit when they were kids. A place like that would be easy to find. Lake Manor didn't sound anywhere near as grand.

Steve was asleep and Lander enjoyed waking him up. He shook his shoulder.

'Where are the maps?'

Steve blinked and looked blank, so Lander repeated. 'The road atlas. Where is it?'

'I've got it.' Steve was still bleary.

'Where is it?'

'What do you want the fucking atlas for at this time of night?'

'I need to find a place.'

'What place? Why do you want to know?'

Lander got exasperated. 'It's my atlas and I want to use it. Where is it?'

'What's going on?' said Magda, emerging blearily from under the shared duvet.

'All right, all right,' said Steve. He told Lander where he'd stowed the atlas in the lead boat.

Lander soon found the village. It didn't seem to be too far away, only a few miles, and it should be easy enough to reach. It didn't look to be very large, so once they got there finding Lake Manor ought to be a doddle.

When he got back to Lisa she'd fallen asleep. Lander took off his fleece and covered her with it. He sat beside her for a long time, until the chill of the night forced him to go back to the boat.

In the morning he talked to Magda. She had gone for a stroll along the canal bank, making her regular check on Joey, and Lander went to meet her. He started straight away with what was on his mind.

'You know this place that Lisa's making for?' he said. 'Well, I talked to her about it. She says it's run by a bunch of women like the lot you were with, except these specialise in medicine and care. She wants to have the baby there. She gave me the address.' He offered Magda the paper but she didn't take it. 'It's in a village and I've looked it up on the atlas. It's not far away, and easy country,' he continued. 'I'm sure it would only take a couple of hours to get to it. I thought I might go check it out, you know, see how the land lies. If we can find out exactly where it is, as soon as Lisa's strong enough we can take her straight to it.'

'Good idea,' said Magda. 'I'll come too.'

The whole thing was settled very quickly. Steve and Lisa would stay with the boats and keep watch on Joey while Magda and Lander would locate Lake Manor, see if the Nightingales were there and, if they were, tell them about Lisa.

'It's only a few miles,' Lander said to Steve. 'It won't take us long. We'll suss the place out and come back.'

'Knock yourselves out,' said Steve.

'Look after Lisa. And Joey.'

'You bet.'

Lander wondered if it might be better to go at night, but Magda pointed out that it would be harder to find their way, and what would they do if they arrived at the place and everyone was asleep?

'Besides,' she said, 'it's the same old problem. Travel at night and there's less chance of being seen, but if we are spotted we'll be much more suspicious. If we look as though we know what we're doing we'll be fine.'

Magda said she'd half a mind to ride Joey but she didn't fancy going all that way bareback. She abandoned the idea when Lander said he wasn't going to be the one to walk.

They each packed a rucksack with things they thought they might need – some food, extra clothing, and a sleeping bag in case their quest turned out to be futile and they had to spend a night in the open. While they did so it started to rain, hard. Lander went to the end of the bridge and looked at the torrent lashing the towpath and splashing into the canal.

'Not good,' said Magda.

'Granddad used to glue himself to the weather forecasts,' said Lander. 'He never missed the Farmers' Forecast on the TV. I never bothered, but I could do with one now. This might go on for ages.'

A drop of icy water fell from the bridge and found the nape of his neck. He shivered. He'd murder a hot drink. He couldn't remember when he'd last had one. They'd only managed to find a few cylinders for their camping stove and they'd not lasted long. As soon as they got back from this trip a top priority would be to find some more. And some drinking chocolate.

They agreed that there was no point waiting for the weather to clear up; they might as well go.

'Looks like we'll be walking in the rain,' said Magda.

Lander grunted. An earworm, an old song their Granddad used to play, started up in his head. *Just walking in the rain, Getting soaking wet, Torturing my heart, By trying to forget.* He remembered the album. It was called Johnnie Ray in Las Vegas. The cover had a picture of the casino where Johnny was performing, as well as his photo. Their Gran had quite fancied him and Granddad used to make fun of her about it. What a lot of daft stuff people used to spend their time on, he thought. Silly, trivial, useless, time-wasting stuff. He'd give anything to have it all back.

After ten minutes they were wondering whether they'd done the right thing. They were drenched, the water trickling off their waterproofs and soaking their fatigue bottoms.

'We'd be better off without these,' said Magda, tugging at hers.

'You mean take them off?'

'Yes. The material just makes a soggy poultice. It's rubbing my leg sore, and the rain won't feel as bad on our bare skin. Might be a bit cold but it will be OK if we keep moving.

They took off their bottoms in a field gateway. There was a bad smell. Lander was conscious that his underwear was far from clean, but it wasn't that.

'What's over there?' he said, seeing a shapeless lump in the field.

It was the body of a dog. Its coat was drenched and rills of dried blood ran from a gunshot wound. The body had started to decompose. Lander poked it with his foot and revealed that it hosted a colony of maggots.

'A wild one,' said Magda, wrinkling her nose. 'The army is shooting them.'

'How do you know that?'

'I've read the PIRPs.'

'The whats?'

'The PIRPs. Post Infection Reconstruction Papers. It's the term for the government's plans to put the country back together again. It's their bible. It covers everything, including culling animals that have gone wild.'

Lander was amazed. It was logical for there to be something like that, some strategy for coping with the chaos and rebuilding the country, but he hadn't imagined anything sensible truly existed. His opinion, and it had been widely shared, was that when the Infection came the government didn't have a clue how to deal with it and thrashed about trying to shut stable doors long after the horses had fled. And once again he was surprised at the amount of information Magda seemed to have.

'How do you know about this "bible"?' he said.

'It's a long story.'

'We've got plenty of time.'

'All right.' She smiled and they started walking again. 'Stop me when you get bored. When the Infection came I was at medical school, in my third year. I wanted to be a doctor. At the start, none of us had a clue what was going on, but all the students agreed we should try to do something to help. I mean we were medics, after all. We weren't fully trained but we knew quite a bit – or we thought we did – and we were sure we could be of some use, so we all volunteered. I thought we'd be sent to work in hospitals. Perhaps some of us were. Not me, though. I was selected – ordered, actually – to join one of the arks. You know about the arks, I heard you telling Steve about them.'

'Yes. Adam told me. Places where groups of people were kept behind protective barriers to isolate them from the virus. He didn't say where they were, though.'

'They were scattered all over the place: in some of the Oxbridge colleges, at military facilities, in stately homes. In some places whole villages were taken over. The one I was sent to was at Hampton Court Palace. Very grand, except I spent most of my time in the cellars.'

'Why?'

'The team I joined was there. We were working on AI.'

'Artificial intelligence?'

Magda laughed. 'Artificial insemination. It was part of a breeding programme. The objective was as soon as the Infection was over to get as many women as possible pregnant.'

'Wow. Better not tell Steve.'

She laughed. 'On the face of it what we were doing isn't a bad idea, but it assumes that all the pre- and post-natal services – the midwives, maternity units, health workers – would be in place to support it. Not to mention the later need for nurseries and schools. But of course, all that had gone, blown away by the superbug. What really killed it, though, was that all the women in the arks turned out to be infertile. Like I told you, all of us exposed to the virus got our ovaries blasted, and while everybody thought the arks would be virus free and foundations for the future, it seems they weren't.'

Lander listened for a touch of emotion in Magda's tone but none was there. It was all very matter-of-fact. It took a moment, but then it dawned on him what Magda's explanation was implying. He said one word. 'Lisa.'

'Yes,' said Magda, 'Lisa. Can you understand how important she is? Can you see why the authorities will be so keen to get her back? Lisa is a rarity, a woman who conceived before the virus struck. There can't be many of those left. Of course, there are loads of questions. Will her baby be born without any disabilities? Once it is born, will her ovaries resume normal egg production or will she be sterile like the rest of us? And if her ovaries are working, will she be able to conceive again? Will the baby be immune to the virus, like its mother? They'll want to get hold of her so that they can discover the answers to all those.'

By now the rain had stopped. It seemed that one effect of the downpour was to inhibit activity elsewhere. There were no patrols or working parties, and there was no sign of anyone else either. They kept up a brisk pace, and soon both were steaming. They came to the first signpost for the village and then they saw it, a small group of houses and a church spire two fields away. They'd have to go around three sides of a rectangle to get there by the road. Lander wanted to take a short cut, but Magda thought that would be too conspicuous.

'We're hoping the Nightingales will be friendly, if they're there, but we can't rely on it. We'll be better off keeping a low profile.'

Lake Manor was easy to spot. There was a large building on a low hill a little way out of the village.

'That must be it,' said Lander. 'There's the lake.'

'Looks like it.'

They headed towards it.

The house was impressive. There was a classical façade above a sweeping flight of steps, with a wing on either side. In front was the lake which gave the place its name, and to the rear was open parkland and a grove of trees. It wasn't exactly a stately home, but it wasn't far off.

'Not bad,' said Lander. 'If Lisa ends up here she should be very comfortable. I can't see anybody about though. Let's go take a look.'

Magda put a restraining hand on his arm. 'Hang on a minute. I think we should take our time.'

Lander frowned. 'Why?'

'Reason one,' Magda said, 'is that even though our fatigues are scruffy they might take us for army, in which case they'll probably hide. Reason two, if they find out I'm a Bonny I don't know how they'll respond. Not all the women's groups get on well with each other. I don't know what relations are like between this lot and us, but I don't want to risk it until we're better acquainted.'

'How would they know you are a Bonny? You're not wearing a badge.'

'Oh yes I am.' Magda pointed to her lower leg; there was a tattoo of a skull and crossbones. Lander had seen it before, but not thought it was anything beyond body art.

'That's the emblem of the Bonnies?' he said. 'I didn't realise.'

'I told you, Anne Bonny was a pirate. You didn't make the connection? Anyway, I think we should put these back on first.'

She tugged her damp fatigue pants out of her backpack, Lander did the same, and they put them on. They were cold and clammy.

'Hold me,' said Magda, and they clung together shivering. After a moment or two she spoke again. 'All right, we can't stay here. Better move.'

They approached the house with caution, but they didn't hide. Magda had pointed out that sneaking up under cover might look threatening, so they walked slowly down the middle of the drive.

The closer they got the more Lander thought their journey was futile. Although the house had looked imposing from a distance, from closer up it was not so impressive. The white paint on the window frames and doors was dirty and flaking, and in many places it was missing altogether. A drainpipe was hanging off the wall. There were signs of neglect in the garden. There was no smoke from the chimneys, no signs of activity outside, and – the clincher – every window was blank, all the shutters closed. The house was abandoned and empty.

'Looks like nobody's home,' said Lander.

'Mm. I'm not so sure,' said Magda. 'Let's get a bit nearer.'

Lander took a step forward, and heard a sound like the crack of a whip. He felt a sharp sting on his buttock. Even as his hand reached down to examine the cause, everything went out of focus and he sank into a black hole.

The last thing he thought as he fell was, oh no, not again.

26

———————

THE NIGHTINGALES

LANDER WAS NOT sure when consciousness returned. He had faded to black, and it was black when he opened his eyes. For some time he stared into the dark. Then he felt an ache in his thigh muscles. It built until it became severe and demanded relief. He must move, but he couldn't. He was fastened to an upright chair, bound with duct tape so tight that it was hard to breathe.

'You awake?' It was Magda.

'Yes. I'm tied up.'

'Me too. Are you all right?'

'I think so. I can't move and I'm getting a cramp in my leg.'

'I'm getting it too. It must be something to do with whatever drug they've given us.'

'What's going on? What happened?'

'I think we were shot with tranquilising darts.'

'Fuck!' Lander spat the word. 'Fuck, fuck, fuck! I can't believe it. Not again.'

'Again?'

'I've been got by one of those things before. I told you. In Snaith.'

Suddenly the convulsion in his leg returned, like a vice squeezing his calf.

'Jesus, it's back,' he snarled through clenched teeth.

'Take deep breaths,' said Magda.

'I can't. I'm strapped too tight.' He gritted his teeth. Gradually the pain retreated. 'Where are we?' he said, panting.

'I don't know, but we must have been captured.'

Lander let out a howl like a stricken dog. 'First jail, then Oxford, then Mickey, now this. I just keep running into people who want to lock me up. Who is it this time? Who's got us?'

'I don't know,' said Magda. 'It could be the Nightingales but it might be somebody else. Anyway, your yelping will have told them we're conscious so we'll soon find out.'

Lander's head throbbed and his throat was parched. 'It can't be the Nightingales,' he said. 'People who are supposed to care for people wouldn't do this.'

'Don't be so sure.'

'When they got me with a tranquilliser in Snaith it was the army. I bet it's them again. We've walked into a trap.'

'It's not the army.'

'How do you know?'

'I just do. Trust me.'

Lander didn't feel like trusting anyone. Anger and frustration boiled.

'Aaagh!' The pain in his leg struck him again, this time worse. His leg muscles contracted and he sucked at the air. 'Oh my God my God my God, it's back. The tape's so tight I can't move to ease it. It's agony. Aaagh!'

Lander writhed and twisted until the attack receded, leaving him sweating and breathless.

As Magda predicted, they soon met the people who had taken them. There was the noise of a door opening and somebody, several somebodies came into the room. Two of them carried torches, which they directed straight into Lander's face. That meant he couldn't see their captors. Another moved behind him, tied a covering across his eyes and knotted it tightly at the back of his head.

'You can put the light on,' somebody said.

Lander saw a fringe of yellow appear around the edges of his blindfold. What was happening was so like what he'd gone through before that he wondered for a crazy moment if this was some kind of fantasy, a groundhog experience, or if he was in some incomprehensible hell where Mickey had been resurrected.

These thoughts were disrupted by the cramp returning, this time in his thigh. It was excruciating. He groaned and tried to move to ease the agony. His leg stiffened and his teeth clamped as his whole body contracted. Their captors seemed to know what was happening because they did nothing, simply waiting until the attack passed. Then one of them spoke.

'I'm going to ask you some questions. If you give me honest answers, truthful ones, then all this can be over very quickly.' It was a woman's voice, without an accent and formal, like a BBC news presenter. It didn't sound cruel or even hostile, but it was firm. It was a voice that was used to giving orders and to them being obeyed. It was not the sort of voice you argued with.

Lander heard the scrape of a chair. The questioner must have sat down in front of him, because when the voice came again it was closer.

'I'm going to start with you, the male,' it said. 'What is your name?'

The old routine, he thought. There was nothing to be gained from hiding who he was. He knew from previous experience that his name was the first thing an abductor wanted to know and that they would go on until he told them.

'Lander,' he said.

'Lander?'

He always had this trouble. 'It's a nickname,' he explained. 'Short for Alexander. Alexander James Shaw.'

The echo of the cramp was still there, lurking beneath the surface and ready to pounce again at any moment. It made it hard to concentrate.

'Good,' said the voice. 'That's your name settled. Now what about your rank and number? Oh, and it would help us, and you, if you told us your unit too.'

She must think we're army, thought Lander, part of a patrol or something. Magda's right, it's not the army that's got us.

'There's no rank or number,' he said. 'Or unit. I'm nothing to do with anything official.'

There was a long pause. Then the woman spoke again. It was very quiet and sounded very patient, as if she were addressing a small child of limited understanding.

'This can take as long as you like,' she said. 'Just so you're fully aware of what's going on, I'll explain. Then you can decide whether you're going to cooperate with us or not.'

Lander let out a strangled gurgle. His whole body tried to arch but the binding meant he couldn't move. The spasm seemed interminable, and when at last it eased he was breathless and soaked in sweat.

'There you have a demonstration of the problem you face,' said the woman. 'You see, we shot you with a tranquilising dart. It's like the ones that are used for rendering wild animals unconscious. The ones used on animals are harmless, but this particular variant has a serious side effect: severe cramping of the muscles. There's an antidote that stops the contractions very quickly, but without that they will get worse. And worse. And worse.'

She paused, as if giving Lander time to take all this in, but he had got the message; he was at this woman's mercy. His pain was her pleasure, its relief in her gift.

'It's rather like tetanus,' she continued. 'The cramps will become more frequent and the spasms will last longer. You will reach a point where it will be pointless for us to question you because you won't be able to speak. Soon after that you won't be able to breathe either, and then you'll die. But that will be many painful hours down the road. And of course, we won't let you die. We'll give you the antidote before that. And then, if we don't have the information we seek, we'll start the whole process again, as many times as we need. Now, we have no desire to cause you pain so let's get this over with. We want to know your number, rank and unit.'

There was a choking sound to Lander's right and he realised that Magda too must be experiencing the cramps.

'Yes,' said the voice, 'in case you are in any doubt, you are both being subjected to the same treatment. We shall see who co-operates first.'

Magda spoke. 'We don't have any of those things you want,' she said, and her voice was tight. 'We're not from the army. We came here because we have a friend who needs your help.'

There was a scraping as the questioner's chair was turned towards Magda.

'Why didn't this "friend" come himself?'

'It's not him, it's her. And she didn't come herself because she's pregnant.'

Lander sensed rather than heard the effect this information had on their torturer.

'Tell me more.'

'Our friend became pregnant before the Infection, which she's survived. She was taken by the authorities for a breeding programme. She escaped and ran into us,' Magda said. 'She'd heard about a group called the Nightingales and was told they were at Lake Manor. She thought they would help her when the time comes for her baby. We said we'd find them.' There was another strangled sound, and a long pause before Magda was able to continue. Then she said, with savage bitterness, 'It's a good job we came alone because if you'd shot her like you shot us you'd have killed her baby.'

There was no immediate response from the woman. Eventually she said, 'What do you think, Christine? Do you go for this, or is it just so much bullshit?'

Another voice spoke, presumably Christine. She sounded older and thoughtful. 'I don't know. They're in army uniforms but they have no badges of rank, no decals, and no ID. That's very suspicious. And they give us a yarn about a pregnant woman, which they know is a story we would want to believe.'

Lander got most of this, but another convulsion wiped out some of it. The attacks were more frequent now.

'If we were army,' said Magda, 'do you think we'd come here in uniform?'

'You might,' said the woman who wasn't Christine.

'Hiding in plain sight,' said a third voice. 'Often the best form of concealment.'

'I can show you I'm not in the army,' said Magda. 'I belong to one of our groups. I'm a Bonny.'

There was an intake of breath.

'Oh yes? Can you prove that?'

'Of course,' said Magda.

'Look at her leg,' said Christine.

There was the shuffle of movement and then the third voice, now low down on Lander's right said, 'It's there. She has the skull and crossbones.'

The first woman spoke. 'That doesn't mean anything. There's nothing to stop an army infiltrator from having that tattoo done as part of their cover, so they can deceive us.'

There was a long pause. The women weren't sure. Lander went into another spasm, the most severe so far. He felt as though his limbs were being pulled apart, each joint dislocated from its neighbour. It was the worst pain he had ever known, far worse than the previous record, which was when he broke his collar bone falling off his bike.

The woman made up her mind. 'Give them the antidote,' she ordered.

Somebody fumbled with Lander's sleeve and he felt a jab in his arm. The effect was almost immediate. There was blissful relief as the drug ran through his body and the pain receded, but every muscle was wounded, affronted by the assault it had suffered. His head fell forward onto his chest. He knew he was drooling, and he sucked in saliva.

'Now listen,' said the woman. 'We are indeed the Nightingales, and for now we're going to give you the benefit of the doubt. However, if anything you tell us turns out not to be true, we'll hit you with the tranquilliser again and this time there will be no antidote. We'll simply shut the door and walk away.'

'Lie and you die,' said one of the others.

'It's easy for us to prove that what I've told you is the truth,' said Magda. 'Let us go, and we'll bring the mother-to-be to you.'

And that's what happened, but it was a long process. First, their blindfolds were removed, and when his eyes got used to the light Lander saw that they were in a cellar. There was a heavy, brown door and walls of a dingy white. There were three women with them. The one who'd spoken first and done most of the talking told them she was called Carole. She looked to be older than Magda but not much, and she had the manner of a school teacher. The one called Christine was considerably older, more

Maisie's vintage. Her grey hair was done in ringlets, which to Lander looked incongruous. The third woman was the youngest of the three, about Lander's age, he guessed. Her name was also Christine but she'd shortened it to Chrissie.

'The three Cs,' said Carole. 'Charity, chastity and chocolate.' They laughed, for the first time since they'd come into the room. 'But we won't tell you which is which.' They laughed more.

While this was going on Chrissie was releasing them from the tape that had held them in their chairs. Magda was able to stand but Lander couldn't.

'We gave you a heavier dose,' Carole said to him, 'being as how you're a big feller.' She got her shoulder under his arm and gently raised him from the chair. His legs were like jelly and wouldn't hold him up. 'Come on, lean on me,' she said. 'Don't be shy. Most men lean on women all the time.'

They were taken out of the cellar, up some stone steps and along a short passage into what must once have been a drawing room. The furniture was grand but faded, and there wasn't much of it. The space was dim because the shutters were closed and the only light came from a couple of oil lamps on tables. They were given drinks of water and a sweet, scented cordial that they were told was elderflower.

'Drink plenty,' said Carole.

'Yes. In effect we poisoned you,' said Christine cheerfully. 'The tranquilliser is toxic, and even the antidote is just another poison. You need to wash them both out of your systems as quickly as possible.' She refilled their tumblers.

Another woman brought in a plate of what, rather incongruously, looked like vol-au-vents, but Lander couldn't face any food. Whatever they had given him had made him nauseous.

The next hour resembled a game of chess; they swapped information like pieces, each side taking a turn to release one item in exchange for another. They learnt that there were currently eighteen Nightingales – 'But our number grows almost daily,' said Christine. All of them were trained medics, or were in the process of undergoing training when the Infection struck. There were four GPs and a couple of consultants – one an obstetrician, the other a rheumatologist. There was a dentist, an optometrist and a trainee dermatologist. The rest were nurses, midwives and health workers of various stages and ages, and there was one girl with a background in alternative medicines and therapies. They were interested to hear that Magda, too, had had some medical training, and wanted to know why she'd joined the Bonnies and not them.

'I didn't know where you were,' said Magda. 'Anyway, the Bonnies seemed to suit me.'

'We Nightingales, named after Florence, you know,' Christine pointed out rather unnecessarily, 'dedicate ourselves to doing good. We try to heal those who are suffering, or at the least to help them if we can't cure them. We're pledged to try to save and preserve lives. All of us have taken an oath to do that.'

'But we also take another oath,' said Carole. 'That is to defend our community and each other from attack by outsiders, by any means possible. Unfortunately, that oath can conflict rather with the first one, as you've found out.'

In return for all this Lander – who was now feeling better and wishing that the vol-au-vents might reappear – and Magda each told them a little about themselves. They added to this where they were going, how, and why. Finally they told them how they'd encountered Lisa and what they knew of her.

'Travelling on the canals? In broad daylight? And you weren't caught?' Carole sounded incredulous.

'We think the imitation army uniforms did that,' said Magda. 'I mean, they fooled you.'

'You were lucky not to be arrested for vagrancy,' said Christine. 'You know that now carries an indeterminate jail sentence? Very lucky indeed.'

It was perhaps because they found this part of their story hard to believe that the women placed strict conditions on the arrangements for fetching Lisa. They agreed that Lander would be allowed to go back to the canal to get her. While he did so Magda would remain with the Nightingales. She wouldn't be locked up, she would be expected to work in the community. However, she would be watched. If Lander didn't return in three days, either with Lisa or with an explanation of why he didn't have her, they would administer the tranquilliser to Magda.

'End of,' said Chrissie helpfully.

27

PARTINGS

GETTING BACK TO the canal was quicker than Lander had expected. He was not surprised that one of the Nightingales was going with him to keep an eye on things, and he'd been pleased when it turned out to be the girl. She was attractive, and he was sure he could chat her up; she wouldn't be any trouble. That was before she showed him a device like a knuckle duster, with finger holes and four spikes.

'This is a stun gun,' she said. 'It may be small but it packs a punch. Want to try it?' She slipped it over her fingers and made a demonstration lunge towards him.

'No thank you,' said Lander, dodging away.

'I should also warn you that I used to be the All-England Under 16 Girls' Taekwondo champion. And I can run too. So no funny stuff.'

'Oh. Right.' Lander had no intention of any funny stuff. Chrissie had made her point.

They walked on in silence for a little way. Then Lander said, 'Are you a student? I mean, were you?'

'No.'

'It's just that you seem a lot younger than the others. You don't look old enough to be a doctor.'

'I'm not. Lake Manor used to belong to my father. Now it's mine. Christine was a family friend. She told me she was starting the Nightingales and asked if they could use the house.'

'So if you're not a medic, what's your job?'

'I help them. And I work on God's plan.'

It was not an answer Lander was expecting and he was thrown. 'God's plan?'

'Yes,' she said. 'His scheme for making a better world.'

Lander was even more bewildered. He'd met two crazy old women. Now it seemed he'd found a crazy young one.

'What scheme?'

'The Infection, of course.'

'You think that what's happened is part of some grand design?'

'Don't you? You've heard the Bible story of the flood, haven't you?'

'Noah and the ark, and the animals going in two by two?'

'Yes. Well, it's not a story. It really happened.'

Lander had an image of a wooden ark and pairs of toy animals that he and Kerryl had played with when they were children. Was she serious?

'You're having me on.'

Chrissie looked hurt. 'No, I mean it. Not the ark and the animals, that's just a myth, but the flood itself was an actual event. It's not just Christian and Jewish scriptures that refer to it. Babylonian, Mesopotamian, Ancient Greek and Hindu writings all mention a great flood, and there's evidence from excavations too.'

Lander had heard something like this before, in fact he thought he might have seen a TV documentary about it, but it was a long time ago and he'd not paid it much attention.

'Why does the Bible say the flood took place?' said Chrissie.

Lander shrugged. 'God made it rain a lot. I think He was supposed to be pissed off because humans weren't doing what He wanted.'

'Exactly. And it's happened again. Think of the world before the Infection. A few people were obscenely wealthy while billions of others had barely enough to get by. Some people starved while the greedy continued to hoard. There were the homeless, who had to sleep on the streets. There were wars that killed not just soldiers but thousands of civilians, many of them children. Terrorists slaughtered people they didn't even know and who had nothing to do with the causes they were pursuing. Countries attacked their neighbours for no reason. We were progressively destroying the planet, our only home, and most people didn't seem to care. They were out for themselves. It was a world of inequality, misery and cruelty. '

'Yes, but there was a lot of good stuff too.'

'There was some, but not enough of it, and we kept missing the opportunities we were given to make things better. Think about it. The lives of some people were so terrible that they had to give up everything and leave their homes. They went on long and dangerous journeys searching for better lives, except when they got there they found that those they were looking to for help turned them away. And lording it over all this were world leaders, strutting around and showing off, more interested in their own wealth and power than in improving the lives of others.' Chrissie's eyes burned with zeal. 'God sent His son to show us how it should be done. It's dead simple: be kind to people; don't take more than you need; feed the hungry, heal the sick, and look after those in trouble. It's not rocket science. But we couldn't hack it, so the only thing God could do was press the reboot button.'

'You mean make the human race start again.'

'Yes. Not surprising, is it?'

Lander was appalled. Did she actually think this? If so she was madder than he'd thought. On the other hand, he sympathised with her analysis of the world before the Infection. If she knew what he did, that it was human beings themselves who had created the Infection in their endless quest to find more effective ways of killing each other, she would be even more convinced. But he was not sure that he believed in God, and if he did it wasn't a God who would do that.

'So what happened?' he said. 'How did God start the virus?'

'Some people think that it was spread deliberately by some very rich and powerful people to slim down the world population.' Chrissie thought for a moment, then she added, 'God works in mysterious ways.'

They continued the rest of their journey in silence. Lander noticed that the stun gun remained in her hand.

They found Lisa sitting on a box at the mouth of the canal tunnel. She was sewing, and the sight of her performing such a simple and homely task in this context seemed incongruous. It was symbolic of the disorder they now endured. She was working on a skirt. It was bright blue, with a butterfly pattern. Lander recognised it. Kerryl loved butterflies and it had been hers.

'It's one of Magda's,' Lisa said. 'She give it me. 'I'm letting it out,' she smiled, shyly.

'It used to be my sister's,' said Lander.

'Oh. Do you mind?'

'No. Help yourself. She won't need it.'

'Where is she?'

Lander told her. He was now getting quite good at telling their story, reducing it to its salient elements to produce a condensed version that he could give without emotion and cover in a few sentences.

Lisa looked at what she'd been doing to the skirt. 'It seems a shame she'll not be wearing it no more,' she said.

'Yes, it is, but I'm sure she'd have been happy for you to have it.'

He turned to Chrissie, who had been waiting behind him, and introduced them.

'Chrissie is one of the women's group you're looking for, the Nightingales. We found them, and they are at the house where you thought they'd be. Magda is still with them.'

She looked both anxious and excited. 'Will they have me?'

'That depends,' said Chrissie, 'but we'd like to talk to you.'

Lander described the house, the set-up and the composition of the group. He didn't go into their hostile reception, the tranquilliser darts, the questioning and the threat that would hang over Magda until he took Lisa to them. He didn't tell her either that Chrissie was a nut case.

Lisa wanted to set out for Lake Manor straight away, but Lander insisted they wait until the following day. There was not much daylight left, and although Lisa was looking better she was not strong. Even the shortened route to Lake Manor was some distance, and she needed to be fresh when she tackled it.

Steve had gone along the canal trying to fish. He came back with nothing but a frown. They dined on tinned luncheon meat, some rather bruised apples, and cream crackers. Steve had found some cider in an abandoned restaurant. He and Lander drank some but Lisa and Chrissie declined. Steve didn't hide his disappointment. It was obvious to Lander, and he guessed to Chrissie too, that he fancied her. Her response was to sit some distance away from him. She still held the stun gun. Steve said nothing about it, but he probably knew what it was because he kept glancing at it.

Now the year had moved on it was getting dark earlier. They didn't want to show a light so they sat in the dark. Eventually, after more of the cider, Steve started telling jokes. They were all bad and many of them were crude. Lander said he was going to kip down, and he got his bedding out of the boat. Magda had taken her sleeping bag with her, but there were some spare blankets and he gave those to Chrissie. He left it to her to decide where she was going to make her bed.

'What do you think?' Steve said in his ear.

'What do I think about what?'

'The bint, Chrissie. Reckon she's up for a bit of pussie, like Magda?'

'I don't know,' said Lander. 'There's one way to find out. Why don't you have a go?'

Lander hoped he would. He had a good idea of the response he would get.

He intended to go along the bank, away from the boats, but it looked like rain so he stayed in the shelter of the tunnel. He fell asleep to the muttered voices of Steve and Lisa. Chrissie was nowhere to be seen.

He woke early, like he always did now, and sat with his back against the brick wall of the tunnel looking at the arch of grey daylight at the mouth. He was cold.

What had happened to him? When he'd been at school he'd developed getting up, dressing and catching the bus into a fine art, reduced to twenty minutes and timed to the second so that he could spend the maximum amount of time in bed. Kerryl had been the early bird, rising before anyone else to do the milking. She'd been praised, while Lander used to get no end of aggro from their Mam for what she called his laziness. The real problem was he'd always been tired. True, he used to stay up far too late using his computer, but going to bed earlier didn't seem to make any difference; he'd still be unable to function effectively before midday. Nowadays, though, he was up before the lark. He sat wrapped in his blanket, watching the mist rise from the water as the drab dawn spread.

Steve had been sleeping further into the tunnel, beside the boats. He stood up, stretched, and came towards Lander.

'A brew?'

'I wish.'

'I mean it. I found a charity shop a bit further along. It had pretty much been stripped but there was a camping stove and some gas cylinders. We've only got tea bags and sugar though, no milk powder.'

They sat for some time listening to the soothing hiss of the stove and waiting for the water to boil.

'You get anywhere last night? With Chrissie?'

Steve didn't say anything but his expression gave the answer Lander had expected. 'Fuck it,' he said, rubbing his eyes. 'I've got cider head.'

'I won't say it serves you right,' said Lander. 'Better get a grip, though. You've got a long walk today.'

'I'm not coming,' said Steve. 'I'm not coming with you and Lisa to this women's place.'

'Why not?'

'No point. You don't need me, and there's nothing for me there. I'd rather get on,' he said.

'Get on where?'

Steve shrugged. 'No idea. Anywhere. See what there is. I fancy being a rolling stone, sort of a gypsy, know what I mean?'

'If you go on without us how will I get to Oxford?'

'You'll manage. It's not that far.'

'It's fucking miles. It must be at least a hundred. How will we cover those?' Lander was annoyed. It was selfish of Steve to carry on without them, and what was worse he seemed to be assuming he would take all their equipment and supplies with him.

Steve shrugged again. 'You'll have Joey. He's a big horse, he'll take both you and Magda. You can ride him along the canal bank.'

'What, and all our stuff too?'

'I'll leave you one of the boats.'

'Kind of you,' said Lander.

'We'll divi up. Split the stuff we've got. You take some and I'll take some.'

Lander wasn't as annoyed as he pretended to be. He would be happy to be rid of Steve. He didn't think he would get on at all well with the Nightingales. More important, though, was that with Steve gone he would have Magda to himself.

Something caught his eye along the bank. It was Lisa, coming towards them, wrapped in a blanket and looking bleary.

'Did you sleep in one of the boats?' Lander asked.

Lisa grunted a yes and sat down beside them.

'I don't know how you do it,' said Lander. 'Weren't you cold?'

She shook her head. 'No, I love it. It's great so long as you're well wrapped up. It's like a water bed.'

'Rather you than me,' said Lander. 'When I tried it I was perished.'

Steve gave Lander and Lisa a mug of hot water and a tea bag each. The tea tasted wonderful.

'I suppose that now we can heat water we can use those camping meals,' Lander said.

'Oh yeah,' said Steve. It hadn't occurred to him.

Lander fetched them and they made their selection. Steve and Lander chose an all-day breakfast and Lisa went for a chocolate pudding.

'Anybody seen Chrissie?' said Lander, when their food was ready and they were settling down to eat.

'She's gone,' said Lisa. 'She said she was done here and she was going back to Lake Manor. She said you knew the way, and she'd see us both there.'

Lander was surprised, but he reminded himself that Chrissie was well aware that Lander had an important incentive to return. He assumed she had decided that having checked his story and seen that there really was a pregnant woman, this part of God's work was done and she could leave them to follow.

As soon as Lisa had finished eating she and Lander put some clothes in a rucksack.

'Okay,' Lander said when they'd finished. 'The parting of the ways.'

'I suppose,' said Steve. He looked thoughtful. 'Hey, you know what I said about you and Kerryl? Well, I'm sorry. I didn't mean it. I was just mouthing off.'

Lander punched his arm. 'Don't worry about it. I'd forgotten it.'

'She was a great chick, your sister. Know what I mean? I liked her a lot. I'm sorry she didn't make it.'

'Me too.'

Lander sighed. How could the death of someone like Kerryl be part of any divine plan? He pulled himself together. He was neglecting his purpose. He was supposed to be going to Oxford, confronting Adam and facing him with what he'd done; and, if it seemed appropriate, making him pay for it. He'd let himself become distracted. As soon as he'd delivered Lisa to Lake Manor he would be off.

'How are you going to move your boat without Joey?' he asked Steve.

'I'll pull it. Maybe sometimes paddle. It won't be hard.'

'Take Joey,' said Lander. 'Me and Magda won't be riding him to Oxford. We need to get there quicker than he can manage, and I don't want to leave him in the field in case something gets him. If you want him, take him.'

Steve grinned. 'What, really?"

Lander nodded. 'He was Kerryl's horse, so look after him or I'll come after you.'

'Right,' said Steve.

'And he's only on loan. Someday I might want him back.'

'Right.'

They bumped fists, Lander shouldered the rucksack and they left.

Lander had expected that Lisa would find the journey hard but she didn't. She was remarkably lively. The result was that they polished off the few miles to Lake Manor more quickly than he'd expected.

Coming back to the commune was for Lander like returning to a different place. Previously the women had treated him and Magda with a mixture of hostility and suspicion. This impression came not only from the initial reception from the three Cs, it was also the way the other women had watched them, sneaking sidelong glances and whispering comments to each other. This time, however, he was greeted like a celebrity. They made even more fuss of Lisa, treating her like royalty. They crowded around her, asking questions, and offering her rest and refreshments. Her nascent bulge held an irresistible fascination for them and they all wanted to touch it. Lander watched in the background until Lisa was led away to a room she'd been given in another part of the house.

'Where's Magda?' he asked one of the women.

'In the library. It's across the hall, at the end of the passage.'

If Magda was ready they could start for Oxford straight away. The sooner they left the better.

The library was a large, oblong room, entered through double doors, which were open. Magda was at the far end. She was deep in conversation with another person. Lander was surprised to see it was a man. He had his back to the door and he was wearing a hoodie, but there was something about the hunched shoulders and the angle of the head that were familiar. They were standing close together, and their positioning and body language said that they were well acquainted. They were friends; good friends. Magda was looking steadily into the man's face and at one point she put her hand on his arm. However, it was not the intimacy of the gesture that shocked Lander, it was the identity of the person she was treating in this manner. He half turned and lowered his hood. There were blond curls and a squarish head. Even from the back, it was easy to recognise him. It was Adam.

28

———

REUNION

LANDER TOOK THREE steps back along the corridor, his head whirling. Magda with Adam? Why? Did they know each other? They must, but how? And why hadn't she told him? What did it mean? And what was Adam doing here with the Nightingales anyway? Bewildered, he retreated towards the hall, and then out through the main door.

He stood on the terrace and looked at the house, struggling to find the meaning of what he had seen. Perhaps the Nightingale women didn't know that Adam was from the authorities. Perhaps he had simply arrived from nowhere and they'd sent Magda to talk to him. But why would they do that? Why Magda rather than Christine, say, or Carole, or even the crazy Chrissie? And why was Adam there?

Another possibility was that Magda was somehow in on this. Maybe she was betraying the Nightingales to the authorities. Is that what she'd been doing with the Bonnies? Infiltrating? She'd lied to Lander before, by omission if in no other way. He'd often had the feeling that she knew more than she was telling him. Could he trust her?

He was angry, and he was hurt. He and Magda had been through a lot together. He liked her, he thought she liked him, and part of him had wondered if they might have some sort of future together, despite her unconventional approach to relationships. He had been jealous when he'd seen her with Steve, and happy that he might now be able to keep her to himself, for a short time at least. And now this. Whatever was going on, Adam seemed to be at the heart of it. Lord Fraud himself.

He turned back towards the door in time to see the hooded figure rounding the edge of the building in the direction of the car park. He was leaving!

Lander raced across the terrace, his feet kicking up the gravel. When he reached the corner, he stopped. Adam was unlocking his car. He looked up, questioningly. There was a beat's pause, then recognition, then an embarrassed grin.

Lander let out a cry of rage. It was a distillation of all the hurt and anger and frustration he'd suffered since he'd left the farm, the days and nights on the road, the times he'd been held by the authorities, Mickey, the Nightingales, his anguish at his sister's death. It was an animal howl, and with it Lander rushed him, hitting Adam so hard that he fell against the car and his head struck the door panel.

They both tumbled to the ground and Lander punched him on the side of the face with a force that jarred his knuckles. Adam tried to defend himself, but Lander was like a thing possessed. He punched and kneed and grabbed, getting his hands around Adam's throat while his enemy writhed to get him off.

'You bastard!' he screamed, shaking Adam's head, his spittle spraying his face. 'You bastard! You fucking, fucking bastard!'

His fingers bit into Adam's neck and he squeezed hard, crushing the windpipe like wringing out a dishcloth. If he'd been left alone he might have killed him, but it didn't get that far.

The explosion was deafening. It jolted Lander and Adam squirmed aside, holding his neck. Magda stood over them. She was holding an automatic pistol.

'Are you crazy?' she yelled at Lander. 'Get yourself together.' She looked at Adam. 'I'll shoot the pair of you if you don't stop this. Don't believe me?' She fired again, into the ground between them, showering them with earth and stinging pebbles. 'I bloody will.'

'You lied to me,' Lander shouted back at her. His ears were ringing from the pistol shot. He pointed at Adam. 'You told me you didn't know this bastard.' He put his head in his hands. He could barely hear anything.

'No I didn't. I just didn't tell you that I did know him.'

'Fucking hypocrite!'

'All right. But remember I saved your life. I could have gone off on my own after I'd done for Mickey and left you to rot in that shed, but I stayed and helped you. I'd no idea then who you were, but if I'd left you behind crackpot Edna would have killed you.'

'What do you mean, you didn't know who I was?'

'You'd given me your name and told me about your sister, but I'd got no idea that Adam was looking for you.'

'In that case, why did you come to Walbrough with me? Why didn't you just piss off to Oxford or Bicester or wherever the hell else it was you came from, so you could be with your slimy friends.'

Magda stuffed the pistol in her waistband and sat on the patch of earth between them. Adam was still massaging his neck. The ringing in Lander's ears was subsiding. He was pleased to see that Adam had an angry-looking red mark on the side of his face. He hoped it would turn into a proper black eye.

'I had to come with you,' said Magda. 'I had no choice. Where else would I go? I was in the middle of nowhere with no transport and no way of getting in touch with anyone. I'd been starved for three months, I'd just been raped, and I'd stabbed a man to death. I was more than half dead. I needed time to get myself together, and going with you was the easiest option. You might remember that I was barely conscious for most of the way back to your home.'

'How did he know where we were?' he said, jerking his thumb at Adam.

'He's known all the time, all the places we've been. On the way to Walbrough I picked up this.' She took a slim phone from her pocket.

'On the way? Where? Anyway, mobiles don't work.'

'Enough questions,' said Adam. 'It's make your mind up time.' His voice sounded strained, constricted and he was still holding his throat. 'You've got to decide whose side you're on.'

'No,' said Magda. 'If he's to make this decision he needs the full picture.' She turned her attention back to Lander. 'Can you remember on the way to your place we went through a village with a war memorial in the middle? And I told you I needed a pee? That was where I got this phone. It uses a completely different protocol and network from the phones you know. It's a system that's been around for a while, reserved for government and emergency use. It was kept going during the Infection to allow communication between the arkies and it's been used since by the army. Spare handsets were hidden in locations all over the country, to be used in case of emergencies. There are more than a hundred of them. We had to learn where they were as part of our training.'

'Helped to pass the long hours while we waited for the abatement,' Adam mumbled.

'Abatement?'

'It's the term we use for the Infection dying down, when it was judged safe for the arkies to come out and for the rebuilding to start,' Magda explained. 'Anyway, when I saw the name of that village on a signboard I remembered there was a handset there, so I asked you to stop for me to pee and went behind the war memorial and got this from its hiding place. As soon as I could I told Adam where I was and where I was going. I also told him about you.'

'Why?'

'I didn't know then that you and Kerryl were special, but I knew that our research people were interested in any survivors, particularly in twins. Of course, as soon as I reported to Adam he knew at once who you were. He knew your home, and he told me what to expect there.'

'Why didn't you tell me? Why didn't you take me directly to him?'

'We were going to do that,' said Adam. 'Magda was on the point of filling you in, but then you found your sister's diaries, you blamed me for her death and you were out for my blood. If we'd met straight away you wouldn't have been in the mood to cooperate. You needed time to cool off. You still do,' he said, rubbing his neck. 'Anyway, when you decided to go to Oxford by canal, that was perfect. We reckoned it would give you a week or more to calm down and come to terms with the changed situation.'

'"Changed situation." Christ! I can't believe you people. Is that all Kerryl's death means to you? A "changed situation"?'

'No, of course not,' Adam said, and Lander was gratified to see that he seemed embarrassed.

'What happened to her, then? What happened to my sister?'

Adam looked at Lander and then very slowly shook his head from side to side. 'I don't know.'

'What do you mean you don't know? Of course you know. You were supposed to be watching her!'

'I was. But I was with you, too. I wasn't with her all the time. I wasn't aware of everything that was going on. It's easy to see what was happening to her when you read her diaries, but I didn't have those. I didn't know she was having hallucinations. I could see she was getting very thin, but I didn't realise she'd been starving herself. I saw her body beside the pool at the Bride Stones. She'd drowned, but exactly why I have no idea. She could have been faint from lack of nourishment and just collapsed into the water. Or she might have done it deliberately, it might have been suicide, that's what her diary seems to say.' He shook his head. 'I don't know.'

'One thing that I know is that you were playing games with her,' said Lander. 'You were pretending to be there, and then not there. She was lonely and she was depressed and she was vulnerable, and you used her to have a bit of fun.'

Adam shook his head, this time more vigorously. 'No, no, no. It wasn't like that. I explained everything to the inquiry. I told them exactly what happened.'

'What enquiry? There was an inquiry?'

'Yes,' said Adam. 'The government put a considerable share of its very limited resources into you and your sister. When things went wrong they wanted to know what had happened. Okay, maybe I misjudged things. Perhaps I didn't see what was coming, but I didn't intend either you or Kerryl to come to any harm. Far from it. For the needs of our programme it was important you both be kept alive. Kerryl's death was a complete disaster, for us as well as for you.'

Adam looked away.

'As soon as Adam knew where you were,' said Magda, 'he came to Walbrough. Straight away. He arrived the night you and Steve went off your heads on the lager, and after I'd put the two of you to bed we met.'

'The extra coffee mug,' said Lander.

'Yes. Smart of you to spot that. Anyway, I showed him the canal route we'd worked out so he could brief the patrols and make sure they left us alone.'

Lander shook his head. So that was why they'd hardly seen any sign of officials, despite sometimes travelling in daylight. That was why, even when they were seen, there'd been no interference. He remembered the bus full of armed soldiers, the way they'd stopped when they'd seen him and Steve on the canal bank. They'd looked as though they were about to step in, but then they just drove off. He'd been manipulated. Operated, like a remote-controlled toy. Adam had moved the joystick, and Magda had made sure he received the commands. He and Steve were puppets.

'And you say you haven't tricked me,' Lander said wearily.

'We neither of us did,' said Adam. 'We fully intended to tell you everything. All we were doing was holding the information back until the time was right. We needed to work out the details and finalise our plans. We hoped that over the couple of weeks it would take you to get to Oxford your grief would die down, you would come to terms with what had happened, and you'd be willing to work with us. We intended that as you got closer, Magda would update you.'

Lander was stupefied. He felt as though he'd been building a structure which he thought was solid, which he believed to be on firm foundations, only to discover when it was almost complete that the whole thing was made of jelly. When he'd read Kerryl's diary he'd become more and more appalled at the cruelty with which she'd been treated. Now these two were trying to explain it, asking him to accept it and move on. He didn't intend to do that.

'You can't read Kerryl's diaries without seeing that being left so alone affected her mind,' said Lander. 'Don't you understand that?'

'Yes, we do,' said Magda. 'But who was it who left her?'

Lander felt something inside him snap. He stood up and faced Magda.

'I left because I thought I was protecting her. That arsehole,' he pointed to Adam, 'knew that. He could see what was going on at the farm. I couldn't because I was being held in prison, or being fed some bullshit in Oxford. So she dies, and then you come along and make the whole thing a thousand times worse.'

Lander's face was inches from Magda's, but she didn't flinch.

'What did your fancy Inquiry say?' said Lander, looking at Adam. 'That you should be locked up for murder?'

'They were concerned, naturally but I had a surprise for them, and I have one for you. What would you say if I told you we could bring your sister back to life?'

29

A PROPOSAL

LANDER WAS THUNDERSTRUCK. What did Adam mean?

'We intended to get you to Oxford and then brief you properly,' said Magda. 'We hoped that when you had the full picture you'd agree to take part in our programme.

Lander felt lost, out of control. He had no idea what they were talking about. How much of what had happened to him since he first left the farm was random, and how much was part of some elaborate plan? It was a different sort of dream walking, a fantasy in which no one was actually what they at first seemed.

'Was Steve in on this?' he said.

Magda snorted and Adam laughed out loud.

'Steve? What do you think?' said Magda. 'He was useful in helping you to navigate the canals, and of course he came up with the idea of using them in the first place, but apart from that, well, he's hardly the fastest horse in the race, is he?' She turned towards Lander and put her hand on his arm. 'I know you think we've organised all this,' she said, 'but we've not. Coming across you at Mickey's was a complete accident.'

'I don't believe you,' he said, moving away.

'Suit yourself, but it's true. Adam knew about you and how important you might be to a programme he was working on, but after you left the hospital in Oxford no one had any idea where you'd gone. Nobody realised at that time how much we did – do – need you, otherwise we'd have tried harder to find you. Adam and I barely knew each other then. I certainly wasn't aware of what he was working on.

Lander felt used, and he couldn't forgive Adam for what he'd done to Kerryl. But what was he talking about? 'You said you could bring my sister back to life,' he said. 'I'm not stupid. I know you can't do that. I don't believe in magic. So what do you mean, and where do your fancy plans go next?'

'I don't believe in magic either,' said Adam. 'But I do think we can give Kerryl some sort of continued existence. Not the Kerryl we knew, you and I. Sadly she's gone from us. But her heritage.'

'And where do I come in?'

'That depends on you,' said Adam. 'Some of what I'm going to share with you now you know already, from *thetruthwillmakeyoufree*, and from what you've discovered since you left home.' He looked to Magda. 'You start. My throat's sore.'

'All right,' said Magda. 'It's like this. When the Infection came we thought it would wipe everyone out, and most of the people who contracted the virus were indeed killed by it. However, there were a few others. You know about them from *thetruth*. In these cases the system resisted the fever but the virus lodged in the brain. The results were all the same: insanity, usually violent insanity. People infected in this way did crazy things, they fought each other, and they took stupid risks. The upshot was that many of them died, just like the others but in different ways. You know them by the term coined by *thetruth*: dream walkers. We prefer to call them "the possessed".

'You and Kerryl were like the possessed,' said Adam. 'You got the virus, avoided the fever, and it migrated to your brains. You might have displayed the classic symptoms but you didn't, because you were different. There were no signs of mental disorder and you both remained calm and rational.

'In Oxford you were in a sheltered situation, so your environment was not a natural one. However, Kerryl was in the real world. And Kerryl was female, whereas everyone else we knew about who'd been infected in this way was male. We needed to observe her and test her responses to what she encountered. We had to see whether she succumbed to hallucinations like the others, so we tried to induce a few. She resisted them, but we noticed something very interesting beginning to happen. Your sister appeared to be constructing a second psyche, another, different Kerryl who existed in the same body, in parallel to the first one but with an independent consciousness. The original Kerryl was there most of the time, but sometimes she was replaced by the other one, the alternative Kerryl. The two operated independently. Neither was aware of the existence of the other.'

Lander remembered the conversation he'd had with Adam and Gwen Matthews, what seemed like a hundred years ago. 'Jekyll and Hyde.'

'Yes,' said Adam. 'Just like the famous Doctor and his alter-ego, one Kerryl could do something and the other Kerryl would know nothing about it.'

'So she was a dream walker.'

'In a way, but she was different from the others. You've seen her diary, you know about the messages she was sending to herself.'

'The ones she thought were coming from you,' said Lander bitterly.

'The tragedy is that she died before we were able to fully understand what was happening to her and could find out the potential of this remarkable quality,' said Magda.

The implications were mind-boggling. Lander could remember a movie he'd seen where the hero didn't know who he was and helplessly followed some programme that the state had planted in his brain. What Adam and Magda were describing seemed like that.

'I still think Kerryl's death was your fault,' he said.

'I can understand you blaming me,' said Adam, 'but I hope you can see that Kerryl dying was the exact opposite of what we wanted. But listen, I meant it when I said that your sister can live again. Or part of her can, and you and she together can help us move towards an incredible future.'

'What do you mean?' said Lander. He still wasn't sure that Adam was completely sane, and he was wary that he might be trying to manipulate him again.

'When the Provisional Government was established it set up the arks, using resources and facilities that had been assembled in case of nuclear war. A small number of elite people were singled out to go into the arks to be safe from the Infection.'

'The arkies. I know,' said Lander.

'Yes,' said Adam. 'Well, the idea was that when the Infection had abated the arkies would march out and start all over again. For that reason, when people were chosen for the arks they were selected not only for the skills they could bring to rebuilding society, but also for what was judged to be a vigorous capacity for breeding. What we didn't know was that everyone who went into an ark would come out sterile. The ovaries of the ark women have ceased to function, and the men all fire blanks.'

'Why? I thought the arks were supposed to be safe.'

'They were. All we can think is that somehow a mutation of the virus that had this effect got around before the arks were sealed. It was probably present amongst one or more of the arkies at the pre-lockdown briefings, it was passed around and some of it got into every one of the arks, where it spread.'

'The divine plan,' said Lander.

'What?'

'Oh, nothing. It was just something one of the Nightingale women said. So what happened?'

'The boffins were desperate,' said Magda. 'It looked like the end of everything. They examined the possibility of extracting eggs from women who had died of the infection, but in all the subjects they tried the samples had been tainted by the virus. When Kerryl's body was found up on the moors behind your house, Adam saw an opportunity. He had her taken immediately to a facility in Manchester, where she was put into cold storage. Now, amazingly, our medics have taken cells from her, and from these they've created oocytes.'

It was a word Lander had heard before. No wonder Magda knew so much about this.

'They can be used to develop ova,' said Adam.

Lander could hardly believe his ears. 'You're going to clone her!'

'No, no, no,' said Adam. He was irritated by the suggestion. 'That would be no use at all. Anyway the artificial cloning of humans is impossible.'

'The South Koreans claimed to have done it back in the early two thousands,' said Magda, 'but they were never able to produce any proof, and as far as we know it can't be done.

'In any case, the whole business of cloning is very iffy,' said Adam. 'There's been some success with a range of animals, but it's not reliable. And there's the age problem.'

'What's that?'

'It's quite simple,' said Magda. 'A cloned subject begins its life at the same age as the organism that provided the cells. So a clone of Kerryl would start out at the same age as she was when we took hers.'

'An eighteen-year-old baby,' said Lander.

'Yes,' said Magda.

'Even if we could do it,' said Adam. 'What I'm talking about is different and really has possibilities. However, it's a one-shot chance, and because so much depends on it, the science has to be spot-on. What we're after is good old-fashioned IVF.'

'I see,' said Lander, although he was not entirely sure he did. 'The baby farms you'd planned, that Lisa told me about, won't work, so you want to make babies in test tubes instead. You've got some eggs you've made from Kerryl, and you want my permission to get them fertilised.'

'We don't need your permission,' said Adam, coldly.

Lander looked as though he was going to have another go at Adam and Magda held up her hand to calm him. 'It's a bit more than that,' she said. 'We do need your permission, because we want you to fertilise them.'

Lander was speechless. What on earth was this mad woman talking about?

'We need your sperm,' she said. 'The tests in Oxford confirmed that you are fertile.'

'But that's crazy. It's ridiculous. You're out of your mind. Anyway, I can't be the only fertile male in the country. There must be others.'

'We want Kerryl's children to have the dual characteristic that she had. There were signs of the same thing coming out in you. When I read Kerryl's diary I saw that the explanation you'd given her for going away was that you were experiencing behaviours like the ones she developed,' said Adam. 'Yours were different, but they were there. This trait is in you, too. If we use sperm from anyone other than you to fertilise Kerryl's eggs, this feature – we call it dual personality syndrome, DPS – most likely won't be replicated. We'll just produce more of the possessed. If we use sperm from you, there's an excellent chance that at least some of your progeny will have this quality.' Adam leant forward. He seemed to have forgotten his injuries and there was passion in his eyes and his voice. 'Don't you see what this means?' he said. 'You and Kerryl can be the founders of a new race. Every member of this race will be two people in one, each of them able to act independently of the other. It will be amazing. It will be the evolution of homo sapiens, a new species of human kind.'

'Homo sapiens will give way to homo duplex,' said Magda.

Lander still couldn't grapple with what was being suggested, but he was starting to see the implications, or some of them. 'But what you're wanting me to do is incest,' he said.

'No, not in the physical sense,' Adam said.

'It's not what Steve was suggesting,' said Magda.

'But it's inbreeding. All it will do is produce idiots.' Lander was remembering the jokes he'd heard about people in isolated communities being mutants and nutters because they were all related to each other.

'Incest has been outlawed and regarded as immoral for societal reasons as much as scientific ones,' said Adam. It's better for the health of society if groups inter-breed. There are biological risks, but we know a lot about gene editing now and we can adjust the DNA of the foetuses to avoid most problems.'

'And if there are any that we can't deal with, sadly we'll have to terminate them,' said Magda.

Lander still couldn't believe what they were saying. It was obscene.

'Imagine it,' said Magda, taking Lander's hand, 'a room full of babies that you and Kerryl have created. I've been talking to the Nightingales. They have agreed to provide host mothers, and they would also care for the infants. We expect some of the other covens will join in too.'

'This is the future,' said Adam.

Is it? thought Lander. It was a sort of future, certainly, but was it a good one? Two people in one? Really? From what he remembered of Jekyll and Hyde, one of the pair was normal but the other was evil. Would the same thing happen here? One could commit terrible acts but the other would be totally innocent, their conscience completely clear. One could be made to carry out whatever lunacies its lords and masters decided were necessary, while its parallel would know nothing about them.

The implications for deception, for crime, for espionage and warfare were huge. It would also be the last word in social control. And presumably these babies, his and Kerryl's numberless offspring, would be immune to the Infection. The virus could be used as the weapon it was originally intended to be.

'It's time to decide,' said Adam. 'Will you be a new Adam to Kerryl's Eve? Will you help us?'

30

____

A DECISION

IT HAD BEEN THE SAME with both Adam and Magda. He had liked them and trusted them, and they had deceived him. Even if what they were proposing was possible, were these the people who should be in control of it? He got to his feet.

'Brave New World, eh?' he said.

'It will be,' said Magda, also standing.

'If you help us,' said Adam. 'Will you join us in making the future?'

Lander paused for a moment. They had power, and so did the people who directed them. There were probably all sorts of ways they could trick or force him into doing what they desired, so his answer needed to have an impact. When they eventually did to him what they would, he wanted them to remember this moment, and that whatever happened was against his will. He looked from Adam to Magda and back, while he chose his words.

'Have you stopped for a moment to think what it was like for Kerry?' he said. 'What you did to her? You've read her diaries.

You know the torment she went through. So how do you imagine the people you propose to create in this obscene way would feel? They would have no free will. They would be lost. They wouldn't know who they were or what was happening to them. They would be more alone than ever Kerryl was. They would be in hell. Help you? Help you to create a race of tortured freaks? No. Not ever.'

Adam looked crestfallen. He was going to say something but Lander had had enough. He turned and walked away across the terrace, the gravel crunching under his feet. He didn't hurry, although he wanted to. He didn't look round, despite feeling their gaze boring into his back.

He reached the grassy slope that skirted the lake and followed the path that led to a small wood. Once hidden from the house he slowed down and took a deep breath. It was a perfect afternoon and the land shimmered in an unseasonal heat haze. A few wispy clouds stippled a cornflower sky. The trees were an autumn carnival – layer upon layer of oranges, yellows, russets, ochres. Was it his imagination, or was everything more vibrant, brighter, and more intense than it had ever been before the Infection?

He sat on the grass, still damp from the morning rain, and soon he felt the moisture seeping through his jeans. He didn't care. The poor start to the day had morphed into a perfect afternoon, and a sweep of wispy clouds stippled a sky of deep, autumn blue. They were like vapour trails, although he knew they couldn't be. The aircraft which used to make such things were gone. Would they ever fly again? Who knew? He looked at the fields beyond the lake. The one nearest had been planted with wheat, at a time when the farmer had thought it would be needed, but there had been no harvest and the ears had dropped so that only chaff and dead stalks were left. They had been beaten down by wind and rain, flattened swathes meandering into the distance.

There was no sign of human activity; nothing moving, no sounds of life beyond insects droning like distant aircraft and bird calls piercing the silence. It was their land now. Would it ever belong to mankind again? Adam had told him that there had been four thousand people in the arks. Then there were the others, people like Adam himself, and Magda, and Gwen, and Steve, and Lisa, and Mickey, and Edna, and Maisie, and Louise, and even Spencer. People who had not been in the arks, but had managed somehow to survive. For now. Adam had been in no doubt that sooner or later some mutation of the virus would get each of them, too, but for the present they were alive. How many were there? A thousand? Two? Even if it were double that, the total of everyone in the country would be less than the population of Walbrough. Fewer than would fill Leeds Arena. A tenth of a home crowd for Manchester United. Certainly not enough to populate and run a country. Kerryl had thought that despite the misery and death the plague brought, life afterwards would be all right. That there would be enough of everything for everybody. She was wrong. Things would run out, and there would be nobody to replace them.

Was it his imagination, or was everything more vibrant, brighter, and more intense since the Infection? Perhaps it was the lurking presence of death that made it seem so. What was it that Roman guy had said? *Carpe diem*; grab it while you can. If the Infection had taught him anything, it had taught him that.

REBOOT SERIES 3
JERICHO ROSE
A GRIPPING ACCOUNT OF FEAR, DANGER AND HOPE
PHILL FEATHERSTONE

1

DOGS

LANDER'S KNUCKLES WERE SORE from when he'd hit Adam, and the bones in his hand hurt. He wondered if maybe he'd broken something. He'd wrenched his wrist too, probably when he'd tried to throttle him.

He sat on the grass, still damp from the morning rain, and soon he felt the moisture seeping through his jeans. He didn't care. The poor start to the day had morphed into a perfect afternoon, and a sweep of wispy clouds stippled a sky of deep, autumn blue. They were like vapour trails, although he knew they couldn't be. The aircraft which used to make such things were gone. Would they ever fly again?

He remembered a trick Granddad used to perform, a favourite when he and Kerryl were small. The focus was a dull brown wad about the size of a baseball. It looked like dead moss, and it was kept in a plastic bag at the back of the airing cupboard. The ritual never varied. Granddad would show them the lifeless lump and get the two children to examine it, and the two children would bend over it, sniffing and prodding.

'What do you think it is?' Granddad would say, picking it up and flourishing it.

'Straw,' Lander would offer.

'Wool,' from Kerryl.

'Granddad would smile and stroke his chin. 'Well you're both wrong,' he'd say. 'It's not straw and it's not wool. It doesn't look like one, but this is a rose. Next question: is it alive or is it dead? What do you think?'

'Dead,' they'd both say.

'Are you sure?'

They'd nod.

'Well then, I'd better bring it back to life. Do you think I can do that? Do you think I can make this rose live again?'

Kerryl and Lander always said no, even though they knew that was the wrong answer.

'Very well,' he'd say. 'In that case, it looks like I might need some magic.'

He'd get one of Gran's cooking bowls from the cupboard and fill it with water from the tap. Next, he'd place it in the middle of the kitchen table, nudging it one way or another to get it in the exact centre. When he was satisfied, he'd hold the wad over the bowl, close his eyes and recite what he said was a secret spell.

> *'Rose, rose, rise from the dead,*
> *Rose, rose, raise your head.'*

Stooping low, he'd place the 'rose' reverentially in the water and wave his hands over it, repeating the spell while the entranced children looked on. After a moment or two something amazing would start to happen. Slowly at first, then more quickly, the dun lump would swell. Tendrils would extend from it, and as they uncurled the brown would become green, and it would grow. Over the next few hours, Lander and Kerryl would keep returning to the table, and at every visit the plant would look bigger, stronger and more alive. This would go on until Gran decided she needed the kitchen table, or perhaps she simply got fed up. Then she'd make Granddad shift the bowl and she'd shoo them all away.

As they grew older, he and Kerryl wearied of the trick. Eventually Kerryl, in a pre-teen strop, said scathingly, 'Why do you call it a rose? It's not a rose. It doesn't look a bit like a rose.'

Granddad shook his head. 'Oh yes, it is a rose,' he said. He got down a battered old encyclopaedia from the bookshelf and opened it. 'Look. There.'

There was a photograph of Granddad's plant looking shrivelled and dry, and another of it green and lush. Beneath them was the caption *Rose of Jericho, also known as The Resurrection Plant*, and a short description saying that it was native to desert regions and could survive long periods of drought by apparently dying, springing back to life when the rains came.

'You see,' Granddad had said, with an air of I-told-you-so. 'It's dead when it has to be, and alive when it can be. It knows how to make the best of things. We could all learn from that.'

That was what the woodland in front of him needed; resurrection. Everywhere did. Lander had heard that the Infection had wiped out ninety-nine per cent of the national population. He couldn't imagine how anyone could know a figure like that or even estimate it, but certainly an unimaginable number of people had gone. Despite that, there still could be more than half a million who had managed to survive. It would surely be enough to rebuild, except...

Over the months since the retreat of the Infection it had become apparent that all the women of childbearing age had stopped having periods. At first premature menopause had been treated light-heartedly, something of a joke, until people began to see how widespread it was, and realised what it meant. However, that wasn't the whole problem; what made it worse was what had happened to men; they were sterile.

Lander knew this because Adam and Magda had told him. Very few other people did. With no social media, limited phone calls and a single radio and TV channel controlled by the government there was no way of spreading the news. So people thought it was something that applied to them and people they knew, not that it was nationwide. Was it worldwide? Was the situation the same in other countries? Why should it be any different?

So there you were: no more babies. There were of course children who had been born before the Infection. The virus had been particularly hard on the very young and the very old, but some had got through. With their parents and carers dead most of the ones that had survived had gone feral, and although it was too soon to tell properly it looked as though they too would be unable to reproduce. So even if the cornfield was resurrected what it grew would not be needed because there would be no more mouths to feed. And what would be the point of rebuilding anything if people knew that their efforts wouldn't be needed beyond their lifetimes? It was an invitation to sink into the sort of nihilism and lawlessness that had been common in towns and cities at the height of the scourge, as their populations collapsed and their structures crumbled.

He was roused by faint drumming. It wasn't an insect, but at first it was no louder than one. As the sound came closer it resolved into the throb of a helicopter. To begin with Lander couldn't see it, but then he located a tiny speck in the dazzling blue distance. As he watched, it grew; then it was joined by another some way behind. They came closer, and he saw that the leader had twin rotors: a Chinook, the choice for military transport. The one following was smaller. It was a fascinating sight. These were the first flying machines he had seen since the Infection took hold and it was exhilarating to see such a demonstration of normality, but it was scary too. Why were they here?

They came towards the house, making a great sweep over the parkland before landing on the terrace where only a short while ago he and Adam had fought. For a second he wondered if they were after him, before realising how ridiculous that was. What would two helicopters be doing looking for him? Then he heard a much more worrying sound: the barking of dogs, rowdy and urgent. There was something about the racket that was threatening. It was time to go.

He got up. The sudden movement made him dizzy, and he had to steady himself on a tree. The noise of the dogs was keener now, and closer. Then he caught sight of them through the trees. There were two of them, big and slobbering, straining against leashes held by two figures in battle fatigues. Had they seen him? It didn't matter, they were following his scent.

The main path was too well trodden, too obvious, so he moved further into the woods and found himself at once in a thicket of tangled undergrowth. Creepers and brambles, tree roots and brushwood, caught, scratched and tripped him. The dense scrub meant he could no longer see the dogs, but he could certainly hear them and they were louder, gaining on him.

There was a stream ahead and he pushed painfully through another thicket towards it. It was three or four metres wide, shallow and running quickly. He'd heard that a fox would use water to put pursuers off its scent, so he splashed into it and headed in the direction of the flow. It was cold and the stones were slippery. He slid, cried out as his damaged hand failed to save him, and there was a flash of pain as his knee struck a rock. He struggled back to his feet and limped on. The dogs sounded even nearer now, baying and snarling, and he could hear their handlers shouting encouragement and crashing about in the brush.

There was a voice through a loud hailer.

'Lander Shaw. You can't get away. We have dogs. Come out and show yourself. We don't mean you any harm.'

No harm? Why the dogs then?

He hurried on, slithering and sliding down the middle of the brook. It would have been easier to run along the tops of the smooth rocks that rose like steppingstones along the shallows at the edge, but he thought the dogs might be able to get his scent from those, so he stuck to the deeper water. With any luck, by the time he climbed out on the other side they might have lost his scent.

Ahead of him the stream ran into a shallow ravine and plunged in a short cascade to a pool below. It looked tricky, but he had to go on. The dogs were on the bank above him and sounded to be only a little way behind. He was exposed. Anyone looking down couldn't miss seeing him. The barking was closer, almost overhead. He jumped towards the pool, landed, fell, righted himself and desperately scanned the bank. To his left was a circular, concrete pipe. It was only just wider than he was. He was afraid of being in confined spaces but he had no choice. He knelt and his injured knee screamed in protest. He ignored it and wriggled into the pipe, drawing his legs in after him. He got them in just as the first dog arrived.

2

———————————

A CHALLENGE

THE TUBE WAS PITCH BLACK. He'd hoped it might be a short, quick escape route but he couldn't see the other end. His body cut out all the light and he was scared to go on. He had no idea where it went. It might not lead anywhere, it could just come to a dead end with no way out. It was dark and damp and he felt like he had in the canal tunnel he'd gone through with Steve on their way south. That had been over a mile long. How long was this? He couldn't crawl a mile, his damaged hand and his injured knee wouldn't put up with it, even if he could stand the mental torture of being enclosed in the dark.

However, the options were simple: either he had to go on, or he must reverse out and face the dogs. There was no choice and he began to wriggle forward. The surface of the pipe was smooth and crawling wasn't too hard. He found he could use his elbows to ease himself along, which meant he was able to protect his hand. However, there was no way of shielding his knee and that hurt, protesting at each contact with the concrete. The pipe was taking some of the water from the stream and his body blocked it, so that a clammy dam soon formed uncomfortably in his crotch.

The culvert amplified his grunting and he could hear nothing else, so he couldn't tell whether the dogs had found the entrance or not. Would he know if they were behind him? Would a dog come into the pipe after him? Might there be a snarling beast between him and the way out? The thought brought on a sudden fit of panic and he froze.

He could see nothing. The conduit seemed to be straight, burrowing into the hillside. What would be at its end? He reasoned that it couldn't be dead because the water had to go somewhere, but it might not be anything he could get out of. How far in was he? It felt like he'd gone a long way, but it might only be a few metres. Suppose the men had worked out where he'd gone and blocked the entrance. It would only take a couple of big rocks to trap him. He shuddered, and forced himself to focus on what he must do now.

Despite the coldness of the water he was hot, sweating from the effort of pulling himself along. He felt again the black hand of claustrophobia, like in the canal tunnel, like in the body scanner in the Oxford hospital where he'd first met Adam. He started to tremble and his head pounded. His impulse was to go backwards as fast as he could, to get out, dogs or no dogs. He fought to control his breathing, to slow his heart, to quell the panic. To lose control now, in here, would be... well, it could be fatal. Deep breaths: in, hold, out; in, hold, out. Slowly the panic eased, his heart rate slowed, and he regained control of his head.

Having moments before been hot, he was now cold, so cold he was shivering. How cold did you have to be to suffer hypothermia? How long did it take? He made himself crawl on in the dark, feeling ahead, breathing in time with each forward reach. The fucking pipe! Where was it going? What was it for? There was a sour smell. It didn't smell like a sewer, more suggestive of ancient, rotting vegetation. It must be some sort of storm overflow, taking water from the stream to ease the risk of flooding below. Earlier he'd noticed that beyond the blue dome of the afternoon sky and the wispy filaments of cirrus, dark clouds were building on the horizon. What would happen if there was a downpour? Would the pipe fill? Would he drown? He felt another wave of fear. Keep calm, he snarled at himself. Don't be a wimp, keep calm.

His leading hand, fumbling forward in the blackness, met an obstruction. There was an instant's terror when he thought the pipe was blocked, before realising that it wasn't, it just turned sharply to the right. The bend was so tight he had to lie on his side to get around it, and even then it was a struggle. He lay still for a moment to get his breath, then looked ahead and saw ... daylight! A slim beam of sunshine struck through a narrow shaft that broke into the top of the pipe a few metres ahead. He could see that beyond it the broad pipe divided into two smaller ones. Neither was big enough for him to get through.

He worked his way towards the sunlight, thankful for the relief from the dark, but his joy was short lived. When he got to the foot of the shaft he rolled onto his back and looked up. He was dazzled at first by the brightness, but then his vision cleared. A couple of metres above him was a barred grating; beyond that the open air, the beautiful sky. But the grating looked solid. Even if he could reach it, could he move it? And before that, there was the problem of getting himself around the angle into the shaft. The pipe was so narrow that movement was only just possible, and the shaft looked even tighter. Still, the sunlight made him feel better and a breeze freshened his face. He tensed his muscles and clenched his teeth. He was going to get out of this fucking place.

His denim jacket was soaked. It had given useful protection to his arms and elbows while he'd been crawling, but it was bulky, and it would be easier to work his way into the shaft without it. Getting his arms out was difficult, but he wriggled and squirmed and eventually, he was free.

He pushed the jacket through his legs and into the pipe behind him and turned his attention to the shaft. It was lined with bricks, fringed at the top with ferns. The bricks were uneven and offered holds for climbing. He reached up with both arms and got his hands around a couple. Tentatively he tried them to see how firm they were. The last thing he wanted was to pull them out of place and for the brick lining of the shaft to tumble down on him. They seemed okay, so he took a deep breath, gathered his strength, and heaved, at the same time twisting to work his shoulders into the shaft.

Whoever had built this thing had joined it up by simply smashing through the concrete pipe, and the edge where they'd done that was rough. His t-shirt was torn, and without his jacket there was nothing between his bare stomach and the jagged surface of the break. He tried to go back to ease the discomfort, but he was stuck.

Yet again he had to fight the fear. His arms were aching and his fingers were numb. He clasped his hands on the bricks and heaved again, and as he did so he jerked his body, ignoring the hurt as his naked skin scraped on the concrete.

He'd managed to get his top half into the shaft, but his legs wouldn't bend in the right direction to get himself properly through the hole. He tried again, and the back of his jeans snagged on the rough edge of the pipe. His arms were over his head and the space was so tight he couldn't get them down to do anything. He struggled and writhed and sucked in his stomach, and as he worked his hips through the hole he felt the jeans being pulled off. They dropped to his ankles and formed a pad of material in the bottom of the shaft. Now he had another problem. His trainers were bulky, and he couldn't get his feet through the legs of the jeans. Until he could manage that he wouldn't be able to get far enough up the shaft to move the grating and get out. He had to get his trainers off, but in the confined space he couldn't reach them to loosen the laces.

He wiggled his foot and managed to get his left toe against the heel of his right shoe. His foot seemed gripped fast in the trainer, but slowly he was able to ease it out. Now he had to do the same with the other one. For the first he'd had the protection of a trainer, but that had now gone and without the buffer he couldn't get enough leverage. In desperation he wedged the back of his foot against the broken edge of the pipe and gave a sudden, hard wrench. With a jerk, his foot came out. He scraped his heel painfully on the jagged edge of the concrete, but he was free.

Without his jeans and footwear he could now get fully into the shaft. He stood on the two protruding bricks he'd used as handholds and reached up to the grating. For a moment he hesitated, too scared to try to move it. It looked depressingly solid. What if it was firmly fast, bolted to the top of the shaft? Suppose it was cemented in. Could he get back the way he'd come?

He told himself not to be an idiot, he'd never get out unless he tried. His hands were trembling as he pushed against the bars. They resisted, but he thought he felt a slight movement. He took a deep breath, pushed again, harder, harder, and gave a yelp of joy as one edge of the grill gave. He heaved, and with a groan of protest it slid aside. There was nothing above him but the glorious, blessed, blissful, joyful open air. He levered himself up until his head and shoulders were out of the shaft, and closed his eyes as the breeze wafted his face. He braced his legs against the sides of the shaft, gave a last push, and he was out.

For several minutes he could do nothing. He lay on his back, panting, flooded with euphoria. Then he felt the cold. He sat up and looked around. He was at the foot of a small slope in the corner of a field. Lake Manor was hidden. He'd lost any sense of direction, but he guessed it must be behind him on the other side of the hill. There were no other buildings in sight. He had no idea how far he'd come underground, it had felt like miles. Everything was quiet; he could hear no dogs, just birdsong and the buzz of insects. He examined his wounds. He had a spread of painful grazes around his waist and sides. His hands, elbows and knees were sore from the crawling and one knee, the one he had fallen on in the stream, had an ugly gash. It was weeping blood, and so was his foot.

He leant over the edge of the shaft and looked down into the hole. He could see his jeans at the bottom, but he couldn't reach them. There was a fallen branch nearby with a fork at the end, and he spent some time trying to hook it around the waistband, but he couldn't. He'd think he'd got it fast, but as soon as he pulled the stick the jeans fell off. No way was he going back into the shaft. He'd manage without them, and his trainers.

He hurled the stick away. Once more events seemed to be repeating themselves. There'd been a time soon after he first left the farm when his trainers had been stolen. Then he'd fashioned foot coverings out of an old rubble sack. There was nothing like that here, and if there was he had nothing to cut it with. There was no sign of any help, either. On the previous occasion a farmer had given him some boots, as well as hiding him from an army patrol. He felt suddenly emotional at the memory of the old man's unconditional kindness and generosity. What had happened to him?

The sun was much lower now. His shirt and underwear were sodden, and he was getting colder all the time. He had some more clothes in one of the inflatables that he'd left on the canal with Steve, and spare trainers too. Steve had assured him that if he decided to go somewhere else he would leave one of the boats behind. Lander hoped that he had remembered his promise and kept to it. He hoped, too, that he would have had the sense to leave Lander's clothes with it.

From the shape of the land, he guessed the canal might be quite close, in a dip a few fields away where he thought he could see a bridge. He started in that direction. It shouldn't be too bad if he could stick to walking on the grass.

3

____

A SUMMONSE

'YOU'RE GOING TO HAVE a black eye.' Magda gently stroked the red swelling on Adam's cheekbone and bent to kiss it.

'It's not too bad. I saw Lander's punch coming and managed to dodge most of it. It's my neck that hurts.'

He pulled aside the scarf that Magda had put around his throat. Angry bruises were already appearing.

'He certainly went for you.'

'True.' Adam shook his head in bewilderment. 'I thought he was going to kill me.'

'So did I for a minute.'

Such uncontrolled rage had not been the response she'd expected from Lander. He'd always seemed pretty laid back, but if she hadn't fired a warning shot in the air he might well have done Adam some serious damage. It looked as though, like many people who seemed easygoing, things brewed and stewed under the surface until they eventually burst out. It seems that finding her with Adam had been the trigger.

She'd spent enough time with Lander to understand how he felt, and she had deep sympathy for the situation that had unfolded around him. When he'd left his home, Paradise Farm, high on the northern hills, he thought he was doing the right thing, he thought he was protecting his family. But it had meant leaving his twin sister, Kerryl. He'd persuaded himself she'd be all right and had intended to return as soon as the Infection was over, but he'd reckoned without the severity of the virus. He'd thought that he'd be able to stay in touch, perhaps by phone, perhaps by email, and hadn't bargained for how quickly and completely everything would collapse. Then he'd met Adam, and that contact had seemed to offer a channel for safeguarding Kerryl. It had turned out to be the opposite. Lander blamed Adam for that and considered himself betrayed. She recognised, too, that he was grieving, and guessed that he himself probably didn't realise this. Even so, his sudden fury had been a shock.

Adam had gone to a mirror where he was examining his throat, pressing it gently. Magda watched him and again was struck by how great he looked, even with a blackening eye. Those blond curls and the square jaw made her heart skip. But of course, Adam knew he was hunky. Unlike Lander, who was good-looking in a different sort of way but seemed unconscious of the impact he had.

'Where do you think Lander's going?' Adam said.

'I don't know, but I expect he'll head back to the canal. That's where the boats that we used to get here will be. I expect his mate, Steve, is there too.'

Adam turned away from the mirror. 'What's this Steve like?' he said.

Magda thought for a moment. 'He's all right. Fairly simple, not too bright, and always out for a good time. I suppose he's a typical lad on the make. He'll do anything you want so long as the price is right, and if there's a bit of skirt involved so much the better.'

'Not principled like our Lander, then.'

'No, definitely not. Mind you, if you're going to get Lander back, you'd better be quick. He won't stay at the canal because he'll expect that's where you'll look for him. He'll be off somewhere else, and I know how well he can dodge.'

'No problem. I've told a couple of my people to bring him in. They've got sniffer dogs so he won't get far. I need to reason with him.' He sat down again. 'He has to understand that I didn't do anything to Kerryl. I honestly didn't mean for her to come to any harm. Just the opposite. I was genuinely studying her, and Lander. It was a unique opportunity, a pair of twins, each with a seeming immunity to the virus. Then, as we looked more closely, we saw that they hadn't escaped the virus, it was just that it had affected them in a different way, and in a way that instead of wiping out the human race could be turned to its advantage. Why can't he see that?'

'I think maybe he can, but he blames you for not seeing what was happening to Kerryl and how isolation was impacting her state of mind. He thinks you should have put yourself in her shoes and been more sensitive. And he finds it hard to understand why you set her problems when it was obvious that she was already suffering from stress. He thinks if you hadn't done those things, his sister would still be alive.'

'But the problems I set were part of the experiment. They were necessary so we could study how what was happening in Lander's brain was paralleling the events in her life.' Adam sounded pained, like a little boy nobody understood.

'Lander doesn't agree that they were necessary. He thinks you were playing games, with both of them.'

Adam sighed. 'He needs to put it behind him,' he said. 'Life has to go on, and there are more important things to think about now. Sooner or later it's going to dawn on somebody that women aren't getting pregnant anymore. None of them. Nobody, but nobody, is expecting.'

'Lisa is, and she said that at the hospital where she was taken there were others too.'

'Yes, but Lisa and the others became pregnant in the very early days of the Infection, before it took proper hold. And we don't know if after they've had their babies they'll be able to conceive again. Added to that, as far as we know all of the male population is sterile. Unless somebody comes up with virgin birth, there will be no more babies. If that were to get out it would spread like wildfire. There'd be mass panic. Our advantage at the moment is that all the communication systems are still down, so there are no opportunities to spread gossip. But the government can't delay restoring the mobile phone network and email forever. As soon as people have access again to social networking, well, that will be the end of it. We've got a tiny window to fix things.'

'Before the Infection, loads of people had sperm and eggs frozen and kept in fertility banks. Can't something be done with those?'

Adam's expression was rueful. 'All lost. When the electricity supplies collapsed there was no power for the cryogenic units. All of the facilities had emergency systems, but they were designed for short-term use in an emergency and not to run permanently. Either the batteries gave out or the generators ran out of diesel and there was no one to tend to them. All the decision makers were hiding from the Infection in the arks, and it never occurred to anybody that such a thing should be a priority. We're still going through the thawed-out batches in the labs, but we haven't yet found any viable samples, and I don't think we will.'

'What's happening in other countries?'

Adam shrugged. 'As far as I know, it's all pretty much the same as here, but it's hard to get anything definite. Foreign governments aren't going to be honest with us about something like that. Their duty is to help their own people, not us. You might just as well ask what's happening on Mars.'

Magda was about to say something more but stopped. She could hear an unfamiliar noise, a throbbing, becoming louder.

'Can you hear that? Surely, it can't be... It sounds like a helicopter.'

She ran to the window. It was. There were two of them, a large one in the lead with a smaller machine in its wake. It was a long time since Magda had seen anything other than birds in the sky, let alone helicopters.

'What's going on?' she said.

'I don't know,' said Adam.

'Are they military?'

'I don't think so. The Chinook has got EA markings. See, there.' He pointed to the three overlapping circles of the Enforcement Agency decal on its body.

'They're coming here.'

They were. The Chinook banked and slid sideways towards the open area in front of the house. Meanwhile the smaller machine performed a large loop above them. She lost sight of it as it passed over the roof. The racket was deafening.

Adam hurried from the library, ran to the hall and took up a position just inside the front door, where he could watch the Chinook land. The big beast touched down only a few metres from the house. As soon as it had, the pilot killed the engines and the rotors slowed. The smaller helicopter landed on the field a little way away. For a few minutes nothing happened. Then two figures got out of the smaller machine and started running towards the house. They were in the black uniform of the EA, wore helmets and flak jackets, and they were armed.

Magda was scared. 'What's happening? We're being invaded,' she said and made to pull Adam away from the doorway.

'No, look,' he said.

The two figures weren't coming to the house but were making for the Chinook. Once there they took up positions on each side of the door. As they did so it opened and a metal ladder extended to the ground. A man in a suit climbed down, buttoned his jacket and walked quickly across the gravel towards the house. From somewhere Magda heard dogs barking. She guessed they were the ones which had been sent to hunt Lander.

The suited stranger reached the door. He was dapper, spruce, lean, and a little older than Adam. He had the air of a civil servant.

'I'm looking for Przemysław Adamski,' he said.

'You've found him,' said Adam. 'That's me.'

'Good,' said the man. 'They told us in Oxford that we'd find you here.'

He held out a paper and Adam took it. Magda craned to see what was written on it. It looked formal and official.

'Would you come with me, sir, please?' the man said.

'What for?'

'This is the official transport of the First Minister of the Provisional Government,' gesturing towards the Chinook. 'He would like to speak with you.'

Magda looked at the windows of the passenger section. They were curtained but blank. Was Gus McFarlane on board? She'd only ever seen him on the television, and then not often. Before the advance of the virus, his role had been to preside over meetings of the Privy Council; nobody had much idea what it or he did, and nobody had taken much notice of him. However, the crisis had put him in a key position. When it became clear that the Infection was a major disaster, Parliament had decided that power should be handed over to a coalition, to a 'provisional government of national unity'. There was no time for the horse trading that such a move would usually have entailed, and the quickest solution was to form the new government from the Privy Council because it contained representatives of all parties and none. Suddenly, Gus McFarlane had found himself to be very important; and now he wanted to see Adam.

Two more armed security people had appeared and deployed themselves at the edge of the field. They were alert, scanning the road, looking for anyone approaching. Beside her, Adam was studying the paper he'd been given. He handed it back to the visitor.

'All right,' he said, and started towards the helicopter.

Magda had no intention of following, but the man held out a suited arm to prevent her in case she tried. 'Not you, ma'am,' he said. 'Just Mr Adamski.'

She stood in the doorway and watched Adam walk across the terrace where, not an hour before, he and Lander had fought. He reached the Chinook. Magda expected him to look back and wave but he didn't. He ran up the ladder, and without so much as a glance in her direction disappeared inside. She might as well have not been there.

In the distance, the dogs sounded more excited. Had they caught Lander? She hoped so, but she also hoped not.

4

————

PODS

THE PUBLIC CELL PHONE NETWORK wasn't working but there was a private one reserved exclusively for official use. Adam had left with Magda a phone adapted to access it. She had been told to contact him only in the direst emergency, and it had so far remained in her bag. It rang now.

There was interference on the line and Adam's voice sounded scratchily distant. 'I'm in Winchester.'

'Winchester? Why?'

'Because that's where the Council is meeting. The First Minister has asked me to address it.'

'Council? What council?'

'It's the heart of the government, like the old cabinet before the Infection.'

'And McFarlane wants you to talk to them? What about?'

'I've been part of a think tank trying to work out what happens now the Infection has died down. Things are pretty chaotic.

There are the people who were protected in the arks who are mostly public servants and are well organised, but there are also some who survived the Infection outside the arks, like your pal Lander. That lot are just drifting about. Most of them are wandering from place to place helping themselves to what they can find and trying to stay alive. It can't go on. I mean, not only is what they're doing illegal, but things will run out.'

It was something that had already occurred to Magda. She'd thought about it on the journey south with Lander and Steve. They'd taken some food with them when they'd left Lander's home but it had soon gone. After that they'd raided stores they'd found on the way, taking what they needed and – she felt guilty about this – sometimes more. In the abstract Magda quite liked the idea of anarchy, but without some sort of organisation there would be a further catastrophe and the few who had scraped through the Infection wouldn't survive. When all the shops had been looted and their stock was either exhausted or rotten there would be a problem. What would people do then?

'We need some order,' said Adam. 'The Provisional Government has to get things under control so that people can be properly cared for. Besides, with all this movement there's a chance of the Infection flaring up again. If it takes hold among these drifters it will only need one or two to transmit it to the rest of us, and we'll be right back where we started.'

'Okay. So what can be done?'

'Ah, that's where my idea comes in.' He sounded pleased with himself. 'The Enforcement Agency is rounding folk up, but they don't know what to do with them. At the moment they're just making them go back to the places where they used to live, but there are plenty who don't want to do that, and those who do go back only slope off again.'

What a surprise, thought Magda. 'It could simply be that people don't want to return to what were their homes because they're afraid they might still be infected. A lot of them will have sad memories of those places, where their family and friends died. Can you blame them for not wanting to go back?'

'I can see that, and it's why we need a plan. I wrote a paper about that and sent it to Gus McFarlane. I didn't think he'd see it, I thought it wouldn't get past his staff, but it made it to the man himself. He likes my proposal and he wants me to put it to the Council.'

'And he sent a helicopter to get you. My oh my, aren't you important?'

He failed to appreciate the irony. Magda had at first put it down to English not being his first language, but she'd by now decided that Adam had almost no sense of humour. It was one of his less attractive features.

'What it is that you're suggesting?' she said.

'Pods.'

'You mean the things you get peas from?'

Again, Adam couldn't see anything funny.

'No, nothing like that. A few weeks ago I was reading an account of the great plague, the one that raged in London in the sixteen hundreds.'

'I know,' said Magda. '1665, the year before the Fire of London.'

'That's it. Well, there was a village called Eyam. It's in Derbyshire and it's still there, or it was before the Infection. One of the Eyam merchants bought some bales of cloth in London and took them home. There were fleas in them that had bitten infected rats, and they carried the plague.'

'And the Eyam villagers caught it. I think I saw a tv programme about it once.'

'Yes, they did. And do you know what they did? In most places the people would have got out of the village as fast as they could, but Eyam folk didn't do that. They realised that if they did they'd simply spread the plague further, so they isolated themselves; no one was allowed out, and no one was allowed in. They sealed themselves off from everywhere else.'

'How did they manage?'

'They had help. Neighbouring villages heard what they were doing and left food for them at the edge of the town, but they didn't enter and the Eyamites wouldn't collect it till they'd gone. They stayed like that, all on their own until the plague had run its course.'

'What happened to them?'

'A lot of them died. But the important thing is that the plague was contained. It didn't spread to anywhere else in their locality.'

Magda was impressed. It would be hard to find bravery and selflessness like that now. 'I'm still not sure what your idea is,' she said.

'The top priority must be to find a vaccine which will work against the virus. That's a given. The people in Oxford are working on it now, night and day, but it will take time. Until we have one we are all vulnerable. My idea is simple. We divide the population into small communities and spread them out. People stay in the places they've been allocated to, and there's no travel between them. Each will be cut off from the others. They'll be new Eyams. If the Infection breaks out in one it will be contained and it won't spread to the rest. These are what I'm calling "pods".'

Magda had a dozen questions. 'Where would they be?'

'The places chosen will need to be small so that they can be controlled, but large enough to have some amenities. They'll have to be a reasonable distance apart, too far for people to be able to get easily between them and far enough to allow the EA to intercept anybody who tries. I've made a list of a dozen or so likely spots spread around the country – Alton in Hampshire, Ludlow in Shropshire, Clitheroe in Lancashire, Hornsea in East Yorkshire, Downham Market in Norfolk – places like that.'

'How can that work? They won't be able to survive on their own.'

'People will be allocated to a pod based on what they can contribute to it. We don't want all the plumbers in one place, all the teachers in another. We'll need to spread the skills around, and train people up in any that are missing.'

Magda could still see plenty of objections.

'Of course, they won't be self-sufficient,' said Adam, anticipating her next question. 'There'll be a strip of land around each pod which the inhabitants will farm. The aim is for them to be as close to self-sufficiency as can be. They won't be able to produce anything exotic, just basics like wheat, root crops, a few cows for milk, chickens. Some of the pods will do better than others, so we'll need a trading arrangement, a system for making up deficiencies and for transferring surpluses from one pod to another. The details need to be worked out, but the beauty of it is, the pod system will stabilise the population and keep individuals in one place while we search for the vaccine.'

'Won't people just wander off again? How will you make them stay in their pods?'

'There'll be incentives. They'll be comfortably housed, fed, entertained, and paid. And there'll be barriers.'

'Barriers?'

'I've discussed this with the Head of the Enforcement Agency. She says she can put casual squads on to setting rings of razor wire around all the pods. She has enough uniformed personnel to allocate guards to each of them, and we can use drones to keep an eye on things too. Finally, there'll be road patrols. It will be against the law to leave your pod without official permission, and those who try will be punished.'

'You mean you'll throw them into another pod called jail.'

'I mean they'll be sent to a correction centre. For life.'

'What?' Magda was horrified.

'To leave your pod for no good reason would be the height of social irresponsibility. It would be in the same category as drunk driving, or even attempted murder.'

'Well, that's one way of looking at it.'

Adam seemed to sense that she was not fully convinced.

'It's the only way to look at it. I can't go into the detail now, but if the Council approves I'll explain more.'

'And what if the Council doesn't approve?'

'It will. Anyway, it doesn't matter. Last week they passed new legislation that gives Gus McFarlane additional powers. He doesn't need Council agreement to take what's defined as "executive action in the national interest".'

'He can do what he likes?'

'Yes, pretty much.'

Magda didn't like the sound of that, but she changed the subject.

'What about Lander? Did your people pick him up?'

'The dogs lost him. I don't know where he is. He's probably back at the canal, like you said. He can't hide, he'll be easy enough to find when I want him. He seems drawn to trouble like a bee to honey.'

Magda smiled to herself. Lander had managed to get away from the dogs. Adam had said that Kerryl had been resourceful, but so was her brother. Although it was true that he did seem to attract trouble, it was also true that he was good at getting out of it.

'How long will you be away?' she asked.

'A few days. I'll let you know.'

5

———

LISA

THAT WAS ALL. Adam had to go. An important man with important things to do, Magda thought, and seemingly becoming more important all the time. She'd always known he was ambitious, that was one of the things about him she liked. Now he had a direct line to the First Minister himself, would he have time for her? It probably depended on how useful he found her. She'd never been dumped, but it would be worse to be pushed into the background, ignored when he had better things to do, brought out when he felt like it. The little woman at home. She didn't intend to let that happen.

She stood up, brushed her hair and straightened her top. One of the things Adam had asked her to do was keep an eye on Lisa. She would have done that anyway because she liked her and she felt sorry for her. The woman had been through a lot.

Lisa had become pregnant just as the Infection struck, and it had wiped out the baby's father. She'd left home and managed to dodge the virus herself. For some time she'd wandered about before ending up in what seemed from her descriptions to be the hospital from hell. She'd run away from that and made her way across the country with no food, no rest, and no proper clothing. She didn't even have a decent pair of shoes. All she did have was some information she'd picked up – no more than gossip really – that somewhere in Shropshire was an old house called Lake Manor where she'd find a group of women who called themselves the Nightingales and might help her. The journey would have been tough at any time, but heavily pregnant it must have been unimaginably gruelling.

Magda had found her stumbling across a field. She had been exhausted, and probably wouldn't have lasted much longer. She'd taken her back to the canal boats where she, Lander and Steve had been living. They'd fed her, given her fresh clothes, and managed to get her to the Nightingales, who had welcomed her and fallen over each other to look after her.

When Magda got to Lisa's room it was in darkness and she was sleeping. Carol, one of the Nightingales' leaders, was sitting with her.

'How is she?'

Carol got up and went towards the door, beckoning Magda to follow. Once on the landing, she whispered.

'She's got a bit of a temperature, and she says she can't feel the baby moving anymore.'

'Is that something we should worry about?'

'I'm not sure. It's fairly usual for the baby to quieten down just before birth, but Lisa hasn't reached that stage yet. I'd say she has a couple of months to go before she gets to full term. And there's no sign of lightening.'

'Lightening?'

'Lightening is the term for when the baby moves down and its head engages in the pelvis. In my experience, it usually occurs a couple of weeks before the onset of labour.'

Magda went back into the room. Lisa was pale and looked weary. She put her palm on her forehead; it felt feverish, clammy and moist.

'Is she going to be all right?'

'We'll do what we can,' said Carol. 'We've carried out some tests, but our facilities are limited. The problem is that our equipment is very basic, and the electricity supply isn't reliable. We get power cuts all the time and that makes things very difficult. Given what she's been through she needs better care than we can give her here. She ought to be in a proper maternity unit.'

'I'm not sure about that. The hospital she was in before I found her sounds awful. The only other option is to take her to Oxford.'

'I suggested that,' said Carol. 'Adam told me he wants her to stay here.'

Magda was going to ask why when Lisa moaned. It was a soft, secret sound, almost apologetic. Carol felt for her wrist. She looked concerned.

'Problem?' said Magda.

'Her pulse is irregular. Can you go downstairs and ask for Margaret? She's a qualified obstetrician and she's had a lot of experience. I think we might need her. We could do with a decent scanner but we don't have one. When's Adam coming back?'

'Not yet.'

'How long did he say he'd be away?'

'Only a few days.'

It was much longer than that.

6

AT THE CANAL

MOVING WARMED LANDER, but the walk wasn't easy. His socks soon wore through, and what was left organised themselves into uncomfortable ridges. He dumped them in the hedge and continued barefoot.

He was relieved when he saw that he'd guessed right and the canal was where he'd thought it would be. He was on a bend and the waterway curved away in both directions. He reckoned that the bridge where he'd left Steve and the inflatables was to his right, opposite the setting sun, and he set off in that direction. He'd limped a couple of hundred yards when he realised that he was wrong, he should have been going the other way. He swore to himself. He must have twisted his leg getting out of the pipe because it was aching and stiffening up. He was cold and he was hungry, his grazed knee was painful and his hand still hurt. Please let Steve not have taken both the boats. Please let at least one of them be there.

It was. In fact, both boats were just where he'd left them, and when he saw their low profiles concealed under the bridge his spirits rose and he quickened his pace. He expected to find Steve in one of them, probably asleep, but there was no sign of him. They'd put Joey, Kerryl's horse that had pulled the boats all the way from home, to graze in a field further along the canal. Lander had told Steve he could take Joey. If the horse was gone it would mean that Steve was gone too. However, he needed to get something on his feet before he went to find out.

He clambered into the boat where his things should be, removed his wet t-shirt and shorts and wrapped himself in a blanket. The blanket was showing signs of heavy use and was smelly, but he put up with that. He found some underwear in his rucksack and some jeans and a sweatshirt and put them on. He pulled the blanket around him again and hugged his knees. Somewhere in their kit was a tin of plasters. When he'd warmed up a bit he'd put one on his knee. He studied his heel. It wasn't still bleeding but there was a nasty scrape and it felt sore. He'd need a plaster for that too, and some antiseptic if he could find any. He examined his spare trainers. They were badly worn, with a split in the side of one. He'd find a new pair as soon as they got to a town.

'They'. He was assuming that he and Steve would travel on together, but would they? When Lander left, Steve had been intending to move on, but he hadn't said where. Lander had found that Steve possessed a talent for getting on his nerves, but he had no particular plans of his own and it made sense for them to stick together, at least for now. The problem was that if they continued on the canal they would be caught by the authorities. There was no doubt about that; the army would have been instructed to find him and bring him in. The only reason they hadn't been nabbed before was because Adam had ordered for them to be allowed to travel south undisturbed.

He found the plasters and the ointment and dressed his injuries. His hand was still painful from where he'd hit Adam, and he felt anger rising in him again, the bitter taste of bile. He had unfinished business with Adam. Would he ever get the opportunity to deal with it?

He'd been betrayed by both Adam and Magda. It was a double hurt. He'd liked and trusted Adam, but Magda's deception was worst because they had been through so much together. Adam wouldn't know he'd gone back to the canal, but Magda would. He needed to find some place to hide. Head over towards Wales and lie low on the borders, miles from anywhere? Return north and go back to Paradise Farm, his home? Or see if he could lose himself in the middle of a city somewhere?

He straightened up and climbed out of the boat onto the canal towpath. He was so wrapped up in his thoughts that he didn't at first see two figures coming towards him in the twilight; when one of them spoke he was startled.

'Hey, Lander, man. I'd given you up. Where've you been?'

It was Steve. There was somebody with him, a girl. His arm was around her and she was standing very close. Steve saw him looking.

'This is Chrissie.'

'Yes, I know,' said Lander. Chrissie was one of the Nightingales who had come from Lake Manor to collect Lisa. It had been obvious then that Steve fancied her.

'Oh, right,' said Steve.

Lander waited for him to go on and explain what Chrissie was doing there now.

'Chrissie's got some ideas about the Infection, about why it all started.'

Chrissie had been staring at Lander and now she spoke. 'Lander knows what I believe,' she said. 'I don't think he agrees.'

That was an understatement. When they'd met before, Chrissie had told Lander that the Infection had been sent by God to punish the human race for its selfishness, cruelty, and careless treatment of the planet. It was a sort of second flood, she'd said. Through it, God had cleared out the human race. There would be a new start. There would be a reboot. Lander had made no secret of what he thought of this idea.

'Anyway, I thought you were staying at this Manor place with Magda?' said Steve. 'What are you doing here? What's happened?'

A great deal had happened, but he didn't want to go into any of it with Steve, so he just said, 'I hung around at the Manor for a bit. Magda wanted to stay but I didn't so I came back here. I was on my way to check on Joey.'

'He's all right,' said Steve. 'We've just been to see.'

They walked back to their makeshift camp beside the canal bridge, Steve and Chrissie in front and Lander behind. Chrissie's hand was hooked in Steve's. When they got to the boats Steve went to the first one and came back with a four-pack of lager. He tossed one to Lander, popped another for Chrissie and kept a third for himself. He took a long slug, then went further under the bridge, where there was an upturned oil drum. There was some kindling and some scraps of wood on top. Steve took out a lighter and put the flame to them.

Lander started forward. 'What are you doing? Are you crazy? Somebody'll see.'

Steve laughed. 'Like who? There's nobody about.'

'But suppose a patrol goes past.'

'They don't patrol out here after dark, you know that. We lit one last night with no problem. Anyway, we have to cook. See what Chrissie brought from the Manor.' He held out a plastic bag and Lander looked inside. It contained steaks, lean and bloody. The smell churned Lander's stomach but Steve licked his lips. 'We're going to have us a barbecue.'

Steve turned out to be a competent cook. They had nothing to go with the meat, so they ate it on its own, off card plates. It was probably very good, but Lander couldn't get over the raw smell.

'You're not going to eat that?' said Steve, eyeing what Lander had left on his plate.

Lander shook his head. Steve's fork made a lightning dart for the meat and hooked it onto his plate.

Chrissie, who'd been squatting on the bank a little detached from the other two, stood up and said, 'I'm going to pray.' She walked along the towpath, back in the direction of Joey.

She was still in sight, and maybe within hearing, when Steve said, 'Well, what do you think?'

'What do I think about what?'

'Her, Chrissie. Fit, isn't she?'

In Lander's opinion Chrissie was in a league way above Steve. Whatever he might think of her religious views, she came across as smart. One of the first things she'd told him was that she'd been a champion schoolgirl sportswoman and it wasn't hard to believe. She was trim, well-proportioned, and moved with an athlete's smoothness and grace. She was also from a different background;

she'd said that Lake Manor had belonged to her family before she'd let the Nightingales have it. What could a girl like that see in a dim loser like Steve?

'Well, what do you think?' Steve said again.

'She's nice enough, good looking...'

'Good looking? Man, she's hot. Hot, hot, hot.'

'Yeah, Okay. But she's also whacky.'

'Whacky?'

'Yeah, nuts. You don't believe all that religious claptrap, do you? About the Infection being God's way to punish us.'

Steve seemed nonplussed. Perhaps it hadn't occurred to him that if he was going to take on Chrissie he might at some stage have to defend her views.

'Well it makes sense, doesn't it? he said. 'She was talking to me about it. Sixty million people were killed in World War Two, and loads more since. The top few have nearly all the world's money but don't share it.' Steve was warming to his theme as he remembered what Chrissie must have said. 'And what about global warming? We knew about it but we did fuck all to stop it. It was getting worse all the time. If the Infection hadn't finished everything off, climate change would have clobbered us for sure. Anyway, I'm happy to go with what she says if it gets me into the sack with her. Know what I mean?' He made an obscene gesture with his forefinger and clenched fist.

Lander sighed.

'She wants to start a movement,' Steve continued. 'Kind of a new church thing. The Reboot Army, she calls it. I'm going to help her.'

'Help her how? What will you do?'

'Whatever she wants. She's going to do preaching. Have you heard her speak? Magic. Gives me a hard-on every time. I'll do what she tells me, look after her stuff, set up the gigs, manage the crowd and that.'

Lander couldn't believe it. If Chrissie really thought that now was the right time to start a new cult, that she could do it, and that Steve was the person to help her, then maybe she wasn't as bright as he'd thought.

'Where are you going to go?' he said. 'You'll need a base. You can't start a new religion from a canal bank.'

Steve laughed. 'That's what I said, but Chrissie said that Jesus did it from the middle of a desert, and so did Mohammed, so where's the problem? Lake Manor would have done but the Nightingales are in there. We'll have to find somewhere else.'

It was clear they'd talked about it, at least in general terms. Then Steve had an idea. 'Hey, we couldn't use your place, could we?'

'My place?'

'Yes, the farm, Paradise Farm. It would be great. Up on the hill, out of the town, plenty of room. Couldn't be better.'

Lander was lost. There were few things he could think of that could be worse: Steve, Chrissie and a bunch of new wave hippies mooning around in the home where he and Kerryl had grown up, where their father had been killed, where their Mam, Gran and Granddad had died of the Infection, where Kerryl had suffered on her own. But then he realised that he didn't care anymore. He had no wish to go back there himself, at least not yet, and it might be useful to have people using it so they could keep out the squatters and looters.

He shrugged. 'I suppose so,' he said. 'Knock yourselves out. There's one condition, though.'

'What's that?'

'You take Joey back there with you, and you look after him.'

'Done,' said Steve. He clapped Lander on the shoulder, popped the fourth can of lager, took a deep swig and passed it over.

7

———

A BIRTH

MICKEY IS LYING ON TOP of her, his vast weight flattening her chest and stopping her breathing. He's groping between her legs, trying to force them apart. She's hidden a knife in the hay, ready for this moment. She reaches for it but can't feel it. It's gone! She panics. Mickey is forcing her. He's hurting her. At last her hand finds the knife, and without thought or aim she plunges it into Mickey's neck, driving hard, again, and again, and again. The knife hits bone and skids. Blood makes the handle slippery and her hand slips so she cuts her fingers on the blade. Mickey's grunts become squeals. Then he's still, and she struggles out from under his dead weight. His blood is sticky, or is it hers? Sticky and slimy and...

'Magda. Magda.'

Someone was shaking her. She was in her bed; her sheets were damp and in a tangle. The foul slaughterhouse of her nightmare receded. She raised her head and forced her eyes open. It was Carol, her hand resting on her shoulder.

'You were dreaming.'

604

'Oh, God. Was I making a noise?'

'You were thrashing about. Was it a bad one?'

'Yeah. Sorry.'

'Don't be. I was coming to wake you anyway. It's Lisa. She's gone into labour.'

Magda swung her legs over the edge of the bed. Her shorts were twisted and her t-shirt was wet.

'Oh my God, so soon. I'll be right there.'

'No hurry. She's only just started so it will be a while yet.'

'Is she okay?'

'Seems to be so far. Are you sure you're all right? You're shaking like a leaf.'

'Yes. I'm cold, that's all. I'll get in the shower.'

She was cold, but it was the memory of the dream that was making her tremble. It had visited her before, and rather than becoming fainter, each time it seemed to be more vivid. She stood under the stream of hot water and let it swill over her, flushing away the filth of her fantasy and trying to forget the feel of Mickey.

She turned off the shower, dried herself, towelled her hair, and put on her underwear. She took several deep breaths and held out both hands in front of her. They were still quivering, although now not as badly. Carol had put a set of green hospital scrubs on the bed and she put them on.

She left her room and went towards the wing the Nightingales had turned into a medical suite. The phantom of Mickey receded with each step, and she was excited by what was about to happen, at the new life Lisa would be bringing into the world. What a moment. This is what they had all been waiting for. It might be the only birth in the whole land since the Infection, and there was so much depending on it. Would the baby be okay? Just as important, would Lisa be able to conceive again?

The suite consisted of a couple of small wards and another room that served as a treatment area. It was fairly basic, but clean, comfortable and bright. That's where she found Lisa, plus what looked like most of the Nightingale community.

Lisa was propped up on the bed and there were several women around her. Carol was there, and Sharon, another leader of the Nightingales. Margaret, the obstetrician, was listening to the dome of Lisa's stomach through a silver tube like a miniature trumpet. Magda recognised another of the women as Hana, who she'd been told was a midwife. There were another two, nurses, hovering in the background. Everyone near the bed was in surgical scrubs. Gathered in the doorway were more Nightingales in ordinary clothing. They were clustered on the threshold, craning to see what was going on inside. It was clear they'd been instructed to keep their distance, and Magda had to push her way through them. The excitement was palpable, and the atmosphere was as charged as the prelude to a thunderstorm.

Just as Magda arrived at the bed, Lisa was seized by a contraction. Carol and Sharon took a hand each while Lisa groaned and moaned. Magda watched her face contort, her teeth clench, and the tendons on her neck stiffen till they were like cords. Everything was frozen for a moment, then the pain ebbed and Lisa's arched body relaxed. Carol pulled her hand away and shook her fingers.

'Hey girl, do you have a grip!'

Hana, who had been timing the contractions, dabbed Lisa's brow with a perfumed towel.

'How are you doing?' Magda said, looking down at the woman on the bed. The eyes that stared back at her burned like coals against her ashen face.

Lisa gulped and nodded. 'All right, I think. I wish it didn't hurt so much. It's been going on for hours.'

Margaret tugged at Magda's sleeve and nodded towards the door.

'Back in a mo',' Magda said, and followed Margaret as she pushed her way through the doorway gaggle into the corridor.

'Carol only just called me,' said Magda. 'Has she been in labour for long?'

'Not really, although it probably seems a long time to her. First deliveries often take a while. The contractions are coming more quickly, but I think there's a problem.'

'Oh?'

'I can't pick up any signs of life from the baby. I can't hear a heartbeat, and Lisa says she hasn't felt any movement since shortly after she was brought here.'

Magda's heart sank. For something to go wrong now, after Lisa had been through so much, would be heartbreakingly cruel.

'Is it all right?'

'It's hard to say. Babies do go quiet before birth, and it might just be lying in a position that makes it hard for me to hear its heart.'

'Don't you have a scanner?'

'We do, but there's something wrong with it. Adam's getting us a replacement from Oxford, but it's not here yet.'

'So you don't know. It could be dead.'

'Yes, but it could be alive too.'

The absurd paradox of Schrödinger's cat leapt into Magda's mind. Until the baby emerged both were true; it was alive, and it was also dead. Would it not be better, then, if it could be left unborn? That was not possible.

'What are the odds?' she said.

'I don't bet,' said Margaret, with a prim expression.

'But if you did?'

'I can't say. Fifty-fifty?'

'Why are you telling me this?'

Margaret looked surprised. 'I thought you'd want to know, being as how you brought Lisa here. Besides, Adam said we were to report to you, that you were in charge.'

Did he? Magda thought. He hadn't told her that. In charge of what?

Magda returned to Lisa's bedside. Another contraction came and went; then another. The group in the doorway dispersed and reformed as its members changed. Outside, the night gave way to a pallid, pasty day. Hana continued to time the contractions, but to Magda's reckoning they were coming no more frequently. They were, however, getting more intense, and each took a greater toll on Lisa's strength. The poor woman looked exhausted.

The day wore on; people came and went. Another Nightingale took over from Hana. Margaret left and said to call her if she was needed. A couple of nurses sponged Lisa and replaced her bedsheets. Carol and Sharon took a break. It was as if the whole world waited, everything in suspended animation, hanging on this single event.

Carol came back just as another contraction struck. When it was over and Lisa lay back against her pillow, she spoke to Magda.

'No change, then.'

'No. None. The spectators have given up.' She indicated the doorway. The women who had been there had all gone and it was now clear.

'You should take a break yourself,' said Carol. 'You look whacked. You must have been here for twelve hours.'

Magda nodded. She did feel weary. She hadn't realised that she'd been at Lisa's side for so long, and that was on top of a restless night.

'Yes, I think I will.' She bent over Lisa, who seemed to have fallen into an uneasy sleep, and kissed her forehead.

'I'm going to take a break and freshen up,' she said. 'I won't be long.'

Lisa's eyes opened. She nodded, but her eyes said, don't go.

Magda had to. She returned to her room and lay on the bed. She supposed she ought to eat something, yet although she hadn't had anything all day she wasn't hungry. Her head and her heart remained with the young woman at the other end of the building. The Nightingales were monitoring her and taking her temperature, blood pressure and pulse regularly. They said she was holding up well, but the longer the process went on the greater the toll it would take. Magda had seen a few live births during her medical training, and every time she'd been astonished by how much a mother could endure. She knew Lisa would be all right, but wasn't it incredible that after so many years of human evolution and after all the advances in modern science and medicine there was no easier way to bring a baby into the world? A woman in a less developed part of Africa, maybe in the very area where the Infection had struck first, might well give birth squatting on the ground. Lisa was in a bed, neat and clean – or it had been when the process started – but nothing else was different. The environment was more fastidious, but as far as Magda could see it didn't make the job of the mother any easier. What the world needed was a magic birthing machine. She began to imagine a foetus inside a transparent sphere filled with clear liquid. It was connected to cables and tubes, and bubbles rose from the base. As her fantasies grew wilder she drifted into sleep.

She dreams of a circular bath full of warm brown mud, the colour of chocolate. Maybe it is chocolate. Babies float in it, rolling and gurgling. She takes one by the arm and pulls it out. Then she holds it under a sprinkler and rinses the mud-chocolate from its body, directing the water into its wrinkles and crevices. When it's clean she wraps it in a towel, lays it on the floor, picks another from the bath and rinses that one too. As soon as she lifts one baby out of the chocolate it's replaced by another. The thing is a baby well, and soon she has a line of newborns beside her on the floor, wriggling and squealing.

Somebody was shaking her again.

'Magda? Magda? I think you should come now.'

Magda blinked up at Carol.

'What? Oh. Is the baby coming?'

'Sort of. You'd better come. Quickly.'

Magda peeled herself off the bed, checked she had her cap and face mask, and followed Carol. Excitement pulsed through her; at last the baby was here.

The atmosphere in the treatment room was very different from when she had left. Sharon was there, so was Margaret and Hana, and a single nurse, but no one else. Lisa was limp on the bed and seemed to be unconscious. Margaret was wiping her face. There was a lot of blood on the plastic sheet that covered the mattress. Magda was suddenly afraid. The baby was born, but where was it?

Then she saw it, a tiny bundle in a plastic crib at the side of the room. Magda went to it and her hand came up to her face. The baby was still, pale as a ghost, its little face like a tiny monkey, screwed in a grimace. She couldn't believe what she was seeing.

'Is it...?'

'I'm afraid so,' said Carol. She was close to tears.

'When?'

'It was like this when it was born,' she said. 'Hana thinks it's probably been dead inside her for several days.'

'Oh, my God.' Magda went to Lisa and took her hand. It was almost as lifeless as her baby. 'You poor, poor thing.'

Lisa managed a slight nod but that was all. Words were beyond her. A tear ran from the corner of her eye and down her cheek; then another. 'I'm sorry,' she said.

8

PARTINGS

CHRISSIE AND STEVE were awake early, and by the time Lander opened his eyes they were busy packing up. Chrissie didn't say much, but she was more cheerful than Lander had seen her before. She clearly liked the idea of her new base. She had probably been regretting offering Lake Manor to the Nightingales. Presumably, she did it before she'd had her Damascus moment, her revelation, or whatever the hell it was that had happened to her. Lander wasn't bothered; she sounded crazy but let her do her thing. She was harmless. And Steve too. Chrissie and Steve; it was hard to imagine a more unlikely couple. However, he had been a little surprised to see that when the two of them settled down the night before they had gone to separate sleeping bags, in different boats.

Lander had assumed that the two of them would return north along the canal in one of the boats, the way he, Steve and Magda had come. However, they'd decided against that.

'We'd be too obvious,' Steve had said. 'There are more people about now than there were when we came down, and the EA are picking folk up. We'll take our chance on the back roads.'

Stave had found a flatbed cart in a farmyard. It was ancient but serviceable. The three of them dragged it onto the bridge under which the boats were hidden. Lander and Steve carried their things up the embankment and put them on the cart, meanwhile Chrissie fetched Joey. They didn't have a proper harness for him but they managed to construct something with ropes and cargo straps that meant he was able to pull the cart. Lander was expecting all the time to see a patrol coming along the road, but there was none. By lunchtime they were ready to go.

Chrissie kissed Lander on the cheek. 'See you,' she said. 'Thank you for the loan of your home. God will bless you for it.'

'Good,' said Lander. 'I could do with a blessing or two.'

Chrissie sensed his scorn and frowned at him.

'Sure you won't come?' said Steve. 'It'll be a gas.'

'I have some things to see to here,' Lander said. 'I may look in on you later. Take care of my house. And look after Joey, too; he meant a lot to Kerryl.'

'You bet.'

The two of them climbed onto the cart, Chrissie shook the makeshift reins and Joey, patient and amiable, moved off.

Lander suddenly thought of something and shouted after them. 'Look out when you go down hills. There's no brake on that cart and Joey won't be able to hold it back.'

Chrissie turned, smiled and waved. Lander had the impression that she knew something about horses.

He watched until the three of them went around a bend and disappeared. Then he sat down on the canal bank and started to pull at the grass.

It wasn't true he had "things to see to". In truth he had no idea what he was going to do or where he was going to do it, he just hadn't wanted to go with the two evangelists. He wasn't anti-religion, just not religious himself, and when he thought about the cruelties, contradictions and perplexities of the world he couldn't believe in a divine creator. He considered it more likely that the whole thing was either a big joke perpetrated by some supernatural prankster, or just plain random.

There were some matters he would have to deal with. He still had to settle things with Adam, but that was down the line. There were things he wanted to settle with Magda too: like what she'd been playing at all the time they'd been together when she'd pretended she didn't know Adam; like exactly whose side she was on. They, too, could wait. In the meantime, he was all right here. There was plenty of food in the boats, and although it was all dried or canned he could easily survive on it. He had his bedding, rather used and in need of washing but it would keep him warm. The boats were well hidden under the bridge and wouldn't be seen unless somebody came along the canal bank, and that was very unlikely. But he couldn't live under a canal bridge for the rest of his life.

The country was in a mess. Somehow things had to be put back together again. Who would do that? The Provisional Government must be doing something, but who knew what? Adam must have a rough idea as he seemed to be close to the establishment, but there was no obvious way that he, Lander, could find out. Even if some of the contacts he'd made online before he left the farm had survived the Infection and were still active, it was impossible to get in touch with them. He had no computer, and in any case he doubted the internet was working yet. His mobile phone had been nicked a long time ago and he'd not bothered to get another. He'd seen them around but there was no coverage, so what was the point?

Was there anything he could do on his own? He knew what he wanted: a new world. What did that mean exactly? He made a mental list: an end to meanness; politicians being honest and not telling lies all the time; everybody looking out for everybody else; things being shared out fairly so that nobody was obscenely rich and nobody really poor; freedom for people to live how they wanted and do what they liked so long as it didn't harm anyone else. Wow, he sounded like Chrissie! But when you came to think about it, it wasn't a bad manifesto (was that the word?). Oh yes, and Yorkshire to win the County Cricket Championship every season, and Leeds United to beat Manchester City 10-0 every time they played, and for them to top the Premier League and run away with the European Championship.

All right, maybe not the last few, but what about the serious stuff? How might he bring about some of the things on his (and Chrissie's?) wish list? Communication was one of the keys. It was necessary to be able to message, to app, to talk. For that you needed the internet, but how could that get started again? And if it was rebooted, how could it be built to benefit everyone and not serve mainly as a channel for narcissist weirdoes, celebrity self-promoters, or as a way to swindle people and pry into their lives?

'I'm sounding like my Granddad,' he said to himself.

A start would be to find people who thought the same way as he did. There was *thetruthwillmakeyoufree*, the website where he'd found the information about dream walking and split personalities that had made him leave the farm. There'd been lots of stuff there about the Infection. They'd given it straight, and told truths that governments wanted hidden. He'd probably be with them now if he hadn't been caught and taken to Oxford for Adam's 'experiments'. Even if the website itself was dead its creators must still be around. He just needed to find them.

His bottom was cold from sitting on the chilly earth. He stood up. He couldn't stay here, a hermit under a bridge. Already, even after only an hour or two, he was bored. It was time to explore, to work out where he was and to make some plans. He went to the boats, found his rucksack, and began to pack it with things he might need. He didn't take much food. Tins were heavy, and it should still be possible to get things to eat as he went along. He would need his sheath knife. And there was the map that they'd used to get here. He still had some clothes that weren't too bad. He'd make it his business to find an empty house where he could wash them and get them dry; that, or find a store that still had some stock and nick some new ones. He thought about taking bedding and decided on just his sleeping bag. It was a quality one, lightweight and warm. The winter was coming on so it wouldn't be usable on its own in the open, but he was sure he'd be able to find places under cover where he'd be able to shelter. He lifted the rucksack and tried its weight. Not too bad.

The boats were a problem. There was nowhere to hide them. The best he could do was disguise them so that if they were seen they wouldn't arouse curiosity, and where he could come back for them if he found he needed them later. He climbed into the emptier of the two and unloaded its contents into the other, stacking and folding to make a neat arrangement. Then he spread a tarp over everything and tied it down. Next, he pulled the empty boat along the canal to where the bank dipped low enough for him to be able to haul it out. It was harder than he expected because it was heavy and cumbersome, but he managed to drag it from the canal and into a field. He tied it to the hedge, and put some heavy stones in it to stop it from flipping over if the wind caught it.

The other inflatable, the full one, was more of a problem. He remembered that a little way back along the canal they'd passed a sort of inlet, like the beginning of an unfinished cutting. It was farther away than he remembered, but when he got there he saw that the towpath didn't go into it and the walkway crossed the opening over a small timber bridge. He pushed the boat under the bridge and then climbed onto the embankment so that he could take the rope and pull it into the cutting. It was tricky. The embankment was at an angle of at least forty-five degrees and he was all the time in danger of slithering down into the water. The rope wasn't long enough either. None of it was easy, but he managed. When he'd got the boat to the far end of the inlet, he scouted around for some broken branches and dropped them on it, together with leaves and dead bracken. Then he went back to the wooden bridge. He was pleased with his work. The boat was well hidden, and if anyone did happen to notice it they'd think it had been there for years. It would be reserve stock, a larder that he could get to if he needed it.

He returned to where he'd left his rucksack and wondered why he hadn't thought to bring it with him; it would have saved him having to go back. Duh!

He consulted the map and worked out the direction for Birmingham. When he'd first left the farm he'd been heading for the coast to get across the Channel to where he understood *thetruthwillmakeyoufree* people had their base. That was still an option, but for now he reasoned that even though in a large city there might be more dangers, there would also be more places to hide and a better chance of finding out what was going on.

He shouldered the rucksack and set off along the towpath, soon settling into an easy rhythm. He'd been going for about an hour when he realised that he was hungry, really hungry. Also, it would soon be dark and he needed to find somewhere to bed down for the night. He stopped and examined his options.

A little way across the fields was a farm. There'd be outbuildings there where he could sleep. Maybe some food too. If there were chickens around there might be a few eggs. He had no way to cook them, but on the journey along the canal he'd got used to having them raw.

He was quite close to the group of buildings before he noticed that there was a dim light showing in one of the rooms. The curtains were drawn, which was why he hadn't seen it before. That meant there was somebody there. It was possible they could be friendly, but they might not be. He remembered Mickey; he wasn't prepared to risk it.

He turned back towards the canal, and froze.

No more than 20 metres away, four uniformed figures faced him in an arc.

9

———

DESTINATION

'STOP!' ONE OF THEM SHOUTED.

Lander threw aside his rucksack and ran. There was a loud crack and he felt a blow high on his thigh, as if someone had clouted him with a hammer. He let out a yell, fell and rolled. The tumble knocked the wind out of him, the pain was excruciating.

He opened his eyes and blinked through tears. Somebody was standing over him, a man, holding a rifle with a stubby attachment on the end of the barrel. A name, Green, and the letters EA were on his chest: the Enforcement Agency, the name for the amalgam of army and police that now imposed the will of the authorities.

'That was a baton round,' the man said. 'If I fire one at you from this close it won't just hurt your leg, it'll break it. Get on your feet.'

Lander felt awful. He was going to throw up. 'I can't.'

'Get the fuck up,' said the man, louder, poking him with his boot.

Lander struggled to his feet and was overtaken by another wave of nausea. He bent over and retched, but nothing came. Green stood back, rifle at the ready. Lander straightened up. Green didn't seem to be much older than Lander himself and had what looked like a failing attempt to grow a beard. He was uncomfortable under Lander's gaze and seemed nervous.

'That way,' he said, jerking his rifle to indicate the road. 'Leave your bag. And put your hands on your fucking head.'

Lander saw that there was a Toyota Avatar on the road, the long wheelbase model, painted in service khaki. It was partially hidden by trees, which was why he hadn't noticed it before. He limped across the uneven ground towards it. Every step was a trial. He felt the same as he had one time when he'd been fielding close in and the batter had slogged a ball straight at him. It had hurt for a week.

There was someone in the Avatar, sitting in the passenger seat. The door was half open and Lander could see that he had sergeant's stripes. As he drew closer the man held up a hand to warn him to stop. He did. He was just close enough to read the man's name tag: Brownrigg. He was much older than Green and had thinning, sandy hair and a moustache. Lander wondered if facial hair was some sort of gang tag for this patrol. Two other men stood at the front of the vehicle. Both held their rifles at the ready.

'Who's this?' said Brownrigg, looking Lander up and down.

'Found him in the field back there,' said Green.

'Did you now? Okay.' Brownrigg made no effort to leave the front seat and fixed Lander with a hard stare. 'Name?'

Lander didn't respond. His leg was hurting badly, and he thought he was going to throw up now. He might feel flattened, but he had enough spirit left to wonder if he could project the vomit onto his questioner's lap.

'I said, what's your fucking name?' Brownrigg said. When Lander still didn't respond he pointed. 'Show me your ID. Put it down on the bonnet there. Don't come near me or any of the others.'

Lander shook his head. However bad he felt he wasn't going to co-operate with these people.

'Where's your fucking ID?' said Green. He was a lot less nervous now he was with his boss. The other two were watching with amusement, clearly enjoying the show.

'I've lost it. It was nicked.'

'Jesus H Christ, not another one,' said Brownrigg, theatrically rolling his eyes. Already Lander had decided that Sergeant Brownrigg liked to put on a show for his squad. 'Listen, do you have a name or not?'

Lander didn't respond. He couldn't prove his ID had been stolen, and obviously Brownrigg had heard the excuse before, it was something anyone who didn't want to be identified would say, but Lander wasn't going to tell him who he really was. Why should he?

'All right,' said the sergeant, 'have it your way. You have no ID so we'd better give you one. But first, you've got to have a name.' He turned to one of the men watching. 'Stubbs, give me a name.'

Stubbs thought for a moment. 'Algernon.'

'I like it,' said Brownrigg, with a chuckle. 'Algernon what?'

'Algernon Pissalot,' said Stubbs. Green laughed loudly, and so did his companion.

'It's good,' said Brownrigg, 'very good, but I think we can do better. Let me see.' He made a show of considering Lander, looking him up and down. 'You look a bit posh to me, sunshine. A posh boy, are you?'

Lander didn't respond.

'I think he is,' said Stubbs.

'He's a posh twat,' said his companion.

'Agreed,' said Brownrigg. 'We all think you're posh, it's unanimous. So, we need a posh name. Let me think.' He made a show of stroking his moustache and contemplating. 'Ah, I've got it. The name for you is Marmaduke. Marmaduke Littledick.'

There was an explosion of laughter. The naming banter looked to be something the squad was used to, a game they probably played whenever they caught someone without ID. Part of Lander shared the humour – in their position he would most likely have joined in – but another part of him thought it was childish, pathetic. How long were they going to make him stand there? His leg was hurting a lot. What were they going to do with him? He had visions of jail again. Well, that wouldn't be too bad if it was like before. He might even get to finish *A Tale of Two Cities*. He'd got that from the library trolley when he'd been imprisoned the first time. It was the only book he'd started for ages and he'd found it all right, one he'd got used to the style. He rubbed his thigh where the round had struck him. He could feel a lump.

The sergeant reached behind him into the vehicle and brought out a small machine. It had a keypad and was a bit like the label printer his Mam had used to price things in the post office where she'd worked, except it was bigger. Brownrigg put it on his knee.

'Now you have a name we'd better do you an ID card,' he said. 'From this moment on and for the rest of your miserable life you are Marmaduke Littledick.' He slid a piece of plastic into the machine and began to type.

'Alexander Shaw,' said Lander.

'Ah,' said the sergeant, looking up in wonder, 'his memory returns. It all comes back to him now.' He smiled at his men. They were all enjoying this. He put the machine aside. 'Let's start again. What's your name? And if you bullshit me I'll have your balls.'

'My name's Shaw. Alexander James Shaw. That's the honest truth. And I really did have my ID card nicked.'

'The truth, is it? Well, we can soon check that. Where do you live, Alexander James Shaw?'

Where did he live? Since leaving home he'd lived all over: he'd been at the hospital in Oxford, he'd stayed with the old lady Maisie in her cottage near Northampton, he'd lived in Mickey's shed, then he'd lived like a nomad on the canal. The truth was that he lived wherever he happened to be at the time, but he could hardly say that.

'Paradise Farm, Walbrough,' he said.

'Walbrough. Never heard of it. Where the fuck's that?'

'It's in West Yorkshire.'

Brownrigg looked sceptical. 'You're a bit off the beaten track, aren't you? If that's home, what are you doing so far from it? You'd better not be shitting me, sunshine.'

The sergeant took another piece of equipment that looked like a large tablet. He tapped the screen and waited. He waited some more, chuntering to himself about "fucking technology". He tapped again. Lander wondered how much longer he'd have to stand. The nausea had gone, but now he felt giddy. The idea of falling in a faint in front of this lot was unthinkable, and he put his hand out towards the Avatar to steady himself. Green jabbed the rifle into his ribs, forcing him back, away from the vehicle. Lander winced.

'Keep your distance,' Brownrigg said.

Lander was puzzled. 'What?'

'Stand away. How do we know you're not infected? We don't know where you've been. Do you think we want to catch the virus from you?'

Lander stood back. The tablet screen came to life.

'Well, it does appear that there's an Alexander James Shaw registered at the address you gave, and the photo I have here looks about as ugly as you.' He consulted the screen again. 'There's no record of your ID being reported missing.'

'I didn't report it,' said Lander.

Brownrigg frowned. 'You know that's an offence, don't you?'

'It's only just happened,' Lander lied. He wished he could sit down.

'There are some more people listed here,' said Brownrigg, going back to the tablet. 'There's a Mary Jane Shaw, noted as deceased.'

'That was my Mam.'

'And there are two more. Gilbert Michael Stanley and Elizabeth Mary Stanley, also deceased.'

'My Grandparents.'

'And we have Cheryl Mary Shaw. She looks a bit like you, poor girl.'

'That's my twin sister. She's dead too.'

'She's not showing here as dead.'

'But she is.'

For the first time the sergeant was sympathetic. 'So you're the last one left. You were lucky.' He gave Lander a long look. 'Or perhaps not. Anyway, you've got a name.'

The tablet on Brownrigg's knee buzzed and the screen changed. He studied it. 'Well, well, well. It seems that you not only have a name, but you're also a person of interest.'

Lander didn't know what he was talking about. Of interest? To who?

'At least that solves the problem of what we're to do with you. You have a destination.'

Brownrigg swapped the tablet for the first machine and again tapped the keys. 'Here.' He pulled a piece of plastic from the back of the machine and tossed it onto the ground beside Lander. He bent painfully and picked it up. It was a new ID card, complete with his name and photo. He put it in his pocket.

Get in,' said Brownrigg, jerking his thumb towards the rear of the vehicle and closing his own door.

'Not there,' said Green, as Lander started towards the second row of seats. 'In the back.'

He went to the rear of the vehicle and opened the tailgate. Lander climbed in and it slammed behind him. He was in a sealed compartment, separated from the rest of the vehicle by a screen of thick plastic. There was a square of foam to sit on, but that was all.

'Comfy?' Brownrigg's voice came through a speaker.

'What is this?'

'It's to keep you isolated, until we get you to where you can be properly de-loused.'

This made no sense, thought Lander. What was he talking about? They must still be worried about the Infection.

'Where are you taking me?' he said.

'To your new home, of course.'

'New home? I've got a home.'

'You had a home, now you've got a new one. Look at your ID. What do you think it's for?'

Lander pulled out the card Brownrigg had given him. The address it gave wasn't Paradise Farm. According to the card he now lived in Pod 9, Ludlow, Shropshire. He'd never been to Ludlow, only vaguely heard of it. And what was Pod 9? Lander still couldn't see any reason for what they were doing.

'Why are you taking me to Ludlow?' he said. 'I don't want to go there.'

'Questions questions questions. Because Ludlow is where we've been given orders to take you. You don't get to choose where you go, the system decides where people are needed. You must have some skills that Ludlow can use, though it beats me what they can be.'

'I expect they're short of wankers.' He heard the voice of Green, and laughter from the others.

'You're lucky,' said Brownrigg, as the Avatar pulled away. 'Normally we'd have taken you to be sanitised and locked you up until transport could be organised. It could have been weeks. At least this way you'll get there quicker.'

Lander wondered if he was supposed to be grateful.

'It's because, according to our records, you've got a green rating. That means somebody important thinks you're special. Now, why might that be?'

Lander had no idea, but it was possible that it might have something to do with Adam.

10

———

BABIES

IT WAS A DIFFICULT DECISION for Magda. Adam had told her that the mobile phone that he'd left with her was for emergencies only.

'It's a secret network,' he'd said, 'for top-level government use. I shouldn't be letting you in on it, but you may need to contact me.'

Was this an emergency? Not really. There was nothing anyone could do for Lisa or for her baby, but Adam had said that she was to report to him on the birth. And he'd left her in charge, although he hadn't bothered to tell her that. In any case, she wasn't sure what being in charge meant; the Nightingales had their own leaders, strong and decisive women, and Magda wasn't confident they would accept her taking over. She hesitated for some time before making the call and waited until late so that she would not be disturbing him in one of his meetings. He took the news she gave in silence. Then he exploded.

'The Goddamned Nightingales! Ignorant bitches! I should never have left her with them. I should have taken her to Oxford.' He

628

was shouting so loud that she had to hold the phone away from her ear.

She was astounded. She'd never heard Adam carry on like that. She'd known he wouldn't be pleased, but she'd thought he would be upset and sympathetic rather than angry; the tirade was unexpected, and completely out of character.

Memories crowded in, of Lisa's interminable labour, the care and attention given by the Nightingale women, herself sitting at the bedside hour after hour after hour. It was fine for Adam to talk, he hadn't been there. She felt resentful at his outburst, but she tried to take the heat out of the situation.

'It wasn't their fault,' she said as evenly as she could. 'I was with them. They did everything they could.'

'Well, it wasn't enough. They were supposed to take care of her. Fucking incompetents. The one natural conception we know about and they can't cope with it. Of course it was their fault. Yours too. What did you do? I left you in charge.'

Magda felt as though he'd slapped her, and her temper rose. 'Hang on a minute. To start with you never told me I was in charge, I had to discover that from Margaret. And what did I do? I saved Lisa and I brought her here in the first place. After what she'd been through – chased, starved, exhausted – it's no wonder her baby didn't make it.'

'You should have watched her. She should have been monitored round the clock.'

'She was monitored. We were watching her.' Adam started to respond but Magda wouldn't let him. She was angry herself now, and the fire built as she spoke. 'We could have done a better job if we'd had the right equipment, like a working scanner. The Nightingales could have watched the baby and done a Caesarean when they saw a problem. You were supposed to be getting them a scanner from Oxford, but I don't see one anywhere.'

There was silence. Then the call went dead.

Early the next morning Adam arrived. He was not alone. Magda watched two other men get out of the black van with him. Adam didn't come over to greet her but stayed by the vehicle, talking to the men. They unloaded a flight case and one of them wheeled it into the hall.

'Video equipment,' he said to the watching Magda.

She was wondering what it was for and waiting to ask Adam when the second man came in. He had a large black canvas sack.

'Babies,' he said, and unzipped it.

There must have been seven or eight of them, all white except for one black one and an oriental one. They were tiny, perfect likenesses of newborn infants. They were so lifelike that Magda was shocked when she saw them. Piling them in a bag like that seemed barbaric and cruel, and she wanted to rush forward and rescue them. She was staring at the babies when Adam came in.

'What's this all about?' she said. She was still angry, angry with Adam for being angry with her. She wanted an apology. It didn't look as though she was going to get one, although he had calmed down since the previous night.

'We're going to shoot some video,' he said. 'I want the Nightingales in bed. At least, all of them who look young enough to get pregnant. Go tell them,' he said, when Magda didn't move.

'Tell them what?'

'Tell them I'm going to make a video. I want ten or so of the younger women in bed, in their nightwear, the sexier the better. Tell them to do it.'

Magda resisted the temptation to tell him to go fuck himself. That would come later. Instead she said very coolly, 'They'll want to know why. What's this all about?'

Adam adopted the tone he might with a slow child. Once more, this was a side of him Magda had not hitherto seen.

'We have a problem,' he said. 'Nobody ever predicted that one of the hidden effects of the Infection virus would be to compromise the male reproductive system. Nobody knew, so nobody said anything or made any preparations. Now rumours are starting. Some women have been trying to conceive but no one has done so. Some of them seem to be infertile too because they've stopped having periods. People are starting to notice that no one is pregnant and they're beginning to talk. If we're not careful there'll be panic, chaos.'

He walked to the window and put his hands on his hips.

'So we have to convince everyone that things are normal,' he said, 'and that what they may experience themselves or see in their immediate area is out of the ordinary. Matt here,' he indicated one of the men with him, 'is going to make a video which will show several women with newborn babies. They'll be holding these dummies,' he poked the sack of babies with his shoe, 'and looking as if they've recently given birth.'

'And you want the Nightingales to be the "mothers"?'

'Got it. Lisa was so important. If we'd been able to include a real living, breathing brat it would have made the scene more convincing. Now we'll have to do without. After the total cock-up the Nightingale women have made, the least they can do is help make this video happen.'

Magda bit her tongue; now wasn't the time to argue. She didn't like Adam's idea or his tone, but she set about doing what he wanted.

It wasn't easy to convince the Nightingales. She began by explaining what the video would show and why. Adam was wise enough not to blame anyone overtly for Lisa's stillbirth, but his mood and demeanour were not pleasant. He radiated an aura of disapproval. Several of the women said that the video was intended to mislead and that was dishonest, and they flatly refused to have anything to do with it. Most of the others were doubtful. Magda had to work hard to convince them that although it was a deception it was for the general good, and it would contribute to keeping people calm and optimistic while scientists worked out a solution to the infertility problem.

It was Carol who showed a lead and unlocked the situation. 'All right,' she said, 'I'll do it. But it's for you, not for him.'

Adam wasn't close enough to hear her and Magda was grateful for that, but even more for the demonstration of comradeship. Carol's support swung it, and after a little discussion more of the Nightingales followed her lead.

Matt was not only the cameraman but the director too. He knew what he wanted and managed everything clearly and briskly.

The first few shots were of "mothers" sitting up in bed with their babies, as if newly born. Tucked up in shawls, it was hard to believe they were not real, even from close in. Matt's colleague with the dolls, who was called Livingstone, did the women's make-up, and he managed to make them appear tired but triumphant. Then Matt had a group of six of the Nightingales stand in a rough circle, some cradling their pretend offspring and others holding them on their shoulders as if patting for wind. These women were in everyday clothes, and the idea was that they should resemble a group of young mums chatting at a post-natal clinic. A few of them were good actors, and next Matt had these in chairs, gazing fondly at the rubber homunculi in their arms while they rocked to and fro and sang lullabies. Livingstone, who was also the sound man, recorded their singing and cooing, and in the background played a soundtrack of babies crying.

There weren't enough of the dolls for the women to have one each, and they had to double up. Magda thought that given the circumstances that was an apt metaphor. Some of them found the experience hard. One, Paula, couldn't stop crying and Matt had to send her away. She came to stand beside Magda.

'Are you all right?'

Paula sniffed. 'I suppose so. It just brings things back. Some of us lost children to the Infection, but at least we know what being a mum feels like. Now no one can get pregnant any more those who've not had kids will never have that experience.' She made a sweeping gesture, taking in the scene Matt was recording, and the other women waiting for their cues. 'Can you think of anything more cruel than making us do this?' She began to cry again.

Magda had never even considered the possibility of giving birth herself. It was a topic that held no interest at all for her. After the initial panic, when she thought she was pregnant, she'd been quite pleased when her periods stopped. She still had her sex drive but now pills, condoms or any of the other paraphernalia of contraception weren't needed any more. The emotion Paula described came as a surprise, but it helped her to understand why so many of the Nightingales had been reluctant to cooperate in Adam's scheme.

Making the video took all day. Most of the women left when their own bit was done, but a few lingered after the last take to view the scenes that had been shot. Adam seemed pleased, moving closer to his usual self, or at least to the self that Magda knew.

'What do you think?' he said.

'It's good,' said Magda. 'If I hadn't seen it made I'd believe it.'

Matt had been careful to ensure that the babies were well covered by blankets and shawls, and the camera had stayed some distance away from them.

Matt and Livingstone packed up their gear and stowed the rubber infants in their bag. They loaded the van and got in. Magda had been expecting Adam to return with them, but it seemed he was going to stay. They stood together and watched the tail lights disappear along the road.

'What happens now?' said Magda.

'I'm not sure,' said Adam. 'Gus, I mean First Minister McFarlane, wants to do an introduction and release it on tv as a public information broadcast. All the pods have tv now, so that would get it around fast. But I think it would be better if we did something less official. We've got some people working on creating a new internet, NewNet we're calling it. It should be up and running soon, and then all the pods will have it. We're getting the mobile networks going again, too. Then we can drop in some clips and organise some sharing, so that the video looks to come from an individual rather than from the government. I think that will be more convincing.'

'You think people will believe it?'

Adam seemed puzzled. 'Why shouldn't they?'

'Some of the women looked sad. They were hardly showing the joy of new motherhood.'

'Mardy cows,' he grunted. 'It's bad enough them not caring for Lisa properly, you'd think they could at least make the video work.'

Magda told him what Paula had said. Adam was unsympathetic.

'Well that's just tough,' he said. 'Everybody's in the same boat.'

Magda wasn't surprised. For Adam the end always justified the means. 'How long do you think it will be before rumours start that the video is a fake?' she said.

Adam shrugged. Magda thought he looked weary. His eyes were red and there were dark shadows under them. 'Why should they?' he said. 'Only a few people know about it. Matt and Livingstone are solid, they won't say anything. We can keep an eye on the people here and make sure the Nightingales don't gossip. Anyway, there'll soon be something else to get everybody's attention.' He became more animated, reminding Magda of the old sparkle that he used to show when he became excited about something. 'The white coats at Oxford say they're making good progress towards producing babies through surrogacy. The tests are going well. The procedures aren't one hundred per cent reliable yet, but they've managed to get a foetus to term.'

Magda was astonished. 'How? I mean, where are the fathers? I thought that all the men you'd tested were sterile.'

Adam laughed. 'That's true, they are. We're working on something completely different.'

11

———

POD 9

LANDER'S JOURNEY TO LUDLOW was dire. The foam pad in the back of the Avatar was useless. Stubbs drove with no care for his passengers, and with each bend it slid around, sometimes tipping Lander onto the metal floor. The scrapes and grazes he'd got from his journey along the stream and through the pipe were still painful but were nothing compared with where he'd been hit by the baton round; that really hurt. They called them rubber bullets, though it had felt more like being struck with a metal bar. Every bump, every jerk, every lurch of the vehicle tweaked the pain. He tried to use his legs to brace himself against the rolling and the pitching, but it was impossible.

The roads were deserted. Night had come on and it was now black, moonless and starless. All he could see through the plastic screen were the triple beams of the Avatar's lights sweeping the road ahead. There were no signs of life anywhere, neither in the villages they passed through nor in any of the roadside houses.

He knew nothing of Ludlow. He had only the vaguest notion of where it was, but he did know he didn't want to go there. What could possibly be there for him? Brownrigg said he'd been allocated to the place. Why? How could he get out of it? He needed to escape, but his guards had guns and he was unable to run. Besides, where would he go? Before the Infection, he'd seen news videos of protests against climate change. The demonstrators had gone in for passive resistance. There had been shots of people lying inert in the road, picked up by the police and carried away. It had taken three policemen to handle some of them. It had looked pretty effective. Could he do that? Could he simply go inert, not actually provoke them by refusing to cooperate but just do nothing? He didn't think so. Brownrigg and the others weren't likely to be anywhere near as easygoing as the policemen had been, with news cameras recording their every move. He didn't fancy subjecting his injured leg to the sort of treatment he guessed Green and Stubbs might give it.

Brownrigg's voice came over the speaker again. 'I'm not apologising that Greeno here fired at you,' he said, 'but I regret it. Do you understand the difference?'

Lander thought he understood but it didn't matter, his leg still hurt. He expected there was a spectacular bruise cooking away under his jeans.

'Why are you taking me to Ludlow?'

'Because that's where Pod 9 is.'

'What's a pod?'

Brownrigg sighed. 'Jesus, where have you been? Pods are where people live now.'

Lander had an image of a row of green tubes filled with people, a bit like the Japanese capsule hotel he'd seen on television. Surely Ludlow wouldn't be like that.

'Are there lots of pods?'

'Fifteen,' said Brownrigg.

'Why can't I choose where I go?'

'Ooh, get you,' said Brownrigg in a stage-gay voice that made the others laugh. 'You go where you're put, that's why. Anyway, it seems that for reasons I can't begin to fathom, Ludlow needs you.'

He heard a click as the speaker was switched off. The conversation was over. Back to the blackness, and the pitching and rolling.

Eventually, he saw faint lights in the distance. Then there were the shapes of houses, all in darkness. The buildings looked old, a couple were half-timbered, and some were boarded up. The Avatar slowed as they passed through a barbed wire fence and came to a gateway. An EA officer waved them through, and they pulled into a car park in front of what might once have been a hotel. Brownrigg got out and went inside. Lander watched through the window, waiting to see what was in store for him.

Stubbs's voice came to him faintly through the screen. 'Well, that's a surprise. I thought they might have a brass band to welcome you, or at least a firework display, being as how you're so fucking important.'

'Or a bunch of cheerleaders,' said Green.

'I wish.'

Brownrigg returned. Two other men were with him: one was small, thin, and weedy looking, with a comb-over that was being badly subverted by the wind, the other was taller, and held something that looked like a cattle prod. The small man was in a jacket and trousers, the other wore a grey one-piece. The three of them stood at the back of the Avatar. Brownrigg signalled to Stubbs, who got out and opened the tailgate.

'Out,' said Brownrigg.

Lander slid down, wincing as his shot leg made contact with the ground.

'This is Mr Wilkinson,' Brownrigg said. 'He's your boss. Do what he tells you, or you'll have me to answer to. And until you're washed keep your distance.' He turned to Wilkinson. 'He's all yours.'

Brownrigg and Stubbs got back into the Avatar and the door slammed. Lander watched the vehicle rumble away. He'd hated the ride, which had been painful in the extreme, but with the departure of the Avatar it seemed a link with the outside world had gone. He was cold, it was dark, and he could hardly see Wilkinson and the other man, who stood a couple of metres from him. Around in the gloom were the dim outlines of featureless buildings. He had no idea where he was or who he was with.

'Follow me,' said Wilkinson. He led the way towards the building outside which they'd stopped.

Lander limped after him. His leg had stiffened on the journey and he could hardly use it. The man with the prod followed. Wilkinson held open the door and motioned Lander to go through.

He was in a long entrance hall. The building wasn't an abandoned hotel; it was a public baths, or it had been, a relic from the days before each house had its own bathroom, a place where people used to go for their weekly clean-up and a swim. At the far end was a door marked "Swimmers Only". On one side was another door, labelled "Males", and opposite it, one marked "Females".

Wilkinson pointed to the male door.

'There's a shower and some towels in there, and a change of clothes. Wash thoroughly, including your hair, but keep it short. Water is scarce. Put on the clothes you'll find in there and leave your own in the bin.'

Lander didn't move. 'Why?' he said. 'What's this all about?'

'All the pods are currently Infection free. We have to make sure they stay that way and that you are not bringing the virus in.'

'But the Infection's over,' Lander protested.

'And that is exactly the way we want to keep it,' said Wilkinson. 'Now go in there and shower, and be quick. We'll wait out here.'

If the man hadn't been polite Lander might have rebelled, but the request was put so reasonably that even though it seemed absurd he followed it. The shower was cold so there was no temptation to prolong it. He was out in less than a minute and grabbed the towel to dry himself. He examined his leg. He was right about the bruise. It was spectacular, a dark core with technicolour rings. It looked cool, but it was sore.

The "clothes" were hanging on a peg. There was a short-sleeved vest, cotton boxers and an orange overall. Were they seriously expecting him to wear that? There was nothing else. He dressed, and put his own clothes in the bin, but before that he fished out the plastic card with his name and photo. It was a statement of his identity, the only thing at the moment that connected him to reality. The feel of the card was confirmation that he was not in a dream. He supposed his clothes would be washed. They were all he had. What had happened to his rucksack? Still in the field where he'd dropped it, probably. It contained everything else he owned. On the bench were socks, and a pair of trainers at least two sizes too big. He put them on, and shuffled towards the door, walking like a clown.

'Ah, there you are,' said Wilkinson. 'Now I can greet you properly.' He held out his hand. 'I am Mr Wilkinson. I am the Mayor of Ludlow, Chief Executive of Pod 9.'

Lander wasn't moved to shake the man's hand, but he did. 'Lander Shaw,' he muttered.

'I know who you are. I've been expecting you. You are welcome.'

Lander looked for the other man, but he'd gone. It was just him and Wilkinson. He could easily push the little man aside and run away, but could he escape? There was barbed wire, and EA people at the gate, and he had no idea where to go.

'Follow me, please,' said Wilkinson. 'I'll take you to your abode.'

Their way led along a dark street. Wilkinson set a fast pace. Only one street light in three seemed to be working; that, the uneven pavement, Lander's bad leg and his oversized shoes made keeping up difficult. He was relieved when they stopped outside a small house in the middle of a terrace. There was no sign of life in the other houses.

'This is your accommodation,' said Wilkinson. 'I think you'll find everything you need. There's food in the fridge, so help yourself. You are the only occupant so there's no need to worry about waking anyone up. I'm sorry about the shoes, we had to guess your size. Someone will be here at nine o'clock tomorrow morning to take you to your briefing. Good night.'

Wilkinson gave a little nod, turned and walked briskly away. Lander was full of questions but he was left on the pavement, watching until the little man disappeared around a corner.

He pushed the door of the house open. There was a smell of disinfectant, which didn't completely mask an underlying mustiness, as if the house hadn't been lived in for some time. He felt around on the wall until he located a light switch. He pressed it without confidence – he'd seen no lighting in any of the houses they'd passed – but the switch worked, and a single naked light bulb came on.

He was in a tiny living room. The bare walls were painted cream, there was a saggy sofa, and in the corner a staircase led to the floor above. A door connected with another room. Lander turned on the light in there too and saw that it was a small kitchen.

He climbed the stairs. They were steep, and his leg complained. The upper floor was no more inviting than the ground. There was a solitary light in each room, hanging shadeless from the centre. One of the two bedrooms had a bed, the other was empty. There were no carpets or rugs, just bare boards. There didn't seem to be a television, radio, or any other entertainment, apart from a few worn paperbacks on a shelf in the living room: *Jane and the Chalet School, Pippi Longstocking, Katy and the Big Snow, Anne of Green Gables.* He'd seen Kerryl with some of these. He bet she'd read the lot. There was *Harry Potter and the Philosopher's Stone.* It was the only story he'd read right through since leaving primary school. He'd quite liked it, but he hadn't bothered with the rest of the series. The movies were better.

All the furniture was old and there wasn't much of it. There was such a lot of newer stuff in abandoned houses and stores that Lander couldn't believe this was the best Ludlow could offer. Were they trying to tell him something? What had Stubbs meant when he said he was important? If this was what the important people got, heaven help the rest.

He went to the fridge and was surprised when a light came on as he opened the door. Did all the pods have electricity? Where did it come from? He knew it was a priority for the government to get the power supplies working again but the system was still patchy and there'd been a generator at Lake Manor.

There was a loaf of sliced bread in the fridge – white, thank God. There were eggs, bacon and milk. Beside the fridge was a portable gas hob with two hotplates and a tube leading to a cylinder under the counter. There was a box of matches beside it. Lander thought that if he was going to stay here he'd move the whole kit to the bedroom so he could make bacon sandwiches in bed. There was a kettle, a mug, a jam jar full of tea bags, and two large water bottles. There were some utensils in a cupboard, including a frying pan. He was hungry, so he took half the bacon, put it in the pan, lit the stove, and fried it. When he'd finished he left the hob lit to warm the room. He made himself a mug of tea and sat on the sofa to eat. The sandwich was good, even without ketchup. The tea was not, there was no sugar, so he left it.

What was going to happen now? He supposed he'd find that out the next morning at the promised "briefing", whatever that was. Did he care? Not really. Until the incident at Lake Manor his aim in life had been to find Adam and face him with what he'd done to Kerryl. Well, he'd found Adam and nothing had been resolved, but what had he expected? An apology? Whatever Adam did wouldn't bring Kerryl back, and in his darker moments he accepted that what had happened to his sister wasn't only the fault of Adam; partly it was his. If he hadn't crept away in the middle of the night, if he'd stayed at the farm, she might still be alive. And now he was in this God-forsaken dump, a town he'd scarcely heard of. He'd been swept up off the street like a stray dog and dropped in a place he didn't know.

Right, he'd had no say in being brought to this rathole, so he was fucked if he was going to cooperate. Briefing at nine o'clock, Wilkinson had said. Time to get some sleep. He turned off the hob but left the frying pan unwashed, his sandwich plate and mug on the living room floor, and dragged himself upstairs where he lay down on the bed.

Nine o'clock the next morning found him fast asleep. When he did finally come to and blinked at his watch it said eleven twenty. He got off the bed and went to the window. Just like the night before, the street was empty. There was nothing anywhere to suggest that any of the houses might be lived in. Where had they put him? The back of beyond? The middle of nowhere? Zombie-town?

He went downstairs. The frying pan, plate and mug were exactly as he'd left them. He'd also not put away the bread, and the unwrapped top slices were curled at the edges.

He put the rest of the bacon in the pan and heated it. Then, in a burst of culinary enterprise, he added two of the eggs. One of them broke but the other survived intact. When everything was cooked, he tipped the contents of the pan onto last night's sandwich plate, set it on the kitchen table, and ate. He drank the rest of the milk. Instead of being in a plastic container, it was in a glass bottle. Weird.

Had somebody come for him at nine? Had they banged on the door, shouted up at the bedroom window and he simply hadn't heard them? Kerryl had always said he could sleep for England, and their Mam had constantly nagged him about getting up in the mornings. The bedroom curtains were navy blue and thick, and they made the bedroom very dark. It was no wonder he'd slept through.

He went to the bathroom. He turned on the tap but there was no water. There was another large plastic bottle beside the basin. He toyed with going downstairs to warm up the water but he couldn't be bothered, so he washed in cold. He examined his bruise. The halo of vivid colours had been replaced by a blotch of rancid yellow. He went downstairs.

Right, he thought. Time to get moving. Time to make some sense of this place.

12

AT HOME

THERE WAS NO KEY so Lander left the house open. It didn't seem there was anybody around to steal from him, even if he had anything worth taking. The street was featureless and deserted. It was also short, and he set out to walk to the junction at its end to see if he could find the town centre, shuffling along in his clown's shoes. He might even be able to locate where he should go for the briefing. He was very late but he was sure that wouldn't matter. After all, nothing else was happening.

He was fifty metres from the junction when somebody crossed it on a bicycle. They too were wearing an orange overall. Lander shouted and waved but the rider didn't see him, or perhaps saw him but chose to ignore him. He ran to the end of the street but by the time he got there, the cyclist had vanished.

The whole place was deserted; it was eerie, a ghost town. It reminded Lander of an old black and white television series he and Kerryl had binge-watched ages ago. It had been about this guy who was kept in some crazy village somewhere. He didn't know why he was there or what he was supposed to have done and he kept trying to escape, but every time he thought he'd got away they caught him and brought him back. Is that what's happening to me? he thought. Am I *The Prisoner?*

He scanned the street. Left, or right? Neither. There was a small shop across the road and Lander made for it, constructing a shopping list in his head. More bacon, more eggs, some baked beans would be nice, coke, chocolate, beer, cereal, milk, burgers, chips, sugar, pizza. And ketchup.

The shop had an old-fashioned bell that tinkled as he opened the door. A woman who was sitting behind the counter glanced up from her book, smiled briefly, and then went back to reading. There was no need here to watch for shoplifting, he thought. She, too, was wearing what seemed to be the regulation one-piece; hers was grey, like the young man's last night.

Lander picked up a basket and started to cruise the shelves. The first disappointment was that the shop had only a few of the items on his list. There were some fresh things – cabbage, leeks, carrots, potatoes, apples – but he didn't fancy much of that and there was nothing canned or preserved, except for jam. There was no ketchup. There was no sugar either, but there were a few small jars of honey. He put one of those in his basket, and bacon and eggs, apples, and currant buns.

He took his selection to the counter. There was no till and the woman added up the items he'd chosen using a pencil and a scrap of paper.

'That's four and a half see yous,' she said. 'But as you're new we'll call it four.'

'See yous?'

'Currency units.'

Lander pulled a couple of crumpled notes and some coins from his pocket and offered them. The woman looked at him sadly and shook her head.

'I'm sorry love. That's old money from before. It's no good anymore. Didn't you know?'

Lander felt a bristle of resentment. What was this place that wouldn't take his money? 'How do you mean, it's no good anymore?'

'It's not legal tender. There was so much theft and looting during the Infection that the whole money system got out of hand. Some people had thousands of pounds, hundreds of thousands, that they'd simply stolen, and other people who had been well off had lost the lot. Because of that, the government banned pounds and pence. Instead, each pod issues its own money. We use LCUs, Ludlow Currency Units. It's a good idea. It keeps things simple, and means that as all the pods are different people are less likely to try to leave because they don't have money they can use anywhere else.' She stopped speaking and waited, as if in anticipation of Lander suddenly producing a fistful of CUs.

'How do I get some of these CU things?'

'They're payment. In return for CTCs.'

Why does this woman have to talk in riddles? thought Lander. Is everyone here like this?

'CTCs?'

'My, you are new, aren't you? CTCs are Community Task Contributions. It's work, but we're not paid by the item or the hour, but for what the Mayor and his advisers judge to be our contribution to the community. They assess what you've done at the end of each week, and then award CUs based on what they think its value is.' She frowned, puzzled. 'Don't you know this? Were you asleep during your briefing?' Then it dawned. 'Ah, you haven't had a briefing yet, have you?'

Lander shook his head.

'Well, you'd better go and get yourself one. That'll explain it all, and you'll be given some CUs to get you started. Then you can come back for your shopping. I'd let you take it now but I'm not allowed to give credit, it's illegal. But I can put it on one side for you to collect later, when you can pay.'

Lander stood for a long moment. He needed to feed himself. Also he'd need soap, toothpaste and a toothbrush, cleaning materials, and for God's sake, some better shoes. It seemed all this depended on him getting some of these CU things. When he was on the canal they'd just taken what they needed from the empty stores they'd come across when they went through towns and villages. Now, though, the days of helping yourself to what you fancied seemed to be gone.

'Where should I go for this briefing?' he asked.

'To the Mayor's office.' Then, when he clearly didn't understand, 'It's along the street, first left, in the square by the castle.' She pointed in the direction the cyclist had gone. 'You can't miss it.'

Last night Lander had been set on a policy of non-co-operation. However, it seemed that if he didn't fall into line he wouldn't be able to eat, so he would play their game; at least, he would for now. He thanked the woman, left the shop and headed in the direction she had shown.

In the centre of the town there were a few people about, all in what seemed to be the uniform onesie, some orange, some grey, and one dark blue. No one took any notice of him. They were strolling from one place to another or chatting together, so he could have asked for directions had they been needed, but the office of the Mayor was obvious. It was an imposing stone building that was the hub of the square, in the shadow of the castle wall. A brass plate said it was the Town Hall.

A short flight of steps led to the entrance. Lander went up them and pushed open the heavy door at the top. He stepped into a dark, high-ceilinged entrance hall. There was a tiled floor, and a hefty mahogany staircase with the treads carpeted in green. In the centre of the space was a large brown desk marked "Reception", and behind it was a young man. It was the same one who had been with the Mayor the night before. In the daylight, Lander could see that he was about his own age, and he suffered badly from acne.

The young man shuffled through a pile of papers. 'Lander Shaw,' he said, taking one. 'Yes, your briefing should have been this morning. It was scheduled for nine-thirty.' He fixed Lander with a stare, waiting for an answer.

Lander studied a particularly fruity zit flourishing on the young man's chin. 'I must have misunderstood,' he mumbled.

'Right, well, you'll have to come back. I'll put you down for the same time tomorrow: nine-thirty.'

'Can't I have the briefing now?'

The young man regarded him as if he'd just asked how many grains of sand it takes to make a desert.

'Do you think the Mayor has been in his office all morning doing nothing else but waiting for you to condescend to turn up? He's a busy man. He has other matters needing his attention.'

'You could ask him.'

'I don't need to. Nine-thirty tomorrow.'

Part of Lander wanted to seize this obnoxious little toad and thump him, but that would achieve nothing. He was simply following his orders. He turned away and left, letting the door slam behind him.

The walk back to the house took less than five minutes, even in the sloppy shoes. As he passed the shop he wondered about going in and pleading with the woman to let him have his shopping. She hadn't seemed unfriendly, but he knew there was no point. He'd already gathered that in Ludlow rules were rules. It was probably the same in the other pods too. It seemed that the First Minister guy, MacSomething-or-other, was laying down the law. If he was the bloke Adam had been working for it went some way towards explaining how he'd become so bossy.

The house was just as he'd left it. The empty milk bottle, the dirty frying pan, the plate, knife, fork, and mug from the night before were exactly where he'd put them. It was obvious no one else was going to clear them away so he ran a bowl of cold water and did his best to get the grease and dried egg off.

He was cold. There'd been a fleece in his rucksack and he wished he had it now. There would probably be a store in Ludlow where he could get some clothes, but that would take CUs. To get those he would have to cooperate. Better not miss tomorrow's briefing. In the meantime, there was the rest of today to get through.

He was bored. Somehow he had to fill the time. What was there to do? He supposed he could go and explore the town, but there didn't seem to be much of it. There must be more shops, but he couldn't buy anything because what he'd thought was money appeared now to be worthless. He wondered how many people were in the pod. He'd hardly seen anybody, and of those he'd met, the woman in the shop had been all right but the spotty little clerk was definitely unfriendly. If there were more like him he'd rather keep away. He got the Harry Potter book and started on it.

After reading for a while he got up and stretched his legs. He made a cup of tea and tried to drink it, but without milk or sugar it was bitter. He read some more until somewhere a clock chimed six. Then he fried the remaining eggs. He wanted some toast, but the only way to make it seemed to be to get the hotplate as hot as he could and lay the slices of bread directly on it. The result was a sort of rusk, but it was all right when dipped in the egg. There were a few slices of bread left, and they were the last of the food. He was still hungry, but he decided to leave them for breakfast. Not great, but at least they were something.

He went back to Hogwarts. After reading for a while he felt chilly again, so he got the hotplate from the kitchen and took it into the living room. At least the electricity supply was working, and it seemed to be unlimited. Would he have to pay for that? Would he need CUs for his heating and cooking?

With the curtains drawn and the doors shut he managed to create what his granddad would have called "a bit of a fug". He heard the distant clock chime eight, then nine. He waited for ten o'clock and went upstairs. He cleaned his teeth with cold water and his finger, splashed his face, and got into bed.

Despite having done very little he was tired, and he was soon asleep.

13

____

A JOB FOR MAGDA

THE NAIL OF MAGDA'S index finger traced the two tiny lines between her eyebrows. She turned her head sideways. There were more lines at the corners of her eyes, and deeper ones running from each side of her nose towards her mouth. Smile lines, her mother had called them, and said they were the marks of a happy life, although she'd been keen enough to get Botox into hers. Was it normal for lines like these to be showing so much at her age? How old was she? Funny, since the Infection nobody seemed to bother about birthdays anymore. Left school at nineteen, three years voluntary work in Botswana, a year temping to try to get some money saved, three years at medical school, and another year since then. That makes me twenty-seven, she thought. No, that can't be right. How pathetic, not to know how old you are.

She studied her reflection again. Oval face, quite pale. Large round eyes. Shoulder length dark hair. It was a face that had seen things; it was the face of someone who had done things.

'Do I have the face of a murderer?' she said, glancing over her shoulder at Adam, standing behind her.

'Don't be stupid. Of course you don't.'

It wasn't stupid. Ever since killing Mickey she'd had nightmares, dreams of that terrible night in the shed, the floor slippery with his blood, her clothes soaked in it. She'd thought that as time passed these visions would fade, but they didn't; they were more vivid than ever, and now she was almost afraid to go to sleep in case they returned. She knew that this was not exceptional, that in cases such as hers imagination fed on memory to create ever more intense evocations. She also knew that they were amplified by her depression, a black cloud on the rim of her consciousness that now seemed to be her constant companion.

'Why not?' she said. 'I've killed somebody, haven't I?'

'Well if you're a murderer, then so am I.'

'What you did isn't the same. Whatever happened with Kerryl was accidental. What I did was deliberate. I meant to kill Mickey.' She shuddered.

Adam gently took her chin and angled her face towards his.

'You had no choice. The way you've told it, Mickey was treating you so badly you would have died if he wasn't stopped. And Lander would have died with you, so you may have taken one life, but you saved another two. Besides, he was raping you. What you did was self-defence. Neither of us has taken life by choice.'

Magda nodded. He was right, of course, but the scene remained strong, and she had no doubt it would be with her forever. She wiped a tear from her cheek.

'Hey,' said Adam.

He leant towards her and his lips met hers. Their mouths were open, but it was a gentle kiss, comforting and calm, not the passionate grappling of the night before.

'Cheer up,' he said.

Adam had turned up late last night, in a completely different mood from the anger and exasperation of his previous visit. The blame was gone, and Lisa and her baby weren't mentioned. He'd taken the video of the Nightingale women and their pretend babies to Winchester and persuaded First Minister McFarlane that his idea for distributing it through social media would be the most effective way of getting it into the public domain.

'The snag is that there currently are no social media,' he'd told her. 'Technically there's no reason why the cell phone network shouldn't be revived. All the gear's there.'

'What's the problem, then?' Magda had asked.

'The problem is Gus McFarlane. It needs his approval to go ahead, and he's hanging back.'

'Why?'

Adam shrugged. 'Perhaps he doesn't want people to be talking to each other yet.'

Magda had never met the First Minister, but she knew enough about him to agree. He had the reputation of being extremely cautious, paranoid even, about allowing people widespread and unfettered interaction. This, she guessed, was because he thought such social behaviour would undo the control he considered necessary for the national rebuilding, and divert attention from the creation of the new order that was going to take all of them the rest of their lives to achieve. It was the same motivation that had made him so ready to accept Adam's idea of the pods. It was nothing to do with isolation from a possible return of the infection, and everything to do with dividing and ruling.

'What about this NewNet that you were talking about? People could chat and message over that.'

'That's a better option as far as the boss is concerned, because it's easier to monitor and posts can be quickly taken down. However, it's not that simple. The technical problems are harder to deal with. We'll get it sorted in the end, but it might take some time. Your boyfriend is one of the people we've lined up to work on it.'

'Boyfriend?'

'Lander.'

Magda had thought about Lander a lot but had no news of him, and given what had happened when they were last together she'd avoided asking Adam about him. She'd just assumed that he was still on the loose somewhere.

'Lander's working for you?' It was hard to believe.

'Well yes, although he doesn't know it's me he's working for. A patrol picked him up a few days ago and he's been given the job of developing the system we need, one that replicates the provisions of the old internet but without the unsavoury free-for-all that went with it; you know, the scams, pornography, trolling, phishing, things like that.'

'Where is he? In Winchester?'

Adam smiled. 'No no no. I don't want him near me or the centre of government at the moment. No, we've sent him to a nice quiet little backwater.'

'Where?'

'It's best for you not to know that at the moment. Maybe when his project's completed you can get together, but for now let him be.' He stood up, stretched and glanced at his watch. 'Got to go. My car will be here soon.'

'Go? But you've only just got here.'

'Duty calls. Gus wants me in Winchester. I'm going to have to spend a lot more time there now. He's made me his Special Adviser.'

'Spend more time there? You couldn't.' Magda felt resentment bubble. What was she supposed to do while Adam was swanning around in Winchester?

'"That's terrific, Adam." "You must be making a great contribution, Adam." "The First Minister thinks a lot of you, Adam." "Congratulations." Aren't those the sorts of things you're wanting to say to me?'

'Yes, of course. Sorry. And yes, congratulations. It's just that I'm bored here on my own. There's nothing to do.'

'Nothing to do? But you're a doctor, at least you were training to be one, and this is a house full of medics. I thought there'd be plenty for you to do taking care of people.'

Magda shook her head, once again baffled by the contradictions that were Adam. On the one hand, he was aware of everything; on the other hand, he noticed nothing.

'It may have escaped your attention,' she said, 'but there are no people here to take care of. Lake Manor is a hospital with no patients. Lisa was the first, last, and only case the Nightingales have ever had.'

'And a fine job you all made of that one.'

Magda felt them edging towards another row. 'Yes, well, let's not go into that now.'

Adam too had seen the warning signs and pulled back. 'I don't think you'd find any more to do in Winchester. Still, you can come if you like.'

She shook her head. 'Can't. I've nothing packed.'

'I don't mean now. In a few days.' He had an idea. 'I might be able to get you a job in one of the government departments. There's an election coming up and there's bound to be some work to do with that.'

'An election?'

'Yes. My idea again. The provisional government was formed across parties to cope with the Infection. Now that's gone it has no real legitimacy. I've persuaded Gus that he needs a proper mandate from the people, so he can form a new government without all the wooden heads from the old Privy Council who keep opposing him. That means an election.'

Magda thought of all the rigmarole that used to go with elections before the Infection: the electoral registers, the leaflets and broadcasts, the news coverage, the canvassing. She couldn't see how it could be done.

'It's simple,' said Adam. 'For starters, there are nowhere near the same number of voters as before. That will make it a lot easier. And people are gathered in pods instead of being spread out. The mayor of each pod will make a list of the people entitled to vote. On the agreed day the election will be held, the votes will be cast and counted in the pods, and the results sent to a central data unit.'

'What about the people who aren't in pods?'

'The bums and layabouts? They won't get a vote, not unless they voluntarily join a pod, or we round them up first. The covens? Well, we'll make special arrangements for useful groups like the Nightingales. As for some of the others, I don't know. It won't make any difference anyway.'

'Why not?'

Adam planted a kiss on her forehead. 'Because, my sweet innocent chick, Gus will win.'

Magda turned away. She thought the kiss patronising, and his tone too. 'How can you be so sure?'

Adam laughed. 'Things will be arranged so that he does. My job, and yours if you come to Winchester, will be to do the arranging. Don't look so horrified. The last thing the country needs at the moment is a change in the administration. We need consistency, continuity, and a firm hand on the tiller. Maybe in a few years, when things are more settled, we can get back to the luxury of democracy, but for now people want stability. They can't cope with uncertainty.'

There had been so many changes, so much upheaval during and since the Infection, that Magda could see why he said that, but she didn't like it. What guarantee was there that Gus McFarlane was the person with the answers to the nation's problems? What guarantee was there that Adam was either? There may be other people better able to fix things. And where did freedom figure in all this? The pod system and the restrictions on movement meant that liberty was already severely limited. Yes, there had to be order, and strong direction, and the possibility of quarantine if the Infection resurfaced, but what Adam was proposing seemed close to dictatorship. And it was dishonest. Did he think no one would realise what was going on?

'Don't be so glum,' he said. 'It will all work out for the best. Trust me.'

And that was the problem. Magda was beginning to wonder if she could.

'While you're waiting, there's something else you can do for me,' Adam said, changing the subject.

'What's that?'

'You can take a look at some fertility research the white coats are doing in Oxford. They're carrying out some interesting work with monkeys, or they say they are. I'd like you to visit, and let me know exactly what's going on there. Here.' Adam rummaged in his document case and handed her a folder. 'That will tell you all about it.'

Something outside caught Magda's eye. A dark blue limousine was crunching over the gravel. It stopped in front of the building.

'That's your car.'

'Indeed it is.'

Adam gave her a quick peck, picked up his case and left the room. He didn't look back and she didn't follow him. She did watch from the window as the limo swept away.

The folder Adam had left contained a bound bundle of papers. They were headed, *Investigation into the feasibility of trans-species reproduction and issues relating to embryo hosting and surrogacy.*

The first part of the report was about the animals they appeared to be using for their experiments. Adam had called them monkeys but they weren't; they were bonobos. She got an encyclopaedia from the library shelves and looked up what they were. Bonobos were apes, very close relatives of chimpanzees but not the same. She went back to the report.

There was a lengthy explanation of why bonobos had been chosen. It seemed that both chimpanzees and bonobos share ninety-nine per cent of human DNA. However, bonobos are different from their better-known cousins. The report described how they have certain characteristics that are more like the traits of humans than of chimpanzees, as well as some features unique to their species. *Bonobo males are almost always subordinate to females,* she read. *They don't compete with each other for dominance or rank, and whereas chimpanzees are aggressive and groups often fight each other, bonobos are peaceful and generally calm.*

The more Magda learnt about these animals the more she was beguiled by their charm. She read that bonobos like to have fun and seem to have something that could be thought of as a sense of humour; they are playful when young and remain so throughout their lives. They indulge in frequent sex, and not necessarily to get the females pregnant but for enjoyment. They often go for same-sex partners, too. In fact, most bonobos seemed to swing all ways. Magda laughed out loud, tickled by the notion of LGBT apes.

The next part of the report was more serious, and had Magda gasping in disbelief.

To begin with, the researchers had tried to infect the bonobos with the I/452 virus. They hadn't succeeded, the creatures remaining resolutely healthy, and it seemed that their immune systems were able to shut out this particular invader. Given the closeness of their DNA profiles to those of humans, the team then speculated on whether it might be possible to somehow combine human and bonobo DNA, to create a new species that would be unsusceptible to the Infection virus and its variants.'

The author of the paper went into a long explanation of their approach to gene editing. To Magda it seemed pure hogwash, but it was powerfully argued. Then there was a description of the desired outcomes. Babies born from the process described would have the appearance of humans but would also have some bonobo attributes. The writers seemed to become more and more excited as their argument developed, predicting a new race which would combine the best features of both species, creatures who would be free from the Infection and would retain many human characteristics, but without the competitiveness and aggression that was a feature of so much human interaction.

Magda put the report aside. She thought the researchers had taken leave of their senses. It was laughable: monkey men, chimp women, Planet of the Apes. Did Adam believe all this guff? That he wanted her to visit the research facility suggested that he did; but he'd asked her to check on what was going on there, so perhaps he was just as sceptical as she. She would see.

14

____

A JOB FOR LANDER

LANDER HAD A BAD NIGHT. He was worried that he might sleep in and miss the briefing yet again, and that would mean no CUs, and no CUs would mean nothing to eat; the result was that he woke up every hour, and eventually got up long before he needed to. He had a wash, again in cold water, put on his orange overall, skipped breakfast – there was only stale bread anyway – and walked to the Mayor's office. It was nine-fifteen by the clock in the square as he climbed the steps.

The same receptionist, who Lander had nicknamed Snotty Spotty, told him to wait, and he sat on a bench against the panelled wall. It was well after ten before Snotty Spotty called over to him, 'The Mayor will see you now,' and pointed to the grand staircase.

Mayor Wilkinson's office was impressive. Glass-fronted cupboards held leather-bound books in rich bindings, and there was a thick Persian carpet. In the centre of the room, a huge desk dwarfed the little man behind it.

'Ah, Shaw,' he said as Lander entered. 'So sorry you couldn't make it yesterday.'

Despite himself and all the resolutions he'd made about not cooperating with these people, not even being nice to them, Lander found himself apologising.

'I'm sorry,' he said. 'I think I must have misunderstood.'

'Yes, perhaps. Well, you're here now.'

That is true, thought Lander, but refrained from saying it. The Mayor didn't strike him as a man with much humour. Nobody in Ludlow did.

'I understand that Audrey, who runs our shop, pre-empted something of my briefing.'

Pre-whated it? That must be the woman he met yesterday. Clearly in this place news travels fast. Or perhaps there wasn't any news, so that anything remotely out of the ordinary went round like a whore in a barracks. He just nodded.

'We have a simple regime here. Everyone works. Everyone. The working day begins at 8 o'clock, there is a half-hour break for lunch – there's usually some flexibility about when you take that, depending on what you are engaged in – and work finishes at 5.30. Before work there are compulsory physical exercises, at 7 am. We have a gym and a soccer pitch, and you will be expected to report to one of those. We put a great store in Pod 9 on health and fitness; *mens sana in corpore sano*.'

Men's what? thought Lander. He liked the idea of football, and of working out in the gym, but not at seven in the morning. He shook his head. What was this man on?

The Mayor continued. 'Three evenings a week there are community activities. My own interest is the choir. Do you sing?'

'No.'

Wilkinson gave the impression that this response was a major failing.

'Very well, there are other options,' he said, tartly. 'We have a drama group, a reading group, a discussion round table, a music society, a crafts club, oh there are plenty of choices, plenty.'

Lander's heart, which had been sinking as the Mayor's briefing went on, reached his boots, or rather his oversize trainers. He could imagine nothing more deadly than the life that was being described. It was worse than school, far far worse. However, Wilkinson hadn't finished.

'This routine obtains for six days of the week,' he said. 'Sunday is a day off, a time for you to catch up with domestic matters – launder your clothes, clean your accommodation, shop for foodstuffs, and so on.'

Lander was speechless. He might as well be in jail. At least there he hadn't had to work for his keep. What would happen if he didn't do any of this stuff? If he simply went on strike? He was sure that he already knew the answer to that.

The Mayor had more to say. 'Audrey explained to you something of the way our money system works, and how you are awarded the Currency Units you need to feed and take care of yourself.'

'Yes, sir.' The sir came out unbidden and Lander immediately regretted it, but the Mayor liked it because he smiled thinly. He pushed an envelope across the desk towards Lander.

'This is an *ex gratia* payment to get you started,' he said.

X what?

'In the envelope are twenty CUs. Any more you receive will depend on what I judge to be the value of your contribution to our community.'

Lander didn't touch the envelope, leaving it where it lay. 'But I don't want to stay here.'

The Mayor gave him a pitying look. 'Where would you rather be?'

Lander shrugged. At the bottom of a septic tank? Hanging by his thumbs from a suspension bridge? Almost anywhere would be better than this.

'You must realise what has happened,' the Mayor said. 'The virus that wiped out the country, indeed the world, is like nothing we have ever encountered before. The Infection it brings is incurable, and there is no defence against it. Until a vaccine is found the priority is to prevent another outbreak. Were there to be one, it would most likely spell the end for us all. To minimise the risk of this, the government has set up fifteen settlements, called pods. Each pod hosts between three and four hundred people. The intention is that everyone will live in a pod, and people who are currently in other places or roaming about, the people who call themselves Drifters, are being rounded up and allocated to them. That's what happened to you. You were found drifting, and you were brought here.'

'But they didn't give me any choice.'

'You mean a choice of which pod you were taken to. Does it matter? I asked you a moment ago where you would rather be, and I received no reply. I take that to mean you have no preference.'

'So I'm supposed to stay here.'

'Not only supposed to, you must. The only way to stop the Infection from taking hold again is to prevent movement. No one may leave his or her pod without special permission, granted by its mayor. And don't think of trying to leave without my permission,' he added. 'The perimeter of the town is sealed, and closely guarded by the Enforcement Agency. The guards have *carte blanche* from the government to do whatever they think fit with anyone they find trying to leave.'

Lander knew the meaning of *carte blanche* but did wonder why this pompous little man couldn't restrict himself to plain English. However, if Wilkinson was the only person who could allow him out, it made sense to keep on the right side of him, although it would mean swallowing the dislike that was already forming.

'Of course,' the Mayor said, 'we all hope that this situation will be quickly over. I am sure that scientists will soon come up with a vaccine against the virus, and therefore that this *modus operandi* will be only temporary. However, until they do we must obey the rules.'

For Lander, the arrangement couldn't end soon enough. Pod 9 was grim, dismal, corseted and old. Despite what the Mayor said escape was a serious temptation. He was sure he could dodge the guards, and if he couldn't, would a correction centre be any worse than staying here?

Lander hadn't been invited to sit and remained standing. His shot leg was starting to ache. Wilkinson leant forward and steepled his fingers.

'It would therefore seem, Mr Shaw, that we are stuck with each other, you with us, and we with you. Therefore, I suggest we make the best of it. Now, what are you good at?'

Lander was stumped.

'What were your best subjects at school?'

'PE, Art, I suppose.'

'Mm. Not much call for either of those here, I'm afraid. However, you seem to be a strong young man. That's the PE, I suppose.' Wilkinson rubbed his chin. 'I am trying to decide how you can best contribute to the common wealth.'

Lander had seen little evidence of wealth in Ludlow, common or other. It was obvious that at one time it had been a prosperous little town, and he remembered hearing before the Infection of a daily paper rating it one of the top places to live, although based on what he'd seen he couldn't think why. There was an old castle, a wide main street, and what must once have been some good pubs, although now they all were boarded up. True, it was several cuts above Walbrough, but then, where wasn't? The problem was that like everywhere else it had taken a pounding during the Infection. Repairs were underway and the rubbish and mess were being cleared, but there was still plenty to do. He didn't want to be involved in any of that. Loading garbage into sacks was a job for people like Steve.

The Mayor was watching him intently, and he realised that if he said nothing he would be given a job that would probably be unpleasant and might even be dangerous. There was a PC on a table in a corner of the room, its screen dark. It was a forlorn object, showing every appearance of being unvalued and neglected. Snotty Spotty obviously kept his records on paper. Audrey in the shop had added up his bill with a pencil and paper. If these were typical of the organisation of Pod 9, there was an opportunity for improvement.

'Computers,' he said. 'I'm quite good with computers.'

Mayor Wilkinson gave him another of his thin smiles. Lander had the uneasy feeling that the Mayor already knew this and for some reason had been waiting for him to volunteer the information himself.

'Exactly how "good with computers" are you?' he said.

Lander wondered how he should respond to that. He'd got decent GCSE grades in two subjects, and Computer Studies was one of them. Was that what the Mayor wanted to know?

'I'm okay,' he said.

'Okay,' the Mayor repeated. 'I've been told you're better than that. Are you aware of...' Wilkinson consulted a note on his desk, '...Hypertext Transfer Protocol?' He pronounced the words carefully, as if trying out a foreign tongue.

'Yes,' said Lander. Of course he was. Who wasn't?

'Please explain it to me.'

Was this some sort of test? 'It's a way that computers use to talk to each other,' he said.

The Mayor waited. He was expecting more.

'It's how the internet works,' Lander went on. 'You need a web browser on your computer. That uses hypertext transfer protocol, http, to send requests to a server for data, like web pages and images and stuff. Usually that links to another server, and then to another, and another.'

'There is no internet now.'

No shit, Sherlock, thought Lander, but said nothing.

'The question is, could the internet be recreated?' Wilkinson asked. 'I don't mean the content, everything that was online all over the world, that would be ridiculous. What I mean is, could this http, this method that, as you say, computers use to talk to each other, could that be used to set up a conversation between two machines?'

'Yes, I suppose so. It's pretty simple really so long as you have the code, just question and answer. The computer asks the server a question, the server answers and then it breaks the connection until it's asked another question. That's how it can deal with loads of users at the same time.'

'Is that possible? Say with that computer on the table over there and another to act as its server?'

Lander thought rapidly. He wasn't sure. He had some coding skills, but he doubted he knew enough. There might be books somewhere that could help him. What was this about?

'I don't know,' he said. 'I know the theory of how it all works, but I've never been under the bonnet. I'd need to get hold of a web browser – Google Chrome, Internet Explorer, Firefox, something like that – and see if I could set up a server that would respond to client requests.'

'Could you do it?'

One of the teachers at King's Heath Boys', one of the very very few that Lander had had any time for, once said, "What you need to get on in life is a 'can do' attitude. So if anybody ever asks you if you can do something, always say yes. If you can't you can always find out how to do it later." The class had thought it a hoot, and one of Lander's mates had said that he should tell that to the girls in St Winifred's down the road. Lander remembered the advice now. Okay, why not take it? What did he have to lose?

'Yes,' he said. 'I'll have a go.'

15

NEWNET

WILKINSON POSITIVELY BEAMED. It was an ugly sight, thought Lander. Was it a bad sign?

'Excellent,' he said. 'I was told you were the person who could deliver what is needed, and my informant was right. Now, you're probably wondering what this is all about. I explained that the pod system is intended to be temporary, while the government's scientists develop a vaccine against the virus. We have no idea how long that will take, but it will not be a swift process. The chief problem is that I/452, the Infection virus, mutates rapidly and constantly. That means that a vaccine which might work today against one strain may well not work tomorrow against another. So we must wait, while the experts search and experiment. In the meantime, the pods provide safe havens. However, their inhabitants must be kept occupied; boredom is a great promoter of discontent.'

Didn't Lander know it; another reminder of Kings Heath Boys'. The Mayor was warming to his theme, clearly working up to a full-scale lecture. Had he been a teacher? Lander thought he

671

probably had because he was showing the relish at a captive audience that in his experience was typical.

'The reason why we, and incidentally all the other pods, have a very full time-table is to keep people busy,' Wilkinson continued. 'However, there is still a considerable amount of leisure time. Also, there is the matter of the pods being isolated from each other. People are allocated to a pod according to the skills they can bring, and unfortunately that means that in some cases families and friendships are divided. Keeping the population of a pod confined within it is a challenge, and it currently relies on enforcement by the EA, backed up by the prospect of punishment. If people were able to communicate with the residents of other pods they would be much less motivated to leave. They could talk to others they knew, and from whom they have been separated. They could exchange messages and ideas. They could play games with them. They could get to know new people and form new friendships. Before the Infection, my daughters were never away from their phones or computers. These are things that used to be key features of people's lives, and they want them back.'

It sounded simple: a means of socialising across and within the pod, and beyond that a way of communicating with people in other pods. Easy to say, but how could it be done?

'So you want a new internet,' Lander said.

'Yes, but with the emphasis on "new". I'm not a computer man myself, but I do not doubt that the internet was an incredible construct, perhaps one of the greatest ever human achievements. I would rank it alongside the discovery of how to make fire, or the invention of powered flight. However, the internet was not perfect and many abused it, which means that any new version needs to be free from what tainted the old one. It needs to be controlled; in other words, there must be some means of regulating the information that is shared.'

Censorship, thought Lander, but he didn't say it.

'My pod, our pod, has been entrusted by the Provisional Government with the task of setting up a new net. Actually, that's what it is to be called: "NewNet". The plan is to begin with communication within this pod, and then replicate the system in all the others. Finally, when that has been done, the separate systems will be connected. We in Ludlow are the pioneers. It starts here. That is the job you have been chosen to do, that is why you have been allocated to Pod 9.'

So that was it. Brownrigg had said something about "green status"? This must be what he meant. Somehow Lander had got labelled as a computer expert. How? Why? There must be those who were better qualified, who knew more. There must have been computer experts in the arks, people who had done courses and got degrees.

Wilkinson interrupted his thoughts. 'I cannot emphasise too much how important this work is. It has been authorised from the very top, by the First Minister himself.'

Lander was surprised, but he wasn't as impressed as Wilkinson seemed to expect him to be. From what he'd heard Gus MacSporran was a prick and he didn't think for a second that he'd had anything to do with it. To him, it sounded more like Adam, but was he that important?

The Mayor rang a small handbell on his desk and after a moment a large black woman came in. She was magnificent, a galleon in full sail breasting the waves, and she advanced as if she owned the room. Every seam of her grey overall was strained. Lander immediately took to her. She wore a perfume so strong that he smelt it the second she appeared. It was eye-watering.

'This is Lander Shaw,' said the Mayor.

The woman looked disappointed. 'You said he was a person of colour.'

'What I think I said was that he is a colourful character.' He turned to Lander. 'This is Monica. She will be your guide. If you have any problems, go to her. Monica knows everything. She will complete your briefing and introduce you to the town. Then she will take you to your workplace. Do you have any questions?'

Lander had a thousand questions, but he shook his head.

'Good,' said Wilkinson. Then to Monica, 'When you've done the introduction, take him to the equipment room and get him started.'

'Oh yes, Massah,' said Monica, with a creole drawl and an ironic curtsey. Wilkinson winced. Lander liked her even more.

'One more thing,' said Wilkinson. He bent down and retrieved something from under his desk. 'I think you will find these a better fit.' He handed Lander a pair of trainers.

They were like nothing Lander would ever have chosen. They were plain black canvas, and there was no logo or brand name on them. They were totally uncool, a symbol of Ludlow, bland, dull and featureless. Nevertheless, it was a kind thought and Lander was touched. Slopping around in his clown's shoes had been a trial, and he'd already decided that he must save up his CUs to replace them.

'Thank you,' he said. 'I appreciate that.'

Wilkinson gave him the most genuine smile he'd yet seen from the man.

'Change into them as soon as you can and give the pair you are currently wearing to Monica.'

Monica winked at him, and Lander followed her out.

Being shown the town by Monica meant sitting beside her while she spread out a map of Ludlow and pointed to where things were.

'We got two stores,' she said. She pointed to what must have been the one where he'd met Audrey. 'This here sells food. This one,' pointing to another spot on the map, 'sells everything else. Though when I say everything, I don't mean everything.' She chortled, and elbowed him in the ribs.

She pointed to other features on the map: the fitness centre and soccer pitch, a meeting hall that doubled as a cinema, a takeaway, a medical surgery, a pharmacy, and she gave one or two bits of basic information, like when they were open and how many CUs a few sample items required.

'Other stuff you'll find when you go there,' she said.

Can't argue with that, Lander thought. 'Any pubs?' he asked, innocently.

'Why you naughty boy,' Monica said, giving his hand a playful slap. 'You don't look old enough to drink.'

'I am.'

'Well that sure is a pity, because there ain't no public houses in this town. There are a couple of gay guys who are trying to start a micro-brewery, but they haven't got much done yet, say they can't get the ingredients. For now, the only ale is Adam's.'

For an instant Lander was thrown, thinking of the Adam he knew, but then he realised that Monica meant water.

'We have a bunch of guys working on the water supply but for now it comes from a well. The deliveries are every other day, and you need to go steady, cos there ain't no top-ups. Right,' she said. 'You ready to do your computing thing?'

'Lead me to it,' said Lander, and stooped to put on his new trainers. Despite their unattractive appearance, they were comfortable. Monica waited while he laced them up.

'Attaboy,' she said. 'After me.'

He followed her down two flights of stairs and into a basement. There were no windows, and the tube lighting was glaring and harsh. She led him into a room that looked rather like a lab, with benches around the walls and along the centre. Lander could hardly believe his eyes. Every square centimetre of space was filled with computers of all types and sizes. Among them were keyboards, mice, screens, routers, hard drives, printers, cables, leads, it was like a yard sale in an IT store. The equipment not only filled the benches, it was stacked on the floor underneath and beside them. There were more things on stools and windowsills.

'There you go,' said Monica, beaming. 'Happy time. Dealing with this lot will keep you out of trouble. And when you're done in here there's another room across the passage exactly like this.'

Lander was gobsmacked. 'What am I supposed to do with all this stuff?'

Monica chuckled. 'Fix it. This is all the IT equipment we could find in the town, and around. There was an order from the government making it illegal for anyone to possess a computer of any sort, and they all had to be handed in. The Enforcement

Agency collected them up, and His Mayorship had them put down here. The problem is, no one knows what we've got. Julian in Reception had a go at making a list. He's a sweet baby, but he doesn't have a clue.'

Julian must be Snotty Spotty, thought Lander. Sweet was not one of the many words he would have used to describe him.

'We need somebody to go through all of this gear and find out what works and what don't, what's worth keeping and what's fit for the bin. Some of it that don't work might be mendable, or it might be useful for spare parts, and we need to know that too. The Mayor hopes there'll be enough working machines here for you to set up his new baby, the Pod 9 internet. Do you think you can do this, boy?'

Normally Lander would have resented being called "boy", but from Monica it seemed fine.

'I'll do my best,' he said.

'You do exactly that. Nobody can ask no more. Anything you need, you come to Monica. Any problems or hassle, anything you're short of, you come to Monica.'

'Right.'

'Except for booze.' She blew him a kiss and wafted out, leaving the heavy imprint of her perfume behind her. Lander looked for some sort of ventilation but there was none.

He took in the collection. Then he crossed the passage to the other room. It was just as full. Only in the movies had he seen so many computers in one place. There were far more than in the IT labs in school, but the ones here were in such a mess. There were towers, there were desktops, there were laptops. There were PCs and there were Apple Macs. There were tablets. There were other things too. Some of it was old, some of it looked battered, but a lot appeared to be in good condition and some of it was high spec and new.

They'd left him to play with all this stuff and they were going to pay him to do it. Well, sort of pay him. He grinned to himself. Maybe life in Pod 9 wouldn't be too bad after all.

16
____

BONOBOS

IT WAS TWO WEEKS before Magda heard again from Adam. His calls always came late at night and that made her feel relegated, as if talking to her was bottom of his to-do list and he'd only just got around to it.

'Of course it's not that,' he said when she told him. 'I call you at night because that's when I miss you most. Where are you?'

'In bed. Where do you think I'd be this late?'

'On your own?'

'Don't be daft. This is a women's commune. There are no men here.'

'You could be in bed with another woman.'

'Well, I'm not.'

'What are you wearing?'

'Nothing. I'm in bed.'

'Mmm, sexy. Are you feeling yourself?'

'No I'm not, I'm trying to get to sleep.'

'I'm feeling myself. Go on, you do it too and tell me about it. Tell me what you'd like me to do to you.'

Part of Magda thought that it might be fun, but she also felt that she was being used.

'I'm not in the mood,' she said. 'If you want to have a wank, go ahead, but I'm tired.'

He laughed. Perhaps he'd been winding her up all along.

'Okay okay okay,' he said. 'What I'm calling about is your trip to the white coats in Oxford. Have you read the report I left you?'

'Yes.'

'What do you think?'

'I think that what they're planning sounds impossible. Mad.'

'I'm not so sure. They put a strong case, and they may have something. Anyway, see what you think when you're there. I've set up your visit for tomorrow. There'll be a car to pick you up at eleven.'

He hadn't checked whether that was convenient, whether she'd be doing anything else. She wouldn't, but it would have been nice to be asked.

The dark blue Lexus arrived at precisely ten-fifty. It looked to be the same car that had collected Adam a fortnight before. Unused to chauffeured transport, Magda assumed she would sit beside the driver, and was pleased to see that it was a woman, hair tied back, white shirt, and crisp black trouser suit. She would be someone to talk to on the journey. However, as she approached the car the woman opened the rear door and held it open for her, blocking off the front passenger door with her body. Magda obediently got in the back of the car and made herself comfortable on the soft leather seat. The Lexus moved away smoothly and without a sound. Magda realised it was electric, which addressed a question that one of the Nightingales had asked the other day: how long would fuel supplies last? The answer was that with electric transport and renewable energy, the availability of petrol and diesel was less important.

Conversation wasn't on the agenda. Magda tried a few openers but all attempts to chat were blocked.

She started with, 'How do you come to be working as a driver?'

'I was selected.'

'Oh, that's interesting. What was the process?'

'It was the usual for a government position.'

'What did you have to do?'

'Tests.'

'Ooh, that sounds tough. What were they like?'

'Reasonable.'

A pause, then Magda tried again.

'It must be great to see different parts of the country. Where do your journeys take you?

'To many places.'

'Where?'

'Here and there.'

The woman had a talent for turning an open question into a closed one; maybe that was a requirement for the job, one of the tests she'd had to pass. Her answers were polite but led nowhere. It was like throwing a ball against a net, it didn't bounce back but simply stuck there. In the end Magda gave up and watched the folded fields and woodlands of middle England roll past the window.

She thought back to the phone call from Adam the night before. He'd felt playful, she hadn't. At one time she'd have joined in phone sex enthusiastically, but not now. Had she changed? No, it was Adam. If it had been Lander it might have been different, but she had a lingering feeling of injustice, a quiet resentment of Adam that wouldn't be silenced. It all came down to Lisa's baby. To blame her, or any of the Nightingales, for what was not their fault was so unfair. He'd never apologised and he hadn't even stayed for the funeral.

But that was Adam. When he fixed on a target he pursued it with a determination that often showed scant regard for others. That was a strength, probably one of the things McFarlane found useful about him; Adam was a man who would get things done. But it was also a weakness. At the very best it could involve hurting other people's feelings. At worst it led to, well, what had happened to Kerryl. Adam was focused and a go-getter, and that was attractive; he was also careless of distress, and that was a profound turn-off.

She couldn't imagine anyone more different from Adam than Lander. They were almost polar opposites. For Lander, the means were much more important than the ends. He was sometimes thoughtless and immature, but he was fair, kind, and sought to avoid causing pain. Despite the apparent ferocity of his attack, there was no way that he would have really harmed Adam. There was no way either that he could have killed Mickey. If Magda had left it to him they would still be slaves on the farm; or more likely they would have been dead by now, worked and starved into their graves.

Adam and Lander were different to look at, too. Adam's sturdy muscularity was in complete contrast to Lander's rangy leanness. When Lander had gone for Adam, surprise had given him an advantage. Adam simply hadn't been expecting the attack. If he had she was sure he could have dropped Lander with ease. Adam had a head of tight, blonde curls. Lander's hair was longer and a glossy brown. It was an appealing look, one that would be the envy of many girls. She could imagine the same hair on Kerryl.

What would Lander be like in bed? Adam was enthusiastic and energetic, but not very inventive. Would Lander be better? Would she get the chance to find out? They had slept together every night when they'd been Mickey's prisoners but there had been no sex. The shabby, stinking shed with its animal reek hadn't encouraged lovemaking; besides, they'd been exhausted from their days of labour. If they were to go to bed now it would be different.

The voice of the driver broke in on her thoughts.

'We'll be there in ten minutes, if you wish to prepare yourself.'

They didn't seem to be going into Oxford, instead skirting it by the ring road. They were on a straight section of dual carriageway, and as they neared an off-ramp the Lexus slowed and took it. There was a sign reading "Ridgeway". The road took them along the crest of a line of hills with plains on each side.

'Where is this?'

'We'll be there shortly.'

Thanks a bunch, thought Magda.

The car turned into a narrow lane that led steeply downhill towards what Magda saw to be a low, modern building. There was no sign or name board to indicate what it was, but she assumed this was the research centre. Several cars were parked outside, and the Lexus joined them. Magda leaned forward to open the door, but the driver beat her to it. She climbed out.

'When I'm done here how can I get back to Lake Manor?' she asked.

'I am to return you when you are finished. The car will be waiting.'

'Oh, thanks.' Magda smiled at the driver, but it was not returned.

The building was anonymous, with tiny windows and a faceless steel door, firmly shut. She pressed the intercom button and waited for a tinny voice of enquiry, but the door opened without that and she walked into a foyer. As she did, a woman came towards her.

'I'm Professor Haynes,' she said, extending a hand. 'Julia. You must be Magda.'

She couldn't have been more than a few years older than Magda herself, but her hair was greying and pulled back tightly in a schoolmarm bun. Glasses rested halfway down her nose. She reminded Magda of a movie, *The Prime of Miss Jean Brodie*, so the Scots accent wasn't a surprise. Everything else was. She'd expected a lab coat, or perhaps a business suit. This woman wore a baggy t-shirt and ripped jeans.

'This way, please.'

She led Magda to a meeting room. There was no preamble or warm-up, no enquiries about the journey or her health; as soon as Magda had taken her seat Julia began.

'How much do you know about the work we're doing here?'

Magda took Adam's report from her bag. 'I was given this to read. I understand that you're trying to mix human genes with those from monkeys.'

'Not monkeys, bonobos,' said Julia. 'They're apes, related to chimpanzees but with significant differences. And we're not trying. We've done it.'

Magda was thunderstruck. She had been convinced that what she'd read in the report was rubbish. If they had done what this woman claimed, it was unbelievable, truly breathtaking. It ran counter to everything she'd understood from her medical training.

'Congratulations,' she said at last. 'That's... amazing.'

Julia held up a hand. 'Thank you, but don't light the celebration fireworks yet. When I say we've done it, I mean that we've managed to create a life form that shares some of the characteristics of both bonobos and humans, yet is different from each. We're testing it to see if it's immune to the Infection, and the early indications are that it is. But it's not the finished article. I should warn you, it's not what you might expect.'

Magda felt a chill in her bones as uneasy memories of science fiction stories rose like spectres. Was she about to meet Frankenstein's monster? Julia must have read something from her expression because she placed a reassuring hand on Magda's arm.

'Don't worry, it's not scary. I'm confident we'll get there in the end, but we have some way to go and we're not as far on as the powers that be would like. I was simply preparing you for what you'll see. But first, we need to get ourselves properly clothed, then we'll go through to the lab.'

Adam referred to the researchers as white coats, but the outfit Magda was given was pale green. It was a one-piece, like a baby grow complete with feet, and made of thin cotton. Following Julia's lead, Magda stripped to her underwear and put it on. She had expected a cap, but instead there was a hood attached to the garment. She pulled it over her head and tucked her hair inside. She watched Julia tighten her drawstring and close the hood around her face, and she did the same. By the time she had put on a mouth mask, goggles, and surgical gloves, no skin was showing. The staff had name tags on lanyards, and she could see why. When fully clothed it was hard to tell people apart.

'Right,' Julia said, 'follow me.'

She led the way to a door, where she punched a code into a keypad. As it opened Magda was conscious of a draft, and she realised that the space they were entering was pressurised, to make sure that any impurities in the air outside would not be drawn in.

The area she entered was long and low, painted white and brightly lit. It was warm, and there was a gentle hum. There were booths and benches with a lot of apparatus. Some of it, microscopes, centrifuges, incubators, she knew well; other equipment was a mystery. There were several large jars in line on a shelf. It took a close examination to see that each contained a baby ape. There was no time to study them because Julia steered her to a curtained alcove on the far side of the room. As they approached the humming grew louder.

'Our most successful experiments have been with bonobo implants in human mothers,' Julia said. 'We wanted to find out whether a sterile human female can host an implanted live embryo. It seems that if the circumstances are right, she can. What you are going to see was brought to term by a human mother who gave birth only a few days ago.'

Magda felt her heart beating faster as she stepped through the curtains behind Julia. What was she going to see?

The space was small, with scarcely enough room for them both to stand. Most of it was taken up by a plastic crib with a transparent cover. She had seen these before, but she had never encountered anything like its occupant. Or, rather, occupants, because there were two of them. Only their heads showed, the rest hidden by a light sheet. Their appearance was human, but they also had ape-like features – protruding jaws and a sparse covering of fine hair. They looked alike and had the wrinkled skin of the newly born. They were tiny, but there was nothing Magda could see to merit the words of caution in Julia's briefing. Then her guide reached inside the incubator and drew aside the covering. The pair lay side by side. Magda couldn't at first see clearly through her goggles and mask, but then she did. The two babies were joined at the hip.

'They've all been like this.' Julia was whispering, as if not to disturb the sleepers.

'You mean conjoined? Do you know why?'

'No. We're trying to find out.'

Magda looked down at the sleeping twins. They were so small, so vulnerable, so innocent.

'What's going to happen to them?' she said.

Our surgical team say they could be separated. They'd probably be able to walk upright, although not very well.'

'How human are they?'

'Genetically they're very close to us. Naturally, we would get to know exactly how human they are as they matured.'

Magda had the fleeting thought that in the circumstances the word "naturally" was wide of the mark. 'Will they behave like humans?'

'That remains to be seen. In theory, there's no reason why they couldn't be taught the basic elements of human conduct.'

'Will they be able to talk?'

'Hard to say. There are probably lots of reasons why bonobos can't talk. One of them is because their vocal cords are too high in their throats. Our early examinations of these two suggest that their vocal cords are lower, more where you'd expect them to be in a regular human newborn. However, we don't know how well they'll be able to process language. Several sections of the brain are used for that – Broca's and Wernicke's areas, for example – and we know that these are present in primates. However, there's more to it than that. Speech depends on integrating many regions of the brain, and the idea of several separate parts that do particular things is rather old hat. There's plenty of evidence that chimps can be taught to sign, so yes, they might be able to talk. In a fashion. If they're bright enough.'

'And are they?'

Julia shrugged. 'Who knows? It could be some time before we found out.'

'What are their names?'

'They don't have any. We don't give names to the subjects of our experiments. We try not to get close, so that when they have to go it's easier.'

'Go where?'

Julia gave Magda an odd look. 'These two won't live. They're not the finished product yet, and the best they could expect is a life as freaks. In a few weeks, when we've got from them all we can, we'll put them to sleep.'

17

CHAT ROOM

LANDER CLIMBED THE FRONT STEPS of the townhouse he was now living in, closed the door behind him and locked it. It was a big improvement on the shabby terrace he'd been allocated when he'd first come to Ludlow. This was just one of several things that had improved since then.

The first perk – and it was a big one for Lander – was being excused from the morning exercises. When told that by the Mayor his first thought had been, great, an extra hour in bed. But after a couple of days, he'd surprised himself by getting up and going to work early. Although it went against his nature, he had to admit that he'd become absorbed in the task he'd been set and was keen to get back to it. He stayed late in the evenings, too, and that brought a second privilege: relief from the expectation to attend the social and cultural activities: the discussion forum, the music society, the drama group, or any of the other horrors Mayor Wilkinson had threatened when he'd first arrived. There were CUs, more than he could spend, and he now wore a grey overall, the colour reserved for higher-level "servants of the community". It had been hinted that he might even graduate to dark blue, which not even Monica had yet managed. The taps worked and there was running water. However, the biggest, most stupendous, awe-inspiring perk of all, the one that almost literally blew him away when Mayor Wilkinson announced it to him, was quietly sitting in the garage: a Honda Meerkat. No bigger than the ancient mini he'd once driven but smoother and quicker.

He'd not asked for it. It had occurred to him that if he was to visit the other fourteen pods and oversee their online interconnection through NewNet, he would need some means of getting to them, but his thinking had gone no further than that. The Meerkat was the Mayor's answer. He needed Wilkinson's approval for every journey – although increasingly that was a mere formality – but it represented freedom. There was the tedious spraying down and temperature testing every time he returned, but that was a small price to pay for the joy of getting out of the dismal pod. Every time he went along the corridor of razor wire at the entrance, sweeping past the guards on the gate and the hovering drones, it was all he could do to stop himself from giving them the finger.

Travelling brought him into contact with the IT Managers of the other pods. He found that with two exceptions they were of the same mind as he: Gus McFarlane – GM in their shorthand – was a disaster; lazy, incompetent, autocratic, a disgrace. Every week some new regulation was imposed to exert even tighter control on the inhabitants of the pods. The authority of the mayors was being strengthened all the time. What was being created was a network of mini dictators governed by a single supreme one. The gossip was that much of this was being driven by McFarlane's special adviser, Przemysław Adamski.

It had to be stopped. Many times Lander was tempted not to return to Ludlow, simply to take off and join the Drifters, but he always came back. The reason was that he knew that there was a better chance of them all achieving what they wanted if for the time being they cooperated with those who were in authority. Rebellion would come later. For now, they'd keep in touch, and Lander had set up a way for them to do that.

He poured himself a glass of milk and went upstairs to his bedroom, turning out the lights behind him. He closed the door, drew the curtains and opened his laptop.

The laptop was a major concession and he'd had to lobby hard to get it. The rule laid down by the government was the same for all the pods, one single PC per household. His own was downstairs, but he'd insisted that he needed a portable machine that he could take with him when he went on the road to the other pods. Wilkinson didn't see why this was, but Lander had begun a long speech about the tools he needed to take with him: trial programs, metadata correction utilities, file transfer protocols, proxy servers, universal resource locators, application layer negotiators, logic analysers, activity monitors, web crawlers. It was a smokescreen, a barrage of garbage, but it did its job; the Mayor's eyes had glazed over and he'd given in, sweetened no doubt by the considerable income from the other pods that Lander's work brought in.

The laptop screen came to life, and Lander entered his password and opened a web browser. This was not Chrome or Explorer or any of the other examples of kindergarten software he'd installed on the household computers. It was Stealth Engine, a very different animal indeed. With a few keystrokes, he navigated to a site that claimed to be an ancient history resource and still under construction. It wasn't, it was the portal of "HushNet", the closed and secret channel Lander had established for communication between selected individuals in all the pods. It had quickly become a tight and focused group.

He entered his online tag, LAN999, and signed in. Several members of the group were already there: TREY740, NOL55, SIMI11, and a few others. He knew them all. TREY740 was Trevor, who managed the IT for Pod 12, Alton. NOL55 was Nolan, who did a similar job in Pod 5 at Downham Market. SIMI11 was Samantha from Retford, Pod 14. They all met in this live chat room once a week.

The last time they'd been dealing with a video which had been sent to Lander to upload on NewNet. It showed happy mums nursing their newborn babies. He'd posted it, and very soon there were tags carrying congratulations and good wishes to the women and their offspring. Lander and the other members of the forum were suspicious. None could confirm any pregnancies or births in their own pods, even though several of them knew couples who were trying for a baby. Then Lander realised that he recognised some of the "mothers". They'd been at Lake Manor, they were Nightingales. It didn't make sense. They talked about it and concluded that the video was fake. The group decided not to make that public, yet.

Tonight's subject was different. Lander began to type.

LAN999: TOPIC IS RECENT ELECTION. AS YOU KNOW, GM'S PEOPLE'S PROGRESSIVE PARTY (PPP) WON BY A LANDSLIDE. SIMI11 HAS QUERIED THIS.

SIMI11: YES. I ADMINISTERED THE VOTE FOR POD 14. PPP CAME THIRD, BEHIND NEW WORLD ALLIANCE (NWA) & LEAP FORWARD (LF). SUCH A BIG DEFEAT THAT THE FINAL RESULT WAS A SURPRISE. I WONDERED WHAT THE PICTURE WAS IN OTHER PODS.

Samantha had flagged this up for review a few days before and had asked members to provide details of the voting in their pods.

The election had been held online, so the IT Managers were in a good position to get the data. The PPP had come second in Ludlow, well behind LF. NWA had been third.

TREY740: SAME IN POD 12. PPP WAY BEHIND.

PAT654: AND HERE.

It was the same story all round. In only one pod had the PPP won; in all the others it had come no better than second, and in most cases a poor third.

FRAN88: HOW COME THEY WON THEN?

SIMI11: THEY DIDN'T. THEY JUST MADE IT LOOK AS IF THEY HAD. GM'S LAPDOGS FIDDLED THE NUMBERS.

There was a long pause while everyone took this in.

PAT654: SO THE WHOLE ELECTION'S FUCKED. WHAT ARE WE GOING TO DO?

Another pause.

LAN999: IDEAS?

TREY740: WE NEED TO GET THIS CHEATING KNOWN ABOUT. GET IT AROUND THE PODS.

SIMI11: AGREED, BUT FIRST WE NEED ACCURATE DATA. SEND ME DETAILS OF HOW ALL YOUR PODS VOTED, I'LL ADD THEM UP & WE'LL SEE WHO REALLY WON. THEN WE CAN DECIDE WHAT TO DO NEXT.

LAN999: THANKS SIMI11, GOOD IDEA. EVERYBODY SEND A SMILING FACE IF YOU'RE HAPPY WITH THAT.

A row of smiling face emojis spread across Lander's screen.

LAN999: GOOD. UNANIMOUS. LET'S DO IT. THANKS EVERYONE.

There were some more smiley faces and thumbs up.

NOL55: BEFORE Y'ALL GO. I'VE HAD A MESSAGE FROM SOMEONE WHO WANTS TO JOIN US.

Lander felt a tingle of alarm. He was uneasy about strangers. So far they'd managed to keep the group tight and its existence a secret, but possible infiltration by the Enforcement Agency was a constant concern.

LAN999: WHO? ONE REP PER POD IS THE RULE AND WE'VE GOT A FULL HOUSE. IS SOMEBODY STEPPING DOWN?

NOL55: IT'S NOT SOMEONE IN A POD. HIS TAG IS REG22 AND HE'S WITH THE FRANKLINS.

Lander knew about the Franklins. It was another of the women's groups, like the Nightingales. They called themselves after Rosalind Franklin who, he'd read, had been a scientist working back in the 1950s. As far as he could discover they were based in a country house near Lincoln. He was even more suspicious.

LAN999: WHAT'S A BLOKE DOING IN A WOMEN'S COVEN?

NOL55: DIDN'T SAY, BUT LUCKY HIM.

SIMI11: SEXIST PIG! A little pink pig emoji oinked across the screen.

LAN999: HOW DID HE FIND YOU?

NOL55: OUR DOC HAD TO VISIT THE FRANKLINS TO GET SOME DRUGS. REG22 ASKED FOR A CONTACT BECAUSE THEY WANT TO LINK UP TO NEWNET. OUR DOC GAVE MY MESSAGE ADDRESS. SHE THINKS REG22 IS GENUINE & I TRUST HER JUDGEMENT.

LAN999: AND THIS REG22 MESSAGED YOU?

NOL55: THE NEXT DAY.

Lander considered. It could be a trap. If the government could penetrate their chat room and identify its members they'd be in big trouble. Some of them were using illegal computers, and that meant a spell in a correction centre if they were caught. The main danger, though, was that their chats were often critical of the government, and sometimes members got carried away and said things that if they got out would bring something worse down on them. However, they were an action group. Their aim was to one day create the conditions for a revolution that would overturn the pod system and sweep away McFarlane's – and Adam's – dictatorship. To achieve that they had to grow by recruiting more people who thought the way they did. Besides, he knew Nolan, and he didn't strike Lander as someone who could be easily taken in.

LAN999: HOW MUCH DOES REG22 KNOW ABOUT US?

NOL55: NOT A LOT. JUST THAT WE'RE A GROUP OF GEEKS WHO LIKE TO CHAT NOW & AGAIN.

LAN999: WHY DOES HE WANT TO JOIN US?

NOL55: HE SAYS THE FRANKLINS ARE RESEARCHING A VACCINE AGAINST THE

INFECTION & ARE CLOSE TO FINDING ONE. HE WANTS US TO HAVE ACCESS TO THAT INFO.

If that was true it was fantastic news, and in any case, having the Franklins on board could be useful. But there were difficulties.

SIMI11: IF THE FRANKLINS ARE RESEARCHING INTO A VACCINE THE GOVT MUST KNOW WHAT THEY'RE DOING.

PAT654: YES. THEY WOULDN'T BE ABLE TO KEEP IT SECRET. THEY COULD BE IN GM'S POCKET.

SIMI11: OR ADAMSKI'S.

Lander stared at the cursor blinking at the end of the last comment. The group was waiting for him to make a decision. He began to type.

LAN999: OK. IF THIS GUY IS GENUINE WE COULD USE HIM. WE DON'T WANT TO PUT HIM OFF BUT WE NEED TO BE CAREFUL. SO HE DOESN'T GET ACCESS TO THE FULL GROUP YET. NOL55, SEND ME HIS LINK & I'LL CHAT WITH HIM & TRY TO FIND OUT IF HE'S FOR REAL. IF HE IS I'LL GIVE HIM A TEMPORARY PASSWORD & WE'LL RUN A TRIAL. ALL OK WITH THAT?

There were more smiley faces, but not everybody sent one. Some members weren't committing themselves, and Lander was cynical enough to realise that they were keeping their distance in case he'd made a bad call.

LAN999: REMINDER - WE DON'T USE REAL NAMES EVER, AND DON'T SHARE YOUR LOCATION WITH ANYONE UNTIL YOU'RE SURE OF THEM. AS FAR AS

THE GOVT IS CONCERNED WE DON'T EXIST. LET'S KEEP IT THAT WAY.

TREY740: GOOD ADVICE.

NOL55: RIGHT ON MAN.

LAN999: OK. TILL NEXT TIME. DON'T FORGET IT'S WEEK 4, SO EVERYONE CHANGE YOUR PASSWORDS.

There were more emojis as the group members logged off: smiley faces, thumbs up, smiling cowboy, smiling demon, pouting lips, a turkey. The list of people logged in was reduced until Lander was left on his own.

He scrolled back over the conversation. The election rigging was sickening, but it didn't surprise him. Did Adam have anything to do with that? He wouldn't put it past him. Regarding REG22, who knew if he was honest or a plant? Maybe he wasn't a single person at all, but a name being used by Enforcement Agency infiltrators. He'd come across a piece of software that was supposed to analyse messages and say whether they all came from a single source or from several. He'd engage this REG22 in some exchanges and see what the software said.

Time would tell.

THE REBOOT ARMY

DESPITE THE CHOKE HOLD of the authorities, Lander had to admit that some things were slowly improving. The sentries on the gate were more relaxed, and one-time Lander had left and there'd been no one on guard at all. When there were watchers at the entrance, a few CUs would persuade them to look the other way. The drones were rarely in the air now. The other pods reported the same; slipping out was getting easier.

One day in conversation with the Mayor he let it slip that he knew Adam. Wilkinson was impressed, but although he pumped Lander to say more about someone who was an influential figure, he managed to dodge the questions. A few days later there followed an invitation to dine with the Wilkinsons, and this was followed by others at about weekly intervals.

Dinner at the Mayor's house was good. He had a cook and she was excellent. Sometimes there would be other guests there, but at least half the time Lander was the only one. The Wilkinsons – mother, father and two daughters – had come through the

Infection in an ark. Lander was interested in how and why they'd been chosen for this special treatment, but all the Mayor would say was that it had been by competitive examination. Lander thought it was probably because he knew the right people. For his part, Wilkinson wanted to know about Adam. Lander gave innocuous answers and made the excuse that he'd only met him a couple of times and didn't know him well. Mrs Wilkinson liked stories about life outside an ark, and Lander provided descriptions of some of the things that had happened to him. These were elaborately embroidered and heavily censored and they went down well, especially with the two daughters.

The younger of the Wilkinson girls, Jemima, was fourteen, dumpy and plain. Her sister, Jocasta, was the opposite: lean, boyish and startlingly pretty. She was seventeen, the age Lander had been when he left home. Given what had happened in and since the ark, and her undoubtedly sheltered life before that, Lander would find himself speculating not on whether she was a virgin, that was obvious, but on whether she'd even been kissed. She would gaze at him with huge, cow-like eyes while hanging on his every word, and he sometimes fantasised about introducing her to sex. There was no chance of that. Common sense told him it was a complete non-starter, and anyway Jocasta would want a relationship. That was not on Lander's list. What he wanted was somebody like Magda might have been, a bedmate who would enjoy a few hours of fun with no questions asked and no expectation of anything to follow. There were no girls like that in Ludlow.

Now that NewNet had been extended to all the pods there was little for Lander to do. There were problems, but they were usually easy to fix. What took up most of his time was setting up the inter-pod events. This was a new initiative introduced since the election, and its declared purpose was to bring the residents of a pod together and promote loyalty. Attendance wasn't compulsory, but absentees had to have a pretty good reason for non-participation.

The first event was opened by Gus McFarlane. He thanked people for their support and trust in electing the PPP by such a huge majority. He assured those who hadn't voted for the PPP that he would have their interests at heart just as much as those of his dedicated supporters. He looked forward to working with the opposition parties. The members of the Provisional Government had all resigned, and his administration would be referred to as the New Government, the NG. He had an exciting programme for getting the country back on its feet and would be happy to receive suggestions and answer questions. The woman next to Lander offered under her breath a suggestion for something McFarlane could do, and Lander registered her as a possible ally.

Next was an inter-pod quiz. Pod 10, Skipton, won. The following week there was a gig played by a band from the Witney pod. They did a few covers and some original stuff and were quite good. The following week a singing group from the Llandindrod pod gave a concert of Welsh folk songs, and the week after that a drama group from the Isle of Wight performed a shortened version of *A Midsummer Night's Dream*.

In between these events, Lander did his best to check out REG22. That was both easy and hard. It was easy to make contact and strike up an exchange, but much harder to get any personal information out of him. Results from the message analysis software were inconclusive. Was REG22 one person or two? Was he above board, or was he – were they – a Trojan horse?

Over several interactions, Lander pieced together that REG22 was a high-level researcher, someone who had an input into running the Franklins, and that they had been working on ways of fighting the virus. Lander asked about the Franklins and was told they were all scientists who had come together shortly after the Infection died down. In the end, he reasoned that the best way forward was to offer REG22 some rope and see if he would hang himself, so he issued a temporary password for the chat group.

The other thing that happened during that period needs a little more detail. It was the first of the two events which told Lander that the time had come to start the move against the New Government.

Since parting from Chrissie and Steve on the canal bank all that time ago he'd heard nothing more, and he had almost forgotten them. There was no news of the movement that Steve said Chrissie would be starting. The two seemed to have disappeared; either they were still at Paradise Farm and managing to keep their heads down, or they'd been picked up and sent to a pod somewhere, perhaps even to two different ones. Then one day he was talking with Monica and she mentioned the Reboot Army.

'Whatever's that?'

Monica was trimming Lander's hair. There were "proper" hairdressers in Ludlow, but Monica was good at it, she was friendly, and she did his for nothing.

'It's a new movement.'

'Not a real army then.'

'Oh no, the opposite. I think they got some good ideas.'

'Like?'

'Like this.' Monica put down the scissors and counted on her fingers. 'Like everybody should be kind to each other. Like you shouldn't take what's not yours. Like you mustn't hurt another person, either in body or mind. Like you should help folks who are down on their luck, give food to those who are hungry, take care of the sick. Like we should all look after the planet. They think the Infection came from God as a way of rebooting the world.'

A lot about this sounded familiar. 'Great,' said Lander. 'What do they do?'

'They hold meetings, they call them gatherings. People go along, and there's this young chick, cute she is, who talks to them. Then people commit themselves to the Big Six Pledges.'

'What are they?'

'It's what I just told you.'

'This cute chick,' he said. 'Is she by any chance called Chrissie?'

'Sister Chrissie,' said Monica, nodding vigorously. 'That's her. Making some waves, she is.'

'Where does she have these meetings?'

'All over. There was one in Hull last week. There's another planned for the end of the month, near Bedford. That one's going to be the first of a whole lot of much bigger ones.'

'But hang on a minute,' said Lander. 'Meetings of any sort outside a pod are illegal.'

'Well so they are,' said Monica, resting her hands on her hips.

'How come she can hold them, then?'

'It's all arranged by word of mouth so the authorities don't know until it's too late. It's the Drifters that spread the messages.'

Drifters. It was a name that kept cropping up, a term used to lump together people who had weathered the storm of the Infection because they'd been miles away from any town, on Scottish islands, in the heart of Wales, places like that. Little was known about them – how many of them there were, whether some had been infected and recovered, where they hid. They were a thorn in the side of the EA, which had the ambition to get them all in pods and constantly sought to round them up. Sometimes they were talked of as an organisation, a group with aims and leadership, but Lander's impression was that they were made up of unrelated bands that formed, split and reformed as events demanded. However, they did seem to have a shared philosophy which was opposed to the way the country seemed to be heading. They also had a method of circulating messages amongst themselves, and Lander had it in mind that if he could discover a way to contact them he might find some allies.

'Well ain't that given you something to think about,' Monica said, reacting to his silence. She had gone back to trimming his hair, and her words brought him back to the present.

'Yeah, I suppose. Doesn't the EA shut the gatherings down?'

Monica sighed, as if explaining to a slow child. 'How many people do you think are in that EA? There were only four thousand of us in the arks. How many would you guess were agents? Three hundred? Four? Four at the very most, and they have to watch the whole country. Do you think they're going to be around to stop a few holy rollers? Here, watch this.'

Monica gave him a movie stick. He hadn't seen one of those for ages. He used to have loads of them – mostly action movies and classic football games – and Kerryl had had a stack of them too. He had no idea what to expect when he plugged it into his PC.

It begins with a slap in the face. A band is playing a track he knows, *Pump It Up*. The sound is loud and the beat is heavy. It's a club scene. A crowd of young people are dancing. The camera homes in on a girl. She wears a bikini top which shows off her flat stomach. Her long, brown legs are topped by a very short skirt. She wears a mask over her eyes that hides her face, but he knows she's familiar. The girl's arms swing, her body jerks and her head snaps from side to side, flicking her long hair. A boy moves in on her and dances beside her. He takes her arm and pulls her towards him. They kiss, swaying suggestively to the music.

Lander froze the picture. Had Monica given him a chick flick? Or even a porn movie? The couple were sexy enough for that. He clicked play again.

The music continues for another couple of seconds, then there's a sound like a car crash and the image splinters. It's replaced by a close-up of a girl looking straight at the camera. It's the same girl, except now her hair is short and she's wearing a white shirt that comes up to her throat. She speaks.

That was me three years ago. I didn't know the boy who comes up to me in the video clip, but that night I slept with him. I had a lot of nights like that. All I was interested in was having a good time. Then the Infection came. It took away my family, the boy I was with, the friend who took the video, and all those you saw dancing. Most people don't know why this happened, but I do.

Chrissie's face fades and is replaced by a sequence of shots of mayhem, cruelty and human carelessness. There's a black and white clip of soldiers being mown down as they try to cross no man's land. There's another of the entrance to Auschwitz, with the cynical and obscene motto over its gate. There are black women holding swollen-bellied children, flies buzzing around their eyes. There are loggers ploughing into a forest with chainsaws, felling majestic giants that were already ancient when their great-grandfathers were born. There's a tableau of sad orangutans in a tree, gazing dejectedly at the plantation of oil palms that covers what was once their home. Then there's the sea. The camera pans across a raft of plastic waste that goes on as far as the eye can see. There are dying turtles, choking in discarded nets. Lastly, there's CCTV footage. It's in monochrome and it's grainy, but the scene is clear enough. A boy hurries along a street. He glances nervously over his shoulder. Two others come up behind him. One grabs him, the other pulls out a long knife. The blade glints in the streetlights. He drives it into the boy's side. He falls to the ground, clutching his wound. The attackers walk on, they don't even run, while their victim's life drains away on the pavement.

Chrissie's voice returns.

That's how we were. That's how we will be again if we let ourselves go that way. More than two thousand years ago a baby was born who grew up to show us all how we should live. His message was clear: be kind to each other, feed the hungry, care for the sick, and look after what God has provided. You'd think it was simple enough, but it turned out to be too difficult for us. Selfishness always won. We killed the young man that baby grew into, and we've been struggling ever since. In the end, God had had enough. He sent the Infection to clear us out, to reboot the world. It was drastic, but it gives those of us who have survived another chance. This time let's get it right.

The screen faded to black.

Lander watched the video again. Then he made a decision. He didn't buy all the religious stuff. He knew from *thetruthwillmakeyoufree* that the Infection wasn't something that had come from nowhere. A country had made the virus as a weapon and it had got loose. And did Chrissie mean no one was to have fun anymore? He couldn't take that. But she did have something. The new world they eventually built couldn't be like the old one, although people like Gus McFarlane, and Adam, and Mayor Wilkinson seemed to think it should be. Something had to be done to stop them.

He would go to Bedford.

19

MAGDA JOINS IN

JULIA'S REMARK, almost the last thing she said before they parted, haunted Magda in the days and nights that followed her trip to Oxford.

'When we've got from them all we can, we'll put them to sleep.'

It was heartless, it made her sad, and it brought on feelings of pity for the bonobo-humans. There was also guilt at what was being done to them.

Were the twins human? They were ape hairy, although she'd seen some newborns almost as furry as that. They were very small. They were helpless and seemed lost. The image of the pair of them lying so close together in the cot, the lips of one puckering in a suck, reached out to her. Julia's casual dismissal of them as expendable was vile. Whether they were human or not, they were being used. Little alien babies, tiny and vulnerable.

Did Adam know what was going on in Oxford? Was he aware that the researchers were creating creatures as they willed and snuffing out their lives when they'd wrung out of them all they could? It was strange, she thought; you might have expected that the Infection would make people value life more. Instead, it seemed to have made them rate it less. The attitude now was that death was a thing that happened, so get over it.

The evening she got back to Lake Manor from her trip she tried to reach Adam. There was no reply and no prompt to leave a voicemail. That was odd. Surely he'd be expecting her to call. He knew she'd be back from Oxford by now; wouldn't he want to hear about what she'd found? She tried again several times in the next couple of hours and got the same result. Perhaps there was a problem with the system, or with his phone. Maybe it needed charging and he hadn't realised yet. Perhaps there was some critical problem in the government that needed Adam's full attention. She put her phone aside; Adam would call her. But he didn't, and eventually she went to bed.

However, she couldn't sleep. Her thoughts were in turmoil and the tiny bonobo faces haunted her. So did the rack of jars she'd seen on her way across the lab, each one containing a small, preserved ape. Rest was impossible.

Why hadn't she been able to contact Adam? She doubted it was a crisis or other work. If it was that he'd have set up voicemail. The only answer was that feedback on what she'd seen wasn't a priority for him. The obvious conclusion then was that he must already know what was going on at the Oxford lab. Which also meant that her trip wasn't necessary, it was just a distraction tossed to her to keep her busy because she'd grumbled that she was bored. If he was aware of the experiments, did he care? Adam was changing. The more important he became the more he was drifting away from the person she'd known. He'd always been determined, but before there'd been a control in place, a governor that had stopped him from going too far. Until now. Since the business with Kerryl, that restraining force had gone.

Eventually she gave up on sleep and got out of bed. There was a faint light on the horizon, a scarcely perceptible tinge of pink. The night would soon be over, thank God. She retrieved from the floor the same clothes she'd flung aside last night, put them on, and went downstairs.

There was a light in the kitchen. It was Carol, reading, a mug in one hand. She put aside her book as Magda came in.

'You can't sleep either.' said Magda. 'I thought I was the only night owl.'

'No,' said Carol, 'I've had some sleep. I'm an early riser. I'm always up well before the others. Something on your mind?'

Magda was on the point of telling Carol what she'd seen, then thought better of it. She settled for, 'I think it must have been all the excitement yesterday. I'm not used to being whisked around in swanky cars.'

'Well, you'd better get used to it. Your boyfriend is going places.' Carol's tone was disapproving.

'Adam's not my boyfriend.' The words came out quickly, almost snappily, and as they did Magda realised that the casual relationship she and Adam had enjoyed, that had suited them both so well, was over. She didn't like the new Adam, and she knew with sudden clarity that they were finished. Did Adam think the same? Had he sensed it? Was that why he hadn't responded to her calls? She didn't think he was that sensitive.

'I thought you might have got up early for the big switch-on,' said Carol. 'It's a special day today. We're joining civilisation.'

'How come?'

'It's the internet. Well, it is, and it isn't. They call it NewNet and it's like the old internet, but the government decides what goes on it. It's been set up to link all the pods, and now they're rolling it out to the covens too. I think the Franklins have got it already, and the Curies. It won't be much fun, but at least we'll be able to talk to each other. Somebody's coming today to set it up for us.'

Magda's heart gave a little start. Would it be Lander? Adam had told her he was involved in this work. As for the system itself, he had told her about that too, and she experienced again the same unease she'd felt before. To her NewNet looked just like the authorities tightening their grip on what people were allowed to say to each other and what they were allowed to know, a device for eavesdropping on private conversations, an endoscope to peer into the innermost workings of the population. The world was being bounded, constricted, and confined.

She declined coffee and left Carol to sit in the Long Room. It had a thick carpet, occasional tables, display cabinets, and four huge sofas. She chose the one with the most cushions and settled into it. It was turning into a beautiful dawn, and shafts of sunlight fell on her through the big windows. She was warm, and suddenly sleepy. Her eyelids grew heavy, her breathing slowed, and she slept.

As the house came to life several people looked in, saw her resting, and left her undisturbed. Except for one.

'Magda?'

The sudden, bluff voice startled her awake. She blinked the sleep from her eyes. Was it? It couldn't be. 'Steve?'

'The very same,' he said, coming into the room. 'Good to see you, how are you doing?'

He strode across and planted a big kiss on her forehead. When they'd been together before, with Lander on the canal, she'd thought Steve a moron, a humper and heaver for whom an idea that didn't involve eating, drinking or screwing was a rare visitor, but now he seemed different. The chubby cheeks and bull neck had gone, his stomach was trimmer, and muscles bulged under his t-shirt. He also seemed more confident, and more in charge of himself.

All this she got from half a dozen words, a few steps, and a kiss.

There was somebody behind him, who now came out from his shadow. Chrissie. The last time she'd seen her she'd been setting off with Lander to bring Lisa to the Nightingales. The first time she'd seen her she'd been strapped to a chair suffering an agony of cramps from a drug that had been given to her. Neither were good memories.

'Chrissie. What are you doing here?' she said, coldly.

Chrissie came forward. 'I could ask you the same. I do own this place, after all.'

Magda remembered having been told that Lake Manor had belonged to Chrissie's family, and with them now all dead from the Infection she was the sole owner and was letting the Nightingales use it.

'I stayed here to help take care of Lisa,' said Magda, 'and I was trying to decide where to go next. You heard about the baby?'

Chrissie nodded.

'Why not come with us?' said Steve.

She was puzzled, but before she could ask him to explain he took a folded paper from his pocket and gave it to her. The cover was a red wall, with a doorway and light blazing from it. The slogan across the top read: *Reboot Army - a new way for a new world.* She opened the leaflet. Its meaning was clear and simple. The old order had failed, now there was an opportunity to make a better life. The new world would be based on kindness, generosity and love. The trouble was that some didn't see this and were intent on putting things back the way they were, complete with all the corruption, cruelty and unfairness that had been common then. Although it didn't say so in as many words the message was revolutionary, implying the removal of the government and its replacement with something new.

Steve and Chrissie joined her on the sofa, one on each side.

'We're starting a crusade,' said Steve. 'We ran some meetings at Lander's farm, but they were small stuff, just trials really.'

'They had to be small because of the travel ban,' said Chrissie. 'We'd set them up at the last minute, and people would get to know by word of mouth, through the Drifters.'

'They were good,' said Steve. 'People took Chrissie's message on board and really went for it. Everybody there made the six pledges. Now we want to grow bigger.'

'What six pledges?'

'It's on the leaflet. I pledge myself to –,' Steve counted them on his fingers, 'one, be kind; two, feed the hungry; three, care for the sick; four, not help myself to things that aren't mine; five, only use what I need and no more; six, always treat other people the way I want them to treat me.'

'And people have to sign up to these?'

'They don't *have* to do anything,' said Chrissie.

'They don't sign either,' said Steve. 'Chrissie reads the pledges out one at a time, and if people agree to commit to them, they cheer. It's okay in small groups but it will be even better in bigger ones, we'll be able to build up more of an atmosphere. In an arena it would be awesome. We want to reach into the pods, and with

NewNet we can do that. The EA goons are more relaxed now about letting people move around, so we're seeing that as a chance to grow.'

Magda had never heard Steve say so much, and certainly not without swearing.

'I'm calling them gatherings,' said Chrissie. 'I think if the powers that be get to know about them they'll find the word gathering less threatening than rally.'

'Good luck,' said Magda, and she meant it.

'Join us,' said Steve. 'Help us.'

He wrapped his arm around her shoulders and squeezed her. She recalled that he'd been quite keen on her when they'd been together on the canal. They had never actually made it, but they'd come close. This gesture, though, was friendly, not sexy. Chrissie clearly had him under control. Magda quite liked the new Steve.

'Join you how? What would I do?' she said.

'Talk with people, gee them along, join in the cheering, help Chrissie get ready, loads of stuff.'

'When are you starting these gatherings?'

'Day after tomorrow.'

'So soon? Where?'

'The first one's in Bedford,' said Chrissie.

Magda hesitated.

'Are you up for it?' said Steve.

She wasn't sure. What was in this for Chrissie and Steve? She looked from one to the other. Chrissie's eyes burned with the passion of the zealot; Steve's burned with passion for Chrissie. And where was the harm? The six pledges were fine. People were being asked to sign up to being nice to each other. How could anyone argue with that? There was no link with any particular god or religion. They were reaching out to everybody, regardless of faith, or lack of it.

'Yes. Okay,' said Magda. 'Count me in. I'll come.'

20

THE GATHERING

THE MUSIC WAS INFECTIOUS and Lander soon found himself moving to its beat. The band was called Reboot Nation. There were driving drums, a tight bass line, a flamboyant lead guitar, and a bouncy female vocalist. The stage was a flatbed truck with a generator, parked in the corner of a field. There was a similar arrangement beside it that Lander assumed was for Chrissie's address, because it bore banners: *Reboot Army - a new way for a new world* and *Make the Big 6 Pledges*.

The crowd must have been a thousand strong, maybe more. Lander hadn't seen so many people together in one place since before the Infection. Where had they all come from? There had only been four thousand people in the arks; this couldn't be a quarter of them. There must be a lot here who hadn't been in the arks and weren't in pods, the ones some people called Drifters. Most of them were about his age. There were more women than men, which wasn't a surprise because Adam had told him long ago that females survived the Infection better than males.

Getting away from Ludlow had been easy. He'd had a story ready about the Letchworth Pod needing some support – he guessed Letchworth was the closest pod to Bedford – but Wilkinson had barely listened and had signed the permit without even looking at the details which Lander had so carefully constructed. As it turned out the permit had not been needed. The Ludlow guards were used to him, and they waved him through the gate without a second glance. He'd met no patrols on the road either.

Lander watched the crowd and felt a sudden upsurge of joy. Music. Dancing. Laughter. People enjoying themselves and each other. Some words came to him: "Oh brave new world that has such people in it." It was a quotation he'd heard from Kerryl. He didn't know where it came from, but it had stuck in his head and it seemed to fit this crowd. Like them, he was lucky. He had survived, and with all its faults this wasn't such a bad place after all. Could they make it a brave new world? Maybe there was just a chance that they could. Maybe Chrissie had something.

The band finished, pretended to go off, played an encore, and then somebody appeared on the other stage, the one with the banners. It took Lander a second or two to realise it was Steve. He'd cut his hair, slimmed down and smartened himself up. Instead of the sloppy t-shirt and scruffy jeans that had been his hallmark, he now wore a white shirt and neatly pressed chinos. He held a microphone and waved to the crowd.

'Hi, Rebooters. Are you all having a good time?'

There was a scattering of shouts.

'I said, are you all having a good time?'

Louder and longer shouts.

'Good. Because that's what the Reboot Army is for. It's not about the church and long faces. It's about having fun.'

That brought a much bigger cheer. Steve carried on. He was speaking fluently, much better than Lander would have expected. It may be a script he'd learnt from Chrissie, but he was handling it well.

'Jesus had fun. When he saw the faces of those people at the wedding in Cana who expected to be swigging water but suddenly found it was wine, don't you think he was pissing himself?'

Laughter and more cheering.

'And when the people at the back of the queue of five thousand, who thought they were going to go hungry because there were only five loaves and two fish to feed the lot of them, when they got to the front and saw there was enough left for them too, don't you think Jesus was in stitches?'

Even louder and more prolonged cheering. Steve let it run on for a moment and then held up his hand. The crowd quietened.

'Yes, the Reboot Army is about having a good time, but more than that, it's about *how* you have a good time. Here to give you the recipe for that is our leader. Friends, brothers and sisters, I ask you to give a big welcome to the founder and inspiration of the Reboot Army, Sister Chrissie.'

There were shouts and whoops and whistles, which reached a crescendo when Chrissie appeared from behind the banner. She looked amazing, wearing the same white shift as in the video Lander had seen, and not much else. There was chanting and there were whistles. Chrissie raised her arms and the racket grew even louder. It was because of the din that nobody heard the vehicles approaching.

At last the crowd settled down and Chrissie took the microphone.

'Brother Steve is right,' she said. 'The Reboot Army is about fun. But in order to have fun, I mean proper fun, not the selfish playtimes of the pre-Infection billionaires, we have to make the world a better place.'

She was speaking more quietly now, in contrast to the rousing tones of Steve, and people had to strain to hear her. They pressed forward until they were in a tight pack, like fish in a seine net. Lander kept to the back.

'Think what it was like before the Infection. There was conflict everywhere. It spread throughout the world. On every continent there were people with guns, trying to kill each other. Families and children living in the desert under plastic sheets were attacked from the air. Hospitals were barrel bombed. And there was conflict inside people's homes, in their living rooms. I don't mean only on the news, I mean in the entertainment they were given and taught to like. Remember the soaps, the reality shows, the blockbuster movies, the drama and crime series? Conflict, violence, brutality, cruelty, murder – models of behaviour for us all to follow. And did the politicians help?'

A chorus of no.

'No. In China and Russia there were dictators who took over their countries and ruled for life. In the middle east there were governments driven by religious fanatics who pretended to be god-fearing but in reality were selfish and cruel. To be the President of the USA you first had to be a billionaire. Even then they often got into power on a minority vote. In Britain we had two big political parties, and if you weren't in one of those you didn't stand a chance of being in government. And the bankers sat in their sties taking from people who were in trouble money they didn't have. All over the world there were systems that kept the rich and powerful just that: powerful and rich.'

The crowd became serious. Some were booing, not directed at Chrissie but in response to the conditions she was describing. They were in the palm of her hand, and she was working up to her main message.

'It's no surprise then that for most people life was a dismal grind. What did you expect when the very rich owned so many houses they didn't have time to visit them all, while the poorest had none and slept, and died, on the streets? What did you expect when the politicians said one thing to get elected and then forgot all about it once they were in power? What did you expect when the whole of life was devoted to getting you to buy things you didn't need with money you didn't have? We have to make our new world better than that. But some people want the same old same old, they want things exactly like they were. We're kept in pens – I'm sorry, I mean pods – run by privileged white men. Gus McFarlane' (some more booing) 'tells us he's trying to make things better. He's wrong. He's trying to make them even worse. He says his government is working on a vaccine, and as soon as they have one the pod system won't be needed any more. Do you believe that?'

Shouts of no.

'Neither do I. In the pods what you get paid depends on what your boss judges to be your value. I know men who have been made to starve for questioning what the mayor tells them to do. I know women who have had to have sex with their mayors to get enough CUs to feed themselves. We can stop all that. Behind me are six pledges. You don't have to sign anything, just affirm them and live by them, but to make them work we have to stop things sliding back to how they were. We have to take on the government and tell them we want something different. We want a reboot.'

The crowd went wild. People were bouncing up and down, chanting, 'Reboot, reboot, reboot.' That was when the blow came.

A gunshot. Two men in the uniform of Enforcement Agents jumped onto the stage. One snatched the microphone and threw it down, the other grabbed Chrissie. Steve dived forward to stop them and a third agent cracked his rifle butt across the side of his head. Steve dropped like a struck tree. More agents flanked the stage and pointed rifles at the crowd. There was shrieking and screaming. People didn't know what was happening, didn't know where to go. They milled about, colliding with each other.

From behind Lander came the sound of whistles, and he turned to see figures in riot gear marching line abreast down the field, swinging batons. People panicked, pushing and scrambling to get away, and they scattered, some straight into the grip of more agents coming from the other side. Somebody tried to grab a baton. He was coshed and fell, bleeding. Lander wanted to help him, but the crowd bore him in the other direction, where people were being herded towards a line of vans waiting at the edge of the field.

He tried to make his way to the stage but he couldn't get through the press of people. He could see Steve lying face down on the platform, a pool of blood swelling around his head. A dark-haired girl was bending over him. Apart from her, nobody was taking any notice. Chrissie had disappeared.

Lander saw a gap in the melee. Somebody was shouting through a loud hailer and a can flew overhead. It landed near him in a swirl of smoke. Tear gas! Even as he realised what it was his eyes began to burn and he felt his throat sting. Blinking and coughing, he backed away.

'Where are you going?'

He was grabbed from behind. He twisted, struggled and freed an arm enough to turn, aiming a kick at his attacker. Somebody wrapped his arms around him. All the other agents were wearing gauntlets but the hand on Lander's chest was bare. He curled and bit it, as hard as he could. With a cry, the man drew back and swung his baton. Lander dodged, but not enough and it struck his elbow. The pain was intense. He broke free, and ran, ducking and weaving through the chaos. He made for the band stage and flung himself under the truck. He was hoping that Chrissie would be at the other side and he'd be able to get near enough to the other flatbed to help Steve, but he couldn't move his right arm. It felt as though the bone was shattered.

He took some deep breaths, rubbed his eyes and came out on the side of the truck away from the battle. No one was there. On the grass was a fragment of white material. Torn from Chrissie's shirt? There was no sign of her, though. He raised his head over the edge of the flatbed. Steve was still there, and a girl was cradling his head. He couldn't see her face, but she looked a bit like Magda. It couldn't be.

In the field part of the crowd had got themselves together to resist the EAs. There were shouts of "pigs" and "fascists". Several of the agents were on the ground and had lost their batons and face masks. A young boy was swiping at them with a carving knife. The EA squad was retreating and trying to reform but they were losing. It seemed as though the Reboot Army might win, then reinforcements arrived in two more vans and the pendulum swung away. Lander watched from behind the truck, helpless as the protesters were corralled and driven towards the EA vans.

He felt sick. His eyes and nose were streaming from the tear gas. He couldn't move his arm without excruciating pain.

'Get in.'

He looked up. Someone was leaning out of the truck cab. It was the girl singer from Reboot Nation.

'Get in. Quick, before they see you.'

Painfully he climbed up into the cab and sat down, cradling his arm. The girl slid across to the driver's seat.

'Are you all right? You look dreadful,' she said.

He wasn't all right, but he nodded.

'Can you drive this thing?' he said.

'Patronising git! Keep your head down. And if you're going to puke, do it out of the window.'

The truck didn't want to start, but after a few sluggish turns the engine fired. There was a grinding noise from the box as the girl got it into gear.

'It's a stubborn fucker, this one,' she said. 'You have to show it who's boss.'

She let the clutch up fast and the truck jerked forward. Lander gasped in pain.

'Hold on tight,' she said and put her foot down.

At first no one seemed to notice, until the banner and its frame crashed from the flatbed behind them onto the field. Then they did. There were more blasts from whistles and something incomprehensible from the loud hailer. The girl might be finding the truck a challenge, but she knew where she was going and she was a good driver. She skirted a mob close enough to make the agents scatter and give the people fighting them a chance, then pointed it at the gateway. Two of the EA stepped into the space, flagging her down. She ignored them, gunning the engine and accelerating as she approached. Just in time, they leapt out of the way, the truck flashed through the gap and sped across the next field.

Lander heard a burst of gunfire and rattling, smacking sounds as shots hit the back of the vehicle.

'They're shooting at us,' he yelled.

''Course they are,' the girl shouted. 'What do you expect them to do? Throw custard pies?'

She zig-zagged rapidly, flinging the truck from side to side to dodge the fire. Lander thought it was going to roll over. They bounced over holes and ruts and his arm hurt so much from the shaking that he was on the verge of passing out.

A wooden gate barred the exit from the field; the girl ignored it and they crashed through, splintered timbers exploding around them.

The jerking eased. They were on a road. The girl glanced in the rear-view mirror.

'Good,' she said, 'No followers, as far as I can see.'

'We should go back,' Lander said weakly. 'Help Chrissie and Steve.'

'Don't be daft,' said the girl. 'What could we do against that lot? Anyway, they've taken Chrissie away, I saw them do it.'

'What about Steve?'

She looked glum and her lips pursed. 'He's in a bad way. That shit who hit him with the rifle butt could have killed him.'

Lander couldn't take it in. He had seen it happen, in front of him, just like that. Like something from a movie, except this was someone he knew, someone who had once been Kerryl's boyfriend.

'I'm Gabby.'

'Oh,' he said, trying to pull himself together. 'Right. My name's Lander.'

'I know who you are. Magda pointed you out and told me to keep an eye on you.'

Magda? *The* Magda?

'Magda? You mean the Magda I know? Was she here?'

'Yes. She was helping Chrissie and Steve.'

Lander tried to get this to sink in. He hadn't seen Magda since his row with Adam at Lake Manor. He'd thought then that she'd been on Adam's side but here she was with his enemies.

'And she said you were to look after me?'

'Yes. Take care of you, keep you out of trouble, get you away.'

'Where are we going?'

'I'm taking you to my place. Where you can get some attention for that arm.'

'Where's that?'

'Claverton Hall. When I'm not prancing around as a rock star, I'm one of the Franklins. I'm taking you to them.'

21

REVELATION

EVERY POTHOLED MILE was agony, and Lander passed out several times. At some point, Gabby brought the truck to a stop.

'What's happening?'

'We're clear now, so I'm going to take off your shirt. It'll hurt, but I think I can make you more comfortable.'

Lander didn't have the strength to argue. Gabby knelt on the seat beside him and gently eased his left arm out of the shirt, then his head, and finally his injured right. It was all bad, but the last bit was the worst.

'What are you doing now?' said Lander, weakly, as she started putting the shirt over his head again.

'Bear with me,' she said. 'This will be better, really it will.'

She got the shirt on with his left arm through the armhole and his right, the injured one, inside it, held against his chest. She sat back on her haunches and studied the result. Then in one smooth move, she whipped off her own t-shirt and did the same with that.

Her shirt was smaller and getting it on hurt even more, but once it was there Lander found it supported his arm well. Lastly, she reached into the back of the cab and brought out a sleeping bag. She rolled it up and put it on his lap so he could use it to support his arm. That felt much better. She adjusted his seat so it was tilted back, and gave him two tablets from her bag.

'We've got no water, but just swallow them with spit, as my mum used to say.'

Lander did.

'Do you think they're following us?'

'No sign of that.'

'Good.' He was relieved. He didn't think he could stand another chase. 'They seem trigger-happy.'

Gabby made a snorting noise. 'Either those arseholes are lousy shots, or they weren't trying.' She started the engine and they moved off again. 'Mind you, it's a good job we've got a steel panel on the front of the flatbed, or else some of those rounds would have come through into the cab.'

Lander barely heard her. There was a dark cloud behind his eyes and a soft weight pressing on his head. He sank into oblivion.

The next thing he was aware of was Gabby shaking his knee.

'Time to rise and shine, sleepy. We're here.'

She dropped from the cab, came around to his side, and opened the door. In a daze, he swung his legs out and she steadied him as he lowered himself. He was wobbly and he almost fell, but there were two more women there. The three of them helped him into the building.

'Welcome to Claverton,' someone said. He was led up a short flight of steps into a large hall where there was a confusion of people, as far as he could see all women, of various ages and sizes.

'I need some clothes. See you later,' said Gabby.

He was surprised that she was in her bra, then remembered she'd given him her t-shirt. Things were a blur. He was supported up a broad flight of stairs and into a large bedroom. There they sat him on the bed, somebody rolled up the sleeve of his good arm, and he felt the prick of a hypodermic. The effect was almost instant.

***

He awoke to find himself in a bed. He felt better, cleaner, and his elbow was now no more than a dull nag, instead of the raging fire it had been before.

It was daylight. It had been just getting dark when he'd arrived so he reckoned he must have been asleep for several hours. He blinked and tried to sit up. The two shirts had gone and his arm had been strapped. His jeans had been removed and he was in cotton boxers. They weren't his own. The Franklins were a female coven. The notion of being undressed by strangers while he was unconscious was disconcerting. There was one man with the Franklins, he remembered: REG22. Perhaps it was Reg who had taken off his old shorts and donated these. He hoped so.

He lay back on the pillows, which were soft and very comfortable. He was in a high room with panelled walls and a ceiling painted with swirls of flowers. Kerryl would have known the style of decoration and been able to name it, but he couldn't. His stomach rumbled. He couldn't remember when he'd last eaten; it must have been breakfast yesterday, before he left for Bedford.

He couldn't just lie there, not after everything that had happened. He needed to get up, and he swung his legs out of bed. But when he tried to stand there was a wave of dizziness and he fell back again. His elbow protested at the sudden movement, reminding him that it wasn't better yet. He was about to try again when the door opened and two women in white coats came in. One of them was Gabby, he didn't know the other.

'You're awake,' said Gabby. 'How do you feel?'

'Better, I think. My elbow doesn't hurt so much, and my headache's gone.'

'Good.' This was the other woman, who was bending forward examining the strapping on his arm. She had oriental features and jet-black hair done in two plaits.

'This is Mei-Ling. She's one of our star researchers,' said Gabby. 'She strapped you up.'

'I don't think your arm is broken,' said Mei-Ling. 'We don't have an x-ray machine here, or not one that can x-ray your arm, so I can't say for sure. We're biologists and scientists, not doctors and nurses — you'd have to go to the Nightingales for those. I think it's just badly bruised, and we can make you comfortable and fix you up. You'll need to rest it for a couple of days.'

'Thank you, but I need to go.'

'Go where?' said Gabby.

Lander didn't know. Not back to Ludlow, that was the first place they'd look for him, but he must do something. The attack had been brutal, the victims innocent. He'd been focused on his own hurt, but he had seen enough, and the images of black-clad figures wading in with batons and gas, beating unarmed young women and men to the ground, were sickening.

'I have to do something about what the EA did. It was brutal.'

But what? His computer with all his contacts was at his house in Ludlow. It would be found as soon as it was noticed that he hadn't returned and somebody went to see where he was. He wasn't too worried about the data on it. It was encrypted and he was sure there wasn't anyone in Ludlow with the skills to hack it. But Adam would be able to find somebody and send them there. If they got into HushNet that would be the end not only of the group but of all those who'd joined it. He must warn them.

'I have to get to a computer,' he said. 'And I must find Steve and Chrissie and help them.'

Gabby sat down on the bed. Mei-Ling smiled and backed away. Gabby waited until she'd left the room before she spoke.

'You have to be careful,' she said. 'The authorities believe there's some sort of unrest brewing, and they're determined to stamp on it before it starts.'

'Where are Chrissie and Steve? Do you know?'

'Chrissie was arrested. The last I saw she was being carried off, and not very gently. I think she was okay, but the pigs had practically stripped her. I expect they'll have taken her to the EA HQ in Welwyn.'

'What about Steve?'

'Not so good, I'm afraid. Magda was with him and I think she was trying to get him to a hospital. There aren't many places where he could be treated. Oxford's probably the nearest, unless they've got somewhere secret.'

Lander had memories of the hospital in Oxford, the one where he'd been kept while Adam conducted his experiments on Kerryl.

The one where he'd played snooker and cards and video games while his sister was being driven to her death. He shuddered.

'Anyway,' said Gabby, 'you said you want a computer. Do you mind me asking what for? I mean, there's stuff that I could do for you.'

Lander didn't stop to wonder whether he could trust Gabby. He knew he could.

'You know all the pods are linked together on NewNet? Well me and some mates have set up a dark shadow of NewNet, a sort of underground. It uses NewNet but it operates in the background. We call it HushNet. The PG, I mean the New Government or whatever it calls itself, doesn't know about it. There's a group of us, and we don't like the way things are going. The pod system stinks. Okay, it makes sense as a way of controlling any re-emergence of the virus, and that's how they sell it to you, but the pods themselves are like prisons. The mayors are all appointed by Gus McFarlane and they're in his pocket. They decide who comes and goes, what everybody does, and even what they get paid for the work they do. Things that ought to be normal are treated as privileges, and if you get in the mayor's bad books you have a lean time. Then there was the election.' He looked at Gabby and raised his eyebrows. 'You know it was rigged?'

Gabby had sat down on the edge of the bed and her expression was rapt. 'There've been rumours, but no one here knew for sure. We don't get to vote anyway.'

Lander was taken aback. 'What? How do you mean you don't get to vote?'

'It's the pod system. It's only the residents of the pods that have full citizens' rights. If you're not in a pod you can't take part in "the democratic process". It's a law that's aimed at the Drifters, but it hits the covens too.'

'But that's outrageous!'

'Yes, it is. Especially as some of the covens, including us, are doing important work for the government. No need to be alarmed,' she said, seeing Lander's panicked expression. 'It's nothing undercover, and the people here hate the authorities just as much as you do, maybe more. The work we're doing is researching a way of stopping the virus that causes the Infection. We're doing it for the good of everybody, not because the government has told us to, but the only way we can get the equipment and supplies we need is by being part of the official research programme.'

Lander felt a sudden unease. 'Does that mean they control you?'

Gabby shook her head. 'They send somebody to inspect us now and again, their research director. She's quite nice actually and not a bit sneaky or threatening. She just gets a report on what we're doing and lists any support – chemicals, samples, equipment – we need. She gives us pretty much everything we ask for. That's all.'

'No one else?'

'No. Not unless they're a mole.' Lander's face fell further. 'I'm joking,' she explained. 'I know all the girls here, they're sisters. I'd trust them with my life.'

Lander was still worried. 'Someone in our group, the one I was telling you about, was contacted by somebody from here wanting to join us.'

'That's interesting. How did they find you?'

'It's a long story, but I was given the job of checking on this person because obviously, we have to be careful. We've had quite a few online exchanges and I'd just come to the conclusion that they were genuine. My next job when I got back to Ludlow was going to be to give them a password and let them into HushNet.'

Gabby stood up. 'Well, you can probably save yourself a job. What's her name? I'll get her.'

'It's not a she, it's a he, and I only have his online tag, REG22, which I guess means his name is Reginald or Reg.'

Gabby shook her head, puzzled. 'This is a women's coven,' she said. 'There are no men here.'

'You're sure?'

'Of course I'm sure. The Franklins are an all female community. Apart from occasional visitors, no man crosses our threshold.'

Lander felt his blood chill. REG22 was a trick after all. REG22 was a spy. Someone in authority had heard of their group and set out to get into it. REG22 was the route they'd chosen.'

'What's wrong?' Gabby asked anxiously. 'You look as though you've just seen a ghost.'

'It's worse than that,' said Lander. 'This contact we've had, pretending to be from here, I think it's a con. I think it's a government agent, and I came so close to letting them in.'

'But surely they wouldn't be stupid enough to use a male tag for someone who's supposed to be in a female coven.'

'They might.'

'Well,' said Gabby, 'there's one way to find out.'

'How?'

'Message this person. See if you can draw them out. Wait here, I'll get you a laptop.'

Gabby left, and Lander sat with his head slumped forward. He was trying hard to remember the details of the exchanges he'd had with REG22. Had he given anything away? He'd tried to appear open and friendly while at the same time being cautious, but these people were clever. He might have let something slip. The contact had come through Nolan. How much had Nolan told REG22? He'd have to get in touch with him and tell him what had happened.

Gabby returned with a laptop under her arm and put it on the table.

'It's all yours. Tell them you're here. That should cause a bit of a stir.'

Lander logged into his account, clicked on the new message icon and began to type. It was hard with only his left hand, so he kept it short and simple.

LAN999: I'M AT CLAVERTON WITH THE FRANKLINS. NOBODY HERE HAS EVER HEARD OF YOU. YOU'RE BUSTED.

He reviewed the message, then pressed send, and closed the link. He didn't want any reply.

'Thanks for this,' said Lander, indicating the laptop. 'I'd better let the others know what's happened. I may have compromised the group and landed us all in the shit. We'll need to put up some new fences, change our user names and passwords, all that sort of thing. I need to start straight away.'

'Okay,' said Gabby. 'I'll leave you to it. When you're done, come downstairs and I'll introduce you to some of the sisters. I expect you're hungry, too. Your clothes are in the cupboard, we've cleaned them up for you.'

Lander opened a new message board and headed it URGENT!! ACTION NEEDED!! But what action? First of all, he ought to explain the situation. It would be embarrassing, but he'd have to own up to how he and Nolan had been conned. Was there anything in any of the group's previous chats that might let an infiltrator know the names of the individuals behind the online tags? Best to relocate the whole group away from their current site. Fortunately, he'd written a protocol for that, which involved sending the group members a link to a reserve site and giving each of them fresh login details. He'd set up some code words that would trigger the procedure to run automatically. The question was, could he remember what they were?

He sat back and sighed. This whole business had made him mistrustful. Were all the rest of the group clean? Might there be other government agents among them, snooping around and waiting for the right time to pounce? What did they call them – sleepers? It seemed unlikely, but that's what spies were good at, seeming authentic while stabbing you in the back. He was exasperated and angry. If he met that REG22 character now he'd flatten him, dodgy arm or not.

He started to type a message to the group, forefinger stabbing angrily at the keys. He was so engrossed that he barely noticed the door open. He glanced up from his keyboard. Then he looked again, longer.

The person who'd come in wasn't Gabby. It wasn't anyone he'd met before. It was, quite simply and without doubt, the most heart-stoppingly beautiful girl he had ever seen.

'LAN999?' she said. 'I'm REG22.'

22

ADAM AND STEVE

MAGDA DISLIKED HOSPITALS, which was strange for someone who had signed up to train as a doctor. She didn't like the antiseptic smell. She didn't like the constant to-and-fro of beds and trolleys. She didn't like the bustle and noise, the fear and anxiety, the pain and tears. That was before the Infection. The hospital in Oxford wasn't like that. It was quiet as a grave; understandable when there were hardly any patients. One of the few was Steve, and Magda sat beside him now, watching the slow rise and fall of his chest.

He hadn't opened his eyes since the EA agent had smashed the butt of an automatic rifle into the side of his head. Magda had seen it from her position behind the banners, where she'd been while watching Chrissie, and had felt the sickening impact. Thinking back, she blamed herself for not at once rushing to help him, but the shock had paralysed her. By the time she was able to react, two black-clad figures were dragging Chrissie away, and Steve was lying in a widening pool of his own blood.

It didn't take medical training to see that he was badly hurt. His cheek was caved in, there was a visible dent in his head, and his eye was bloated like a frog's. There was little she could do. She couldn't apply pressure to stem the bleeding for fear of pressing bone splinters into his brain. It needed experts to move him. If she tried it on her own she might kill him. She jumped off the truck to find help, and it was then she saw Lander.

Her first response was to get to him so he could help her with Steve. Then she saw one of the agents thwack him with his baton and he fell. Lander now needed help himself and she couldn't deal with both him and Steve. Gabby had been clearing up after the Reboot Nation set and Magda ran to her.

'The guy there with those agents, the one with the hurt arm. He's called Lander, he's a friend. See what you can do to help him.'

'What about Steve?'

'He needs a hospital but I can't move him yet, not with all this going on.'

'He's going to bleed to death.'

Magda knew that. She took a risk, climbed back onto the truck and cradled Steve's head. An agent saw her. She thought he was going to come for them but all he did was shout.

'You're wasting your time, he's dead.'

The other agents were busy fighting the crowd, and she was pleased to see it wasn't all going their way.

She couldn't have told you how long she sat there, Steve's blood soaking her jeans. The fighting moved away from the trucks and she saw the other one drive off, threatening to mow down a posse of agents. She thought it was Gabby at the wheel but she wasn't sure. She couldn't see Lander anywhere. Was he safe?

Most of the crowd had run away. Some were hiding behind a hedge in the next field, a few were being thrown into EA vans. After almost all the vehicles had gone some of the people who had been hiding came over to the truck. Steve was still breathing and had a pulse, but only just. She didn't know how long he could last.

'He needs a hospital. Help me.'

She lowered Steve's head as gently as she could and slid off the truck. The air was thick with the smell of blood and her hands were sticky with it. It reminded her of the night she killed Mickey.

She ran to the van she and Gabby had arrived in earlier, on a morning of excitement and promise. It had some first aid equipment, including a folding stretcher in the back. One of the crowd had come after her, and together they assembled the stretcher and got it to where Steve lay. They put it beside his inert body on the truck.

'Keep him warm,' she said, and took off her fleece to cover him. A couple of the others did the same with theirs.

She supervised the volunteers, setting two at Steve's feet and two at his shoulders and directing them to lift him slowly, and very gently move him onto the stretcher. She held his head, doing her best to keep the motion smooth. When he was on his back on the stretcher she put a rolled-up fleece on each side of his head to limit movement.

Two of the biggest of the boys took the stretcher, manoeuvred it off the truck and carried it to the van.

'Easy,' she said, as they edged it in. It was just an ordinary van, not an ambulance and not equipped for someone so seriously injured.

'Where are you taking him?' said one of the boys.

'Oxford,' she said.

'That must be fifty miles.'

'He needs a hospital. It's the nearest. There's no choice.'

'I'll come with you.'

'What? Sure?'

'Yes, sure.'

She was so grateful she felt like hugging him.

'Thank you. Get in the back and try to steady the stretcher to keep it from sliding around. What's your name?'

'Ajay,' said the boy.

'You're a star.'

He smiled a little sheepishly and got in with Steve. She closed the doors.

The drive left her emotionally shredded. There was a harrowing conflict between the imperative to get Steve to the hospital as quickly as possible and the need to proceed smoothly and limit the g-forces of bends and the judder of bumps. There was also the ever-present threat of running into the EA. Meanwhile, it grew dark.

It seemed to take hours to get to Oxford and she thought they'd never make it, but at last they did. Two hospitals were signposted, and Magda knew that only one functioned. Shit, which? At least they were both in the same direction so if she picked the wrong one it wouldn't be far to go to the other. She opted for the Churchill and prayed she'd made the right choice. It probably didn't matter, she told herself sadly; she was resigned to Steve being dead by the time they got there.

He wasn't, but his pulse was even fainter, and irregular.

'Has he moved or said anything?' she asked.

'No, just the same,' said Ajay. 'I kept him as steady as I could.'

'Thank you. Stay with him, please. I'll go get some paramedics. Talk to him, see if you can get him to answer, but don't touch him.'

Paramedics were hard to find. She located the two who were supposed to be on duty drinking hot chocolate in a staff room towards the rear of the building. They seemed pleased to have a break in their monotony and hurried with Magda to the van. On the way, one of them put out a call for help.

The hospital's resources and staff were limited, but they moved with polished choreography to attend to what was now a rare emergency. There followed two hours of procedures. The urgent need was for a blood transfusion, but first it was necessary to determine Steve's blood group. It was O-positive, the most common type and the same as Magda's own.

Once the bleeding had been arrested and the lost blood replaced, Steve was prepared for the operating theatre. By now a team had assembled, all in green scrubs. Magda told the leader that she'd had medical training and asked if she could assist, but she was told it would be best if she waited outside. She watched the trolley disappear through the double doors and felt a sudden loss. She hadn't stopped to think since the raid in the field. Now she had nothing to do but think. The hospital was silent, the beds empty. Someone had given her an orderly's uniform and she changed out of her ruined clothes. She took her jeans and t-shirt, now stiff with dried blood, and dropped them in a bin for incineration.

She went into the waiting room. She was surprised to see Ajay still there.

'Is he going to be OK?' he said.

'I don't know. They're operating now.' She felt suddenly tearful and blinked them back. 'I'm so grateful for your help, I can't thank you enough. I could never have got Steve here without you.'

'No problem.'

'You must have come a long way out of your way. How are you going to get home?'

Ajay grinned. 'I am home. I'm a Drifter. Wherever I happen to be is home.'

'Do you want to stay here?'

'In the hospital?' Ajay shook his head.

'Where will you go?'

'My people. There'll be some more Drifters in this town. We're everywhere, and when you're a Drifter yourself you pick up ways of finding others, wherever you are. Every Drifter must offer food and somewhere to sleep to another Drifter if they need it. It's the way we do things.'

'There's a place called Lake Manor,' Magda said. 'It's a big house near Shrewsbury. If you're ever in the area there'll be food and a bed for you there.'

Ajay nodded. 'I may take you up on that someday.' He took one last look at Magda, and left her alone.

The lights were dim, and Magda suddenly realised how tired she was, but she couldn't rest. What was happening in the operating theatre? Would Steve pull through? It must have been three hours between him getting hit and receiving treatment. Could he survive that?

It was a long time before she heard a noise in the corridor and the trolley was wheeled past her into a single room. Steve was prone, tubes coming out of him, a dressing on his face and his head in bandages. She waited anxiously for the surgeon to finish and come to her.

'Well, there's good news and there's bad news,' he said. 'Your friend's cheekbone was fractured, and we've been able to put that back together. He has a compound cranial fracture but as far as we can see there's no significant intracranial hematoma. That's bleeding in the brain.'

'I know. And the bad news?'

'Well, he's going to be laid up for quite some time. His jaw's wired so he's going to be off solids. The dent in his skull isn't good and ideally I'd like to straighten it out, but I think that given the circumstances it will be best to leave it for now. It may be we can treat it non-operatively. Anyway, I'd like him to be a bit stronger before putting him through anything more.'

The surgical team was dispersing. The surgeon said he'd be back later to see how things were going, and a nurse told Magda she'd be just outside and to call if needed. After they'd all gone there was a blissful calm. Steve had an airline to his nose and was hooked up to a machine monitoring his heart rate, temperature, and blood pressure.

There was a spare bed in the room. Magda kicked off her shoes and lay down. The rhythmic beeping of the equipment reassured her, confirming Steve was alive.

She was roused by a new noise. Somebody was bending over the bandaged, anonymous figure in the next bed.

'And this is the famous Steve?'

'Adam?' Magda swung her legs off the bed. 'When did you get here?'

'Just now. I had a quick word with the nurse and then came in.' He studied Magda's scrubs. 'So this is what you'd have looked like if you'd finished your qualification.'

'No, it would have been ordinary clothes for me. I'd have made consultant by now.' She had an uneasy feeling, and although she didn't want confirmation of what she suspected would be the answer, she had to ask. 'Did you know the Reboot gathering was going to be broken up like that?'

Adam dodged the question. 'It was their own fault. It was an illegal meeting.'

Magda persisted. 'But did you know the EA were going to go in with all guns blazing?'

Adam dodged again. 'The Reboot lot were asking for trouble. They were promoting rebellion. They were warned about what would happen if they carried on.'

'But did you know?'

'I knew the Enforcement Agency would act, of course I did. Maintaining law and order is their job.'

'And you didn't think to tell me? Even though you knew my friends were involved?'

Adam sighed. 'This is getting ridiculous. Did I need to tell you? You know that unauthorised assembly is forbidden. They know that unauthorised assembly is forbidden. What did you all expect? That the EA would say, "Oh, they're Magda's mates, so we'll let it go"? Chrissie has been arrested and will face trial. Steve will too, when – if – he gets better. There was a girl there too, a singer who was seen getting away in one of the trucks and nearly killed some of the agents in the process. We don't know who she is, but we'll find her and she'll join the others in jail. I hear that your special friend Lander put in an appearance as well. He's gone AWOL from his pod, so he's in double trouble. We'll catch him too, and then I shall have great pleasure in putting him away.'

Magda didn't reply. It was like talking to somebody from another planet. Adam's view of the rights and wrongs of the situation, his belief that it was justified to brutally attack a group of unarmed people who were holding a peaceful meeting, sickened her. There was no point talking to him; she had nothing to say. She got up and left the room, walked along the corridor and went down to the ground floor and out into the open. The cold revived her after the artificial warmth of the hospital, and it was good to get some fresh air.

She wasn't gone for long, just enough time to let her temper cool. Walking out on Adam wouldn't achieve anything. She had to talk to him. She started back to the ward.

She knew something was wrong the second she stepped out of the lift. The strident tone of the monitor alarm echoed along the corridor, persistent and urgent. She ran to Steve's room.

Adam had gone, and Steve was no longer breathing.

23

REG22

LANDER HAD ALWAYS been good at talking to girls. He had somehow missed out on the tongue-tied embarrassment that all his friends seemed to have experienced as they approached puberty, and had instead become a master of the chat-up. He had a simple formula: girls couldn't resist talking about a) themselves, or b) other girls. If you tossed them an opening which allowed for either of those, and then put on your best listening face, you were well away. All that was needed was the occasional prompt to keep the stream of consciousness flowing. If you did it right, within a very short time the girl would be treating you as her best buddy, the only person who properly understood her. The technique had worked for him many times.

It was no good now. His mouth had dried, his brain had gone numb and he couldn't think of a thing to say.

She was beautiful. It was a tired word, worn out by over use, but there was no other.

'REG22' she said, more slowly and louder, as if speaking to someone who might have a problem with communication.

She came fully into the room and held out a hand. She even, Lander realised, had the sensitivity to see that his right arm was bandaged, and she kept the black glove on her right hand and offered him her left. He took it, almost afraid to in case she was a vision and vanished at the touch of a mere mortal.

When Lander still said nothing, she said, 'You messaged me to tell me you were here, but I knew. I would have come to meet you before now, except there was an experiment I needed to finish.'

At last Lander found his voice. 'REG22? But you're a woman.'

She smiled. 'Thanks for noticing.'

Lander felt himself blushing. He hadn't felt like this in front of a girl since his pre-teens. Her eyes were a greenish blue, and now she was close he could see fine lines at their corners. Girl was maybe not the right term. She was a few years older than he was. Not too many, he hastily assured himself. She was wearing the same type of blue jumpsuit that Gabby had. It was a uniform and probably intended to be sexless. It wasn't.

'Sorry,' he said. 'I thought you were... I mean, I didn't expect... that is, I thought you'd be...'

'I can understand the confusion. You thought I would be a man. Sorry to disappoint you.' She smiled again.

There was no way Lander was disappointed. He'd expected Reg to be nerdy, and probably very boring. He could never have guessed it would be somebody like this. She was watching him closely with an amused expression, waiting for him to say something. She really did have the most fabulous smile.

'Why did you say you were Reg?'

'REG22's one of the online names I used before the Infection to protect my identity. I found I got less hassle and unwanted attention if I pretended to be male. I've just carried on with it since.'

She took a pace back and half turned. Was she going? Was he boring her? Quick, think of something to say to keep her here, ask her another question. Reg was maybe her father? Or her brother? Please let it not be her boyfriend. Or even worse, her husband.

'Why Reg?'

'It's a long story.'

'I've got time.' Daft thing to say. He had time, but did she? Stupid. Stupid.

'All right,' she said. She sat down. 'I didn't realise my tag would be such a big deal for you.'

Oh God, she thinks I'm being anal. 'It's not. It isn't. I mean, it's not my business.'

She ignored him and carried on. 'Reg is short for regina. The Reginas was a band I was in before the Infection and REG seemed a good tag. What's funny?'

Lander hadn't realised he must be smiling. 'Nothing, It's not. I mean, it's just the word regina. It was kind of a joke thing when I was at school. Because it sounds like vagina.'

She looked unimpressed and he immediately wished he hadn't said that.

'Was it? It means queen. There were four of us: me, another girl called Rebecca, and two guys, Rick and Rob. Beccy and I were the queens, but it was a play on words because the two boys were gay.'

He didn't know where this was going but he had to keep her talking.

'What sort of stuff did you do?'

'Kind of Indie Rock with a girlie twist. Beccy was the drummer. Rick and Rob were on guitars.'

Ask another question. 'What did you play?'

Her gloved right hand had been in her lap. Now she put it on the table and peeled off the glove. The hand was a prosthesis.

'I did think about learning to play keyboards left-handed, but actually I was the singer,' she said.

Lander felt embarrassed, although there was no way he could have known, and anyway it wasn't his fault. 'Oh. I'm sorry,' he said.

She seemed genuinely surprised. 'What about? Oh, this. Don't be. I've never had a right hand so it's not as if I miss it.'

There was a pause. Lander didn't know what to say. Sympathy wasn't right, and anyway she didn't seem to want any. He went back to the music.

'Were you any good?'

It was a daft question. What was she going to say? Yes, they'd got five Grammy Awards? No, they were rubbish? Despite that, she took it seriously.

'I think so. We were starting to make an impression, getting a good number of downloads on Musegram and Soundhouse. We had a manager and we were talking to a record company about releasing an album. Then the virus came.'

It had been the same with Kerryl; all set to go to Cambridge, then wham. In a few months her world, this girl's, everybody's, had been trashed, and their plans turned upside down. Everybody's but his. He'd had no plans, so he'd not lost anything. He supposed he was lucky.

'Will you get the band back together again, now the Infection's died down?'

She shook her head and the corners of her mouth turned down. 'The other three are dead.'

Stupid again. It would have been surprising if they'd all come through. He did the mental equivalent of kicking himself. Why couldn't he say something sensible?

'Beccy was one of the first people in England to get the Infection,' she said. 'She died very early on. When she did, Rick and Rob decided to take off. They were heading for Scotland but got involved in a big rave in the north, Leeds, I think. It had a gothic name, Death's Doorway, or something like that. They QuickChatted me a couple of times. They wanted me to go up there and join them to do some of our numbers, but I didn't and then they stopped answering my messages. I don't expect they survived. The pictures they sent looked ghastly.'

'I heard about it too. I think it was grim.' Steve had been there, Lander remembered. Kerryl had mentioned his description of it in her diary, and described the photos he'd sent her.

There was silence.

'What are you staring at?'

'What?'

'You're gaping at me.'

'I wasn't.'

'You were. I thought I'd got a bogey on my cheek or something.'

Lander realised that he had been staring. It was because this girl reminded him of Kerryl. The similarities weren't obvious. Kerryl had been dark, she was fair. Kerryl's hair had been thick and wavy, hers was silky and straight. You wouldn't have confused them for a second, but despite that there was something about the angle at which she held her head, her dimpled smile, her full mouth, and the way she moved, that echoed his sister. And her voice. She didn't have Kerryl's northern inflexion, but the pitch, the rich tone and the texture were the same. It was uncanny.

'I'm sorry,' said Lander, pulling himself together. 'I didn't mean to stare. It's just that you look a bit like someone I used to know. Well, my sister actually.'

She seemed puzzled. 'You "used to know" your sister?' Then she realised. 'Oh, I see. Silly of me. I'm sorry. Were you close?'

'We were identical twins. Well, not identical obviously because she was a girl, but we were very alike.'

'And I remind you of her?'

'In a way, yes.'

'So that means you must think that you and I resemble each other.' She looked at him closely. 'Really?'

'Well no, of course not. I mean, not in the way you'd expect.' He couldn't explain. 'It's complicated,' he said, trailing off.

'It does seem to be.' She was thoughtful. 'It's an odd coincidence, but I'm a twin too.'

Lander was intrigued. The idea of another like her was disturbingly erotic.

'I had a brother. He's gone too, although not from the Infection. He had an accident.'

'My sister as well. She died in an accident.'

The girl looked surprised. 'This gets more and more interesting. We must compare notes, but later.'

'Yes.' Lander sighed. Comparing notes with her was exactly what he wanted to do. He was surprising himself at how drawn to her he was, and that "later" seemed like a promise. If somebody had told him about a girl with a missing hand he'd have felt sorry for her, he wouldn't have thought it an attraction. But it was. It made her seem vulnerable, and made him want to look after her.

'Right,' he said, focussing. 'When you contacted my mate, Nolan, and told him you wanted to join our group you said the Franklins were looking for a vaccine against the Infection virus, and you thought you'd found one.'

She shook her head vigorously. 'Did I say that? No no no. You must have misunderstood. We're nowhere near.'

Lander was taken aback. The messages from REG22 had been so clear. They'd left no doubt that the means to combat the virus were close at hand. He was about to protest but she held a finger to her lips as a sign to be quiet. She pulled a notepad from the middle of the table towards her and used her false hand to steady it. Then she took a pencil in her other hand, wrote quickly and turned the pad round for Lander to read. She'd written in capitals.

THIS ROOM IS BUGGED. AGREE WITH ANYTHING I SAY BUT DON'T BELIEVE IT! WILL EXPLAIN LATER.

After he'd read it she tore the sheet from the pad and put it down the front of her jumpsuit. She put her finger to her lips again and shook her head. Lander was taken aback. What was this all about? Was she serious? Room bugged? Why? Who was bugging it? He couldn't see any sign of anything that might be a microphone or a camera, but he didn't know what he was looking for. When the heroes in films he'd seen had searched a room for bugs they'd known exactly where to find them, and the things were huge. Nowadays they were tiny.

'We thought we had an answer, a viable vaccine,' she said. Her voice was louder than before, and rather weary. 'That was when I first contacted you. It was all going well, but the tests failed.'

Lander was bitterly disappointed. REG22's news had held out the prospect of a possible return to normality, the chance for people to break free from their pod prisons. Now it seemed it had been a dream. Except she'd said he was not to believe her.

'If you're interested I can take you to the labs and show you what we're doing. We're making some progress, but it's a very tricky problem, and false starts I suppose are inevitable. We were hoping to beat the other IEU to it but now it looks as though we won't, at least, not yet.'

'IEU?'

'Infection Eradication Unit. The government has two organisations researching the Infection, this one here at the Franklins, and another. Their brief is to concentrate on a cure, we're tasked to find a vaccine. Although it amounts to the same thing, really.'

She rose and moved towards the door. Lander rushed to open it for her, and his reward was a smile that set his hormones racing. She was a step away. He could close the gap, put his arm around her waist, and run his fingers through that wonderful hair. It was all he could do to stop himself. He told himself not to be so stupid. Like most young men, he found it hard to believe that his advances might not be welcome, but there was that possibility. Anyway, she'd only met him half an hour ago, they barely knew each other. The online stuff didn't count; then she had been a bloke.

'About seven?' she said.

'Seven what?'

'Seven o'clock. For me to take you to see the labs.'

'Oh, yes.' Had they arranged that? She must think I'm a complete idiot, he thought.

'I have a couple of things to see to first. I'll come up here and get you when I'm ready.'

She left, and it was only by an effort of will that Lander didn't follow her through the door to watch her go along the corridor. Instead, he examined the room, paying particular attention to the corners. He could see nothing unusual. Was it really bugged? If so, what on earth for? He tried to remember the conversation he'd had with Gabby. He thought they'd both said things critical of the government, and he'd talked about the HushNet group. Had they been overheard? What would happen if they had?

He looked out of the window, where the afternoon sun threw the shadows of trees across the grass. Claverton was bigger than he'd expected. He'd thought it would be like Lake Manor, a substantial country home yet not stately, but this place was huge and surrounded by rolling parkland. He wasn't even sure where it was. He'd been in such a state when Gabby had driven him here that he'd not been able to concentrate on where they were going. On a low rise half a mile away was a folly that looked like a tower of Hogwarts. A straight drive led to a courtyard immediately below his window.

His elbow was beginning to hurt again, and he took a couple of the tablets Mei-Ling had left for him.

One thing was settled; REG22 was not a government agent. He saw her face again, the intense green-blue gaze under long lashes. Other images paraded before him, disturbing ones: the set of her shoulders, her trim body, her delicacy and poise. Who was she? What was she? Why was she there? Why had she come to see him?

He could answer none of those questions. He knew nothing about her; not even her real name.

24

ARREST

THE VAN WAS EXACTLY where Magda had left it, and the keys were dangling from the steering column. She wasn't in a fit state to drive. She was trembling with anger and shock, and she was still in her hospital scrubs.

She sat behind the wheel and silently wept, the tears dropping from her chin onto her lap. How long had she been out of Steve's room? Five minutes? Ten? Surely no longer than that. When she came back the duty nurse was not at her station. Had she been there when Magda had left? She couldn't remember. She'd been so furious with Adam that she hadn't noticed.

She'd heard the steady tone of the monitoring equipment before she reached the room, and when she rounded the door she froze while she took in the scene. Steve was still, lying on his back, heavily bandaged, with all the tubes in place. He didn't look any different. She felt his neck. There was no pulse – of course not, that's what the flatline on the monitor was telling her. He wasn't breathing. She could do CPR but couldn't be sure that was suitable for someone with such severe injuries.

She rushed out of the room and shouted, her voice echoing along the corridor. There was no response. Frantic, she ran to the place she'd found help when she'd first arrived at the hospital, the paramedic's restroom. It was to the rear of the building and she sprinted to get there. There were two more paramedics on duty, different ones. Breathlessly she told them what had happened and where Steve was, and they hurried away. She didn't follow. She knew it was too late to save her friend now. Steve was lost. She went to the van.

There were so many questions. How long had Adam been alone with Steve? Why had he left? When? Surely Steve would have been alive then, otherwise Adam would have raised the alarm, and he would have stayed in the room. Wouldn't he? She could barely bring herself to think about the alternative: that Adam was responsible for the state in which she'd found Steve. That Adam had done something to end his life. But for what reason? It couldn't have been intentional, surely. Adam wasn't like that. Even if it had been his fault, Kerryl's death hadn't been deliberate. When Lander had attacked him, he had defended himself but he hadn't fought back. She couldn't see him as a killer. Or could she? He had shown no regret at the mayhem caused by the EA when they broke up Chrissie's gathering. It had been so brutal that Steve probably wasn't the only one to have been badly hurt. And the facts were there. She'd left Steve and Adam together. At that time Steve had been alive and stable. When she came back he was dead, and Adam had vanished.

She had to get away. It was a long way from Oxford to Lake Manor, and she didn't know if in her distressed state she could make it. Was there anywhere nearer she could go? Gabby would have gone back to the Franklins, but she didn't know where they were. She thought somebody had said they were somewhere in Lincolnshire, but it was a big county and she didn't know where to start looking. Ajay had told her he knew people in Oxford, other Drifters, but she had no way of contacting him either. No, it had to be Lake Manor, the place she had started to think of as home.

The journey passed in a blur. She knew roughly the right way to go from her ride in the limo a few days before, but there was neither moon nor stars, and the night was dark. It was like driving into a curtain of black velvet. It didn't get any easier to pick out the route until the first fingers of dawn began to lift the sky; even then she still had a long way to go. Several times she found her eyelids closing and came to with a start. Twice she stopped for what she intended to be power naps, but they weren't. Her emotions were in turmoil, and after some uneasy twisting and turning to try to get comfortable she gave up and carried on. The thing in her favour was that there was nothing else on the road at all, so her sometimes erratic steering wasn't a problem.

At last she came to the turning for the village, and drove down the rise to the hump-back bridge over the canal. Lake Manor was less than a mile away. Although she was so close to the end of her journey, she stopped. She had to have some air, had to unknot her aching back. She got out of the van and leant over the parapet, staring at the opaque water only a few feet below. That was where she and Lander and Steve had ended up, having come all those miles from Paradise Farm. That was where she'd met Lisa, and where Steve had stayed while she and Lander took her to Lake Manor. The rubber dinghies that they'd hidden under the bridge were gone. She glanced to the left, towards the field where they'd put Joey, Kerryl's horse, to graze. He'd gone too.

She got back into the van and was overcome by an almost unbearable weariness. It was like a thick, heavy blanket. She'd had enough. Adam, whom she'd trusted, had changed. He was a different person from the one she'd known. Whether this new side of him was an attitude learnt from Gus McFarlane and others in Winchester, or whether it had been there all along but concealed, she didn't know. Whatever, the old Adam had gone. Of her other friends, Steve was dead, and she had no idea where Lander was. She could still see in her mind's eye the baton smashing into his arm. Was he all right? Had Gabby managed to help him? If Adam could do what he'd threatened, Lander would soon be in jail. It was all hopeless.

She looked down again at the inky canal and thought about her options. Had she been on a bridge over a wide river she might have run the van off the edge into the obliterating water, with herself strapped inside. There was no chance of using this narrow, shallow channel for that. The opportunities that rural England offered for a spectacular suicide were limited. There was a railway not far away. She could curl up on the track and go to sleep but she could remember hearing no more than two or three trains in a whole day so it could be a long wait. She restarted the engine and drove the last few miles to Lake Manor.

The Nightingales were lovely, but they'd be curious, and solicitous. They'd ask her questions and fuss around her. They'd want to know about Chrissie and Steve. She couldn't face that. She didn't want to meet anyone, so she parked the van a little way away from the house, behind the woods. She approached from the rear, covered the last few open metres at a dash, and got in through the back door. She managed to reach her room without anyone seeing her. She locked the door and fell onto her bed.

She was exhausted and slept for a long time, soundly, obliviously, without dreaming. When she did open her eyes the day had gone and it was dark again. She got out of bed, washed, and searched for some fresh clothes. Her favourite jeans were the ones that had become soaked in Steve's blood and she'd thrown them away. The thought of that brought a sudden stab of pain at the remembered vision of him prostrate on the truck, and later lying immobile and lifeless in the hospital bed. The thought of him dying there, alone in a strange place, was heartbreaking. The notion that Adam might be responsible was almost more than she could bear.

She blew her nose and made an effort to pull herself together. She brushed her hair and put on some makeup to hide the black shadows under her eyes. She realised she was hungry. In fact, when she thought about it she was ravenous. She hadn't eaten since breakfast the day before, well over twenty-four hours ago. She went downstairs to search for food.

Magda found Carol in her usual spot in the kitchen, this time with a couple of the other Nightingales. She looked up in surprise as she came in and seemed genuinely pleased to see her.

'Well hello, stranger,' she said. 'We were just talking about you and wondering how you were. I'm glad to see you back safely.' Then, as Magda came closer, 'You don't look too good. Are you all right?'

Magda nodded. She wasn't all right, but she said, 'I'm fine. Just tired.' She joined them at the table.

'We heard that there was some trouble at the Reboot Army do and people were hurt,' said one of the women.

'Yes, it was bad. Things were fine until the EA turned up and started clubbing people. Chrissie was arrested and her friend, Steve, was hurt.'

'Chrissie, oh no,' said the woman. 'Is she okay? Where have they taken her?'

Magda shook her head. She didn't know the answer to either question.

'We've been wondering what we could do to help, maybe by looking after some of the people who need attention,' said Carol. 'We've made some extra beds ready in the clinic and sent a message to Medical Services, but we've not heard anything from them.'

Magda didn't expect they would. The EA wouldn't be inclined to take much notice of the injured. 'How did you find out about it?' she said.

'There was a young lad here, a Drifter,' said Carol. 'He told us. He was asking about you.'

'Ajay?'

'He didn't give a name, but he said he'd been at the gathering. He said the EA were heavy. He said you and he had taken one of the injured to hospital.'

'Yes, that was Steve. When did Ajay call?'

'Mid-afternoon. He stayed a while, didn't leave till around six. You must have only just missed him. He wanted to know if there was any news of the person the two of you helped.'

Magda would have liked to have seen Ajay again. She was dismayed that she must have been sleeping all the time he'd been talking to Carol downstairs. She couldn't bring herself to say anything about Steve because she knew if she mentioned him she would start crying again.

'I suggested he should come back later,' said Carol. 'He said he would.'

'When?'

'You mean when will he come back? Who knows? You know Drifters, they don't bother with calendars or clocks. But I think he will. He seemed keen to talk to you.'

'I'm going to get you something to eat,' said one of the women. 'You look done in.'

It was soup, with crusty bread. At first Magda didn't think she had the appetite to eat it, but once she started she found she couldn't stop. She was on her second bowl when a bell clanged, followed by heavy and insistent banging on the front door.

Carol tutted her disapproval. 'Who on earth can that be at this time of day?'

'Perhaps it's Medical Services with some of the wounded,' someone suggested.

Carol rose from the table, but before she could get to the door another woman came in. She seemed surprised to see Magda.

'What's all the racket?' said Carol.

'There are two Enforcement Agents at the door. They're asking for Magda. I didn't know she was back, I told them she wasn't here.'

'Where are they now?' said Carol.

There was no need for the woman to answer. The two agents appeared in the doorway behind her. They were in the black riot uniform that Magda had seen at the gathering. It was more intimidating than the khaki denim they usually wore. Had these two been in the field? Had they clubbed the Rebooters?

'We're looking for Magda Gelashvili,' said the taller one.

'You've found her, that's me,' said Magda. 'What is it you want?'

'You're Magda Gelashvili?'

'Yes, I said so, didn't I?'

His colleague came forward and pinched Magda's arm in a firm grip.

'Magda Gelashvili,' he said, 'I'm arresting you for the murder of Steven Barnes. You do not have to say anything now, but anything you do say will be recorded. It may harm your defence if you do not mention now something you later rely on at your trial.'

Magda's arms were tugged behind her back and she felt the cold, steel grip of handcuffs.

25

———

SMITTEN

SHE CAME FOR HIM a little before seven. There was a tap on the door, but instead of coming in like before she waited. Lander opened it. She was still in the pale blue jumpsuit, but now her hair was tied back, and he caught a faint trace of perfume – he hadn't noticed any before – and she was wearing lipstick. His heart leapt. He'd been thinking about her all the time and she was just as wonderful as he remembered. He hadn't been able to tidy himself as he would have liked. He didn't have a razor, or deodorant, or fragrance, or anything for his hair. He was showered, but he felt scruffy and poorly prepared to meet such an amazing creature again.

'Rachel,' she said. And when he didn't reply, 'That's me. Rachel. I know your name, but it occurred to me that when we met earlier that I never told you mine.'

She seemed embarrassed by her omission, but for Lander there was no need. She couldn't possibly do anything that was not perfect. What was the word his Gran would have used? Smitten. That was it. He was well and truly smitten.

'Not Reg, then,' he said.

She laughed, a sound that to Lander was like music. 'No, not Reg.'

Rachel. He'd not known a Rachel. He remembered there'd been a book about a Rachel on Kerryl's shelves, somebody's cousin, he thought.

'We'll use the back stairs,' she said. 'Come this way.'

Lander followed her along the passage outside his room to a small door at the rear of the building. The back stairs must have been intended for use by servants because they were steep and too narrow for them to descend side by side. Lander came behind her, looking down at her golden head.

She paused on the first landing.

'Sorry about the melodrama when we met before,' she said. She spoke very softly, and Lander had to lean close to hear. He caught her perfume again, a delicate, gentle scent that reminded him of washing dried on a summer's day. 'The thing is, most of this building is under surveillance. They didn't bother to install any of their spyware on these stairs, but all the main spaces and work areas have listening devices, and some have cameras too.'

'Why? What for?'

'It's the government. Their people are paranoid about the research we're doing. They want to know everything that's going on here.'

'Why?'

'It's complicated. I'll tell you when we get downstairs.'

'How do you know about this?'

'Because they told us: "Everything you say, everything you do, we'll know." It's a threat, to keep us on our toes.'

'They could be lying.'

'We were here when they came to install the equipment,' said Rachel. 'And we have a technician who does periodic sweeps. That's how we know where all the bugs are. They don't know that we know, though.'

For a beat Lander's eyes locked on hers. He wanted to kiss her, but he'd not known her for an hour yet. Not that this would normally have been a problem for him. His record was arriving at a party and making out with a girl he'd met only ten minutes before, but Rachel was different.

'Come on, I'll take you to meet our Director of Research,' she said. 'She tells me she knows you.'

She carried on down the stairs and Lander followed, wondering how it could be that somebody here might know him.

Gwen Mathews had changed; she was thinner, older, and more careworn. Lander had first met her at the hospital in Oxford a long time ago. At that time the Infection had not yet peaked. At that time Kerryl had been alive. If he'd not met Adam she might still be. And who had introduced him to Adam? Gwen Mathews.

She stood up as Lander came in and studied him warily. She was expecting trouble, and he saw that her fingers were holding on tight to the edge of the desk, as if she was relying on it for support.

'I didn't expect it to be you,' Lander muttered.

Gwen bent her head and held up a hand as if to ward him off. 'Please. Sit down,' she said.

Lander toyed with walking out. He toyed with wiping everything off the desk and trashing the room. Then he caught Rachel's expression, anxious and concerned.

'I know there's a lot you have to get off your chest,' Gwen said, 'and you'll get your chance, I promise. But before you do, hear me out. Will you? Please?'

Gwen and Adam had sat in her room in the Oxford hospital and talked to him about Kerryl. They had said how he and his sister were exceptional, not because they were twins but because they possessed some quality that made their bodies able to resist the worst effects of the virus. There seemed to be a special link between them, they said, and they had to discover what that was, because it might be useful in helping others to combat the Infection. They presented it to him as if he had a duty to do what they wanted and to refuse would have been antisocial in the extreme.

But the plan had had a flaw. It had not taken account of the mental toll on Kerryl of being completely alone when everyone around her had died. The effect had been catastrophic and had led to her death. In Lander's view there was nothing this woman could say that might excuse what she and Adam had done; there was nothing she could say that would relieve the guilt he felt at his own part in it.

'Sit down. Please.' Gwen indicated a trio of chairs away from her desk. 'Please.'

He was reluctant, but there must be a reason why Rachel had brought him here. For her sake, he'd hear what Gwen had to say.

He took one of the chairs. Gwen looked relieved, and she and Rachel sat down too.

'There's a lot of baggage between us,' she said, 'and I want to start by saying how very sorry I am for what happened to your sister, sorrier than you can imagine. Adam and I both thought that the programme we devised would generate important information that would help us against the virus. The last thing we wanted was for any harm to come to either of you.'

Lander sighed. Harm had come. It was Gwen's fault, and Adam's, but if he'd stayed on the farm and not left Kerryl on her own all this would never have happened. The guilt for that would be with him forever.

Rachel was sitting a little apart, her gaze anxiously switching from one of them to the other. Gwen noticed Lander looking.

'Incidentally, Rachel knows nothing of this,' she said, 'it's all news to her.'

That was good. He couldn't believe that Rachel could have any idea what they were talking about, and he was glad for this reassurance that she didn't.

Gwen was looking less tense now, probably thankful that Lander hadn't walked out, or worse. 'Everything was going so well,' she continued. 'We were making real progress. Then I was reassigned to work on the arks. Choosing who was to go in them, setting them up, and organising the screening so that no one who was incubating the Infection was admitted, all took time. I travelled the country and was seldom in Oxford. However, I kept in touch with Adam from a distance, and he assured me that things were fine. It was not until I got back to my base that I found out that they were not, that he'd pushed Kerryl too far.'

'So that's your excuse, is it? Blame Adam.'

Gwen winced, but she took it. 'No, both of us were at fault. Me for not keeping a closer eye on things and Adam for elaborating on the programme we had agreed.'

'Elaborating!'

'He thought he was acting for the best by taking the experiment further. Kerryl was dealing very well with the problems he set her, and quality data was coming from your brain scans. But he wasn't properly aware of your sister's mental state.'

'You mean that she was loopy?'

An expression of distaste crossed Gwen's face. 'I mean, he didn't know that she had a history of eating disorders, or that she was subject to periods of anxiety. She seemed to be well-balanced and cheerful, and our studies suggested she enjoyed spending time on her own. That meant he didn't pick up on how badly isolation was affecting her. What Adam did might have been careless, but it wasn't deliberate. He didn't mean for Kerryl to die.'

Lander shook his head. 'The difference between manslaughter and murder doesn't matter much to the person who's dead,' he said.

'No, but it should matter to those who are left behind. Adam is guilty and so am I, and believe me we have both paid for that.'

Lander was doubtful. The last time he'd seen Adam he'd been as cocky as ever, and now he'd got a top job in the government. It seemed unlikely that he'd suffered at all.

'Look,' Gwen went on, 'Adam's motives are sound. He wants to eradicate the virus and he wants to ensure the survival of the human race. Who could argue with that? There can't be anything more important. Some of his schemes are working out well. Setting up the pods was a brilliant idea. There have been no major outbreaks of the Infection since, and so long as they're maintained we are safe, while we find a more sustainable solution. But sometimes he gets carried away. For example, his plan to use oocytes from Kerryl to create some sort of immune super-race able to resist the Infection is crazy. Now he has an idea to create a new species by merging humans and apes. That's pure science fiction and could never work. It's just another of his hare-brained schemes.'

Two influences played in Lander's mind. The first was that Gwen's remorse seemed genuine. He had liked her when they'd first met, and he decided that he still did. The second, and to him more important one, was that he was sitting near Rachel; she was watching him closely, and he wanted her to think well of him. Could he forgive Gwen? He remembered looking for her in the Oxford hospital and being told that she'd gone away, so he believed her when she said that she'd not been close enough to Adam to control what he was doing. Could he forgive Adam? That was much harder.

What would Kerryl have done?

He knew what Kerryl would have done. Kerryl was kind. Everybody said so, and he knew it. She would have accepted that Adam meant her no harm. She would have been able to trust his motives, even though what he had done was dangerous and inept. She would have grasped Gwen's predicament and sympathised with the difficult situation in which she'd been placed. She would have forgiven them.

'All right,' he said. 'Let's move on.'

He sensed the atmosphere in the room change. Gwen relaxed visibly. He wondered why what he thought should matter to her. Did she want something from him? He looked about him. There were no conspicuous cameras or listening devices, but of course, if there were any they wouldn't be obvious.

'There's no surveillance in here,' said Rachel, who must have noticed his eyes wandering around the room. 'This office isn't bugged.'

'It was,' said Gwen, 'but our sweeper found it and neutralised it. We've got to have some privacy.' It was almost a snort. 'That's why we brought you in here, so we can talk openly.'

Rachel leant forward. Her hair fell over her face. He wanted to brush it gently aside and kiss her eyelids. This impulse was new to him; he had never felt this way before. If one of his mates at school had been acting towards a girl in the way he was responding to Rachel they would all have stuck two fingers down their throats to show their nausea at such mawkish behaviour, Lander among them. Yet here he was, and here she was, and he didn't want to be anywhere else, ever.

26

———

VACCINE

'WHAT I TOLD YOU earlier about the vaccine was rubbish,' Rachel said. 'We do have something that's effective against the virus, or we think we do.'

Lander felt a tingle of excitement, but he was confused. First, there was a vaccine, then there wasn't, and now there was again. Rachel was telling him not to believe what she'd said upstairs. Should he believe her now?

'It's probably helpful if I give you some background,' said Gwen. 'You already know that Adam identified two priorities following the Infection. In terms of urgency, though not of importance, the first was to ensure that virus I/452 couldn't become established again. For that, he came up with the idea of the pods. The other was to find a way to stop it permanently; in other words, a vaccine. Adam sold McFarlane the idea that there should be two teams and they would perform best if they worked in competition with each other. One was set up in the hospital in Oxford and the other here, with the Franklins. I was given the job of supervising the two, making sure not only that they stayed on track but that they really did keep apart and there was no backdoor sneaking of methods or data. Rachel, tell him about the Franklins.'

'Right,' said Rachel. 'Well, you know about the women's groups, the covens.'

'Yes.' Lander did. He'd already met the Nightingales at Lake Manor, and Magda had told him she had belonged to another group. 'They're bands of women who came together during or right after the Infection. They've each got their own special interest and they call themselves after women who were important in their areas.'

'Very good,' said Rachel, and smiled. Lander felt a glow of approval. 'One of them formed here at Claverton. It was made up of physicists and chemists, mostly university types but also including several from private companies. Others joined them, also some biologists, and they decided to name themselves after Rosalind Franklin. You know who she was?'

Lander didn't. 'No, sorry.'

'Don't be, not many people do. She was a British chemist who worked in London in the 1940s and 50s and made some important discoveries about DNA, RNA, and viruses. Crick and Watson would never have understood the double helix structure of DNA without her work, and many of us think she should have shared the Nobel Prize with them.'

'Why didn't she?'

'Crick and Watson got it in 1962. Franklin was dead by then.'

'Bummer,' said Lander.

'And she was a woman,' said Gwen.

'That too,' said Rachel. 'I came to the Franklins by accident. I did Biomedical Sciences at Leeds, and then spent three years on a doctorate at Johns Hopkins in Baltimore. After that, I came back to the UK and took a post at Imperial College in London. That's where I was when the Infection hit.'

Lander did some mental calculations: three years as an undergraduate, another three on her doctorate, maybe two more doing research, then the time since. He studied Rachel's face. She could be ten years older than he was. She could be thirty. Maybe even more. Would she be interested in somebody so much younger? Then it occurred to him with a sickening thump that Rachel probably had somebody already. A girl like her, of course she would.

'The work I was doing at Imperial wasn't glamorous,' she was saying. 'It was to do with trying to find a cure for the common cold. I spent my life dealing with snuffling people. I had an almost permanent cold myself.' She laughed. 'I used to put in bulk orders for Kleenex.'

'How much do you know about viruses and what they do?' Gwen said.

'Not a lot,' said Lander. 'At least, not about your viruses. I know a bit about computer ones.' Computer viruses were malevolent and destructive and usually placed by someone else. He assumed that pathological viruses were the same, malicious little bugs programmed to attack, like micro-wasps but worse.

'Well,' said Rachel, 'viruses are both very simple and very complicated, so please don't mind if I cut a few corners and just give you the general idea.'

'Cut corners are fine,' said Lander, and was rewarded with another of her sensational smiles.

'Right then, start with the basics. First of all, there are billions of viruses. Literally. They're everywhere.'

Lander looked around uneasily.

'Next,' said Rachel, 'they're tiny. They're so small that most of them can't be seen through even the most powerful light microscope.'

'How do you know they're there, then?'

'Electron microscopes. They can be examined through those. Next, they're inert. They have no thought, no will, and they can't even move on their own.'

'So how do they get about?'

'By hitching a ride on other organisms, or by being sprayed through the air, or by being carried when they've landed on a receptive surface.'

'Coughs and sneezes spread diseases.'

'Exactly. They can't move on their own and all they can do is hang around until they're picked up by something that can move them. They're able to remain in their inert state in the atmosphere or on surfaces for some time, but it's only when a virus finds a host that it can progress. This has led some scientists to suggest that they're not really alive at all, but others disagree with that and the jury's out.'

The word host gave Lander a mental picture of a jovial landlord welcoming customers; he couldn't think of the virus that had killed his family and so many of his friends in that way.

'So without what you call a host, a virus is harmless,' he said.

'Completely, and very many viruses are harmless anyway. In fact, you've got loads of them in and around you at this very minute.'

Lander couldn't prevent a shudder. He'd once seen at school a video of mites that lived on people's skin, and in his imagination he pictured himself crawling with similar visitors.

'Whether harmless or not,' said Rachel, 'they all behave in more or less the same way. Once a virus finds a host it starts to do things. It's the host that enables it to reproduce.'

'How does it do that?'

'By merging with the host's healthy cells and taking them over. Often that's only a small problem, but in some cases it's huge. With me so far?'

Lander nodded.

'Good.' That smile again.

Gwen took over. 'As soon as a host becomes aware that it's picked up a virus its defences set about trying to neutralise it. I'm talking about animal hosts. There are viruses that exist in plants, insects and fish, but for now let's stick to humans. The immune system sends what we call antibodies against it, either ones that are already in its armoury or ones that it makes especially to head off the new intruder. Once its immune system has manufactured an antibody for a particular virus, the body keeps it and can bring it into play again if needed. That's why it's rare to catch some viral diseases more than once. Measles and mumps, for example, are usually one-offs.'

Lander was impressed. 'Jesus, that's amazing.'

'Yes, it is isn't it?' said Rachel. 'And it happens all the time. There are an immense number of viruses, and we pick them up all day every day. Most aren't harmful, and those that are we usually deal with easily, scarcely knowing anything about it. Some, like cold viruses, cause minor problems. Others, like polio, Ebola and the

Infection are much more serious and bring about such damage that the body can't continue to function as it did. And to make it worse, these viruses can be caught more than once because they mutate. That means that as they reproduce they undergo minor changes, and eventually these get to the state where antibodies created for their predecessors won't work on them. You're frowning. What's the problem?'

Lander hadn't realised he was frowning, but he was finding a major difficulty with what Rachel was saying. 'What happens to the virus when the body dies? Doesn't it die too?'

'Sort of. Once the host dies, the viruses in it are stuck. If they're to go on they must establish themselves in a new host. That's why everyone who died of the Infection was cremated, to destroy all the viruses their corpse might be holding. You're still frowning.'

'It seems to me that viruses are pretty dim,' said Lander. 'What's the point of a virus killing its host? Wouldn't it be better for it to keep the host alive so it could carry on using it?'

'That's human logic,' said Gwen. 'A virus can't think, it has no brain. It doesn't *try* to find a host, it's all random. And it doesn't *will* harm to the host it finds. It's simply that it doesn't have everything it needs to reproduce, so it's evolved to fasten onto a living cell and hijack it to make more copies of itself until eventually the cell ruptures and these new daughter viruses burst out to invade more cells.'

'Some viruses live quite happily with some hosts,' Rachel added. 'The rabies virus exists in bats and does them no harm. But when it spreads to wolves, coyotes, dogs and humans it can be fatal. Same with waterfowl and the bird flu virus. Okay for one host but a real problem for another.'

To Lander, the answer seemed simple. 'It looks like all we need are the right antibodies.'

'Exactly, but it's not that easy. We inherit some antibodies from our mothers, and we add to those ones we make ourselves until we have an extensive collection, but we never have all the antibodies we need. Inevitably we'll come across some viruses against which we have no defence.'

'Why can't our bodies just make some more?'

Rachel shrugged. 'Sometimes we simply can't, or we can't make them fast enough.'

'Can't we be given them?'

'Some vaccines work just like that,' said Gwen. 'There are different approaches to developing them, and one of the most common is to create a weakened version, not powerful enough to make you ill but enough to stimulate your body to produce an antibody for it. That's the approach the group in Oxford have been taking. The problem is, as I expect you know, that the Infection is very unusual. Unlike almost all the other viruses, which have evolved over millennia, I/452 was created by human beings, almost certainly as a weapon. They did that by combining some of the characteristics of enteroviruses – they're the family that causes things like flu and polio – with the virus that causes Ebola.'

'Whatever you think of the morality,' said Rachel, 'you can't help wondering at the science. It was an astonishing achievement, real Nobel Prize stuff, if there were one for that sort of thing.'

'Why did they bother?' said Lander. 'Why not just use Ebola on its own.'

'Nowhere near effective enough for the guys who were behind this,' said Rachel. 'The Ebola virus is deadly but it's fairly stable, it doesn't change much and there are vaccines against it. Enteroviruses change all the time and different strains evolve. That's why people need new flu jabs every year.'

Gwen took up the story. 'At least fifty variants of I/452 have been found, and we're still coming across new ones. That makes it extremely difficult to make a vaccine.'

'Whack-a-mole,' said Lander.

'What?' said Gwen.

'I know what he means,' said Rachel. 'It's that game where a toy creature pops its head out of a hole and you have to whack it. Usually, you're not quick enough and before you can get it, it ducks back and comes out of a different hole.'

'Oh,' said Gwen, unimpressed. 'It's not really like that, but I see the analogy. The Infection mole is very hard to whack. That's why when Rachel came to the Franklins with her experience of research into the common cold, we decided to try something different.'

'Yes,' said Rachel. 'As I said, a virus can't reproduce on its own. It does it by attaching itself to its host's cells and using their proteins. You know what proteins are?'

'Kind of body-building stuff?' said Lander.

Rachel nodded. 'Well, that's part of it. Proteins are essential for developing muscle mass, but they do a lot of other things too. The important thing here is that a virus is partly made up of proteins. It can't make its own, so if it's to reproduce it needs to get more of them. If we can stop it from getting proteins we can stop it from making copies of itself. That was what we tried at Imperial. We started with human cells and then used gene editing to turn off the instructions inside the DNA to make the particular protein the virus needs. We then let a range of enteroviruses loose on these doctored cells and bingo; they couldn't replicate. That was all in test tubes, so we moved on to mice. We left some of the mice as they were and changed others so they were unable to produce the protein the virus needs, and then we tried to infect them all. And what do you know?'

'The same?' said Lander.

'You got it. The mice that lacked that protein were totally protected.'

'But isn't just turning stuff off dangerous?'

'You might think so, but it seems not. The mice were healthy for their whole lives, despite lacking the protein. They could manage without it.'

Visions of mutants from all the science fiction films he'd ever seen rose up in Lander's imagination. 'You're talking about genetically modifying people?'

'No,' said Gwen, 'of course not.'

'Well if you're not going to modify people, how can you do it?'

'Ah,' said Rachel, 'that's the breakthrough. We've managed to develop a molecule that can block the virus and interfere with its ability to hook itself onto new proteins. You've seen pictures of viruses?'

'Yes, round and spikey, like a sea mine.'

'Right. Not all viruses are like that, but the ones we're talking about are. The virus swills about inside the body until one of them runs into the proteins on a cell, and then it locks one of its spikes onto it. From there it can start to work its way inside. The molecule we have stops that. It blocks the spikes so the virus can't attach itself to a cell. If it works on people we can stop the Infection!'

Lander didn't know how to respond. It was fantastic news, obviously, but should he applaud? Cheer? Dance around the room? Why couldn't Rachel have told him this at the outset, when they were upstairs? Why the secrecy? Why keep news like this from the government?

'So, what happens now?' he said. 'How do people get this molecule thingy?'

'It's early days yet,' said Rachel. 'We've taken it as far as we can in the lab and with animals. Now we need to try it on humans.'

'The trouble is,' Gwen continued, 'a human trial is risky. What we'd be asking people to do is take the molecules and then deliberately infect themselves with as many strains of the virus as we can find, and trust that they won't get the Infection. It's a big ask, particularly of people who have seen what this group of viruses can do and have managed to escape so far. In a proper clinical trial, we'd have a lot of people, it would be carefully regulated and it would take a long time. However, we don't have a lot of people and we don't have a long time, so we've decided to go ahead with just two volunteers. We already have one.'

'Who's that?' said Lander.

'Me,' said Rachel.

27

______

JUSTICE

ON THE MORNING of Magda's second day in jail she was taken from her cell to another part of the same building. It was set up like a courtroom but there was just her, a guard, a clerk, and an older woman in a smart business suit.

'I'm the Examining Magistrate,' the woman said. 'In the past, a murder trial would have been a grand affair. It would have involved barristers and a jury and would have taken days, sometimes weeks. There aren't the people to do that now, so under the current arrangements an experienced legal professional is appointed to hear the evidence, reach a judgement and, if appropriate, pass sentence. I am that person. Despite being a streamlined operation, this is a proper court of law. Its decisions are binding, and although there is a system for appeals they are rarely allowed. We don't have people taking oaths in here, but every statement you make is assumed to be made under oath, and you are guilty of perjury if it turns out to be untrue. Do you understand all that?'

'Yes,' said Magda.

'Do you want any of it repeating?'

'No.' She could accept that there just weren't the resources to support the old system of trial by jury, and this woman seemed all right. It would be a relief to be able to explain to her what had happened and so put an end to this silly nonsense.

'Good.' The Magistrate glanced down at her notes. 'You are Magda Gelashvili?'

'Yes.'

'Gelashvili. That's not an English name, is it?' It sounded a little like an accusation.

'My family were originally from Georgia in the former Soviet Union. My father and I were born in this country and we are British citizens.'

'I see. Which pod are you allocated to?'

'I'm not in a pod. I'm a member of a coven. The Nightingales, at Lake Manor, near Shrewsbury.'

'And that is where you were arrested.'

'Yes.'

'Where had you been immediately before that?'

'The Churchill Hospital in Oxford.'

'Why were you there?'

'I was with a young man who'd been hurt.'

The Magistrate consulted her notes again. 'That would be Mr Steven Barnes.'

'Yes.'

'Miss Gelashvili, you are accused that on the tenth of this month at the Churchill Hospital in Oxford you murdered Mr Steven Barnes. How do you plead?'

Magda's temper rose and so did her voice. 'It's complete rubbish. Steve was my friend, I tried to save his life, I…'

There was a loud bang that startled Magda. The Magistrate had brought her gavel down hard on her desk.

'The accusation of murder often elicits an emotional response,' said the woman, tersely. 'However, I cannot tolerate that sort of outburst in my court. Any more behaviour like that and you'll be returned to your cell and I'll proceed without you. If you want to hear the evidence against you and to have the opportunity to question the witnesses, behave yourself. Now, how do you plead? Guilty, or not guilty?'

'Not guilty,' said Magda, firmly.

She felt uneasy. What witnesses? There were no witnesses because she hadn't done anything. There was a pause while the Magistrate organised her papers. Then she looked to the attendant. 'Call the first witness,' she said.

Magda didn't recognise the man who came in. Then she realised that the last time she'd seen him he'd been wearing surgical scrubs.

'Your name?' said the Magistrate.

'Robert Cooper.'

'And your profession?'

'I am a qualified medical practitioner specialising in surgery. Before the Infection I was a Senior Consultant at the Churchill. I have particular expertise in repairing damage caused by trauma.'

'Thank you, Mr Cooper. Now tell me, were you in attendance at the Churchill Hospital on the tenth of this month?'

'I was.'

'And did you carry out any surgical procedures on that day?'

'Yes. Towards the end of the afternoon I was called to attend to a young man who presented with severe head and facial injuries. He had been struck with a blunt object.'

'He'd been clubbed with a rifle butt,' said Magda, 'I saw it happen.'

'Miss Gelashvili,' the Magistrate said sternly.

Magda looked down, hoping that would show a repentance that she certainly didn't feel.

'Please continue, Mr Cooper.'

'Yes, well, the patient had been struck by a blunt object, there was nothing to indicate what it was. It had caused considerable damage. He had a mandible fracture and a temporomandibular dislocation. That's a dislocation of the jaw. In addition, he was exhibiting a compound cranial fracture. I relocated his jawbone and wired the jaw. He appeared to be stable, so I decided to defer a decision on whether to operate on his skull fracture until I had had the opportunity to observe him further.'

There was something wrong with the sound of this. To Magda, it seemed too glib, as if it was a script he had learnt. She could imagine the smooth-talking Cooper practising it in front of a mirror.

'What was Mr Barnes's condition when he was returned to the ward?' said the Magistrate.

'He was stable. I had seen no evidence of intracranial hematoma. If I had, that would have required immediate intervention.'

'Did you see any reason why Mr Barnes might not last the night?'

'No, I did not.'

The Magistrate turned to Magda. 'Do you have any questions for Mr Cooper, Miss Gelashvili?'

She had none. The doctor had told it as it was. Steve had been all right when he came out of the theatre. Just as he'd been all right when she left him.

'No,' she said.

The Magistrate dismissed the witness and he left. Magda realised that throughout his testimony he had not looked at her once.

The next to come in was a nurse. She said she'd been on duty on the night Steve had been admitted. Magda didn't recognise her, but it was possible. She'd been under a lot of stress and so concerned for Steve that there was probably a great deal she hadn't taken in.

The nurse confirmed Cooper's story and said that after the operation she had remained on duty at the nurses' station outside Steve's room. She said she had been there for about an hour when a young man arrived, and she showed him into the room. Then she had taken a toilet break. Before she left, she checked that the equipment monitoring Steve was functioning and concluded that his condition had not changed.

'Miss Gelashvili and the young man were with him, so I considered it safe to leave.'

It was all Magda could do to restrain herself from interrupting again. She'd not seen the nurse carrying out this check and was sure she'd never come into the room. But it would be just her word against the nurse's. She bit her tongue.

The nurse's story for being so long away from her post was that the symptoms of a stomach upset had started to trouble her, and that made her absence longer than she'd intended. When she did return and approached her station she heard the monitor alarms.

'I ran to Mr Barnes's room but I found him dead, and Miss Gelashvili and the young man had gone.'

This, too, sounded like a speech that had been learnt by heart, except that this girl was less convincing than the doctor had been. Magda had no questions; what the girl said proved nothing. The more this went on the greater her conviction that she knew who had killed Steve.

The third witness was a total shock; such a shock that for a second or two Magda felt giddy.

'Your name?' said the Magistrate.

'Przemysław Adamski. But please call me Adam, it's simpler.'

The Magistrate smiled. All pals together in this great palace of fun, thought Magda. At least Adam had the grace to avoid eye contact with her. Her faintness was being replaced by anger.

'And your profession?'

'I am Special Adviser to the First Minister.'

The Magistrate appeared to be impressed. 'Very good, Mr Adam. Please give your account of the events at Churchill Hospital on the tenth of this month.'

'Thank you, ma'am. I was in the Oxford area at the time, the government has several facilities there which I'd been visiting, when I heard that there had been an altercation near Bedford. A group had been attempting to hold an anti-government rally. It had turned into a riot and had been broken up by the Enforcement Agency. One of the demonstrators, Mr Barnes, had been seriously injured. I had not met him but I knew of him, and I learnt that he had been brought to the Churchill Hospital by somebody I did know, Miss Gelashvili. I hurried to the hospital to see if there was anything I could do, and found that Mr Barnes had undergone surgery and was in a recovery room. Miss Gelashvili was with him.'

'In what condition was Mr Barnes?'

Adam gave an apologetic little smile. 'I regret that I am not a medical expert, ma'am, but to me he appeared to be stable. He was unconscious, but his breathing was regular and the readings on the monitors beside his bed suggested that his pulse and blood pressure were satisfactory.'

'He was not dying?'

'Not at that point, as far as I could see, ma'am.'

'Very well. What happened next?'

Magda leant forward. This was going to be the crunch. What would he say?

'I remained in the room for a time, talking to Miss Gelashvili, but then I realised that I was due at a meeting where my attendance was required. Mr Barnes seemed fine and the nurse was at her station close by, so I left.'

'And was Miss Gelashvili in the room when you went?'

'Yes, ma'am.'

'So she was alone with Mr Barnes.'

'Yes, ma'am.'

Magda was speechless. It was a complete fabrication. She had left first, leaving Adam alone with Steve, not the other way round. She opened her mouth to protest but saw the glare from the Magistrate. How could she prove it?

'One more thing, Mr Adam. Can you confirm without any doubt that Mr Barnes was alive when you left?'

'Yes, ma'am, I can.'

'That will be all. Thank you.'

Magda stood up. 'May I ask a question?' she said.

The Magistrate nodded.

'Mr Adam,' she said in a voice heavy with sarcasm. 'You say you left the room first. That's a lie. I left first, not you.'

Adam looked to the Magistrate, a thin smile on his lips.

'Ma'am, is this a question?'

'It doesn't sound like one to me,' said the Magistrate. 'Do you have a question, Miss Gelashvili?'

Magda felt powerless. The whole thing was arranged, stacked against her. 'He's lying,' she mumbled, and sat down.

Adam made a shallow bow and left, again without looking at Magda. It had been a polished performance, and it was obvious that he had made a strong impression on the Magistrate.

Magda's evidence came last. The Magistrate told her to give an account of what had happened. She told how she had rescued Steve, who had been badly beaten by an Enforcement Agent, and with the help of another young man had taken him to the hospital in Oxford. There had been the operation, and she'd had a meeting with the surgeon, Mr Cooper. She was in the recovery room with Steve when Adam arrived. He didn't seem to have much sympathy for Steve and believed he'd brought what had happened on himself. They'd quarrelled, and because Magda was angry and she didn't want to risk disturbing Steve by arguing in the room, she had left to cool off. She hadn't noticed if the nurse was at her station when she left. When she did return, Adam had gone, and Steve was dead.

She was asked if she wanted to call any witnesses. There were none. Ajay might have testified how well she'd tried to care for Steve in getting him to Oxford, but she had no way of contacting him.

There was a long pause while the Magistrate organised her papers. Then she said, 'Very good, that concludes our business. I need a little time to consider the evidence and reach my verdict. The court is adjourned until tomorrow morning.'

Magda had hoped for a resolution, she'd hoped to hear the truth. Neither wish had been realised. Her fate was in the balance, and she faced a sleepless night before she would know which way the scales would tip.

28

PARADISE FARM

LANDER HAD VOLUNTEERED immediately, without thinking for a second. If Rachel asked him to jump with her into a pool full of sharks he would, so there was no possibility of him not grasping with both hands the chance to be the second guinea pig. However, as soon as he had done so the thought came that he might have been set up, that they'd brought him to Claverton, gone through all the explanation of the research, and dangled Rachel in front of him purely to make him volunteer for the human trial. Why would they do that? Because there weren't any males at the Franklins and they needed one for the trial. Don't be a prick, he told himself. They wouldn't do that. Would they?

There was another problem.

'I will do it,' he'd said, 'but there's no point.'

'What do you mean?'

'There's no point you trying your protein-blocking stuff on me. I'm immune to the Infection. Like Kerryl was.'

'That's only partly true,' Gwen said. 'You and your sister were extremely resistant to the I/452 virus, or at least to the strains of it that you'd met so far, but both of you were affected. You had some experiences of what you called "dream walking", carrying out actions in a state of trance and not being aware later of what you'd done. It's likely, too, that Kerryl's abnormal mental state when she appeared to be sending messages to herself was due to the Infection.'

'What Adam called the Jekyll and Hyde syndrome.'

'Exactly. You have shown some responses to the virus, although not the more usual ones. That doesn't mean you're immune. There are probably variants that if you encountered them would bring on the common symptoms – cramps, diarrhoea, high temperature, bleeding – you know them as well as I do. We have about fifty different strains of the virus in the lab. We'll give each of you twenty-five. I wouldn't mind betting that among your share will be some that you haven't struck before, and that they'll be able to get through whatever defences your body can put up. Without the blocker, that is.'

So that had been it. He and Rachel would be the subjects for the trial.

Gwen had also settled another issue, one that had been puzzling Lander for some time.

'This seems an amazing discovery,' he said. 'Why are you keeping it to yourselves? Why don't you want the government to know about it?'

'We do want them to know,' Gwen had said. 'But we don't want them to know yet. It would be a bad idea to make a big song and dance about this until we're sure it works.'

'There's another thing too,' Rachel added. 'If we have found a way of making people immune there's a decision to be made, and that is how it will be used. It can't be given to everyone at once, so who will be first to get it? And following on from that, who decides? The government will inevitably want to be the ones to take control of this, and they'll want their own people to be at the head of the line. They may even decide to keep it a secret. We don't agree. We think it should be the people who decide what is done with this, and before we announce our success, if that's what it turns out to be, we need to figure out how we can make that happen.'

'That means nobody must know about it for now,' said Gwen, 'and there's to be no mention of it in any other part of the building. Not until the blocker molecule is proved to be effective and we're sure it really will stop the virus.'

'And when we are sure,' said Lander, 'well, then we see to it that absolutely everybody knows about it.'

'Yes, we do.' Rachel nodded. They were on the same page.

'And that everyone can have it.'

'Of course.'

So that was it. The final thing to be settled was where the two of them would go for the trial. They must be isolated, and although there were plenty of spare rooms at Claverton, they couldn't stay there. Apart from the bugging, it was too busy and too public. Everyone would be bursting to know if the trial was proving successful. They didn't want to be a circus, and that meant they had to find a location which would ensure that they were completely cut off. There were several cottages on the Claverton lands, the former homes of estate workers. Gwen suggested using those, but Rachel rejected them because she thought they were too close to the house and wouldn't be much different from staying in the main building.

'No,' she said. 'We need somewhere completely off the beaten track, where we can go out without fear of meeting anyone else or being seen. We're going to be stuck there for two weeks. We have to be able to look after ourselves, get into the open air, go for walks, and if by any chance the molecule doesn't do its job, we need to be in a place where we can wait for the inevitable.'

For Lander the choice was obvious.

'The farm,' he said.

'Which farm?'

'Paradise Farm. My home, where Kerryl and me used to live. It's a thousand feet up on the Yorkshire Pennines, miles from anywhere. I told Chrissie and Steve they could use it as a base for the Reboot Army, but I don't know if they did. Anyway,' he added bitterly, 'they won't be there now.'

Rachel thought Paradise Farm would be ideal, and so did Gwen.

All Lander's belongings were at his house in Ludlow. He couldn't get them, so he would have to manage without. That meant he had little to pack. Rachel had more, because as well as her own things there was the equipment that would be needed to monitor their health and their responses to what would be happening to their bodies. A couple of the other Franklins put together boxes of food and household necessities. Lander reflected that in his gran's time none of that would have been needed; she always kept the larder stocked as if she was expecting a siege.

It took two days to organise all the kit, but at last they were ready. They decided to take Rachel's car; it was an automatic, with adapted controls so it could be driven with one hand. That suited Lander, whose elbow was still sore and sometimes painful.

'What happens if we're stopped by an EA patrol?' Lander asked.

Gwen shook her head. 'Then you're in trouble. You, Lander, could say you were on the way back to Ludlow to give yourself up, but that wouldn't explain all the medical gear.'

'We'd better make sure we're not stopped, then,' said Rachel.

They said little to each other on the journey. Now it came to it, Lander had to admit to himself that he was scared, and each time his mind returned to what they were about to do his pulse quickened. They might be driving to their deaths. On the positive side, there was the fact that he would be spending two weeks alone with Rachel. It was a situation he would have paid anything for, and he didn't have to, it had simply happened. He'd not managed to find out yet whether Rachel had a "significant other", as Kerryl might have put it. It would be a simple question – have you got a boyfriend/girlfriend? – but to come up with it out of the blue, with no lead-up or preamble, seemed like prying, and their conversations so far hadn't provided any opportunity to go in that direction. And he had to admit he was afraid of her possible answer. Suppose she said yes, I'm in a long-time relationship. A further thing was that Rachel had said and done nothing to suggest that she was at all interested in him sexually or romantically.

As it turned out the journey was uneventful. They saw little traffic and nothing that looked like an EA patrol. They reached Walbrough easily and were soon heading up the hill out of the town. Lander was apprehensive about what they might find at the farm. What state would it be in? He didn't know whether Chrissie and Steve had been there or not, and if they had used it for the Reboot Army he didn't know what effect that would have had. Would it look as though a bunch of hippies had been living there? Or, if they had left it empty, might idiots have got in and trashed the place?

He needn't have worried. The first reassurance he got was a view of Joey grazing peacefully in the top field. That meant that Steve at least, and therefore probably Chrissie too, had been there. Next was the yard. As soon as he turned in he could see that it was changed from when he'd last been there. Then Steve had been living at the farm on his own and it had been a dump; there'd been things scattered around, black bags of rubbish ripped open by animals, a broken window poorly patched with cardboard. Now, though, the mess had been cleared up, the window repaired, and it was as ordered as it had been when Lander and his family had lived there before the Infection. The main difference was that there were no animals. The cows had gone and so had their dog, Buster, but everything else was eerily normal. Even the wind turbine that had caused Kerryl such trouble towards the end was spinning steadily, beating a firm rhythm.

He'd left his keys in the car he'd taken to Bedford so heaven alone knew where they were now, but there was a spare house key in its usual place in the barn. It turned easily in the back door. Lander took a deep breath and stepped inside.

He'd expected signs of occupancy, some mess, a musty odour, but there was none of that. The air smelt sweet, the surfaces were clear; the whole place was immaculate, just a little dusty. On the hall table was a pile of leaflets, with the red and yellow starburst and the slogan, *Reboot Army - a new way for a new world*. Inside were the six pledges.

He went into the parlour. The black plastic urn and the cardboard boxes containing the ashes of his and Kerryl's grandparents and their mother had been on the mantelpiece. Somebody – Chrissie? – had put them on a shelf in the cupboard, safe behind glass doors, with a candle on each side. The candles were not new, they'd been lit. He was touched by that simple fact. Where were Chrissie and Steve now? He hoped they were all right.

He went to the window and looked out at the front field sloping away from the house, and beyond it the sweep of the valley. It was a view he'd seen every day of his childhood. He'd missed it and he had a pang of nostalgia. How was it that you only realised how important things were when they were over, not while they were happening? Why did life have no action replay, so you could relive the good bits, and maybe fast-forward past those parts that were not so hot?

Rachel came and stood beside him.

'What an incredible view,' she said. She slipped her hand through his arm. 'Thank you.'

Lander's heart leapt. It was the first time they had touched, apart from casual, accidental connects when he handed her something or helped her put something in the car. This contact had an intimacy the others lacked. And it had come from her, she had initiated it. He felt like singing.

'Thank you for what?'

'For this. For bringing me to this lovely place. For volunteering to test the molecule with me.'

He turned to her and she faced him. Her eyes were bright, and her lips parted. The afternoon sun raised highlights in her hair. Afterwards, he went over the scene a thousand times in his memory, but he couldn't say which of them moved first. He put his hand around her waist and leaned into her. Or was it the other way round, did she start it? Whichever, his mouth rested for a heartbeat only millimetres from hers. There was that giddying, dizzying instant of anticipation and excitement, like being at the top of a rollercoaster plunge; then they kissed.

Lander had been out with some very pretty girls, but when he'd come to kiss them it had sometimes been disappointing. There'd been a clash of teeth; or the nose problem; or she'd had gum in her mouth; or he'd opened his eyes to see hers wide and bored. Not this kiss. It was long, and moist. Each tongue probed and explored the other. His good hand rested in the small of her back and pressed her firmly to him. She moved against him.

They stopped for breath and she stepped back. Her eyes were wide, and she was panting a little. She looked surprised. At what they'd done? Or the way they'd done it? Her hand tucked some stray hair behind her ear. He wanted to say something cool, something witty, but he could think of nothing. As if she understood this, she shook her head, smiled and took his hand.

'Show me around your beautiful home,' she said.

29

ULTIMATUM

'THE JUDGEMENT IS that you're guilty.'

Adam was standing in the doorway to Magda's cell. He looked self-satisfied, complacent. She would have liked to throw herself on him and scrape her nails down his face, but there was a particularly hefty prison guard standing behind him.

She'd been back in her cell for less than an hour, so the news had travelled fast. Early that morning she'd been taken before the Examining Magistrate. The proceedings had been short, but certainly not sweet. The Magistrate had given a brief summary of the evidence as she saw it. It was firstly that the surgeon saw no reason why Mr Barnes should not have recovered from his injuries; next, Mr Barnes had been alive the last time the nurse had seen him, when she and Mr Adam had both been in the room; lastly, and most tellingly according to the Magistrate, she had been the last to leave, and soon after that Mr Barnes had been found dead. The Magistrate concluded that Magda must have killed him, although she didn't suggest how she might have done that, or why she would bother getting him all the way from

Bedford to a hospital in Oxford only to then finish him off. None of it made any sense, but that didn't interfere with her verdict. Magda could hear the chilling words now.

'Magda Gelashvili, I find you guilty of the murder of Steven Barnes at the Churchill Hospital, Oxford, on the evening of the tenth of this month. You are remanded in custody and will be returned to me for sentencing in three days. You should prepare yourself for a long period in a correction centre.'

That was it. It was such a lot of nonsense, and Magda swung between disbelief and despair. A visit from Adam was the last thing she either expected or wanted.

'Cat got your tongue?' he said.

Magda thought that was the silliest term she had ever heard. 'I have nothing to say to you,' she answered.

Adam sat down on the edge of her bunk. She hadn't invited him to, and she made a point of moving to the other end, as far away from him as she could get.

'You think I killed Steve, don't you?' he said.

'Of course I do. You were with him when I left, and he was alive then.'

He shook his head. 'Why would I? I didn't know him. He was in a hospital bed with no chance of moving, and as soon as he was well enough he would have been taken straight from there to jail to await trial for his part in holding an illegal assembly. What on earth would have been my reason for killing him?'

'What would have been mine? I tried to save his life.'

'I don't know what had gone on between you and Steve. I don't know what motive you might have had.'

'Nevertheless, you think I'm guilty.'

'Well, you've killed a man before so it wouldn't be the first time. You have, as they say, form. Anyway, it doesn't matter what I think. The important thing is what the Magistrate believes, and her view is that you did it.'

A new wave of anger coursed through Magda. Of course the Magistrate thought that. Adam had played her like a fish. 'Yes ma'am' this and 'No ma'am' that. He'd practically had his head in the old crow's lap. Her fists clenched.

'It doesn't have to be like this, you know.' Adam sounded genuinely conciliatory. Magda waited to see what was coming next. 'The evidence against you…'

'Such as it is.'

'Yes, such as it is, the evidence against you is all circumstantial. It's simply that you were there and Steve was alive, then you were gone and Steve was dead. The finger points to you, but nobody saw you do anything.'

This was too much. 'I fucking know that, you moron!' she shouted. 'Nobody saw me do anything because there was nothing to see.'

'Okay, okay,' said Adam, holding up a hand. 'What I'm saying is that I think I can do something to get you out of this.'

Magda scowled. What was he up to now? 'You mean confess that you did it?' she said.

'I mean I think I can persuade Gus McFarlane to have a word with the Justice Secretary and tell her to declare the verdict unsafe.'

'What will that mean?'

'Well, it could mean a retrial, but it won't. It will simply mean that the charge against you will be dropped and you'll be free. It'll be as if it never happened.'

So that was it. Adam was willing to bend the system. If he honestly thought she was innocent he could have done something sooner. He could have told the Magistrate the truth, that it was she who had left first. He hadn't been prepared to do that, so why this? What was the catch? She didn't have to wait long to find out.

'Of course, the whole thing would go through much more smoothly if I could tell Gus that you were volunteering to contribute to something for the public good.'

'I don't have any money.'

'I don't mean that sort of contribution. I mean something you could do.'

'Such as?'

'There are several possibilities.' Adam pretended to think. 'I think what would carry the most weight is if you volunteered to host a bonobo embryo.'

Magda thought she hadn't heard him right. Then she realised she had, and it was as if she'd been tipped off a cliff.

'Host? Do you mean be a surrogate mother? To one of those pitiful little creatures I saw at the research unit?' One, she thought, or maybe even two.

'Yes.'

'But it's insane. I'm sterile. I'm not producing eggs and I'm not having periods.'

'It doesn't matter. You don't have to be fertile yourself to host an embryo. We can make sure you have all the necessary hormones.'

'It's crazy. You're out of your mind.'

'Am I? Think about it. In three days you'll be sentenced for murdering a defenceless young man as he lay in his hospital bed recovering from a serious injury. You'll be given the maximum penalty. You'll be an old woman before you're out of jail. Or you can do what I ask, spend nine months in a comfortable clinic, followed by an easy birth – the bonobo hybrids are very small – and then it's all over. Get on with the rest of your life. In addition, you'll not only be helping the government, you'll also be helping humanity. Unless we can find some way of reproducing human beings, we're finished as a race.'

'We're finished anyway. Those ghoulish experiments they're conducting aren't about us. The embryos aren't human.'

'Strictly speaking, no, they're not. But they're very close, and the white coats assure me that when the whole thing is perfected the result will be a new species that looks human, that can do the things humans do, but has some of the gentler characteristics of bonobos. Think of that, a species that's as bright as we are but lacks our aggression and cruelty. Do you think the Infection virus would have been created and released if these new bonobo-human hybrids had been in charge? No, that was definitely the work of Homo Sapiens.'

He made it sound reasonable, but it was lunacy. It was as if Adam had written off the human race and it was already gone, finished, soon to be extinct. But it wasn't the hollow logic of the thing that appalled Magda, she found the whole idea nauseating. She remembered the pathetic little bundle she'd seen in the natal unit at the lab; she remembered the sad creatures preserved in the jars. It was obscene. Could she do it? Could she prostitute herself like that?

'Give it some thought,' said Adam. 'I'll be back after your sentencing.' He left.

There followed two seemingly endless days followed by restless, tiring nights, the sort where she got up more exhausted than she was when she turned in. On the third morning she was out of bed very early. She smartened herself up as best she could and sat in her cell waiting. She was both exhausted and frightened. After a long time she heard movement outside, the door was unlocked and she was led through to the courtroom. She expected to be handcuffed and held out her wrists, but the guard shook her head; there was nowhere she could run to.

It was the same set-up as before: guard, clerk, and then, after another wait, the Magistrate. She scowled, and Magda prepared herself for the worst.

The woman repeated that she had found Magda guilty of murder, and went into a long lecture about what a despicable act it was to kill an already sick man who lay defenceless in a hospital bed. She had satisfied herself that Magda had a motive, which was that she and Steve were lovers and Magda's action had been prompted by jealousy when he took up with Chrissie. Where on earth had she got that from? Magda had a good idea.

It was preposterous. Magda had told herself that whatever happened she must be silent, but it was all she could do to keep her resolve. Then came the bombshell.

'Magda Gelashvili, you have committed a serious crime. I sentence you to be taken from here to a government correction centre, where you will remain for the rest of your life.' Then to the guard, 'Take her down.'

Life. Life? Magda was shell-shocked. She could barely stand. Adam had warned her that the sentence would be a long one but she'd thought he'd been exaggerating.

'Don't worry, you'll be out in thirty years,' the guard said as she was led back to her cell, and laughed.

Adam was already there, waiting for her.

'Well?' he said.

He seemed to be enjoying the situation. Magda boiled with rage. She wanted to kill him. She was to serve life for a murder she hadn't committed; this one would be worth it. Adam sensed her anger and remained at a safe distance.

'Don't forget,' he said, 'before the Infection people serving prison sentences often contributed to medical research. It's very likely that if you turn down my offer and choose to spend the rest of your life in jail, you'll be conscripted for the vaccine programme anyway. That would be worse. So why not do what I ask?'

'Do I have a choice?'

'Oh, there's always a choice.'

Magda snapped. 'You smug, supercilious git,' she yelled, and ran at him, fists flying. He was expecting it, caught her wrists, and shoved her hard onto the bunk. He stood over her.

'Easy with the long words, young lady.'

'Yes, I suppose "git" does seem a long word to you!' Magda spat.

Adam's response was a mocking smile. It came to her that the whole situation, all of it, was an elaborate fabrication – the murder, the trial, the verdict, the sentence, everything, all of it a set-up.

'Why me?' she said. 'There are plenty of women you could have picked to do this. You could have paid them. Some would have jumped at it.'

'I'm doing you a favour. I'm saving you from wasting your life. And it may help you in establishing your priorities.'

'And what are my priorities?'

'Deciding how you can best serve your country, and where your loyalties should lie.'

There was no point arguing about it. Whether it was planned or not, Adam had won.

'All right,' she said wearily. 'I'll do what you want, but don't expect me to be grateful to you.'

'I won't, but I'm pleased you've seen sense. I'll speak to Gus tomorrow, your conviction will be quashed in a few days, and then we'll take you to Oxford.'

When Adam had gone she lay on her bunk, her emotions swaying between anger and misery. And then it came to her what this was all about. Adam had offered her a job working for the government. It had been to supervise the rigging of the election, ensuring that however the pods voted, Gus McFarlane and his cronies would get in. She'd considered it scandalous and had had no intention of taking part. She'd ignored Adam's invitation to go to Winchester and join the team, and when he'd sent a car to Lake Manor to pick her up she'd told one of the Nightingales to say she'd gone for a walk. The driver had waited three hours, while Magda watched from an upstairs window. After that, Adam spent more and more time away, and she became involved with Reboot. They'd never discussed it, but she knew he'd felt let down and disappointed. It seemed he'd been angry too, and this was his revenge.

30

SETTLING IN

WHEN LANDER THOUGHT LATER about how his relationship with Rachel developed, he tended to divide its progress into BK and AK; before the kiss and after the kiss.

Following the meeting with Gwen, Rachel had explained how the trial would work. It had all been calm, cool, and transactional. She had been friendly and had smiled a lot, but there had been no indication that they might be anything other than partners in a scientific experiment, and he'd been coming to the conclusion that either she wasn't interested in him, or maybe not in men at all. But then they'd stood together at the window, she'd slid her arm through his and looked at him with a new expression in her eyes. How long had the kiss lasted? Thirty seconds? A minute? Two? Lander had no idea. All he knew was that it had ended too soon.

They had separated and she'd seemed slightly embarrassed, and Lander's mind raced. Did she regret it? What did she feel? But it was as if they'd decided that neither would mention it, and they had carried on as before.

Or not quite as before; there was a hidden charge, an undercurrent of suppressed emotion. They edged around each other as if any touch or any reference to that sudden intimacy might upset some delicate balance. They'd unloaded the car and stored their food, enough for two weeks. Then he had shown her the house: the parlour with its sagging sofa where Granddad used to sit to watch the television, the seldom-used dining room, and the kitchen, the hub of the house, where Gran had been queen, even if her rule was occasionally challenged by their Mam.

He'd been prepared for the upstairs arrangements to be tricky. There were four bedrooms: two, his and Kerryl's, had single beds; their grandparents and their Mam's both had doubles. With most of his previous girlfriends, Lander would have ploughed ahead on the cheerful assumption that they would share one of the doubles, but Rachel was different. The kiss had been without restraint, there had been no holding back, but he didn't want to run the risk of taking anything for granted. What should he do? Have a mature, adult conversation at the top of the stairs in which he would suggest that they might sleep together? In fact, events steered him towards a way out of the dilemma; neither of the double beds was made up, both the singles were.

'I guess you'll have your room and I'll take your sister's,' Rachel had said. Had there been a trace of disappointment in her tone? He was certainly disappointed, not realising at the time that there was a very good reason why they should keep apart.

Rachel had had the presence of mind to bring a prepared meal from the kitchen at Claverton, and all they had to do was heat it. They ate in more or less silence and drank water from the spring. Then they watched television. There were only two channels; one was mostly government information, news and propaganda, and the other showed a stream of pre-Infection soaps and sitcoms.

They were soon bored, and it was not long before Rachel said she was going to bed to read.

Lander left time for her to have unhurried use of the bathroom, then went upstairs himself. The door to Kerryl's room was closed, and he went into his own. He found it strange being back there again, and spent a long time awake, thinking about the girl only a couple of metres away on the other side of the wall. Was she awake too, thinking about him? At one stage he got out of bed and almost went onto the landing to tap on her door, hoping she'd invite him in. Had she locked it? Whether she had or not would give him a clear message. But he stayed in his room.

Lander was not in the habit of analysing his feelings and it was unusual to find himself thinking about how he should behave, but he did now. What did Rachel expect? What might she want? He was not experiencing some sort of newly acquired chivalry; it was simply that he didn't want to do anything she might find difficult. She was vulnerable, confined in an isolated house with a male she hardly knew. He didn't want her to feel threatened, he must respect her situation. And then there was the age gap. He knew that wasn't an issue for him, but it might be for her. If there was to be anything between them he wanted it to be her call. Was this love? he wondered. Or at least the beginnings of it?

In the morning they breakfasted together, behaving as if they'd done that a thousand times. Then they walked to a neighbouring farmhouse higher up the hill. Lander had known the family that had lived there well. He and Kerryl had played, and later hung out, with the two older children, and although they'd lost that closeness when they all went to different schools, they still used to see them about. The parents had been straightforward, northern farming stock, kind and honest. It was a shock now to see their home empty, weeds in the yard, and the tattered remains of biohazard tape flapping around the doors and windows.

They turned away and walked along the crest of the hill, taking in the landscape. Lander pointed out the features – the wind farm across the valley that Granddad had hated so much; the small town in the valley bottom; the railway line winding its way towards Manchester; the canal where he'd set off on the journey south with Magda and Steve; and, on the edge of the moor, the sombre grandeur of the Bride Stones, the last place Kerryl had visited.

They sat together on a flat rock, warmed by the sun.

'When are we going to start?' Lander said.

She gave him a quizzical look. 'Start what?'

'The trial. When are we going to take the stuff?'

Rachel became serious. 'What we're going to do is very dangerous. I can't guarantee the molecules will be effective. You know what the Infection virus can do, you've seen it. It's not too late to pull out of the trial, and I won't think any the less of you if you do. I'd probably admire your common sense. Are you sure you want to put yourself through this?'

Lander thought for a moment. She was offering him a way out, but there was no way he was going to take it.

'Yes and no,' he said. 'No, I don't want to do it, but yes, I'm completely sure I'm going to. I shouldn't think you want to either. But if you can, so can I.'

There was a long pause. A cloud passed before the sun and there was a sudden chill. Rachel shuddered and got up, pulling her fleece around her. She wasn't wearing her prosthetic hand, and Lander could see that her arm finished a couple of inches above where her wrist would have been. He'd known a neighbour, a farmer, who'd had an accident and his leg had been amputated below the knee. Even when healed the wound it had looked ugly. His skin had been scarred, puckered and distorted where it had been stretched over the bone. Rachel's arm was nothing like that. There was no disfigurement; it simply came to a stop, smooth and rounded, like an elbow. It seemed to him as if it was always meant to be like that, as if that was normal and it was his arms with their flappy hands and dangly fingers that were odd.

'Time to make plans,' she said. She walked away from him, down the hill towards the farm.

Back in the kitchen, Lander made coffee while Rachel brought her medical bag downstairs from her room. She put it on the table, opened it and took out two small plastic specimen containers. She sat down and poured herself a coffee. The two phials lay before her on the table. Her face was serious.

'What's in these jars is probably the scariest thing ever devised by human beings. It's far more lethal than a nuclear bomb. Each contains around twenty-five variants of the Infection virus. One lot is for you and the other is for me. Like Gwen told you, just because you haven't been seriously infected yet doesn't mean that there's not a strain of the virus in one of these with your name on it.'

'Same for you, isn't it?' he said.

'Yes. We've both been lucky, so far.'

'It's weird,' Lander said, peering at the phials. The liquid in them was clear, with a slight milkiness. 'It doesn't look like anything special. It could be water.'

'Well it's not, it's our enemy and we have to beat it, but we also have to respect it. Here's how the trial will work. The first thing we'll do is take the molecule that's intended to stop the viruses fixing on to our cells.'

'That's the stuff that locks the pantry door so the little buggers starve to death.'

Rachel smiled. 'Kind of. We'll need to leave it for three days to give it time to get thoroughly absorbed in our bloodstreams. We can treat that as a holiday. We can't go anywhere where there might be other people, but we can walk on the moors, you can show me where you and your sister used to hang out when you were kids, and I'd love to ride Joey, if that's all right.'

'Yeah, 'course.' He wondered how she would manage Joey with only one arm, but she seemed able to handle everything else and he had no doubt Rachel could do whatever she put her mind to.

'Then we take the bugs?' he said.

'Yes, then we take what you call the bugs. I'll inject the contents of one of these phials into you, and the other one into me. Which of them do you want?'

'You mean I get to choose?'

'Yes.'

Lander hesitated. It was a biological version of Russian roulette. 'It should be ladies first,' he said. Rachel shook her head. 'Okay. Might as well be that one.' He pointed to the phial nearest to him.

Rachel took it, steadied it with her blunt right arm and with her left hand wrote the initial L on the label. Then she took the other and wrote R on that. Lander had an image of the two initials together, linked by a heart. Soppy, he thought to himself. I'm getting soft-headed.

She put the phials back in her bag. 'Once I've injected us with the viruses it's essential that we are isolated.'

'We are,' said Lander, glancing out of the window. 'We're on our own. There ain't nobody going to bother us up here.'

'No,' she said. 'I mean isolated from each other. The two phials are not the same. They both contain the Infection virus, but they're different strains. We must avoid any possibility of cross-contamination, so we must keep apart. We need to be no closer than three metres, and preferably not even in the same room.'

Lander's spirits sank. He'd imagined that while they waited to see what happened they'd spend their time together. He'd assumed they'd share a bottle or two, cuddle on the sofa while they watched tv, maybe more.

'We'll have to keep ourselves to ourselves,' Rachel continued. 'And we need to protect ourselves: scrubs, face masks and surgical gloves at all times. I've got plenty in my kit. We'll divide the food into yours and mine and self-cater, and we'll use separate cutlery and crockery. We can arrange the use of the kitchen so we're not both wanting to be in there at the same time. We must each wipe the surfaces with antibacterial wipes when we're done. Same with the bathroom.

He rolled up his sleeve and held out his arm. 'Let's do it,' he said. 'Let's take the molecule.'

'Really?'

He pointed at his arm. 'Really.'

'All right then.'

She took two syringes from her bag. They were already loaded and sealed in plastic. She opened one, took the cap off the needle, held it vertically and tapped it gently on the edge of the table. She gave an experimental squeeze and watched the fine mist, then bent over him. She was so close he could smell her hair, warm and female. He wanted to take her in his arms again and repeat the kiss, but she seemed blind to that possibility. She moved back to the table and prepared the other syringe in the same way. She set it down, put her foot on the chair, lifted her skirt and pushed the needle into her thigh. It was a turn-on. Lander couldn't take his eyes off what she was doing, but again she didn't seem to notice.

'That it?' he said. She nodded.

They cleared the table and washed the coffee mugs like a couple who had lived together for years.

That night Lander gave Kerryl's diaries to Rachel to read. The next morning he was downstairs before she was, sitting at the kitchen table. She paused in the doorway, the diaries in her hand. He stood up, and she ran into his arms.

31

THE TRIAL

THE THREE DAYS PASSED frighteningly quickly. They walked, they talked, and they read. Rachel rode Joey, and when there was nothing else left to do they watched tv. A couple of times they kissed, but nothing more. It seemed that they were both focused on what was to come, and neither felt it right to go further yet.

Lander thought that when they took the virus they should do something to mark the occasion; raise a glass, drink to the prospect of them getting successfully through the trial. However, Rachel was much too businesslike for such a thing. They'd had breakfast together, as on the previous mornings, but today they said very little. Neither of them had eaten much. He was nervous and had little appetite, and he supposed it was the same for her. If Rachel is anxious, and she's a scientist and knows what's going on, he thought, I must be stupid to be doing this. He knew it was not too late to pull out, but he also knew there was nowhere he would rather be, and no one he would rather be with.

They arranged to meet in the parlour after Rachel had gathered what would be needed for the procedure. Lander was there first, and he sat at the table fidgeting. It was a few minutes before she came in, already in her scrubs. She was wearing glasses, which surprised him because he'd not seen her in them before. They gave her a scholarly, academic look.

Lander stayed at the table and slipped off his shirt to bare his upper arm.

'Well, this is it,' he said, trying to project a cheeriness he didn't feel.

'Yes, it is.'

'Good luck, Rachel,' he said.

'Thanks. Good luck to you too, Lander.'

She bent and kissed him, a quick peck, like a parent sending a child off to school. She took out the two phials and selected the one with an L.

'You're sure you want this one?' she said.

'It's as good as any.'

'Yes.' She smiled. 'Or as bad.'

There was no answer to that.

She broke out a hypodermic and inserted the needle through the bung that sealed the phial. Lander watched with his heart racing as she filled the syringe. Scary tabloid headlines ran through his head: Needle of Death, Curtains Cocktail, Killer Jab. Rachel looked at him and raised her eyebrows. He took a deep breath and nodded. She slid the needle into his arm and squeezed the syringe. It was uncomfortable, as if the device was filled with something thick and sticky. Lander clenched his teeth and thought that if this was the Angel of Death he couldn't imagine a lovelier one.

She stood back and put the hypodermic in a plastic case which she sealed. She did all this smoothly, efficiently and one-handed.

'What are you going to do with that?' he said, meaning the remains of the virus brew still in the phial.

'Pour it down the drain,' she said, then smiled at his horrified expression. 'Only joking.'

She put it in another plastic case and sealed that too. For an awful moment it occurred to Lander that Rachel could walk away now, leaving him infected. There was no way he could purge the injection from his system. He could be the trial, just him, the guinea pig, and she would observe what happened to him. He was ashamed at the thought, more so when she took the second phial, held it between her knees and filled a fresh syringe.

'Steady my arm,' she said, then gave him the syringe. 'Here,' she said, pointing to a spot above her elbow.

Lander hesitated. He'd seen lots of injections, in animals as well as humans, but he'd never been on the delivery end.

'Come on,' she said. 'It isn't rocket science.'

His hand was trembling. He didn't want to do this to her, but he took a deep breath and eased the needle into her arm. Then, smoothly and gently, just like she'd done, he depressed the plunger. He withdrew the needle, handed it to her and she put that and the phial in yet more plastic boxes, and then put all four of them into a transparent bag and sealed that too. She took a marker and wrote the dates and their names on the bag.

'Right, what do we do now?' said Lander.

'You get into your scrubs and mask, then we go to our own areas and we wait.'

They had spent some time making preparations for the waiting. They'd flipped a coin to decide who would have which downstairs room; he'd got the parlour, and that pleased him because it was bigger than the dining room. He felt guilty about that, but not guilty enough to offer to swap with her. Instead he'd moved one of the two sofas from the parlour into her room. Then he dragged downstairs the two single mattresses, first Kerryl's for Rachel, then his own, and they made them up.

There was no television in the dining room, so he brought down the one that had been in his grandparents' room and set it up. He thought it would be nice to have, although neither of them would want to watch the endless stream of inane gameshows, brainwashing and propaganda on the two channels. He remembered that Kerryl had had a huge collection of moviesticks. He found them in a shoe box in her wardrobe. There were enough to keep them occupied for weeks. Rachel told him that as they couldn't share, they would have to choose immediately which ones they wanted and stick to those. They spent an enjoyable half hour taking turns to pick, like two captains choosing their school teams. It was the same with the books, although considerably easier. Rachel would have the fiction in Kerryl's room, and Lander would have the books on football, computing, cars, bikes, and war that had been in his own room or had belonged to their Granddad.

Then Rachel had spent half a day cooking, preparing some dishes for the following days, and when he wasn't doing jobs to help, Lander checked that the wind turbine and solar panels were functioning properly and the connection to the electricity main was in order. The landline wasn't working, which meant that they had no way of connecting to NewNet, or to HushNet. He hadn't shared anything about his trip to Bedford or Claverton with the HushNet group. They didn't know where he was and he was worried that his long silence would cause concern and start enquiries, but there was nothing he could do about that. Their mobile phones were able to pick up a signal, but they'd agreed with Gwen that they wouldn't use them in case they were traced; it was no secret that the new system was being monitored by the government, and so there was the ever-present danger of eavesdroppers.

After the injections, they went to their rooms and closed the connecting door. Lander listened to the sounds of Rachel moving about next door before falling asleep on his sofa.

He was woken by discomfort in his upper arm. He rolled up his sleeve and examined it; it was red and swollen. He called through the door to Rachel, and she called back that the same had happened to her and it was to be expected. As the day went on the pain got worse, and that night it took him a long time to get to sleep. In the morning his arm was less inflamed, but it still hurt. What with the aftermath of the injection affecting his left arm and the lingering discomfort from the blow to his elbow troubling his right, he felt thoroughly miserable and sorry for himself.

During the next morning they had a few long-distance exchanges from their separate rooms, but it wasn't easy and in any case it seemed strange. Neither of them wanted to talk about the vaccine, and chatting about anything else seemed irrelevant, so the conversations gradually died away.

Rachel had left a complete kit for him on the sideboard – a blood pressure monitor, a clinical thermometer, syringes – and she'd checked that he could use them. Daily blood samples were to be left in a tray on the kitchen table for her to collect and analyse. For the rest, there was a supply of printed sheets on which he was to write his two hourly blood pressure and temperature readings, and a notebook in which she said he should record several times a day how he felt. 'Everything,' she told him. 'Ups, downs, highs, lows, headaches, cramps, bowel movements, let's have it all.'

This was the first of several similar days. The routine kept him occupied for half an hour, and then the chasm of unfilled time would open before him. He was bored. It hadn't occurred to him that there would be a sterile boundary between him and Rachel. He'd thought that he would be spending his time closer to her, and that had been one of the things that had been in the back of his mind when he'd volunteered to join her in the trial. As a result, he hadn't made any plans for what he might do to fill the void while he waited to see if the molecule worked.

Each day dragged, and he thought it would never end. It was worse than the dullest, most tedious lesson he had ever snored through at school. The television was flat and uninteresting and showed nothing that seemed remotely relevant to him. There was a book on the Falklands War that had belonged to Granddad. He could remember finding it fascinating before the Infection, but now it seemed a pointless waste. All that fuss over a few sheep! The only interesting thing about the Falklands was that they were islands, which meant they might have escaped the Infection. Or perhaps not. Perhaps now the sheep were all that was left. There were some magazines, but they were old and from the time before, a different world. He tried some music on his phone, and games on the tv, but nothing held his attention for more than a few minutes. He wished he had his laptop with him.

When he and Rachel had shared out the moviesticks he'd gone for action and adventure. Several of the ones he'd chosen were dystopian, telling tales of some dark Armageddon. He tried one now, but he couldn't settle to it and he swapped it for another. That was just the same. Robots strode the earth, obliterating everything in their path with ray guns. How little the people who had made that movie knew. The actual apocalypse hadn't been at all like that. Destruction wasn't brought about by artificially intelligent androids, from this world or any other. It had been caused by human beings in their mindless search for more efficient ways to kill their enemies. The supreme irony was that the instrument they had chosen for their slaughter was not even truly alive, and perversely it couldn't itself exist without the human hosts it was destroying.

He turned off the television and browsed the shelves again. There was a stack of paper and several pens which Rachel had put there. What did she expect him to do with them? Make a diary, like Kerryl? Come on, he could never do that. His sister had been the bookish one; he had never been either a writer or a reader. Kerryl had loved English at school. She'd liked nothing better than to curl up with a book, reading, reading, reading. As far as he was concerned, English was the least interesting thing on the unappetising menu his school had offered. Art, though, was different. He'd enjoyed that, and been quite good at it too. His teacher had told him that he could have got a top grade if he'd bothered to do the assignments and produce some sketch books; as it was, he'd done okay.

He took some of the paper and a pen and sat down. Suppose he were to write a diary; what would he put in it? He started with a list of girls he had known. He put their names in columns. First were the ones he'd fancied. Some of those were friends of Kerryl that he'd never even got close to but had lusted after, girls like Suzy Simmonds and Charlene Brooker. Then there were those he'd managed to get to know and gone out with. That was a much shorter list. Finally, there were the few he'd had sex with. He got stuck with one of them. Her name had been Janice something or other, he couldn't even remember her second name now. They'd been in her house and on the brink of making out when her parents had returned unexpectedly, so they'd never actually done it. Which column should she go in?

He threw the pen down. How stupid this was! How pitiful, how immature! What would Rachel think if she found him doing this? He caught sight of his reflection in the mirror over the mantle. 'You poor sod,' he said to it. 'You poor pathetic sod.'

'Are you all right?' It was Rachel. 'I thought I heard you call.'

'I'm fine,' he said. 'Just talking to myself. Are you okay?'

'Yes,' she said. 'I was reading one of Kerryl's books. Your sister had good taste.'

'Yes,' said Lander.

'How do you feel?'

'All right. Normal, I suppose. What about you?'

'I feel well. No ill effects so far. We'll do some more blood samples tomorrow and I can then see if anything's happening with either of us.'

He tore up the list of girls, shredding it into tiny, illegible pieces.

There was a set of pencils on the shelves with the paper, and he took one of them now, and a fresh sheet. For a moment he looked at it as if it were a foreign object, then he made a few experimental marks. At school he'd been quite good at drawing people, their faces, not their bodies. The bodies he drew always appeared to be deformed and out of proportion, but the faces were much better. His art teacher had given him some help, telling him to start with an oval, work out the position of the ears, around halfway down the oval, and then put in the eyes level with the ears. Add the hair and the mouth. Noses were hard and he had a problem making them convincing. He worked quietly, concentrating: oval, ears, large eyes, long hair tied back, slanting fringe, full lips. He held his work up to study. Then he realised; he had drawn Rachel.

32

LEFT TILL CALLED FOR

IT HAPPENED AS ADAM had said, though not as quickly and not without some difficulty.

Instead of being taken to a correction centre, which she had been dreading, Magda remained in her cell at the courthouse. She had perhaps at some stage in her life been more bored, but if that was so she couldn't remember when. There was nothing at all to do; no books or magazines, no television, no pen, paper, laptop, phone, none of any of the things that she took for granted and thought of as entitlements. She spent hours lying on her bed, and when she wasn't doing that she did bends and stretches and ran on the spot.

The enormous guard was thawing out and now gave her an occasional smile when she brought in one of her three daily meals. She had a lank-looking ponytail, which emphasised her round face, and she usually wore a scowl, but after a week she must have decided that she could trust Magda and began to relax. She allowed her to leave her cell for meals and eat in a sort of communal area. At least, that was what it appeared to be but there was no one else there apart from the guard, who sat in a corner and watched every mouthful.

A day or two later she was allowed to go into an enclosed courtyard. It was plantless, paved and tiny, sterile, but at least it was outside, away from the tiny cell with its odour of dampness and its barred window.

As she reached the end of the third week of her incarceration, Magda decided she had to do something. She'd seen and heard nothing from Adam. She didn't know whether her case had yet been presented to the Justice Secretary or if it had what the outcome had been. Was no news good news? The guard knew nothing either; nor did there seem to be anyone else she could ask. How long would this torture go on? She settled on the only thing she could do to attract some attention, and decided to start at the first opportunity. It came soon.

The guard had taken to leaving her cell door unlocked during the day and so there was no rattle of keys to announce her arrival. Instead, she just came in.

'Your dinner's ready,' she announced.

Magda didn't reply at once but paused for effect.

'I'm not having it,' she said.

'Oh,' said the guard. She was surprised, and disappointed. The meals were brought in from a nearby restaurant and they were varied and tasty. She couldn't handle the idea that someone might turn down the offer of food like that. 'Oh dear. Not hungry, are we?'

'No,' said Magda.

'Sure?' She adopted a wheedling tone. 'It's a chicken casserole, and baked jam roll for pudding.'

'I'm sure,' said Magda. She liked both those things, especially the baked jam roll, and almost wavered, but she told herself that it would do her good to miss a meal or two. Her largely sedentary lifestyle combined with a high calorie diet was making her feel sluggish, and when she pinched her waist she could feel a roll of fat.

The guard looked in again before lights out that night.

'Do you want anything, love? I've got a few biscuits.'

It was a kind gesture, but Magda declined.

The following morning the guard unlocked the cell at the usual time and Magda rose, showered and dressed.

'Breakfast,' said the guard enthusiastically. 'Scrambled eggs today. I bet you're hungry after yesterday.'

'No, not really,' Magda said, even though she was ravenous.

The guard was puzzled and went away; although the woman was clearly disappointed, Magda was sure that the eggs would not go uneaten. It was when she also declined lunch that the guard began to show concern.

'Are you all right? You're not ill, are you? You young girls are all the same, always thinking about your figures.'

'It's not that,' said Magda. 'I'm not going to eat anything until I get some news about what's going to happen to me. It's been three weeks since I was sentenced. They can't keep me here forever.'

'You mean a sort of hunger strike?' The guard said.

'That's exactly what I mean.'

'Holy shit.' The guard could scarcely believe her ears; to her, refusing food was sheer madness.

Magda was relying on the idea of a hunger strike being so alien to the guard that she would quickly pass the news up the line. For now, she could do nothing but wait.

It took longer than she expected. The first change was that the guard's mood altered. Every mealtime she brought food and every time Magda refused it the woman treated it as a personal rejection. The atmosphere between them became chilly. The cell door was still left unlocked during the day, but now the guard seldom spoke to her. As the days passed, Magda began to feel weakened. She had no energy and spent most of her time lying on her bunk.

It was day five – or maybe day six, Magda had lost count – when the Examining Magistrate appeared. She was in a brisk, no-nonsense mood.

'Your guard tells me you're on hunger strike. Why?'

Magda explained her reason.

'I see,' said the Magistrate. 'You refuse to eat until your friend Mr Adamski persuades the Justice Secretary to decree that my judgement was wrong. You refuse to eat until you have managed to undermine the authority of my court and made me appear incompetent.'

Magda hadn't seen it like that, but yes, that's what it amounted to. All she said was, 'Mr Adamski is not my friend.'

The Magistrate ignored it. 'You realise I have the power to order you to eat, and to instruct court staff to force feed you if you refuse.'

Magda hadn't thought of that. She'd seen force-feeding in movies, and had a vision of her jaws being prised open and a tube thrust down her throat. The idea was horrifying and it frightened her, but she said nothing.

'Very good,' said the Magistrate, with prim resignation. 'Have it your way.'

Magda did. The following day a driver appeared and said she'd been instructed to take Magda to the bonobos research facility, but only on condition that she broke her fast first. Magda knew she had to be careful, so she drank some milk and ate a little oatmeal, which was all she could manage, while the driver, the same woman who'd taken her from Lake Manor, waited, sour-faced.

Magda knew better than to try to engage the driver in conversation, and she was silent for the whole journey. For most of the way she was nauseous, which she thought must be to do with suddenly taking food after a long spell without any. They reached the facility just in time to prevent her from throwing up over the back seat of the Lexus.

Julia was expecting her and treated her, if not like an old friend, at least with warmth. She led Magda straight to the meeting room where she'd had her initial briefing. There was a plate of chocolate biscuits on the table and she found it hard to stop herself from grabbing a handful and cramming them into her mouth.

'Adam says you're here to help us,' Julia said.

Was that what Adam had told them? 'Yes,' she said.

'You've volunteered to be a surrogate mother.'

'Not quite,' said Magda. She decided it was best to tell Julia the truth, so she gave a short account of the deal Adam had forced on her. 'But I'm not prepared to do anything until I have it in writing from the Justice Secretary that my conviction has been overturned.'

'There's plenty of time for that,' said Julia. 'You see, what Adam probably didn't realise is that there's a hold up.'

'Why is that?'

She shrugged. 'We've run out of apes. The pair you saw died, and anyway they were both females. We need a male to enable us to fertilise the human ova that we want to use.'

Magda was surprised. On her previous visit Julia had said nothing about any snags in the programme, it had all looked to be running smoothly.

Julia sighed. 'It's Adam. He's not a scientist. He did history and politics at uni and he has no background in this sort of thing. But he's read some pop science and he thinks he knows it all. What we're attempting here has never been done before. The Russians and the Chinese both claimed some success in creating chimp-human hybrids back in the 1950s and 60s, but it's pretty certain that they never actually managed it. And a bit later, in the USA, there was a chimp called Oliver who had a number of human characteristics, including being attracted to human females. His owners claimed that he was a hybrid, but DNA analysis showed he was pure chimp. What we're trying to do is at the very limit of what's biologically possible. Maybe it's beyond it, but all Adam says when I tell him that is "GDSR".'

'What's that mean?'

'It's a stupid, irritating mantra that's his answer to everything. "Get the Damn Science Right." He knows so little about it he thinks it's easy.'

Adam misinformed? Arrogant? Tell me something I don't know, thought Magda. 'What is it they say about a little knowledge?'

Julia was now wound up. 'Exactly. Like I said when you were here before, humans, bonobos, chimps and gorillas have huge biological similarities. They're as close as horses are to donkeys. Horses and donkeys interbreed easily, and the result is a mule. And the trouble with mules is...?'

'They're stubborn.'

'They're sterile.'

'Oh, my God. Oh, I see.' It was a game-changer. If the bonobo-human hybrid was infertile anyway, what was the point of what Julia and her team were being told to do? And more importantly for Magda, why was she there?

'Yes. We haven't yet been in a position to do any proper tests, but the general opinion is that what we produce would be the same. If, that is, we manage to get the hybrids to survive for more than a few days.'

The news was a huge relief. Magda had been dreading the surrogacy that Adam had forced on her. If there were no apes, that couldn't happen. But it also created uncertainties. Would she be taken back to jail to serve her sentence? Or would she be expected to stay at the facility until more apes were available? And if the outcome was likely to be sterile offspring, what was the point?

Julia answered at least one of those questions.

'We have a room for you here, and we can make you comfortable. We've been told to let you walk in the garden if you wish, but you are not allowed to leave the premises. And we're to watch you at all times. Sorry, but...' Julia shrugged.

"Sorry but..." about summed it up for Magda. It had Adam written all over it.

'I need to get in touch with Mr Adamski,' she said.

'You and me both,' said Julia. 'He wants to come here for an update on the current state of play, and I have some questions about our future and progress that I need answered. So he'll be here, but I don't know when.'

When the big, important man could fit it into his oh-so-busy schedule, Magda thought bitterly. 'Do you have a phone?'

'I do, but I can't let you have it,' said Julia. And then, when she saw Magda's frown, 'Sorry again, but it's not my decision. I think if Adam had wanted you to contact him in that way he would have made it easy, don't you?'

Yes, she did. The message was obvious. Magda was now Adam's tool, his chattel, to be shelved until he was ready to use her. She was to be left till called for, or until she might be required for other duties. She was certainly not expected to have any will of her own.

The days that followed were tedious, but nowhere near as bad as being in her jail cell. The weather was good, and she spent a lot of time enjoying the garden. It was small and it was surrounded by a thick hedge and a high, chain-link fence, but she could peer through them and see fields. That lifted her spirits; there was a world beyond the one in which she was being held captive. Best of all, there were flowers, roses, the scent of liberty. Sometimes she sunbathed, stripping to her underwear and lying on the lawn.

In the evenings she read or watched one of the stupefying tv channels. She went to bed early, slept well, and ate well.

She tried to exercise every day and devised a strict regime of running on the spot, star jumps, press-ups, twists and stretches that left her hot and breathless. She didn't like doing these in public and chose a spot in a quiet corner of the garden at the laboratory end of the building. Here the windows were frosted, which meant she couldn't be overlooked.

She'd been at the facility for a little over a week and was doing her exercises. It was very early; she'd not yet had breakfast and there was no one else around. It had been a clear night and the temperature had fallen so there was a chill in the air, and such a heavy dew on the grass that her trainers were soon soaked.

She was coming to the end of her routine when she heard a sound behind her. It startled her and she froze, immobile and panting. Then she heard it again, a metallic scraping as if someone was sawing at the fence. Slowly she turned around, and saw a face watching her through the wire mesh. It was someone she knew; someone she was very pleased to see.

'Hi,' the face said. 'They told me you'd be here.'

33

———

RESULT

IT WAS PROBABLY Rachel's simple act of providing art materials that stopped Lander from being driven by tedium to do something desperate. He drew for hours. He drew endlessly. He drew the view from the window. He drew Buster, his old dog, copying from a photograph beside the cupboard. He tried Joey, but horses are difficult and the result didn't do the original justice. And he drew Rachel. He didn't have a photo of her, not even one on his phone, and none of his attempts turned out as well as the first one when he hadn't been meaning to draw her. He often wondered what Rachel was doing, how she was passing the time. There were occasional unidentifiable noises from next door but apart from that, nothing. Sometimes they spoke, but they had to raise their voices to be heard through the closed door, and that didn't encourage conversation.

He was conscientious about the record keeping, the personal notes, and about putting on a fresh pair of surgical gloves and mask before going into the shared areas of the kitchen and the bathroom. The discarded ones he put in a tough plastic sack which he kept sealed and in the sideboard cupboard, as Rachel had instructed. Every evening as he prepared for bed he wondered if he'd just had his last day as a normal, healthy human being, whether he'd reached the end of his time.

Each morning, as soon as he awoke, before he even tied to move, he conducted an appraisal of his condition. Aches? Not really; a bit of a twinge from the elbow but that was still after-effects from the baton blow. Stiffness? No, but see "Aches". Cramps? Sore throat? Headache? Sniffle? No to all. With each day that passed he drew closer to the end of what would be the incubation period for the virus, and his disquiet increased. He was scared. He was scared for himself but he was even more scared for Rachel. What would he do if she got it and he didn't? He had only known her a couple of weeks, but already the idea of being without her was unbearable.

He said nothing to her about these thoughts. Did she perhaps guess? She was smart enough to. Maybe she was having them too. As soon as he heard any movement from next door he would call to her to make sure she was all right. So far she had been.

By day five he was feeling awful. Not from the Infection, he knew it wasn't that, but just from being indoors all the time. He felt dull and lethargic. He called through the connecting door to Rachel.

'I'm going crazy in here. Do I have to stay in?'

'In your room? Yes, you most definitely do. We can't either of us wander around the house.'

'I meant outside. What about outside?'

There was a pause before she answered, and then she said, 'You mean go for a walk?'

'Yes. I was thinking of a run actually.'

There was another pause.

'Do you have any kit?'

'I've got my t-shirt and jeans, the stuff I was wearing before I changed into the scrubs. And I've got my trainers.'

'All right,' she said, her voice muffled by the closed door, 'but there are some rules. First of all, you must keep your scrubs, mask and gloves on until you're out of the house. Get changed out there, in the yard. You must not bring the clothes that you run in, that you will have touched unprotected, back into the house. Put them in an outbuilding. Also, if you see anybody don't go near them, and whatever you do lead anyone back here.'

'Fair enough,' he said.

He collected his clothes and went over to the barn to change. As soon as he stepped out, the cold air on his face made him feel better. He started up the hill, following the steep packhorse trail to the edge of the moor and the track through the heather to the Bride Stones. He was pleased that although he was panting hard before he reached the summit he could manage the gradient without stopping, and at a respectable pace too.

It was a grey morning, with low clouds only just clearing the top of the hill. In this light the Bride Stones were dark and forbidding. He imagined Kerryl walking this same path, wearing her bridal dress, clutching her best shoes, thinking she was going to meet a lover and dreaming of what would happen when she did. Her presence was almost physical. He could see her staggering from clump to grassy clump, breathless, eyes bright with anticipation.

He stopped at the long, rectangular slab of the Bride Stone itself. It was here, so the tale said, that a girl might sit and see the one who would be her true love. It was here that Kerryl had sat on her last day.

He looked into the peaty pool beside the stone. He stepped into it, and though his feet sank into the mud on the bottom, it came only halfway up his shins. How could she have drowned in this? What exactly happened when she came here for the last time? Had she killed herself, forcing her face under the surface until with a gasp her lungs filled? Had she taken something that knocked her out, and then accidentally slid into the pool? Did she faint? Did she collapse in a coma and fall face first into the water? Had someone else been there, watching her from behind a rock and moving in when they saw their chance?

Lander shuddered, and splashed out of the water. He ran back down the hill to the farm. He felt better physically, but not mentally. He was still jumpy, frustrated and worried.

The next day he was awake earlier than usual. He didn't get up but lay staring at the ceiling, thinking again about the cocktail of viruses he'd taken. What would you call a virus cocktail? All the good names – like Apocalypse Now, Zombie, Last Dance – had been taken. How about Sudden Death? That might be appropriate if that was what was happening inside his body. But death from the Infection wasn't sudden; it was drawn out over days of agony as the virus replicated itself and took over the body of its host. Had the molecules they'd taken managed to block the proteins the virus needed to do that?

When she'd administered the injection Rachel had reminded him that the usual incubation period before signs of the Infection became obvious was around ten days. However, after five she'd be able to tell from their blood samples whether any of the viruses they had absorbed was reproducing. This was day six. When they'd said their usual good nights through the closed door the previous evening there'd been a strange atmosphere, one of unspoken anxiety and trepidation. She'd told him it was important that he take a blood sample first thing in the morning. After that there was silence. He often heard the muffled sound of the television from her room, but not tonight. He wasn't surprised; he didn't feel like watching anything either. He'd stood at the door and whispered, 'I love you.' Had she heard?

He got up and sat at the table where he usually took his blood. How did he feel? His throat was dry. Was that significant, or was it just that he'd slept with his mouth open? He had aches in his thighs and calves. That might be from the unaccustomed running, but it might not. He thought of Kerryl going through this same self-analysis, wondering day after day if the virus had crept up behind her like an assassin in the night, whether she would soon be sweating and bleeding. Alone. Once more he felt the piercing dagger of guilt at leaving the farm, abandoning her to manage by herself. It was no less intense, no less raw for being familiar; in fact, the more time passed the worse it seemed to get. It would be with him all his life, however long, or short, that might be.

He took the strip of elastic that he always used, and slowly and carefully wrapped it around his bicep. It was tricky because he was trembling. He slapped the inside of his elbow with two fingers to raise the vein, the way Rachel had showed him. Then he took the syringe, broke it from its plastic wrapper, and carefully eased the needle into his vein. He watched fascinated as the crimson liquid oozed into the tube. It looked full of life, bursting with health. Was that a deception? Was it really a sludge thick with active viruses?

Rachel had said that there was no need to fill the syringe, half would be plenty, so when his blood reached what he judged to be the appropriate mark he took it off the needle and put it in a kidney dish. He withdrew the needle and put that in a plastic disposal box. Then he released the binding on his arm and dabbed the needle entry point with cotton wool. He took a pen, but his hands were shaking too much to write. He inhaled deeply, trying to slow his heartbeat, and after a while he felt enough in control to go on. He labelled the syringe with his initial and "Day 6"; the writing was shaky but legible. Then he adjusted his face mask, put on fresh gloves, and went to the kitchen.

The kidney dish with Rachel's sample was already on the table. So was her microscope, a couple of other pieces of equipment he couldn't identify, and some small bottles of liquids. Although he hadn't heard her, she must have been up before him. He put his dish beside hers, went back to the parlour and closed the door. He was tempted to call to her, but he didn't. Instead, he stood by the mantelpiece and studied the small gallery of family photos: Gran, Granddad, Mam. There was one of their father, taken a long time ago, before he had his accident in the bottom field when the tractor rolled over and crushed him. It was a family group, at the seaside. He looked happy, with no idea of how brutally and painfully he would soon die. Lander remembered a verse from the Bible that Granddad used to quote: "Lord, let me know my end and the number of my days." Thank God I don't, he thought.

He moved along the shelf to where there were pictures of him and Kerryl, mostly together, rarely separate. He was struck yet again by how much Rachel reminded him of her, and still he couldn't place exactly why. There was no way they would have been taken for sisters, but there was something about the curve of their mouths, the arch of their brows, the shape of their eyes, and the directness of their gaze that linked one to the other. What the photo couldn't show was how like each other they were as people.

He sat down on his mattress and put his head in his hands, and for the first time in many years he prayed; it was not for himself he prayed, but for the girl in the room next door. Silently he began to weep, the tears running down his cheeks and trickling through the fingers that supported his chin. Please God let her be all right, he prayed. Please.

How long did he wait? He didn't time it. He wanted the whole thing to be over, to know the outcome. But then he wanted the opposite; fearful of what the result might be, he wanted the waiting to go on.

He went across the yard to the barn and put on the jeans, t-shirt and trainers he'd left there. He went towards Joey's field. It was a blustery morning, and an ill-tempered and erratic wind jostled and chilled him. The turbine spun and dark clouds raced, threatening a downpour. Before the end of the day there would be one of the vicious storms which were characteristic of those hills, with a gale blowing rain horizontally across the fields. The old horse stood with his back to the wind. He, too, knew what was coming.

How long should he wait? Rachel had said that analysing their blood wouldn't take long, but how long was long? An hour? Two?

He went back to the barn, collected some brushes, called up Joey and spent some time grooming him. He brushed vigorously, working up a sweat until his coat shone. Joey liked it and kept nudging him with his muzzle. He took the brushes back to the barn, and then checked the meters showing the outputs from the solar panels and the wind turbine. The turbine was going crazy in the high wind. He took a broom and swept out the stalls where their cows had been. They hadn't been used in a long time and didn't require his attention. None of these jobs needed doing, but they filled the time; however, they couldn't take his mind off what Rachel might be discovering.

When he could think of nothing more to do he changed back into his scrubs and walked across the yard to the house. His feet were like lead. Would there be news?

He went into the parlour, and for a long time regarded the landscape through the windows. He'd been right about the rain. It was starting now, sweeping across the fields, beating on the flagstones and lashing the windowpanes.

There was a noise behind him. He turned. Rachel stood in the doorway to the hall.

'I've got the results,' she said. He felt his heart lurch. Her face was solemn. Was it good news? Bad? She waited. 'You are showing no sign of active viruses,' she said. 'You're all clear.'

There was an even longer pause. He said nothing but his mind was in turmoil, a mixture of relief and terror. And? And? And? What about her?

'You're clear,' she said. Then she smiled. 'And so am I. It seems that the molecules have done their job. All the viruses have reached a dead end.'

Lander stood staring at her, frozen to the spot. Then in two strides he was in front of her. He ripped off his mask, wrapped his arms around her and hugged her, squeezing until she laughed and pulled away, panting and complaining she couldn't breathe.

'Is that it?' said Lander. 'Do we go now?'

'We could, but I think we should leave it a little longer, just to be sure.'

'But we don't need to keep apart, do we?'

She glanced at his hand resting on her shoulder and his face close to hers. 'I think it's a little late for that now.'

She kissed him.

34

THE DRIFTERS

MAGDA PEERED AT THE FACE looking through the mesh fence. 'Ajay?'

It shone with a toothy grin. 'Right in one.'

'Ajay. My God. What are you doing here?'

'Looking for you.'

Magda pushed further into the bushes so she could see him better. The last time they'd met she'd been distracted by trying to get Steve to the hospital and she had barely noticed him, but she remembered the mop of black hair and the broad smile.

'How did you know to find me here?' she said.

'There's not much gets past us Drifters,' he said. 'I went to the hospital and they told me about Steve and that you'd been arrested. By the time I got to the courthouse, the trial was over and you'd gone. They wouldn't say where you'd been taken, but I put the word out I was looking for you. Some local Drifters have been keeping an eye on this place and they got a message to me that you were here.'

'Oh.' Magda had heard before about the mysterious network of communication between the Drifters. They seemed to know more than anyone about what was happening, and where. She was impressed. But there was something she had to get straight. 'I didn't do it,' she said.

Ajay looked at her and shook his head. 'I know. Why would you go to the trouble of driving the guy all that way to the hospital if you wanted him dead? Anyone with half a brain would see that it wasn't you.'

'That's exactly what I said to the Magistrate, but she wouldn't have it.'

'Moaning Margaret? No, she wouldn't'

'You know her?'

'Oh yes. We Drifters know everybody, and a couple of us have been up before her. She decides on her verdict before hearing the evidence, and then she chooses what she does hear to make it fit. I think probably somebody got to her.'

Magda could believe that, and she could make a good guess at who that "somebody" might have been. They both reacted to a sound from the building, Ajay shrinking back, Magda turning. Someone was calling her name.

'I think I'm wanted,' she said.

'Don't go to bed,' he whispered.

'What?'

'Tonight. Don't go to bed. We're going to get you out of here. Keep your clothes on, and be prepared to move fast. And as soon as it gets dark flash your light three times, so we know which room is yours.'

Magda hurried back to the building. The person calling her wasn't Julia, but a woman she'd not seen before.

'Ah, there you are.'

'Yes.' Magda smiled, but it wasn't returned; the woman didn't seem friendly. 'I was just taking some air.'

'How nice.' Still no smile. 'We'd prefer it if you remain in sight at all times. If you go into the garden, stay in view of the windows.'

Magda nodded. She resented the instruction, but if Ajay meant what he'd said it wouldn't be relevant. Could he really get her out? Was he alone or were there other Drifters with him? She hadn't seen anyone else.

'My name is Dr Williams,' the woman said. 'You're here to assist us with our research, but as you know, we can't implant you yet because we have no apes. However, there's a zoo in Frankfurt that has some bonobo semen and they're sending us a sample. It should be here in a day or two, then we can go ahead. We have the human ova, so there won't be any delay.'

This was the first time since the Infection gripped that Magda had heard any reference to anything happening outside the UK, in fact, outside England. There was nothing in news reports, no mention in official channels. The rest of the world might just as well have ceased to exist. Until now she thought it had, but from what this woman said it seemed that other places had survived and that they and we were organised enough to be able to communicate. It was heartening, but she didn't like what the doctor was saying.

'We're going to start preparing you now. We'll fertilise the ovum in vitro and as soon as that's succeeded we'll implant you, but before that, you need to have fertility medication. Most treatments are intended to stimulate ovulation, but we don't want that with you. However, they also raise hormone levels, which we do want. I expect you know that with any surrogacy it's important to get the timing right, so you're to come with me now to the lab for tests.'

Williams turned away and went back into the building. She didn't check that Magda was following, there was no need; she knew she had no choice.

The afternoon was unpleasant. Magda had her blood pressure and temperature taken several times. There were swabs, there were blood and urine samples, but most of the time there was nothing, and Magda found herself spending long periods sitting in a less than comfortable armchair waiting for the next invasion. The worst part was the vaginal examination. This was carried out by Williams, with rather less tender care than Magda would have liked or expected. She couldn't suppress sharp intakes of breath when the doctor's pushing and prodding hurt, and she thought that this was an aspect of her work that the woman enjoyed. Finally, there was an injection. Nobody said what it was, but she guessed it was part of the treatment. She couldn't be bothered to ask; by then she was past caring.

At last she was allowed back to her room, but this time she was locked in. She stood at the window, looking out on the garden, the hedge and the fields beyond. Were Ajay and his friends still out there? She could see no sign, but she would have been surprised if she could. It stood to reason that the ability to move around without being seen was a key skill for the Drifters. Could they really get her out? How? Her door was locked. When? What would happen if they did? What if they didn't?

She remained at the window for a long time, while the sun dipped, the shadows lengthened, and twilight wrapped the building. As soon as she judged it dark enough she turned her bedroom lights on, then off, then on again, then off, then on. Would they have seen that? To be on the safe side, she repeated the signal. Then she moved away from the window and lay on her bed. As Ajay had instructed, she remained fully dressed, including her shoes.

She had a television but she didn't want to watch it. There were half a dozen tattered paperbacks on a shelf but none took her fancy. She fell into a light doze. She thought she heard an owl, but the sound wasn't repeated. Later there was another sound, short and sharp, the yelp of a vixen. She checked her watch frequently but wasn't convinced it was working properly, the time seemed to go so slowly. At some point, she must have slept.

Suddenly she was wide awake and jumping from her bed. She didn't know what had woken her, but she knew that something was happening. She could smell burning. She flicked the light switch. Nothing, no light came on. The red stand-by on the television was absent too. It was very dark. She stood in the centre of the room, not knowing what to do. She groped her way to the door. It was still locked. There were shouts from downstairs, and a female cry. Then a pounding in the corridor outside.

'Stand back,' somebody called. 'We're coming in.'

The door shuddered under a hefty kick. There was another, and then it gave, wrenching the hinges and splintering the frame. Three masked figures came in, together with a lot of smoke. Behind them was the red-orange flicker of fire. Their torches dazzled her as they raked the room. One of the figures gave her something damp.

'It's a wet sheet. Wrap it around you, and over your head. And put this over your mouth and nose. For the smoke.'

It sounded like Ajay, but it was impossible to tell. Whoever it was helped her to quickly drape the sheet over her head and shoulders and took one of her hands to lead her out. With the other, she held the wet cloth to her face.

Already the smoke was stinging her throat and eyes, and tears blurred her vision.

'This way.'

Blindly she stumbled after her guide. Thoughts raced. What was happening? Where were Julia and Dr Williams? Where was she being taken?

She fumbled along in the dark, down some stairs, then through an open door and into the car park. It was better here, but her throat was raw and she couldn't stop coughing. There were more people around now though she could barely see them, just shadows. She turned; the whole building was ablaze, flames raging at the laboratory end, lively but less vigorous in the part she'd just left. There was an unbelievable racket, the roar of the flames, pops and bangs from different parts of the building, a crash as a beam collapsed. She'd never realised that a big fire made so much noise. At the edge of her vision there were half a dozen women. She recognised one as Julie, another as Williams and a third as one of the domestic staff. They were being made to sit on the ground, and somebody was binding them with duct tape. Were they going to do that to her?

A tall figure strode out of the confusion, flung back his hood and removed his mask. Ajay. He wrapped his arms around her.

'Hi. I said we'd get you out. Come with me.'

Before she could say anything, before she could thank him or ask what was happening or anything, she was pulled towards a van. The sheet fell and almost tripped her. She dropped the wet cloth she'd used for her face. She was bundled into the front seat and Ajay got behind the wheel.

She looked at the research building. It was blazing spectacularly now. Somebody was shouting at people to get back, and others were trying to move a couple of parked cars out of range of the heat. The bound women sat in a row, seemingly at a safe distance.

'Let's get out of here,' Ajay said. He leant out of the window and shouted. 'Time to go, guys. There'll be fire trucks here in five minutes, and the EA probably sooner than that. Leave the women there on the grass, they'll be fine. I mean now.'

He started the van, slammed it in gear, and raced out of the car park. Neither of them said anything until the burning building was little more than a glow in the sky behind them.

Ajay spoke first, 'You okay?'

'I think so.' Her eyes were still stinging and her throat was sore, but the coughing had eased. 'Thank you for getting me out.'

Ajay looked at her and winked. 'You're welcome. Mind you, that turned out to be a bit more spectacular than we'd planned. I never thought the place would go up like that. It must be made of matchwood.'

'There was probably a lot of flammable stuff in the labs.'

'You think? I threw a Molotov in there and it was like a firework display.'

'What about the women, the ones you were tying up?'

'They'll be fine. The EA will pick them up in no time.'

'Was that all?'

'All what?'

'Was that everyone in the building? Just those three?'

Magda was pleased to see the place destroyed, together with the grotesque drama that it had housed, but she didn't wish harm to the people who had been working there, apart maybe from Williams.

'Yes, two doctors and four domestics. And you, of course. We got them to confirm there was no one else in there, and we searched anyway. Hold on.' Suddenly he killed the lights and at the same time flung the van into a deep gateway and turned off the engine.

There was a moment's silence, and then Magda saw headlights sweeping the road and a vehicle speeding towards them. As it passed she saw the fluorescent decals on its side. It was an EA Avatar. A few seconds later it was followed by another.

'Do you think they saw us?'

'Those guys? Not a chance. They couldn't see a candle in a cave, believe me.'

Magda wasn't so sure, but Ajay seemed confident; he also seemed to be the sort of person who would know.

'Why did you do it?'

'Do what?'

'Burn it down.'

Ajay snorted. 'We've been watching it. It was a scummy place, evil. We knew what was going on in there, and them taking you was the last straw. We had a meeting and agreed it was time.'

They waited a few minutes, presumably to be sure there were no more EA vehicles, and then Ajay started the engine, turned on the lights again, and backed out of the gateway onto the road.

'Right,' he said. 'Let's get there.'

'Get where? Where are you taking me?'

Ajay looked at her and winked again. 'You'll be surprised,' he said.

35

RETURN

LANDER AND RACHEL STAYED for another week at Paradise Farm.

When Lander later recalled those days he thought of them as their honeymoon. They did little. They talked, and he learnt a lot about Rachel: who she was, where she had been, what she had done. It turned out that as well as the scientific work she'd been selected to train for the Special Olympics and had made the squad as a discus thrower. The Infection had killed all that, as it had killed so much else. The virus had robbed Kerryl of her future and it seemed that it had snatched away Rachel's dreams too, or at least some of them. Work, training, plans, hopes, preparations, ambitions, interests, loved ones, and obligations, all snuffed out by a single strand of RNA.

She asked him about himself, but he was evasive, embarrassed at how little he had achieved compared with Kerryl's entry to a top university and Rachel's prospects for Olympic glory. Add to that, she was bloody clever, what with all that study and her understanding of what made viruses tick; or rather, what stopped them ticking. Reluctantly he told her about his cricket, how he'd played for Yorkshire Colts and taken a lot of wickets against Derbyshire, and been awarded the match ball and offered a place at the Yorkshire Cricket Academy.

'But I never went.'

'Why ever not?'

'It was our Mam. She said it wasn't secure. She said that if it turned out I wasn't good enough to be a professional cricketer I'd be stuck, so I ought to get some qualifications behind me.'

'And did you?'

Lander shook his head, embarrassed. 'No. When she wouldn't let me go I gave up. I stopped bothering about school, stopped doing any work, and often I didn't even go.' As he said it he realised how pathetic it sounded. 'I went into a spectacular sulk, without realising that the only person I was hurting was me.'

He fell silent. Rachel took his hand.

'The match ball, do you still have it?'

'No. I threw it away.'

She hugged him, and kissed him on the forehead. He'd known before, but he really knew now: he could have made it, he could have become a professional cricketer, playing for Yorkshire, perhaps even England. You needed the talent, of course you did, but lots of people had that. What made it work was the dream; the dream, the will and the effort. You had to have the dream, and you had to have the determination to trudge those miles to make it come true. If he'd had Rachel then he would have done that. Now he did have her, he could, he would, do something that would make her proud of him.

The thing that had troubled him at first, the difference in their ages, didn't come up. It turned out that she was thirty-two, eleven years older than he was. It didn't matter to him. Did it to her? Nothing she did or said indicated that it might. Jokingly she asked him about previous girlfriends. He mentioned two or three names and was surprised to find himself blushing. The physical contacts had been hurried and clumsy. None of the relationships – if you could call them that – had meant anything to him, although when he considered it they may have meant something to the girls, and he felt guilty at not having thought about that before. He asked Rachel about boyfriends. She shrugged and smiled. 'Later,' she said.

They walked on the moors, returning to the Bride Stones.

'I don't know why I keep bringing you here,' he said.

'I do. It's because of Kerryl.'

'Yes, but it's sad. This is where they found her body.'

'Yes, that's sad, but the place isn't. It's beautiful. It's a lovely spot to remember her.'

They explored other areas too. There was a dell in the woods where John Wesley, the 18th Century preacher, used to hold prayer meetings. It reminded them of Chrissie's gatherings, and Rachel told Lander that often Wesley's meetings had been broken up by the authorities too, just as the Reboot Army had. Why couldn't people leave each other alone? he asked. Why were there always people trying to stop you from doing what you thought was right?

They talked about going down the hill into Walbrough. Lander wanted to find out what was going on and to see what of the town had survived, whether any of it was being rebuilt. When they'd driven through it on the way to the farm it had looked grim, and he wanted to know if that impression was correct. However, Rachel thought that they should avoid meeting other people yet. 'Besides, I don't want to break the spell,' she'd said. So they remained close to the farm. Rachel rode Joey, and Lander saddled and groomed him. They walked, they talked, and they worked together in the kitchen. The rest of the time they spent in bed. Lander had never been happier.

They would have stayed there for more than a week. They would have stayed there forever, but they were both aware of their responsibility to the Franklins. The women at Claverton would be desperate for news; they deserved to know how things had gone. As Rachel pointed out, the limited test that they had done was a million miles from the large-scale field trial that was needed for something like this, and perhaps they had just been lucky. Perhaps the mixture of virus variants that they'd each taken simply hadn't contained one that could settle in them. Perhaps if he had taken the contents of Rachel's phial and she had taken his, the outcome would have been different. There were many perhaps, but what they had experienced was a start, an indication that Rachels' research was on to something. They owed it to the other women to help them move it forward. They owed it to the rest of the coven, and to everyone else too, be they people in pods, in covens, or Drifters.

They loaded the car, made sure Joey could get in and out of his stable, and locked the door of the house. Then they stood in the yard and took a long look around. The wind turbine spun lazily in a gentle breeze. There was the barn where their few cows had been kept, and behind it the pit where Kerryl had cremated Buster. Beyond that was the hillside path where she had written in her diary that she'd seen a fair-haired young man watching her. Had it been Adam? It seemed likely but he'd said not. Would anyone ever know?

Rachel leaned in and kissed him. 'Can we come back here sometime?' she said.

'Of course we can. We will, I promise.' There was nothing Lander wanted more.

Rachel drove to Claverton. She was an excellent driver, but the main reason was so that Lander could duck and hide if they ran into an EA patrol. Ludlow would have reported him missing long ago, and by now his photo would have been widely circulated and his ID cancelled. However, concealment wasn't necessary. They saw hardly any other vehicles on the way, and those they did see paid them no regard.

Back at the house there was both a reunion and a party. Everyone greeted them like returnees from space, which Lander supposed in a way they were. He experienced considerable jealousy because the women mobbed Rachel and he couldn't get near her, but he also received plenty of attention himself. Gabby and Gwen were overjoyed and hugged him endlessly. He recognised amongst the crowd Carol and Christine from the Nightingales.

'What are you doing here?' Lander said.

'That's a fine greeting,' said Carol. 'I'm very well, thank you.'

'I'm sorry, I didn't mean to be rude. I was surprised to see you, that's all.'

She laughed and poked him in the ribs. 'I was joking. We've come over from Lake Manor because the Nightingales and the Franklins have decided to merge. We're in the same line of business, more or less. It makes sense to come together and we have a plan to get some of the other women's groups to join us. The more of us there are working together the better chance we've got of bringing down McFarlane.'

There was someone else at Claverton that Lander was even more surprised to see. Magda. He listened with growing astonishment and anger as she told him about her rift with Adam and what had happened to her and Steve.

'Adam killed Steve?'

Magda shook her head. 'I don't know. Perhaps Steve's body just gave up the struggle after everything he'd been through. Adam denies he had anything to do with it and I can't see why he would do it, but who knows? The closer he gets to McFarlane and the government the harder it becomes to take what he says at face value. It's almost as if he's been put under a spell.'

A spell, thought Lander. If so it was one of Adam's own making, driven by his ambition. He supposed it was possible that Steve had finally given in. He was a strong guy, but Lander had seen the savage blow that had felled him. He felt for Steve, missed him, and he hated that the identity of the vile agent who had struck him would never be known, and the man would never be made to face what he'd done.

'Adam blames you though. I can't believe that.'

Magda gave a rueful smile. 'Neither can I, but it was all part of his plan. He wanted me punished.'

'What for?'

'I've been trying to work that out.'

'Bastard.'

'Perhaps. But I remember how he used to be. He was well-meaning and he wouldn't have intentionally hurt anyone. I'm sure that part of him is still there somewhere. We just need to give him cause to find it again.'

That evening Lander and Rachel gave an account of everything that had happened at Paradise Farm; well, not everything, but everything the others needed to know. The bags of samples, the empty and full syringes, the swabs, and all the other paraphernalia they'd accumulated over the days of their trial, were taken to the labs for examination later. This was more of a first update.

Gwen took the lead.

'As you can see,' she said to them, 'a lot has happened while you've been away. The Franklins and the Nightingales have agreed to join together and we're reaching out to other covens. The Curies, the Obamas, the Kellers, and the Franks have all said they're interested in joining us. We've also made some good links with the Drifters. Their communication network is proving very useful and extremely effective. Lander's HushNet can reach the pods, but the Drifters can get to everybody else. It's the Drifters we must thank for rescuing Magda. And now, Rachel and Lander, we have you. We're relieved to see you back safe and sound. Tell us all about it.'

It took a long time. Using the notes they'd kept, they each gave an hour by hour account of everything they'd felt. There'd been the nervous apprehension at the start, when they'd gone to sleep each night wondering whether they would wake the next morning to the first deadly symptoms. That was a given; the women were more interested in what the two of them had felt physically. In Lander's case that had been nothing, and it came as a surprise when Rachel told them she'd experienced several bouts of aches and stiffness, and had a couple of sessions of nausea. He was ashamed that he'd not asked her about this himself; he'd just assumed she had felt the same as he had. He made a mental note that this had not been, and certainly in the future would not always be, the case. He had to think of her more, to be aware that the ways she was experiencing the world would often be different from his. All this, of course, was on the assumption that they had a shared future. They'd not talked about it; he'd just supposed that now they'd connected they would always be together. Did Rachel think that too? He couldn't ask her now, not in this room full of people.

It was agreed that another trial was urgently needed. Gabby was among the first to volunteer, followed by half a dozen others. They would start the following day, this time isolating themselves in the estate cottages, where they could be easily monitored.

'Of course, we're not there yet,' said Gwen. 'Assuming this second trial works, there's still the issue of fertility, or rather, infertility. We might have managed to save the people who are alive now, but there's also the matter of the survival of the race.'

Lander felt Rachel's hand reaching for his under the table and squeezing it. He looked at her and she smiled. He smiled too and squeezed her hand in return. Was that a celebration of successfully surviving the ordeal of the trial? Or did it mean something more?

'First, we have to make sure that everyone has access to the vaccine,' said Gabby.

Lander wanted to go to all the pods and give out phials of the molecule. The others were wary of that and cautioned a different approach.

'We know what McFarlane's like,' said Carol. 'He'll see this as a heaven-sent opportunity. He'll grab it and pretend it's his, and the result will be that a grateful population will keep him in office forever.'

'They might,' said one of the other women, who Lander thought was called Lucy. 'In fact, they probably would take it and claim the credit, but that wouldn't be the worst thing. The trouble is that they wouldn't let everyone have it. The Drifters wouldn't get it, and most likely neither would us lot in the covens. It would go to those who the government wanted to reward and preserve. It would be a prize for doing what the authorities wanted, like the honours lists in the old days.'

'Yes,' said Christine, 'and do you realise what would follow from that? Once the government was happy that all its supporters and lackeys were safe it could release the virus again and let the Infection take care of its enemies, wipe out everybody who wasn't on the side of Gus McFarlane.'

There were expressions of horror and disbelief. It was a terrible thought, the more so because everyone had the suspicion that it was plausible.

'We need to talk to Adam,' said Rachel. 'He pulls McFarlane's strings, so why not see if we can negotiate with him?'

Lander was incredulous. 'Negotiate with Adam? There's not much chance of that.'

'What makes you think he'll talk to us?' said Gabby.

'Tell him we've discovered something that will stop the virus. That should get him,' said Gwen.

'It might not. He might just send somebody else to meet us.'

'Or an EA squad to take it,' said Lander.

'I'll go,' said Magda. 'I can persuade him. Let's talk about what we have to offer, and what we want in return.'

36

BAIT

IT SEEMED A GOOD IDEA. Magda knew Adam better than any of them and probably had the best chance of success.

They agreed that she would wait until the end of the second trial. Then, assuming it was successful, she would go back to Lake Manor. From there she would call Adam and tell him that she had information about the fire at the bonobo research centre, important information that would lead to arrests, but she would only tell him in person. Would he come? Who could tell? She just hoped the bait would be tasty enough to tempt him.

It was. She left a message and got a brief one back to say that he would be there the next day.

As she waited for Adam to arrive she went over what could go wrong. Adam might arrive with a hit squad, seize her and throw her back in jail. There were no grounds for that, she had the paper from the Justice Secretary declaring her conviction quashed, but he could disregard that. He might ignore what she was planning to tell him, go back to Winchester and carry on trying to deal with the unrest starting to ferment in some of the pods, the government's inability to control the Drifters, and a system that was showing signs of collapsing. Or of course, he might not turn up at all.

He arrived in the middle of the afternoon, alone, just him and his driver. He looked careworn, and he didn't seem to notice that the Nightingales had gone, and Lake Manor was empty apart from her. There were mechanical greetings. He kissed her awkwardly on the cheek and she asked him how he was. She gave him time to pour himself a drink and settle down, then decided there was no point delaying.

'I asked you to come here to tell you about the fire at the lab,' she said.

'Yes, you said you know who was responsible.'

'I did, I do, but that's not the real reason I want to talk to you.'

Adam looked surprised and peered at her over the rim of his glass. 'Oh no? What is it, then?'

'It's this. One of the women's covens has found a way to neutralise the virus.'

Adam carefully put down his glass and sat very still. 'The Franklins,' he said.

'I can't tell you.'

'It must be. Only two groups were looking for a vaccine, them and the Oxford clinic.'

'Yes,' she said, 'the Franklins.'

Adam drained his glass and refilled it. 'I don't believe you.'

'Why would I lie about something like that?'

'Why would they send you? If it were true, Gwen Mathews would have contacted me.'

Adam looked very tired. Perhaps after all things were not going his way as well as they had. Magda had read enough history to know that it was inevitable that sooner or later any dictator's right-hand man would fall. That was the way such things went.

'I can prove it,' she said. 'They want you to meet them so they can explain to you what they've done.'

'They can come to Winchester,' said Adam. 'Tell them to book an appointment through my secretary.' He refilled his glass.

'It's not going to work like that,' Magda said. 'They want you to go to them.'

He snorted. 'Oh do they? Why should I?'

'Because they have the vaccine, and if you don't go you won't get it. And there are some other things they want to talk to you about, some things they want in exchange.'

'Which are?'

She handed him the list that Carol and Gwen had compiled in discussion with the others. Adam read it twice, and for a long time said nothing. Then at last he spoke.

'Holy fuck,' he said. 'McFarlane will never agree to this.'

'McFarlane won't have to. You have to because you're the person who can make it happen.'

'What if I refuse?'

'The vaccine disappears. The Franklins will treat themselves and a few others, but then they'll destroy it, together with every last trace that might give a clue to how to create it. It's a completely different approach from the one the clinic in Oxford has been taking. They're a million miles from it. They may come up with something, but it will be nowhere near as effective as this. One treatment, that's all anyone needs, whereas the best you can expect from Oxford is having to vaccinate the entire population every year, and still some of them would die from new strains of the virus.'

'I could take their precious vaccine, if they have one. I could just come in and arrest them all.'

Magda shook her head. 'Of course you could. You're the big, powerful man, aren't you? But it wouldn't do you any good. They wouldn't tell you anything.'

He laughed, but it was dry and humourless. 'I think I could persuade them. I could start shooting them, one a day until they did.'

She knew that this was just bravado. He was getting desperate. The list of demands she'd given him was extreme, but he was beginning to see that he might have to agree to at least some of them. He was also starting to realise that what was being proposed had big advantages for him.

'You're not that stupid,' she said. 'There are twenty-three Franklins. You don't know who knows what. The one you shoot first might be the one who knows the most. Besides, you'd be surprised how determined they are.'

There was another pause. Then he said, 'Go back to them. Tell them I'll be there the day after tomorrow.'

He poured himself another glass and drained it in one. Magda studied him. 'You don't look particularly excited,' she said.

Adam raised an eyebrow. 'Should I be? I'll believe it when I see it,' he said.

37

AGREEMENT

AJAY WANTED TO SET booby traps to "get the bastard". Fortunately for everyone, Adam's arrival was sudden, so there was no opportunity to do that. Sudden, but not unheralded. It was the motorbikes that made the most noise, four of them, two leading the official car and two behind it.

'Look at him,' said Lander, as he watched the long, black Mercedes come along the Claverton drive towards the house. 'Who the fuck does he think he is?'

'Now, now,' said Rachel, at his side. 'You told me you used to get on well with him once. This meeting is about building bridges, let's not forget that.'

Lander nodded. Rachel was right, but the chasm that he saw between him and Adam looked too wide to ever be bridged. Nevertheless, for her he would try.

Things got off to a bad start. Sweeping in behind the Mercedes came an EA truck, which skidded to a halt in front of the house with a dirt-scattering flourish. A dozen agents jumped from it and fanned out in a semi-circle facing the main door, each of them on one knee, carbines at the ready. To every one of the people inside the house, this was terrifying.

'What the...?' Magda exclaimed. 'They must know the people in here are unarmed. Why threaten us in this way? Is he planning just to come in and take over?'

'Looks like it,' said Gwen.

'If he is,' said Carol, 'remember what we discussed. Non-co-operation. He doesn't know what we know, and he doesn't know who knows it. We all say that we weren't involved in the research and we have no information. For most of us, that's true.'

The driver held open the door of the Mercedes and Adam got out. Next, there was an argument. Adam wanted to bring eight armed EA personnel into the house with him but the women refused and formed a human barrier across the entrance.

'You realise I don't need your permission to do this,' Adam snarled. 'My people could just walk in.'

Gwen gave him a gentle smile. 'You could, but you wouldn't, would you? Where would that get you?'

Lander remembered that way back, when he'd first met them, Adam and Gwen had been working together. There still seemed to be a connection between them, even though they were now on different sides. The compromise was that a couple of armed guards would be allowed into the building but they would remain at the back of the room where Adam and the others were to meet, and their weapons would be kept out of sight.

A large oval table had been made ready in the library. Gwen seated herself on one side and Adam was given the chair opposite. He was still ruffled by the argument about his guards, and seemingly wounded by what he saw as a failure to get his own way. Lander thought that he looked weary, as if everything was becoming too much for him. He'd put on weight, and there were dark shadows under his eyes.

'You've changed your tune,' he said to Gwen. 'I thought you were supposed to work for me.'

'I work for our country,' said Gwen. 'For everybody.'

Adam made a dismissive gesture. 'Very worthy,' he said with heavy sarcasm. 'You suppose that I don't? Why don't I simply arrest the lot of you? You,' pointing at Lander, 'are absent from your pod without leave. You,' pointing at Magda, 'may have had your murder conviction overturned, but I could charge you with aiding an illegal meeting, and possibly with arson too.' He looked around the room. 'I'm sure I could get the rest of you for something. I saw a bunch of scruffs outside who I guess are Drifters. There are some in here too.' He scowled at Ajay and a couple of his friends who were hanging back in the shadows. 'Drifting is classed as vagabondage,' he went on, 'and is outlawed. That in itself means a spell in correction, but some of the Drifters are suspected of other things too.' He became exasperated. 'Harbouring Drifters is an offence. Why don't I just lock you all up?'

There was a long pause. Some of the women looked at the table, some at the ceiling, none at Adam, while they digested this outburst.

In the end Gwen spoke. 'Because if you did lock us all up, you wouldn't get what you came here for.'

'Your vaccine.' He said it with a dismissive snort, as if such a thing was beneath contempt. 'I have my own. My people in Oxford have one already.'

Gwen shook her head. 'You forget that I've been monitoring the Oxford group too, so I know that's not true. What you have there is the first stage in what might possibly turn out to be some way to make some people immune to some strains of the virus, but it's nowhere near ready yet, and when it is it will be very hit-and-miss. Because I/452 mutates so easily, the best you'll be able to do will be to keep half a step behind it, like vaccinations against flu, which don't always work and need to be constantly updated.'

Adam shrugged.

'It's simple,' Rachel joined in. 'We have something that works. It's been thoroughly tested and it's ready now. Besides, we have something else too.'

She rummaged under the table and took from her bag a plastic container. Inside it was a small, white cylinder with a blue cap. 'There.'

There was a stupefied silence. Then Carol spoke. 'Is that what I think it is?'

'I expect so,' said Rachel, and she pushed the container across the table. 'I took another test as well as the anti-virus one. I'm pregnant.'

There was an amazed silence. Lander was swamped by a tumult of emotions. Joy: he was to be a father! Puzzlement: why had she kept it secret? Hurt: why hadn't she told him first? The joy won, and he found himself grinning. The women clapped.

Adam reached forward and looked at the container. 'It's faked,' he said.

'It's not a fake,' said Rachel. 'I have another kit here and I'll do the test again. You can watch if you like, if you need proof it's genuine.'

Lander was gratified to read from Adam's face that the suggestion embarrassed him.

'No need for that,' he said. 'But I could just take you, ransack the place for the vaccine you say you've got, and go.'

'You could,' said Rachel, 'but you wouldn't?'

'Oh, and why not?'

'Because,' said Gwen, 'if you did you would die.'

There was a sudden fuss at the back of the room as the guards snatched their weapons and held them at the ready.

Adam looked at Gwen, his sneer a classic. 'You think?' he said.

'I know,' said Gwen. 'You see this?' She held up a clear glass tube. 'It's a cocktail of the fifty or so different strains of the I/452 virus that we've collected since the Infection began. Before you arrived, we smeared it on the door handles here. We also sprayed it on the area of the table where we've put you, and on the cup that you're holding. You're one of the people who appears to have some natural protection, but do you want to risk that among those fifty strains there isn't one to which you are not immune, against which you have no defence? If there is, you'll leave here and in ten or so days you'll feel the first symptoms of the Infection. Your head will ache, your joints will ache, and you'll get cramps. Next, you'll feel nauseous and you'll get diarrhoea. Finally, you'll start to bleed from your nose, ears, eyes, anus, and internally. This will happen to you, and to your two guards here.' There was a clatter as one of the rifles was dropped.

'You're bluffing.' Adam's voice was barely audible.

'I'm not,' said Gwen, 'but anyway do you want to risk it? There's only one way to be sure you'll live.'

'How?' Adam's whole attitude had changed, so fast. He was a shadow of the blusterer they had seen only a few minutes before.

'We treat you. You see, all of us here have already had our vaccine, so we're protected. Rachel and Lander were the first to test it and came through maximum exposure to all the strains unscathed. Since then Gabby and some of the other girls have also tested it, with one hundred per cent success. We have no doubt it's effective.'

'Give it to me. I demand it.' The swagger was coming back, but the voice sounded choked.

Gwen slowly shook her head. 'You're not in a position to demand. Why don't you instead tell us what you can offer us, what you're prepared to do to buy your life?'

'Buy my life? Are you serious?' There was silence. 'All right, if I believe you and go along with what you're saying, tell me what you want.'

'Easy. It's all written down on the list Magda gave you. To remind you, here's a copy.' Gwen pushed a sheet of paper across the table to him. Adam looked at it suspiciously. 'Yes,' said Gwen, 'that sheet of paper will be contaminated too, so let me read it to you.'

She took another paper and held it up.

'The things we want are both straightforward and simple. One, the result of the last election is to be declared invalid owing to irregularities in the voting. This will be followed by two, the resignation of Gus McFarlane and his whole administration. Three, we want the formation of a new government that will be representative of the whole country, made up of representatives chosen by the pods, the covens and the Drifters. You will chair this new government, but you will be its servant, not its master. Four, our vaccine will be made available to everyone, and that means everyone, regardless of social status, gender, race, colour or anything else. Every single living human being will have free and open access to it. We'll set up facilities to produce it in large quantities, and we will as far as possible, make it available to other nations too. Five, there will be unconditional pardons for Lander, Magda, and all the Drifters, every single one of them. Drifting will no longer be a crime. Six, you will free Chrissie, pardon her, and allow the Reboot Army to hold open and unrestricted gatherings. Seven, there will be an official funeral for Steve. Eight, a statue of Kerryl Shaw will be erected at a place to be decided by Lander. Nine, Rachel and Lander will be awarded the George Medal. Ten, the women who have created this vaccine will be awarded the Francis Crick Prize for Science.'

There was a long, long pause while Adam read through his copy, poking it distantly with his finger as if afraid it might burn him.

'Don't you see?' said Magda. 'The only way forward, the only way we can drag civilisation out of this trough and rebuild it, is if we all work together. A dictatorship where somebody like Gus McFarlane makes all the rules and people have no freedom can't work. A lot of people will be hurt while it exists, and a lot more when it collapses, as it surely will.'

'Sign that,' said Gwen, 'and you and your guards will receive immediate treatment. It would have been better for you to have taken our medication before being exposed to the virus rather than after, but Rachel, who's an expert in this field, says it should work.'

'Provided it's done now, without delay,' said Rachel.

Another pause.

'There's one more thing,' said Gwen, 'and we don't mind you taking the credit for this if you can think of a way to do so. A hidden and unexpected side effect of the virus is that men who have been exposed to it are sterile. That's just about the whole male population. As you know, there's already considerable unrest about this. Now, a bonus of the procedure we've devised is a reversal of that sterility. We didn't know this, but we vaccinated some of the Drifter men and, to put it bluntly, it seems that they're no longer firing blanks.'

'Right on,' said Ajay.

'Get your people to present this properly,' said Rachel, 'and you could be seen as the saviour of the race.'

'Yes, forget your poor, pathetic little bonobos,' said Magda, bitterly.

Adam pulled the paper towards him. 'I suppose I have no choice.'

'Oh, there's always a choice,' said Magda. Adam glared at her.

'One thing before you sign,' said Gwen. 'We want two copies, and they'll be kept under strict security in different locations. If you ever go back on anything these documents contain, if you ever depart in the tiniest, smallest way from what they say or from their spirit, we'll make them public. We'll broadcast them widely, together with an account of all of the selfish, stupid, cruel and short-sighted things you've either initiated yourself or done as McFarlane's lapdog. And just to be absolutely sure, we've been video recording this whole meeting.'

Ajay waved his mobile phone.

Adam hesitated a moment longer. Then he picked up the pen that had been given to him and signed first one paper, then the other. Gwen took them, folded them and put them in separate envelopes.

'One of these is, for now, going in our safe here. The other is being handed over to the Drifters. They will pass it from group to group, moving it about the country. You will never know exactly where it is at any time, but they will.'

Gabby took one of the envelopes and left the room. Gwen gave the other to Ajay.

Rachel advanced on Adam with a needle. 'Right,' she said. 'Take off your jacket and turn up your shirt sleeve.'

'How do I know this isn't poison?'

Rachel didn't answer but rolled her eyes. Adam watched as the clear liquid was injected into his arm.

'Is that it?' he said.

'Yes, that's it.'

He took the pad of cotton wool and held it to where the needle had gone in. 'Hard to believe,' he said, 'that's all it takes to stop the plague.' He stared at his arm. Then, for the first time, he smiled.

'What's funny?' said Magda.

'I've got to think of a way to tell my former boss that he's lost his job.'

He grinned again, and for a second it was the old Adam, the one that Lander had known and liked when he'd first gone to Oxford, the one that had haunted Kerryl's imagination and she'd fallen in love with. In time perhaps Lander would be able to forgive him for what he'd done. For now, they had to work together.

38

COMMEMORATION

LANDER WENT TO THE FIRST remembrance ceremony, but after that he didn't bother. There were in his view too many people swanning around taking credit for things they hadn't done. However, even though he had always turned down his invitation to the event he did every year follow it on television, and he sat on the sofa now, looking at the screen as the proceedings reached their climax.

He'd devised his own way of commemorating the terrible scourge that five years earlier had devastated the planet. It was a ritual that had arisen by accident. He had been trying to fix a joint behind the hot water cylinder. He hated plumbing, and he was hot and bothered and fed up with trying to reach into the tight space when his fingers found something. It was an old paper bag, dusty, brown and wrinkled with age. It must have been there for years. He looked inside and knew at once what it was: Granddad's Jericho Rose. He fingered the crisp, dry bundle and remembered the old man's performance, and how he and Kerryl had been fascinated by what for a long time they had taken to be magic.

The world was rebuilding, with a spirit of cooperation that hadn't been there before. Nationally people had come together, moved by a realisation that whatever their differences, in the face of a killer virus everyone was equal. Granddad's ritual seemed to symbolise the movement towards bringing life back to the world, and the annual ceremony to commemorate the defeat of the Infection was the right time to resurrect it.

On the screen, a drone camera showed an aerial view of a vast circle, with the flags of the 197 countries recognised as nations of the world around its perimeter. At its centre was a gigantic slab of slate, with a single flame that burned night and day throughout the year. It was the memorial to all those who had died from or as a result of the Infection. The flags were at half-mast.

It was a grey day, with an edgy wind that made it clear that the winter was not yet over. A man in a long overcoat stepped down from the VIP dais and walked slowly to a lectern. It was festooned with microphones, and on its front was a logo made up of a circle of figure sixes. The camera cut to a close-up of the man, showing a fresh face topped by tight blond curls. The man opened a black leather folder, looked steadily at the camera, and read. His delivery was measured, balanced and dignified.

'Sisters, brothers, friends. It is now five years since virus I/452, what came to be known as the Infection, swept our country and the world. We gather here today at the National Arboretum as we do every year, to remember not only those who died from the virus but all those who suffered from it in other ways too. And that is all of us, because there is not a person here or anywhere else who was untouched by this menace.

'For some the outcome was obvious: they perished. Others survived but in an altered state. All of us here today and watching at home lost people who were dear to us. We are the fortunate few, privileged to be alive, and that privilege carries obligations: the responsibility to rebuild, and to do better.

'The world will never be the same as it was before. That is sad, but it is also a good thing because there was much in the world which preceded this one that was wrong. There was much that was cruel, careless, selfish, and evil. There was much that deserved to be swept away. However, there was also much that deserved no such thing. We owe it to those who paid with their lives, or their sanity, to ensure that we never return to the way things were before, and to ensure that we take the opportunity which has been given to us to make a better world. To rebuild. To reboot. I ask you to dedicate yourselves to this noble task. I dedicate myself to helping you to achieve it.'

The speaker turned away from the lectern and beckoned to the young woman he'd been sitting beside, who stood and came towards him. She was dressed all in white. They faced the crowd, hand in hand, waving and smiling.

'Chrissie looks well.' It was Rachel, who flopped down on the sofa beside him.

'Yes, she does,' said Lander. 'So does Adam.'

'Oh Adam, he always looks well.'

'The golden couple.'

Rachel snorted a laugh. 'The unlikely couple.'

'I suppose they are. Chrissie's a clever girl, though. After what happened to her and Steve at that rally I thought all she'd want from Adam was his head on a spike. But she saw an opportunity. She knew Adam would never go for the religious aspect of the Reboot Army, but she's managed to get him to take on her message without that. That speech was pure Chrissie.'

Rachel thought for a moment. 'Do you wish you were there, with them?'

Lander looked out to the garden where their children were engrossed in a game. They had lost interest in watching the inert blob in the bowl of water and gone out into the garden to play, telling him to summon them when it was 'ready'.

He squeezed Rachel's hand. 'There? With them? Are you mad? Of course not.'

They both of them looked again at the screen. Adam and Chrissie had gone back to their places. A lone trumpeter played as the flags of the nations were slowly raised, every one of them reaching the top of its pole at exactly the same instant.

'Is that it, then?' Rachel said.

'Yes, over for another year.'

'Right.' She stood up. 'Picnic time. I'll get the food, you fetch the kids.'

Rachel left in the direction of the kitchen and Lander went into the garden. He stood for a moment on the terrace, watching the two bent heads.

'Come on, twins,' he called.

The children ran over to him. He was struck, as he was every time he saw them, by how much they resembled their mother, and behind and beyond that, by the ghostly echo of Kerryl.

The children were excited.

'Is it ready? Has the Jericho Rose come back to life?' said the girl.

'Come and have a look,' said Lander.

They went back into the parlour and he lifted the bowl down from the mantelpiece.

'It's gone all green,' said the boy.

'It's like salad,' said the girl.

'Can we eat it? said the boy.

'Yuk!' said the girl.

'Picnic,' said Rachel, coming in from the kitchen with a large basket.

'Where are we going?' said the girl.

'Where we always go on this day,' said Lander.

'The Bride Stones,' said the boy.

'Right, the Bride Stones,' said Rachel.

So that was where they all went, to sit at the edge of the pool, beside the statue of Kerryl.

Writers love to talk about writing, how they do it and why. You'll know this if you've ever been unfortunate enough to get close to one at a party. One of the greats, I think it was EM Forster, said that writing is both an extremely selfish and extremely lonely activity. He was right, it is. It's lonely not only because the writer shuts herself or himself off to write, but also because a writer is often alone when they're in company. When I'm developing a book, from the first germ of an idea through to the final edit, I am often ribbed by my family for dropping out of conversations and missing what's going on around me because my mind is elsewhere, on some scene, a snatch of dialogue, or an emerging character.

That was until I found myself writing a tale about a killer virus in the middle of an actual pandemic. Then everything seemed rather too immediate! I've written elsewhere about where the initial idea for Paradise Girl came from. It was intended to be a one-off, but the response from readers prompted me to follow it up, which I did in Aftershocks. That story reached an inconclusive ending (which some reviewers pointed out), and I felt there was a need for a more settled resolution of what happened to Lander, Magda, Adam and the others. It was also necessary for Lander to finish growing up, a process he started in Aftershocks but still had some way to go. This was the aim in Jericho Rose. I hope I've done that, and that my readers feel I've brought the series to a satisfying conclusion.

A Note on Viruses

I am not an expert on viruses, although having completed this book in the middle of the Covid-19 pandemic I know more about them now than I did; as I suspect do many others. I approached Professor Shamshad Cockcroft of UCL for a view on the credibility of my account of viruses and what they can do. She kindly introduced me to a wonderful book, *Virology* by Frank Ryan. This work manages to do what so many similar efforts fail to achieve; it doesn't pull any punches on the science front, but it remains accessible and extremely readable. His views are both fascinating and disturbing. The conversation in Chapter 25 where Rachel and Gwen explain to Lander how they intend to combat the I/452 virus is informed by his work, and by several magazine and newspaper reports and articles (try Googling 'molecule to block virus replication' for a selection).

Is the virus I describe in REBOOT possible? The short answer is not at the moment, although the notion of a rogue power devising a deadly infection as a weapon of war is not only credible but has probably already happened. It is also true that the same virus may affect people in dissimilar ways, so the notion that Lander and Kerryl have symptoms different from those displayed by family, friends and others is not unreasonable. Can a virus make men sterile? The answer is that some do. Is it true that viruses mutate? Many do, the most obvious being those that carry influenza and the common cold. It's unlikely that one virus has all these attributes; that is my fiction, at least for now.

ACKNOWLEDGMENTS

Many people have helped, advised and supported me while I've been writing this book. Some of them don't even know they've done it. Several I must thank by name, but there are far too many to list them all.

Firstly, there is my family, who have to get used to me inflicting on them embryonic plot ideas, character speculation and half-finished drafts. They are my son, John, and my daughter, Sarah. This book is dedicated to them.

Just as important, to me and to them, are their partners, Kathy Featherstone and Jeff Durber. Thank you to both of them for their interest in and support for my writing. Their children, Hailey and Ella Featherstone and Bruce and Lenny Durber have also been involved, reading my work, talking to me, or simply by being there. Hailey and Ella live in the USA so are harder to reach. Bruce and Lenny are closer, and it is they who have helped me in my efforts to get inside the mind of a teenager, even if they don't know it.

As always, my deepest thanks go to Sally Featherstone, my wife, my business and creative partner, and my very best friend. She helps me with ideas, reads drafts, suggests improvements, and encourages me to fly, but she also knows when I should keep my feet on the ground. I am endlessly grateful to her for helping me to do what I do. Most important, being an author herself she knows what it's like when you have a book in your head and it won't leave you alone.

I feel very fortunate to have a number of friends who are interested in my work and prepared to discuss it with me. Thank you to Rod and Helen Collett, Mark Edwards, Judith Shorrocks, Catherine Corry, Lynn Broadbent, Laurence and Shamshad Cockroft, Chris and Michelle O'Gorman. I am grateful to you all.

When I published the first edition of Paradise Girl it was not in my mind to write a companion or a sequel. However, a number of Facebook friends, bloggers and Amazon and Goodreads reviewers were kind enough to say they would like to read more. So I opened my laptop and started to tell the story of Lander. My thanks go to all of them for their encouragement and support.

BOOKS BY PHILL FEATHERSTONE

<u>Novels</u>

Paradise Girl (REBOOT series book 1)

After Shocks (REBOOT series book 2)

Jericho Roase (REBOOT series book 3)

REBOOT - the complete collection

The God Jar

I know What You're Thinking

What Dreams We Had

The Poisoned Garden (Leopards Bane Book 1)

The Rhymer's Daughter ((Leopards Bane Book 2)

<u>Short Stories</u>

Undiscovered Countries

<u>Education</u>

Various books for teachers of very young children, written in partnership with Sally Featherstone and published under the Featherstone Education imprint by Bloomsbury Publishing plc.

ABOUT THE AUTHOR

Thank you for reading my book. If you enjoyed it would you leave a review on Amazon? And if you can on Goodreads too? Reviews are important to independent authors because they let other readers know about our work. And if you did like it please tell your friends, both in person and on social media.

You can find details of all my books on my website, together with plot summaries, book covers, buying options, and questions for book discussion groups –

www.phillfeatherstone.net

While you're there please consider joining my email list. When you sign up you'll be able to download a free book of short stories, and you'll receive a monthly email giving news, my thoughts about writing, and special offers.

Finally, would you follow me on Facebook, Instagram and Twitter?

facebook.com/PhillFeatherstone-author

twitter.com/@PhillFeathers

instagram.com/phillfeathers

www.ingramcontent.com/pod-product-compliance
Lightning Source LLC
Chambersburg PA
CBHW072032190726

48294CB00005B/1237